Tales of the City
More Tales of the City
Further Tales of the City

An Omnibus

ARMISTEAD MAUPIN

Chatto & Windus
LONDON

Published in 1989 by
Chatto & Windus Ltd
30 Bedford Square
London WC1B 3SG

Tales of the City, *More Tales of the City* and *Further Tales of the City* have all been published in somewhat different form in the *San Francisco Chronicle*.

A CIP catalogue for this book is available from the British Library.

ISBN 0 7011 3429 1

Typeset at The Spartan Press Ltd,
Lymington, Hants
Printed in Great Britain by
Mackays of Chatham plc,
Chatham, Kent

TALES OF THE CITY
MORE TALES OF THE CITY
FURTHER TALES OF THE CITY
An Omnibus

Introduction by the Author

The three novels in this omnibus have their origins in a daily newspaper serial which began in 1976 in the *San Francisco Chronicle*. I wrote *Tales of the City* by the seat of my pants, often pounding out Monday's installment on the previous Friday, much to the exasperation of my editors. The pace was nerve-racking, to say the least, but with it came an unexpected dividend: current events could be mined for subject matter almost as soon as they occurred. Through the imaginary residents of 28 Barbary Lane I could comment on the follies of the moment in a way that journalists wouldn't dare.

This had been done before, of course – most notably by Dickens and Thackeray – but storytelling hadn't been attempted in an American daily for decades, and I was ill-prepared for the uproar which followed. Defenders of 'serious' journalism, anticipating the worst, fired off angry letters of protest to the editor. Bored society matrons, discovering this naughty new diversion in their midsts, invited me to dinner with people they were *absolutely positive* I was writing about.

If my fan mail could be believed, reading *Tales* aloud became a commonplace ritual among white-collar Californians, some of whom made furtive runs to the office copier to reproduce the day's installment for friends in other places. A saloon in San Francisco's financial district named a drink The Anna Madrigal after the serial's dope-smoking landlady, while a startling number of born-again Christians – I know this because they told me so – prayed daily for my deliverance from hell.

Jan Struther, the brilliant English writer whose *Mrs Miniver* was serialized on the court page of *The Times*, once remarked on the curiously depersonalized experience of writing fiction directly for a mass readership. 'I feel,' she said dryly, upon receiving yet another letter addressed to her title character, 'rather like a ventriloquist whose doll has suddenly struck up a direct conversation with the audience.'

I know the feeling well. Less than a year into *Tales* I stopped being its author and became sort of a second landlord at Barbary Lane, a dubious and shadowy figure entrusted only with the continued safekeeping of the lodgers. Indeed, when Michael Tolliver, the main gay character, was endangered by illness in the second book, he received his own flowers and cards, thank you, while his harried creator was the subject of veiled threats. 'I'm nothing but a middle-aged housewife from Moraga, with two little machos of my own,' wrote one indignant reader, 'but if you kill Michael Mouse, I'll never subscribe to the *Chronicle* again.'

After significant revisions, the first year's worth of episodes took shape as a novel, published in 1978 by Harper & Row. The original plan had been to release it in hardcover, but a last-minute decision by the editors caused it to debut as an oversized paperback – a pioneer, I'm told, of the boom that was to follow. The book floundered, then disappeared, and an appalling number of them were returned to the publisher. The teaser I'd appended to the last page – 'End of Book One' – seemed brutally literal at the time.

It was not until 1980, when Harper & Row risked *More Tales of the City*, that the tide began to turn. Outlanders who'd been privy to the 'Xerox editions' – as I'd come to think of those early samizdats from San Francisco – began, slowly, to buy the books and urge them on their friends. Encouraged by a leap in sales, I signed on for another stint at the newspaper and started work on *Further Tales*, which, after the usual rewrite, hit the bookstores in 1982.

The success which followed could hardly be termed meteoric, but the books have been 'steady sellers', as they say, ever since. Today, as I complete *Sure of You*, the sixth and final volume of the series, almost half-a-million copies of the earlier books are in print around the world – some of them in German and Spanish.

In the UK a Corgi (now Black Swan) paperback series has spawned 'Barbaryphiles' of disarming orthodoxy, prompting Chatto & Windus to publish my latest, *Significant Others*, in hardcover. There, as elsewhere, the fans of *Tales* seem to be a loyal lot, re-reading on a seasonal basis, forgiving me my trespasses when I deal too harshly, or too infrequently, with their favorite characters.

To those of you who discovered, and championed, these novels in softcover – sometimes of necessity reading them out of order -- I offer my heartfelt thanks for your faith. I hope you enjoy the heft of this handsome new edition as much as I do and that you'll pass on those paperbacks to a friend. If, on the other hand, you're a newcomer to the lane, let me be the first to welcome you to the neighborhood.

A.M.
January, 1989
San Francisco

Tales of the City

For my mother and father
and my family at The Duck House

It's an odd thing, but anyone who disappears
is said to be seen in San Francisco.

OSCAR WILDE

Taking the Plunge

Mary Ann Singleton was twenty-five years old when she saw San Francisco for the first time.

She came to the city alone for an eight-day vacation. On the fifth night, she drank three Irish coffees at the Buena Vista, realized that her Mood Ring was blue, and decided to phone her mother in Cleveland.

'Hi, Mom. It's me.'

'Oh, darling. Your daddy and I were just talking about you. There was this crazy man on *McMillan and Wife* who was strangling all these secretaries, and I just couldn't help thinking . . .'

'Mom . . .'

'I know. Just crazy ol' Mom, worrying herself sick over nothing. But you never can tell about those things. Look at that poor Patty Hearst, locked up in that closet with all those awful . . .'

'Mom . . . long distance.'

'Oh . . . yes. You must be having a grand time.'

'God . . . you wouldn't believe it! The people here are so friendly I feel like I've . . .'

'Have you been to the Top of the Mark like I told you?'

'Not yet.'

'Well, don't you dare miss that! You know, your daddy took me there when he got back from the South Pacific. I remember he slipped the bandleader five dollars, so we could dance to "Moonlight Serenade", and I spilled Tom Collins all over his beautiful white Navy . . .'

'Mom, I want you to do me a favor.'

'Of course, darling. Just listen to me. Oh . . . before I forget it, I ran into Mr Lassiter yesterday at the Ridgemont Mall, and he said the office is just falling apart with you gone. They don't get many good secretaries at Lassiter Fertilizers.'

'Mom, that's sort of why I called.'

'Yes, darling?'

'I want you to call Mr Lassiter and tell him I won't be in on Monday morning.'

'Oh . . . Mary Ann, I'm not sure you should ask for an extension on your vacation.'

'It's not an extension, Mom.'

'Well, then why . . .'

'I'm not coming home, Mom.'

Silence. Then, dimly in the distance, a television voice began to tell Mary Ann's father about the temporary relief of hemorrhoids. Finally, her mother spoke: 'Don't be silly, darling.'

'Mom . . . I'm not being silly. I *like* it here. It feels like home already.'

'Mary Ann, if there's a boy . . .'

'There's no boy . . . I've thought about this for a long time.'

'Don't be ridiculous. You've been there five days!'

'Mom, I know how you feel, but . . . well, it's got nothing to do with you and Daddy. I just want to start making my own life . . . have my own apartment and all.'

'Oh, *that*. Well, darling . . . of *course* you can. As a matter of fact, your daddy and I thought those new apartments out at Ridgemont might be just perfect for you. They take lots of young people, and they've got a swimming pool and a sauna, and I could make some of those darling curtains like I made for Sonny and Vicki when they got married. You could have all the privacy you . . .'

'You aren't listening, Mom. I'm trying to tell you I'm a grown woman.'

'Well, act like it, then! You can't just . . . run away from your family and friends to go live with a bunch of hippies and mass murderers!'

'You've been watching too much TV.'

'OK . . . then what about The Horoscope?'

'What?'

'The Horoscope. That crazy man. The killer.'

'Mom . . . The Zodiac.'

'Same difference. And what about . . . earthquakes? I saw that movie, Mary Ann, and I nearly died when Ava Gardner . . .'

'Will you just call Mr Lassiter for me?'

Her mother began to cry. 'You won't come back. I just know it.'

'Mom . . . please . . . I will. I promise.'

'But you won't be . . . the same!'

'No! I hope not.'

*

When it was over, Mary Ann left the bar and walked through Aquatic Park to the bay. She stood there for several minutes in a chill wind, staring at the beacon on Alcatraz. She made a vow not to think about her mother for a while.

Back at Fisherman's Wharf Holiday Inn, she looked up Connie Bradshaw's phone number.

Connie was a stewardess for United. Mary Ann hadn't seen her since high school: 1968.

'Fantabulous!' squealed Connie. 'How long you here for?'

'For good.'

'Super! Found an apartment yet?'

'No . . . I . . . well, I was wondering if I might be able to crash at your place, until I can . . .'

'Sure. No sweat.'

'Connie . . . you're single?'

The stewardess laughed. 'A bear shit in the woods?'

Connie's Place

Mary Ann dragged her American Tourister into Connie's apartment, groaned softly and sank into a mock zebra-skin captain's chair.

'Well . . . hello, Sodom and Gomorrah.'

Connie laughed. 'Your Mom freaked, huh?'

'God!'

'Poor baby! I know the feeling. When I told *my* mom I was moving to San Francisco, she had an absolute hissy-fit! It was a zillion times worse than the summer I tried to join Up With People!'

'God . . . I almost forgot.'

Connie's eyes glazed nostalgically. 'Yeah . . . Hey, you work up a thirst, hon?'

'Sure.'

'Sit tight. I'll be right back.'

Thirty seconds later, Connie emerged from the kitchen with two airlines glasses and a bottle of Banana Cow. She poured a drink for Mary Ann.

Mary Ann sipped warily. 'Well . . . look at all this. You're practically a native, aren't you? This is . . . quite something.'

'Quite something' was the best she could manage. Connie's apartment was a potpourri of plastic Tiffany lamps and ankle-deep shag carpeting, needlepoint Snoopy pictures and 'Hang in There, Baby' kitten posters, monkey pod salad sets and macramé plant hangers and – please, no, thought Mary Ann – a Pet Rock.

'I've been lucky,' Connie beamed. 'Being a stew and all . . . well, you can pick up a lot of art objects in your travels.'

'Mmm.' Mary Ann wondered if Connie regarded her black velvet bullfighter painting as an art object.

The stewardess kept smiling. 'Cow OK?'

'What? Oh . . . yes. Hits the spot.'

'I love the stuff.' She downed some more of it to demonstrate her point, then looked up as if she had just discovered Mary Ann's presence in the room. 'Hey, hon! Long time no see!'

'Yeah. Too long. Eight years.'

'Eight years . . . Eight years! You're lookin' good, though. You're lookin' real . . . Hey, you wanna see something absolutely yucky?'

Without waiting for an answer, she leaped to her feet and went to the bookshelf made of six orange plastic Foremost milk crates. Mary Ann could make out copies of *Jonathan Livingston Seagull*, *How to Be Your Own Best Friend*, *The Sensuous Woman*, *More Joy of Sex* and *Listen to the Warm*.

Connie reached for a large book bound in burgundy vinyl and held it up to Mary Ann.

'Ta-*ta*!'

'Oh, God! *The Buccaneer*?'

Connie nodded triumphantly and pulled up a chair. She opened the yearbook. 'You'll absolutely *die* over your hair!'

Mary Ann found her senior picture. Her hair was very blond and meticulously ironed. She was wearing the obligatory sweater and pearl necklace. Despite the camouflage of an airbrush, she could still remember the exact location of the zit she had sprouted on the day of the photograph.

The inscription read:

MARY ANN SINGLETON
'Still Waters Run Deep'
Pep Club 2,3,4; Future Homemakers of America 3,4;
National Forensic League 4;
Plume and Palette, 3,4

Mary Ann shook her head. 'Rest in peace,' she said and winced.

Connie, mercifully, didn't offer her own biography for examination. Mary Ann remembered it all too well: head majorette, class treasurer for three years, president of the Y-Teens. Connie's waters had run fast and shallow. She had been popular.

Mary Ann struggled back into the present. 'So what do you do – like for fun?'

Connie rolled her eyes. 'You name it.'

'I'd rather not.'

'Well . . . for instance.' Connie bent over her hatch-cover coffee table and dut out a copy of *Oui* magazine. 'You read that?' asked Mary Ann.

'No. Some guy left it.'

'Oh.'

'Check out page seventy.'

Mary Ann turned to an article entitled 'Coed Baths – Welcome to the World's Cleanest Orgy.' It was illustrated by a photograph of intermingling legs, breasts and buttocks.

'Charming.'

'It's down on Valencia Street. You pays your money and you takes your chances.'

'You've been there?'

'No. But I wouldn't rule it out.'

'I'm afraid you'll have to count me out, if you're planning on . . .'

Connie laughed throatily. 'Relax, hon. I wasn't suggesting we . . . You're a new girl. Give it time. This city loosens people up.'

'I'll never be that loose . . . or desperate.'

Connie shrugged, looking vaguely hurt. She took another sip of her Banana Cow.

'Connie, I didn't . . .'

'It's OK, hon. I knew what you meant. Hey, I'm hungry as hell. How 'bout a little Hamburger Helper?'

After dinner, Mary Ann napped for an hour.

She dreamed she was in a huge tile room full of steam. She was naked. Her mother and father were there, watching *Let's Make a Deal* through the steam. Connie walked in with Mr Lassiter, who was furious at Mary Ann and began to shout at her. Mary Ann's mother and father were shouting at Monty Hall's first contestant.

'Take the box,' they screamed. 'Take the box . . .'

Mary Ann woke up. She stumbled into the bathroom and splashed water on her face.

When she opened the cabinet over the sink, she discovered an assortment of after-shave lotions: Brut, Old Spice, Jade East.

Connie, apparently, was still popular.

A Frisco Disco

The discotheque was called Dance Your Ass Off. Mary Ann thought that was gross, but didn't tell Connie so. Connie was too busy getting off on being Marisa Berenson.

'The trick is to look bored with it all.'

'That shouldn't be hard.'

'If you wanna get laid, Mary Ann, you'd better . . .'

'I never said that.'

'Nobody ever *says* it, for Christ's sake! Look, if you can't deal with your own sexuality, hon, you're gonna get screwed but good in this town.'

'I like that. You should make it into a country-western song.'

Connie sighed in exasperation. 'C'mon. And *try* not to look like Tricia Nixon reviewing the troops.' She led the way into the building and staked out a battered sofa against the wall.

The room was supposed to look funky: brick-red walls, revolving beer signs, kitschy memorabilia. Henna-rinsed women and rugby-shirted men clustered decoratively along the bar, as if posing for a Seagram's ad.

While Connie was buying their drinks, Mary Ann settled uncomfortably on the sofa and commanded herself to stop comparing things with Cleveland.

Several yards away, a girl in cowboy boots, sweat pants and a red squirrel Eisenhower jacket stared haughtily at Mary Ann's polyester pantsuit. Mary Ann turned away from her, only to confront another woman, looking blasé in a macramé halter, black finger-nails and a crew cut.

'There's a dude at the bar who looks *exactly* like Robert Redford.' Connie was back with the drinks. A tequila sunrise for herself, a white wine for Mary Ann.

'Warts?' asked Mary Ann, taking the wine.

'What?'

'That guy. Does he have warts. Robert Redford has warts.'

'That's sick. Look . . . I feel like a little heavy bumping. Wanna hit the disco?'

'I think I'll just . . . soak it in for a while. You go ahead.'

'You sure now?'

'Yeah. Thanks. I'll be OK.'

'Suit yourself, hon.'

Seconds after Connie had disappeared into the disco, a long-haired man in a Greek peasant shirt sat down next to Mary Ann on the sofa. 'Mind if I join you?'

'Sure . . . I mean no.'

'You're not into boogying, huh?'

'Well, not right now.'

'You're into head trips, then?'

'I don't know exactly what . . .'

'What sign are you?'

She wanted to say, 'Do Not Disturb.' She said, 'What sign do you think I am?'

'Ah . . . you're into games. OK . . . I'd say you're a Taurus.'

He rattled her. 'All right . . . How did you do it?'

'Easy. Taureans are stubborn as hell. They *never* want to tell you what sign they are.' He leaned over close enough for Mary Ann to smell his musk oil, and looked directly into her eyes. 'But underneath that tough Taurus hide beats the heart of a hopeless romantic.'

Mary Ann moved away slightly.

'Well?' said the man.

'Well, what?'

'You're a romantic, right? You like earth colors and foggy nights and Lina Wertmuller movies and lemon candles burning when you make love.' He reached for her hand. She flinched. 'It's all right,' he said calmly. 'I'm not making a pass yet. I just wanna look at your heart line.'

He ran his forefinger gently across Mary Ann's palm. 'Look at your point of insertion,' he said. 'Right there between Jupiter and Saturn.'

'What does that mean?' Mary Ann looked down at his finger. It was resting between her middle finger and forefinger. 'It means that you're a very sensual person,' said the man. He began to slide the finger in and out. 'That's true, isn't it? You're a very sensual person?'

'Well, I . . .'

'Do you know you look exactly like Jennifer O'Neill?'

Mary Ann stood up suddenly. 'No, but if you hum a few bars . . .'

'Hey, hey, lady. It's cool, it's cool. I'll give you space . . .'

'Good. I'll take the other room. Happy hunting.' She headed for the disco in search of Connie. She found her in the eye of the storm, bumping with a black man in Lurex knickers and glitter wedgies.

'What's up?' asked the stewardess, boogying to the sidelines.

'I'm beat. Could I have the keys to the apartment?'

'You OK, hon?'

'Fine. I'm just tired.'

'Hot date?'

'No, just . . . could I have the keys, Connie?'

'Here's an extra set. Sweet dreams.'

Boarding the 41 Union bus, Mary Ann realized suddenly why Connie kept an extra set of keys in her purse.

Mary Ann watched *Mary Hartman, Mary Hartman*, then turned off the television and fell asleep.

It was after 2 A.M. when Connie got home.

She wasn't alone.

Mary Ann rolled over on the sofa and buried her head under the covers, pretending to be asleep. Connie and her guest tiptoed noisily into the bedroom.

The man's voice was fuzzy with whiskey, but Mary Ann knew immediately who he was.

He was asking for lemon candles.

Her New Home

Mary Ann crept out of the apartment just before dawn. The prospect of sharing Trix for three at breakfast was more than she could take.

She wandered the streets of the Marina in search of For Rent signs, then ate a mammoth breakfast at the International House of Pancakes.

At nine o'clock she was the first customer of the day at a rental agency on Lombard Street.

She wanted a View, a Deck and a Fireplace for under $175.

'Jees,' said the rental lady. 'Awful picky for a girl without a job.' She offered Mary Ann 'a nice Lower Pacific Heights studio with AEK, wall to wall carpeting and a partial view of Fillmore Auditorium.' Mary Ann said no.

She ended up with three possibles.

The first one had an uptight landlady who asked if Mary Ann 'took marijuana'.

The second was a pink stucco fortress on Upper Market with gold glitter in the ceiling plaster.

The last was on Russian Hill. Mary Ann arrived there at four-thirty.

The house was on Barbary Lane, a narrow, wooded walkway off Leavenworth between Union and Filbert. It was a well-weathered, three-story structure made of brown shingles. It made Mary Ann think of an old bear with bits of foliage caught in its fur. She liked it instantly.

The landlady was a fiftyish woman in a plum-colored kimono.

'I'm Mrs Madrigal,' she said cheerfully. 'As in medieval.'

Mary Ann smiled. 'You can't feel as ancient as I do. I've been apartment-hunting all day.'

'Well, take your time. There's a partial view, if you count that little patch of bay peeping through the trees. Utilities included, of course. Small house. Nice people. You get here this week?'

'That obvious, huh?'

The landlady nodded. 'The look's a dead giveaway. You just can't wait to bite into that lotus.'

'What? I'm sorry . . .'

'Tennyson. You know: "Eating the lotus day by day, To watch the crisping ripples on the beach, And tender curving lines of creamy spray; To lend our hearts and spirits wholly to the influence of" . . . something, something . . . You get the point.'

'Does the . . . furniture go with it?'

'Don't change the subject while I'm quoting Tennyson.'

Mary Ann was shaken until she noticed that the landlady was smiling. 'You'll get used to my babbling,' said Mrs Madrigal. 'All the others have.' She walked to the window, where the wind made her kimono flutter like brilliant plumage. 'The furniture is included. What do you say, dear?'

Mary Ann said yes.

'Good. You're one of us, then. Welcome to 28 Barbary Lane.'

'Thank you.'

'Yes, you should.' Mrs Madrigal smiled. There was something a little careworn about her face, but she was really quite lovely, Mary Ann decided. 'Do you have any objection to pets?' asked the new tenant.

'Dear . . . I have no objection to anything.'

Elated, Mary Ann walked to the corner of Hyde and Unicorn and phoned Connie from the Searchlight Market. 'Hi. Guess what?'

'You got kidnapped?'

'Oh . . . Connie, I'm sorry. I've been looking for a place . . .'

'I was freaked.'

'I'm really sorry. I . . . Connie, I've found this darling place on Russian Hill on the third floor of the funkiest old building . . . and I can move in tomorrow.'

'Oh . . . that was quick.'

'It's so *neat*! I can't wait for you to see it.'

'Sounds nice. Look, Mary Ann – like, if there's any problem with money or anything, you can stay with me until . . .'

'I've got some saved. Thanks, though. You've been wonderful.'

'No sweat. Hey . . . what's on for tonight, hon?'

'Let's see. Oh, yeah. Robert Redford is picking me up at seven, and we're going to Ernie's for dinner.'

'Ditch him. He's got warts.'

'For what?'

'The hottest spot in town. Social Safeway.'

'Social *what*?'

'Safeway, dink. As in supermarket.'

'That's what I thought you said. You sure know how to show a girl a good time.'

'For your information, dink, Social Safeway just happens to be . . . well, it's just the . . . big thing, that's all.'

'For those who get off on groceries.'

'For those who get off on *men*, hon. It's a local tradition. Every Wednesday night. And you don't even have to look like you're on the make.'

'I don't believe it.'

'There's only one way to prove it to you.'

Mary Ann giggled. 'What am I supposed to do? Lurk behind the artichokes until some unsuspecting stockbroker comes along?'

'Meet me here at eight, dink. You'll see.'

Love with the Proper Shopper

A dozen cardboard disks dangled from the ceiling of the Marina Safeway, coaxing the customers with a double-edged message: 'Since we're neighbors, let's be friends.'

And friends were being made.

As Mary Ann watched, a blond man in a Stanford sweatshirt sauntered up to a brunette in a denim halter. 'Uh . . . excuse me, but could you tell me whether it's better to use Saffola oil or Wesson oil?'

The girl giggled. 'For what?'

'I don't believe this,' said Mary Ann, taking a shopping cart. 'Every Wednesday night?'

Connie nodded. 'It ain't half bad on weekends, either.' She grabbed a cart and charged off down a busy aisle. 'See ya. It works better if you're alone.'

Mary Ann strode to the produce counter. She intended to *shop*, Connie's pagan mating ritual notwithstanding.

Then someone tugged on her arm.

He was a puffy-faced man of about thirty-five. He was wearing a leisure suit with a white vinyl belt and matching shoes. 'Are those the things you use in Chinese cooking?' he asked, pointing to the snow peas.

'Yes,' she said, as uninvitingly as possible.

'Far out. I've been looking for some all week. I've really been getting into Chinese cooking lately. Bought a wok and everything.'

'Yeah. Well, those are the ones. Good luck.' She wheeled sharply and headed for the check-out counter. Her assailant followed.

'Hey . . . like, maybe you could tell me a little about Chinese cooking?'

'I doubt it very seriously.'

'C'mon. Most chicks in this town are really into Chinese cooking.'

'I'm not most chicks.'

'OK. I can dig it. Different strokes for different folks, right? What *are* you into, anyway?'

'Solitude.'

'OK. Skip it, just skip it.' He hesitated a moment, then delivered his exit line. 'Get off the rag, bitch!'

He left her standing in the frozen food department, white knuckles clamped around the rim of the freezer, her breath rising like a tiny distress signal. 'Jesus,' she said in a frosty whisper, as a single tear plopped onto a box of Sara Lee brownies.

'Charming,' said a man standing next to her.

Mary Ann stiffened. 'What?'

'Your friend there . . . with the sparkling repartee. He's a real prince.'

'You heard all that?'

'Only the parting endearment. Was the rest any better?'

'Nope. Unless you get off on discussing snow peas with Charlie Manson.'

The man laughed, showing beautiful white teeth. He was about thirty, Mary Ann guessed, with curly brown hair, blue eyes and a soft flannel shirt. 'Sometimes I don't believe this place,' he said.

'Really.' Had he seen her crying?

'The hell of it is that the whole goddamn town talks about relating and communicating and all that Age of Aquarius shit, and most of us are *still* trying to look like something we aren't . . . Sorry. I sound like Dear Abby, don't I?'

'No. Not at all. I . . . agree with you.'

He extended his hand. 'My name is Robert.' Not Bob or Robbie, but Robert. Strong and direct. She gripped his hand. 'I'm Mary Ann Singleton.' She wanted him to remember it.

'Well . . . at the risk of sounding like Charlie Manson . . . how about a little culinary advice for a hapless male?'

'Sure. No snow peas?'

He laughed. 'Not snow peas. Asparagus.'

Mary Ann had never found the subject so exciting. She was watching Robert's eyes respond to her hollandaise recipe when a young man with a mustache approached with his cart.

'Can't leave you alone for a minute.' He was talking to Robert.

Robert chuckled. 'Michael . . . this is Mary Ann . . .'

'Singleton,' said Mary Ann.

'This is my roommate, Michael. She's been helping me with hollandaise, Michael.'

'Good,' said Michael, smiling at Mary Ann. 'He's awful at hollandaise.'

Robert shrugged. 'Michael's the master chef in the house. That entitles him to make life miserable for me.' He grinned at his roommate.

Mary Ann's palms were sweating.

'I'm not much of a cook, either,' she said. Why in the world was she siding with Robert? Robert didn't need her help. Robert didn't know she was there.

'She's been a lot of help,' said Robert. 'That's more than I can say for some people.'

'Temper,' Michael grinned.

'Well,' said Mary Ann feebly. 'I guess I'd better . . . finish up.'

'Thanks for your help,' said Robert. 'Really.'

'Nice to meet you,' said Michael.

'Same here,' said Mary Ann, pushing her cart in the direction of the paper-supplies aisle. When Connie rounded the corner several seconds later, she found her friend standing glumly by herself, squeezing a roll of Charmin.

'Hot damn!' said the stewardess. 'This place is Pickup City tonight!'

Mary Ann threw the toilet paper into her cart. 'I've got a headache, Connie. I think I'll walk home. OK?'

'Well . . . hang on a sec. I'll come with you.'

'Connie, I . . . I'd like to be alone, OK?'

'Sure. OK.'

As usual, she looked hurt.

Connie's Bummer Night

Connie came home from the Marina Safeway an hour after Mary Ann did.

Noisily, she dropped her groceries on the kitchen counter. 'Well,' she said, walking into the living room, 'I'm ready for Union Street. I suppose you're ready for bed?'

Mary Ann nodded. 'Job-hunting and moving tomorrow. I need my strength.'

'Abstinence causes pimples.'

'I'll remember that,' said Mary Ann, as Connie stalked out the door.

*

21

Mary Ann ate dinner in front of the television. She had steak, salad and Tater Tots, the fare that Connie swore by for keeping men happy. She checked out Connie's record collection (The Carpenters, Percy Faith, 101 Strings), then looked at the pictures in *More Joy of Sex*. She fell asleep on the sofa shortly before midnight.

When she awoke, the room was filled with light. A garbage truck rumbled along Greenwich Street. A key chain was clinking against the front door.

Connie lumbered in. 'I cannot *believe* the assholes in this town!'

Mary Ann sat up and rubbed her eyes. 'Bad night, huh?'

'Bad night, bad morning, bad week, bad year. Weirdos! God-dammit, I can pick 'em. If there's a weirdo around for a hundred goddamn miles, good ol' Connie Bradshaw will be there to make a date with him. Fuck!'

'How 'bout some coffee?'

'What's the matter with me, Mary Ann? Will you tell me that? I have two tits, a nice ass. I wash. I'm a *good* listener . . .'

'C'mon. We both need coffee.'

The kitchen was too perversely cheerful for an early-morning soul-baring. Mary Ann winced at the Doris Day yellow walls and the little windowed boxes full of dried beans.

Connie devoured a bowl of Trix. 'I think I'll become a nun,' she said.

'They'll love your outfit at Dance Your Ass Off.'

'Not funny.'

'OK. What happened?'

'You don't wanna know.'

'Yes I do. You went to Union Street, right?'

'Perry's. Then Slater Hawkins. But the *real* bummer was at Thomas Lord's.'

Mary Ann poured her a cup of coffee. 'What happened?'

'Fuck if I know. I was having a perfectly innocent drink at the bar when I noticed this guy sitting over by the fire. I recognized him right away, because him and me did a little number last month on his houseboat in Sausalito.'

'A little number?'

'Fucked.'

'Thank you.'

'So . . . I walked over to where this guy was sitting. Jerry something. A German name. Buckskin pants and a turquoise squash blossom necklace and a pair of those John Denver-type glasses. *Gorgeous*, in a

22

. . . you know . . . Marin kind of way. And I said, "Hi, Jerry, who's keeping the houseboat warm?" and the asshole just stared at me like I was some whore on Market Street or something. I mean, like he didn't even *recognize* me. I was *mortified.*'

'I guess so.'

'So, finally, I said, "Connie Bradshaw from the Friendly Skies of United." Only, I said it in . . . like a really bitchy tone of voice so he'd get the point.'

'But he didn't?'

'Fuck, no! He just sat there looking stuck-up and spaced out. He finally asked me to sit down, and he introduced me to this friend of his named Danny. Then the asshole just got up and walked out, leaving me with this Danny person, who had just finished his goddamn est training and was spouting all this shit about making a space, et cetera.'

'What on earth did you do?'

'What *could* I do? I went home with Danny. I sure as hell wasn't gonna let *him* get up and leave me there munching pretzels all by myself. There's such a thing as pride!'

'Of course.'

'Anyway, Danny had this really neat redwood apartment in Mill Valley, with lots of stained glass and all, but he was an absolute *nut* about ecology. As soon as we smoked a joint, he started babbling about saving whales in Mendocino and screwing up the ozone layer with feminine hygiene spray.'

'*What?*'

'You know. Aerosol can. The fucking ozone layer. Anyway, I was really bent out of shape at that point, and I said I thought it was a woman's unalienable . . . inalienable . . . which is it?'

'Inalienable.'

'Inalienable right to use a feminine hygiene spray if she wanted to, ozone layer or no ozone layer!'

'And . . .'

'And he said that just because I have some *bizarre* notion that my . . . you know . . . smells bad is no reason for me to expose the rest of the world to ultraviolet rays and skin cancer. Or something like that.'

'Well . . . delightful evening.'

'I mean, get *him.* Not only does he subject me to all this ecology crap, but . . . nothing happened.'

'Nothing happened?'

'Nada. Zilch. He drives me all the way across the bridge just to talk. He says he wants to *relate* to me as a person. Ha!'

'So . . . what did you say?'

'I told him to drive me home. And you know what he said?'

Mary Ann shook her head.

'He said, "I'm sorry you sprayed for nothing."'

Later that day, Mary Ann moved out of Connie's apartment into 28 Barbary Lane. The move involved only a suitcase. Connie was visibly depressed.

'You'll still come see me, won't you?'

'Sure. And you'll have to come visit me.'

'Cross your heart?'

'Hope to die.'

Neither one of them believed it.

The Employment Line

On her first morning at Barbary Lane, Mary Ann scanned the Yellow Pages for the key to her future.

According to a large, daisy-bedecked ad, the Metropolitan Employment Agency was 'an individualized job placement service that really cares about your future.'

She liked the sound of it. Solid yet compassionate.

Gulping an Instant Breakfast, she put on her low-key navy-blue suit and caught the 41 Union to Montgomery Street. Her horoscope today promised 'matchless opportunities for a Taurus who takes the bull by the horns.'

The agency was on the fifth floor of a yellow-brick building that smelled of cigars and industrial ammonia. Someone with an eye for contemporary Californiana had decorated the walls of the waiting room with Art Nouveau posters and a driftwood-and-copper sculpture of a seagull in flight.

Mary Ann sat down. There was no one in sight, so she picked up a copy of *Office Management* magazine. She was reading an article about desktop avocado gardening when a woman appeared from a cubicle in the back.

'Have you filled out a form yet?'

'No. I didn't know . . .'

'On the desk. I can't talk to you until you've filled out a form.'

Mary Ann filled out a form. She agonized over the questions. Do you own a car? Will you accept employment outside San Francisco? Do you speak any foreign languages?

She took the form to the woman's cubicle. 'All done,' she said, as cheerfully and efficiently as possible.

The woman grunted. She took the form from Mary Ann and readjusted her chain-guarded glasses on a small, piglike nose. Her hair was done in a salt-and-pepper DA.

As she examined the form, her fingers manipulated an executive desk toy. Four steel balls suspended on strings from a walnut scaffolding.

'No degree,' said the woman at last.

'Like . . . college?'

The woman snapped. 'Yes. Like college.'

'I had two years at a junior college in Ohio, if that . . .'

'Major?'

'Yes.'

'Well?'

'What?'

'What did you *major* in?'

'Oh. Art history.'

The woman smirked. 'We've certainly got enough of *those* for a while.'

'Does a degree really matter that much? I mean . . . for secretarial work?'

'Are you kidding? I've got PhD candidates doing clerical work.' She used the first person as if these struggling scholars were her personal serfs. She wrote something on an index card and handed it to Mary Ann. 'This is a small office-supply company on Market Street. The sales manager needs a Girl Friday. Ask for Mr Creech.'

He turned out to be a red-faced man of about fifty. He was wearing a burgundy polyester jacket with an over-sized hound's-tooth pattern. His trousers and tie were the same color.

'You ever done sales work before?' He smiled and leaned back in a squeaky swivel chair.

'Not . . . well, not exactly. For the past four years I've worked as a secretary for Lassiter Fertilizers in Cleveland. I wasn't exactly *in* sales, but I had a lot of . . . you know . . . contacts and all.'

'Sounds good. Steady work. Always a good sign.'

'I was also an admin assistant for the past year and a half, and I was attached to several of . . .'

'Fine, fine . . . Now, I suppose you know what a Girl Friday is?'

'Sort of a gofer . . . right?' She laughed nervously.

'Pay's good. Six fifty a month. And we're pretty relaxed around here . . . this being San Francisco.' His eyes were fixed on Mary Ann's face. He began to chew the knuckle of his forefinger.

'I like . . . an informal office,' said Mary Ann.

'You like Vegas?'

'Sir?'

'Earl.'

'What?'

'Name's Earl. Informal, remember?' He smiled and wiped his forehead. He was sweating profusely. 'I asked if you like Vegas. We go to Vegas a lot. Vegas, Sacramento, LA, Hawaii. Lotsa fringe benefits.'

'Sounds . . . really nice.'

He winked at her. 'If you're not . . . you know . . . uptight.'

'Oh.'

'Oh, what?'

'I'm uptight, Mr Creech.'

He plucked a paper clip off the desk and tore it apart slowly without looking up. 'Next,' he said quietly.

'Sir?'

'Get out.'

She went home to her new apartment and cried, falling asleep as the afternoon sun spilled in the window. She woke up at five and scoured the kitchen sink for therapy. She ate some blueberry yogurt and made a list of things she would need for her apartment.

She wrote a letter to her parents. Optimistic, but vague.

There was a noise outside her door. She listened for a moment, then opened it. Plum-colored silk fluttered at the tip of the stairway and descended out of sight.

There was a note on Mary Ann's door:

26

Something from my garden to welcome you to your new home.
          Anna Madrigal
P.S. I'll shoot you if you write your mother about this.

Taped to the note was a neatly rolled joint.

Enter Mona

The woman down by the garbage cans had frizzy red hair and was wearing a country-chic cotton sharecropper's dress.

She dropped her Hefty bag with a disdainful wrinkle of her nose and smiled at Mary Ann. 'Garbage, you know, is *very* revealing. It beats the shit out of tarot cards!'

'What would you say about . . . let's see – four yogurt cartons, a Cost Plus bag, some avocado peels and assorted cellophane wrappings?'

The woman pressed her fingers to her forehead like a psychic. 'Ah, yes . . . the subject takes care of herself . . . nutritionally, that is. She is probably on a diet and is . . . furnishing a new apartment?'

'Uncanny!' Mary Ann smiled. 'She also . . . likes growing things. She didn't throw out the avocado pit, so she's probably rooting it in her kitchen.'

'Bravo!' Mary Ann extended her hand. 'I'm Mary Ann Singleton.'

'I know.'

'From my garbage?'

'From our landlady. The Mother of Us All.' She shook Mary Ann's hand firmly. 'I'm Mona Ramsey . . . right below you.'

'Hi. You should have seen what Mother taped on my door last night.'

'A joint?'

'She told you?'

'Nope. It's standard procedure. We all get one.'

'She grows it in the garden?'

'Right over there behind the azaleas. She's even got names for the plants . . . like Dante and Beatrice and . . . Hey, want some ginseng?'

'What?'

'Ginseng. I'm brewing some upstairs. C'mon.'

Mona's second-floor apartment was adorned with Indian wall

27

hangings, assorted street signs, and Art Deco light globes. Her dining table was an industrial cable spool. Her armchair, a converted Victorian toilet.

'I used to have curtains,' she smiled, handing Mary Ann a mug of tea, 'but after a while paisley bedspreads seemed so . . . Sixties Vassar.' She shrugged. 'Besides . . . like . . . who am I hiding my body from?'

Mary Ann peeped out of the window. 'What about that building over . . .'

'No . . . I mean . . . you know . . . *nobody's* really hiding anything from the Cosmos. Beneath the rays of the White Healing Light, we are all . . . like . . . capital *N* Naked. Who gives a shit about the little *n*?'

'This tea is really . . .'

'Why do you want to be a secretary?'

'How did you know?'

'Big Mother. Mrs Madrigal.'

Mary Ann couldn't hide her irritation. 'She gets the news out quick enough, doesn't she?'

'She likes you.'

'She told you that?'

Mona nodded. 'Don't you like her?'

'Well . . . yes . . . I mean, I haven't really known her long enough to . . .'

'She thinks you think she's weird.'

'Oh, great. Instant rapport.'

'*Do* you think she's weird?'

'Mona, I . . . yeah, I guess I do,' she smiled. 'Maybe it's my fault. We don't have people like that in Cleveland.'

'Maybe so.'

'She wants you in the family, Mary Ann. Give it a chance, OK?'

Mona's condescension irked Mary Ann. 'There's no problem here.'

'No. Not now.'

Mary Ann sipped the weird-tasting tea in silence.

The best news of the day came minutes later. Mona was a copywriter for Halcyon Communications, a well-respected Jackson Square ad agency.

Edgar Halcyon, chairman of the board, needed a woman to replace the personal secretary who had 'gotten pregnant on him.'

Mona arranged an interview for Mary Ann.

'You're not planning to run back to Cleveland, are you?'

'Sir?'

'You're staying put?'

'Yes, sir. I love San Francisco.'

'They all say that.'

'In my case, it happens to be the truth.'

Halcyon's huge white eyebrows leaped. 'Are you that sassy with your parents, young lady?'

Mary Ann deadpanned. 'Why do you think I can't go back to Cleveland?'

It was risky, but it worked. Halcyon threw back his head and roared. 'OK,' he said, regaining his composure. 'That was it.'

'Sir?'

'That's the last time you'll see me laugh like that. Go get some rest. Tomorrow you'll be working for the biggest son-of-a-bitch in town.'

Mrs Madrigal was weeding the garden when Mary Ann returned to Barbary Lane.

'You got it, didn't you?'

Mary Ann nodded. 'Mona call you?'

'Nope. I just knew you would. You always get what you want.'

Mary Ann smiled and shrugged. 'Thanks, I think.'

'You're a lot like me, dear . . . whether you know it or not.'

Mary Ann headed for the front door, then stopped and turned around. 'Mrs Madrigal?'

'Yes?'

'I . . . Thank you for the joint.'

'You're welcome, dear. I think you'll like Beatrice.'

'It was nice of you to . . .'

The landlady dismissed her with a wave of her hand. 'Go say your prayers or something. You're a working girl now.'

The Ad Game

Halcyon Communications had been a food-processing warehouse in an earlier incarnation. Now its mellow brick walls blazed with supergraphics and rental art. Matrons shopping for Louis Quinze

29

bargains in Jackson Square often mistook its secretaries for top fashion models.

Mary Ann liked that.

What she didn't particularly like was her job.

'Is the flag out, Mary Ann?'

That was Halcyon's first question of the morning. Every morning.

'Yes, sir.' She felt less like Lauren Hutton every second. Who would make Lauren Hutton raise the American flag before nine o'clock in the morning?

'Are we out of coffee?'

'I set it up for you in the conference room.'

'Why in God's name would . . . Oh, Christ . . . Adorable's here?'

Mary Ann nodded. 'Nine o'clock conference.'

'Goddammit. Tell Beauchamp to hustle his butt up here on the double.'

'I've already checked, sir. He's not in yet.'

'Christ!'

'I could check with Mildred, if you want. Sometimes he has coffee down in Production.'

'Do it.'

Mary Ann did it, feeling vaguely like a fifth-grader who had snitched on a classmate. She *liked* Beauchamp Day, actually, despite his irresponsibility. She may have even liked him *for* his irresponsibility.

Beauchamp was Edgar Halcyon's son-in-law, the husband of post-post-debutante DeDe Halcyon. A graduate of Groton and Stanford, the handsome young Bostonian had been a natural for the Bachelors when he moved to San Francisco as a Bank of America trainee in 1971.

According to the social columns, he had met his wife-to-be at the 1973 Spinsters Ball. Within months, he was savoring the delights of pool parties in Atherton, brunch on Belvedere and ski treks in Tahoe.

The Halcyon-Day courtship had been whirlwind. DeDe and Beauchamp were married in June 1973 on the sunlit slopes of Halcyon Hill, the bride's family estate in Hillsborough. At her own insistence, the bride was barefoot. She wore a peasant dress by Adolfo of Saks Fifth Avenue. Her maid of honor and Bennington roommate, Muffy Van Wyck, recited selections from Kahlil Gibran, while a string quartet played the theme from *Elvira Madigan*.

After the wedding, the bride's mother, Frannie Halcyon, told reporters: 'We're so proud of our DeDe. She's always been *such* an individualist.'

Beauchamp and DeDe moved into a fashionable Art Deco penthouse on Telegraph Hill. They entertained lavishly and were frequently seen at philanthropic extravaganzas . . . by almost everyone, it seemed, but Mary Ann Singleton.

Mary Ann had chatted with DeDe once at an inter-agency softball game (Halcyon vs Hoefer Dieterich & Brown). Mrs Day didn't strike the secretary as snobby, but Mary Ann concluded that a Dina Merrill hairdo looks *ridiculous* on a twenty-six-year-old.

Beauchamp, on the other hand, had looked magnificent that afternoon, transforming the pitcher's mound into a mini-Olympus.

Blue eyes, black hair, brown arms glistening under a faded green Lacoste . . .

She was right. He was drinking coffee in Production.

'His Majesty requests your presence in the royal chambers.' She didn't hesitate to use that kind of irreverence with Beauchamp. She was sure he was a kindred spirit.

'Tell him the Bastard Prince is on his way.'

Within seconds, Beauchamp was standing next to her desk, flashing his self-assured post-preppie grin. 'Don't tell me. I screwed up the Adorable account, right?'

'Not yet. There's a conference at nine. He was nervous, that's all.'

'He's always nervous. I didn't forget.'

'I know you didn't.'

'You think I'm OK, don't you?'

'As an account executive?'

'As anything?'

'Not fair. Want a Dynamint?'

Beauchamp shook his head and slumped into a Barcelona chair. 'He's a real fart, isn't he?'

'Beauchamp . . .'

'How about lunch tomorrow?'

'I think he's booked.'

'Not him. You. Will he let you out of your cage for an hour?'

'Oh . . . sure. Dutch?'

'Italian.'

Mary Ann giggled, then jumped as Halcyon buzzed her. 'I'm ready for him,' said her boss.

Beauchamp rose, winking at Mary Ann. 'Well, it ain't bloody mutual.'

31

Edgar Blows Up

Edgar glared at his son-in-law, wondering how anyone so well-groomed, articulate and generally *presentable* could be such a royal pain in the ass.

'I think you know what this is about.'

Beauchamp leaned forward and brushed a speck of dust off his Guccis. 'Yeah, the pantyhose bitch. I think we might as well forget about the Bicentennial angle.'

'I'm talking about DeDe and you know it!'

'I do, huh?'

Edgar's eyes narrowed. His fist tightened around the neck of a mahogany decoy Frannie had bought him at Abercrombie's. 'Where were you last night, Beauchamp?'

Silence.

'I don't get a big bang out of this you know. It doesn't thrill me to remember that my own daughter called me up last night, crying her eyes out . . .'

'Frankly, I don't see what business this . . .'

'Goddammit! Frannie spent two hours on the phone with DeDe, trying to calm her down. What the hell time did you get in last night, anyway?'

'Why don't you ask DeDe? I'm sure she wrote it in the log!'

Edgar spun his chair around and faced the wall. He studied a hunt print and tried to calm himself. He spoke quietly, deliberately, knowing that tone implied the greatest menace.

'One more time, Beauchamp. Where were you?'

The answer was addressed to the back of his head. 'I had a committee meeting at the club.'

'Which club?'

'University. Not *quite* as grand as PU, but Nob Hill nonethe . . .'

'You were there till midnight?'

'We had a few drinks afterwards.'

'We? You and some chippie from Ruffles?'

'That's Ripples. And I didn't pick up any . . . what's that quaint word? I was at the club. Ask Peter Cipriani. He was there.'

'I'm not running a detective agency.'

'You could have fooled me. Is that all?'

Edgar massaged his forehead with his fingertips. He didn't turn around. 'We have a conference.'

'Right,' said Beauchamp, leaving.

Promptly at noon, Mary Ann headed for the Royal Exchange with Mona.

'Shit,' groaned the copywriter over a Pimm's Cup. 'I am *so* spaced today.'

Not surprising, thought Mary Ann. Mona was *paid* to be spaced. She was the resident freak at Halcyon Communications. Clients who weren't immediately impressed with her creativity changed their minds when they saw her office: an assortment of hookah pipes, an oak icebox which served as a bar, an antique wheelchair, a collage of *Playgirl* beefcake photos, and a neon martini glass from a Tenderloin bar.

'What's the matter?' asked Mary Ann.

'I did mescaline last night.'

'Oh?'

'We went to Mission Street and tripped through all those godawful tacky furniture stores with the tasseled lampshades and round beds and . . . you know . . . those phony waterfall things in the glass tubes. It was so *plastic*, but . . . you know . . . like *cosmic* plasticity . . . and in a weird way it was sort of, like, spiritual, you know.'

Mary Ann did *not* know. She avoided the issue by ordering a turkey sandwich and a bean salad. Mona ordered another Pimm's cup.

'Guess what?'

'Yeah?'

'I'm going to dinner at Mrs Madrigal's tonight.'

'Congratulations. She likes you.'

'You already told me that.'

'Well . . . then she trusts you.'

'Why do I have to be trusted?'

'Nothing . . . I just meant . . .'

'How should I handle it, Mona?'

'Handle what?'

'Her. I don't know . . . I feel like she *expects* something of me.'

'Bourgeois paranoia.'

'I know . . . but you're really close to her, and I thought you might be able to tell me . . . you know . . . her quirks.'

33

'She's decent. That's her quirk. She also makes a fabulous rack of lamb.'

Mona left work at four o'clock, deliberately skirting Mary Ann's alcove near the elevator. When she got home, she found Mrs Madrigal in the garden.

The landlady was wearing plaid slacks, a paint-smeared smock and a straw hat. Her face was ruddy from exertion. 'Well . . . home so early from the fields, dear?'

'Yeah.'

'Just so many things you can say about pantyhose, eh?'

Mona smiled. 'I wanted to tell you something. It's no big deal, really.'

'Fine.'

'Mary Ann's been asking about you.'

'Have you told her anything?'

'I figure that's *your* business.'

'You think she's too green, don't you?'

Mona nodded. 'Right now, yeah.'

'We're having dinner tonight.'

'She told me. That's why . . . well, I didn't want you to be embarrassed, that's all.'

'Thank you, dear.'

'I should mind my own business, shouldn't I?'

'No. I appreciate your concern. Would you like to come tonight?'

'No, I . . . no, thank you.'

'You're very special to me, dear.'

'Thank you, Mrs Madrigal.'

Anguish in Bohemia

After work, Edgar swilled a double scotch at the Bohemia Club.

The rules of a well-ordered life were never enough when other people refused to obey them. Beauchamp was only one of many.

The Cartoon Room was crowded. Edgar sat alone in the Domino Room, preferring silence. The dread had begun to grow again.

He rose and went to the telephone. His hands grew slippery around the receiver.

The maid answered.

'Halcyon Hill.'

'Emma . . . is Mrs Halcyon available?'

'Just a moment, Mr Halcyon.'

Frannie's mouth was full. 'Uhhmm . . . darling . . . marvelous cheese puffs I doggy-bagged from Cyril's party! And Emma's whipped up a divine *blanquette de veau*! When are you coming home?'

'I have to pass tonight, Frannie.'

'Edgar! Not those damn pantyhose again?'

'No. I'm at the club. There's a . . . committee meeting.'

Silence.

'Frannie?'

'What?' She was icy.

'I have to do these things. You know that.'

'We do what we *want*, Edgar.'

Blood rushed to his face. 'All right, then, goddammit! I *want* to go to this meeting! That make you happy?'

Frannie hung up.

He stood there, holding the phone, then put it down and mopped his face with a handkerchief. He took several deep breaths. He reached for the directory and looked up Ruby Miller's phone number.

He dialed.

'Evening. Ruby here.' She sounded more grandmotherly than ever.

'Edgar Halcyon, Mrs Miller.'

'Oh . . . how nice to hear your voice. Gracious, it's been a long time.'

'Yes . . . you know . . . business.'

'Yes! Busy, busy.'

His brow was drenched again. 'Can I see you tonight, Mrs Miller? I know it isn't much notice.'

'Oh . . . well, just a minute, Mr Halcyon. Let me check my book.' She left the phone. Edgar could hear her rummaging around. 'All right,' she said at last. 'Eight o'clock, OK?'

'Thank you so much.'

'Not at all, Mr Halcyon.'

He felt much better now. Ruby Miller meant hope to him, however vague. He decided to have a drink at the bar in the Cartoon Room.

35

'Edgar, you old bastard, why aren't you home pruning the rosebuds?'

It was Roger Manigault, senior vice president of Pacific Excelsior. The Manigault tennis courts bordered on the Halcyon apple orchard in Hillsborough.

Edgar smiled. 'Past *your* bedtime, too, Booter.' The nickname was a hangover from Stanford days, when Manigault had been beatified on the gridiron. Nothing since then had pleased him.

He was currently angered by the demise of the Stanford Indian.

'Everybody's so goddamn *sensitive* nowadays! Indians aren't Indians anymore . . . oh, no! They're Native Americans. I spent ten years learning to say "Negroes" right, and now they've turned into Blacks. Goddammit, I don't know *what* to call the maid anymore!'

Edgar took a slug of drink and nodded. He had heard it all before.

'Now, you take the word "gay", Edgar. That used to be a perfectly normal word that meant something wholesome and *fun*, goddammit! Jesus God! Look at it now!' He polished off his scotch and slammed the glass down. 'A decent young couple is almost embarrassed to mention they've been to the Gaieties!'

'Good point,' said Edgar.

'Damn right! Say . . . speaking of that, Roger and Suzie say they bumped into Beauchamp and DeDe at the Gaieties. Beauchamp's a damn good dancer, Suzie says . . . hustling or whatever they call it.'

Hustling is probably the word, Edgar thought. He had wondered about Beauchamp and Suzie on several occasions. 'Excuse me, Booter. I promised Frannie I'd be home early tonight.'

For the lies she required, Ruby Miller might as well have been Edgar's mistress.

Up the hill at the University Club, Beauchamp sought solace from Peter Cipriani, heir to a fabled San Mateo flower fortune.

'I'm getting paranoid, I guess.'

'The Old Man again?'

'Yeah. He put the screws to me about DeDe.'

'He's suspicious?'

'Always.'

'What does DeDe think?'

'You're assuming she knows how to.'

'She's a tad thick, but she *does* pay for your Wilkes Bashford addiction . . . and she's got a nice box.'

Beauchamp frowned.

'At the *opera*, Beauchamp.'

'Very funny.'

'I thought so.'

'I didn't come here to talk about my wife, Peter.'

'Hmm . . . that's funny. Everybody else did.'

Silence.

'Sorry. Cheap shot. Wanna hear about the Bachelors Ball?'

'Do I look like I do?'

'Well, we missed you, anyway. Actually, we missed your Navy dress whites. They were always just the right touch. Very Gilbert and Sullivan.'

'Thank you.'

'The Prune Prince wore his great-uncle's opera tails this year.'

'John Stonecypher?'

'The one. Are you ready for this? He spilled a bottle of amyl in the breast pocket.'

'C'mon!'

'*While* he was dancing with Madge!'

'What did she do?'

'Oh . . . she just kept waltzing around like a Cotillion deb, presumably pretending that all her dance partners smell like dirty sweat socks . . . You're going to her do tonight, aren't you?'

'Shit!'

'Forgot, huh?'

'DeDe will shit a brick!' He downed his drink. 'I'm off.'

'More than likely,' said Peter.

The Wrath of DeDe

DeDe was sitting at her Louis Quinze *escritoire* making notations in her Louis Vuitton checkbook.

'You forgot about Marge's party, didn't you?'

'I hauled ass to get here.'

'It starts in half an hour.'

'Then we'll be late. Pull in your claws. Your old man's been bitching at me all day.'

'Did you make the Adorable presentation?'

37

'No. He did.'

'Why?'

'Why don't *you* tell me?'

'I don't know what you're talking about.'

'He was pissed, DeDe. Royally.'

Silence.

'You know why, of course.'

DeDe looked down at her checkbook.

Beauchamp persisted. 'He was pissed because his darling daughter called him up last night and told him I was a son-of-a-bitch.'

'I didn't do anything of . . .'

'Bullshit!'

'I was worried, Beauchamp. It was after midnight. I tried the club and Sam's and Jack's. I . . . panicked. I thought Daddy might know where you were.'

'Of course. Little Beauchamp doesn't make a fucking *move* without checking with the Great White Father!'

'Don't talk about Daddy like that.'

'Oh . . . fuck him! I don't need his permission to breathe. I don't need him for a goddamn thing!'

'Oh? Daddy would be interested to hear that.'

Silence.

'Why don't we call him up and tell him?'

'DeDe . . .'

'Me or you?'

'DeDe . . . I'm sorry. I'm tired. It's been a bitch of a day.'

'I'll bet.' She moved to the hall mirror and made last minute adjustments to her makeup. 'How's Little Miss Whatshername?'

'Who?'

'Daddy's secretary. Your little . . . afterwork amusement?'

'You've gotta be kidding?'

'No. I don't think so.'

'Mary Ann Singleton.'

'Is that her name? How quaint.'

'Christ! I hardly know her.'

'Apparently that hasn't stopped you before.'

'She's your father's secretary!'

'And she's not exactly an eyesore.'

'I can't help that, can I?'

DeDe pursed her lips to blot her lipstick. She looked at her husband. 'Look . . . I've had it with this. You dropped off the face of the earth last night.'

'I told you. I was at the club.'

'Well, *quelle coincidence*! You were at the club when you stood me up for the reception at the de Young last Wednesday *and* last Friday when we missed the Telfairs' party at *Beach Blanket Babylon.*'

'We've seen it five times.'

'That isn't the point.'

Beauchamp laughed bitterly. 'You are too much. You really are . . . Where in God's name did you dig *this* one up?'

'I've got eyes, Beauchamp.'

'Where? When?'

'Last week. I was shopping with Binky at La Remise de Soleil.'

'How very chic of you.'

'You were crossing the street with her.'

'Mary Ann.'

'Yes.'

'That *is* incriminating.'

'It was lunchtime, and you were looking *very* chummy.'

'You missed the good part. You should have been there earlier when I ravaged her in the redwood grove behind the Transamerica Pyramid.'

'You're not gonna smartass your way out of this one, Beauchamp.'

'I'm not even trying.' He snatched the keys to the Porsche from the hall table. 'I stopped with you a long time ago.'

'Tell me,' said DeDe, following him out the door.

The Landlady's Dinner

Mary Ann stopped by Mona's on her way to Mrs Madrigal's for dinner.

'Wanna mellow out?' asked Mona.

'It depends.'

'Coke.'

'I'm on a diet. Have you got a Tab or Fresca?'

'I don't *believe* you.' Mona placed a hand mirror on her cable spool table. 'Even *you* must have seen *Porgy and Bess?*'

'So?' Mary Ann's voice cracked. Mona was spading white powder from a vial with a tiny silver spoon. The handle of the spoon was engraved with an ecology emblem.

39

'Sportin' Life,' said Mona. 'Happy Dust. This stuff is an American institution.' She made a line of powder across the surface of the mirror. 'All the silent film stars snorted. Why do you think they looked like this?' She moved her head and arms spastically, like Charlie Chaplin.

'And now,' she continued, 'all we need is a common, ordinary, all-purpose food stamp.' She flourished a ten-dollar food stamp like a magician, presenting both sides for Mary Ann's examination.

'Do you get food stamps?' asked Mary Ann. She makes four times what I do, thought the secretary.

Mona didn't answer, absorbed in the operation. She rolled the food stamp into a little tube and stuck it in her left nostril. 'Stunning, eh? Very sexy!'

She went after the powder, like an anteater on the rampage. Mary Ann was horrified. 'Mona, is that . . .'

'It's your turn.'

'No, thank you.'

'Aw . . . go ahead. It's good for social occasions.'

'I'm nervous enough as it is.'

'It doesn't make you *nervous*, dearheart. It . . .'

Mary Ann stood up. 'I have to go, Mona. I'm late.'

'God!'

'What?'

'You make me feel like such . . . an addict.'

Mrs Madrigal looked almost elegant in black satin pajamas and a matching cloche.

'Ah, Mary Ann. I'm grinding the gazpacho. Help yourself to the hors d'oeuvres. I'll be right back in two shakes of a lamb's tail.'

The 'hors d'oeuvres' were arranged symmetrically on two plates. One held several stuffed mushrooms. The other, half a dozen joints.

Mary Ann chose a mushroom and gave the apartment a once-over.

Two rather gross marble statues flanked the fireplace: a boy with a thorn in his foot and a woman holding a jug. Silk fringes dangled everywhere, from lampshades, coverlets, curtains and valances, even from the archway that led to the hall. The only photograph was a picture of the 1915 Panama-Pacific Exposition.

'Well, what do you think of my little bordello?' Mrs Madrigal was posing dramatically under the archway.

'It's . . . very nice.'

'Don't be ridiculous. It's depraved!'

Mary Ann laughed. 'You planned it that way?'

'Of course. Help yourself to a joint, dear, and *don't* bother to pass it around. I *loathe* that soggy communal business! I mean . . . if you're going to be degenerate, you might as well be a lady about it, don't you think?'

There were two other guests. One was a fiftyish, red-bearded North Beach poet named Joaquin Schwartz. ('A dear man,' Mrs Madrigal confided to Mary Ann, 'but I *wish* he'd learn to use capital letters.') The other was a woman named Laurel who worked at the Haight-Ashbury Free Clinic. She didn't shave under her arms.

Joaquin and Laurel spent dinner discussing their favorite years. Joaquin believed in 1957. Laurel felt 1967 was where it was at . . . or where it *had* been at.

'We could have kept it going,' she said. 'I mean, it had a life of its own, didn't it? We shared *everything* . . . the acid, the music, the sex, the Avalon, the Family Dog, the Human Be-In. There were fourteen freaks in that flat on Oak Street, fourteen freaks and six sleeping bags. It was fucking beautiful, because it was . . . was, like, history. *We* were history. We were the fucking cover of *Time* magazine, man!'

Mrs Madrigal was polite. 'What do you think happened, dear?'

'They killed it. Not the Pigs. The Media.'

'Killed what?'

'Nineteen sixty-seven.'

'I see.'

'Nixon, Watergate, Patty Fucking Hearst, the Bicentennial. The Media got bored with 1967, so they zapped it. It could have survived for a while. Some of it escaped to Mendocino . . . but the Media found out about it and killed it all over again. Jesus . . . I mean, what's left? There's not a single fucking place where it's still 1967!'

Mrs Madrigal winked at Mary Ann. 'You're being awfully quiet.'

'I'm not sure I . . .'

'What's *your* favorite year?'

'I don't think I have one.'

'Mine's 1987,' said Mrs Madrigal. 'I'll be sixty-five or so . . . I can collect social security and stash away enough to buy a small Greek island.' She twirled a lock of hair around her forefinger and smiled faintly. 'Actually, I'd settle for a small Greek.'

*

41

After dinner, on the way to the bathroom, Mary Ann lingered in the landlady's bedroom. There was a photograph on the dresser in a silver frame.

A young man, a soldier, standing beside a 1940s car. He was quite handsome, if a little awkward in his uniform.

'So you see, the old dame does have a past.'

Mrs Madrigal was standing in the doorway.

'Oh . . . I'm prying, aren't I?'

Mrs Madrigal smiled. 'I hope it means we're friends.'

'I . . .' Mary Ann turned back to the photograph, embarrassed. 'He's very good-looking. Is that Mr Madrigal?'

The landlady shook her head. 'There's never been a Mr Madrigal.'

'I see.'

'No you don't. How could you? Madrigal is . . . an assumed name, as they say in the gangster movies. I cleaned up my act about a dozen years back, and the old name was the first to go.'

'What was it?'

'Don't be naughty. If I'd wanted you to know it, I wouldn't have changed it.'

'But . . .'

'Why the Mrs?'

'Yes.'

'Widows and divorcees don't get . . . what's Mona's word? . . . hassled. We don't get hassled as much as single girls. You must have figured that out by now.'

'Who's hassled? I haven't had so much as an obscene phone call since I moved to San Francisco. I could use a little hassling, frankly.'

'The town is full of charming young men.'

'To each other.'

Mrs Madrigal chuckled. 'There's a lot of that going around.'

'You make it sound like the flu. I think it's terribly depressing.'

'Nonsense. Take it as a challenge. When a woman triumphs in this town, she *really* triumphs. You'll do all right, dear. Give it time.'

'You think?'

'I *know*.' The landlady winked and put her arm across Mary Ann's shoulder. 'C'mon, let's go join those *tedious* people.'

Rendezvous with Ruby

Ruby Miller's house was on Ortega Street in the Sunset district, a green stucco bungalow with a manicured lawn and a bowl of plastic roses in the picture window. A Rambler parked in the driveway bore a bumper sticker that said: HONK IF YOU LOVE JESUS.

Edgar parked the Mercedes across the street. He was locking the doors when he saw Mrs Miller waving from the window.

He returned the wave. Christ! He felt like a shoe salesman coming home to the wife.

Mrs Miller turned on the porch light, took off her apron and fussed with a strand of gray hair. 'You're a sight for sore eyes, you are! I'm a mess . . . I didn't plan . . .'

'I'm sorry. I hope it's not too much trouble.'

'Don't be silly. I'm tickled to death.' She gave his hand a pat and led him into the house. 'Ernie . . . look who's here!'

Her husband was seated in front of the television set in a Danish Modern chair. His arms were the shape and color of provolone cheese.

'Hiya, Mr Halcyon.' He didn't get up. He was engrossed in the box before him.

'How's everything, Ernie?'

'Bob Barker just reunited a Marine with his loved one.'

'I'm sorry . . .'

'*Truth or Consequences.* They brought this Marine back from Okinawa and reunited him with his fiancée. She was dressed up like a frog. They made him kiss her . . . blindfolded.'

Mrs Miller took Edgar's arm. 'Isn't that sweet? You don't watch much TV, I guess.'

'No. I'm afraid not.'

'Well, enough chitchat. Let's get to work. Something to eat first. Hi-C, maybe? Fritos?'

'I'm fine, thank you.' At the last minute, out of nervousness, he had gorged himself on chicken livers at the club. 'I'm ready whenever you are.'

'Then let's you and me go out to the garage. Ernie, don't you play the TV too loud, hear?' Her husband grunted his reply.

Mrs Miller led Edgar through the kitchen. 'That Ernie and his TV! I guess it relaxes him . . . and it's much more Christian than the movies these days, what with . . . you know . . . all that nasty stuff . . .'

'Mmm,' he said vaguely, trying to sound polite but disinterested. Mrs Miller could slip into a monologue with all the precision of a New York cabby or an Italian barber. Edgar didn't want to spend this session hearing about Smut in the Cinema.

In the semidarkness of the garage, she went about her business. She cleared muddy garden tools off the pingpong table and removed a couple of candle stubs from an old MJB can. Humming softly to herself, she donned the familiar purple velveteen robe.

'Have you noticed any changes?'

'In the garage?'

Mrs Miller chuckled. 'In *you*. This is your fifth visit. You should be feeling . . . changes.'

'I'm not sure. I may . . .'

'Don't force it. It will come.'

'I wish I shared your confidence.'

'*Faith*, Mr Halcyon.'

'Yes.'

'Faith is different than confidence.'

She was beginning to irritate him. 'Mrs Miller . . . my wife is expecting me home shortly. Could we . . .'

'Of course.' She was all business now. She brushed some imaginary lint off the front of her robe and kneaded her fingers for a moment. 'Assume the posture, please.'

Edgar loosened his tie and climbed on to the pingpong table. He lay down on his back. Mrs Miller lit a candle and placed it on the table near Edgar's head.

'Mr Halcyon?'

'Yes?'

'Forgive me, but . . . well, I was wondering if . . . You mentioned Mrs Halcyon. I was wondering if you told her.'

'No.'

'I know you don't like to talk about it . . . but sometimes it helps if a loved one joins in and . . .'

'My family is Catholic, Mrs Miller.'

She was visibly jarred. 'Oh . . . I'm sorry.'

'That's all right.' He waved it away.

'I didn't mean I was sorry you're Catholic. I mean . . .'

'I know, Mrs Miller.'

'Jesus loves Catholics too.'

'Yes.'

She pressed her fingertips against Edgar's temples and made small circular strokes. 'Jesus will help heal you, Mr Halcyon, but you must believe in Him. You must become a little child again and seek refuge in His bosom.'

A motorcycle roared down Ortega Street, spluttering blasphemously, as Ruby Miller began the incantation that Edgar Halcyon now knew by heart.

'Heal him, Jesus! Heal thy servant Edgar. Heal his failing kidneys and make him whole again. Heal him, Jesus! Heal thy servant . . .'

The Boy Next Door

Mary Ann left Mrs Madrigal's just after ten o'clock. Back at her own apartment, she put her feet up, sipped a Tab and checked her mail.

There was a short gloomy note from her mother, a Contemporary Card from Connie implying desertion, and a box containing her Scenic San Francisco checks from Hibernia Bank.

The personalized message on her checks was 'Have a Nice Day'.

Despite her pathetic income, the choice of a bank had somehow seemed crucial to the establishment of her identity in the city.

In the beginning, she had wavered between the Chartered Bank of London and Wells Fargo. The former had a wonderfully classy name and a fireplace in the lobby, but only one branch in the entire city. The latter had a nice Western ring to it and lots of branches.

But she had never considered Dale Robertson all *that* cute.

In the end, she had gone with Hibernia.

Their jingle promised they would remember your name.

Someone rapped on her door.

It was Brian Hawkins, who lived across the hall. He was a waiter at Perry's and they had chatted briefly only once or twice before. His hours were extremely irregular.

'Hi,' he said. 'Mrs Madrigal just called.'

'Yeah?'

'What is it? Furniture?'

'I'm sorry, Brian. I don't . . .'

'She said you needed help with something.'

'I can't imagine what . . .' The light dawned. Mary Ann laughed, shaking her head, taking stock once more of Brian's chestnut curls and green eyes. Mrs Madrigal was pushy, but her taste wasn't bad.

Brian looked vaguely irked. 'You wanna let me in on it.'

'I think Mrs Madrigal is matchmaking.'

'You *don't* need furniture moved?'

'It's kind of embarrassing. I . . . well, I just finished telling her there weren't enough straight men in San Francisco.'

He brightened. 'Yeah. Ain't it great?'

'Oh, Brian . . . I'm sorry. I thought you . . .'

'Relax, will ya? I'm straight as they come. I just don't like *competition*.'

He invited her over for a nightcap. His tiny kitchen was decorated with empty Chianti bottles and Sierra Club posters. The carcass of a neglected piggybank plant hung grimly from a pot on the window sill.

'I love your stove,' said Mary Ann.

'Funky, huh? Anywhere else it's called squalor. Here we pass it off as Old World charm.'

'Did it come with the apartment?'

'Are you kidding? The stereo and the incline board are mine. The rest belongs to Dragon Lady.'

'Mrs Madrigal?'

He nodded, looking her over. 'She's trying to fix us up, huh?' His smile was approaching a leer.

Mary Ann chose not to deal with it. 'She's a little strange, but I think she means well.'

'Sure.'

'Has she always had this place?'

He shook his head. 'I think she used to run a bookstore in North Beach.'

'Is she from here?'

'Nobody's *from* here.' He refilled her glass with Almadén Pinot Noir. 'You're from Cleveland, aren't you?'

'Yeah. How did you know.'

'Mona told me.' The green eyes were burning into her.

She looked down at her glass. 'Well, no secrets at *all*.'

46

'Don't count on it.'

'What?'

'We've *all* got secrets in this town. You just have to dig a little deeper for them.'

He's being mysterious, she thought, because he thinks it's sexy. She decided it was time to leave.

'Well,' she said, rising. 'Work tomorrow. Thanks for the wine . . . and the tour.'

'Anytime.'

She was sure he meant exactly that.

The Matriarch

When Edgar got home at eleven-fifteen, it was clear that Frannie had been drinking.

'Well, how was the club, darling? You make like a little hooty owl?'

She was perched on the sofa on the sun porch. Her legs were curled up under her Thai silk muumuu. Her wig was askew. She smelled of rum and Trader Vic's Mai Tai Mix.

'Hello, Frannie.'

'Awful long committee meeting.'

'We were planning for the Grove Play.' He tried to sound nonchalant about it, though Frannie was too far gone to appreciate the effort.

'Lotta work, huh?'

'We had a few drinks afterward. You know how those things go.'

Frannie nodded, stifling a hiccup. She certainly knew how those things went.

He changed the subject. 'How about you? You have a fun day?' His tone was that of a kindly father to a small child. What had happened to the debutante who once looked like Veronica Lake?

'I had lunch with Helen and Gladys at that *darling* place on Polk Street . . . The Pavilion. Then I bought a ceramic duck. *Precious.* Maybe it's a goose. I think it's supposed to be for soup, but I thought it would look darling in the den with some ivy or something.'

'Good.'

'Annnd . . . I went to my Opera Guild meeting this afternoon and made the most marvelous discovery. What do you think it is?'

'I don't know.' Christ, how he hated this game!

'C'mon. One eensy-weensy guess.'

'Frannie, I've had a long day . . .'

'Don't you wuv me?'

'For Christ's sake!'

'Oh, all *right*! If you're going to be a grouch about it . . . Guess who's in town?'

'Who?'

Frannie sustained the suspense as long as possible, shifting her torso on the sofa and adjusting her wig. She needs attention, thought Edgar. You haven't been giving it to her.

'The Huxtables,' Frannie said at last.

'The who?'

'Really, Edgar. Nigel Huxtable. The conductor. His wife is Nora Cunningham.'

'It's coming back to me.'

'You slept through their *Aïda*.'

'Yes. Marvelous evening.'

'They're here to do a benefit for Kurt Adler. Practically *nobody* knows they're staying at the Mark . . . and we're going to give a party for them!'

'We are?'

'Aren't you excited?'

'We threw a party last month, Frannie.'

'This is a *coup*, Edgar! The Farnsworths will just *die*. Viola's been gloating for two months over that absurd little barbecue she gave for Baryshnikov.'

'I don't even remember it.'

'Yes you do. She hired those seedy Russian waiters from some place on Clement Street, and they served Russian dressing and Russian tea, and the organist played "Lara's Theme" when Baryshnikov made his entrance. It was too ghastly for words!'

'You just did fairly well.'

'Edgar . . . the Huxtables make Baryshnikov look like . . . Barney Google. I *know* I can get them, darling.'

'Frannie, I just don't think . . .'

'Please . . . I didn't complain when you wouldn't let me have Truman Capote or Giancarlo Giannini.'

Edgar turned away. He couldn't face that Emmett Kelly expression. 'All right. Try and keep the cost down, will you?'

*

Emma warmed up some leftover quiche for him. He ate it in his study, while he scanned the new book he had ordered: *Death as a Fact of Life*.

'Watcha reading, darling?' Frannie was propped against the doorway.

He closed the book. 'Consumer research. Boring.'

'You coming to bed?'

'In a minute, Frannie?'

She was out cold and snoring when he got there.

Stranger in the Park

Edgar spoke to Mary Ann on the intercom. 'I need the Adorable script as soon as possible. I think Beauchamp has a copy.'

'He's out right now, Mr Halcyon.'

'Check with Mona, then.'

'I don't think she . . .'

'Ask her, goddammit! Somebody's got one!'

As soon as Mary Ann was gone, Edgar dialed Jack Kincaid's number.

'Dr Kincaid's office.'

'Is he in?'

'May I tell him who's calling?'

'No, you may not!'

'One moment, please, Mr Halcyon.'

Kincaid's tone was much too jovial. 'Hello, Edgar. How's the pantyhose game?'

'When can you see me?'

'What about?'

'The tests. I want new ones.'

'Edgar, that won't make a damn bit of . . .'

'I'll pay for them, goddammit!'

'Edgar . . .'

'You were wrong about Addison Branch. You told me so yourself.'

'That was different. His symptoms weren't so pronounced.'

'Symptoms can change. It's been three months.'

'Edgar . . . look . . . I'm telling you as a friend. Stop fighting this thing. You're beating your head against a brick wall. You're not being fair to yourself or the people who love you.'

'What the hell has fairness got to do with it?'

'Face it, Edgar. You've got to. Tell your family. Buy yourself a yacht and take Frannie on a cruise around the world. Hell . . . rent a castle in Spain or run off with a whore or keep right on raising hell in Jackson Square . . . but face it! For God's sake . . . no, for *yours* . . . make these next six months count.'

When Mary Ann returned, he was sitting waiting at her desk. 'I'm going out. If anyone wants me, I'm at lunch with a client.'

'Doro's?'

'Never mind where. Just say I'm out.'

He strode out of the building, furious that a contract he had never signed was being carried out anyway.

Tell Frannie? Christ! What kind of mileage could she get out of *that* one in the social columns?

Frances Halcyon, Hillsborough hostess par excellence, scored another triumph Friday night with an intimate little dinner for operatic greats Nora Cunningham and Nigel Huxtable. Frannie, who just saw *A Chorus Line* in New York ('Adored it'), delighted some very well-bred palates with beef roulades and potato puffs. Hubby Edgar (he's the advertising giant) surprised the assembled guests with the announcement of his impending death . . .

He headed away from Jackson Square, up Columbus into the frantic heart of North Beach. Carol Doda's electric nipples winked at him cruelly, flaunting a revolution in which he had never even been an insurgent.

In front of The Garden of Eden, a walleyed derelict bellowed: 'It's all over. It's time to make peace with the Lord. It's time to get right with Jesus!'

He needed a place to clear his head.

And time to do it. Precious time.

He sat down on a bench in Washington Square. Next to him was a woman who was roughly his age. She was wearing wool slacks and a paisley smock. She was reading the Bhagavad Gita.

She smiled.

'Is that the answer?' asked Edgar, nodding at the book.

'What's the question?' asked the woman.

Edgar grinned. 'Gertrude Stein.'

50

'I don't think she said it, do you? No one's *that* clever on a deathbed.'

There it was again.

He felt a surge of recklessness. 'What would *you* say?'

'About what?'

'The end. Your last words. If you could choose.'

The woman studied his face for a moment. Then she said: 'How about . . . "Oh, shit!" '

His laughter was cathartic, an animal yelp that brought tears to his eyes. The woman watched him benignly, detached yet somehow gentle.

It was almost as if she knew.

'Would you like a sandwich?' she asked when he stopped laughing. 'It's made from *focaccia* bread.'

Edgar said yes, delighting in her charity. It was nice to have someone taking care of *him* for once. 'I'm Edgar Halcyon,' he said.

'That's nice,' she said. 'I'm Anna Madrigal.'

Relating at Lunch

Back at the agency, Mary Ann was glossing her lips when Beauchamp approached on little cat feet.

'Has the Blue Meanie gone to lunch yet?'

'Oh . . . Beauchamp . . .' She dropped the lip gloss into a wicker pocketbook she had decoupaged with frogs and mushrooms.

'He's . . . he left over an hour ago. I think he was upset about something.'

'News.'

'This was different.'

'Maybe they asked him to be a wood nymph in the Grove Play.'

'What?'

'Nothing. We've got a lunch date, remember?'

'Oh . . . that's right.'

She had thought of nothing else all morning.

At MacArthur park, they both ordered salads. Mary Ann nibbled hers half-heartedly, put off slightly by the restaurant's caged birds and Urban Organic aloofness. Beauchamp sensed her discomfort.

'You're freaked, aren't you?'

'I . . . how do you mean?'

'You know. This. Us.'

'Why do you say that?'

'Uh uh. You have to answer first.'

She killed time by hunting for a chunk of avocado. 'It's . . . new, I guess.'

'Lunch with a married man?'

She nodded, avoiding his French Racing Blue eyes. 'Could I have some ice water, Beauchamp?'

He signaled for a waiter without shifting his gaze from her. 'You shouldn't be nervous, you know. You're the one who's free. There's a lot to be said for that.'

'Free?'

'Single.'

'Oh . . . yeah.'

'Single people can call the shots.'

The waiter appeared. 'The lady would like some ice water,' said Beauchamp. He smiled at Mary Ann. 'You don't mind being called a lady, do you?' She shook her head. The waiter smirked and left.

'You know what?' said Mary Ann.

'What?' The eyes were locked on her now.

'I used to pronounce your name "Bo-shomp" instead of "Beechum."'

'Everybody does that.'

'I felt so dumb. Mildred finally corrected me. It's English, isn't it?'

He nodded. 'My parents were shamelessly affected.'

'I think it's nice. You should have told me when I said it wrong.'

He shrugged. 'It doesn't matter.'

'I even said Greenwich Street wrong when I first got here.'

'I called Kearny "Keerny."'

'Did you?'

'And Ghirardelli "Jeerardelli" and . . . blasphemy of blasphemies . . . I called the cable cars trolleys!'

Mary Ann giggled. 'I *still* do that.'

'So big deal! Fuck 'em, if they can't take a joke!'

She laughed, hoping it would cover her embarrassment.

'We're all babes in the woods,' said Beauchamp. 'At one point or another. Use it to your advantage. Innocence is very erotic.' He picked a crouton out of his salad and popped it in his mouth. 'It is to me, at least.'

The waiter was back with her water. She thanked him and sipped at it, considering a new course for the conversation. Beauchamp beat her to it.

'Have you ever met my wife?'

'Uh . . . once. At the softball game.'

'Oh, yeah. What did you think?'

'She's very nice.'

His smile was wan. 'Yes . . . very nice.'

'I read about you two a lot.'

'Yes. Don't you?'

She was squirming. 'Beauchamp . . . I think Mr Halcyon's gonna be back in . . .'

'You want a scoop you won't find in the social columns?'

'I don't want to talk about your wife.'

'I don't blame you.'

She dabbed at her mouth with a napkin. 'This has been really . . .'

'We haven't slept together since the Fol de Rol.'

She decided not to ask what the Fol de Rol was. 'I think we should go, Beauchamp.'

'DeDe and I aren't even *friends*, Mary Ann. We don't talk like you and I do. We don't *relate* . . .'

'Beauchamp . . .'

'I'm trying to tell you something, goddammit! Will you stop being so fucking . . . Middle American for about ten seconds?' He dropped his head and rubbed his forehead with his fingertips. 'I'm sorry . . . God . . . please, help me, will you?'

She reached across the table and squeezed his hand. He was crying.

'What can I do, Beauchamp?'

'I don't know. Don't leave . . . please. Talk to me.'

'Beauchamp, this is the wrong place for . . .'

'I know. We need time.'

'We could meet for a drink after work.'

'What about this weekend?'

'I don't think that would . . .'

'I know a place in Mendocino.'

A Piece of Anna's Past

The sun in the park was warmer now, and the birds were singing much more joyously.

Or so it seemed to Edgar.

'Madrigal. That's lovely. Aren't there some Madrigals in Philadelphia?'

Anna shrugged. 'This one came from Winnemucca.'

'Oh . . . I don't know Nevada too well.'

'You must've been to Winnemucca at least once. Probably when you were eighteen.'

He laughed. 'Twenty. We were late bloomers in my family.'

'Which one did you go to?'

'My God! You're talking about the Paleolithic period. I couldn't remember a thing like that!'

'It was your first time, wasn't it?'

'Yes.'

'Well, then you can remember it. Everybody remembers the first time.' She blinked her eyes coaxingly, like a teacher trying to extract the multiplication tables from a shy pupil. 'When was it – 1935 or thereabouts?'

'I guess . . . it was 1937. My junior year at Stanford.'

'How did you get there?'

'Christ . . . a dilapidated Olds. We drove all night until we reached this disappointing-looking cinder-block house out in the middle of the desert.' He chuckled to himself. 'I guess we wanted it to look like the Arabian Nights or, at least, one of those gaslight-and-red-velvet places.'

'San Franciscans are spoiled rotten.'

He laughed. 'Well, I felt we deserved more. The house was ridiculously tame. They even had a photo of Franklin and Eleanor in the parlor.'

'One has to keep up appearances, doesn't one? Do you remember the name now?'

Edgar's eyebrows arched. 'By God . . . the Blue Moon Lodge! I haven't thought of that in years!'

'And the girl's name?'

'She was hardly a girl. More like forty-five.'

'That's a girl. Believe me.'

'No offense.'

'What was her name?'

'Oh, Christ . . . No, that one's impossible.'

'Margaret?'

'Yes! How did you . . .'

'She read me all the *Winnie-the-Pooh* books.'

'What?'

'Are you sure you want to hear this?'

'Look, if I've . . .'

'My mother ran the Blue Moon Lodge. That was my home. I grew up there.'

'You're not making that up, are you?'

'No.'

'Christ!'

'Don't you *dare* apologize. If you apologize, so help me, I'll take my sandwich and run home.'

'Why did you let me go on like that?'

'I wanted you to remember who you were then. You don't seem too happy with who you are now.'

Edgar stared at her. 'I don't, huh?'

'Nope.'

He took a bite of his sandwich. His own present made him much more uneasy than this woman's questionable past. He shifted the focus. 'Did you ever . . . you know . . .'

She smiled. 'What do you think?'

'No fair.'

'OK. I ran away from home when I was sixteen several years before you patronized the Blue Moon. I never worked for my mother.'

'I see.'

'I'm currently running a house of my own.'

'Here?'

'At 28 Barbary Lane, San Francisco, 94109.'

'On Russian Hill?'

She gave up the game. 'I'm a garden-variety landlady, Mr Halcyon.'

'Ah.'

'Are you disappointed?'

'Not a bit.'

'Good. Then tomorrow . . . *your* turn to buy lunch.'

55

Mona's New Roomie

The uncosmic jangle of the telephone brought an abrupt end to Mona's mantra.

'Yeah?'

'Hi. It's Michael.'

'Mouse! Jesus! I figured you got kidnapped by the CIA!'

'Long time, huh?'

'Three months.'

'Yeah. That's about my average.'

'Oh . . . you got the shaft?'

'Well, we parted amiably enough. He was terribly civilized about it, and I sat in Lafayette Park and cried all morning. Yeah . . . I got the shaft.'

'I'm sorry, Mouse. I thought this one was gonna work out. I kinda liked . . . Robert, was it?'

'Yeah. I kinda liked him too.' He laughed. 'He used to be a Marine recruiter. Did I ever tell you that? He gave me this little key ring with a medallion that said, "The Marines Are Looking for a Few Good Men."'

'Sweet.'

'We used to jog every morning in Golden Gate Park . . . right down to the ocean. Robert had a red Marine tank top, and all the old mossbacks would stop us and say how nice it was to know there were still some decent, upstanding young men left in the world. Boy, we'd laugh about that . . . usually in bed.'

'So what happened?'

'Who knows? He panicked I guess. We were buying furniture together and stuff. Well . . . not exactly *together*. He'd buy a sofa and I'd buy a couple of matching chairs. One has to plan on divorce at all times . . . still, it was a landmark of sorts. I'd never gotten to the furniture-buying stage before.'

'Well, that's *something*.'

'Yeah . . . and I never had anyone read me German poetry in bed before. In German.'

'Hot stuff!'

'He played the harmonica, Mona. Sometimes when we were

56

walking down the street. I was so fucking proud to be with him!'

'Talk much?'

'What?'

'Could he talk? Or was he too busy playing the harmonica?'

'He was a nice guy, Mona.'

'Which is why he dumped on you.'

'He didn't dump on me.'

'You just said he did.'

'It just wasn't . . . meant to be, that's all.'

'Bullshit. You're a hopeless romantic.'

'Thanks for the words of comfort.'

'All I know is I haven't laid eyes on you in three months. There are other people in the world besides Mr Right . . . and we love you too.'

'I know. Mona, I'm sorry.'

'Mouse . . .'

'I really am. I didn't mean to . . .'

'Michael Mouse, if you start crying on me, I'll never boogie with you again!'

'I'm not crying, I'm being pensive.'

'You've got ten seconds to snap out of it. Jesus, Mouse, the woods are full of jogging Marine recruiters. Christ! You and your Rustic Innocent trip! I'll bet that asshole had a closetful of lumberjack shirts, didn't he?'

'Lay off.'

'He's down at Toad Hall right now, stomping around in his blue nylon flight jacket, with a thumb hooked in his Levi's and a bottle of Acme beer in his fist.'

'You're a real hardass.'

'Just your type. Look . . . if I learn a little German poetry, will you come stay here till you find a place? There's plenty of room in this barn. Mrs Madrigal won't mind.'

'I don't know.'

'You're out on your can, right? You've got money?'

'A couple of thousand. Saving account.'

'Well, I'm sick of playing Edna St Vincent Millay. It's perfect. You can live here till you find another studio . . . or another harmonica player. Whichever comes first.'

'It'll *never* work.'

'Why the hell not?'

'You're into T M and I'm into est. It'll never work.'

That night, he moved all his earthly goods into Mona's apartment:

The literary works of Mary Renault and the late Adelle Davis. Assorted work boots, overalls and denims from Kaplan's Army Surplus on Market Street. An Art Deco lamp in the form of a nymph perched on one foot. Random sea shells. A T-shirt that said DANCE 10, LOOKS 3. A hemostat roach clip. An exercise wheel. An autographed photo of La Belle.

'The furniture's at Robert's,' he explained.

'Fuck him,' said Mona. 'You've got a new roomie now.'

Michael hugged her. 'You've saved my life again.'

'Don't mention it, Babycakes. Let's just get the ground rules worked out, OK?'

'I squeeze the toothpaste from the bottom.'

'You know what I'm talking about, Mouse.'

'Yeah. Well . . . we've each got a bedroom.'

'And the living room is off limits for tricks.'

'Of course.'

'And if I bring any switch hitters home with me, it's hands off, right?'

'Do I look like that kind of cad?'

'What about that Basque gardener last summer?'

'Yeah.' Michael smiled. 'He was all right, wasn't he?'

Mona stuck her tongue out at him.

Their First Date

Anna suggested they lunch at the Washington Square Bar & Grill. 'It's a hoot,' she laughed over the phone. 'Everybody's trying to be so godawful literary. For the price of a hamburger, you can look like you've just completed a slim volume of verse.'

Edgar was wary. 'I think I'd prefer something less boisterous.'

'More private, you mean?'

'Well . . . yes.'

'For God's sake! This isn't a shack-up! If one of your cronies spots us, you can say I'm a client or something.'

'My clients don't look as good as you do.'

'You naughty man!'

*

They ended up sitting two tables away from Richard Brautigan. Or someone who was trying to *look* like Richard Brautigan.

'That's Mimi Fariña over by the bar.'

Edgar drew a blank.

'Joan Baez's sister, you philistine. Where have you been all your life? The Peninsula?'

He grinned sleepily. 'You're mightly uppity for a slum lord.'

'Slum lady.'

'Sorry. I'm not very good on celebrities.'

Anna smiled at him unaccusingly. 'Doesn't your wife entertain them all the time?'

'You read the papers?'

'Sometimes.'

'My wife *collects* things, Anna. She collects porcelain ducks, old wicker furniture, nineteenth-century French Provincial birdcages that look like the château at Blois . . . She also collects people. Last year she collected Rudolf Nureyev, Luciano Pavarotti, several Auchinclosses and a bona-fide, first-edition Spanish prince named Umberto de Something-or-Other.'

'You can't hardly get them no more.'

'She also collects bottles. Rum bottles.'

'Oh.'

'Shall we stop talking about her?'

'If you like. What *would* you like, by the way?'

'I'd like a good-looking . . . how old are you?'

'Fifty-six.'

'I'd like a good-looking fifty-six-year-old woman to walk on the beach with me and tell me a few jokes.'

'How soon?'

'Right away.'

'Crank up the Mercedes.'

The beach at Point Bonita was almost empty. At the north end, a group of teenagers was flying a huge Mylar kite with a shimmering tail.

'Goddammit,' said Edgar. 'Remember how much fun that used to be?'

Anna trudged along beside him through the coarse black sand. '*Used* to? I fly kites all the time. It's *delicious* when you're stoned.'

'Marijuana?'

59

Anna arched an eyebrow wickedly. She dug into her tapestry shoulder bag and produced a neatly rolled joint. 'Please observe the cigarette paper. I thought it might appeal to your stern businessman's heart.'

The paper was a counterfeit one-dollar bill.

'Anna . . . I don't mean to be a spoilsport . . .'

She dropped the joint back in the bag. 'Of course you don't. Well! Let's have a nice little stroll, shall we?'

He was hurt by her artificial cheeriness. He felt older than ever. He wanted to reach out to her, to establish some link between them that would last.

'Anna?'

'Yes?'

'I think you're incredible for a fifty-six-year-old woman.'

'Bullshit.'

'I do.'

'This is *exactly* what a fifty-six-year-old-woman is *supposed* to be like.'

He laughed weakly. 'I wish you approved of me.'

'Edgar . . .' She took his arm for the first time. 'I approve of *you*. I just want *you* to climb out of that tough hide of yours. I want you to see how wonderful you . . .'

She let go of his arm and ran down the beach toward the teenagers. In less than a minute she was back, trailing the great silver kite behind her.

She presented the string to Edgar. 'It's yours for ten minutes,' she panted. 'Make it count.'

'You're insane.' He laughed.

'Maybe.'

'How did you talk them into it?'

'Don't ask.'

At the end of the beach, the teenagers were huddled in a circle, watching Anna's bribe go up in smoke.

Off to Mendocino

Beauchamp's silver Porsche careened down a Marin hillside like a pinball destined for a score.

Mary Ann fidgeted with her Mood Ring. 'Beauchamp?'

'Yeah?'

'What did you tell your wife?'

He smiled like an errant Cub Scout. 'She thinks I'm sending a kid to camp.'

'What?'

'I told her the Guardsmen were having a weekend for under-privileged kids on Mount Tam. It doesn't matter. She wasn't listening. She and her mother were planning a party for Nora Cunningham.'

'The opera star?'

'Yes.'

'Your family knows a lot of famous people, don't they?'

'I suppose.'

'You didn't tell Mr Halcyon, did you?'

'About what?'

'About us . . . going off?'

'Christ! Are you crazy?'

She turned and looked at him. 'I don't know. Am I?'

The place was located on a wooded bluff overlooking the Mendocino. There were half a dozen cabins in varying states of repair. It was called the Fools Rush Inn.

The lady innkeeper kept winking at Mary Ann.

When she had gone, Mary Ann said, 'There's only one bed?'

'Yeah. I'll get her to bring in a rollaway.'

'She'll think we're really weird.'

'She will, won't she?'

'Beauchamp, you said we wouldn't . . .'

'I know. And I meant it. Don't worry. I'll tell her you're my sister or something.'

He built a fire in the fireplace while Mary Ann unpacked her bag. Out of habit, she had packed the tattered copy of *Nicholas and Alexandra* she had been reading for the past three summers.

'Scotch?' he asked.

'I don't think so.'

'It helps me to unwind.'

'Go ahead, then.'

'I really appreciate this, Mary Ann. I needed the space.'

'I know. I hope it helps.'

He sat on the hearth and sipped his scotch. She sat next to him. 'You don't have many friends, do you?'

He shook his head. 'They're all DeDe's friends. I don't trust any of them.'

'I want you to be able to trust me.'

'So do I.'

'You *can*, Beauchamp.'

'I hope so.'

She put her hand on his knees. 'You *can*.'

They drove into the village at nightfall and ate dinner at the Mendocino Hotel.

'It used to be wonderful,' said Beauchamp, surveying the dining room. 'Funky and cheap and the floors slanted . . . the real thing.'

Mary Ann looked around. 'It looks fine to me.'

'It's too precious. It knows what it is now. The charm is gone.'

'They have sprinklers on the ceiling, though.'

He smiled. 'Perfect. That was the perfect thing for you to say.'

'What did I say?'

'You're the same way, Mary Ann. Like this building. You should never know what you are . . . or your magic will disappear.'

'You think I'm naïve, don't you?'

'A little.'

'Unsophisticated?'

'Oh, yes!'

'Beauchamp . . . I don't think that's . . .'

'I worship it, Mary Ann. I worship your innocence.'

When they returned to the cabin, there were still a few embers glowing in the fire. Beauchamp knelt down and threw a pine log onto the grate.

He stayed there immobile, golden as a Maxfield Parrish faun. 'They haven't brought the rollaway. I'll check at the office.'

Mary Ann sat down next to him on the floor. Gently, she stroked the dark hair on his forearm.

'Forget about the rollaway, Beauchamp.'

Brian Climbs the Walls

Brian rang Mary Ann's buzzer three times, muttered 'Fuck' to no one but himself, and skulked back across the hall to his own apartment.

It figured.

A girl like that didn't spend Saturday night sacking out with Colonel Sanders and Bob Newhart. A girl like that was gettin' down . . . boogying and boozing and nibbling on the Brut-flavored ear of a junior Bechtel exec with a 240 Z, a trimaran in Tiburon, and a condominium at Sea Ranch.

He stripped off his blue denim Perry's shirt and did two dozen feverish push-ups on the bedroom floor. What point was there getting a mental hard-on over Mary Ann Singleton?'

She was probably a dumb cunt, anyway. She probably read *Reader's Digest Condensed Books* and swapped chain letters and dotted her *i*'s with little circles.

She was probably *dynamite* in the sack.

He climbed into the shower and sublimated his sex drive in a Donna Summer song.

So what would it be tonight? Henry Africa's. It was far enough away from Perry's and Union Street to provide at least *token* escape. Some of the girls there had been known to master witticisms beyond 'Really!' and 'Far out!' Two, at least.

He couldn't get into it.

He was dying of fern poisoning. O D'ing on Tiffany lamplight. He was sick of the whole plastic-fantastic scene. But where else . . . ?'

Christ! The Come Clean Center.

He had picked up some *hot* women there last month. Hot women flocked to the Come Clean Center like lemmings headed for the Sea of Matrimony. But you didn't have to marry 'em to nail 'em!

Perfect! He toweled off hurriedly and climbed into corduroy Levi's and a gray-and-maroon rugby shirt. Why the hell hadn't he thought of it before?

He slapped his belly in front of the closet mirror. It made a solid sound, like a baseball hitting a mitt. Not too shabby for thirty-two!

He headed for the door, then stopped, remembering.

He grabbed a pillowcase off the bed, returned to the closet and stuffed the pillowcase with dirty boxer shorts, shirts and sheets.

He almost sprinted down Barbary Lane.

The Come Clean Center squatted unceremoniously at the intersection of Lombard and Fillmore, across the street from the Marina Health Spa. It was blue and Sixties Functional bland enough to have sprouted up in Boise or Augusta or Kansas City. A sign by the doorway said: NO WASHING AFTER 8 P.M. PLEASE.

Brian smiled at the notice, appreciating the management's chagrin. Some people stayed until the bitter end. He checked the time: 7.27. He had to work fast.

Inside, along a wall of tumbling Speed Queens, a dozen young women pretended to be engrossed in their laundry. Their eyes darted briefly toward Brian, then back to their machines. Brian's heart felt like a Maytag agitator.

He took stock of the men he could see. Not much competition really. A couple of leisure suits, a bad toupee, a wimp with a rhinestone in his ear.

Tucking in his shirt and sucking in his belly, he moved with pantherlike grace toward the detergent dispenser. Every detail mattered now, every ripple of a tendon, every flicker of an eyelid.

'Psst, Hawkins!'

Brian spun around to see Chip Hardesty grinning his worse game show grin. Chip was a bachelor who lived in Larkspur and practiced dentistry in a converted warehouse on Northpoint. His office was full of stained-glass panels and silken Renaissance banners. People frequently mistook it for a fern bar.

Brian sighed peevishly. 'OK . . . so this turf's already staked out.'

'I'm leaving. Don't get your bowels in an uproar.'

That was pure Chip Hardesty. *Don't get your bowels in an uproar*. He may *look* like a TV sportscaster, thought Brian, but his wit is straight out of the Chi Psi Lodge, circa 1963.

'No luck?' asked Brian, goading him.

'I wasn't looking.'

'You weren't, huh?'

Chip held up his laundry basket. 'See?'

'I guess they don't have laundromats in Larkspur.'

64

'Look, man, I've got a date tonight. Otherwise I'd be scarfing up on a sure thing.'

'In here?'

'As we speak, ol' buddy.'

'Where?'

'Hey, man, do your own legwork.'

'Fuck you very much.'

Chip chuckled and cast his eyes to the corner of the room. 'She's all yours, ol' buddy. The one in orange.' He slapped Brian on the shoulder and headed for the door. 'Don't say I never did you any favors.'

'Right,' muttered Brian as he regrouped for the attack.

Post-mortem

'Beauchamp?'

'Yeah?'

'Is that side OK for you?'

'Yeah. It's fine.'

'Are you sure? I don't mind changing.'

'I'm sure.'

Mary Ann sat up in bed and chewed her forefinger for a moment. 'You know what I think would be neat?'

Silence.

'I saw a sign out on the highway for one of those rent-a-canoe places. We could pack a picnic lunch and rent a canoe and spend a nice lazy Sunday morning paddling up . . . What's the name of that river, anyway?'

'Big.'

'The Big River?'

'Yes.'

'Well, *that* could be improved on, but I'm an expert paddler, and I could recite all the poetry I wrote during my senior year in . . .'

'I have to get back early.'

'I thought you said . . .'

'Mary Ann, could we get some sleep, huh?' He rolled away from her, inching closer to the edge of the bed. Mary Ann remained upright and kept silent for half a minute.

Finally:

'Beauchamp?'

'What?'

'Are you . . .'

'What?'

'It doesn't matter. My mind was wandering.'

'What, goddammit!'

'Are you . . . upset about tonight?'

'What the hell do you think?'

'It doesn't matter, Beauchamp. I mean, it may matter to you, but it doesn't matter to me at all. You were probably just tense. It was a fluke.'

'Terrific. Thank you very much, Dr Joyce Brothers.'

'I'm only trying to . . .'

'Skip it, will you?'

'You could've had too much to drink, you know.'

'I've had three fucking scotches!'

'Well, that's enough to . . .'

'Skip it, goddammit!'

'Look, Beauchamp, I personally resent the implication that . . . this . . . was the purpose of this trip. I came here because I *like* you. You asked me to help you.'

'Fat lot of good it did!'

'You're just concentrating too hard. I think your troubles with DeDe probably . . .'

'I don't wanna talk about DeDe!'

'Well, what if *I* wanna talk about her, huh? I'm the one who stands to get burnt in this deal, Beauchamp! I'm the one who's sticking my neck out. You can run home to your penthouse and your wife and your goddamn society parties. I'm stuck with . . . computer dating . . . and singles dances at the goddamn Jack Tar Hotel!'

She leaped out of bed and headed for the bathroom.

'What are you doing?' asked Beauchamp.

'Brushing my teeth! Do you mind!'

'Mary Ann, look . . . I . . .'

'I can't hear you. The water's running.'

He shouted. '*I'm sorry, Mary Ann!*'

'Mrrpletlrp.'

He joined her in the bathroom, standing behind her, stroking her stomach appeasingly. 'I said I'm sorry.'

66

'Would you mind getting out of the bathroom?'
'I love you.'
Silence.
'Did you hear me?'
'Beauchamp, you're making me spill the Scope!'
'I love you, goddammit!'
'Not *here*, for God's sake!'
'Yes, here!'
'Beauchamp, for God's sake. Beauchamp!'

She propped her chin on her elbow and studied his sleeping Keane-kid face. He was snoring so softly that it sounded like a purr. His right arm, tanned and dark-furred, was flung across her waist.

He was talking in his sleep.

At first it was gibberish. Then she thought she heard a name. She couldn't make it out, though. It wasn't DeDe . . . and it wasn't Mary Ann.

She leaned closer. The sounds grew more obscure. He rolled over on his stomach, withdrawing his arm from her waist. He began to snore again.

She slipped out of bed and tiptoed to the window. The moon was slashing a silvery wake across the ocean. 'That's a Moon River,' her brother Sonny had told her when she was ten. She had believed him. She had also believed that someday she would be Audrey Hepburn and someone would come along to be George Peppard.

For the next two hours, she sat by the fire and read *Nicholas and Alexandra*.

Coming Clean in the Marina

Brian's prey was sitting in a plastic chair in the Come Clean Center's shag-carpeted waiting area. She was wearing orange slacks that could have protected a road crew at night.

Her Mao Tse-tung T-shirt was stretched so tightly across her chest that the Chairman was grinning broadly.

And she was reading a *People* magazine.

Brian hesitated a moment in front of the dispenser, feigning indecision. Then he turned around.

'Uh . . . excuse me? Could you tell me the difference between Downy and Cheer?'

She looked up from an article on Cher and peered at him through cobalt-blue contacts. Chewing the cud of her Care-free Sugarless she sniffed out the new bull who had pawed his way into her pasture.

'Downy's a fabric softener,' she smiled. 'It makes your clothes all soft and sweet-smelling. Here . . . wanna try some of mine?'

Brian smiled back. 'Sure you got enough?'

'Sure.'

She dug a bottle of Downy out of her red plastic laundry basket. 'See? It says here . . .'

Brian moved next to her. 'Where?'

'Here . . . on the label under . . .'

'Oh, yeah.' Her cheek was *inches* away. He could smell her Charlie. 'I see . . . April fresh.'

She giggled, reading from the label. 'And it helps eliminate static cling.'

'I *hate* to cling statically, don't you?'

She turned and looked at him quizzically, then continued to read. 'Whites white and colors bright.'

'Of course.'

'Softens deep and luxurious.'

'Mmm. Deep . . . and luxurious.'

She jerked away from him suddenly, then faced him, grinning coyly. 'You are *fresh*, you know that?'

'April fresh, I hope?'

'You're too much!'

'That's what they tell me.'

'Well, you can just . . .'

'You must not be from around here, huh?'

'Why?'

'I don't know. You just have a kind of . . . no, forget it.'

'What?'

'It'll sound like a line.'

'Will you just let me be the judge of that?'

'Well, there's something kind of . . . cosmopolitan about you.'

After blinking at him for a moment, she looked down at her T-shirt, then back at him.

'Why did you do that?' he asked.

'I couldn't remember if I was wearing my *Paris Match* T-shirt.'

He chuckled smoothly. 'It's not your clothes. There's just . . . something . . . an air. Oh, forget it.'

'Are you from around here?'

'Sure. Third drier from the right.'

'C'mon!'

'I know it doesn't *look* like much, but it's really pretty inside. Crystal chandeliers, flocked wallpaper, Armstrong linoleum . . . Where do you live?'

'The Marina.'

'Near here, huh?'

'Yeah.'

'How quick could we walk it?'

'I don't think . . . five minutes.'

'You don't think what?'

'Nothing.'

'Good. Shall we?'

'Look, I don't even know your name.'

'Of course. How stupid. Brian Hawkins.'

She took his hand and shook it rather formally. 'I'm Connie Bradshaw. From the Friendly Skies of United.'

. . . and Many Happy Returns

The floor around Connie's bed was littered with the bodies of its daytime occupants: a five-foot plush Snoopy dog, a chartreuse beanbag frog, a terry-cloth python with eyes that rolled (Forgive her, Sigmund, thought Brian) and a maroon pillow that said: SCHOOL SPIRIT DAY, CENTRAL HIGH, 1967.

Brian was propped against the headboard. 'Do you mind if I smoke?'

'Go ahead.'

He chuckled. 'That's very New Wave, isn't it?'

'What?'

'You know . . . the couple sacked out afterwards with . . . It doesn't matter.'

'All right.'

'Would you like me to leave?'

'Did I say that, Byron?'

'Brian.'

'You can go if you want.'

'Are you pissed or something?'

Silence.

'Ah, methinks the lady is pissed.'

'Oh . . . you're *such* an intellectual, aren't you?'

'My *brain* offends you?'

Silence.

'Look, Bonnie . . .'

'Connie.'

'So we're even. Look . . . I'll be guilty if you want. I'm the quintessential liberal. Ring a bell, I'll salivate, flog myself, feel guilty for *weeks*. Just tell me what I *did*, will you?'

She rolled over and hunched into a fetal position. 'If you don't know, there's no point in discussing it.'

'Bonnie! Connie!'

'Do you treat all your bed partners that way?'

'*What* way?'

'Wham, bam, thank you, ma'am!'

'Well, that's getting to the point.'

'You asked me.'

'So I did.'

'I don't think it's *abnormal* to require a little tenderness.'

'"She may be weary, women do get weary . . ."'

'Blow it out your . . .'

'"Wearin' the same shabby dress . . ."'

'You're really an asshole, you know that? You are truly a . . . *pathetic* human being! You've got about as much warmth as . . . I don't know what!'

'Nice smile.'

'Go fuck yourself!'

She was up now, sitting at her French Provincial vanity, brushing her hair with a vengeance.

'I'm sorry,' he said. 'OK?'

'What's to apologize for? We don't even know each other.'

'We shared a fabric softener. Doesn't that mean anything to you?'

'Yeah. The end of a horrible day.'

'Jesus. What *else* happened to you today?'

'Nothing. Not a goddamn thing.'

70

'So?'

'So it's my birthday, dink!'

He held her until she had stopped crying, then dried her eyes with a corner of her Wamsutta floral.

'I'm hungry,' he said. 'How 'bout you?'

She didn't answer. She sat on the edge of the bed like a broken Barbie Doll. Brian left for the kitchen.

He was back several minutes later, holding a tin plate with mock solemnity. 'Don't those North Beach bakeries do a nice job?' he said.

From the top of a triple-decker peanut butter and jelly sandwich four kitchen matches were blazing festively.

'Make a wish,' he said, 'and no wisecracks!'

Mrs Day at Home

DeDe was ticked. It was already midafternoon Sunday and Beauchamp wasn't home from his Guardsmen weekend on Mount Tam.

She slammed around the penthouse in search of something to occupy her mind. She had already read *Town and Country*, watered the ficas, walked the corgi, and chatted with Michael Vincent about the twig furniture for the living room.

There was nothing left but bills.

She sat down at her *escritoire* and began to disembowel windowed envelopes. The latest tally from Wilkes Bashford was $1,748. Daddy would be *livid*. She had already got three advances on her allowance that month.

Screw it. Beauchamp could sweat out the bills for once. She was sick to death of it.

Angrily, she rose and went to the window, confronting a panorama of almost ludicrous exoticism: the sylvan slope of Telegraph Hill, the crude grandeur of a Norwegian freighter, the bold blue sweep of the bay . . .

And then . . . a sudden slash of electric green as a flock – no, *the* flock – of wild parrots headed north to the eucalyptus trees above Julius Castle.

The birds were a legend on the hill. Once upon a time they had belonged to human beings. Then, somehow, they had fled their separate cages to band together in this raucous platoon of freedom

71

fighters. According to most accounts, they divided their time daily between Telegraph Hill and Potrero Hill. Their screeching en route was regarded by many locals as a hymn to the liberated souls.

But not by DeDe.

In her opinion, the parrots were annoyingly arrogant. You could buy the most beautiful one in town, she observed, but that wouldn't make it love you. You could feed it, care for it and exclaim over its loveliness, but there was nothing to guarantee that it would stay home with you.

There had to be a lesson there somewhere.

She locked herself in the bathroom and poured half a cup of Vitabath into the tub. She soaked for an hour, trying to calm her nerves. It helped to think of old times, carefree days in Hillsborough when she and Binky and Muffy would snitch the keys to Daddy's Mercedes and tool down to the Fillmore to tease the black studs lurking on the street corners.

Good times. Pre-Cotillion. Pre-Spinsters. Pre-Beauchamp.

But what was there now?

Muffy had married a Castilian prince.

Binky was still living it up as the Jewish American Princess.

DeDe was stuck with a Shabby Genteel Bostonian who thought he was a parrot.

Lying there in the warm, fragrant water, she realized suddenly that most of her ideas about love and marriage and sex had solidified when she was fourteen years old.

Mother Immaculata, her social studies teacher, had explained the whole thing:

'Boys will try to kiss you, DeDe. You must expect that, and you must be prepared for it.'

'But *how?*'

'It's as close as your heart, DeDe. The scapular you wear around your neck.'

'I don't see how . . .'

'When a boy tries to kiss you, you must pull out your scapular and say, "Here, kiss this, if you must kiss something."'

DeDe's scapular bore a picture of Jesus or St Anthony or somebody. Nobody ever tried to kiss it.

Mother Immaculata knew her stuff, all right.

*

DeDe climbed out of the tub and stood in front of the mirror for a long time, smearing her face with Oil of Olay. The flesh under her chin was soft and spongy. Nothing drastic. It could still pass for baby fat.

The rest of her body had a certain . . . voluptuous quality, she felt, though it would certainly be nice to have an outside opinion again. If Beauchamp didn't want her, there were still people who did. There was no goddamn reason in the world why she had to act like Miss Peninsula Virgin of 1969.

She found her address book and looked up Splinter Riley's number.

Splinter of the massive shoulders and molten eyes. Splinter, who had begged her one balmy night on Belvedere (1970? 1971?) to follow him to the Mallard's boathouse, where he brutalized her Oscar de la Renta and took his manly pleasure with gratifying thoroughness.

God! She had forgotten none of it. The mingled odors of sweat and Chanel for Men. The scrape of the damp planks against her fanny. The distant strains of Walt Tolleson's combo playing 'Close to You' up on the hillside.

Her hand trembled as she dialed.

Please, she prayed, don't let Oona be at home.

The Chinese Connection

Mercifully, it was Splinter who answered the phone.

'Hello?'

'Hi, Splint.'

'Who's this, please?'

'Here's a hint: "Sittin' on the dock of the bay, wastin' tiiiiime . . ." '

'DeDe?'

'I thought that might remind you.' Her tone was tantalizing, but ladylike, she felt.

'Good to hear from you. What have you and Beauchamp been up to?'

'Not much. Beauchamp's off with the Guardsmen.'

'Shit! Did I miss a meeting?'

73

'What?'

'Beauchamp and I are on the same committee. They'll skin my ass if I . . .'

'It may not have been the Guardsmen, Splint . . . come to think of it.' Well, that answered *that*.

'I hope to hell not. What can I do for you?'

'I can remember when it used to be the other way around.'

Silence.

'Beauchamp's away till this evening, Splint.'

'DeDe . . .'

'No strings attached.'

'I don't think . . .'

'Is Oona there? Is that it?'

'No. DeDe, look . . . I'm flattered to death, honest to God . . .'

'No emotional commitments. I've changed a lot, Splint.'

'So have I.'

'What could have changed that much?'

'I'm in love with Oona.'

She hung up on him.

Almost immediately, she picked up the phone and dialed Jiffy's Market. She ordered half a gallon of milk, a box of Familia and some bananas. There was something very comforting about cereal. It made her think of childhood at Halcyon Hill.

The delivery boy arrived in fifteen minutes.

DeDe knew him. It was Lionel Wong, a muscular eighteen-year-old suffering from a Bruce Lee fixation.

'Shall I put it in the kitchen, Mrs Day?'

'Thanks, Lionel. I'll get my purse out of the bedroom.'

'No sweat, Mrs Day. We can put it on your tab.'

'No . . . I want to give you something for your trouble.'

She went into the bedroom, returning with a dollar bill.

'Thanks a lot!'

DeDe smiled. 'Have you seen the exhibit at the de Young?'

'What?'

'The People's Republic exhibit. It's *stunning*, Lionel. You should be very proud of your people.'

'Yes, ma'am.'

'Truly stunning. The culture is amazing.'

'Yeah.'

74

'Would you like something to drink, Lionel? I don't have any Cokes in the house. How about a bitter lemon?'

'I've got a couple more stops, Mrs Day.'

'Just for a little while?'

'Thanks a lot, but . . .'

'Lionel, please . . .'

Half an hour later, Beauchamp arrived home. He met Lionel at the elevator.

'Working Sundays, Lionel? That's a bummer.'

'No sweat.'

'Anything for the Days?'

'Yeah . . . Mrs Day needed a few things.'

'How's the Kung Fu coming?'

'Fine.'

'Keep it up. You're getting some nice definition.'

'Thanks. See you later.'

'Take it easy. Don't do anything I wouldn't do.'

Upstairs, DeDe was basking in her second Vitabath of the day.

Confession in the Nude

The parking lot at Devil's Slide was jammed with vehicles; flowered hippie vans, city clunkers, organic pickups with shingled gypsy houses, and a dusty pack of Harley-Davidsons.

Mona had to park her '64 Volvo almost a quarter of a mile from the beach. 'Shit,' she groaned. 'It must be wall-to-wall flesh down there.'

'I hope so,' leered Michael.

'That's sexism, even if you *are* talking about men.'

'So I'm sexist.'

They trekked along the dirt road with dozens of other wayfarers headed for the beach. 'This reminds me of the Donner Party,' said Mona.

Michael grinned. 'Yeah. Drop by the wayside and you get eaten.'

When they reached the highway, Mona gave the ticket-taker a dollar for both of them.

'This is on me,' she said. 'You're in mourning.'

Michael skipped down to the stairway on the cliff. 'Just watch me recover, Babycakes!'

Two minutes later, they were standing on a broad stretch of white sand. Michael flung a pebble into the air. 'Where shall we go? The gay end or the straight end?'

'Let me guess.'

Michael grinned. 'It's less windy down at the gay end.'

'I'm not real crazy about climbing over those rocks.'

'I shall carry you, my lovely.'

'You're one helluva gentleman!'

They headed, arm in arm, for the sandy cove that nestled amid the rocks at the north end of the beach. On the way they passed five or six frolicking bathers, all naked and brown as organic date bars.

'Look at them!' sighed Mona. 'I feel like a goddamn fish belly.'

Michael shook his head. 'That's no good. They haven't got a tan line.'

'A what?'

'A tan line. The contrast between brown and white when you take off your trunks.'

'Who needs it? I haven't taken off my trunks before an audience in ages. I'd rather be brown all over.'

'Suit yourself. I want a tan line.'

'You're a prude, that's what.'

'Five minutes ago, I was a sexist.'

She snatched a piece of seaweed off the sand and draped it over his ear. 'You're a sexist, faggot prude, Michael Mouse.'

There were thirty or forty naked men on the tiny patch of beach. Mona and Michael spread a towel. It displayed the words *Chez Moi ou Chez Toi?* and a life-size picture of a naked man.

Mona looked around her, then down at the towel. 'How redund-and. Aren't you afraid people will make comparisons?'

Michael laughed, stripping off his sweatshirt, tank top and Levi's. He stretched out in his green-and-yellow satin boxing trunks.

Mona removed her own Levi's and tank top. 'How do you like my impression of the Great White Whale?'

'Bullshit. You look fabulous. You look like . . . September Morn.'

'A fat lot of good it'll do me here.'

'Don't be so sure. There's a nasty epidemic of heterosexuality afoot. I know lots of gay guys who're sneaking off to the Sutro Baths to get it on with women.'

'How bizarre.'

'Well . . . everything gets old after a while. I personally get a little sick of wrecking my liver at The Lion for the privilege of tricking some guy whose lover is in L A for the weekend.'

'So you're going straight?'

'I didn't say *that*.'

Mona rolled over on her stomach and handed Michael a bottle of Bain de Soleil. 'Do my back, will you?'

Michael obeyed, applying the lotion in strong circular strokes. 'You do have a nice bod, you know.'

'Thanks, Babycakes.'

'Don't mention it.'

'Mouse?'

'Yeah?'

'Do you think I'm a fag hag?'

'*What?*'

'I do. I'm sure of it.'

'You've been eating funny mushrooms again.'

'I don't mind being a fag hag, actually. There are worse things to be.'

'You are *not* a fag hag, Mona.'

'Look at the symptoms. I hang around with you, don't I? We go boogying at Buzzby's and The Endup. I'm practically a *fixture* at The Palms.' She laughed. 'Shit! I've drunk so many Blue Moons I feel like I'm turning into Dorothy Lamour.'

'Mona . . .'

'Hell, Mouse! I hardly know any straight men anymore.'

'You live in San Francisco.'

'It isn't that. I don't even *like* straight men. Brian Hawkins repulses me. Straight men are boorish and boring and . . .'

'Maybe you've just been exposed to the wrong ones.'

'Then where the hell are the *right* ones?'

'Hell, I don't know. There must be . . .'

'Don't you *dare* suggest one of those mellowed-out Marin types. Underneath all that hair and patchouli beats the heart of a true pig. I've been *that* route.'

'What can I say?'

'Nothing. Not a damned thing.'

'I love you a lot, Mona.'

'I know, I know.'

'For what it's worth . . . sometimes I wish that were enough.'

Two hours later, they left hand in hand, parting a Red Sea of naked male bodies.

They ate dinner at Pier 54, boogied briefly at Buzzby's, and arrived back at Barbary Lane at ten-thirty.

Mary Ann passed them on the stairs.

'How was your weekend?' asked Mona.

'Fine.'

'You go away?'

'Up north. With a friend from school.'

'Have you met Michael Tolliver, my new roommate?'

'No, I . . .'

'Yes.' Michael smiled. 'I believe we have.'

'I'm sorry, I don't . . .'

'The Marina Safeway.'

'Oh . . . yes. How are you?'

'Hangin' in there.'

Back at the apartment, Mona asked, 'You met Mary Ann at a supermarket?'

Michael smiled ruefully. 'She tried to pick up Robert.'

'You see?' said Mona. 'You see?'

Miss Singleton Dines Alone

After unpacking her suitcase, Mary Ann padded restlessly through her apartment in the pink quilted bathrobe her mother had sent her from the Ridgemont Mall.

She *hated* Sunday nights.

When she was a little girl, Sunday nights had meant only one thing: unfinished homework.

That's how she felt now. Anxious, guilty, frightened of recriminations that were certain to follow. Beauchamp Day was homework she should have finished. She would pay for it. Sooner or later.

She decided to pamper herself.

She quick-thawed a pork chop under the faucet, wondering if it was sacrilegious to Shake 'n Bake meat from Marcel & Henri.

Lighting a spice candle on the parsons table in the living room, she dug out her Design Research cloth napkins, her wood-handled stainless flatware, her imitation Dansk china, and her ceramic creamer shaped like a cow.

Solitude was no excuse for sloppiness.

She scrounged in the kitchen for a vegetable. There was nothing but a Baggie full of limp lettuce and a half-eaten package of Stouffer's Spinach Soufflé. She decided on cottage cheese with chives.

She supped by candlelight, bent over a *Ms* article entitled 'The Quest for Multiple Orgasms.' Music was provided by K C B S - F M, the mellow station:

> Out of work, I'm out of my head.
> Out of self-respect,
> I'm out of bread,
> Underloved and underfed,
> I wanna go home . . .
> It never rains in California,
> But, girl, don't they warn ya,
> It pours, man, it pours.

After dinner, she decided to try the 'monster mask' formula from her herbal cosmetics book. She cooked a saucepan of the glop – using oatmeal, dried prunes and an overripe fig – and smeared it relentlessly over her face.

For twenty minutes, she lay perfectly still in a sudsy tub.

She could feel the mask drying, chipping off in gross, leprous flakes and sinking into the water above her chest. This would kill another ten minutes. Then what?

She could write her parents.

She could fill out her application to the Sierra Club.

She could walk down to Cost Plus and buy another coffee mug.

She could call Beauchamp.

Lurching out of the bathtub like a reject from a Japanese horror film, she examined her face in the mirror.

She looked like a giant Shake 'n Bake pork chop.

And for what?

For Dance Your Ass Off? For Mr Halcyon? For Michael

79

Whatshisname downstairs? For a married man who mutters strange things in his sleep?

She would *not* call him. The love he offered was deceitful, destructive and dead-end.

He would have to call *her*.

She fell asleep just before midnight, with *Nicholas and Alexandra* in her lap.

Over on Telegraph Hill, DeDe was eyeing Beauchamp malevolently as he adjusted the ship's clock in the library.

'I talked to Splinter today.'

He didn't look up. 'Mmm.'

'Apparently he had forgotten about your little Guardsmen function on Mount Tam.'

'Oh well . . . Did he call here?'

'No.'

'I don't get it.'

'I . . . I called Oona. He answered the phone.'

'You *detest* Oona.'

'We're doing a League project together. The Model Ghetto Program in Hunters Point. Beauchamp, why do you suppose Splinter forgot such an important meeting? He says you two are in the same committee.'

'Beats me.'

She grunted audibly. Beauchamp turned and whistled to the corgi, half asleep on the couch. The dog yelped excitedly when his master opened a desk drawer and produced his leash.

'I'm taking Caesar for his constitutional.'

DeDe frowned. 'I've walked him twice already.'

'OK. So I need the air myself.'

'What's the matter? Not enough air on Mount Tam?'

He left without answering, stopping by the bedroom on his way downstairs. He closed the door quietly and dug in his underwear drawer for an object he had brought with him from Mendocino.

Then, slipping it into the breast pocket of his sports coat, he descended into the dark garage, where he planted it in the glove compartment of the Porsche.

A nice touch, he told himself as Caesar led him up the Filbert Steps to Coit Tower.

A very nice touch.

Mona vs. The Pig

On the worst of all possible Monday mornings, Mona stopped by Mary Ann's desk en route to a conference with Mr Siegel, the president of Adorable Pantyhose.

'What's the matter with *you*, Babycakes?'

'Nothing . . . everything!'

'Yeah. The moon's in ca-ca. Speaking of which, I have a dog-and-pony show for Fartface Siegel this morning. Have you seen Beauchamp?'

'Nope.'

'If you see him, he's got ten minutes to get down there. Hey . . . are you OK, Mary Ann?'

'I'm fine.'

'I have a Valium, if you want one.'

'No. Thanks. I'm fine.'

'I probably should have taken it myself.'

Mona stood next to Beauchamp, her hand clamped rigidly to the storyboard.

'Our approach should be carefree,' she explained. 'We're not backtracking . . . we're simply *improving*. The only nylon crotch wasn't unsafe. The new one is simply . . . better.'

The client's expression didn't change.

'The youth image is important, of course. The cotton crotch is young, vibrant, hip. The cotton crotch is for with-it women on the go.'

Buddha would have to forgive her.

She revealed the first card on the storyboard. It showed a young woman with a Dorothy Hamill haircut hanging off the side of a cable car. The copy read: 'Under my clothes, I like to feel Adorable.'

Mona gestured with a pointer. 'Notice we don't mention the crotch in the headline.'

'Mmm,' said the client.

'The idea is there, of course. Hygienic. Safe. Functional. But we don't come right out and say it. The effect is subtle, low-key, subliminal.'

'It's not clear enough,' said the client.

'The crotch comes in later – down here in the fourth paragraph. We don't want to hit people over the head with the crotch.'

Hit people over the head with the crotch? *This* was the woman who was going to be another Lillian Hellman?

The client grunted. 'We're not selling subtlety, honey.'

'Oh? What *are* we selling . . . honey?'

Beauchamp squeezed Mona's arm. 'Mona . . . Perhaps we could move the crotch up to the first paragraph, Mr Siegel?'

'The young lady doesn't seem to be pleased with that.'

'*Woman*, Mr Siegel. Young *woman*. Please don't call me a lady. I wouldn't *dream* of calling you a gentleman.'

Beauchamp was scarlet. 'Mona, goddammit . . . Mr Siegel, I think I can handle these revisions myself. Mona, I'll talk to you later.'

'Don't you patronize me, you prick! I'm not married to *my* job.'

'You're *way* out of line, Mona.'

'Thank God for that! Who the hell wants to be in line with that fat, sexist, capitalist sack of . . .'

'Mona!'

'You want crotch, Mr Siegel. Is that it? Well, I'll give you crotch. Crotch, crotch, crotch, crotch, crotch, crotch . . .'

She stormed to the door, stopped and wheeled around to confront Beauchamp. 'Your karma is *really* fucked!'

That evening, she broke the news to Michael.

'What are you going to do, Mona?'

She shrugged. 'I don't know. Collect unemployment. Join a woman's collective. Shop at the dented-can store. Give up coke. I'll manage.'

'Maybe Halcyon would reconsider if you . . .'

'Forget it. That was my finest hour. I wouldn't take it back for nothin'!'

'Maybe I could get my job back at the P.S.'

'We'll hack it, Mouse. I can free-lance. Mrs Madrigal will understand.'

Michael sat down on the floor, slipped off Mona's Earth Shoes and began massaging her feet. 'She's crazy about you, isn't she?'

'Who? Mrs Madrigal?'

'Yeah.'

'Yeah . . . I guess so.'

'It shows. Have you told her about getting fired yet?'

'No . . . I'll have to, I guess.'

Where Is Love?

Despite her defiance, Mona was clearly depressed over losing her job. Michael tried his usual ploy for cheering her up: He read her the classified from the 'Trader Dick' section of *The Advocate*.

'God! Listen to this one! "Clean-cut, straight-looking court reporter, 32, sick to death of bars, baths and bitchiness, seeks a permanent relationship with a *real man* who's into white-water rafting, classical music and gardening. No fats, fems or dopers, please. I'm *sincere*. Ron."'

Mona laughed. 'Are you *sincere*?'

'Who the hell isn't?'

'You'd leave me in a second, wouldn't you?'

Michael thought for a moment. 'Only if he had a cottage on Potrero Hill with a butcher-block kitchen, a functioning fireplace and . . . a golden retriever in the small but tastefully designed garden.'

'Don't hold your breath.'

'You know . . . when I moved here three years ago, I had never seen so many faggots in my whole goddamned life! I didn't know there were that many faggots in the *world*! Jesus! I thought all I had to do was go to a party and pick somebody out. Everybody wants a lover, right?'

'Wrong.'

'OK . . . So *almost* everybody. Anyway, I thought I'd be snapped up in six months. At the very most!'

'You were. Hundreds of times.'

'Not funny.'

'What about Robert?'

'Affairettes don't count.'

'What if I grew a mustache?'

Michael grinned and tossed a paisley pillow at her. 'C'mon. Let's go to the movies or something.'

'I don't know . . .'

'There's a Fellini double bill at the Surf.'

'Downer.'

'Nah. Lotsa big tits and pretty boys and dwarfs. Very up.'

'You go ahead. Take the car, if you want.'

'What are *you* gonna do?'

Mona shrugged. 'Curl up with Anaïs Nin, take a Quaalude. I don't know.'

'Is my MDA still in your stash box?'

'Yeah. Christ, you don't need that for a movie!'

'I might not *see* a movie, Mother!'

'Ah.'

'I hate movies when I'm alone.'

'Michael, I just don't feel like . . .'

'I hear you.'

'Where are you going?'

'Here and there.'

'Trashing, huh?'

'Maybe.'

'Be careful, will you?'

'What?'

'Don't do anything risky.'

'You read the papers too much.'

'Just be careful . . . and cheer up. Someday your prince will come.'

Michael blew a kiss to her from the door. 'Same to you, fella.'

She rattled around the apartment for half an hour, talking to her rosy fishhooks cactus and fiddling with her Ching coins.

She decided against a Quaalude. Quaaludes made her feel sleazy. What was the point in feeling sleazy if you had no one to sleaze with?

Could you conjugate that? To sleaze. I sleaze. You sleaze. We all have sleazen.

Words constantly annoyed her like that, reminding her of the gulf between Art and Making a Living. 'Mona's good with words,' her mother used to say matter-of-factly, 'if she can just learn to Make a Living at it.'

Her mother Made a Living in real estate.

Mona hadn't spoken to her in eight months, not since mother had joined the Reagan campaign in Minneapolis and daughter had written home breezily about her Sexual Awareness Retreat at a Cosmic Light Fellowship.

It didn't matter.

More and more it seemed that Mona's *real* mother was a woman so in tune with creation that even her marijuana plants had names.

So Mona trudged downstairs to tell Mrs Madrigal the news.

If the Shoe Fits

Michael decided against the MDA. There were rumors afoot that someone on MDA had dropped dead at The Barracks the week before. It probably wasn't true, but what point was there in pressing your luck?

Actually, there were *lots* of murky legends like that among gay people in San Francisco. God only knew where they originated!

There was the Doodler, a sinister black man who sat at the bar and sketched your face . . . before taking you home to murder you.

Not to mention the Man in the White Van, a faceless fiend whose unwitting passengers never found their way home again.

And the Dempster Dumpster Killer, whose S & M fantasies knew no limit.

It was almost enough to make you stick with Mary Tyler Moore.

Once again, he ended up in the Castro. True, he badmouthed the gay ghetto at *least* twice a day, but there was a lot to be said for sheer numbers when you were looking for company.

Toad Hall and The Midnight Sun were wall-to-wall flannel, as usual. He passed them up for The Twin Peaks, where his crew-neck sweater and corduroy trousers would seem less alien to the environment.

Cruising, he had long ago decided, was a lot like hitchhiking.

It was best to dress like the people you wanted to pick you up.

'Crowded, huh?' The man at the bar was wearing Levi's, a rugby shirt and red-white-and-blue tigers. He had a pleasant, square-jawed face that reminded Michael of people he had once known in the Campus Crusade for Christ.

'What is it?' Michael asked. 'A full moon or something?'

'Got me. I don't keep up with that crap.'

Point One in his favour. Despite Mona's proselytizing, Michael was not big on astrology freaks. He grinned.

Go ahead, Michael told himself. Ply him with cheap jokes. Have no shame.

'Don't tell anybody, but the moon's in Uranus.'

The man stared dumbly, then got it. 'The moon's in your anus. That's a riot!'

The man obviously liked him. 'What are you drinking?'

'Calistoga water.'

'I figured that.'

'Why?'

'I don't know. You're . . . healthy-looking.'

'Thanks.'

The man extended his hand. 'I'm Chuck.'

'Michael.'

'Hi, Mike.'

'Michael.'

'Oh . . . You know what, man? I gotta tell you the truth. I scoped you out when you walked in here . . . and I said, "That's the one, Chuck!" I swear to God!'

What *was* it with this butch number? 'Keep it up,' Michael grinned. 'I can use the strokes.'

'You know what it was, man?'

'No.'

The man smiled self-assuredly, then pointed to Michael's shoes. 'Them.'

'My shoes?'

He nodded. 'Weejuns.'

'Yeah?'

'And white socks.'

'I see.'

'They new?'

'The Weejuns?'

'No. I just had them half-soled.'

The man shook his head reverentially, still staring at the loafers. 'Half-soled. Far fucking out!'

'Excuse me, are you . . . ?'

'How many pairs you got?'

'Just these.'

'I have six pairs. Black, brown, scotch grain . . .'

'You like 'em, huh?'

'You seen my ad in *The Advocate*?'

86

'No.'

'It says . . .' He held his hand up to make it graphic for Michael. ' "Bass Weejuns." Big capital letters, like.'

'Catchy wording.'

'I get a lotta calls. Collegiate types. Lotta guys get sick of the glitter fairies in this town.'

'I can imagine.'

The man moved closer, lowering his voice. 'You ever . . . done it in 'em?'

'Not to my recollection. Look . . . if you've got six pairs, how come you're not wearing any tonight?'

The man was aghast at his *faux pas*. 'I always wear my Tigers with my rugby shirt!'

'Right.'

He held his foot up for examination. 'They're just like Billy Sive's. In *The Front Runner.* '

Sherry and Sympathy

Mrs Madrigal seemed oddly subdued when she opened the door.

'Mona, dear . . .'

'Hi. I thought you might like company.'

'Certainly.'

'That's a lie, actually. I thought *I* might like company.'

'Well, it works both ways, doesn't it? Come in.'

The landlady poured a glass of sherry for her tenant. 'Is Michael out?'

Mona nodded. 'Taking the vapors, I think.'

'I see.'

'God knows when he'll be back.'

'He's a sweet boy, Mona. I approve of him wholeheartedly.'

Mona sniffed. 'You make it sound like we're *married* or something.'

'There are all kinds of marriages, dear.'

'I don't think you understand the trip with me and Michael.'

'Mona . . . lots of things are more binding than sex. They last longer too. When I was . . . little, my mother once told me that if a married couple puts a penny in a pot for every time they make love the first year, and takes a penny out every time after that, they'll never get

87

all the pennies out of the pot . . . Damn! I haven't thought of that in years.'

'That's a trip.'

Mrs Madrigal smiled. 'It's also a comfort to those of us who never put in too many pennies in the first place.'

Mona sipped her sherry, embarrassed.

'Have you and Michael talked, dear?'

'About you?'

The landlady nodded.

'I . . . no. I think that's up to you.'

'You're very close. He must have asked you questions.'

'No. Nothing.'

'I don't mind, you know . . . with him.'

'I understand . . . but I think it's up to you.'

'Thank you, dear.'

'I lost my job,' Mona said at last.

'*What?*'

'The old son-of-a-bitch fired me.'

'Who?'

'Edgar Halcyon. His son-in-law put the badmouth on me, and the old man tossed me out on my can.'

'Mona . . . why on earth would he . . .'

Mona snorted. 'You don't know Edgar Halcyon. He's the biggest asshole on the Barbary Coast.'

'Mona!'

'Well, he *is*. It was a relief, actually. I *loathed* that job . . . all that crap about demographics and consumer profiles and . . .'

'Did you . . . do something, Mona?'

'I was honest with a client. The Ultimate No-No.'

'What did you say?'

'It doesn't matter.'

'Mona! It matters to me!'

'Jesus! What's with you?'

'I . . . I'm sorry. I didn't mean . . . Are you all right, Mona? Financially, I mean?'

'Yeah, sure. I can pay the rent.'

'I didn't mean that.'

'I know. I'm sorry. I didn't mean to snap. I'm fine, Mrs Madrigal, really.'

She wasn't fine. She left ten minutes later, returned to her apartment and took the Quaalude. It put her to sleep.

Michael was back at one-thirty. He woke her on the couch. 'You OK, Babycakes? Don't you wanna go to bed?'

'No. This is OK.'

'This is Chuck, Mona.'

'Hi, Chuck.'

'Hi, Mona.'

'Sleep tight, Babycakes.'

'You too.'

The two men went into Michael's bedroom and closed the door.

The Rap About Rape

DeDe found her mother on the terrace at Halcyon Hill, aghast over the 1976 San Francisco Social Register.

'I don't believe it! I *don't* believe it!'

'Mother, will you put that down for a . . .'

'They *are* listed. They are actually *listed.*'

'Who?'

'Those dreadful people who bought the old Feeney place on Broadway. Viola told me they were listed, but I simply couldn't . . .'

'He speaks seven languages, Mother.'

'I don't care if he *tap-dances.* They used to live in the *Castro,* DeDe . . . and now they're living with his boyfriend . . . or is it *hers?*'

'Binky says it's both of theirs.'

'No! Do you think? Of course, they never take *him* anywhere . . . and he's even got a side entrance, so his address is different . . .'

'Mother, I need to talk to you.'

'Viola says they even have different *zip codes*!'

'Mother!'

'What, darling?'

'I think Beauchamp has a mistress.'

Silence.

'I'm sure of it, in fact.'

'Darling, are you . . . ? You poor baby! How did you . . . ? Are you . . . ? Hand me that pitcher, will you, darling?'

*

89

DeDe dug into her Obiko shoulder bag and produced the offending scarf. Frannie studied it at arm's length, sipping her Mai Tai all the time.

'You found it in his car?'

DeDe nodded. 'He walked to work on Monday. Binky and I drove the Porsche to Mr Lee's at noon, and I found it then. I tried to act like nothing was . . .' Her voice cracked. She began to cry. 'Mother . . . I'm sure this time.'

'You're sure it's hers?'

'I've seen her wearing it.'

'He could have given her a ride home, DeDe. Anyway . . . don't you think your father would have noticed, if she was . . . carrying on with . . .'

'Mother! I know!'

Frannie began to sniffle. 'The party was going to be *so* lovely.'

DeDe went to lunch at Prue Giroux's townhouse on Nob Hill.

Under the circumstances, she might have canceled, but this wasn't just *any* lunch.

This was The Forum, a rarefied gathering of concerned matrons who met monthly to discuss topics of Major Social Significance.

In previous months, the topics had been alcoholism, lesbianism and the plight of female grape-pickers. Today the ladies would discuss rape.

Prue's cook had whipped up a *divine* crab quiche.

DeDe was nervous. This was her first lunch at The Forum, and she wasn't sure of protocol. For guidance, she sat next to Binky Gruen.

'Keep your eye on Prue,' whispered Binky. 'When she rings that little silver bell, it means she's heard enough and you're supposed to stop talking.'

'What am I supposed to *say*?'

Binky patted her hand. 'Prue will tell you.'

DING-A-LING!

The ladies dropped their forks and leaned forward, a dozen thoughtful faces hovering intently over the asparagus.

'Good afternoon,' Prue beamed, surveying her guests. 'I'm delighted you could be here today to share your personal insights into a subject of grave importance.' Her face fell suddenly, like a jarred soufflé. 'Our very special guest today is Velma Runningwater, a

90

Native American who successfully defended herself against an attempted gang rape by sixteen members of the Hell's Angels in Petaluma.'

Binky whistled under her breath. 'This is better than the day she brought the bull dyke in!'

'Pass the rolls,' whispered DeDe.

'But before we hear Ms Runningwater's truly remarkable tale, I would like to try a very special experiment with those of us assembled here at The Forum . . .'

'Here it comes,' said Binky, nudging DeDe under the tablecloth. 'She's always got a kicker.'

'Today,' said Prue, pausing dramatically, 'we are going to rap about rape . . .'

Binky pinched DeDe. 'Can you believe this?'

DeDe gnawed nervously on her roll. Dark circles had begun to form under the arms of her Geoffrey Beane shirtwaist. She *hated* public speaking. Even at Sacred Heart, it had terrified her.

'This is going to be difficult,' continued Prue, 'but I want each of you to share an experience that you have probably tried to block from your memory . . . a time when your . . . person . . . was violated against your will. This is a time for openness, an opportunity for sharing with your sisters.'

'Shugie Sussman is not my sister,' whispered Binky. 'She puked in my Alfa after the Cotillion.'

'Shhh,' hissed DeDe. She was counting the seconds until the moment of truth. What could she say? She had never been raped, for Christ's sake! She had never even been *mugged*.

'Perhaps it would help,' purred Prue, sensing the reticence of her guests, 'if I began by sharing my own tale with you.'

Binky giggled.

DeDe kicked her.

'This is the first time,' continued Prue, 'that I have told this story to a living soul. Not counting Reg, of course. It happened, not in the Tenderloin or the Fillmore or the Mission, as you might think, but in . . . Atherton!'

The ladies gasped in unison.

'And,' said the hostess, aborting a pregnant pause, 'it was someone you all know *very well* . . .'

Prue lowered her head. 'It serves no purpose to dwell on the morbid details . . . Now perhaps someone else would like to share with us. What about you, DeDe?'

Shit. It never failed.

DeDe rose haltingly, folding and refolding her napkin. 'I . . . I'm . . not sure.'

Binky tittered.

Prue rang the silver bell gently. 'Please . . . DeDe is going to share with us. We're your sisters, DeDe. You can be up front with us.'

'It was . . . awful,' DeDe said at last.

'Of course it was,' Prue said sympathetically. 'Can you tell us where it happened, DeDe?'

DeDe swallowed. 'At home,' she said feebly.

Prue clutched the front of her sari. 'Not . . . an intruder?'

'No,' said DeDe. 'A grocery boy.'

When she got home, she picked up the phone and dialed Jiffy's, ordering a box of doughnuts and a can of Drano.

Lionel was up in ten minutes.

Romance in the Rink

Mona celebrated her first day of freedom with a leisurely morning cappuccino at Malvina's. When she returned to Barbary Lane, Michael was in the shower.

'Christ! Didn't you get enough steam at the tubs last night?'

Michael stuck his head around the curtain. 'Oh . . . sorry. Open a window, OK? No, here . . . I'll do it.' He climbed out of the stall, dripping wet, and cranked open the window.

'Uh . . . Michael, dearheart?'

'Huh?'

'Why are you doing that?'

'Doing what?'

'Wearing your Levi's in the shower.'

'Oh . . .' He laughed, hopping back into the stall. 'I'm wire-brushing my basket. See?' He picked up a wire brush from the floor of the stall. 'Just the thing for achieving that well-worn shading in just the right places.' Scraping the brush gingerly across the crotch of his jeans, he screwed his face into an expression of mock pain. 'Arrrggh!'

Mona was bland. 'Do-it-yourself S & M?'

Michael flicked water at her. 'They'll be *devastating* when they're dry.'

'Where'd you pick that one up? *Hints from Heloise?*'

'This is *no* frivolous matter, woman. These babies have to be perfection by tonight.'

'Date with Chuck?'

'Who . . . Oh, no. I'm going to the Grand Arena.'

'New bar?'

'Nope. A skating rink.'

'*You're* going ice-skating?'

'Roller-skating. Tuesday is Gay Night.'

Mona rolled her eyes. 'Now I *know* I'm gonna kill myself.'

'It's a scream. You'd love it.'

Michael climbed out of the shower, shucked the wet jeans and toweled off. 'Some fag hag, *you* are.'

'I didn't hear that,' said Mona, heading into the hallway.

He didn't make it to the Grand Arena until eight o'clock, so he was prepared for the worst.

It happened, of course.

They had already run out of men's skates.

Small wonder. The giant South San Francisco rink was jammed with flannel-shirted men, circling the floor in predatory delight.

Michael caught his breath.

He shed his navy-blue cotton parka, submitted to the indignity of women's skates (white, with nelly-looking tassels) and clopped his way awkwardly to the edge of the rink.

He grinned when he recognized the recorded organ music: 'I Enjoy Being a Girl.'

There were half a dozen girls on the rink. Four of them were under twelve. The others beehived Loretta Lynn lookalikes in sherbet-colored skating costumes. They were welded to sherbet-colored partners of the opposite sex, who propelled them across the floor like Brisbane's answer to Baryshnikov.

The other hundred men were less graceful.

Arms flailing and teeth flashing, they rolled around the rink in a swelling tide of denim. Some were alone; others snaked along merrily in lines of four or five. For Michael, it was a magical sight.

He waited for a moment, steeling himself.

When *was* the last time? Murphy's Skating Rink . . . Orlando, 1963.

93

He murmured a short, conventional Baptist prayer. Werner was never there when he needed him.

He wasn't half bad, actually.

A little wobbly on the turns, but nothing to snicker at.

After five minutes, he had gained enough confidence to concentrate on serious cruising.

So far, his favorite was a blond guy in chinos and a blue Gant shirt. He looked like the vice president of every high school class in northern Florida. He probably *still* drove a Mustang.

And he was skating alone.

Michael moved in the direction of his quarry, overtaking two small black kids in Dyn-O-Mite T-shirts. The only hindrance now was a couple of sherbet straights, doing a very showy Arthur Murray routine less than ten feet away.

The couple heeled like a yacht in a gale, drifting off to the left, clearing the way for Michael . . .

He felt like a roller derby star, moving in for the kill.

Fixing his sights on the target, he accelerated at the turn . . . and realized, too late, what was about to happen. The blond man wasn't turning.

He was stopping.

And Michael had forgotten how to stop.

Clutching desperately at the air, his hands sought anchorage at the sacred oxford-cloth shirttail. His right leg buckled under him, as he skidded unceremoniously into the iron railing, dragging his Galahad behind him.

The two black kids backtracked momentarily, studied the carnage with undisguised glee, and skated off again.

Michael's face was covered with blood. The blond man helped him to his feet.

'Jesus. Are you all right?'

Michael poked his face cautiously with his fingertips. 'It's my nose. It's OK. It bleeds if you don't talk nice to it.'

'Are you sure? Can I get you a Kleenex?'

'Thanks. I think I'll hobble off to the head.'

When he returned, the blond man was waiting for him. 'They just announced "couples only,"' he grinned. 'You man enough for that?'

Michael grinned back. 'Sure. Just tell me when you're gonna stop.'

94

So this time they moved as a unit, hand gripped in hand, under the twirling mirror ball.

'My name is Jon,' said the blond man.

'I'm Michael,' said Michael, just as his nose started to bleed again.

Coed Steam

Valencia Street, with its union halls and Mexican restaurants and motorcycle repair shops, was an oddly squalid setting for the gates of heaven.

For Brian, though, that was part of the turn-on.

He *basked* in the squalor, the teenager-in-Tijuana feeling that came over him whenever he caught sight of that seedy neon sign:

FOR BETTER HEALTH — STEAM BATHS.

Behind the façade, in a tiny entrance alcove, he flashed his laminated photo ID card and forked out five dollars to the guy in the admission booth.

Four dollars for admission.

One dollar for The Party.

The Party made Mondays special at the Sutro Bath House.

Women were admitted free, and tonight there were at least a dozen.

There were twice as many men, mingling with the women in a space that seemed strangely reminiscent of a rumpus room in Walnut Creek: rosy-shaded lamps, mis-matched furniture, and a miniature electric train that chugged noisily along a shelf around the perimeter of the room.

A television set mounted on the wall offered *Phyllis* to the partygoers.

On the opposite wall a movie screen flickered with vintage pornography.

The partygoers were naked, though some of them chose the shelter of a bath towel.

And most of them were watching *Phyllis*.

Brian stripped in the locker room. Overhead, in a plastic arbor, a mechanical canary twittered incessantly. He smiled at it, then

95

wrapped a towel around his waist and headed back to the television lounge.

In the hallway, he met one of the hostesses.

'Hi, Frieda.'

'How's it goin', Brian?'

'Just got here. Any hassles tonight?' Frieda's job was to ensure that women at the baths weren't harassed by the men . . . unless they wanted to be.

She shook her head. 'Mellow as ever.'

'That's too bad.'

Frieda grinned, pinched him on the butt. 'Go play with yourself, pig.'

Then she was off again, walking her rounds in a T-shirt that said: WE DARE YOU.

Brian decided it was still to early to head for the orgy room. The Party was going full tilt. Most people would chow down on cheese and cold cuts before heading upstairs. And *Phyllis* wasn't over.

Adjusting his towel, he sauntered up to a blond woman with an all-over-tan.

'Can I buy you some salami?'

'Now *that's* a new one.'

He grinned. 'I swear I didn't mean it that way.'

'I'm a vegetarian.' She smiled back.

'Me too.' He extended his hand. 'Put it there.'

She studied him for several seconds, then asked flatly: 'What kind?'

'Uh . . . you know, strict.'

'With occasional lapses into lacto and ovo, huh?'

'Yep. Except on weekends and nights when I'm stoned. Then I'm a steako-lacto-ovo . . . or maybe a porkchopo-lacto-ovo . . .'

She smirked at his fraud. 'You're a turko . . . that's what you are!'

'I knew we'd hit on it.'

'Actually, I almost *never* make it with vegetarians.'

'The woman has taste.'

'We've met before, haven't we?'

'I like my line better.'

'No . . . I'm serious. Didn't we play Earth Ball together at the New Games this year?'

'No, but I . . .'

'You into whales?'

'What?'

'Whales. Saving whales.'

Brian shook his head apologetically, wishing to hell he'd saved a whale or two.

'Baby seals?'

'Nope. I used to be into lots of things. Now I'm into this.'

'That's up front, anyway.'

'Thank God for small favors.'

'Hey . . . are you making fun of me?'

'Hell, no. I just feel like I'm . . . applying for a position, that's all.'

She smiled again. 'You are.'

They both laughed. Brian decided it was time to take the initiative. 'Look . . . I don't have a room, but maybe we could . . . you know . . . go upstairs.'

'I can't handle the exhibitionism trip.'

'Then maybe we could . . .'

'It's cool,' she smiled. 'I've got a room.'

Hillary's Room

Brian was wrecked. She was a *goddess*. A younger sister of Liv Ullmann, maybe . . . and Christ almighty, she had a room!

The girl meant business!

'I'm Hillary,' she said, closing the door. The room was no bigger than a walk-in closet.

'You would be.'

'Huh?'

'It fits you. You fit it.'

'You don't have to compliment me. I've processed through all that.'

'I mean it.'

'What's your name?'

'Brian.'

She patted a spot next to her on the bed. 'Sit down, Brian.' She sounded oddly clinical, despite her nakedness. 'Have you done this often?'

'Come to the baths?' She *couldn't* mean fuck.

'No. I mean got it on with girls . . . women?'

He flashed his best Steve McQueen grin. 'A fair amount.'

97

'How long have you been gay?'

'*What?*'

'It's cool if you don't wanna talk about it.'

'Uh . . . I think you've made a mistake.'

'Fine . . . whatever.' Her look was professionally compassionate. It irritated the piss out of him.

'No, Hillary . . . not fine. I'm not gay, understand?'

'You're not?'

'No.'

'Then what are you doing here?'

'I'm losing my mind! What am I doing here, she asks? What the fuck do you *think* I'm doing here?'

'A lot of guys who come here are gay . . . or at least bi.'

'Well, I'm not, got it? I have a well-rehearsed but limited repertoire.' Gently, he placed his hand on her leg.

Gently, she removed it.

'All of us are a little homosexual, Brian. You must not be in touch with your body.'

'It's not *my* body that I want to be in touch with!'

'You don't have to be macho all the time, you know.'

'Who's trying to be macho? I'm trying to get laid.'

'Right. A heartless, mechanical exploitation of . . .'

'Look . . .' He adopted a softer tone. 'I don't think you're being entirely fair when you imply that I'm a male chauvinist or something. I mean, we're equals, aren't we? Look at us. You invited me to your room . . . and I accepted. Right?'

She stared at the wall. 'I thought you needed help.'

'I *do*! Oh, God, do I need help!'

'It's not the same.'

'Can I help it if I'm weird? I've had this perverse craving for women as long as I can remember.'

'Don't be so goddamn flip! You're not any better than a gay person, you know.'

'Did I say that, Hillary? Did I, huh? I like gay people. I *accept* gay people. Christ almighty, don't make me say that some of my best friends are gay!'

'I wouldn't believe you if you did.'

'Hillary, look . . .'

'I think you'd better leave, Brian.'

'Would you please just . . .'

'Don't make me call Frieda.'

He stood up, retrieving his towel from the floor. He wrapped it around himself. She was at the door now, holding it open for him.

'Once,' he blurted, 'when I was twelve, this guy who was in my scout troop and I took off our . . .'

'That doesn't count,' she said.

He stood in the doorway and watched wistfully as she pulled the door closed again.

Venus reentering the clam shell.

Breakfast in Bed

Michael woke with cottonmouth.

He slipped out of bed as quietly as possible and went to the bathroom, squeezing Aim onto his toothbrush with his sterling Tiffany toothpaste roller. He brushed with the door closed.

When he tiptoed back to the bedroom, the shape under the sheets spoke to him, 'You cheated.'

Michael crawled back into bed. 'I thought you were asleep.'

'Now I'll have to brush *my* teeth.'

'No you won't. I'm paranoid about *my* breath, not yours.'

Jon threw back the covers and headed for the bathroom. 'Well, there's something *else* we have in common.'

Mona knocked at the wrong time.

'Uh . . . yeah . . . wait a minute, Mona.'

Mona shouted through the door. 'Room service, gentlemen. Just pull the covers up.'

Michael grinned at Jon. 'My roommate. Brace yourself.'

Seconds later, Mona burst through the doorway with a tray of coffee and croissants.

'Hi! I'm Nancy Drew! You must be the Hardy Boys!'

'I like her,' said Jon, after Mona swept out. 'Does she do that every morning?'

'No. I think she's curious.'

'About what?'

'You.'

'Oh . . . Are you two . . . ?'

'No. Just friends.'

'You've never . . . ?'

Michael shook his head. 'Never.'

'Why not?'

'Why not? Well . . . let's see now. How about . . . I'm queer as a three-dollar bill.'

'So?'

'So I'm a virgin with women. A perfect Kinsey six.'

'Oh.'

'That freaks you?'

'No, I just . . . How old are you?'

'I hope you're not a chicken queen. I'm twenty-six.'

'I'm twenty-eight . . . and I'm not a chicken queen.'

'That's a relief.'

'What about high school?'

'B-minus average.'

Jon smiled. 'I mean *girls* in high school. Didn't you ever get it on with them?'

'All I ever did in high school was tool around with the guys and a six-pack of Bud, looking for heterosexuals to beat up.'

'Is that right?'

Michael nodded. 'You can't miss 'em. They walk funny and carry their books against their hips. That's what you did, wasn't it . . . when you were a heterosexual?'

Jon studied his face for a moment. 'Don't be so defensive. I wasn't criticizing you.'

'If it helps any, I didn't come out until three years ago. I was a eunuch in high school.'

'I wish I'd known you then.'

'As opposed to now?'

'In *addition* to now.' Jon tousled his hair. 'I *like* you, turkey!'

Michael was abuzz after Jon left. 'He's *incredible*, Mona. He's well-adjusted and self-assured . . . and he's a goddamn *doctor*! Can you imagine me with my very own live-in doctor?'

'He's proposed?'

'Don't get technical.'

'What kind of doctor?'

'A gynecologist.'

'That oughta come in handy.'

Michael slapped her on the fanny. 'Just let me fantasize, will you?'

'You're gonna wanna move out, aren't you?'

'Mona!'

'Well?'

'You're my *friend*, Mona. We'll always be together in one way or another.'

'Oh, yeah? What are you gonna do? Adopt me?' She walked to the door and opened it, addressing an invisible guest. 'Oh, hi, Mrs Plushbottom! May I present my father, Michael Tolliver, the famous raconteur and bon vivant, and my mother, the gynecologist!'

Michael shook his head, laughing. 'I'd marry you in a second, Mona Ramsey.'

'If you were the only boy in the world, and I were the only girl. What else is new?'

He kissed her on the forehead. 'Don't worry. I'll screw this up.'

'It sounds like you want to.'

'Spare me the Jungian analysis.'

'Take out the garbage, then. If it happens, it happens.'

The Maestro Vanishes

The P R woman was almost as shaken as Frannie was.

'Mrs Halcyon . . . believe me . . . we've tried our best to . . .'

'The party *starts* in two hours. I've notified *Women's Wear Daily*, the *Chronicle* and the *Examiner*, Carson Callas . . . How on God's green earth can you *lose* a conductor?'

The opera publicist's voice turned starchy. 'The Maestro is not . . . lost, Mrs Halcyon. We've simply been unable to locate him. We've left word for him at the Mark, and there's a good chance he'll . . .'

'What about Cunningham? She'll come without him, won't she?'

'We're trying to find an alternate escort, in the event that . . . We're doing our best, Mrs Halcyon. Miss Cunningham is not generally compatible with tenors.'

'Are you telling me she won't . . . ? Oh, God . . . Really, this is the shoddiest excuse for . . . What am I supposed to tell my guests?'

Beauchamp and DeDe arrived at Halcyon Hill later than planned.

DeDe had popped the zipper on her Galanos. Beauchamp, to survive the ordeal, had downed four jiggers of J & B.

'Mother must be *dying*,' said DeDe.

'Stop trying to cheer me up.'

'God . . . Carson Callas is here already. He *loves* to write no-show stories. He absolutely humiliated the Stonecyphers with that article about . . . Beauchamp, would you please try not to look so bored?'

'There's Splinter.'

'I want a drink, Beauchamp.'

'Help yourself. I'll be talking to Splinter.'

'Beauchamp, Beauchamp! I don't want to . . . talk to Oona.'

It was too late. The Rileys were next to them now, radiating marital bliss. DeDe forced a smile. Her gown felt like a sausage casing.

'So where's the diva?' Splinter asked cheerfully. 'That's the right word, isn't it?'

Oona smiled and squeezed her husband's arm. 'He's such an oaf! How did you manage to marry an intellectual, DeDe?'

The message came through loud and clear. An *impotent* intellectual.

Splinter had told Oona about the phone call. DeDe was sure of it.

Beauchamp broke the silence. 'Well, this intellectual needs to kill a few brain cells. Join me at the bar, Splinter?'

The men walked off together.

Oona remained, smiling at DeDe, but only around the mouth.

'I'm sorry, DeDe.'

'What about?'

'Your ordeal.'

'What ordeal?'

'Oh . . . I see. I'm sorry. I guess we should talk opera or something.'

'I haven't the slightest idea what you're talking about.'

'Forget it. You must think me *terribly* insensitive.'

'Oona, will you please . . .'

'The grocery boy, darling. The *Chinese* grocery boy.'

Silence.

'Shugie told me about The Forum, and we *all* feel for you dreadfully. It must have been awful.' Oona smiled diabolically. 'It *was* awful, wasn't it?'

'I have to go, Oona.'

'I won't say a *thing*, darling. We Sacred Heart girls have to stick together, don't we?'

'Besides,' she added, tucking DeDe's bra strap back under her dress, 'a girl has to make do *somehow*.'

Frannie Freaks

Frannie had begun wobbling slightly. 'Edgar, what am I gonna *do*?'

'I'd say it was in the lap of the gods.'

'Don't be ridiculous! We can't just stand here and let things . . . go to hell.'

'They look as if they're having a good time.'

'Of course they're having a good time! They're *crucifying* me, Edgar. Look at Viola. She hasn't stopped giggling with Carson all evening!'

'Frannie . . . look . . . if you need entertainment or something, I could call the accordionist who plays at the club. It's late notice, but maybe he'd . . .'

Frannie groaned. 'You don't just *swap* an accordionist for the greatest soprano in the world, Edgar!'

'I didn't know she was going to sing.'

'She doesn't have to *sing*, Edgar! God! Do you do that on purpose?'

'What?'

'Act like a philistine.'

'I *am* a philistine.'

'You are not a . . .'

'My father ran a department store, Frannie.'

'He bought a box at the opera!'

'He ran a department store.'

Beauchamp chatted with Peter Cipriani on a quiet corner of the terrace.

'So what's *your* theory on La Grande Nora?'

Peter shrugged. 'Who cares? I didn't come for that. My new passion is Troyanos.'

'Your pupils are dilated.'

'They'd better be. Psilocybin.'

'Jesus.'

'I'm dating Shugie Sussman, for Christ's sake.'

'Is that your excuse for altered consciousness?'
'Got a better one?'
'I pass.'
'I hope the little darling can drive. I had two drinks at The Mill before I picked her up.'

'I'm *so* bored,' said Margaret van Wyck Montoya-Corona.

DeDe fish-eyed her. 'Mother will be so glad to hear that.'

'Oh, no, DeDe . . . not *here* . . . I mean, in general. Jorge's been in Madrid for three weeks. It's *no* fun being married to a contraceptive czar, lemme tell you.'

'I can imagine.'

'It's the company I miss mostly.'

'Get a dog, then.'

Muffy smirked. 'I've thought about getting a Samoan.'

'You mean a Samoyed.'

'No. I mean a *Samoan.* Penny and Trinka have *both* got Samoans. Matching Samoans. They're mechanics in the Mission . . . and, my dear, they are *big.*'

DeDe grimaced. 'I don't like fat men.'

'Not fat.' She held her hands up. 'Big.'

'Oh. I see.'

'Well, it's a helluva lot better than sending away for one of those plastic doohickies.'

Edgar pulled his daughter aside. 'I need your help,' he whispered.

'What?'

'Your mother's locked herself in the john.'

'Again?'

'Would you mind, DeDe? She's upset over . . . that singer.'

Upstairs, DeDe bellowed at her mother through the bathroom door. 'Mother!'

Silence.

'Mother, goddammit! You are *not* Zelda Fitzgerald. This act gets *real* old.'

'Go away.'

'If you're freaked over Nora Cunningham . . . I talked to Carson Callas. He says she does this all the time.'

'It doesn't matter.'

'He's giving you nine inches, Mother. Nine inches.'

'What?'

'In *Western Gentry*. He's devoting most of his column to . . .'

The bathroom door swung open. Frannie stood there, red-eyed, holding a Mai Tai. 'Did you ask him to stay for breakfast?' she said.

The Case of the Six Batons

The caterers made scrambled eggs for the remnants of the party at Halcyon Hill. While Frannie was cornering Carson Callas, Edgar slipped away to his den and placed a phone call to Barbary Lane.

'Madrigal.'

'It's me, Anna.'

'Hello, Edgar.'

'I'm sorry about Mona, Anna.'

'You don't need to apologize.'

'Yes I do. I shouldn't have snapped at you this morning.'

'I . . . you have a job to do, Edgar.'

'If I had known how much Mona means to you . . .'

'I shouldn't have called. I meddle too much.'

'I have a free day next week. We could beach it again.'

'Fine.'

'Thank God!'

'Go on, now. Get back to your guests.'

Back to Barbary Lane, Mona was prone on the sofa with *New West* when Michael dragged in.

'Well,' she said. 'How's the wonderful world of gynecology?'

'I wasn't with Jon.'

'My! How soon the flame of love can die!'

'He had a meeting tonight.'

'So you went to the tubs?' She frowned at him, only half-jokingly.

'It isn't good to put all your eggs in one basket.'

'So to speak.'

He grinned. 'Yeah.'

'My lips are sealed.'

He wriggled onto the sofa next to her. 'Guess who was there?'

'The Mormon Tabernacle Choir.'

'OK, if you don't wanna dish, we won't dish.'

'No. Go ahead. I want to.'

'No. First I have to tell you about Hamburger Mary's.'

'I hate it when you punish me.'

'I'm setting the stage, Mona. Relax. Pretend I'm your guru. Maharishi Mahesh Mouse. I bring you the Keys to the Kingdom of Folsom Street. The Holy Red Bandanna That Sitteth on the Left Hand of the Levi's. The . . .'

'Michael, you fucker!'

'All right, all right. There I was at Hamburger Mary's, eating a bean sprout salad and wondering if my new Sears work boots looked *too* new, when this couple waltzed in and took a seat in the middle of a heavy biker contingent.'

'A couple of guys?'

'Hell, no. A guy and his wife, slumming. Radical chic, vintage 1976. She was wearing a David Bowie T-shirt to show where her sympathies lay, and he was looking *grossly* uncomfortable in a Grodins sports ensemble. I mean, five years ago you could have caught these turkeys down in the Fillmore, chowing down on chitlins and black-eyed peas with the Brothers and Sisters. Now they're into faggots. They want *desperately* to relate to perverts.'

'It's nothing but heartbreak, I can tell 'em!'

'OK, so this scene gets more rough-trade by the minute. And then this dude sits down next to them and he's wearing a ring in his nose and a Future Farmers of America jacket and Mr Grodins Ensemble is freaking out so badly that he may have to split for El Cerrito *any* minute.'

'What about the wife?'

'Oh, God . . . *extremely* PO'd that hubby's not getting off on the decadent ambience. Finally, she looks at him intently and says, in a voice *fraught* with meaning: "Which do you think you'd prefer, Rich? S or M?"'

'And?'

'He thought it was something to put on the hamburger.'

'So who did you meet at the tubs, Mouse?'

'Well . . . I met him after I'd been there a couple of hours. I was walking down the hall, looking into rooms, and this gray-haired guy motioned me to come into his room. He seemed pretty old, but he had a nice body. So I went in and sat down on the edge of his bed, and he said, "Had a busy night?" and I immediately knew who it was by his accent. I also recognized him from his album covers.'

'Who?'
'Nigel Huxtable.'
'Yep.'
'The conductor?'
'Yep. Nora Cunningham's husband, no less.'
'Did you two . . . ?'
'Are you kidding?'
'Well, I didn't . . .'
'I got out of there as soon as I saw what he had in his bag.'
'Go on, go on.'
'A cassette recorder . . . a tape of his lovely wife singing the "Casta Diva" . . . a piece of gold brocade cord which he *said* came from the curtain at La Scala . . . and six rubber batons!'
'Jesus Christ!'
'I didn't do anything, Mona. With anybody.'
'Tell that to your gynecologist!'

Back to Cleveland?

Days dragged like weeks at Halcyon Communications.

Beauchamp would smile as he passed Mary Ann's desk, and sometimes even wink at her in the elevator, but there were no more invitations, no more anguished pleas for friendship.

It was as if Mendocino had never happened.

Fine, thought Mary Ann, if that's the way he wants it. There were lots of other outlets for her energies . . . and miles to go before she slept.

She cleaned out Edgar Halcyon's coffee machine.

She bought a glass-cutter and made a wine-jug terrarium for her desk.

She created a 'personal corner' of her bulletin board, filling it with *Peanuts* cartoons, fortune cookie messages and postcards from friends on vacation.

Once a morning, she sat perfectly still at her desk, closed her eyes, and uttered the brave new litany of the seventies:

'Today is the first day of the rest of my life.'

One night, Michael showed up at her door, bearing a clay pot shaped like a chicken.

'It's half of my *poulet Tolliver*,' he grinned, pronouncing his name *toe-lee-vay*. 'Mona's out either raising her consciousness or lowering her expectations, and I thought . . . well, here.'

'Michael, that's very sweet.'

'Don't get gushy until you've seen it. It looks like a seagull that tangled with a 747.'

'It smells delicious.'

'Shall I put it on the parsons table?'

'Fine. Thanks.'

He set the crock down, then smiled, shaking his head.

'What?' asked Mary Ann.

'They do this in the South when somebody dies. Bring food, I mean.'

'Well, you're close.'

'What do you mean?'

'Are you – have you eaten the other half of that chicken yet?'

He shook his head.

'Would you like company?'

Michael rolled his eyes. 'Sometimes to the point of obsession.'

Mary Ann made a salad, while Michael was retrieving his half of the chicken.

They dined by candlelight.

'This is my first formal dinner – for a guest.'

'I'm honored.'

'I hope you like Green Goddess.'

'Mmm. Next time we'll have asparagus and you can show me your hollandaise recipe.'

'How did you know I . . . oh . . .'

Michael nodded. 'Robert. I lost the recipe in the divorce settlement.'

Mary Ann reddened. 'It's easy.'

'I shouldn't have brought up ancient history. I'm sorry.'

'It's OK. I've always felt a little dumb about that.'

'Why? Robert's a hot number. I would have done it. Hell, I *did* do it. Where do you think *I* met him?'

'The Safeway?'

'Not *that* one, actually. The one on Upper Market. From *my* standpoint, it's a lot cruisier.' He slapped his own cheek. 'Stop that. You're embarrassing the girl.'

She laughed. 'Do I look that out of it?'

'No, I . . . yeah, sometimes.'

'Well, I am.'

'It's very becoming, actually.'

'I've heard *that* one before.'

'Oh . . . who?'

'It doesn't matter.'

Michael smiled wryly, studying her expression. 'Is that why you're close to death?'

'Michael, I . . .'

'Look . . . let's plan a big night next week. We can go out to someplace impossibly straight . . . like the Starlight Roof or something. You haven't lived until you've done business with the Tolliver Gigolo Service.'

She managed a grin. 'That might be nice.'

'Try to control your ecstasy, will you?'

'I might not be here, Michael.'

'Huh?'

'I think I'm going home to Cleveland.'

Michael whistled. 'That's not close to death. That *is* death.'

'It's the only thing that makes sense right now.'

'You mean' – he threw his napkin down – 'I just wasted a whole chicken making friends with a transient?' He stood up from the table, walked over to the sofa, sat down and folded his arms. 'Come over here. It's time for a little girl talk!'

Michael's Pep Talk

Mary Ann stood up uncertainly, ill at ease with Michael's new role as mentor. She was sorry she had ever mentioned going home to Cleveland.

'Can I get you some crème de menthe?'

'Why are you leaving, Mary Ann?'

She sat down next to him. 'Lots of reasons . . . I don't know . . . San Francisco in general.'

'Just because some turkey dumped on you . . .'

'It isn't that . . . Michael, there's no stability here. Everything's too easy. Nobody sticks with anybody or anything, because there's always something just a little bit better waiting around the corner.'

'What did he *do* anyway?'

'I can't handle all this, Michael. I want to live somewhere where you don't have to apologize for serving instant coffee. Do you know what I like about Cleveland? People in Cleveland aren't "into" anything!'

'Boring, in other words.'

'I don't care what you call it. I need it. I need it badly.'

'Why go home? We have boring people here. Haven't you ever been to Paoli's at lunchtime?'

'There's no point . . .'

The phone rang. Michael jumped up and grabbed it. 'The boring residence of Mary Ann Singleton.'

'Michael!' Mary Ann jerked the phone away from him. 'Hello.'

'Mary Ann?'

'Mom.'

'We've been worried sick.'

'What else is new?'

'Don't talk to me like that. We haven't heard from you in *weeks.*'

'I'm sorry. It's been hectic, Mom.'

'Who was that man?'

'What man? Oh . . . Michael. Just a friend.'

'Michael what?'

Mary Ann covered the receiver. 'What's your last name, Michael?'

'De Sade.'

'Michael!'

'Tolliver.'

'Michael Tolliver, Mom. He's a real nice guy. He lives down-stairs.'

'Your daddy and I have been talking, Mary Ann . . . so hear me out on this. We both agree that you deserved a chance to . . . try your wings in San Francisco . . . but the time has come now . . . well, we can't just sit by and watch you throw your life away.'

'It's *my* life to throw away, Mom.'

'Not when you apparently don't have the maturity to . . .'

'How would you know?'

'Mary Ann . . . a strange man answered your phone.'

'He's not a strange man, Mom.'

'Who says?' grinned Michael.

'You don't even know his last name.'

'We're more informal out here.'

'Apparently . . . if you have no more judgment than to invite some perfectly . . .'

'Mom, Michael is homosexual.'

Silence.

'He likes *boys*, got it. I know you've heard of it. They've got it on TV now.'

'I think you've completely lost your . . .'

'Not completely. Gimme another week or two.'

'I can't believe I'm . . .'

'Mom, I'll call you in a few days, OK? Everything is fine. Night-night.'

She hung up.

Michael beamed at her from the sofa.

Mona was the second assault wave.

'Christ, Mary Ann! No wonder you're miserable. You sit around on your butt all day expecting life to be one great big Hallmark card. Well, I've got news for you. There's not a single goddamn soul out there who cares enough to send the very best.'

'So what point is there in . . .'

'You've got to *make* things work for you, Mary Ann. When you're down to the seeds and stems, get out there and grab life by the . . . Get a pencil. Take down this address . . .'

War and Peace

A platoon of sandpipers patrolled the beach at Point Bonita, pecking at the poptops in the shiny black sand. The water was sometimes blue, sometimes gray.

Edgar slipped his arm around Anna's waist. 'I'll take her back, you know.'

'Who?'

'Mona . . . if you tell me to, Anna, I will.'

Anna shook her head. 'I wouldn't do that. Furthermore, she wouldn't come back, even if you *did* change your mind.'

'I'm a horse's ass, then?'

'No. Your son-in-law.'

'She told you that?'

Anna nodded. 'Is she right?'

'Absolutely.'

'I thought she might be.'

'Have you told her, Anna?'

'About you?'

'Yes.'

Anna shook her head. 'This is us, Edgar. Just us.'

'I know, but . . .'

'What?'

'She's like a daughter to you, isn't she?'

'Yes.'

'Isn't it hard *not* to tell her?'

'Yes.'

'I want to tell the whole goddamn world.'

Anna smiled. 'Not so much as a memo to your secretary.'

'She'll figure it out before Mona does.'

'I hope not.'

'Why? I have more to lose than you do.'

Anna gazed at him for a moment. 'C'mon. Let's get the blanket out of the car. It's colder than a witch's titty out here.'

Edgar chuckled. 'I didn't know nice girls knew that expression.'

'They don't.'

'We used to say that in France. During the war.'

'That's when I learned it.'

'What are you talking about?'

'I was in the Fort Ord campaign.'

'You were a WAC?'

'I typed munitions requests for a colonel who was drunk most of the time. Hey, are we gonna get that blanket or not?'

They huddled together behind a sand dune, out of the wind. 'What was it like growing up in a whorehouse?' Edgar asked.

Anna pursed her lips. 'What was it like growing up in Hillsborough?'

'I didn't grow up in Hillsborough. I grew up in Pacific Heights.'

'Oh, my! You *have* been a gypsy, haven't you?'

'C'mon. I asked you first.'

'Well . . .' She scooped up a handful of sand and let it trickle through her fingers. 'For one thing, I was fourteen years old before I realized that American currency does *not* bear the inscription "Good for all night."'

Edgar laughed.

'Also, I developed a number of quaint superstitions that hound me to this very day.'

'For instance?'

'For instance . . . I can't abide cut flowers, so don't send me a dozen longstems, if you want to maintain our strange and wonderful relationship.'

'What's wrong with cut flowers?'

'Ladies of the evening consider them to be a sign of impending death. Beauty cut down in its prime and all that.'

'Oh.'

'Not pleasant.'

'No.'

Anna looked down at the sand, tracing a line there with her finger. And it seemed to Edgar that she not only sensed, but shared his pain.

Once More into the Breach

The Bay Area Crisis Switchboard was located in a renovated Victorian house in Noe Valley. Its exterior was painted persimmon, mole, avocado, fuchsia and chocolate. A sign in the window informed visitors that the building's occupants did not drink Gallo wine.

Mary Ann felt weird already.

She rang the buzzer. A man in a Renaissance shirt came to the door. Mary Ann's gaze climbed from the shirt past a scraggly red beard to the place where his left ear should have been.

'I . . . called earlier.'

'Far out. The new volunteer. I'm Vincent.'

He led her into a sparsely furnished room dominated by a gargantuan macramé hanging that incorporated bits of shell and feather and driftwood. She had no choice but to comment on it.

'That's . . . really wonderful.'

'Yeah,' he beamed. 'My Old Lady made it.'

She assumed he didn't mean his mother.

To her great relief, he turned out to be a very nice guy. He worked the Tuesday to Thursday shift at the switchboard. He was an artist. He fixed her a cup of Maxim, without apologizing.

'We'll probably . . . like . . . work together,' he explained. 'We get enough calls between eight and eleven to keep us both pretty busy.'

'Are they all . . . trying to kill themselves?'

'No. You'll learn to psyche out the regulars.'

'The regulars?'

'Loonies. Lonelies. The ones who call just to talk. That's cool too. That's what we're here for. And some of 'em just need referral to the proper social agency.'

'For instance?'

'Battered wives, gay teenagers, senior citizens with questions about social security, child abusers, rape victims, minorities with housing problems . . .' He rattled off the list like a Howard Johnson's employee reciting the twenty-eight flavors.

'Then what about the suicides?'

'Oh . . . we get maybe two or three a night.'

'You know, I haven't had any special training in . . .'

'It's cool. I'll handle the hairy ones. Most of the time they're just trying to get your attention.'

Mary Ann sipped her coffee, drawing strength from Vincent's casual confidence. 'It's pretty rewarding, isn't it?'

Vincent shrugged. 'Sometimes. And sometimes it's a real drag. It depends.'

'Has it been . . . hairy lately?'

'I don't know. I've been off for a couple of weeks.'

'Vacation?'

He shook his head, holding up his right hand. Mary Ann had already noticed that his little finger was bandaged . . . but not the fact that it appeared to have been severed at midpoint.

'You poor thing! How did that happen?'

'Aww . . .'

The ear . . . the finger . . . She was suddenly embarrassed.

Vincent saw her redden. 'I get on downers.'

'Pills?'

He smiled. 'No . . . just downers. Depressed. Bummed out.'

'I'm afraid I don't . . .'

'No big deal. I'm gettin' it together. Hey, hey! Almost eight o'clock. All set?'

'Yeah. I guess so.' She sank into the chair in front of the telephone. 'I guess I'll just . . . play it by ear.'

She could have bitten her tongue off.

Fantasia for Two

After watching *Young Frankenstein* at the Ghirardelli Cinema, Michael and Jon walked onto the pier at Aquatic Park.

The pier was dark. Clusters of Chinese fishermen broke the silence with laughter and the tinny blare of transistor radios. A helicopter made a *whup-whup* noise in the sky over Fort Mason.

The couple sat at the end of the pier on the mammoth concrete bench.

'It's a question mark,' said Michael.

'What?'

'The pier. It's a giant question mark.'

Jon looked across the black lagoon defined by the curve of the pier. 'No it's not. It bends the other way. It's a backwards question mark.'

'Doctors are so literal.'

'Sorry.'

'I never told you about my chimp, did I?'

'As in monkey?'

'Uh, huh. Do you wanna hear it?'

'By all means.'

'Well . . . ever since I was a kid I've always wanted a chimp. I used to fantasize about training a chimp to burst into my fifth-grade classroom and throw water balloons at my teacher, Miss Watson.' He laughed. 'She was probably a dyke, come to think of it. I should've been nicer to her . . . Anyway, I *never* outgrew it . . . the desire to own one . . . and last year I happened to mention this to my ex-lover . . . I mean, he's my ex-lover now . . . He was my lover at the time.'

'Stick to the chimp.'

'O K . . . The *big* coincidence was that Christopher had had this *exact same* fantasy ever since *he* was a kid. Sooo . . . we talked about it for a while and decided we were two responsible adults and there was no reason in the world why we shouldn't have one. Anyway, Christopher contacted this friend of his at Marine World who knew how to handle all the red tape and everything and eventually . . . we ended up the proud parents of a teenaged chimp named Andrew.'

Jon smiled. 'Andrew, Michael and Christopher. Very nice.'

'We thought so. And it worked out *beautifully*, after we got past the toilet-training and all. We took him *everywhere*. Golden Gate Park, the Renaissance Faire . . . and the *zoo*. Christ, he *adored* the zoo! Then one day our friend at Marine World asked if we would . . . like . . . mate him with a lady chimp that belonged to a friend of his. Naturally, we were pretty excited about this, since it would make us grand-parents, in effect.'

'In effect.'

'So the big day came . . . but Andrew didn't.'

'Oh, no!'

'Hell, he wouldn't go in the same *room* with her.'

'OK, let me guess.'

Michael nodded soberly. 'Queer as a goddamn three-dollar bill!'

'Now wait a minute!'

'I could handle it OK, because I really *loved* Andrew, but Christopher took it personally. He was *convinced* that if he had played more ball with Andrew . . .'

Jon began to laugh. 'You're too much!'

'It was *awful*, I tell you! Christopher accused me of mollycoddling Andrew and taking him to too many Busby Berkeley movies and . . . letting him see the men's underwear section of the Sears catalogue!'

'Stop it!'

Michael grinned finally, forsaking the game altogether. 'You like that one, do you?'

'Do you always make things up?'

'Always.'

'Why?'

Michael shrugged. 'I want to deceive him just long enough to make him want me.'

'What's that from?'

'Blanche DuBois. In *Streetcar*.'

Jon threw an arm around Michael's neck. 'Come over here, Blanche.' They kissed for a long time, pressed against the cold concrete.

When they separated, Michael said, 'Would it sound better if the lover was named Andrew and the chimp Christopher?'

'You made up the lover too?'

'Oh . . . *especially* the lover.'

116

The Mysterious Caller

The wind was rising on the beach, so Anna readjusted the blanket that sheltered them. 'Here, Edgar . . . cover up. Somebody might see your Brooks Brothers ensemble.'

'Watch it.'

'Say . . . those socks are adorable . . . pardon the expression. I understand *everybody* in St Moritz is wearing charcoal over-the-calves these days!'

'That tickles, Anna. Cut it out.'

'Ticklish? Edgar Halcyon? Is *nothing* sacred?'

'Anna, I'm warning you . . .'

'Tough talk for a city boy!' She jumped up suddenly, giving his loosened tie a yank, and pranced down the beach. Edgar chased her back into the dunes, then tackled her with a Samurai yelp.

They lay there together, laughing and gasping.

'C'mon,' said Anna, taking his hands. 'Let's go find some flotsam and/or jetsam.'

'Wait a minute, Anna.'

'Are you all right?'

'Yes, I . . .'

'I keep forgetting you're an old buzzard.'

'I'm two years older than you.'

'Right. An old buzzard.'

The sky cleared at four o'clock. They walked barefoot up the beach.

'This reminds me of something,' Edgar said.

'A bourbon commercial?'

He smiled and squeezed her hand. 'When I was nineteen, my parents sent me to England for the summer. I stayed with some cousins in a village called Cley-next-the-Sea. I used to walk on the beach looking for carnelians.'

'Stones?'

'Beautiful red ones. Orangish-red. One day I met an old lady on the beach. At least, I *thought* she was old at the time. Her daughter was with her. She was eighteen and beautiful. They asked me to walk with them. They were looking for carnelians too.'

'Did you do it?'

'What do you think?'

'I think Edgar was too busy . . . or too embarrassed.'

Edgar stopped and turned to face her. He looked like a lion with a thorn in his paw. 'It's too late, isn't it, Anna?'

She dropped her shoes in the sand and wrapped her arms around his neck. 'It's too late for the girl, Edgar. The old lady's a pushover.'

They were under the blanket again.

'We should get back, Anna.'

'I know.

'I told Frannie I would . . .'

'Fine.'

'Are we making a big mistake?'

'Oh, I hope so.'

'You don't know much about me.'

'No.'

'I'm dying, Anna.'

'Oh . . . I thought you might be.'

'You've known about . . .'

Anna shrugged. 'Why else would Edgar Halcyon do this?'

'Jesus.'

She toyed with the white curls on the back of his neck. 'How much time have we got?'

Back at Barbary Lane, Anna soaked in a hot tub. She was humming a very old tune when her buzzer rang.

She dried off, slipped into her kimono, and buzzed in her visitor.

'Who is it?' she shouted down the hallway.

'A friend of Mary Ann Singleton's,' came the reply. It was a young woman's voice.

'She's out, dear. At the Crisis Switchboard.'

'Would it be all right if I waited here? In the foyer, I mean. It's kind of important.'

Anna walked into the hallway. The young woman was blond and plump, with the face of a lost child. She was carrying a Gucci tote bag.

'Have a seat, dear,' said the landlady. 'Mary Ann should be home soon.'

Back in the tub, Anna puzzled over the visitor. She looked familiar somehow. Something about the eyes and the line of the jaw.

Then it hit her.

She looked like Edgar.

So Where Was Beauchamp?

The woman's face was in the shadows. She had gained so much weight that Mary Ann didn't recognize her immediately.

'Mary Ann?'

'Oh . . .'

'Beauchamp's wife. DeDe. Your landlady let me in.'

'Yes. Mrs Madgrigal.'

'She was very nice. I hope you don't mind. I was afraid I'd miss you.'

'No . . . that's fine. Can you come up for a drink?'

'You're not expecting . . . company?'

'No,' said Mary Ann, already denying the accusation.

DeDe sat in a yellow vinyl director's chair, folding her hands across the surface of her tote bag.

'Would you like some crème de menthe?' asked Mary Ann.

'Thank you. Do you have white?'

'White what?'

'Crème de menthe.'

'Oh . . . no . . . just the other.'

'Oh . . . I think I'll pass.'

'A Tab or a Fresca?'

'Really. I'm fine.'

Mary Ann sank to the edge of the sofa. 'But not *that* fine.' She smiled feebly.

DeDe looked down at her hands. 'No, I guess not. Mary Ann . . . I'm not here to make a scene.'

Mary Ann swallowed, feeling her face turn hot.

'I wanted to bring you this.' DeDe fumbled in the tote bag and produced Mary Ann's brown-and-white polka-dot scarf. 'I found it in Beauchamp's car.'

Mary Ann stared at the scarf, dumbfounded. 'When?'

'The Monday after you went to Mendocino with him.'

'Oh.'

'He told me about that.'

'I see.'

'It's yours, isn't it?'

'Yes.'

'I don't care. I mean . . . I *care*, but I've stopped . . . exhausting myself over it. I've dealt with it. I think I even understand how he . . . got you involved.'

'DeDe, I . . . Why are you here, then?'

'Because . . . I'm hoping you'll tell me the truth.'

Mary Ann made an impotent gesture with her hands. 'I thought I just had.'

'Were you with him last weekend, Mary Ann?'

'No! I was . . .'

'What about Tuesday before last?'

Mary Ann's jaw dropped. 'DeDe . . . I swear to God . . . I was with Beauchamp one time and one time only. He asked me to go to Mendocino with him because . . .' She cut herself off.

'Because of what?'

'It sounds dumb. He . . . said he wanted someone to talk to. I felt sorry for him. I've barely talked to him since.'

'You're with him every day.'

'In the same building. That's about it.'

'You *did* sleep together in Mendocino?'

'I . . . yes.'

DeDe stood up. 'Well . . . I'm sorry to bother you. I think that's enough of this soap opera for both of us.' She turned and headed for the door.

'DeDe?'

'Yes?'

'Did Beauchamp tell you I was with him last weekend and . . . whatever the other time was?'

'Not in so many words.'

'He implied it?'

'Yes.'

'I wasn't, DeDe. I want you to believe me.'

DeDe smiled bitterly. 'I do. Isn't *that* the pits?'

Back on Montgomery Street, DeDe tore ruthlessly into the mail she had ignored all day.

There were new bills from Wilkes and Abercrombie's, the latest issue of *Architectural Digest*, a plea for money from the Bennington Alumni Association, and a letter from Binky Gruen.

She took Binky's letter into the kitchen, where she fixed a bowl of Familia and milk. She opened the envelope with a butter knife.

The letter was written on Golden Door stationery.

DeDe Dear,

Well, there's old Bink, wallowing in luxurious misery at America's most elegant fat farm. We get up at some godawful hour of the morning to jog through the boonies in very unflattering pink terrycloth jump suits called 'pinkies'. (Please, darling, no jokes about Binky in her Pinky.) I've lost six pounds already. Trumpet fanfare. Movie stars everywhere you turn. I feel déclassé if I don't wear my Foster Grants in the steam room. Try it, you'll hate it.

Love and kisses.

Binky

Beauchamp walked into the kitchen. 'Where did you go tonight?'

'Junior League.'

He looked at the cereal bowl. 'They didn't feed you?'

'I had a *small* bowl, Beauchamp!'

'Suit yourself. It's too late to get in shape for the opening of the opera, anyway.' He smiled maddeningly and walked out of the room.

DeDe glowered at him until he was out of sight. Then she picked up Binky's letter and read it again.

What the Simple Folk Do

The beast in the doorway made Mary Ann's flesh crawl.

Its face was chalk white with lurid spots of rouge on the cheekbones. It was bare-chested and furry-thighed, and two gnarled goat horns rose hideously from its brow.

It spoke to her.

'How horny can ya get, huh?'

'Michael!'

'*Wrong*, O boring one. I am the Great God Pan.'

'You scared me to death!'

'But I am a gentle, playful creature . . . the spirit of forests and shepherds . . . Screw it! How can anybody stay in character with you?'

Mary Ann smiled. 'A costume party?'

'No. Actually, I'm meeting my Aunt Agnes at the Greyhound station.'

'You're going to the bus . . . ? Why do I even *talk* to you?'

'Aren't you gonna invite me in?'

She giggled. 'My mother would love you.'

'This may come as a rude shock to you, but I don't particularly *want* your mother to love me. Look . . . if you don't let me out of the hallway, that man on the roof is gonna have a heart attack.'

'Come on in. *What* man on the roof?'

Michael bounced into the room and sat down, adjusting the brown Afro wig that held his horns. 'The new tenant. Somebody Williams. I saw him on the steps to the roof a little while ago. He nearly freaked.'

'There's an apartment on the roof?'

'Sorta. I call it a pentshack. It doesn't rent very often, but it has a *gorgeous* view. He moved in a couple of days ago. Hey, can I have something to drink?'

'Sure . . . there's some . . .'

'Say crème de menthe and I'll gore you!'

She wiggled one of his horns. 'White wine, Your Holiness.'

'Sure . . . no, I take it back. I've gotta leave soon. I kinda hoped you'd go with me.'

'As what? A nanny goat?'

'A shepherdess. I've got a neat-looking peasant dress with a ribboned bodice and . . . Don't look at me like that, woman. It's Mona's!'

Mary Ann laughed. 'I'd love to, Michael . . . but tonight's my night at the Crisis Switchboard.'

'This *is* a crisis! Lonely, horned homophile with hairy legs seeks attractive but boring lady for free-wheeling evening of . . .'

'What about the guy I saw you with?'

'Jon?'

'Blond hair?'

Michael nodded. 'Tonight's the opening night of the opera.'

'Oh . . . you don't like opera, huh?'

'No . . . well, that's true, as a matter of fact . . . but that isn't it. Jon bought season tickets with a friend. But you're right . . . I can't really handle opera. I don't think I would've . . . you know.'

She kissed him cautiously on his rouged cheek. 'How about a rain check?'

He stood up, sighed and readjusted his horns. 'That's what they *all* say.'

'Where's the party?'

'Not far. The Hyde and Green Plant Store. I'm gonna walk it.'

'Dressed like that?'

'Don't be so . . . Cleveland. Half the people on Russian Hill look like this.'

'Well, be careful.'

'Of what?'

'I don't know . . . Other people who look like that, I guess.'

'Have fun with the suicides.'

'Thanks.' She pushed him playfully out the door. 'Go find yourself a nice billy goat.'

Intermezzo

Meanwhile, at the opera house, the gentlemen came and went in the shadows, preening their plumage amid the red leather and dark wood and gleaming fixtures of the men's room at The Boxes. For the next two hours, it would be the most elegant toilet in town.

'Guard the door,' ordered Peter Cipriani.

'What?' said Beauchamp.

'The *last* thing we need is one of those tight-assed old dinosaurs stumbling in here ripped to the tits!'

From his pocket Peter took a Gump's envelope embossed with the Cipriani crest. He dug into it with a tiny gold spoon and lifted the spoon to his left nostril.

'Ah! Uncut! The way I like my coke *and* my men.'

Beauchamp was nervous. 'C'mon! Hurry up!'

'Ladies first.'

The spoon went down and up again, catering to Peter's other nostril. Beauchamp followed suit, then inspected his tails for lint in front of the mirror.

'God, this is dreary!'

Peter grinned at him. 'Are you going to L'Orangerie with the Halcyons afterwards?'

'Check with DeDe. She and her mother are calling the shots tonight.'

Peter extracted a Bill Blass bronzer from his breast pocket and began to touch up his cheekbones. 'Why don't you split with me at intermission and go to The Club?'

'The club has something planned?'

Peter groaned. 'You poor naïve heiress! I'm talking about the one at Eighth and Howard.'

'I think you're on your own tonight, Peter.'

'*Chacun à son goût.* Personally, I'm sick of these pseudo-patricians. I'm ready for a few pseudo-lumberjacks.'

Ryan Hammond swept into the room. Ryan was an Englishman, or at least *talked* like one. He was renowned in the social columns as an escort of widows and a star of musical comedies on the Peninsula.

'Well,' purred Peter, 'haven't the walkers crawled out of the woodwork tonight?'

Beauchamp glared at his friend.

Ryan ignored him, heading for the urinals.

'Your date's real cute, Ryan. How old is she? A hundred and eight?'

'Peter!' snapped Beauchamp.

Going about his business, Ryan fixed Peter with his best George Sanders evil eye. 'Good evening, Mr Cipriani. I didn't know Massenet was your cup of tea.'

'Well, not ordinarily . . . but opening night is such a spectacle, isn't it? Hell, it's the only night of the year that *you* wear less jewelry than your girlfriends.'

The bathroom was empty again when Edgar entered with Booter Manigault

Booter was adorned with his European Campaign ribbons and the earplug of a transistor radio. He was listening to the Giants-Cincinnati game.

The two men faced the wall. 'Almost time for ducks again,' Edgar said expressionlessly.

'What? . . . Sorry, Edgar.' He pulled out the earplug.

'I said it's almost time for ducks again.'

'Yeah . . . the old tempus really fugits, doesn't it?' Booter chuckled to himself. 'Who says we haven't got seasons in California? Just about now the hookers are leaving their nests in Rio Nido and migrating to Marysville. I'd say that was a sure sign of fall, wouldn't you?'

Silence.

'Edgar . . . are you all right?'

'Yeah . . . I'm fine.'

'You look a little white.'

'Opera.' He forced a grin.

Booter reinstated the earplug. 'Goddamn right!'

Vincent's Old Lady

Michael uncapped a tube of Dance Arts clown white and repaired his Pan face in the foyer of 28 Barbary Lane. He loved that foyer, with its tarnished Deco ladies and gilt mirrors and pressed-tin ceiling full of thirties hieroglyphics.

Somehow it made him feel debonair – gay in the archaic sense of the word – like Fred Astaire in *Top Hat* or Noel Coward off to meet Gertie Lawrence at the Savoy Grill.

Thank heavens, he thought, for Mrs Madrigal, a landlady of almost cosmic sensitivity who had never felt called upon to defile the building with polyethylene palm trees or Florentine stick-on mirror tiles from Goodman Lumber.

He gave himself a thorough inspection and smiled in approval. He looked damned good.

His horns were outrageously realistic. His mock-chinchilla Home Yardage goat haunches jutted out from his waist with comic eroticism. His belly was flat, and his pecs . . . well, his pecs were the pecs of a man who hardly ever cheated on a bench press at the Y.

You're hot, he told himself. Remember that.

Remember that and hold your head up later when your parents call from Orlando and wonder if you've met any 'nice girls' . . . when that cute trick from The Midnight Sun turns out to have a lover on the diving team at Berkeley . . . when someone at the tubs says, 'I'm just resting right now' . . . when the beautiful and aloof Dr Jon Fielding furrows his Byronesque brow and declines to step out of his white porcelain closet.

125

Well, eat your heart out, Dr Beautiful! Pan is on the rampage tonight!

When Mary Ann arrived at the Bay Area Crisis Switchboard, Vincent seemed to be on a bummer.

She checked his extremities for recent ravages.

He was still wearing a bandage on his truncated little finger, but nothing else – other than his left ear – was missing. Mary Ann heaved a secret sigh of relief and sat down in front of her phone.

'Bad day, huh?'

Vincent smiled wistfully and held up a string of Greek worry beads. 'I haven't let go since breakfast.'

'What's the matter?'

'I don't think . . .' He turned away from her, nervously twisting a Rolodex with his good hand. 'I don't like to lay heavy trips on people.' His sad eyes and scraggly red whiskers reminded Mary Ann of some pitiful zoo animal on the verge of extinction.

'Go ahead,' she smiled. 'It's good practice for this.'

She patted the telephone.

Vincent stared at her. 'You are really . . . a very far-out person.'

'C'mon.'

'No. I really mean it. When I first met you, I thought you were just another Hostess cupcake. I thought you were probably . . . like . . . slumming here, doing your bit for the Junior League or something . . . but you're not like that at all. You're really altogether.'

Mary Ann reddened. 'Thank you, Vincent.'

Vincent smiled at her warmly, scratching his stub.

His problem, it turned out, was his Old Lady.

He had met his Old Lady when he was a house painter and she was a waitress in an organic pizzeria called The Karmic Anchovy. Together, they had fought for peace, forging their love in the fires of zealotry. They had named their first child Ho and joined a commune in Olema.

A union made in Nirvana.

'What happened?' asked Mary Ann softly.

Vincent shook his head. 'I don't know. The war, I guess.'

'The war?'

'Vietnam. She couldn't take it when it was over. She fell all to pieces.'

Mary Ann nodded sympathetically.

'It was the biggest thing in her life, Mary Ann, and nothing after that quite fulfilled her. She tried Indians for a while, then oil spills and PG&E, but it wasn't the same. It just wasn't the same.'

He looked down at the worry beads twined around his fingers. Mary Ann hoped he wouldn't start crying.

'We tried everything,' Vincent continued. 'I even sold our food stamps to send her to an awareness retreat on the Russian River.'

'A what?'

'You know. A place to go to get centred. Feminist therapy, bioenergetics, herbology, transcendental volleyball . . . It didn't work. Nothing has worked.'

'I'm really sorry, Vincent.'

'It isn't fair, is it?' said Vincent, blinking back tears. 'There ought to be an American Legion for pacifists.'

Now Mary Ann was certain that *she* was going to cry.

'Vincent . . . it'll work out.'

Vincent just shook his head in desolation.

'It *will*, Vincent. You love her, and she loves you. That's all that matters.'

'She left me.'

'Oh . . . well, then run to her side. Tell her how much she means to you. Tell her . . .'

'I can't afford to go to Israel.'

'She's in Israel?'

Vincent nodded. 'She joined the Israeli Army.'

Abruptly, he pushed back his chair and fled from the room, locking himself in the bathroom.

Mary Ann listened at the door, white with fear.

'Vincent?'

Silence.

'*Vincent*! Everything is going to work out. Do you hear me, Vincent?'

She heard him rummaging in the bathroom cabinet.

'Vincent, for God's sake! Don't cut anything off!'

Then her phone rang.

The Anniversary Tango

'So where's our wandering boy tonight?' asked Mrs Madrigal, pouring Mona a glass of sherry.

'Michael?'

'Do you know any other wandering boys?'

'I wish I did.'

'Mona! Have you two quarreled or something?'

'No. I didn't mean it like that.' She ran her palm along the worn red velvet on the arm of the chair. 'Michael's gone to a costume party.'

The landlady pulled her chair closer to Mona's. She smiled. 'I think Brian's at home tonight.'

'Christ! You sound just like my mother!'

'Stop avoiding the issue. Don't you *like* Brian?'

'He's a womanizer.'

'So?'

'So I don't need that right now, thank you.'

'You could have fooled me.'

Mona gulped her sherry, avoiding Mrs Madrigal's eyes. 'Is that your answer for everything?'

The landlady chuckled. 'It isn't *my* answer for everything. It's *the* answer for everything. C'mon, Calamity Jane, get your coat. I've got two tickets to *Beach Blanket Babylon*.'

Warmed by a pitcher of sangria, the two women unwound amid the rococo funk of Club Fugazi. When the revue was over, Mrs Madrigal stayed seated, chatting easily with the wine-flushed strangers around her.

'Oh, Mona . . . I feel . . . immortal right now. I'm very happy to be here with you.'

Sentiment shot from the hip embarrassed Mona. 'It's a wonderful show,' she said, burying her face in a wineglass.

Mrs Madrigal let a smile bloom slowly on her angular face. 'You'd be so much happier if you could see yourself the way I see you.'

'Nobody's happy. What's happy? Happiness is over when the lights come on.'

The older woman poured herself some more sangria. 'Screw that,' she said quietly.

'What?'

'Screw that. Wash your mouth out. Who taught you that half-assed existential drivel?'

'I don't see why it should matter to you.'

'No. I suppose you don't.'

Mona was puzzled by the hurt look in her companion's eyes. 'I'm sorry. I'm a bitch tonight. Look . . . let's go somewhere for coffee, OK?'

The sight of the Caffè Sport gave Mona an instant shiver of nostalgia.

Mrs Madrigal had planned it that way.

'God,' said Mona, grinning at the restaurant's Neapolitan bric-a-brac. 'I'd almost forgotten what a trip this place is!'

They took a small table in the back, next to a dusty 'Roman ruin' bas-relief which a loving, but practical, artist had protected with chicken wire. A tango was playing on the jukebox.

Mrs Madrigal ordered a bottle of Verdicchio.

When the wine came, she lifted her glass to Mona. 'To three more,' she said merrily.

'Three more whats?'

'Years. It's our anniversary.'

'What?'

'You've been my tenant for three years. Tonight.'

'How in God's name would you ever remember a thing like that?'

'I'm an elephant, Mona. Old and battered . . . but happy.'

Mona smiled affectionately, raising her glass. 'Well, here's to elephants. I'm glad I chose Barbary Lane.'

Anna shook her head. 'Wrong, dear.'

'What?'

'You didn't choose Barbary Lane. It chose you.'

'What does that mean?'

Mrs Madrigal winked. 'Finish your wine first.'

Bells are Ringing

Letting the crisis phone ring, Mary Ann pounded on the bathroom door.

'Vincent, listen to me. Nothing's as bad as you think it is! Do you hear me, Vincent?'

She made a hasty inventory of the items in the cabinet over the sink. Were there scissors? Or knives? Or razors?

RRRRINNNGGGG!

'Vincent! I have to answer the phone, Vincent! Will you just say something? Vincent, for God's sake!'

RRRINNNNGGGG!

'Vincent, you are a child of the universe! No less than the trees and the stars! You have a right to be here, Vincent! And whether or . . . whether or not . . . Today is the first day of the rest of your life . . .'

Nausea swept over her in waves. She ran from the bathroom door and lunged at the telephone. 'Bay Area Crisis Switchboard,' she panted.

The voice on the other end was high-pitched and wheezy, like some Disney forest creature receding into senility.

'Who are you?'

'Uh . . . Mary Ann Singleton.'

'You're new.'

'Sir, could you hold . . . ?'

'Where's Rebecca? I always talk to Rebecca.'

She held her hand over the mouthpiece. '*VINCENT!*'

Silence.

'*VINCENT!*'

The reply was strangely subdued. 'What?'

'Are you all right, Vincent?'

'Yes.'

'This guy wants somebody named Rebecca.'

'Tell him you're Rebecca's replacement.'

Mary Ann spoke into the phone. 'Sir . . . I'm Rebecca's replacement.

'Liar.'

'Sir?'

'Stop calling me sir! How old are you anyway?'
'Twenty-five.'
'What have you done to Rebecca?'
'Look, I don't even *know* Rebecca!'
'You *don't*, huh?'
'No.'
'You wanna suck my weenie?'

Vincent stood in the middle of the room like a frightened rodent, his sad eyes blinking rhythmically above the brush pile of his beard.

'Mary Ann?'

She didn't look up. She was still on her knees over the wastebasket.

'Can I get you something, Mary Ann? A Wash'n Dri, maybe? I think there's a Wash'n Dri in the desk drawer.'

She nodded.

Vincent handed her the moist towelette, placing his hand lamely on her shoulder.

'I'm sorry . . . I really am. I didn't mean to freak you out. God, I'm really . . .'

She shook her head, pointing to the dangling telephone receiver. It was beeping angrily. Vincent returned it to its hook.

'Who was that?'

She straightened up warily, assessing Vincent. Everything seemed to be there. 'He . . . a crank, I think.'

'Oh . . . Randy.'

'Randy?'

Vincent nodded. 'Rebecca called him that. I should have mentioned him.'

'He calls a lot?'

'Yeah. Rebecca figured if he called *anybody* it might as well be us.'

'Oh . . .'

'It's like . . . we're here for everybody, and . . .'

'What happened to Rebecca?'

'Oh . . . she OD'd.'

Once again they sat by the phones.

Vincent offered her a kindly smile. 'You a junkie or something?'

'What?'

He picked up her box of Dynamints. 'You've eaten half a box in five minutes.'

131

'I guess I'm edgy.'

'Have some of mine.' He handed her a bag of trail mix. 'I got it at Tassajara.'

'In Ghirardelli Square?'

He smiled indulgently. 'Near Big Sur. A Zen retreat.'

'Oh.'

'Lay off the sugar, OK? It'll kill ya.'

The Landlady Bares her Soul

'OK,' said Mona, downing her Verdicchio. 'What was the cryptic comment all about?'

Mrs Madrigal smiled. 'What did I say?'

'You said Barbary Lane *chose* me. You meant that literally, didn't you?'

The landlady nodded. 'Don't you remember how we met?'

'At the Savoy-Tivoli.'

'Three years ago this week.'

Mona shrugged. 'I still don't get it.'

'It wasn't an accident, Mona.'

'What?'

'I engineered it. Rather magnificently, I think.' She smiled, swirling the wine in her glass.

Mona thought back to that distant summer evening. Mrs Madrigal had come to her table with a basket of Alice B. Toklas brownies. 'I made too many,' she had said. 'Take two, but save one for later. They'll knock you on your ass.'

A spirited conversation had followed, a long winy chat about Proust and Tennyson and the Astral Plane. By the end of the evening, the two women were solid friends.

The next day Mrs Madrigal had called about the apartment.

'This is the madwoman you met at the Tivoli. There's a house on Russian Hill that claims it's your home.'

Mona had moved in two days later.

'But why?' asked Mona.

'You intrigued me . . . and you were also a celebrity.'

Mona rolled her eyes. 'Right.'

132

'Well, you were. *Everybody* knew about your swimwear campaign for J. Walter Thompson.'

'In New York?'

Mrs Madrigal nodded. 'I read the trade journals from time to time.'

'You blow me away sometimes.'

'Good.'

'What if I had said no?'

'About the apartment, you mean?'

'Yeah.'

'I don't know. I would have tried something else, I guess.'

'I guess I should be flattered.'

'Yes. I guess you should.'

Mona felt herself reddening. 'Anyway, I'm glad.'

'Well . . . here's to it!'

'Uh uh,' said Mona, watching the landlady's upraised glass. 'Not until I find out what "it" is.'

Mrs Madrigal shrugged. 'What else, dear? Home.'

Mary Ann was already there, recuperating from her night at the switchboard.

She had installed her new walnut-grained shelf paper, scrubbed the ick off the back of the stove, and replaced the blue-water thingahoochie in the toilet tank.

When Mona stopped by, she was hunched over the kitchen table.

'What the fuck are you doing?'

'Alphabetizing my spice rack.'

'Jesus.'

'It's therapeutic.'

'The switchboard was supposed to be your therapy.'

'Don't even bring it up.'

'Why? What happened?'

'I don't wanna talk about it.'

'That's right. Repress it. Keep all that prom queen neurosis locked up inside, so . . .'

'I was *never* a prom queen, Mona.'

'It doesn't matter. You were the type.'

'How do *you* know? How the hell do you know *what* type . . .'

'Ladies, ladies . . .' It was Michael, standing in the doorway. His furry Pan legs were matted and wine-stained.

'Mouse . . . you're back.'

133

'You think it's *easy* getting picked up dressed like this?'

Suppressing a smile, Mona moved next to him and touched the mock chinchilla. 'Yuck!'

'OK, OK. So Nair doesn't work for everybody.'

At the Fat Farm

Sagebrush and avocado trees shimmered in the afternoon heat as the huge gold limousine sped north through the hills of Escondido.

DeDe settled back in the seat and closed her eyes.

She was bound for The Golden Door!

The Golden Door! America's most sumptuous and blue-blooded fat farm! A jeweled oasis of sauna baths and facials, pedicures and manicures, dancing lessons, herbal wraps and gourmet cuisine!

And not a moment too soon.

DeDe was *sick* of the city, sick of Beauchamp and his deception, sick of the guilt she had suffered over Lionel. Furthermore, she had had it with the puffy-cheeked wretch who stared at her morosely from mirrors and shop-windows.

She wanted the old DeDe back, the DeDe of Aspen and Tahoe, the golden-maned temptress who had teased the Phi Delts, tantalized the Bachelors and devastated Splinter Riley not *that* many years ago.

She had done it before.

She could do it again.

The driver peered over his shoulder at her. 'Your first time, madam?'

DeDe laughed nervously. 'I look that far gone, do I?'

'Oh, no, madam. It's just that your face is a new one.'

'I guess you see some pretty famous faces.'

He nodded, apparently pleased she had brought up the subject. 'Just last week, Miss Esther Williams.'

'Really?'

'The Gabors were here last month. Three of them, in fact. I've also driven Rhonda Fleming, Jeanne Crain, Dyan Cannon, Barbara Howar . . .' He paused, though presumably only for effect; DeDe was sure he had memorized the list. 'Also, Mrs Mellon and Mrs Gimbel, Roberta Flack, Liz Carpenter . . . I could go on and on, Mrs Day.'

The sound of her own name jolted her, but she tried not to show it.

134

The Gabors would *never* have shown it.

A stately row of Monterey pines lined the highway on either side of the security gates. The driver mumbled something into an intercom and the gates swung open.

The driveway beyond was a sinuous downhill sweep, flanked on one side by the spa's private orange grove and on the other by thickets of pine and oak.

Then The Door appeared, gleaming in the sunshine like the gates of Xanadu.

DeDe felt like Sally Kellerman on the brink of Shangri-La!

Her Calvin Klein T-shirt was already two shades darker under the arms.

The driver parked at a gatehouse next to The Door, collected her luggage, and led the way through the mythical gates. On the other side, DeDe crossed a pussy-willowed stream by means of a delicate Japanese bridge, then passed through shoji screens and finally a massive wooden door.

The reception area was an elegantly sparse chamber of bamboo furniture and Japanese silk paintings. After a short but pleasant interchange with a fortyish directress, DeDe Halcyon Day signed her name to one of the world's most rarefied registers.

Her $2,500 transformation had begun!

Her room, as arranged, opened onto the Camellia Court. ('Don't let them stick you in the Bell Court or the Azalea Court,' Binky had warned. 'They're OK, but very Piedmont, if you know what I mean.')

DeDe wandered amid her private Oriental splendor, checking out her tokonoma (a niche housing a bronze Buddha) and her 'moon-watching deck' overlooking the garden. On her night table lay a copy of Erich Fromm's *The Art of Loving*, which she perused idly, totally transported from the agonies of San Francisco.

Then the phone rang.

Would she kindly report to the weigh-in room at her convenience?

The weigh-in room!

She grabbed a handful of fanny flab, said a small prayer and braced herself for the cold, steel reality of the Toledo.

135

Michael's Shocker

Lunch for Mona and Michael consisted of two cheesedogs and an order of fries at The Noble Frankfurter on Polk Street.

'I should have changed my nail polish,' said Mona.

'Beg pardon, ma'am?'

'Green nail polish at a weenie stand is not Divine Decadence. It's just plain tacky.'

Michael laughed. 'It's very *Grey Gardens*, actually. It makes you shabby genteel.'

'Well, you're half right. We are bordering on financial embarrassment, Mouse. My unemployment check will not keep us living in the style to which we have become accustomed.'

She was only half kidding, and Michael knew it.

'Mona . . . I signed up with an Agency this week. They might be coming up with a waiter's job for me really soon. I don't want you to think I'm just sitting around on my ass mooching off . . .'

'I know, Michael. Really. I was just thinking out loud. It's just that we're already a month behind on the rent, and I feel funny about Mrs Madrigal. She'll overlook it . . . but she's gotta pay taxes and all, and I . . .'

'Aha!' said Michael, raising a french fry as an exclamation point. 'I haven't told you about my instant cash plan yet!'

'God! Am I ready for this?'

'A hundred bucks, Babycakes! In one night!' He popped the french fry into his mouth. 'Think you can handle that?'

'Won't it get a little chilly, working the corner of Powell and Geary?'

'Very funny, Wonder Woman. Do you wanna hear my plan or not?'

'Shoot.'

'I, Michael Mouse Tolliver, am going to enter the jockey shorts dance contest at The Endup.'

'Oh, please!'

'I'm serious, Mona.'

And he was.

Across town, at Halcyon Communications, Edgar Halcyon called Beauchamp Day into his office.

'Sit down.'

Beauchamp smirked. 'Thank you.' He was already seated.

'I think we should talk.'

'Fine.'

'I know you think I'm a horse's ass, but we're stuck with each other, aren't we?'

Beauchamp smiled uncomfortably. 'I wouldn't exactly put . . .'

'Are you serious about this business, Beauchamp?'

'Sir?'

'Do you give a good goddamn about advertising? Is this what you want to do with your life?'

'Well, I think I've amply demonstrated . . .'

'Never mind what you've *demonstrated*, goddammit! What do you *feel*. Can you honestly stomach a lifetime of pushing pantyhose?'

The thought made Beauchamp cringe, but he knew what the answer should be. 'This is my career,' he said forcefully.

Edgar looked weary. 'It is, is it?'

'Yes sir.'

'You want my job, don't you?'

'I . . .'

'I don't *hire* men who don't want my job, Beauchamp.'

Beauchamp uncrossed his legs, now totally unsettled. 'Yes sir, I can understand that.'

'I want to talk to you while DeDe's out of town. Are you free for drinks tonight at the club?'

'Fine. Yes sir.'

'What I'm going to tell you is in the strictest confidence. Do you understand that?'

'Yes sir.'

The Family Myth

Anna was waiting for him at the Seal Rock Inn.

'Did the desk clerk give you a funny look?' she asked.

'No, goddammit. I've never been so insulted.'

She grinned at him. 'My ego's a little bruised too. I thought maybe you'd had second thoughts and run off with a nude encounter girl from Big Al's.'

'I'm sorry,' he said, kissing her forehead. 'Beauchamp and I had a couple of drinks at the Bohemian club. It took longer than I planned.'

'What?'

'Nothing. Nothing important. Business . . . God, you look good!'

'A trick of the light.' She took his arm and led him to the window. 'There's the best example I know anywhere.'

Beyond the dark trees, Seal Rock gleamed eerily against the ocean, white as an iceberg under the moon.

'Magic,' she said, squeezing his arm.

Edgar nodded.

'That's what I mean,' she winked. 'In the right light, even seal shit looks good.'

'Anna?'

'Mmm?'

'Thanks.'

'Anytime.'

'I feel . . .'

'I know.'

'Let me finish.'

'I thought you had.'

'Will you let me be serious?'

'Not for a second.'

'I love you, Anna.'

'Then we're even, OK?'

'OK.'

She leaned on her elbow and studied his face. 'I'll bet you don't even know where your name came from?'

'Something to do with birds, right?'

'You know the legend?'

'I heard it once, but I've forgotten it. Tell it to me, why don't you?'

'All right. Once upon a time there was a just and peaceful ruler named Ceyx, who reigned over the kingdom of Thessaly. Ceyx was married to Halcyone, daughter of Aeolus, keeper of the winds . . .'

'Where in God's name did you learn all this?'

'Margaret used to read to me from *Bulfinch's Mythology*.'

'Margaret?'

'At the Blue Moon Lodge. The lady who got first crack at you. Stop interrupting now.'

'Sorry.'

'Anyway, Ceyx went off on a sea voyage to consult an oracle because his brother had died and he was convinced that the gods had it in for him. Halcyone, on the other hand, had a terrible premonition that Ceyx would die during the voyage and begged him not to go.'

'But he went anyway, of course.'

'Of course. He was a busy executive, and she was an hysterical female. Naturally, there was a godawful storm and Ceyx was killed. Halcyone found his body several days later, floating offshore at the very spot where he had set sail.'

'Delightful.'

Anna pressed her fingers to his mouth. 'Here comes the sweet part. Suddenly, Halcyone was transformed into a beautiful bird. She flew to her lover's body and lighted on his chest, and instantly he became a bird, and Aeolus decreed that for one week each winter the seas would be calm, so that the halcyon birds could build build their nest on a raft of twigs and hatch their young and live happily ever after.'

'That's nice,' said Edgar, looking up at her. 'My father had more imagination than I gave him credit for.'

'You just lost me.'

'He made up the name. The real one was Halstein.'

'Why on earth?'

Edgar smiled and kissed her. 'He wanted to be a Bohemian, I guess.'

DeDe Triumphs

Submerged in four feet of warm water, DeDe Halcyon Day gripped a volleyball uneasily between her knees.

'Stay there,' she muttered, gritting her teeth. Twice in ten minutes she had torpedoed the movie star exercising next to her.

The movie star smiled gamely, indicating no hard feelings. 'It's a bitch, isn't it? I feel like I've got the *Hindenburg* between my legs.'

Somehow still clutching the volleyball, DeDe went through her gyrations again, swinging her arms frenetically above her head. Every muscle in her body was screaming in pain.

'Stretch it!' shouted the instructress at the edge of the pool. 'Strrrreeetch that gorgeous body.'

'Gorgeous?' groaned the movie star. 'My ass is so waterlogged it looks like a Sunsweet prune.'

DeDe grinned at her companion, delighting in the earthiness of a woman who had always seemed larger than life on the screen. Up close, the tracheotomy scar at the base of her neck testified to her mortality.

But her eyes *were* violet.

This was her second week at The Golden Door. For six rigorous days she had driven her body to its limits, rising at six forty-five to flop about the countryside in a pale-pink sweatsuit, her face stripped of makeup, her hair drab and icky in a thick coat of Vaseline. It was murder, but she was getting there.

Wasn't she?

Well, at least she *felt* better. Breakfast in bed was enhanced by the fact that she actually looked forward to her nine o'clock Leonardo da Vinci exercises. Then there was the Jump for Joy session and the morning facial and yoga and a Kneipp Herbal Wrap and . . . goddammit, something *must* have been happening!

At twilight, she would soak in the fan-shaped whirlpool bath, giggling happily with the movie star and half a dozen other members of the elite sisterhood. She felt like a girl again, placid and simple and whole. Her pride had returned, and somehow, miraculously, so had her self-control. Not once, but twice, she had talked the movie star out of leading a raid on the orange grove.

She was over the hump now.

The old DeDe . . . the pre-Beauchamp DeDe – was running her life again, and it felt damn good!

'God, I can't believe it!'

'If it's good,' the movie star scowled, 'I *don't* wanna hear it.'

DeDe stepped off the scales, then on again, fiddling with the weights. 'Look at that, would you? Would you just look at that? Eighteen pounds! I've lost eighteen pounds in two weeks!'

'That's abnormal. You should see a doctor.'

'It's a miracle.'

'What the hell do you expect for three grand?' The movie star gave up the tough façade and burst into a radiant smile, enveloping DeDe in her still flabby arms. 'Oh, I hope it makes you happy, DeDe!'

For a moment, DeDe thought she would cry. Here was this idol –

this goddess – and *she* was envious of DeDe! Nobody at home would ever believe it!

They would simply have to believe their eyes.

She felt like a different woman on the flight from San Diego to San Francisco.

Her skin was tanned and glowing, her eyes danced with self-esteem. Her peach-colored T-shirt clung to her waist – her waist! –as if she had nothing to hide.

In the seat next to her, an aggressive sailor made inane conversation about 'Frisco,' boring her with endless details about his tour of duty on Treasure Island.

It didn't matter. She was enjoying the warm friction of his legs against her. She felt deliciously single, free from Beauchamp's petty intrigues and the dreary quagmire of her marriage.

Well, why shouldn't she? Beauchamp hadn't missed her. She was sure of that. And she sure as hell hadn't missed him. Period.

Period?

Dear God. She had missed her period.

Boris Steps In

On a warm autumn Saturday at Barbary Lane, Mary Ann stretched lazily in bed, savoring the musk from the eucalyptus tree outside her window.

A fat, tiger-striped cat lumbered into view along the window ledge, scratching its back against the open sash. Bored with that exercise, it took several half-hearted swats at the stained-glass butterfly hanging from the curtain rod.

Mary Ann grinned and tossed a pillow at the cat. 'Boris . . . don't!'

Boris accepted the gesture as an invitation to play. He landed with a muffled plop on Mary Ann's mock flokati and sauntered in the direction of the bed.

'Lucky ol' Boris,' said Mary Ann, scratching the cat behind his ears. Boris, she couldn't help thinking, was beautiful, independent and loved. He belonged to no one in particular (at least, no one at 28 Barbary Lane), but he moved freely through a wide circle of benefactors and friends.

Why couldn't *she* do that?

She was sick and tired of being dumped on – romantically, emotionally and every other way. Wasn't it time to take control of her life again? To deal with her problems directly and experience each moment to the fullest?

Yes! She bounded out of bed, startling Boris, and twirled around the room on her toes. God, what a day! Here in this magical city, here on this storybook lane! Where little cable cars climb halfway to the stars and cats crawl in your window and the butcher speaks French and . . .

Boris darted past her, intent on avoiding this lunatic altogether.

He raced through the living room, only to find the front door closed.

'You want out, Boris? Is that what you want, baby?' Mary Ann opened the door for him, instantly recognizing the folly of that decision. Boris sped down the hallway and sought the protection of elevation by heading up the stairway to the roof.

The house on the roof.

Downstairs on the second floor, Michael was serving Mona breakfast in bed: poached eggs, nine-grain toast, Italian roast coffee and French sausages from Marcel & Henri. When he set the tray on the bed, he was whistling 'What I did for Love.'

'Well,' said Mona, grinning at him, 'a little nookie does you a world of good.'

'You said it, Babycakes!'

'Where's Jon? Ask him in. We can all have breakfast together.'

'He's at home. I stayed there last night.'

'You little dip! Did you come all the way back to fix me breakfast?'

'I have to drop off my laundry, too.'

'Drop off your laundry, my ass!'

'Sorry. Mr Lee only does shirts and sheets.' He leaned over and kissed her on the forehead. 'O K . . . so I missed you a little.'

Michael's evening had begun at a cocktail party given by *After Dark* magazine at the Stanford court. 'What can I tell you, Mona? It was sheer piss-elegance!'

Next to 'affairette,' 'piss-elegance' was Michael's favourite word.

'Jon got the invitation, actually. I didn't know a soul . . . unless you count Tab Hunter, of course.'

'Of course.'

'He looked damn good for forty-five, and I kinda wanted to talk to him, but he was *surrounded* by G Q types, and what the hell do you say to Tab Hunter, anyway? "Hi, I'm Michael Tolliver, and I always liked you better than Sandra Dee"?'

'It doesn't read. You're right.'

'Sooo . . . I gorged myself on pizza canapés and did my best to avoid the guy from Brebner's who once told me I was too average-looking to make it as a model.'

'Poor Mouse!'

'Well, he was right! Christ, Mona, you should have *seen* the beauties in that room! There was so much hair spray they probably had to make an Environmental Impact Report before they could hold the party!'

'Is the plan still on?' Mona asked after breakfast.

'What plan?'

'The jockey shorts dance contest.'

'I've been practicing all *week*, woman. You're coming, aren't you? It's tomorrow at five-thirty.'

'What the hell for?'

'I don't know . . . moral support, I guess.'

'Jon'll go with you.'

'No. I'd rather Jon didn't know about this, Mona.'

'OK,' she said quietly. 'I'll go.'

Renewing Vows

Beauchamp was waiting for her at the PSA terminal, surrounded by stewardesses in pink-and-orange miniskirts. When DeDe caught his eye, he smiled phosphorescently and pushed his way through the crowd to her side.

He was deeply tanned, and his eyes danced with genuine surprise. 'You look great!' he beamed. 'God, you're a new person!'

It's possible, she thought, that I am *two* new people. But even that prospect couldn't dim the triumph she felt at Beauchamp's reaction.

She had planned on being cool with him, but one look at his face melted her Catherine Deneuve icicle.

'It wasn't easy,' she said finally.

Then he crushed her in his arms and kissed her passionately on the mouth. 'I swear to God I've missed you!' he said, burying his face in her hair.

It was almost more than she could take. Was *this* what he had needed all along? Two weeks alone in the city. Enough time to put things in perspective, to discover what she had meant to him.

Or was he simply intrigued by her new body?

On the way back to Telegraph Hill he briefed her on the fortnight she had missed.

The family was fine. Mother had spent several days at the house in St Helena, catching up on correspondence while Faust received treatment from the family vet. Daddy seemed in good spirits. He and Beauchamp had chatted amiably over drinks. Several times.

DeDe smiled at that. 'He really likes you, Beauchamp.'

'I know.'

'I'm glad you got a chance to talk . . . man to man, I mean.'

'So am I. DeDe?'

'Uh huh?'

'Is there anything I can do to let you know I still love you?'

She turned to study his profile, as if uncertain that the words had come from him at all. His hair was swept back in the wind: his eyes were fixed firmly on the freeway. Only his mouth, boyishly vulnerable, betrayed the turmoil within.

DeDe reached over and placed her hand gently on his thigh.

Beauchamp continued. 'Do you know when I missed you the most?'

'Beauchamp, you don't need . . . When?'

'In the morning. Those few terrible moments between sleeping and waking when you're not sure where you are or even *why* you are. I missed you then. I *needed* you then, DeDe.'

She squeezed his thigh. 'I'm glad.'

'I want to make things better between us.'

'We'll see.'

'I *do*, DeDe. I'm going to try. I promise you.'

'I know.'

'You don't believe me, do you?'

'I *want* to, Beauchamp.'

'I don't blame you. I'm an asshole.'

'Beauchamp . . .'

144

'I am. I'm an asshole. But I'll make it up to you, I promise.'

'A day at a time, OK?'

'Right. A day at a time.'

At Halcyon Hill a dying sun slipped behind the trees as Frannie strolled in the garden with her only confidante.

'I don't know what's happened to Edgar,' she said, sipping disconsolately at her Mai Tai. 'He used to care about things . . . about us . . . You know, it's funny, but when Eddie was in France during the war, I used to miss him terribly. He wasn't *with* me, but he was, you know . . . Now he's with me, but he's not . . . and goddammit, I like missing him the other way more!'

Her eyes were brimming with tears now, but she didn't brush them away. She was lost in another time, when loneliness wasn't barren but beautiful, when snapshots and love letters and the honeyed voice of Bing Crosby had eased her gently through the most difficult winter of her life.

But now it was summer, and Bing lived just over the next hill. Why hadn't things worked out?

'"I'm . . . dreammminnngg . . . of a . . . whiiite . . . Chrissssmusss . . . juss like the ones I usssse to knooow . . .'

Her tears kept her from finishing. 'I'm sorry,' she whispered to her companion. 'I shouldn't burden you with this, baby. You're *so* patient . . . so good . . . If it weren't for you, I'd be like Helen . . . yes, I would . . . lunching with her *decorator*, for God's sake! C'mon. There's a teensy-weensy little bit of Mai Tai left in the pitcher.'

She poured some Mai Tai into a large plastic bowl on the terrace.

Faust, her Great Dane, lapped it up with relish.

The Man on the Roof

Boris's tail marked time like a metronome as he sped down the hallway and up the stairs to the roof.

Mary Ann slipped into her bathrobe and set off in pursuit of the unofficial tenant, fearful that he might get trapped in the building.

The steps to the roof were uncarpeted, painted with dark-green deck enamel. At the top, next to an ivy-choked window, a bright-orange door blocked the cat's escape. Boris was indignant.

'Here, kitty . . . come on, Boris . . . nice Boris . . .'

145

Boris was having none of it. He stood fast, answering her with a terse saber rattle of his tail.

Mary Ann climbed higher, now less than a yard away from the door. 'You really are a *pain*, Boris! You know that, don't you?'

The door banged open, grazing Boris's side, sending the startled cat bounding down the steps with a howl. Mary Ann stiffened.

Before her stood a large, middle-aged man.

'Sorry,' he said uncomfortably. 'I didn't hear you out here. I hope I didn't hurt your cat.'

She struggled to regain her composure. 'No . . . I don't think so . . .'

'He's a nice-looking cat.'

'Oh . . . he's not my cat. He sort of belongs to everybody. I think he lives down at the end of the lane. I'm sorry . . . I didn't mean to intrude.'

The man looked concerned. 'I scared you, didn't I?'

'It's OK.'

He smiled, extending his hand. 'I'm Norman Neal Williams.'

'Hi.' She returned his shake, noticing how huge his hand was. Somehow, though, his size made him seem especially vulnerable.

He was wearing baggy gray suit pants and a short-sleeved drip-dry shirt. A little tuft of dark-brown hair spilled over the top of his clip-on-four-in-hand tie.

'You live just below, don't you?'

'Yeah . . . oh, sorry . . . I'm Mary Ann Singleton.'

'Three names.'

'Excuse me?'

'Mary Ann Singleton. Three names. Like Norman Neal Williams.'

'Oh . . . do you go by Norman Neal?'

'No. Just Norman.'

'I see.'

'I like to say Norman Neal Williams first off, because it flows nice, you know.'

'Yes, it does.'

'Would you like some coffee?'

'Oh, thanks, but I've got lots of things . . .'

'The view's real nice.'

That got her. She *did* want to see his view, as well as the layout of the Lilliputian rooftop house.

'OK,' she smiled. 'I'd love to.'

The view was dazzling. White sails on a delft-blue way. Angel Island, wreathed in fog, faraway and mystical as Bali Ha'i. Wheeling gulls over red tile rooftops.

'That's what you pay for,' he said, obviously apologizing for the size of the place. There was nowhere to sit but the bed and a kitchen chair next to the window facing the bay. The coat of his suit was folded over the back of the chair.

Mary Ann sighed at the panorama. 'You must *love* getting up in the morning.'

'Yeah. Except I'm not here that much.'

'Oh.'

'I'm a salesman.'

'I see.'

'Vitamins.' He indicated a carrying case in the corner of the room. Mary Ann recognized the company logo.

'Oh . . . Nutri-Vim. I've heard of those.'

'Completely organic.'

She was sure his enthusiasm was strictly professional. There was nothing about Norman Neal Williams that struck her as organic.

That Ol'-time Religion

On Sunday morning Mona went to church.

In the old days – post-Woodstock and pre-Watergate – she had gone to church a lot. Not just *any* church, she was quick to point out, but a *People's* church, a church that was Relevant.

That was a long time ago. She'd had it with the People, and Relevance was as obsolete as puka shells. Still, there was something nostalgically *comfortable* about returning to Glibb Memorial.

Maybe it was the light show or the rock ensemble . . . or the Afro-aphrodisia of the Reverend Willy Sessums, bojangling the bejeezus out of Third World Socialism.

Or maybe it was the Quaalude she took at breakfast.

Whatever.

Today she felt mellow. Together. A karmic cog in the great,

147

swaying mechanism of Glibb Memorial. She sang out with the fervor of a Southern Baptist, flanked by a Noe Valley wood butcher and a Tenderloin drag queen in a coral prom gown.

> He's got the Yoo-nited Farm Workers
> In His hands!
> He's got the Yoo-nited Farm Workers
> In His hands!

'That's right!' shouted Reverend Sessums, darting through his flock with a leather pouch full of black juju dust. 'Chairman Jesus loves you, brother! And he loves you too, sister!'

He was talking to Mona. *Directly* to her. He smiled radiantly and embraced her, sprinkling her with juju dust.

Even with the Quaalude, Mona stiffened. She hated herself for it, for the cynicism that cloaked her embarrassment over anything personal. She wanted him to go away.

He would not.

'Do you hear me, sister?'

She nodded, smiling feebly.

'Chairman Jesus loves you! He loves all of us! The black and the brown and the yellow and the white . . . and the lavender!' The last color was directed to the man in the prom gown.

Mona looked at the drag queen, praying that Sessums had shifted his focus.

He had not.

'If you believe Willy . . . If you believe that Chairman Jesus loves you more than the oil companies, more than Big Business and Male Chauvinists and the House Armed Services Committee . . . and if you believe that, sister, then let ol' Willy hear a "Right on!"'

'Right on.'

'Make it *loud*, sister, so Chairman Jesus can hear you!'

'*Right on!*'

'Make it *loud*, sister, so Chairman Jesus can hear you!'

'*Right on!*'

'*Awwwwwwriiiight!* You're *beautiful*, sister!' He began to sway and clap to the music again, winking privately at Mona like a nightclub comedian who had just had harmless fun at her expense.

The band broke into 'Love Will Keep Us Together' as Sessums moved on.

'This is to die over,' said the drag queen, recognizing the song. 'Don't you absolutely *adore* the Captain and Tennille?'

Mona nodded, collecting herself.

Her fellow churchgoer fumbled in his purse and produced a bullet-shaped inhaler. He handed it to her.

'Have a popper, honey.'

After church, she drove back to Barbary Lane and fell into a black, contemplative mood.

She was thirty-one years old. She needed a job. She was living with a man who might leave her at any moment for another man. Her mother in Minneapolis had somehow lost the power to communicate with her.

Her only *real* guardian was Anna Madrigal, and the landlady's interest had recently assumed an intensity that made her nervous.

Seeds and stems, seeds and stems.

The phone rang.

'Yeah?'

'Mona.'

'Right.'

'This is D'orothea.'

'Jesus. Where are you?'

'Here. In town. Are you glad?'

'Of course, I'm . . . Are you on vacation?'

'Nope. This is it. I did it. I'm here for good. Can I see you?'

'I . . . sure.'

'Try not to sound so ecstatic.'

'I'm just a little surprised, D'or. What about lunch tomorrow?'

'I was hoping for dinner tonight.'

'I can't, D'or. I'm going to . . . a dance contest.'

'Good reason.'

'I'll tell you about it tomorrow.'

'What time?'

'Noon? Here?'

'Twenty-eight Barbary Lane?'

'Yeah . . . OK?'

'I've missed the hell out of you, Mona.'

'I've missed you too, D'or.'

149

Child's Play

Mary Ann stopped by Mona's just before noon. She was wearing what Michael referred to as her 'Lauren Hutton drag'.

Levi's and a pink button-down shirt from the boy's department at Brooks Brothers . . . with a pale-blue crew-neck sweater knotted cavalierly around her neck.

'Hi,' she chirped. 'Do you guys feel like brunch at Mama's?'

Mona shook her head. 'Michael's not eating. The big contest is tonight, and he thinks he's fat.'

'Where is he?'

'Down in the courtyard . . . bronzing his fat.'

Mary Ann laughed. 'What about you, then?'

'Thanks. I think I'll pass.'

'Are you . . . O K, Mona?'

'Don't I look it?'

'Sure . . . I didn't mean . . . You look . . . distracted, that's all.'

Mona shrugged and looked out the window. 'I just hope it's not terminal.'

The line at Mama's snaked out of the building and up Stockton Street. Mary Ann was considering alternative brunch spots when a familiar figure in the crowd signaled her sheepishly.

'Oh . . . hi, Norman.'

'Hello. I've been saving your spot.' He winked at her rather obviously, fooling no one around him. Mary Ann slipped into the line behind him.

A little girl tugged on Norman's leg. 'Who's she?' she asked.

Norman smiled. 'She's a friend, Lexy.'

'Well,' said Mary Ann, looking down at the child. 'Where did *you* come from?'

'My mommy.'

Mary Ann giggled. 'She's *precious*, Norman. Does she belong to you?'

Before he could answer, the child reached up and tugged at Mary Ann's sweater. 'Are you breaking in line?'

'Well, I . . .'

Norman laughed. 'Alexandra . . . this is Mary Ann Singleton. We live in the same building . . . right up there on that big hill.' He winked at Mary Ann. 'She belongs to some friends of mine in San Leandro. Sometimes I give them a breather on Sundays.'

'That's sweet.'

Norman shrugged. 'I don't mind. I get the best of both worlds.' He tugged playfully on one of the child's braids. 'Isn't that right, Lexy?'

'What?'

'Never mind. Tell ya later.'

'Can I feed the pigeons, Norman?'

'After breakfast, OK?'

Mary Ann knelt down in front of the child. 'That's a *beautiful* dress, Alexandra!'

The child stared at her, then giggled.

'Do you know what it's called, Alexandra?'

'What?'

'Your dress. It's called a Heidi dress. Can you say that?'

Alexandra looked slightly put out. 'This is a *dirndl*,' she said flatly.

'Oh, well . . .' Mary Ann stood up, grinning at Norman. 'I asked for that, didn't I?'

The trio dined on omelets at Mama's. Alexandra ate in silence, studying Mary Ann.

Afterwards, in Washington Square, the grownups talked, while Alexandra chased pigeons in the sunshine.

'She's very bright, isn't she?'

Norman nodded. 'She gives me a complex sometimes.'

'Have you known her parents long?'

'About . . . oh, five years. Her father and I were in Vietnam together.'

'Oh . . . I'm sorry.'

'Why?'

'Well . . . Vietnam . . . It must have been awful.'

He smiled, holding up his arms. 'No wounds, see? I was a chief yeoman in Saigon. Office job. Navy intelligence.'

'How did you get interested in vitamins?'

He shrugged. 'I got interested in making a living.'

'I see.'

'I'm afraid there's nothing very interesting about me, Mary Ann.'

'Oh, no . . . I think you're very . . .'

151

'There's a movie I'd like to see tonight, if you haven't already . . .'

'What is it?'

'An oldie. *Detective Story*. Kirk Douglas and Eleanor Parker.'

'I'd love to,' she said.

What Are Friends For?

Beauchamp and DeDe spent a leisurely Sunday morning in Sausalito, brunching at the Altamira.

They were a pair again, a matched set – bronzed and blooded and beautiful. People looked at them with hungry eyes, whispering speculations over Ramos fizzes in the brilliant sunlight of the hotel terrace.

And DeDe loved every minute of it.

'Beauchamp?'

'Mmm?' His eyes were *exactly* the color of the bay.

'Last night was . . . better than our wedding night.'

'I know.'

'Was it . . . ? Is it me that's changed, or you?'

'Does it matter?'

'It does to me. A little.'

Beauchamp shrugged. 'I guess I've . . . sorted out my priorities.'

'It confuses me a little, Beauchamp.'

'Why?'

'I don't know. Things are . . . working now and . . . well, I just wanna know what I'm doing right, so I can keep on doing it.'

He rubbed his knee against hers. 'Just keep being yourself, OK?'

'OK,' she smiled.

Back at Montgomery Street, Beauchamp clipped a leash on the corgi. 'I think I'll take Caesar up to the Tower. Feel like a walk?'

'Thanks. I should catch up on my letters.'

As soon as he had gone she called Binky Gruen.

'Bink?'

'DeDe?'

'I'm back.'

'Well?'

'Well, what?'

'How much, dummy? How much did you lose?'

'Oh . . . eighteen pounds.'

Binky whistled. 'That sounds like anorexia to me!'

'Binky, I need . . .'

'I am *convinced*, by the way, that Shugie Sussman has anorexia. I mean, there's no doubt in my mind. She's wasting away to *nothing*, and nobody can persuade her that she's isn't *obese*. It's too tragic, DeDe. We may have to ship the poor thing off to the Menninger Clinic in a Manila envelope!'

'Binky, as much as I'd like to hear about Shugie Sussman . . .'

'Sorry, darling. Did you have a marvelous time? I mean, aside from those godawful Leonardo da Vinci exer . . .'

'I need your help, Binky.'

'Sure.'

'I . . . need a doctor.'

'Oh, God! You *are* sick! Jesus, I am such a . . .'

'No, not sick. I just need a doctor.'

'Oh.'

'I was thinking about the one you saw last spring.'

'Uh oh.'

'It isn't an item yet. I'm not sure. I'd just feel better if . . .'

'It may have been the exercise, DeDe. Sometimes a physical change like that can screw up your cycle.'

'I've considered that.'

'Hell, it could even be anorexia.'

'Will you *stop*? It could be almost anything. I just want . . .'

'Almost anything but Beauchamp, huh?'

Silence.

'You want a gynecologist who doesn't know the family, right?'

'Yes.'

'OK. This guy's a prince. Gentle, discreet, and a *treat* to look at. Got a pencil?'

'Yeah.'

'Jon Fielding. The Jon doesn't have an *h*. He's at 450 Sutter. You can tell him I sent you.'

The Beach Boys

Mrs Madrigal's tenants had dubbed that corner of the courtyard 'Barbary Beach'.

Well, thought Michael, spreading his towel on the bricks, it ain't Sunday at Lake Temescal, but it'll have to do.

In less than seven hours he would be on the platform at The Endup.

He needed all the rays he could get.

'Hi,' said a voice somewhere between him and the sun.

He looked up, shielding his eyes. It was the guy from the third floor. Brian something. He was carrying a towel imprinted with a Coors label.

'Hi. Come on in. The water's fine.'

Brian nodded and tossed his towel on the ground. Five feet away, Michael noted. Close, but not *too* close. A perfect HBU. Hunky But Uptight.

'Think it's worth it?' asked Brian.

'Probably not, but what the hell? Who are we to disappoint all those *other* pink bodies in the bars?'

Brian laughed, obviously catching the irony of the remark. OK, thought Michael, he knows we're not heading for the same bars. Much less the same bodies. Still . . . he knows, and he knows that I know he knows. It's OK.

'You're Brian, and I'm Michael. Right?'

'Right.'

They shook hands, still on their bellies, reaching out over the void in order to touch.

Michael laughed. 'We look like something off the ceiling of the Sistine chapel!'

Fifteen minutes later, Michael felt like talking again.

'You're single, right?'

'Yeah.'

'This must be a great town to be single in. I mean . . . for a straight guy.'

'Oh?'

'Well, I mean . . . there are so many gay guys that a straight guy must be a hot property with the women. At least . . . you know what I mean.'

Brian grunted. He was on his back now, his hands folded behind his head. 'I spent four fucking hours at Slater Hawkins last night, trying to plug a chick I wouldn't have sneezed at in college.'

'Yeah,' said Michael, somewhat jarred by the remark. 'It kinda gets to be a game, doesn't it? Unwrapping the package is more fun than the package itself. At least, sometimes . . .' He looked over at Brian, wondering if they were communicating at all. 'Do you know Mary Ann Singleton?'

'Yeah.'

'Well, Mary Ann and I had this really heavy session where she told me she wanted to go back to Cleveland, and I gave her the whole est trip about taking control of her life and all . . . but the creepy thing is that sometimes I think she's right. Maybe we should all go back to Cleveland.'

'Yeah. Or go live in a farm town in Utah or something. Get back to basics.'

'Uh huh. I have that one too. A mountain village in Colorado, maybe, with just the bare essentials. One nice French restaurant and a branch of Design Research.'

They both laughed. Michael felt instantly more comfortable with him.

'The thing that bugs me,' said Brian, 'is that you never really know what women are like . . . not for a long time, anyway. They only show you what they want you to see.'

Michael nodded. 'So you fantasize over all the wrong things.'

'Yeah.' Brian began to tear blades of grass from between the bricks.

'Christ! That happens to me all the time,' said Michael. 'I meet some person . . . male-type . . . at a bar or the baths, and he seems really . . . what I want. A nice mustache, Levi's, a starched khaki army shirt . . . strong . . . Somebody you could take back to Orlando and they'd never know the difference.

'Then you go home with him to his house on Upper Market, and you try like hell not to go to the bathroom, because the bathroom is the giveaway, the fantasy-killer . . .'

Brian looked confused.

'It's the bathroom cabinet,' Michael explained. 'Face creams and shampoos for *days*. And on the top of the toilet tank they've all always got one of those goddamn little gold pedestals full of colored soap balls!'

Ebony Idol

The black woman ate Sunday dinner alone in the back room at Perry's.

She was an image of grace and sophistication, dark and sleek as a patent-leather dancing slipper. She was avoiding her french fries, Brian noticed, and her eyes seldom wandered from her plate.

'More coffee?'

She looked up and smiled. Wistfully, he thought. She shook her head and said, 'Thanks.' She was devastating.

'What about dessert?'

Another no.

OK, he thought, so much for the standard conversation ploys. It's time for the heavy-duty back up patter.

'Didn't like the french fries, huh?'

She patted her tiny waist. 'I'm allergic to them. They look wonderful, though.'

'One or two won't hurt you.'

'I've never seen round ones like that. They look like potato chips with a thyroid condition.'

He chuckled manfully. *Now* we're getting somewhere, kiddo. But keep it loose as a goose. Nothing heavy. And move slow, for God's sake, move slow . . .

She folded her napkin across her plate. Shit! She was going to ask for her check!

She smiled again. 'May I . . . ?'

'Do you know you look exactly like Lola Falana?'

Subtle as shit. If *that* didn't scare her off, nothing would.

Her face didn't change, though. She was still smiling. 'You want to buy me a drink, don't you?'

'Uh . . . yeah, as a matter of fact.'

'What time do you get off work?'

'Ten o'clock.'

'It's a date, then.'

'You bet. My name is Brian.'

'I'm D'orothea,' she said.

Across town at The Endup, Michael Tolliver threaded his way through a forest of Lacoste shirts. Mona was with him.

'Well, that clinches it, Mouse.'

'What?'

'I am *definitely* a fag hag.'

'Oh, for Christ's sake!'

'Look around the goddamn room, would you? I'm the only woman here!'

Michael grabbed her shoulder, spinning her around to face the bar. A robust-looking woman in Levi's and a work shirt was tending bar. 'Feel better now?'

'Terrific. Look . . . are you gonna change or what?'

'I think I'm supposed to register. Will you be all right if I leave you here?'

'Probably. Goddammit.' She winked and slapped him on the behind. 'Give my regards to Bert Parks.'

The bartender directed Michael to a man in charge of registration. The man took Michael's name and vital statistics and issued him a numbered paper plate on a string.

He was Number 7.

'Where do I . . . uh . . . change?'

'In the ladies' room.'

'Figures.'

There were already three guys in the ladies' room. Two of them had stripped down to their jockey shorts and were placing their clothes in plastic bags provided by the management. The third was smoking a joint, still decked out in recycled Vietnam fatigues.

'Hi,' said Michael, nodding to his fellow gladiators.

They smiled back at him, some with more calculation than others. They reminded him of his competition in the 1966 Orlando High School Science Fair. Artificially flippant. And hungry for victory.

Well, he thought, a hundred bucks is a hundred bucks.

'Can we . . . are we supposed to stay in here until our turn comes up?'

A blond in Mark Spitz briefs smiled at Michael's naïveté. 'I don't know about you, honey, but I'm gonna mingle. They might be giving out a Miss Congeniality award.'

So Michael slipped into the crowd, wearing only his paper plate and the jockey shorts he had bought at Macy's the day before.

Mona rolled her eyes when she saw him.

'I'll pay the rent,' said Michael.

'Don't get too cocky. I think I just saw Arnold Schwarzenegger come out of the ladies' room.'

'You're such a comfort, Mona.'

She snapped the elastic in his shorts. 'You'll do all right, kid.'

D'orothea's Lament

As arranged, Brian met her at the Washington Square Bar & Grill.

She was draped decoratively against the bar, brown eyes ablaze with interest as she chatted with Charles McCabe. The columnist seemed equally fascinated.

'You know him?' asked Brian, when she broke away to join him.

'I just met him.'

'You work fast, don't you?'

She gave him a playful shove. 'Haven't you figured *that* out yet?'

D'orothea was a model, he learned. She had worked in New York for five years, peddling her polished onyx features to *Vogue* and *Harper's*, Clovis Ruffin and Stephen Burrows and 'everybody else who was hopping on the Afro bandwagon.'

She had made money, she admitted, and lots of it. 'Which ain't half bad for a girl who grew up in Oakland B A.'

'B A?' asked Brian.

She smiled. 'Before Apostrophe. I used to be Dorothy Wilson until Eileen Ford turned it into Dorothea and stuck an apostrophe between the *D* and the *o*.' She arched an eyebrow dramatically. 'Very chic, don't you think?'

'I think Dorothy was good enough.'

'Well, so did I, honey! But it was either the apostrophe or one of those godawful African names like Simbu or Tamara or Bonzo, and I'd be goddamned if I'd go around town sounding like Ronald Reagan's chimpanzee!'

Brian laughed, noticing that her face was even more beautiful when animated. He was silent for several seconds, then asked soberly: 'Was it tough growing up in Oakland?'

She did a slow take, staring at him through heavy-lidded eyes. 'Oh, I get it! A lib-ber-rull!'

He reddened. 'No, not exact . . .'

'Gimme a hint, then, a Vista Volunteer, maybe? A civil rights lawyer?'

Her accuracy annoyed the hell out of him. 'I did work for the Urban League in Chicago, but I don't see what that . . .'

'And all that guilt exhausted you so much that you decided to hell with it and chucked it all for a waiter's job. I hear you, baby. I hear you.'

He downed his drink. 'I don't think you're hearing a goddamn thing but your own voice.'

She set down her glass of Dubonnet and stared at him expressionlessly. 'I'm sorry,' she said softly. 'I guess I'm nervous about being back here.'

'Forget it.'

'You have a nice face, Brian. I need somebody to talk to.'

'A therapist.'

'If you like. Does that bother you?'

'I'd hoped for something more basic.'

She ignored the implication. 'Sometimes it helps to tell things to strangers.'

He signalled the bartender for another drink. 'Go ahead, then. The doctor is in.'

She told her story without embellishment, seldom meeting his eyes.

'Four years ago, when I was just beginning to catch on in New York, I met this person who was working on a swimsuit campaign at J. Walter Thompson. We were together almost all the time, shooting at locations all over the East Coast. It took us about three weeks to fall in love.'

Brian nodded, abandoning his hopes.

'Anyway, we moved in together, fixing up this wonderful loft in SoHo, and I experienced the happiest six months of my life. Then something happened . . . I don't know what . . . and my lover accepted a job in San Francisco. We corresponded some after that, never completely losing touch, and I just kept on . . . making money.'

She sipped her Dubonnet and looked at him for the first time. 'Now I'm back home, Brian, and all I want is to have this person back in my life again. But that's completely up to . . .'

'Her.'

She smiled warmly. 'You're quick,' she said.

'Thanks.'

'This drink's on me, OK?'

The Winner's Circle

The master of ceremonies for the jockey shorts dance contest was someone called Luscious Lorelei. His platinum wig hovered over his rotund frame like a mushroom cloud over an atoll.

Michael groaned and readjusted his shorts. 'What the fuck am I doing here, Mona? I used to be a Future Farmer of America!'

'You're paying the rent, remember?'

'Right. I'm paying the rent, I'm paying the rent. *This* is a recording . . .'

'Just take it easy.'

'What if I lose? What if they laugh? Jesus! What if they don't even *notice* me?'

'You're not gonna lose, Mouse. Those assholes can't dance, and you look better than any of 'em. You've gotta believe in yourself!'

'Thank you, Norman Vincent Peale.'

'Cool it, Mouse.'

'I think I'm gonna throw up.'

'Save it for the finale.'

Five contestants had already vied for the hundred-dollar prize. Another was competing now, thrashing across the plastic dance floor in nylon leopard-skin briefs.

The crowd howled its approval.

'Listen to that, Mona. It's all over.' Michael chided himself silently for selecting the standard white jockey briefs. This mob obviously went in for flash.

'C'mon,' said Mona, pulling him through the crowd to the edge of the dance floor. 'You're next, Mouse.' She stayed by his side as they waited in the glow of an electrified American flag.

Luscious Lorelei moved to the microphone when the applause for Contestant Number 6 had subsided. 'How about that, guys? Could you *BUHLIEVE* the pecs on that humpy number? I mean, *PULLEASE*, Mary!' He gripped the contours of his sequined bosom. 'Rice bags never looked so good.'

Michael felt the color leave his face.

'Call Mary Ann,' he whispered to Mona. 'I'm going back to Cleveland with her.' Mona reassured him with a pat on the rump.

'OK,' bellowed Lorelei, 'our next contestant is . . . Contestant Number 7! He hails from Orlando, Florida, where the sun shines bright and they grow all those *BEE-YOOTIFUL* fruits, and his name is Michael . . . Michael Something . . . Honey, I can't read your handwriting. If you're out there, how 'bout telling Lorelei your name?'

Michael raised his hand half-heartedly and said, 'Tolliver.'

'What, honey?'

'Michael Tolliver.'

'*OKAAY*! Let's hear it for Michael Oliver!'

Now bright red, Michael climbed onto the dance platform as Lorelei slipped back into the darkness. The revelers at the bar turned in unison to assess the newcomer. The music began. It was Dr Buzzard's Original Savannah Band doing 'Cherchez la Femme.'

Michael slipped his body into gear and his mind into neutral. He moved with the music, riding its rhythm like a madman. He was merely having that dream again, that ancient high school nightmare about appearing in the senior play in his . . . jockey shorts!

His eyes unglazed long enough to see the crowd. The shining, tanned faces. The muscled necks. A hundred tiny alligators leering from a hundred chests . . .

Then his blood froze.

For there in the crowd, somber above a silk shirt and Brioni blazer, was the one face he didn't want to see. It linked with his, but only for a moment, then wrinkled with disdain and turned away.

Jon.

The music stopped. Michael leaped off the stage into the crowd, oblivious of the congratulatory hands that grazed his body. He pushed his way through a fog of amyl nitrite to the swinging doors in the corner of the room.

Jon was leaving.

Michael stood in the doorway and watched the lean figure retreat down Sixth Street. There were three other men with him, also in suits. A brief burst of laughter rose from the foursome as they climbed into a beige BMW and drove away.

An hour later, he got the news.

He had won. A hundred dollars and a gold pendant shaped like a pair of jockey shorts. Victory.

Mona kissed him on the cheek when he climbed off the platform. 'Who *cares* if there's a doctor in the house?' Michael smiled wanly and held on to her arm, losing himself in the music.

Then he began to cry.

Fiasco in Chinatown

Leaving the Gateway Cinema, Mary Ann and Norman headed west up Jackson toward Chinatown.

When they reached the pagoda-shaped Chevron station at Columbus, a thick pocket of fog had begun to soften the edges of the neon.

'On nights like this,' said Norman, 'I feel like somebody in a Hammett story.'

'Hammond?'

'Hammett. Dashiell Hammett. You know . . . *The Maltese Falcon*?'

She knew the name, but not much else. It didn't matter, however.

The only Falcon in Norman's life was parked at the corner of Jackson and Kearny.

'Do you have to get home straight away?' He asked it cautiously, like a child seeking permission to stay up late.

'Well, I should . . . no. Not right away.'

'Do you like Chinese food?'

'Sure.' She smiled, suddenly realizing how much she liked this bumbling, kindly, Smokey the Bear man with a clip-on tie. She wasn't particularly *attracted* to him, but she liked him a lot.

He took her to Sam Woh's on Washington Street, where they wriggled through the tiny kitchen, up the stairway and into a booth on the second floor.

'Brace yourself,' said Norman.

'For what?'

'You'll see.'

Three minutes later she made a discreet exit to the rest room. There was no sink in the cramped cabinet, and she was halfway back to the table before she discovered where it was.

'Hey, lady! Go wash yo' hands!'

Thunderstruck, she turned to see where the voice had come from. An indignant Chinese waiter was unloading plates of noodles from the dumbwaiter. She stopped in her tracks, stared at her accuser, then looked back toward the rest room.

The sink was outside the door. *In the dining room.*

A dozen diners were watching her, smirking at her discomfort. The waiter stood his ground. 'Wash, lady. You don' wash, you don' eat!'

She washed, returning red-faced to the table. Norman grinned sheepishly. 'I should have warned you.'

'You *knew* he would do that?'

'He specializes in being rude. It's a joke. War lord-turned-waiter. People come here for it.'

'Well, *I* didn't.'

'I'm really sorry.'

'Can we go, Norman?'

'The food's really . . .'

'Please?'

So they left.

Back in the dark canyon of Barbary Lane, he took her arm protectively.

'I'm sorry about Edsel.'

'Who?'

'That's his name. The waiter. Edsel Ford Fong.'

She giggled in spite of herself. 'Really?'

'I meant it to be fun, Mary Ann.'

'I know.'

'I really blew it. I'm sorry.'

She stopped in the courtyard and turned to face him. 'You're very old-fashioned. I like that.'

He looked down at his black wing-tips. 'I'm very old.'

'No you're not. You shouldn't say that. How old are you?'

'Forty-four.'

'That's not old. Paul Newman is older than that.'

He chuckled. 'I'm not exactly Paul Newman.'

'You're . . . just fine, Norman.'

He stood there awkwardly, as her palm slid gently along the contour of his jaw. She pressed her cheek against his. 'Just fine,' she repeated.

They kissed.

Her fingers moved down across his chest and clutched at the ends of his tie for support.

It came off in her hand.

Starry, Starry Night

There were mornings when Vincent felt like the last hippie in the world.

The Last Hippie. The phrase assumed a kind of tragic grandeur as he stood in the bathroom of his Oak Street flat, fluffing his amber mane, to conceal his missing ear.

If you couldn't be the first, there was something bitter-sweet and noble about being the last. The Last of the Mohicans. The Last Supper. The Last Hippie!

He had mentioned the concept once to his Old Lady, just hours before she had run off to join the Israeli Army, but Laurel had only sneered. 'It's too late,' she said, lifting the hair on the left side of his head. 'You're only seven eighths of The Last Hippie.'

She hadn't always been that way.

During the war, she had been coming from a different place. Her Virgoan anal retentiveness had been channeled into positive trips.

Astral travel. Sand candles. Macramé.

But postbellum, things had got heavy. She had enrolled in a woman's self-defense course and would practice holds on him while he was saying his mantra. Later, despite the efforts of her instructors at an Arica forty-day intensive, she developed an overnight obsession for Rolfing.

But not as a patient. As a practitioner.

That budding career came to an abrupt end when a dentist from Marin threatened to have her arrested for assault and battery.

'He was paranoid,' Laurel claimed afterward.

'He said you were getting into it,' Vincent replied quietly.

'Of course I was getting into it! It's my *job* to get into it!'

'He said you said things while you Rolfed him.'

'Like what?'

'Let's drop it, Laurel.'

'Like what?'

'Like . . . "Bourgeois pig" and "Up against the wall." '

'That's a lie!'

'Well, he said . . .'

'Look, Vincent! Who are you gonna believe, anyway? Me or a goddamn paranoid bourgeois pig?'

Well, she had gone now. She had left Amerika for good.

That's the way she had spelled it. With a *k.*

The very thought of that quirk made him tearful now, clinging desperately to the last vestiges of their life together.

He shuffled into the kitchen and stared balefully at his Day-Glo 'Keep on Truckin'' poster.

Laurel had put it there. A hundred years ago. It was yellow and cracked with age now, and its message seemed a cruel anachronism.

He had stopped truckin' a long time ago.

Lunging at the poster with his five-fingered hand, he crumpled it into a ball and hurled it across the room with a cry of primal anguish. Then he stormed into the bedroom and did the same to Che Guevara and Tania Hearst.

It was time to split.

The switchboard, he decided, was the best place to do it. It was neutral ground somehow. Public domain. It had nothing to do with him and Laurel.

He arrived there at seven-thirty and made himself a cup of Maxim from the tap in the bathroom. He tidied the desk, emptied the wastebaskets and cleaned his scalpel with a Wash'n Dri.

Mary Ann would arrive at eight o'clock.

There was time to do it properly.

He made a last entry in the log book, feeling a twinge of remorse for the tortured souls who would call tonight seeking his solace.

What would Mary Ann tell them?

And what would she do when she found him?

165

The scalpel wasn't fair, he decided, fingering his worry beads for the last time. There had to be a cleaner way, a method that would lessen the horror for Mary Ann.

Then he thought of it.

The News from Home

Before leaving for the Crisis Switchboard, Mary Ann stopped by Mona and Michael's.

A red-eyed Michael opened the door.

'Hi', he said quietly. 'Welcome to Heartbreak Hotel.'

'Company?' A stereo was playing in the bedroom.

'I wish.'

'Michael . . . is something the matter?'

He shook his head, forcing a smile. 'Come on in. I want you to hear something.'

He led her into his bedroom and pointed to a chair. 'Sit down and have a good cry. This woman is God's gift to romantics.' He held up an album cover. Jane Olivor's *First Night*.

Mary Ann propped her head on her hand and listened. The chanteuse was singing 'Some Enchanted Evening,' wrenching still more tears from Michael.

'Every faggot in town adores her,' explained Michael. 'It's real washing-up music.'

'Washing-up music?'

'You know. Post-whoopie. You play it afterwards, while he's lighting a cigarette and . . . washing up.'

Mary Ann reddened. 'Why not before?'

'Uh . . . good question. I guess it's . . . a threat before. Afterwards, there's no danger.'

'Oh.' She laughed nervously.

Michael flopped on the bed and stared at the ceiling. 'I hope I don't become cynical.'

'You won't.'

'Do you believe in marriage, Mary Ann?'

She nodded. 'Most of the time.'

'Me too. I think about it every time I see a new face. I got married four times today on the 41 Union bus.'

There was embarrassment in Mary Ann's laugh.

'I know,' said Michael unaccusingly. 'A bunch of fairies in caftans, tripping through Golden Gate Park with drag bridesmaids and quotations from "Song of the Loon" . . . That's not what I mean.'

'I know.'

'It would be like . . . friends. Somebody to buy a Christmas tree with.'

'Sure.' She tried in vain to picture herself choosing a Scotch pine with Norman.

Mona had been gone all day. Her absence began to gnaw at Michael again as soon as Mary Ann had left. Mona wasn't much fun these days, but she was at least a distraction.

She kept him away from Lands End.

Big deal, he thought, turning off the stereo and skulking into the kitchen. *Your whole goddamn life is at Lands End.* You belong to nobody, and nobody belongs to you. Your sacred chastity doesn't mean *shit*.

He foraged in the refrigerator for munchies, emerging with a grapefruit half and a flat Tab. Next to the ice tray, a bottle of Locker Room sat in stoic isolation, waiting for the next time.

He glared murderously at the squat brown bottle and slammed the freezer door. 'Freeze your ass off, you little mother!'

'Mikey?'

'Mama?'

'How are you, Mikey?'

'Fine, Mama. There hasn't been . . . ? Everything's all right, isn't it?'

'Oh . . . fair to middlin', I guess. Papa and I've got a surprise for you, Mikey.'

His fingertips traced the furrows of his brow. Please God, don't do this to me. 'What, Mama?'

'Well, you know Papa's been trying for *years* to wangle one of those trips with Florida Citrus Mutual . . .'

Come *on*, God! I'll join the church of my choice! I'll never lust in my heart again!

'So guess what happened just this afternoon?'

'You got the trip.'

'Uh huh. And guess where?'

'Fire Island.'

'What?'

'Nothing, Mama. I was being silly. You're coming to San Francisco, right?'

'Isn't it wonderful? We've got four whole days to visit, Mikey! And we've already got the hotel reservations and everything!'

The reservations, it turned out, were at the Holiday Inn on Van Ness. October 29 through November 1.

The horrible significance of those dates didn't hit Michael until he checked a calendar.

Mr and Mrs Herbert L. Tolliver were forsaking their orange groves, their Sizzlers and their Shakey's and their *Saturday Evening Posts*, to spend four fun-filled days in Everybody's Favorite City.

On Halloween weekend.

Jesus H. Christ.

A Place for Strays

Anna's bedroom had been carefully groomed for Edgar's arrival.

The linens were fresh, the ferns were misted, and the photograph that usually stayed on the dresser was tucked away in the bottom of the lingerie drawer.

'No waterbed?' Edgar grinned slyly, surveying the room for the first time.

'Sorry.' Anna shrugged. 'It's in the shop for repairs. I had a gentleman caller last night and we nearly drowned the cat!'

'What cat?'

She threw a pillow at him. 'You're supposed to say, "What gentleman caller?" goddammit!'

'OK. What gentleman caller?'

'I've forgotten. There've been so many!'

He wrapped his arms around her and held her for half a minute, then leaned down and kissed her lightly on the eyelids. When he was done, Anna looked up and said, 'Fitzgerald.'

'Ma'am?'

'That was from *The Great Gatsby* . . . "She was the kind of woman who was meant to be kissed upon the eyes." Something like that, anyway . . . Do you want something to drink, or are you already drunk?'

'Anna!'

She nudged him in the ribs. 'You smell like expensive scotch.'

'I've been to a cocktail party at The Summit.'

'With Frannie?'

Edgar nodded.

'How did you . . .'

'DeDe took her home.'

'Edgar . . . surely she *notices* when you . . .'

'She was barely conscious, Anna.'

Anna rested her hand on his chest and pointed a long, delicate fore-finger towards the window.

'There,' she said, adjusting the pillow under his head. 'You want proof?'

He rolled over to face the window and saw a plump tiger-striped cat inching along the ledge. The animal stopped for a moment, mewed at Anna, then moved on.

'His name is Boris,' said Anna.

'You don't let him in?'

'He doesn't belong to me.'

'Ah . . . then it doesn't count.'

'I love him,' she said flatly. 'That counts, doesn't it?'

'There's a theory,' said Anna, handing him a cup of tea as she climbed back into bed, 'that we are all Atlanteans.'

'Who?'

'Us. San Franciscans.'

Edgar grinned indulgently, bracing himself for another yarn.

Anna caught it. 'Do you want to hear it . . . or are you getting stuffy on me?'

'Go ahead. Tell me a story.'

'Well . . . in one of our last incarnations, we were all citizens of Atlantis. All of us. You, me, Frannie, DeDe, Mary Ann . . .'

'Are you *sure* she's out of the building?'

'She's gone to her switchboard. Will you relax?'

'OK. I'm relaxed.'

'All right, then. We all lived in this lovely, enlightened kingdom that sank beneath the sea a long time ago. Now we've come back to this special peninsula on the edge of the continent . . . because we *know*, in a secret corner of our minds, that we must return together to the sea.'

'The earthquake.'

Anna nodded. 'Don't you see? You said *the* earthquake, not *an* earthquake. You're expecting it. We're all expecting it.'

'So what does that have to do with Atlantis?'

'The Transamerica Pyramid, for one thing.'

'*Huh?*'

'Don't you know what dominated the skyline of Atlantis, Edgar . . . the thing that loomed over everything?'

He shook his head.

'A pyramid! An enormous pyramid with a beacon burning at the top!'

When Edgar slipped into the lane an hour later, Anna was watching him from the window. She rapped once, but he didn't hear her.

Someone else was watching too, concealed in the shrubbery at the edge of the courtyard.

Norman Neal Williams.

Hanging Loose

Mary Ann was running late, but the Mercedes parked at the foot of Barbary Lane stairway caught her eye. Its personalized plates said FRANNI. She recognized it instantly as Edgar Halcyon's.

A small town, she thought. Smaller, in a lot of ways, than Cleveland. She wondered which celebrated Russian Hill hostess was serving cocktails to the Halcyons tonight.

'Off to the body shops?'

It was Brian Hawkins striding down Leavenworth with a *definite* smirk on his face.

'I'm late for the switchboard,' she said crisply.

'Oh . . . the suicide place.'

She frowned. 'That's only part of it.'

'What time are you off?'

'Pretty late.'

'I see. OK . . . Well, if you feel like it, come on up for a joint afterwards.'

'I'm usually pretty tired, Brian.'

He brushed past her, heading up the stairway. 'Right. Can't get much plainer than that, can you?'

*

As usual, the J Church streetcar was a zoo.

Once past the scowl of the conductor, Mary Ann inched through a cloud of Woolworth's cologne to an empty seat in the back. She sat next to an old woman in a pink cloth coat and a battered brown wig.

'Warming up.'

'Ma'am?'

'Seems to be getting warmer.' A talker, thought Mary Ann. It never fails.

'Yes, ma'am. It does.'

'Where you from?'

'Cleveland.'

'My sister went to Akron once.'

'Oh . . . Akron's very nice.'

'I was born and raised here. Castro Street. Before all the you-know-whats moved in.'

'Yes, ma'am.'

'Have you found Jesus yet?'

'Ma'am?'

'Have you accepted Jesus as your personal Saviour?'

'Well . . . I'm . . . I was raised a Presbyterian.'

'The Bible says until ye be born again, ye shall not enter into the Kingdom of Heaven.'

If there's a God, thought Mary Ann, He must get his jollies by bringing these people into my life. Fundamentalist crones. Hare Krishna flower peddlers. Scientologists offering 'personality tests' on the corner of Powell and Geary.

When the streetcar stopped at Twenty-fourth Street, Mary Ann wasted no time in heading for the door.

The old woman reached into the aisle and said, 'Praise Jesus,' handing her convert a dog-eared pamphlet. Mary Ann accepted it with a blush and a nod of thanks.

As the streetcar departed, she stood on the corner and read the pamphlet's boldly emblazoned headline: JIMMY CARTER FOR PRESIDENT.

The world was changing, she decided. Even to her untrained Midwestern eye. Twenty-fourth Street seemed almost quaintly anachronistic. Men still wore their hair in ponytails here, and women slumped around in vintage granny dresses.

'Far out' had the sound of 'Oh, you kid.'

171

So what's next? she wondered. What will come along to take the place of free clinics and crisis switchboards and alternative newspapers and macrobiotic everything?

The entrance hall of the Switchboard was dark. A sliver of light from the back room guided her feet to the sound of a ringing phone.

'I'm here, Vincent. I'm really sorry! I just lost track of the time. I know you must be . . . *No!* . . . *Oh, God, Vincent, No!* . . . *You didn't?*'

His tongue was the worst part, protruding from his mouth like a fat black sausage.

He was swinging very slowly from the ceiling, his neck a hideous mass of twine and shells and feathers. Laurel's macramé had finally served a purpose.

He had died as organically as possible.

Nightcap

The policeman who dropped her off at Barbary Lane was so young that he had zits. But he was gentle and he seemed to be genuinely worried about her.

'You sure you're gonna be OK?'

'Yes. Thank you.' She had come very close to inviting him up for a crème de menthe . . . Anything to keep from being alone tonight.

Bounding up the stairway into the dark lane, she found herself praying that Mona or Michael would be at home. But no one answered their buzzer.

Upstairs, she fumbled in her purse for her key, then noticed the light spilling under Brian's door. She reversed her course without a moment's hesitation.

He was wearing boxer shorts and a sweatshirt when he opened the door. His face was shiny with sweat.

'Sit-ups,' he grinned, jerking his head toward his incline board.

'I'm sorry if I . . .'

'It's OK.'

'I . . . Does that offer for a joint still hold?'

He listened to her account of the horror with a face almost devoid of expression. When she had finished, he whistled softly. 'He was a good friend?'

172

She shook her head. 'Not at all.'

'That's the part that hurts, doesn't it?'

'God, Brian, if I had only *talked* to him a little more . . .'

'No. It wouldn't have done any good.' He shook his head, smiling ruefully. 'So we've *both* had a good day.'

'What happened to *you*?'

'Not much. A house party at Stinson Beach.'

'You didn't like it?'

He took a toke off the joint. 'Picture this, OK? Five young married couples and me. Well . . . semi-young. Thirty to thirty-five. Still in Topsiders, mind you, but driving an Audi now and sending a couple of rug rats to the French-American School and swapping notes on their Cuisinarts . . .'

'Their what?'

He handed her the joint. 'Next image: a beach full of pink people, the women on one side, chattering about hot tubs and cellulite and the best place for runny Brie . . . and the guys out by the volleyball net, huffing and puffing in twelve-year-old Madras bermudas their wives have let out at least twice . . . and all these yellow-haired kids fighting over who gets to play with Big Bird and G I Joe . . .'

Mary Ann smiled for the first time. 'I got it.'

'So here's our hero in the middle of all this . . . wondering if he can get food stamps if he quits at Perry's . . . hoping to hell the Clap Clinic doesn't call this week . . .' He stopped, seeing the look on her face. 'A joke, Mary Ann . . . And then this guy runs out of the house with his guitar slung around his neck like some refugee from *Hootenanny*, only he is a *lawyer*, right? . . . and he drops down in the sand and starts singing "I don't give a damn about a greenback dollar" . . . and everybody claps along and sings and jiggles kids in their laps . . .'

She nodded, confused by his cynical tone. The whole thing sounded rather *sweet* to her.

'Christ! I went back to the house when the singalong started and sat in an empty bedroom and smoked a joint and thanked my fucking lucky stars I wasn't trapped in that *pathetic*, middle-class prison!'

'I see.'

'This kid . . . about six years old . . . walks into the room, right? She asks me why I'm not singing and I say I'm a lousy singer and she says that's OK because she is too.'

'How cute.'

'She was all right.'

173

'Did she stay there with you?'

'She asked me to read her a story.'

'Did you?'

'For a little while. Hell, I was stoned.'

'Well, that doesn't sound so bad.'

'Her old man and I went to George Washington together.'

'Where?'

'Law school. He was the one who didn't give a damn about the greenback dollar.'

'You were a lawyer?'

The roach was so short that it burned his fingers. He threw it on the floor and stepped on it. 'Oh yes . . . only I *really* didn't give a damn about the greenback dollar. I was everybody's favorite freebie.'

'You didn't charge?'

'Not if you were black in Chicago . . . or a draft resister in Toronto or an Indian in Arizona . . . or a Chicano in LA.'

'But you could've . . .'

'I *hated* law. It was the causes I loved . . . and . . . well, I ran out of them.' He looked down at his hands dangling between his knees. 'Ol' Vincent and I would have gotten on like a house on fire.'

'Brian . . .'

'Go on.'

'Thanks for listening.'

'Out. Gotta finish my sit-ups.'

Words of Comfort

Mr Halcyon was nicer than she expected when she asked for the day off.

'I'm sorry about your friend, Mary Ann.'

'He wasn't really a *friend* exactly . . .'

'Just the same.'

'I really appreciate it.'

'It's not easy living in Atlantis, is it?'

'Sir?'

'Nothing. Take your time. I can call Kelly Girl.'

She was more out of it than ever. She sat on her wicker sofa, munching a Pop-Tart and watching the bay. The water was so *blue* . . . but was the price too high?

How many times now had she threatened to go home to Cleveland?

How many times had the lure of family china and split-level security beckoned her from the slopes of this beautiful volcano?

Would she *ever* stop feeling like a colonist on the moon?

Or would she wake up one morning to find herself a cloth-coated old lady, tottering about Russian Hill in slightly soiled gloves, prolonging her choice of a single lamb chop at Marcel & Henri, telling the butcher or the doorman or the nice young gripman who helped her onto the cable car that any day now, when her social security check came in, when the weather turned, when she found a home for her cat . . . she was going home to Cleveland?

Her buzzer rang.

When she opened the door, the face of her visitor was obscured by a huge pot of yellow mums.

'Hello, Mary Ann.'

'Norman?'

'I didn't wake you up, did I?'

'No. Come in.'

He set the flowers on one of her teak nesting tables from Cost Plus. 'Are those for me?' she asked.

He nodded. 'I heard about last night.'

'How sweet . . . Who told you?'

'That guy across the hall. I ran into him in the courtyard this morning.'

'Brian.'

'Yeah. Look, are you sure I'm not . . .'

'I'm delighted to see you, Norman. Really.' She pecked him on the cheek. 'Really.'

Norman flushed. 'I thought you might like the yellows better than the whites.'

'Yes.' She touched the flowers appreciatively. 'Yellow's my favorite. Hey, can I fix you some coffee?'

'If it's not too much trouble.'

'Of course not. I'll be right back.' She dashed into the kitchen and began fussing with her French stainless-steel-and-glass Melior pot from Thomas Cara Ltd. She had paid thirty-five dollars for it a month ago . . . and used it exactly twice.

175

She was almost positive that Norman was a Maxim-type person, but there was no point in risking it.

Norman seemed to like the coffee. 'Boy!' he grinned, looking up from his cup. 'Brian showed me what the landlady grows in the garden.'

'Oh . . . the grass, you mean?' She marveled at the matter-of-fact tone of her voice. Her growing sophistication sometimes astounded her.

'Yeah. I guess that's pretty common around here, huh?'

She shrugged. 'She only grows it for us . . . and herself. Well, you know . . . you got one when you moved in, didn't you?'

'One what?'

'A joint . . . taped on your door?'

Norman looked puzzled. 'No.'

'Oh . . . well.'

'She taped a joint on your door when you moved in?'

Mary Ann nodded. 'It's a house custom, sort of. I guess she must've . . . forgotten or something.'

Norman smiled. 'My feelings aren't hurt.'

'You don't smoke, huh?'

'No.'

'Well, maybe she could tell. She's awfully intuitive.'

'Yeah . . . maybe. Brian says she used to work in a bookshop in North Beach.'

Mary Ann failed to see the connection. 'Yeah. He told me that too. I've never asked her.'

'She's not from around here, is she?'

'Are you kidding?' said Mary Ann, grateful for the chance to use the line herself. '*Nobody's* from around here.'

'She sounds Midwestern to me.'

'Yeah . . . she and Mona talk a lot alike, I think.'

'Mona?'

'The red-headed woman on the second floor.'

'Oh.'

He looked a little lost, Mary Ann felt. Poor thing. *Someday*, she hoped he would learn to feel part of the family.

The Clue in the Bookshop

Norman left Mary Ann's apartment just before noon.

He spent the next three hours exploring bookshops, with no success. Finally, on Upper Grant, he discovered a dusty hole-in-the-wall sandwiched between a leather shop and an organic ice cream parlour.

He sniffed around for several minutes before approaching the old man in the back.

'Anything on sky-diving?'

'Huh?'

'Sky-diving. Parachuting.'

'Sports?'

'Yeah. A sport.'

The old man lifted his cardigan to scratch his side, then pointed to a shelf just above eye level. 'That's all we got on sports.' He conveyed an air of mild disgust, as if Norman had asked him for the pornography section.

'Well, it doesn't matter, anyway. I just wanted to get a look at the old place. I used to come here a long time ago. You've fixed it up real nice.'

'Think so?'

'Yeah. Real tasteful. You don't see many places like this anymore. It's nice to know some people still have respect for the past.'

The old man chuckled. 'I got plenty of past . . . I guess I oughta have plenty of respect.'

'Yeah . . . but you're young at heart, aren't you? That's what counts. You're a lot easier to deal with than that woman who used to run the place.'

The old man eyed him. 'You knew her?'

'Not well. She struck me as a real disagreeable lady.'

'Never heard *that* about her. A little peculiar, maybe.'

'Peculiar as hell. You bought the place from her?'

The old man nodded. 'About ten years ago. Been here ever since.'

'That's nice to hear. A place like this needs some . . . stability. I guess Mrs Whatshername went back East . . . or wherever she came from?'

'Nope. Still here. I see her off and on.'

'I wouldn't have figured that. She didn't seem too happy here. She was always gabbing about . . . hell, *someplace* back East. Where was she· from, anyway?'

'I guess you could call it back East. She was from Norway.'

'Maybe Denmark. Yeah . . . Denmark.'

'I guess I've got her mixed up with somebody else.'

'Name Madrigal?'

'Yep. That was it.'

'She was from Denmark, I'm sure. Born here . . . I mean the States . . . but she lived in Denmark before she bought the shop. I guess that's where she picked up her funny customs.'

'She had some funny ones, all right.'

The old man smiled. 'See that cash register?'

'Yeah?'

'Well, when I took the place over . . . the day I moved in . . . I found a note pasted there that said, "Good luck and God bless you" . . . and you know what else?'

Norman shook his head.

'A cigarette. A hand-rolled cigarette. Stuck up there with a piece of tape.'

'Peculiar.'

'Mighty peculiar,' said the old man.

As Mona and D'orothea entered Malvina's, Norman was striding down Union Street towards Washington Square.

Mona nodded to him, but the gesture went unnoticed.

'He's in our building,' she explained. 'He's afraid of his own shadow.'

'I can tell.'

'He watched me, though. He doesn't talk much, but he watches me.'

Upstairs at Malvina's, they sipped cappucinos and reconstructed the missing years.

'I've lost track,' said Mona. 'What happened to Curt?'

'Lots . . . *Sleuth* for a year or so. A couple of new soaps, then one of the big roles in *Absurd Person Singular*. He's done all right.'

'And so have you?'

'So have I.'

178

'I lost my job.'

'I know.'

'How the . . . ?'

'I'm doing some modeling for Halcyon. Beauchamp Day told me.'

'Small fucking world.'

'I'm finished with New York, Mona. I want this to be my home again.'

'Comin' home to go roamin' no more, huh?'

'You sound so cynical.'

'Sorry.'

'I need you, Mona.'

'D'or . . .'

'I want you back.'

Mona Moves On

The morning was bright and blustery. Michael tossed a pebble into the bay and flung an arm across Mona's shoulders. 'I love the Marina Green,' he said.

Mona grimaced and stopped in her tracks, scraping an ancient Earth Shoe against the curb. 'Not to mention the Marina Brown.'

'You're such a romantic!'

'Fuck romanticism. Look where it gets *you*.'

'Thanks, I needed that.'

'Sorry. I didn't mean it to sound that way.'

'Well, you're right.'

'No. I'm not. I'm a coward. I'm scared shitless. One of these days, Mouse, something really nice is going to happen to you. And you'll deserve it when it comes, because you never stop trying. I gave up a long time ago.'

Michael sat down on a bench and dusted off the space next to him. 'What's bugging you, Mona?'

'Nothing in particular.'

'Bullshit.'

'You don't need another downer, Mouse.'

'Says who? I *thrive* on downers.'

She sat down next to him, fixing her eyes glassily on the bay. 'I think I may move out, Mouse.'

His face was blank. 'Oh?'

'A friend of mine wants me to move in with her.'

'I see.'

'It's got nothing to do with you, Mouse. It really doesn't. I just feel like *something's* gotta change soon or I'll freak . . . I hope you . . .'

'Who is it?'

'You don't know her. She's a model I used to know in New York.'

'Just like that, huh?'

'She's really nice, Mouse. She's just bought this beautiful remodeled Victorian in Pacific Heights.'

'Rich, huh?'

'Yeah. I suppose.'

He stared at her without a word.

'I need . . . some sort of security, Mouse. I'm thirty-one years old, for Christ's sake!'

'So?'

'So I'm sick of buying clothes at Goodwill and pretending they're funky. I want a bathroom you can clean and a microwave oven and a place to plant roses and a goddamn dog who'll recognize me when I come home!'

Michael bit the tip of his forefinger and blinked at her. 'Arf,' he said feebly.

They walked for a while along the quay.

'Was she your lover, Mona?'

'Uh huh.'

'How come you never told me?'

'It never really seemed important, I guess. I wasn't exactly . . . into that scene. I was a lousy dyke.'

'But you aren't now, huh?'

'It doesn't matter.'

'The hell it doesn't.'

'She's a sweet person, and . . .'

'She'll take good care of you and you can stay at home and eat bonbons and read movie magazines to your heart's . . .'

'That's enough, Mouse.'

'Christ! Maybe you *did* give up a long time ago, but I'm not going to stand by and watch you throw your life away. You're not even being fair to *her*, Mona! What the hell does she need with some half-assed lover who's got the hots for tile bathrooms?'

'Look, you're not . . .'

'Nothing's free, Mona! Nothing!'

'Oh, yeah? What about your rent?'

The words stung harder than she expected, silencing Michael completely.

'I didn't mean that, Mouse.'

'Why not? It's the truth.'

'Mouse . . . I don't care about that.' He was crying now. She stopped walking and reached for his hand. 'Look, Mouse, you'll have the whole place to yourself, and Mrs Madrigal is bound to give you some slack on the rent until you can find a job.'

He rubbed his eyes with the back of his hand. 'Why does this sound like the end of a B-movie affair?'

She kissed him on the cheek. 'It does, doesn't it?'

'Some affair. You didn't even stick around long enough to meet my parents.'

At the Gynecologist's

The waiting room was the same shade of green that once oppressed DeDe at the Convent of the Sacred Heart. There were clowns on the walls – weeping clowns – and nothing to read but a July 1974 issue of *Ladies' Home Journal*.

She might as well have been waiting to get a tooth pulled.

The receptionist ignored her. She was ravaging a bag of barbecue potato chips while she read the *Chronicle*.

'Will it be much longer?' DeDe asked, hating herself for sounding apologetic.

'What?' This chinless Bryman School graduate was plainly irked that her reading had been interrupted . . . 'Uh . . . the doctor will be with you in a moment.' She brightened a little, holding up the paper and pointing to a serial on the back page. 'Have you read this today?'

DeDe stiffened. 'I don't read that.'

'Ah . . . c'mon.'

'I don't. It's nothing but trash. A friend of mine almost sued him once.'

'Far out. Have you ever . . .' She cut off the sentence and covered the newspaper with an IUD catalogue, just as a door swung open next to her booth.

DeDe looked up to see a lean, blond man in a blue oxford-cloth shirt, chino pants and a white cotton jacket. He reminded her instantly of Ashley Wilkes.

'Ms Day?'

That was one point in his favor. She hadn't explained her marital status on the telephone. She had said simply that she was a 'friend of Binky's,' sounding as quaintly furtive as a flapper approaching a speakeasy.

'Yes,' she said colorlessly, extending her hand.

Obviously sensing her discomfort, he led her out of the waiting room and into the room with the stirrups.

'Any nausea recently?' he asked softly, going about his work.

'A little. Not much. Sometimes when I smell cigarette smoke.'

'Any foods bother you?'

'Some.'

'Like?'

'Sweet and sour pork.'

He chuckled. 'But half an hour later you feel fine.'

That was *not* funny. She froze him out . . . or as much as she could in that position.

'Have you felt tired lately?'

She shook her head.

'How's Binky?'

'What?'

'Binky. I haven't seen her since the film festival.'

'She . . . I guess she's fine.' It enraged her that anyone could talk about Binky Gruen at a time like this.

When he was done, he came away from the sink with a smile on his smooth, Arrow collar face. 'It's yours, if you want it.'

'What?'

'The baby. There's no point in waiting for the urinalysis. You're going to be a mother, Mrs Day.'

She wondered later if some automatic defense mechanism had dulled her response to the announcement. Most women, surely, would not have chosen that particular moment to dwell on the luminous blue pools of their doctor's eyes.

*

She warmed to him after that, freed from embarrassment by his loose-limbed easiness, his toothy, prepschool smile. She could trust him, she felt. Baby or no baby. She was certain that he sensed the delicacy of the situation.

'When you make up your mind,' he said, 'give me a call. In the meantime, take these.' He winked at her. 'They're pink and blue. It's a subtle propaganda campaign.'

He said good-bye to her in the waiting room, turning to the receptionist as DeDe headed for the door.

'Through with the paper?'

She nodded, handing him the *Chronicle*.

He opened the newspaper at the same page that had occupied the receptionist. A slow smile crept over his face, and he began to shake his head.

'Sick,' said the doctor. 'Really sick.'

The Diagnosis

Stupefied, Frannie stared at her daughter.

'God, DeDe! Are you sure?'

DeDe nodded, fighting back the tears. 'I talked to him this morning.'

'And . . . he's sure?'

'Yes.'

'Dear God.' She clutched at the trellis in the morning room, as if to support herself. 'Why didn't . . . we know before? Why didn't the *tell* us?'

'He wasn't sure, Mother.'

Frannie's voice grew strident. 'Wasn't *sure*? Who gave him the right to play God? Don't we have a right to know?'

'Mother . . .'

Frannie turned away from her daughter, hiding her face. She fidgeted with a pot of yellow spider mums. 'Did the doctor . . . did he say how long he has?'

'Six months,' said DeDe softly.

'Will he . . . be uncomfortable?'

'No. Not until the end, anyway.' Her voice cracked. Her mother had begun to cry. 'Please don't, Mother. He's awfully old. The vet says it was time.'

'Where is he now?'

'On the terrace.'

Frannie left the morning room, brushing the tears from her eyes.

Out on the terrace, she knelt by the chaise longue where Faust lay sleeping.

'Poor baby,' she said, stroking the dog's graying muzzle. 'Poor, sweet baby.'

Later that day, Frannie poked morosely at her cheese soufflé and raised her voice over the noontime din at the Cow Hollow Inn.

'I said . . . I hope I can prepare myself for it.'

'Of course you do.' Helen Stonecypher was busying herself with a wet napkin, removing a chunk of Geminesse lipstick from her front tooth.

'Am I being maudlin?'

'Not at all.'

'I thought I might have his dish bronzed . . . as a kind of . . . memorial.'

'Sweet.'

'You *know* how I abhor women who get hysterical about their dogs . . . but Faust was . . . is . . .' Her voice trailed off.

Helen patted her hand, jangling their bangle bracelets in unison. 'Darling, do whatever makes *you* feel best. You remember Choy, don't you? My grandmother's cook in the big house on Pacific?'

Frannie nodded, blinking back the tears.

'Well, ol' Choy was Nana's dearest friend in the world . . . and when he died . . .'

'I remember that. Wasn't he wheeling her around the fair at Treasure Island?'

Helen nodded. 'When he died, Nana had his queue cut off and made into a choker.'

'A . . . ?'

'A necklace, darling . . . with three or four *very* understated little ivory beads worked into the strands. It was quite lovely, actually, and Nana *adored* it. As a matter of fact, she was wearing it when she died in our box in 1947.'

'I remember,' said Frannie, smiling bravely. '*Götterdämmerung.*'

Helen dropped her compact back in her purse. 'C'mon, darling. Let's go pour a stiff one at Jean's.'

184

'Helen . . . not just yet.'

'Darling, you *are* down!'

'I'll be all right in a . . .'

'He was an old, old pooch, Frannie.'

'Is.'

'Is . . . Frannie, look at it this way. He's had a full, rich life. *No* dog's had it as good as he has.'

'That's true,' said Frannie, brightening somewhat. 'That's very, very true.'

The Tollivers Invade

All things considered, Halloween weekend had gone quite well.

So far.

Michael's parents had rented a Dodge Aspen upon their arrival in the city, so it was easy enough to fill up their time with Muir Woods and Sausalito, The Crooked Street and Fisherman's Wharf.

But now it was Sunday. The Witches' Sabbath was upon them.

If he was careful, very careful, he could ease them through it, protect their fragile, *Reader's Digest* sensibilities from the horror of The Love That Dare Not Speak Its Name.

Maybe.

In *this* town, he thought, The Love That Dare Not Speak Its Name almost never shuts up.

His father chuckled when he saw the apartment for the first time. 'Took you all weekend to clean it up, huh?'

'I'm neater than I used to be,' Michael grinned.

'Looks like a lady's neatness, if you ask me.' He winked at his son.

Michael's mother frowned. 'Herb, I told you not . . .'

'Aw, it's OK, Alice. Christ, we're not a couple of old fuddy-duddies. I remember what I was like at Mike's age. Hell, son . . . I hope you didn't move her out on our account.'

'Herb!'

'Your mother's too old-fashioned, Mike. Go snoop around the kitchen, Alice. I'm surprised you could hold off this long.'

Michael's mother pushed out her lower lip and trudged out of the room.

185

'Now,' said his father. 'What the hell's going on? Your mother and I thought you'd like to introduce us to . . . what's her name?'

'Mona . . . Papa, she's only . . .'

'I don't give a damn *what* she is, Mike. Frankly, I'm a little disappointed you felt you had to hide the poor little thing. I've seen *Hustler*, son. I know a thing or two about 1976.'

'Papa . . . she moved out. She wanted to.'

'Because of us?'

'No. She just wanted to. She found another roommate. There's no hard feelings.'

'You're a damned idiot, then! She just up and left you and there's no hard feelings? Jesus, Mike . . .'

He stopped talking when he heard his wife return. She was standing in the kitchen doorway with a small brown bottle in her hand.

'What's this stuff, Mikey?'

Michael went white. 'Uh . . . Mama, that's something . . . my roommate left behind.'

'In the freezer?'

'She used it to clean her paintbrushes.'

'Oh.' She looked at the bottle again and returned it to the refrigerator. 'You need to scrub your vegetable bin, Mikey.'

'I know, Mama.'

'Where do you keep your Ajax?'

'Mama, can't we just . . .'

'It's disgusting, Mikey. It won't take me a second.'

'Alice, for God's sake! Leave the boy alone! We didn't come three thousand miles to scrub his goddamn vegetable bin! Look, son, your mama and I want to take you out to dinner tonight. Why don't you show us one of your favorite places?'

Peachy, thought Michael. We'll just boogie on down to The Palms, sip Blue Moons in a window seat, and watch the Cycle Sluts wave leather dildos at the traffic cops.

The Aspen was parked up on Leavenworth, near Green. Michael's mother was out of breath by the time they reached Union. 'I've never seen a street like that in my life, Mikey!'

He squeezed her arm, taking sudden pleasure in her innocence. 'It's an amazing city, Mama.'

Almost on cue, the nuns appeared.

'Herb, look!'

'Goddammit, Alice! Don't point!'

'Herb . . . they're on roller skates!'

'Goddamn if they aren't! Mike, what the hell . . . ?'

Before their son could answer, the six white-coifed figures had rounded the corner as a unit, rocketing in the direction of the revelry on Polk Street.

One of them bellowed at Michael.

'Hey, Tolliver!'

Michael waved half-heartedly.

The nun gave a high sign, blew a kiss, then shouted: '*Loved* your jockey shorts!'

Trick or Treat in Suburbia

Mary Ann tugged on her driver's arm. 'Oh, Norman . . . beep will you?'

'Who is it?'

'Michael and his parents. Mona's roommate.'

Norman tapped on the horn. Michael looked towards them as Mary Ann blew a kiss from the window of the Falcon. He smiled feebly and pretended to yank out a handful of hair. His parents were charging ahead, oblivious.

'Poor baby!' said Mary Ann.

'What's the matter?'

'Oh . . . it's complicated.'

'He's queer, isn't he?'

'Gay, Norman.'

Lexy poked her head over the seat. 'What's queer?'

'Sit down,' said Norman.

Mary Ann turned around and fussed with Lexy's Wonder Woman cape. 'You look so *nice*, Lexy.'

The child bounced on the back seat. 'Why don't *you* have a costume?'

'Well . . . I'm a grownup, Lexy.'

The child shook her head vehemently and pointed out the window to three men dressed as high school majorettes. '*Those* grownups have costumes.'

Norman chuckled, shaking his head.

Mary Ann sighed. '*How* old did you say she was?'

It was almost dark by the time they reached San Leandro. Norman parked the car in a pseudo-Spanish subdivision and opened the door for Lexy.

The little girl bounded down the sidewalk with a mammoth plastic trick-or-treat bag.

'Are you sure she'll be all right?' asked Mary Ann.

Norman nodded. 'Her folks live over in the next block. I told them I'd . . . you know . . . let her get this out of her system.'

'I hope they appreciate all this.'

'I wouldn't do it if I didn't like it.' He grinned sheepishly. 'Rent-a-kid, you know.'

'Yeah. It's kinda nice, isn't it?'

'It isn't boring for you?'

'Not at all.'

He looked at her solemnly for a moment, then squeezed her hand.

'Norman?'

'Yeah?'

'Have you ever been married?'

Silence.

'I'm sorry. It's just that you're so good with kids that . . .'

'Roxanne and me were gonna have kids. That was the plan, anyway.'

'Oh . . . she died?'

Norman shook his head. 'She ran off with a ceramic-tile salesman from Daly City. When I was in Nam.'

'I'm sorry.'

He shrugged. 'That was a long time ago. About the time Lexy was born, in fact. I got over it.'

She looked out the window, embarrassed by this new insight into his personality. Was Lexy his only link with a vanished dream? Had he given up all hope of building a home again?

'Norman . . . I don't see how *anyone* could leave you.'

'It doesn't matter.'

'Of course it matters, Norman! You're a gentle, kind, loving man, and no one should . . . Norman, you've got *so* much love to give someone.'

His hands were fidgeting in his lap. He looked down at them. 'Someone,' he repeated vacantly.

He needed a sign from her. He was *pleading* for a sign.

She was reaching up to touch his sad bear's face when a hand on her shoulder made her yelp.

Lexy was back.

'Oh, Lexy . . .' Mary Ann laughed, somewhat relieved. 'How did you do?'

'A crummy apple.'

'Well, apples are good. I'll eat it if you don't want it.'

The child looked at her for a moment, then produced the apple and sunk her teeth into it defiantly.

Norman shouted in horror. 'Lexy . . . no!'

Lexy grinned at him as the juice dribbled down her face. 'It's OK,' she said. 'I already checked it for razor blades.'

Chip off the Old Block

Michael ended up taking his parents to the Cliff House. It was the straightest place he could think of.

It was also far enough away from the Halloween madness of Polk Street that roller-skating nuns were not likely to invade the family circle again.

The nuns, he explained as cavalierly as possible, were 'some crazy friends of Mona's.' And yes, they were men.

'Fruits?'

'Herb!' Michael's mother dropped her fork and glared at her husband.

'Well, what the hell do you want me to call them?'

'That's not a very nice word, Herb.'

'Why not? I'm a citrus grower, Alice. We *raise* fruits.' He laughed raucously.

'You just shouldn't talk that way about people who can't help themselves.'

'Can't help themselves! Who the hell can't help skatin' down the middle of the street dressed up like a goddamn nun?'

'Herb . . . don't raise your voice. There might be Catholics in the room.'

Michael looked up from his plate, speaking as offhandedly as possible. 'It's kinda like Mardi Gras, Papa. There's a lot of crazy stuff going on. A lot of people do it.'

'A lot of fruits.'

'Not just . . . them, Papa. Everybody.'

His father snorted and reattacked his steak. 'I don't notice *you* out there making a goddamn fool of yourself.'

'He's with *us*, Herb. Maybe he'd *like* to be out there . . . going to a party or something. It sounds like a lot of fun to me.'

'Well, you two go right ahead. I'll just sit here and finish my steak with the normal people.'

A waiter refilling Herbert Tolliver's water glass caught the remark and rolled his eyes in pained forbearance.

Then he winked at Michael.

Back at Barbary Lane, Alice Tolliver recapped the social history of Orlando for the past six months.

A new shopping mall had been built. The Henleys' daughter, Iris, was addicted to pot and living with a professor in Atlanta. A coloured family had bought the McKinneys' split-level down the road. Aunt Miriam was doing fine, despite her overlong recovery from a female operation, and everybody in Central Florida agreed that Earl Butz would never have been fired if he had made that remark about an Irishman.

They weren't expecting an early frost.

Herbert Tolliver sat quietly through the telling of this saga, embellishing only occasionally with a chuckle or a nod of his head. He was mellower now, softened by the wine at dinner, and he beamed at his son in open affection.

'Is . . . everything goin' OK for you, Mike?'

'Pretty good, Papa.'

'Don't you worry about your ladyfriend, you hear?'

'I won't, Papa.'

'Your mama and I are gonna miss you at Christmas.'

'Now, Herb, he's grown up now, and he's got friends of his . . .'

'I know that, goddammit! I just said we'd miss him, didn't I?'

His wife nodded. 'We will, Mikey.'

'I'll miss y'all too. It's just so expensive to fly back there for . . .'

'I know, Mikey. Don't you worry about that.'

'Mike . . . if we can help out a little bit until you can find a job . . .'

'Thanks, Papa. I think I can manage. I've picked up a little on odd jobs.'

'Well, you let us know, OK?'

'OK, Papa.'

'We're mighty proud of you, son.'

Michael shrugged. 'Not much to be proud of, is there?'

'Don't be a damn fool! You're as good as the best of 'em! Some things take a little time, son. You'll work it out before you know it. Hell, I kind of envy you, son. You're young and you're single and you're livin' in a beautiful town full of beautiful women. You got no sweat at all, son!'

'I guess you're right.'

'Course I'm right. Smooth sailin' all the way.' He chuckled and grazed his son's cheek with a playful fist. 'Long as you can keep those fruits away.'

Michael made a manly grin. 'I'm not their type, anyway.'

'Attaboy!' said Herbert Tolliver, tousling the hair of his pride and joy.

DeDe's Growing Dilemma

When DeDe called Beauchamp at work, he was briefing Halcyon's hottest new model on the Adorable Christmas campaign.

'Look, I'm right in the middle of . . .'

'Sorry, darling. I just . . . I was afraid you'd forget about Pinkie and Herbert's opening tonight.'

'Shit.'

'You forgot.'

'What time do we have to be there?'

'I can meet you after work. We just need to make an appearance.'

'Six o'clock?'

'Fine . . . I love you, Beauchamp.'

'Me too. Six o'clock, then?'

'Yeah. Be good.'

'Always.'

He hung up and winked at D'orothea. 'My wife. Sometimes I think God put women on this earth to remind men of cocktail parties.'

D'orothea merely grunted.

'Ah,' Beauchamp grinned. 'That makes me sound like a chauvinist pig, I guess.'

'No,' she said coldly. 'Do you want to?'

*

The Hoover Gallery was jammed with patrons, a canvas of kelly green and pink. The women were decked out in understated Lilly Pulitzers, while their blue-blazered husbands expressed their individuality in madras patchwork trousers.

Beauchamp and DeDe headed directly to the bar, wearing identical smiles and flaunting their new-found bliss like Tahitian tans.

DeDe was still clinging to Beauchamp's arm when Binky Gruen intercepted them.

'Oh, thank God you two showed up! Beauchamp, quick, gimme a kiss! I have to look occupied.'

Beauchamp pecked her on the cheek. 'I've heard better excuses, Ms Gruen.'

'Keep talking, goddammit! He's looking this way!'

'Who?'

'Carson Callas. He's been blowing pipe breath at me for the past fifteen minutes, telling me how sexy he is! Yecchh!'

Beauchamp recoiled in mock surprise. 'You don't think Carson Callas is sexy?'

'Sure. If you get off on midgets in puka shells.'

'Naughty, naughty. He won't put you in his column, Binky.'

'Or vice versa, if *I* can help it. Look, be an angel and fill this up with scotch. I feel an attack of ennui coming on. Your skinny wife looks thirsty too.'

Beauchamp took Binky's glass, then turned to DeDe. 'Champagne, Skinny Wife?'

'Please.' Her tone was deliberately chilly. She *hated* it when Binky and Beauchamp did their Lombard and Gable routine.

By the time Beauchamp had disappeared into the crowd, Binky was ready to pounce.

'Well?'

'Well, what?'

'Did you see Dr Fielding?'

'Binky . . . this is hardly the place.'

'Yes or no?'

'Yes.'

Binky whistled. 'I've got a good abortion man, if you need one.'

'Binky . . . will you just shut up, please!'

'Well, *pardonnez-moi*! I thought you could use a friend about now. I guess I was mistaken.'

'Binky, I . . . Look, I'm sorry . . . it's just that you make it sound so . . . A good abortion man, for heaven's sake! Does he cater parties too?'

Binky giggled. 'No, but he's *marvelous* with windows and floors!'

'That's not funny.'

'Well, I think you're getting *much* too heavy about this whole business.' She patted DeDe's stomach. 'No pun intended, darling. Look . . . if all that nasty Catholic guilt is gonna be too much for you, why don't you just go ahead and have the little bastard?'

'I thought you had that one figured out already.'

'What the hell? Beauchamp can play along. He needs an heir, doesn't he? Who's gonna know the difference?'

'Binky . . . you don't know what you're talking about . . .'

'Don't tell me it would *show*?'

DeDe glared at her for several seconds, then nodded.

'Hair?' asked Binky, her eyes fairly dancing with excitement. 'A different color hair?'

'No.'

'Not *skin*?'

Another nod.

'Oh, you poor baby! Oh, DeDe, I didn't mean to be so . . . What color?'

DeDe pointed to her daffodil Diane von Furstenberg and burst into tears.

After repairing her mascara in the bathroom, she emerged with the mob again. Beauchamp was waiting with lukewarm champagne.

'I'm with Peter and Shugie,' he said. 'Wanna join us?'

She shook her head with a watery smile. 'Not right now, Beauchamp. Binky and I are catching up.'

Alone again, she plastered a smile on her face and headed toward the corner where Binky had been holding court. A hand stopped her, clamping onto her forearm.

'Well, doesn't Mrs Day look good enough to eat?'

If her arm had been free, she might have crossed herself. It was the society editor of *Western Gentry* magazine.

Carson Callas.

Mrs Madrigal and the Mouse

Michael was shifting half of his clothes into Mona's closet when Mrs Madrigal phoned.

'Michael, dear. Could you come down for a moment?'

'Sure. Three minutes, OK?'

'Take your time, dear.'

Well, he thought, hanging up the phone, here it comes. Eviction time. She's been more than lenient about the rent so far, but enough is enough.

He slipped into corduroy trousers and a white shirt, brushed his teeth, Pro-Maxed his hair into place, and ran a wet towel across his Weejuns.

There was no point in *looking* like a deadbeat.

The landlady's angular face, usually so mobile, was locked into the smile of a corporate receptionist.

She seemed artificially restrained, moving with such deliberate dignity that her kimono looked as dowdy as a housecoat.

'Mona's left, hasn't she?'

He nodded. 'Yesterday.'

'For good?'

'So she says. But you know Mona.'

'Yes.' Her smile was off-kilter.

'I'm gonna stay, Mrs Madrigal. I mean . . . I'd *like* to. Mona's gonna pay off the rest of this month's rent, and I've registered with an employment agency, so if you're worried . . .'

'Where did she go, Michael?'

'Oh . . . uh . . . a friend's house. In Pacific Heights.'

Mrs Madrigal walked to the window, where she stood motionless, keeping her back to Michael. 'Pacific Heights,' she echoed.

'Didn't she . . . talk to you, Mrs Madrigal?'

'No.'

'I'm sure she planned to. Things have been kinda hectic for her lately. Anyway, *I'm* still here. It's not like she's breaking a lease or anything.'

'Do you know this person, Michael?'

'Who? . . . Oh . . . no, I've never met her.'

'A woman?'

He nodded. 'Somebody she knew in New York.'

'Oh.'

'Mona says she's really nice.'

'I'm sure . . . Michael, you don't have to answer this if you don't want to . . .'

'Uh huh?'

'Is this woman . . . are she and Mona special friends?'

'Uh . . .'

'Do you understand me, dear?'

'Sure. I don't know, Mrs Madrigal. They *used* to be . . . in New York. I think they're just . . . regular friends now.'

'Well . . . then why on earth . . . ? Michael, has Mona ever said anything to you about me? Anything that . . . might make you think she was unhappy here?'

'No, ma'am,' he said earnestly, reverting to Central Floridian custom. 'She was *crazy* about Barbary Lane . . . and she liked you a lot.'

Mrs Madrigal turned to face him. 'Liked?' she asked.

'No. Likes. She's *very* fond of you, I'm sure she'll call. Really.'

The landlady turned crisply businesslike again. 'Well, *you're* staying. That's something.'

'I'll try to be better about the rent.'

'I know. Look, dear, I've got a brand-new lid, and the night is young. Will you join me?'

Her fingers trembled noticeably as she worked the roller. She set it down, drew a breath, and massaged her forehead with both hands. 'I'm sorry, Mouse. I'm being awfully silly.'

'Please don't . . . where did you hear that name?'

She chewed her lower lip for a moment, observing him. 'I'm not the only one that Mona was fond of.'

'Oh . . . yeah.'

'My stupid fingers won't behave! Would you do the . . . ?'

He took the roller from her, avoiding her eyes as they began to fill with tears. 'Mrs Madrigal, I wish I could say . . .'

She moved no closer, but her long, slender hand came to rest on his knee as she pressed a handkerchief to her face. 'I hate *weepy* women,' she said.

195

The Shadow Knows

The rat-faced man in the safari suit moved so close to DeDe that she could smell the Cherry Blend on his breath. 'You've lost weight,' he smirked, flashing an uneven row of Vuitton-colored teeth.

DeDe nodded. 'How have you been, Carson?'

'Hangin' in there. A fat farm, huh?'

'The Golden Door.' She smiled when she said it, without elaborating. He was pumping her, she knew, and she didn't relish the thought of reading about her weight problem in *Western Gentry* magazine.

'Well, it looks darn good.'

'Thanks, Carson.'

'What do you think of the artist?'

That threw her for a moment. Paintings were the *last* thing she noticed at an opening. 'Oh . . . a very individual style. Quite sensitive, I think . . .'

'You and Beauchamp in the market?'

'Oh . . . no, I don't think so, Carson. Beauchamp and I are into Western art.'

He sucked on his pipe, never taking his tiny eyes off her face. 'This man's Western,' he said finally.

'I mean . . . you know . . . the old stuff.'

'Yeah, the old stuff. Sometimes the old stuff's better.' He winked at her, chewing methodically on his pipestem until she acknowledged the joke with a thin smile.

'Excuse me, will you, Carson? I think Beauchamp . . .'

'I was hoping you'd tell me about the Fol de Rol.'

'Oh . . . sure.' Her spirits brightened instantly. This could be a *coup* that would drive Shugie Sussman up the wall!

Callas pulled a pad and pencil from the pocket of his safari suit. 'You're on the committee, right?'

'Yeah. Me and a few others.'

'Who's performing this year?'

'Oh, it's *fabulous*, Carson! The theme is "Wine, Women and Song" and we've got Domingo, Troyanos and Wixell . . .'

'First names?'

'Placido Domingo . . .'

'Oh, sure . . .'

'Tatiana Troyanos and Ingvar Wixell.' She stopped herself from spelling the names, remembering Callas' vanity. He could look them up when he got back to his office.

The columnist returned the pad and pencil to his pocket. 'Fun evening, huh?'

'Should be.'

'But not as fun as most of yours?'

'Uh . . . what, Carson?'

The leer was back again. 'I think you heard me, sweetheart.'

The crowd in the gallery had grown thicker and noisier, but now the din seemed oddly remote. DeDe swallowed and forced herself to look blasé.

'Carson, really! Sometimes you can be *too* much!'

'I think we've got a lot in common.'

'Carson, I don't know what . . .'

'Look . . . we're both grownups. Nobody ever accused me of not knowing my way around an orgy . . . and I think I can recognize a kindred spirit when I see one.'

God, she thought, how many times had he used *that* one?

It was a standing joke in town that Callas had once unsuccessfully propositioned the entire cast of a local musical revue, starting with the women and working down to the less attractive men.

'Carson . . . I love chatting with you, but I think I need a drink.'

'One more question about the Fol de Rol?'

'Sure.'

'Are you gonna have the abortion before or after?'

The glass slipped from her hand almost instantly, shattering as a punctuation to the horrid question. Callas dropped to his knees and helped her gather the pieces in a cocktail napkin.

'Ah, c'mon! It's not that bad, DeDe. I'm sure we can work it out . . . if you'd like to talk about it some night.' He stuffed his business card into the belt of her dress and stood up again.

'Your friends are *concerned*,' he added. 'Surely there's nothing wrong with that?'

She didn't look up, but continued picking up the pieces in silence.

Discretion was too much to expect of Binky Gruen.

197

How to Cure the Munchies

Brian crashed at midnight after a grueling shift at Perry's, only to wake up five hours later with a bitch of an appetite.

Stumbling into the kitchen in his boxer shorts, he rummaged through the refrigerator for something to placate his growl.

Ketchup. Mayonnaise. Two bluish Ball Park franks. And a jar of cocktail onions.

Had he been stoned, he might have hacked it. (Once, after smoking half a joint of Maui Wowie, he'd been reduced to using Crisco as a dip for Ritz crackers.)

But not tonight.

Tonight – hell, five o'clock in the morning! . . . he lusted for a Zim-burger. And a fat, greasy side-order of fries, and maybe a chocolate malt or a . . .

He excavated in his laundry bag until he found a rugby shirt that would pass the sniff test, climbed into Levi's and Adidas, and almost sprinted out of the house into Barbary Lane.

Hyde Street was freakishly quiet. Asleep in its iron cocoon, the ancient cable seemed more intrusive than ever. From the crest of Russian Hill, the wharf was a colorless landscape, a black-and-white postcard from the forties.

Even the Porsches parked on Francisco suggested abandonment.

It felt like the last scene of *On the Beach*.

Zim's, by contrast, was jarringly cheery. The all-night eatery was humming with efficient waitresses, frazzled insomniacs and the remnants of parties that couldn't stop.

Brian's waitress was dressed in commercial country-western. Orange blouse and jumper. Orange-checked kerchief. Her name tag said 'Candi Colma'.

'"The City of the Dead."' Brian grinned as she slapped a napkin and fork in front of him.

'What?'

'You're from Colma. Cemeteryland.'

'South San Francisco, really. Just over the border. South San Francisco was too long to put on the name tag.'

'Candi Colma sounds nicer, anyway.'

'Really.' Her smile was nice, implying an intimacy that didn't exist. She was in her late thirties, Brian guessed, but it showed only around the eyes. Her waist was small and firm, her legs wickedly long.

Never mind the teased blond hair, he thought. You can't get picky at five o'clock in the morning.

After she had taken his order, he watched her move across the room. She walked like a woman who knew she had an audience.

'Zimburger OK?'

'Fine. Perfect.'

'Anything else? Dessert, maybe?'

'Whatcha got to offer?'

'It's on the menu there, sugar.'

He flapped the menu shut and gave her his best Huck Finn grin. 'I bet it's not . . . sugar.'

Moving closer to him, she tapped her pencil against her lower lip, cast her eyes left and right, and whispered, 'I don't get off till seven o'clock.'

Brian shrugged. 'It's not *when* you get off, is it? It's *how*.'

Candi's Camaro was parked around the corner next to the Maritime Museum. It was plum-colored and its bumper sticker said: I BRAKE FOR ANIMALS.

When the seat-belt buzzers had stopped, she looked at him apologetically. 'I'd feel better if we went to my place.'

'Colma?'

She nodded. 'If you don't mind.'

'Christ, that's a half hour's drive!'

'The traffic's not bad when you're going this direction.'

'How the hell am I gonna get home?'

'I'll drive you. Look . . . I've got a roommate.'

Brian slammed his palm against his forehead. 'Oh, shit.'

'No. It's a girl. It's cool, really. It's just that she'll worry if I'm not home.'

'Call her, then.'

She shook her head. 'I'm sorry, Brian. If you'd like to forget it, I'll understand.'

'No. Let's go.'

'You don't have to, if . . .'

'I said let's go, didn't I?'

She stuck the key in the ignition. 'I live in a trailer. I hope you don't mind.'

He shook his head and stared out at the pewter surface of the early-morning bay.

He was sure of it now.

This had all happened before.

The Hungry Eye

Norman was wolfing down a breakfast of cold egg rolls when the telephone rang.

The noise startled him. He wasn't used to receiving calls in the little house on the roof.

'Hello.'

'Mr Williams?'

He recognized the grating Midwestern twang immediately. 'I hope this is important.'

'Well, I . . . I was just wondering how it was going.'

'Look, I gave you the number of my answering service, right?'

'Mr Williams . . . I've left three messages with your service in the last two . . .'

'Do you think you're my only client?'

'Of course not . . . but I don't see why you can't . . .'

'You're perfectly free to find another man, if you want.' He knew it was safe to say that. He was too valuable to her now.

'I have the utmost confidence in your . . .'

'I'm working on *three* different husbands right now . . . plus a runaway kid from Denver and more guys messing around on their wives than I can . . . You're paying me by the job, remember? Not by the hour.'

'I know.' Her tone was placating.

'You could've blown the whole thing by calling me here. I've got no privacy at all in this cracker box. There could've been somebody sitting two feet away from me who would've figured out the . . .'

'I know, Mr Williams. I'm sorry I . . . Could you just tell me if you've found out anything?'

He waited for a moment, then said. 'It's going OK.'

'Do you think . . . ?'

'I think she's the one.'

That rocked her. 'God,' she said incredulously.

'I have to go slow, though. It's ticklish.'

'I understand.'

'People are sticky out here about privacy, you know.'

'Of course.'

'It should be a matter of weeks. I can tell you that.'

'I hope you can understand why I'm so . . .'

'Look . . . look at it this way, OK? You've waited thirty years already. Another month or so won't kill you.'

'I thought you said two weeks.'

'Mrs Ramsey!'

'All right. OK. Did you find out if the name is . . .'

'Yeah. Phony. It's an anagram.'

'Anna Madrigal? You mean it spells . . . ?'

'Look, lady! Will you wait for my goddamn report!'

'I won't bother you again, Mr Williams.'

She hung up.

The call unsettled him for the rest of the morning. Who the hell was he kidding?

The kid from Denver had shown up *weeks* ago, canceling the most potential lucrative job of his career. Most of his missing-persons clients had switched to slicker agencies, and he hadn't been offered a philandering-husband case since 1972.

He prolonged the Ramsey case because it was his *only* case . . . and he couldn't confront the reality of failure.

If things kept up like this for long, he might be selling Nutri-Vim for real.

'Paul?'

'Yeah?'

'It's Norman.'

'Hey, man . . . the proofs aren't ready yet. I'll call you when they're ready, OK?'

'I didn't call about that. I thought . . . well, I thought you might wanna schedule the next session.'

'Nah. Too soon. Besides . . . I think we're gonna film this week.'

'How's it pay?'

'Not bad. You wanna . . . ?'
'Yeah. I can arrange it.'
'How much notice do you need?'
'Coupla days.'
'Can do.'
'I want the money in advance, Paul.'
'You got it.'

Trauma in a Travel-Eze

The Treasure Island Trailer Court was a dreary little encampment just off El Camino Real at the Colma-South San Francisco border.

It's nearest neighbor was Cypress Lawn Cemetery.

As Candi's Camaro swung off the highway into the court, Brian winced at the ugly row of Monopoly board houses snaking along a distant hillside.

Rows.

Peninsula people often condemned themselves to rows, thought Brian. Rows of houses, rows of apartments, rows of tombstones . . .

Ah, but not so at the Treasure Island Trailer Court. The Treasure Island Trailer Court had *rues*.

French. Much classier.

Rue 1, Rue 2, Rue 3 . . . Candi's home was a faded pink Travel-Eze mired in a bed of succulents on Rue 8. An engraved redwood sign out front said: CANDI AND CHERYL.

And that was all he needed to know.

'Uh . . . Candi. There's something I should tell you.'

'Uh huh?'

'You're not gonna believe this, but . . . I think I know your roommate.'

'Cheryl?'

'Does she work at Zim's too?'

Candi grinned. 'The morning shift. That's OK, Brian. We hardly ever see each other.'

'I've been here before, Candi.'

She squeezed his thigh. 'I said it was OK, didn't I?'

Apparently it was OK with Cheryl too.

Wolfing down a breakfast of Froot Loops, she looked only mildly surprised when Brian slumped in with Candi. 'Well, look what the cat drug in.'

She was younger than Candi. Considerably. Brian did a heavy déjà vu number on her pouty Bernadette Peters mouth. He would have swapped on the spot, given the chance. 'Small world, huh?'

She grinned lewdly. 'Not particularly. I'd say you've just run out of material.'

Candi slammed her way into the bedroom, shouting over her shoulder at her roommate. 'You're late again, Cheryl. I'm not gonna keep making excuses for you. It's gettin' embarrassing.'

'I was waiting for my fuckin' *wig*, if you don't mind!'

Silence.

'Did you hear me?'

The voice from the bedroom was low and menacing. 'Cheryl, come in here a minute.'

'I'm finishing my Froot . . .'

'Goddammit, Cheryl!'

Cheryl pushed her chair back noisily, rolled her eyes at Brian and left the room. A muffled catfight followed. When Cheryl reemerged several minutes later, she was wearing a Zim's uniform and Candi's head of hair.

'Don't break the bed,' she purred to Brian, goosing him as she walked out the door.

'Brian?'

'Huh?'

'Would you like something to drink? A Pepsi or something?'

'Hey. You're off duty, remember?'

'I just thought . . . well, you know. Sometimes people get thirsty afterwards.'

'I'm fine.'

'Was I . . . ? Do you think I'm as pretty as Cheryl? I mean . . . I know I'm older and all, but, you know, like for my age . . . do you think I look OK?'

He wiggled her earlobe and kissed the tip of her nose. 'Better than OK. Even without that damn wig.'

She beamed. 'You know what? I've got the whole day off, and the Camaro's full of gas . . .'

'I've gotta get home, Candi. I'm expecting a phone call.'

'It wouldn't take long. I could show you a pumpkin patch. They're beautiful right now.'

He shook his head, smiling.

'Do you want me to drive you home?'

'There's a bus, isn't there?'

'Yeah. If you want. It's no trouble for me, Brian.'

He climbed out of bed. 'I don't mind the bus.'

'I'd like it if you'd call me.'

'Sure. You in the book?'

She nodded.

'I'll call you, then.'

'It's Moretti.'

'OK.'

'Two *t*'s.'

'Good. I'll give you a buzz in a week or so.'

He got out without giving her his last name, but not without noticing a photograph framed on the bathroom wall.

Cheryl in a high school cap and gown.

Candi in street clothes, giving her a hug.

And this inscription: 'To the best Mom in the whole wide world.'

And Baby Makes Three?

A Wagnerian fog was settling over the Avenues when DeDe drove away from Carson Callas' house in her husband's silver Porsche.

Done.

She shivered a little, thinking of it. That icky little body. The yellowed fingernail digging into her flesh. The . . . thing . . . he kept in the bedside table.

Her secret, however, was still intact, and she doubted very seriously that the columnist would demand a repeat performance. By the time she reached Upper Montgomery Street the horrid indignity of it all seemed as dim and distant as Cotillion days.

Riding the elevator to the penthouse, she felt almost noble about it. She had sacrificed something, bitten the bullet . . . for the sake of her marriage, for the sake of the Halcyon family name.

'How were the whales?' asked Beauchamp.

'Same as before,' she lied. 'We're still trying to set a date for the benefit.'

'I think you'd be better off in Leukemia.'

'Muffy does Leukemia. It's not very original.'

'Crippled children, then.'

'God, no. We went to at *least* three crippled children tea dances last month. Anyway, you don't have to have your picture taken with whales.' She sat in his lap and planted a kiss on his mouth. 'You don't look like you missed me that much.'

'I've been reading.'

'What?'

'You're sitting on it.'

'Oh.' She shifted onto the arm of the wing chair as Beauchamp held up a copy of *Some Kind of Hero*.

'James Kirkwood,' he said.

DeDe studied the book jacket. 'It's about Vietnam?'

'Yeah. Sort of.'

'Beauchamp?'

'Huh?'

'Take me to bed, will you?'

'It's been a long day, DeDe.'

'Just to cuddle, OK?'

He dropped the book on the floor and smiled at her. 'OK.'

'Beauchamp?'

'Mmm?'

'We're doing better, don't you think?'

'At what?'

'You know . . . living together.'

'What do you want? A Good Housekeeping Seal of Approval?'

'Really, though, I think . . .'

'Marriage is a bitch, DeDe . . . for *everybody*. Other people don't do much better than we do. I've told you that all along.'

'Still . . . I think we're learning more . . . growing.'

'OK. If that makes you feel any better.'

'I suppose.'

'Before . . . I really didn't think we were *mature* enough to raise children.'

'Jesus Christ!'

'Well, you have to admit we've weathered . . .'

'How many times do I have to tell you, DeDe? I have no intention of ...'

'You! *You*! It's *my* body! What if I *want* a baby? What about *that*, huh?'

He sat up in bed and smirked at her. 'Fine. Go get somebody else to knock you up.'

'You're disgusting!'

'Don't expect me to pay for it, though. *Or* to live with it.'

'It? It's not a thing, Beauchamp. It's a *human being*!'

His eyes burned into her. 'Christ! Are you pregnant?'

'No.'

'Well, shut up, then ... and go to sleep. I've got a long day tomorrow.'

Ties That Bind

Mary Ann spent her lunch hour at Hastings, picking out just the right tie for Norman. The hint might not be terribly subtle, she decided, but *somebody* had to do something about that gross, gravy-stained clip-on number.

Walking back to Jackson Square, she watched as a big yellow Hertz truck parked on Montgomery Street in a commercial zone.

The burly driver sauntered to the back of the truck and opened the double doors.

Inside were at least two dozen young women, packed as tightly as cattle in a disinfectant chamber. They were giggling nervously, and most of them appeared to be dressed for office work.

'OK,' said the driver. 'Stand on the lift. Six at a time.' He returned to the front of the truck, as the young women waited obediently to be lowered to the street. When the last of them had stepped off the hydraulic lift, the driver came back to issue them each a cardboard box with a neck strap attached.

The boxes contained complimentary mini-packs of Newport Lights.

Mary Ann shuddered. So *that's* where they came from! Those pathetic creatures who stood on street corners, pushing free cigarettes and lucky wooden nickels and garish fliers for yet another soup-and-sandwich spot.

There were worse jobs than hers. Plenty of them.

She quickened her pace. She was already fifteen minutes late.

Back at the agency, she breathed a sigh of relief. Mr Halcyon was still in conference with Adorable.

She opened the tie box and looked at her purchase again. It was silk, with maroon and navy stripes. Conservative but . . . sharp. Just the thing Norman needed.

She doodled on a note paid with a Flair, ending up with this:

> don't listen when they scoff
> that you are old and i am young,
> for i am old enough to know better
> and you are young enough not to care.

Not bad, she concluded. And poetry was fabulous therapy, taking her back to simpler days at Central High when she cranked out anguished, e.e. cumming-style verses for the *Plume and Palette*.

But *this* poem made her uncomfortable somehow, touching a little too close to the defensiveness she felt about her relationship with Norman.

What relationship? So far, they had only kissed. A perfectly tame good-night kiss, at that. Norman was like . . . a big brother? No . . . and not exactly an uncle, either.

She felt toward Norman what she felt toward Gregory Peck when she was twelve and saw *To Kill a Mockingbird* five times . . . just to experience that goose-bumpy, dry-throated, shivery feeling that came over her whenever Atticus Finch appeared on the screen.

But Norman Neal Williams was no Gregory Peck.

She tore up the poem.

Mr Halcyon was still in conference when Beauchamp sidled up to her cubicle.

'Rough day?'

'Not particularly,' she answered with deliberate blandness.

'You look a little . . . bummed out.'

'I guess it's my biorhythms.' She wasn't exactly sure what that meant, but it kept things impersonal.

'Can I buy you a drink tonight?'

She stared at him icily. 'I don't believe you. I really don't.'

'Just trying to be nice.'

'Thank you very much. I have a date tonight.'

'Aha! Where's the lucky man taking you?'

She slipped a piece of paper into her typewriter. 'I don't see why you should care about . . .'

'Oh, c'mon! I'd like to know.'

She began to type. 'Some place called the Beach Chalet.'

'Ah.'

'You know it?'

'Sure. You'll love it. The VFW meets there.'

She looked up to see a smirk curl across his face. He headed into the hallway again, where he saluted her crisply. 'Don't OD on Beer Nuts, toots!'

New York, New York

Riveted to the receiver of her antique French telephone, D'orothea wielded a gold-tipped Sherman like a conductor's baton.

She was talking to New York again.

The fourth time in two days.

Mona watched in cynical silence, curled up comfortably on their new buff suede Billy Gaylord banquette. She was sick of competing with New York.

'Oh, Bobby,' shrieked D'orothea, 'that's the third time this month you've taken Lina to The Toilet . . . Well, I know, honey, but . . . Well, look, Bobbie. Once is slumming, three times is just plain *sick* . . . It isn't *all* like The Anvil. The Anvil was fun in the old days. I mean, Rudi went there, for God's sake! . . . I never saw that . . . They weren't, Bobby. I never saw any of that business with the fists . . . Anyway, The Toilet is just plain flat-out *scuzzy*. I totaled a perfectly good pair of Bergdorf Goodman shoes . . .'

It went on like that for ten minutes. When D'orothea hung up, she smiled apologetically at Mona. 'Shit, I got out just in time. The Big Apple's getting too wormy for words.'

'Is that why you need a progress report every night?'

'It *isn't* every night.'

'We have depravity here too, you know . . . and what the hell's The Toilet?'

208

'It's a bar.'

'Of course.'

'It's in *Vogue* this month.'

'How gauche of me not to . . .'

'Hey . . . what is it with you, Mona?'

'I'm just sick of dealing with New York, that's all. I mean, you've moved back here now, and it seems to me that you could . . .'

'That isn't it, Mona. You've been brooding about something.'

'I'm not brooding. I'm always like this.'

'I think you miss Michael.'

'Don't overanalyze things.'

'Hon, if we don't talk about it . . .'

'It's nothing. I'm in a bitchy mood. Forget it.'

'I'm a little claustrophobic myself. C'mon . . . let's take a walk.'

Back at Barbary Lane, Brian Hawkins was boiling a bag of frozen chow mein. When it was ready, he gulped it down at the kitchen table while he leafed through his mail.

Not much. An Occupant notice about a new pizzeria. A circular from the Chicago Urban League. A garish pink envelope listing the Treasure Island Trailer Court as the return address.

This envelope contained a note card bearing the face of a Keane child, a sugary nymphet staring mawkishly from a tenement window.

Dear Brian,

They gave me your address at Perry's. I hope you don't mind. I just wanted to tell you what a fabulous time I had with you. You are a real sweet guy, and I hope you will call me some time. I can't call you cuz I'm not aggressive. Ha ha. Seriously, you are really a neat person. Don't feel like you have to write back.

Luff ya,
Candi

She had dotted the *i* in 'Candi' with a Happy Face.

He dumped the mail into his garbage bag, left the dishes in the sink, and went into the bedroom to roll a joint. There was a little Maui Wowie left. Enough for a good buzz, anyway.

He lay on his back on the Busvan sofa, sorting out the half-assed little escapades of the last six months. Mary Ann Singleton, who *still*

209

tormented him . . . Connie Bradshaw, a veritable museum of kitsch . . . that chick at the Sutro Baths . . . and now a goddamn mother-and-daughter team!

He laughed out loud at himself.

Either he was a masochist or God was a sadist.

Minutes later, he was up again, changing into Levi's and a khaki army shirt. He headed for the door, stopped, and returned to roll another joint.

Then he bounded downstairs to the second-floor and rang Michael's buzzer.

Full Moon in Seacliff

Jon Fielding couldn't help but feel a twinge of envy when the Hampton-Giddes' houseboy offered him a stuffed mushroom.

Harold was an absolute *find.*

Efficient, courteous and intelligent. With just enough café au lait skin and gray at the temples to make him seem like an old family retainer . . . a spare servant that Mother had shipped from Bar Harbor.

'He's a gem,' Jon said to Collier Lane as soon as Harold had moved on.

Collier nodded. 'Perfect. Sort of a gay Uncle Ben.'

'He's gay?'

'Better be. He's the one who shows the movies.'

'Here?'

'Over there. In front of that Claes Oldenburg that looks like a couple of Hefty bags. A screen comes down. They're showing *Boys in the Sand* after cigars and brandy.'

The Hampton-Giddes, Jon observed, hadn't skimped on any thing. Brown suede walls. A chrome bin for the fireplace logs. Travertine marble for *days* and a lighting system that would have functioned nicely for a smallish production of *Aïda.*

The doctor grinned at his lawyer friend. 'Somebody told me they've even got the television on a dimmer switch.'

Collier smiled back. 'They've got their whole *life* on a dimmer switch.'

There were eight people at the dinner party. Rick Hampton and Arch

Gidde (the Hampton-Giddes), Ed Stoker and Chuck Lord (the Stoker-Lords), Bill Hill and Tony Hughes (the Hill-Hugheses), and Jon Fielding and Collier Lane.

Jon and Collier sought refuge in the Hampton-Giddes' black onyx bathroom.

'Christ, Jon, aren't you sick of hearing about remodeled kitchens?'

'Have a line,' said the doctor. 'Things go better with coke.'

The Hampton-Giddes had provided the cocaine for their guests. In the bathroom only. Out of sight from the servants. Collier snorted a line.

'Let's go to the tubs,' he said, straightening up.

'We can't just walk out, Collier.'

'Who can't? I'm bored shitless.'

'Have another line, then.'

'Where are the twinks, anyway? They usually have the decency to provide one or two decorative twinks . . . Jesus, who needs to waste a night staring at these tired old Gucci queens.'

'I can't leave now. Maybe after the movie . . .'

'Fuck the movie! Whatever happened to the real thing? My God, there's a full moon tonight! Can't you imagine the tubs . . . ?'

Jon tweaked Collier's cheek. 'There's such a thing as social obligation, turkey.'

'You're a jellyfish, Fielding.'

Jon smiled. 'Take a cold shower. It'll keep.'

'So,' said William Devereux Hill III, passing the braised endive to Edward Paxton Stoker, Jr, 'Tony and I checked the St Louis Social Register, and they are *not* in it. Neither one of them.'

'Jesus.'

'And let's face it, honey. In St Louis, it's *not* that difficult!'

'How about the eighth?' asked Archibald Anson Gidde.

Charles Hillary Lord checked his black leather Hermès appointment book. 'Sorry. Edward's taking Mrs Langhurst to hear Edo that night. Once again, I'm a symphony widow.'

'What about the following Wednesday?'

'That's our ACT night.'

'I give up.'

'It's mad, isn't it?' sighed Charles Hillary Lord.

*

'How's the twink?' asked Richard Evan Hampton, smirking across the travertine table at Jon Philip Fielding.

'Who?'

'The twink in the jockey shorts. At The Endup.'

'Oh . . . I haven't seen him for a while.'

'Well, he was hardly your type, was he?'

'Oh?'

'Well, I mean, how many people do you know who enter jockey shorts dance contests?'

'I knew *him*. And I liked him, Rick.'

'Well, pardon me, Mary.'

'No, pardon me.'

'What?'

'It's a full moon, Mr Hampton, and I've had just about as much of this DAR meeting as I can take. Will you excuse me, gentlemen?' He pushed back his chair, stood up and nodded to his friend. 'I'll get a cab,' he said.

'The hell you will,' said Collier Lane.

They wore their Brioni blazers to the tubs.

Norman Confesses

After three white wines at the Beach Chalet, Mary Ann felt much better about the bar's Archie Bunker ambience.

'I like this place,' she told Norman honestly. 'It's very . . . down-to-earth.' Beauchamp could just go to hell with his snotty crack about the VFW.

'I thought you might get a kick out of the muriels,' said Norman.

'The . . . ?'

'The paintings on the walls.'

'Oh . . . yes, they're beautiful. Art Nouveau, right?'

Norman nodded. 'Good ol' Mr Roosevelt and the WPA. Hey, how about a little walk on the beach?'

The idea didn't particularly appeal to her. It was cold outside and there was something really cozy about the glowing beer signs and the bowling-jacketed patrons bellied up to the bar.

She smiled at him. '*You'd* like to, wouldn't you?'

'Yes.'

'Is something the matter, Norman?'

'No. I'd just like to take a walk, OK?'

'Sure.'

He smiled and touched the tip of her nose.

She took Norman's arm when they reached the sand, fortifying herself with his warmth. Beneath a full moon, the Cliff House gleamed like a mansion out of Daphne du Maurier.

She was the first to speak.

'Do you want to talk?'

'I wish . . . never mind.'

'What, Norman?'

'I wish I was better-looking.'

'Norman!'

'The *old* part wouldn't be so bad, if . . . forget it.'

She stopped walking and made him turn to face her. 'In the first place . . . you are *not* old, Norman. There's no reason for you to go around apologizing for that all the time. And in the second place, you are a *very* strong, masculine and . . . appealing man.'

He acted as if he hadn't heard any of it. 'Why do you go out with me, Mary Ann?'

She threw her hands up and groaned. 'You're not even *listening*.'

'Lots of guys are after you. I've seen the way Brian Hawkins looks at you.'

'Oh, please!'

'Don't you think Brian's handsome?'

'Brian Hawkins thinks any woman who goes to bed with him is . . .' She cut herself off.

'Is what?'

'Norman . . .'

'Is *what*?'

'A whore.'

'Oh.'

'Norman . . . I wish I could show you the things you've got going for you.'

'Don't strain yourself.'

'Norman, you are *gentle* . . . and considerate . . . and you believe in a lot of . . . traditional values . . . and you don't make me feel like I'm out of it all the time.'

He laughed bleakly. 'Because I'm more out of it than you are.'

'I didn't say that. And thanks a lot!'

'Do you think I could make you happy, Mary Ann?'

She had been afraid of that one. 'Norman . . . I always have a good time with you.'

'That's not what I asked.'

'We haven't known each other very long.'

The line was so weak she was instantly sorry she had used it. She studied his face for damage. He seemed to be struggling with something. His features were strangely distorted.

'I don't push pills, Mary Ann.'

'What?'

'I don't sell Nutri-Vim. I just told you that to . . . I just told you that.'

'But what about the . . . ?'

'I'm coming into a lot of money really soon. I can buy you anything you want. I know I must look like a failure now, but I'm . . .'

'Norman,' she said as gently as possible, 'I don't want you to *buy* me anything.'

His face had eroded completely. He stared at her in desolation.

'Norman . . .' She reached up and readjusted his new tie. 'It looks . . . real nice on you.'

'I'll take you home.'

'Please don't feel like . . .'

'It's OK. I just . . . want too much sometimes.'

He said almost nothing on the way back to Barbary Lane.

What D'or Won't Tell Her

A fluorescent phone booth glowed like ectoplasm against the black slope of Alta Plaza as Mona and D'orothea strolled west up Jackson Street.

Mona shuddered. 'What a creepy place to make a phone call!'

'You afraid of the dark?'

'Terrified.'

'I never would've guessed.'

'I thought everybody was afraid of the dark. It's the only thing that distinguishes us from animals.'

D'or grinned. 'Not me. Black is Beautiful, remember?'

'It looks good on *you*, anyway.'

D'or stopped walking and took Mona's hands in hers. 'Hon . . . would you still . . . ?'

'What?'

'Nothing.' She dismissed the thought with a wave of her hand and began walking again. 'No big deal.'

Mona frowned. 'I hate that.'

'What, hon?'

'The way you weed out things you think I can't handle.'

'I don't mean to seem . . .'

'I'm not all that fucking fragile, D'or. Don't you think you could *communicate* a little more?'

'Fine.' D'or looked hurt.

'And I don't need to hear that you love me. I *know* you love me, D'or. The thing is . . . you don't really share your . . . your thoughts with me. Sometimes I feel like I'm living with a stranger.'

Silence.

'I'm sorry. You asked what was bothering me.'

'You want to move out. Is that it?'

'No! I never expected miracles, D'or . . . ever. I just . . .'

'Is it the sex part? I've told you that isn't important to me if . . .'

'D'or . . . I *like* you a lot.'

'Ouch.'

'Well, goddammit . . . that's a lot, isn't it? I mean, I'm not sure I even need a lover, male *or* female. Sometimes I think I'd settle for five good friends.'

They walked in silence for several minutes. Then D'orothea said: 'So what do we do?'

'I want to stay, D'or.'

'But I have to shape up. Is that it?'

'I didn't say that.'

'Look, Mona . . . you're bitching about *something*.'

Mona glared at her. 'Do you really think it's my function in life to sit here on my ass all day while you're out there making another hundred thou off the same son-of-a-bitch who fired me?'

'Mona . . . I could talk to Edgar Halcyon about . . .'

'You do and I'll pack tomorrow.'

'Well, *what* then? What do you want me to do?'

'I don't know . . . I feel cut off, somehow. I can't hack all these blue-haired old ladies with Mace in their pocketbooks, marching their poodles endlessly up and down the . . .'

'There's nothing I can do about . . .'

'You could let me share your life, D'or. Introduce me to your friends . . . and your family. Christ, your parents are in Oakland and I've never even *seen* them!'

D'orothea's tone grew chilly. 'Let's not drag my parents into this.'

'Ah!'

'What's *that* supposed to mean?'

'It means you're *petrified* that Mommy and Daddy will find out you're a dyke!'

'It does not.'

'Well, what, then?'

'I don't . . . talk to my parents. I haven't exchanged a word with them since I got back from New York. Not a word.'

'C'mon!'

'Have you seen me do it? When have I talked to them?'

'But why?'

'When did you last talk to *your* mother?'

'That's different. She's in Minneapolis. It wouldn't take that much for you to . . .'

'You haven't the slightest *idea* what it would take, Mona.'

Mona stopped walking and turned to confront her. 'Look, I know you must be a lot more . . .' She cut herself off.

'A lot more what?'

'I don't know . . . sophisticated?'

D'orothea laughed ruefully. 'That ain't the half of it, honey!'

'Well, so what? Do I look like a snob to you? I've done a thing or two for Third World people, you know!'

'My father is a baker in the Twinkie factory, Mona!'

Mona stifled a grin. 'You made that up.'

'Drop it, will you?'

'No. You think I can't relate to older black people, don't you? Racist *and* agist, in spite of myself!'

Silence.

'That's it, isn't it?'

'I think you're very good with people. Now let's drop it, OK?'

So Mona shut up.

Her liberal consciousness, however, wouldn't permit her to discard the issue.

There couldn't be *that* many Wilsons working at the Twinkie factory.

Michael's Visitor

Michael was making his bed when the door buzzer rang. He sped up the procedure, laughing at himself. He never made his bed for *himself*. He did it for others . . . or the hope of others.

The same reason, really, that he kept the toilet clean and a fresh guest toothbrush in the bathroom cabinet. You never knew for sure when you were auditioning for the role of housewife.

He opened the door on the second ring, prepared once more to be a sympathetic ear for Mary Ann.

'Brian!'

'I'm not . . . interrupting anything?'

'As a matter of fact, Casey Donovan is languishing in my boudoir.'

'Oh, I'm . . .'

'A joke, Brian. Esoteric. What can I do for you?'

'Nothing . . . I . . . I've got some Maui Wowie. I thought you might like to smoke a little and . . . rap for a while.'

Such a quaint word, thought Michael. Rap. Straight people still *longed* for the Summer of Love.

The grass took hold quickly.

'Jesus,' said Michael. 'How much *is* this stuff, anyway?'

'Two hundred a lid.'

'Please!'

'Swear to God.'

'My teeth are numb.'

'Who needs 'em?'

Michael laughed. 'Damn right! Is this stuff *local*, Brian?'

'Uh uh. L A.'

'Good ol' Lah!'

'Huh?'

'Lah. L A . . . get it?'

'Oh . . . yeah.'

'LA is Lah. SF is Sif.'
'Is it ever!'
They laughed. 'Jesus, Brian. One more toke and I'll see God.'
'Too late. He moved to Lah.'
'God's in Lah?'
'Who you think sold it to me?'

'Sometimes,' said Brian, 'I get the feeling that the New Morality is over. Know what I mean?'

'Sorta.'

'I mean . . . like . . . what's left? You know?'

'Yeah.'

'Guys and chicks, chicks and chicks, guys and guys.'

'Right on.'

'But now . . . you know . . . the pendulum.'

'Yeah . . . the fucking pendulum.'

'I mean, Michael . . . I think . . . I think it's gonna be all over, man.'

'What?'

'Everything.'

'Sodom and Gomorrah, huh?'

'Maybe not that . . . dramatic, but something like that. We're gonna be . . . I mean people like you and me . . . we're gonna be fifty-year-old libertines in a world full of twenty-year-old Calvinists.'

Michael winced. 'Lusting in their hearts like Jimmy . . . but nowhere else.'

'Yeah . . . Are you horny?'

Michael's heart stopped. 'Uh . . .'

'Grass always makes me horny.'

'Yeah . . . I know what you mean.'

'Why don't we . . . do something about it?'

The room was so still that Michael could hear the hair growing on Brian's chest.

'Brian . . . that's kind of . . . complicated, isn't it?'

'Why?'

'Why?' repeated Michael. 'Well, I . . . you and I aren't exactly coming from the same place, are we?'

'So? There must be *some* place in this fucking city where they've got straight chicks *and* gay guys.'

'You want us to . . . go cruising together?'

'Kind of a kick, huh?'

Michael looked at him for several seconds, then broke into a slow grin. 'You're really serious, aren't you?'

'Fuckin' A.'

'It's truly twisted.'

'I knew you'd get into it.'

'Maybe,' said Michael, turning into Pan again, 'we could break up a couple.'

Three Men at the Tubs

Leaving the Hampton-Giddes', Jon filled his lungs with the cleansing fog that had spilled into Seacliff from the bay.

Collier grinned at him. 'I knew you'd OD, sooner or later.'

'Shut up.'

'You're stuck on that Tolliver kid, aren't you?'

'I'm not *stuck* on anybody, Collier. I just get sick of that bitchy talk about twinks. That's just a queen's way of being a male chauvinist pig!'

'Can I send that to Bartlett's *Quotations*?'

'Just drive, will you?'

'The tubs, right?'

'That's what you want, isn't it?'

'I could drop you off at the twink's house.'

'Collier, if you mention that one more . . .'

'The tubs it is, milord.'

Jon kept silent on the long ride to Eighth and Howard. He hated these unsettled moments when the stuffiness of the Hampton-Giddes and the aimlessness of the Michael Tollivers seemed equally inapplicable to his own life.

At times like this, the tubs was an easy way out.

Discreet, dispassionate, noncommittal. He could diddle away a frenzied hour or two, then return unblemished to the business of being a doctor.

It was really his only choice.

Decorators, hairdressers and selected sheriff's deputies were *expected* to be gay in San Francisco.

But who wanted a gay gynecologist?

Most women, he observed, expected their gynecologist to be detached in dealing with their most intimate specifics. They did *not*, however, expect detachment to come easy. In their heart of hearts lurked the tiniest hope that they were driving the poor devil mad.

Gay was not Good in OB/GYN.

The television lounge of the Club Baths was jammed with terry-cloth Tarzans.

For once, they were genuinely engrossed in the television.

'Forget about the orgy room,' said Collier. 'It empties during *Mary Hartman.*'

Jon grinned, already feeling better. 'I'm hungry, anyway. We never got past the braised endive, remember?'

They microwaved a couple of hot dogs, laughing over the oven's obligatory warning about pacemakers. A pacemaker at the Club Baths was about as common as an Accu-Jac at the Bohemian club.

Then they parted, each seeking his own private adventure in Wonderland.

Jon prowled the corridors for fifteen minutes, finally settling on a dark-haired number in a room near the showers. He was resting on his elbows in bed.

His towel was still on, his rheostat turned up.

A good sign, thought Jon. The desperates invariably kept their lights down and their towels off.

When they had finished, Jon said, 'Let me know when you want me to leave.'

'No problem,' said the dark-haired man.

'It's nice to rest.'

'Yeah. It's a mob scene out there.'

'Full moon.'

'I like it better on slow nights. I mean . . . sometimes I come here just to . . . get away.'

'Me too.'

The dark-haired man folded his hands behind his head and stared at the ceiling. 'I wasn't even particularly horny tonight.'

'Neither was I. I usually tell myself I'm here for the steam, but it never seems to work out that way.'

The man laughed. '*Quelle coincidence*!'

Jon sat up. 'Well, I guess I'd better . . .'

'Can I buy you a cup of coffee?'

'Thanks. I'm here with a friend.'

'A lover?'

Jon laughed. 'God, no!'

'Are you . . . one of the reachables?'

'Sure.'

'Can I give you my phone number?'

Jon nodded, extending his hand. 'My name's Jon,' he said.

'Hi. I'm Beauchamp.'

Cruising at The Stud

For his night on the town with Brian, Michael settled on The Stud. The Folsom Street bar was suitably mega-sexual, and its pseudo-ecological décor would probably be the least intimidating to Brian.

It might even remind him of Sausalito.

'It reminds me of The Trident,' he said, as they walked in the door.

Michael grinned. 'That's the Code of the Seventies, isn't it? It doesn't matter what you do, as long as you do it in something that looks like a barn.'

'Christ! Look at those tits by the bar!'

'Yeah. He's gotta been pumping iron since junior high school, at least!'

'The chick, Michael!'

'Hey,' said Michael. 'You look at your tits and I'll look at mine!'

The other patrons were grouped undramatically around the central bar, some in knots of three or four. They laughed in short, stony spasms, while a scruffy-looking band imitated Kenny Loggins singing 'Back to Georgia'.

'Here's the plan,' said Michael in a stage whisper. 'If I run into anything that might interest you, I'll send it your way.'

'Not *it*, Michael. *Her*.'

'Right. And you do the same for me.'

'Don't worry.'

'See anything you like?'

'Yeah. Ol' Angel Tits over there.'

'You'll have to pry her away from that guy she's with.'

'Maybe he's gay.'

'Forget it. He's straight.'

'Now, how can you tell?'

'Look at the size of his ass, Brian!'

'Gay guys don't have fat asses?'

'If they do, they don't go to bars. That's the *other* Code of the Seventies.'

The woman who sat down next to Brian was wearing a beige French T-shirt that said 'bitch' in discreet lower-case letters.

'You guys here together?'

'Yeah. Well . . . not exactly. He's gay and I'm straight.'

'How nice for you.'

'I didn't mean it like that. Michael's a friend.'

'What do you do?'

'Me and Michael?'

'No. You. For a living, like.'

'I'm a waiter. At Perry's.'

'Oh. Heavy.'

That irked him. 'Is it?'

'Well, I mean . . . that's kind of . . . plastic, isn't it?'

'I like it,' he lied. No radical-chick cunt in a bitch T-shirt was calling *his* job plastic.

'I work for Francis.'

'The Talking Mule?'

She rolled her eyes impatiently. 'Ford Coppola,' she said.

Michael was standing alone by the bar when Brian rejoined him.

'Any luck?'

Brian took a swig of his beer. 'I didn't stick around long enough to find out. She was weird.'

'How so?'

'Aw, forget it.'

'C'mon. Gimmie the dirt. Bondage and Discipline? Water sports? Satin sheets?'

'She wanted to know if I was into . . . cockrings.'

222

Michael almost shrieked. 'You're kidding!'

'What the hell do they do, anyway?'

'A cockring? Well, Jesus . . . lemme see. It's this steel ring about . . . yea big . . . although sometimes it's brass or leather . . . and you put it around your . . . equipment.'

'Why the fuck would you do that?'

'It helps you to keep it up longer.'

'Oh.'

'Isn't life interesting.'

'Do you have one?'

Michael laughed. 'Hell, no.'

'Why not?'

'Well . . . it's just one more thing to remember. Christ, I can't hang on to a pair of *sunglasses* for longer than a week.' He laughed suddenly, thinking of something. 'I used to know this guy . . . a very proper stockbroker, in fact . . . who wore one *all* the time. But he soon got cured of *that*.'

'What happened?'

'He had to fly to Denver for a conference, and they caught him when he passed through the metal detector at the airport.'

'God! What did they do?'

'They opened his suitcase and found his black leather chaps!'

Brian whistled, shaking his head.

'It's not too late for a cup of coffee at Pam-Pam.'

'You got a date, man!'

She is Woman, Hear Her Roar

Shortly after seven, Beauchamp stumbled out of bed and into the bathroom.

DeDe rolled over and continued to breathe heavily, pretending to be asleep.

This time she didn't want to hear his excuse. She was numb from excuses, drained by the effort it took to believe in him.

He had come in at 4. A M. Period.

There might not be Another Woman, but there were definitely other women.

Her response to that fact must be forceful, reasoned and

intrinsically feminine. She tried to imagine how Helen Reddy might have handled it.

The phone woke her at nine-fifteen.
  'Hello.'
  'You asleep, darling?'
  'Not exactly.'
  'You sound down.'
  'Do I?'
  'Look . . . if it's about the you-know-what . . . well, it's a simple little procedure and you . . .'
  'Binky, I . . .'
  'It's not like the old rusty coat hanger days.'
  '*All right*, Binky!'
  Silence.
  'Binky . . . I'm sorry, OK?'
  'Sure.'
  'I . . . had a bad night.'
  'Of course. Look . . . I called with a juicy one. Wanna hear it?'
  'All ears.'
  'Jimmy Carter is a Kennedy!'
  'Uh . . . once more.'
  'Isn't that the absolute *ripest* gossip you've heard in *months*?'
  'Rank is more like it.'
  'Look . . . I'm only telling you what *everybody* was talking about at the Stonecyphers' last night. Apparently there's been some hush money paid to make sure that . . .'
  'What *are* you talking about?'
  'Miss Lillian used to be Joe Kennedy's secretary.'
  'When?'
  'Oh, don't be such a spoilsport, darling. I think it's a divine story.'
  'Divine.'
  'Well, it explains all those *teeth*, doesn't it?'

When she finally got off the phone, she headed for the bathroom with a shudder.
  A half-hour conversation with Binky was like eating a Whitman Sampler in one sitting.
  Avoiding the kitchen, she dressed hastily in a cashmere turtleneck and Levi's, throwing on her Ann Klein suede jacket as an afterthought.

She wanted to walk. And think.

As usual, she went to the Filbert Steps, where the gingerbread houses and alpine cul-de-sacs provided a Walt Disney setting for her woes.

She sat down on the boardwalk at Napier Lane and watched the neighborhood cats promenading in the sun.

Once there was a cat who fell asleep in the sun and dreamed she was a woman sleeping in the sun. When she woke, she couldn't remember if she was a cat or a woman.

Where had she heard that?

It didn't matter. She didn't feel like a cat *or* a woman.

All her life, she had done as she was told. She had moved, without so much as a skipped heartbeat, from the benevolent autocracy of Edgar Halcyon to the spineless tyranny of Beauchamp Day.

Her husband ruled her as certainly as her father had, manipulating her with guilt and promised love and the fear of rejection. She had never done *anything* for herself.

'Dr Fielding?'

'Yes?'

'I'm sorry to bother you at home.'

'That's all right. Uh . . . who is this, please?'

'DeDe Day.'

'Oh. How are you?'

'I . . . I've made up my mind.'

'Good.'

'I want the baby, Dr Fielding.'

The Doctor Is In

Beauchamp decided to drink his lunch at Wilkes Bashford.

There, amidst the wicker and lucite and cool plaster walls, he downed three Negronis while he tried on a pair of $225 Walter Newberger boots.

He was fitted by Walter Newberger himself.

'How does it feel?' asked the designer.

'Heaven,' said Beauchamp. '*Exactly* the right amount of Campari.'

'The *boots*, Beauchamp. You *can* stand up, can't you?'

Beauchamp grinned roguishly. 'Only when completely necessary . . . Look, where's your phone?'

'There's one in the mirror room.'

Beauchamp lurched into the mirror room and dialed Jon's office at 450 Sutter.

'Hi, Blondie.'

'Good afternoon.'

'I'm in the neighborhood, Hot Stuff. Why don't we rent a room at the Mark Twain and have a nooner?'

'I'm quite busy right now. If you'll check with my receptionist later, I'm sure . . .'

'Oh, I get it!'

'Good.'

'You've got a customer in the office with you?'

'That's correct.'

'Is she cute?'

'I'm sorry . . . I can't discuss . . .'

'Awww . . . c'mon! Just tell me if she's cute.'

'I have to go now.'

'She *can't* be cuter than me, can she?'

The doctor hung up.

Beauchamp laughed out loud, leaning against the stuffed cotton cactus in the mirror room. Then he sauntered back to the bar, where the shoe designer was standing.

'Charge 'em,' said Beauchamp.

The Old Man was apparently still having lunch at the Villa Taverna.

Beauchamp ambled into the executive suite and made a few mental notes to himself.

The space wasn't bad, actually. Clean lines and fairly decent track lighting. Once you got rid of those *godawful* huge prints and tired Barcelona chairs, Tony Hail could probably do something really stunning with baskets and a few ficus trees and maybe some ostrich eggs on the shelf behind the . . .

'Is there something you're looking for?'

It was Mary Ann, being *very* territorial about the Old Man's lair.

'No,' he said flatly.

'Mr Halcyon won't be back until two.'

Beauchamp shrugged. 'Fine.'

She stood stonily in the doorway until he had walked past her and back to his own office down the hall.

That night Mary Ann submitted to an urge that had plagued her all week.

She told Michael about Norman . . . and the weird night at the Beach Chalet.

Michael shrugged it off. 'What's the big deal? You're a foxy lady. You break hearts. That's not *your* fault.'

'That's not the *point*, Mouse. I just can't shake the feeling that he's . . . up to something.'

'Sounds to me like he's blowing smoke.'

'What?'

'Trying to impress you. Have you talked to him since then?'

'Once or twice. Just superficial stuff. He bought me an ice cream cone at Swensen's. There's something terribly . . . I don't know . . . desperate . . . about him. It's like he's biding his time . . . waiting to prove something to me.'

'Look . . . if you were forty-four years old and selling vitamins door to door . . .'

'But he *isn't*. I'm sure of that. He *told* me he isn't . . . and I believe him.'

'He sure carries that stupid Nutri-Vim case around with him enough.'

'He's *fooling* people, Michael. I don't know why, but he is.'

Michael grinned devilishly. 'There's one way to find out.'

'What?'

'I know where Mrs Madrigal keeps the extra keys.'

'Oh, Mouse . . . no, forget it. I couldn't.'

'He's gone out tonight. I saw him leave.'

'Mouse, no!'

'OK, OK. How 'bout a movie, then?'

'Mouse . . . ?'

'Huh?'

'Do you really think I'm a foxy lady?'

Not Even a Mouse

The city itself, not the weather, let Mary Ann know that winter had finally come.

Ferris wheels spun merrily on the roof of The Emporium. Aluminum cedars sprouted in the windows of Chinese laundries. And one bright morning in mid December a note appeared on her door.

Mary Ann,
    If you haven't made plans, please join me and the rest of your Barbary Lane family for a spot of eggnog on Christmas Eve.
Love
A.M.
    P.S. I could use some help in organizing it.

That news – and the joint attached to the note – boosted her spirits considerably. It was good to feel part of a unit again, though she rarely regarded her fellow tenants as members of a 'family'.

But why shouldn't Mrs Madrigal be permitted that fantasy?

The Christmas party became Mary Ann's new obsession.

' . . . and after we light the tree, maybe we could have some sort of caroling thing . . . or a *skit*! A skit would be *fabulous*, Mouse!'

Michael deadpanned it. 'Great. You can be Judy Garland and I'll be Mickey Rooney.'

'Mouse!'

'OK, then. *You* be Mickey Rooney and *I'll* be Judy Garland.'

'You're not into this at all, are you?'

'Well, *you* certainly are. You've been running around for three days acting like Gale Storm organizing a shuffleboard tournament.'

'Don't you *like* Christmas?'

He shrugged. 'That isn't the point. Christmas doesn't like *me*.'

'Well . . . I know it's gotten commercial and all, but that's not . . .'

'Oh, *that* part's OK. I *like* all the tacky lights and the mob scenes and the plastic reindeer. It's the . . . gooey part that drives me up the wall.'

'The gooey part?'

'It's a conspiracy. Christmas is a conspiracy to make single people feel lonely.'

'Mouse . . . *I'm* single and . . .'

'And *look* at you . . . scrambling like mad to make sure you've got someplace to go.' He swept his hands around the room. 'Where's your tree, if you're so crazy about Christmas? And your wreath . . . and your mistletoe?'

'I might get a tree,' she said defensively.

'It wouldn't make sense. It wouldn't make a damn bit of sense to trek down to Polk Street to pick out some pathetic little tabletop tree and spend two days' pay decorating it with things you used to like back in Cleveland, just so you could sit there alone in the dark and watch it blink at you.'

'I have friends, Mouse. *You* have friends.'

'Friends go home. And Christmas Eve is the most horrible night of the year to go to bed alone . . . because when you wake up it's not going to be one of those Kodak commercials with kids in bunny slippers . . . It's going to be just like any other goddamned day of the year!'

She slid closer to him on the sofa. 'Couldn't you ask Jon to the party?'

'Hey . . . drop that, will you?'

'I think he liked you a lot, Mouse.'

'I haven't seen him since . . .'

'What if *I* called him?'

'Goddammit!'

'All right . . . all *right*!'

He took her hand. 'I'm sorry. I just . . . I get so sick of the We People.'

'The what?'

'The We People. They never say I. They say, "We're going to Hawaii after Christmas" or "We're taking the dog to get his shots." They wallow in the first person plural, because they remember how shitty it was to be the first person singular.'

Mary Ann stood up, tugging on his hand. 'C'mon, Ebenezer.'

'What for?'

'*We're* buying Christmas trees. Two of 'em.'

'Mary Ann . . .'

'C'mon. Don your gay apparel.' She giggled at the inadvertent pun. 'That's funny, isn't it?'

He smiled in spite of himself. 'We are *not* amused!'

Enigma at the Twinkie Factory

After weeks of worrying about it, Mona finally embarked on her secret plan to reunite D'orothea with her parents.

There wasn't much to go on.

She learned that Twinkies were made by the Continental Baking Company and that there were two locations in the Bay Area. One was the Wonder Bread bakery in Orlando. The other was on Bryant Street.

'Thank you for calling Hostess Cakes.'

'I . . . do you make Twinkies?'

'Yes, we do. Also Ho Hos, Ding Dongs, Crumb Cakes . . .'

'Thank you. Do you have a Mr Wilson there?'

'Which one?'

'Uh . . . I'm not sure.' She almost said 'the black one', but somehow it sounded racist to her.

'Donald K. Wilson is a wrapper here . . . and we have a Leroy N. Wilson, who's a baker.'

'I think that's the one.'

'Leroy?'

'Yes . . . may I speak to him, please?'

'I'm sorry. The bakers work the night shift. Eleven to seven.'

'Can you give me his home number?'

'I'm sorry. We're not allowed to divulge that information.'

Christ, she thought. What is this? A nuclear power plant or a fucking Twinkie factory. 'If I came down there . . . tonight, I mean . . . would it be possible to talk to him?'

'I don't see why not. On his break or something?'

'Around midnight, say?'

'I guess so.'

'You're on Bryant?'

'Uh huh. At Fifteenth. A big brown brick building.'

'Thanks a lot.'

'May I leave a message for him or anything?'

'No . . . Thanks, anyway.'

*

D'orothea got home at eight o'clock, devastated by a ten-hour session before the cameras.

'If I *never* see another plate of Rice-a-Roni, it'll be too soon!'

Mona laughed and handed her a glass of Dubonnet. 'Guess what's for supper?'

'I'll kill you!'

'Hang on . . . pork chops and okra!'

'What!'

Mona nodded, smiling. 'Just like your mother probably used to make.'

'What a shitty thing to say about somebody's mother!'

'Well . . . your foremothers, then.'

'Have you been reading *Roots* again?'

'I *like* soul food, D'or!'

D'or scowled at her. 'Would you like *me* if I weren't black?'

'D'or! What a thing to say!'

After studying Mona's face for a moment, D'or ended the discussion with a smile and a wink. 'I'm just tard, honey. Les go eat dem poke chops.'

After dinner, they lay by the fire and looked at color transparencies of D'orothea modeling Adorable Pantyhose.

It seemed like a good time to tell her.

'D'or . . . Michael's asked me to go out with him to a late show at the Lumiere tonight.'

'Good.'

'You won't mind if . . . ?'

'You don't need to ask my permission to go to movies.'

'Well, normally I'd want you to come along . . .'

D'orothea patted her hand. 'I'm gonna crash in ten minutes, hon. You go have a good time, OK?'

Shortly after midnight, Mona's heart was pounding so fast that the Twinkie factory might as well have been the House of Usher.

The waiting room reminded her of the lobby of an ancient Tenderloin hotel.

She rang a buzzer at the information desk. Several minutes later, a man who appeared to be a baker asked if he could help her.

'Do you know Leroy Wilson?' she asked.

'Sure . . . wanna talk to him?'

'Please.'

The man disappeared into the back, and another ten minutes passed before Leroy Wilson presented himself to a mystified Mona Ramsey.

The baker was dusted with a fine coating of powdered sugar.

And his skin was as white as the sugar.

Anna Crumbles

The couple trudged up the dark mountainside along a narrow mud path that was slick from similar pilgrimages.

'What time is it?' he asked.

She checked her watch. A man's Timex. 'A little before midnight.'

Something other than the fog caused him to shiver as they moved through the eucalyptus forest. His companion seemed unperturbed.

'You're a stout-hearted woman, Anna.'

'What's the matter? Can't you keep up? This little jaunt was your idea, remember?'

'I don't know what the hell got into me.'

She didn't say anything. He looked down at her and brushed a strand of hair away from her face.

'Yes, I do, Anna. Yes I do.'

At the crest of Mount Davidson, they caught their breath beneath the giant concrete cross.

Edgar swept his arm over the city beneath them.

'All my life . . . all my goddamn life and I never came up here.'

'Pretend you were saving it.'

He took her hand and pulled her next to him. 'I swear it was worth it.'

Silence.

'Anna?'

'We didn't come here to neck, did we, Edgar?'

He sat down on the ledge under the cross. 'I . . . no.'

She joined him. 'What is it?'

'I don't know exactly. I got a call today.'

'About what?'

'A man who wants to talk to me about madrigals.'

'What?'

'That's what he said. That's *all* he said, actually. "I'm a friend and I want to talk to you about madrigals." He was maddeningly coy about it.'

'Do you think he . . . ?'

'What else? He wants money, I guess.'

'Blackmail?'

Edgar chuckled. 'Quaint, isn't it? Six months ago that might have shaken me up real bad.'

'But how would he know?'

'Who knows? Who *cares*?'

'*You* do, apparently. You just marched me up Calvary to tell me about it.'

'That wasn't the reason.'

'Will you see him?'

'Long enough to memorize his face and kick his ass down the steps.'

'Are you sure that's wise?'

'Hell, what can he do? I'm a goner. Christ, I never thought that would come in handy someday!'

Anna picked up a twig and traced a circle in the damp earth. 'We're not the only ones to consider, Edgar.'

'Frannie?'

Anna nodded.

'He won't go to her. Not when he sees how little it matters to me.'

'You don't know that for certain.'

'No . . . but I'm not losing sleep over it, either.'

'Are you sure it's blackmail?'

'Positive.'

Anna stood up and walked away from the cross, closer to the lights of the city. 'Did he tell you his name?'

'Just Williams. Mr Williams.'

'When does he want to see you?'

'Christmas Eve afternoon.' He grinned. 'Gothic, eh?'

Anna didn't smile. 'I don't want to hurt your family, Edgar. Or you.'

'Me? Anna, you've *never* caused me a single moment of . . .'

'I *could*, though, Edgar. I could hurt you very badly.'

'Bullshit!'

'Your family needs you now, Edgar. It isn't right or fair for me . . .'

233

'What the hell is the matter with you? Christ, *I'm* supposed to be the nervous one in this relationship! I brought you up here to ask you to go away with me!'

She spun around to face him. 'What?'

'I want you to go away with me.'

'But we . . . Where?'

'Any place you want. We could take a cruise to Mexico. I could make it look like a business trip. Look at me, Anna! You can see how much time I've got left!'

There were tears in her eyes. 'I can see . . . a beautiful man.'

'It's yes, then?'

'You can't do that to Frannie.'

'Would you let me worry about that!'

'I don't . . .' Her voice choked up. 'I don't want you caught up in this, Edgar.'

'I'm *already* caught up in it, goddammit!'

'It's not too late. You can tell Mr Williams . . . you can tell him . . . Hell, I don't know . . . deny it. He can't have positive proof about us. If we never see each other again . . .'

He grasped her shoulders and looked into her eyes. 'You're way out of line, lady.'

'God help me . . . I know!' She was sobbing now.

'Anna, please don't . . .'

'I'm a liar, Edgar. I love you with all my heart, but I'm a liar.'

'What the hell are you talking about?'

She composed herself somewhat and turned away from him. 'It's worse than you think,' she said.

The Baker's Wife

For a moment, Mona was speechless, confronting this stranger at the Twinkie factory at midnight.

This *white* stranger.

'Yes, ma'am,' he said pleasantly. 'What can I do for you?'

'I . . . excuse me . . . I think I must want the other Mr Wilson.'

'Don? The wrapper? I'll get him, if you'd . . .'

'No. Wait, please . . . Do you have a daughter named Dorothy?'

Leroy Wilson's face went whiter still. 'Oh, my God!'

'Mr Wilson, I . . .

'You're from the Red Cross or something? Something's happened to her?'

'Oh, no! She's fine. Really! I saw her tonight.'

'She's in San Francisco?'

'Yes.'

The relief in his expression gave way to bitterness. 'I wouldn't expect we'd hear from her.'

'She lives here now, Mr Wilson.'

'Who are you?'

'I'm sorry . . . Mona Ramsey. I room with your daughter.'

'What do you want from me?'

'I want to . . . Wouldn't you like to see Dorothy, Mr Wilson?'

He snorted. 'What *we* want doesn't have much to do with it, does it?'

'I think . . . I think Dorothy would really like . . .'

'Dorothy doesn't even *approve* of me and her mother.'

So *that* was it, thought Mona. The sophisticated Miss D'orothea Wilson was the product of a lower-class interracial marriage. And it bugged the hell out of her.

Which explained, among other things, D'orothea's semi-Caucasian features and her fierce reluctance to deal with her African heritage.

She was, in short, an Oreo.

Leroy Wilson bought Mona a cup of coffee in the bakery's second-floor snack bar. Obviously wounded by his daughter's behaviour, he allowed his visitor to do most of the talking.

'Mr Wilson, I don't know why Dorothy decided to . . . cut off communications with you and Mrs Wilson . . . but I think she's changed now. She wants to live in San Francisco, and I'm sure that means . . .'

'I don't even remember the last time Dorothy wrote us.'

'It's easy to lose touch in New York, especially if you're a model and . . .'

'C'mon. Get to the point.'

Mona set her cup down and looked him in the eye. 'I want you and your wife to come to dinner this week.'

He blinked at her, slack-jawed.

'It would be just the four of us.'

235

'Dorothy knows about this?'

'Well, uh . . . no.'

'I think you'd better run along home.'

'Mr Wilson, please . . .'

'What do *you* get out of this, anyway?'

'Dorothy's my *friend*.'

'That's not all of it.'

'It's such a *waste*, dammit!'

He stared at her soberly, and Mona sensed a sort of primitive intuition at work. 'Do you talk to your daddy?'

'Mr Wilson . . .'

'Do you?'

'I . . . never knew him.'

'He passed away?'

'I don't know. He left my mother when I was a baby.'

'Oh.'

'Go ahead. Psyche out my motives, if you want. All I . . .'

'OK. When?'

'What?'

'When do you want us to come?'

'Oh, I'm so . . .' She flung her arms around his neck and hugged him, then backed off, embarrassed. 'Is Christmas Eve OK?'

'Yeah,' said Leroy Wilson. 'I guess so.'

Old Flames

Christmas. Some years it happens. Others it doesn't.

This year, thought Brian, finishing off a bottle of Gatorade, it isn't going to happen.

Not if it snows on Barbary Lane. Not if you OD on eggnog. Not if Donny and Marie and Sonny and Cher and the whole fucking Mormon Tabernacle Choir show up on your doorstep with a partridge in a pear tree . . . it isn't going to happen.

As far as he was concerned, Mrs Madrigal's pary would be just like any other.

'Cheryl?'

'Yeah.'

'Brian.'

'Uh . . . Brian who?'

'Hawkins. From Perry's. The one who nailed your mother, dingbat!'

'Oh . . . Hi!'

'What's up?'

'Oh . . . not much.'

'Still living in the trailer park?'

'Yeah . . . *I* am.'

'Swell.'

'Candi's left. She's working in Redwood City now. At Waterbed Wonderland.'

'Terrific.'

'She's got an old man now. A hot-shit celebrity. Larry Larson.'

'Don't know him.'

'You know . . . Channel 36?'

'No.'

'The Wizard of Waterbeds.'

'Oh.'

' "We'll help you make a splash in bed"?'

'Got it.'

'Larry might let her do a commercial soon.'

'Well . . . star time. Look, Cheryl . . . you wanna go to a Christmas party?'

'When?'

'Christmas Eve.'

'Oh . . . I'd *love* to, but Larry's taking us to Rickey's Hyatt House for turkey with all the trimmings.'

'Oh.'

'I could check with Larry. He might not mind if you came along.'

'That's all right.'

'I hate for you to be alone on . . .'

'I won't be alone, Cheryl.'

'I'd try to get out of it, but Larry's called ahead for Mateus and everything.'

'Ol' Larry thinks of everything.'

'Yeah. He's real nice.'

'Well, I hope you find one for yourself . . . some rich asshole in a leisure suit who can buy you all the Mateus and . . . Mediterranean furniture and . . . steel-belted radials . . .'

237

'You're still as fucked up as ever, aren't you?'

'And you're about as liberated as a goddamn hamster.'

'I *never* said I was liberated!'

'Right you are!'

'I am really, really sorry for you!'

'I can tell.'

'You really hate women, don't you?'

'What makes you think you're a woman?'

She slammed the phone down.

'Connie?'

'Just a sec. Lemme turn down the stereo.' The Ray Conniff Singers were murdering 'The Little Drummer Boy' in the background.

'Hi,' she said, returning. 'Who's this?'

'Your birthday boy.'

'Byron?'

'Brian.'

'Oh . . . sorry. Long time no see, huh?'

'Yeah, look . . . It might turn out to be a big bore, but I'm invited to this Christmas party my landlady's giving and . . . well, that's it.'

Silence.

'Whatdya say?'

'Was that an invitation, Brian?'

'Yeah.'

'I see. When?'

'Uh . . . the twenty-fourth.'

'Just a sec, OK?' She left the phone for a matter of seconds. 'Sure,' she said finally. 'The twenty-fourth is fine.'

A Lovers' Farewell

The noontime Perry's crowd was thicker than usual. Beauchamp pushed his way to the far end of the bar and nodded to the blue-blazered maître d'.

'I'm meeting a friend,' he said.

Jon was waiting for him at a table in the tiny back courtyard.

'Sorry,' said Beauchamp. 'I got tied up in pantyhose again.'

The gynecologist smiled. 'Still trying to wreck my business, huh?'

'That's funny. I hadn't thought of that.'

'I ordered you a Bullshot.'

'Perfect.'

'I can't stay long, Beauchamp.'

'Fine. Neither can I.'

'I don't think this is such a good idea, anyway.'

Beauchamp frowned. 'Look, there's no goddamn reason in the world why two men can't have a perfectly . . .'

'You don't consider a wife a *reason?*'

'Don't start on that again!'

'I hadn't planned to.'

'Anyway . . . why should *you* care, if I don't. DeDe doesn't know you from Adam. You could be *anybody*. You could be a friend from the club, for all she knows!'

'That isn't the point.'

'Well, what the hell *is* the goddamn . . . ?'

'Can I take your order now?' The Bullshots had arrived, along with a waiter whose green eyes and chestnut hair temporarily diverted both men from the crisis at hand.

Beauchamp flushed and chose the first thing he saw on the menu. 'Yeah. The shepherd's pie.'

'Same here,' Jon said.

The waiter left without a word.

'Surly bastard,' said Beauchamp.

Jon shrugged. 'But pretty.'

'You *would* notice that, wouldn't you?'

'Didn't you?'

'Not when I'm with somebody I care about!'

Jon looked down at his drink. 'I think you're expecting too much of me, Beauchamp.'

Silence.

'I think this should be . . . it.'

'Just like that, huh?'

'It isn't "just like that" and you know it. It's been coming on for a long time.'

'It's DeDe, isn't it?'

'No. Not entirely.'

'Well, *what*, then?'

'I'm not sure exactly.'

'Yes you are.'

'Beauchamp . . . I don't think I *trust* you.'

'Jesus!'

'I *know* DeDe can't trust you. Why should I trust you?'

'That's different.'

'It's *not* different. She hurts the same way you and I do.'

'Look, what is this shit with DeDe? What the hell has DeDe got to do with . . . ?'

'She's pregnant, Beauchamp.'

Silence.

'She's a patient of mine.'

'Fuck.'

'Well, *somebody* did.'

'Jesus Christ.'

'He's as good a possibility as any, I suppose.'

'How can you *joke* about this, Jon?'

'It isn't *my* joke, Beauchamp. It's yours. I'm not gonna be part of this.'

The food arrived. Neither of them spoke until the waiter had gone.

'I still wanna see you, Jon.'

'It figures.'

'There's a party at the club on Christmas Eve.'

'I have plans on Christmas Eve.' He pushed his chair back and stood up, dropping a ten-dollar bill on the table. 'I'm not hungry. It's on me.'

Beauchamp grabbed his wrist. 'Wait a minute, goddammit! Did you tell DeDe about us?'

'Let go.'

'I wanna know!'

Jon jerked his arm free and straightened his tie. 'She's a nice woman,' he said. 'She could have done better than you.'

Edgar on the Brink

The cramps had begun again.

Edgar stood up from his desk and stretched his arms out slowly, arcing them from his body like a tired semaphorist.

He repeated the exercise four or five times, long enough to realize that it wasn't working, then confronted the mirror in his office washroom. His face was waxy white.

Chronic pyelonephritis. Renal disease. Toxic products that would back up just so long until one day . . . acute pericarditis would cause his heart to stop.

A lot of fancy words for bum kidneys.

Mary Ann buzzed him from the outer office. 'Mildred called from Production. She wants to talk to you about the mailboy.'

'For Christ's sake! Can't you keep that old bat off my neck long enough . . .'

'I'm sorry, Mr Halcyon. She was really upset, and I didn't know what . . .'

'Did he flip her the bird again?'

Mary Ann giggled. 'You're not gonna believe it.'

'The suspense is killing me.'

'She caught him Xeroxing his . . . privates.'

'What!'

'She came in early this morning and found him on top of the Xerox machine . . . with his pants down.'

Edgar began to laugh. So hard, in fact, that he broke into a coughing jag.

'Are you all right, Mr Halcyon?'

'That's the funniest . . . goddamn thing I've . . . What was he going to do with it?'

Now Mary Ann broke up. 'He's . . . he's been doing it for *weeks*, Mr Halcyon.' She paused for a moment to collect herself. 'Everybody in Production called him the Xerox Flasher, but nobody knew who it was. Mildred . . .' She began to giggle again, losing control.

'Mildred what?' Christ, he thought. Am I gossiping with my secretary?

'Mildred thought it was somebody from Creative . . .'

'Mmm. Perverts all.'

'Anyway . . . he always made a lot of copies and left them in the secretaries' desks every morning . . . until Mildred found out about it.'

'Hell, he's the only person in the building who isn't guilty of false advertising!'

'Well, not exactly.'

Edgar began to laugh. 'Oh, God! Don't tell me . . .'

'Yes, sir. He was using the enlarger.'

Frannie called after lunch, obviously distraught.

'Edgar, I want you to do something about those people at Macy's.'
'What is it this time?'
'I have *never*, Edgar . . . in all my life . . . been so *humiliated* . . .'
'Frannie . . .'
'I went to Loehmann's this morning, out at Westlake . . .'
'I thought you said Macy's?'
'Let me finish. I went to Loehmann's because I wanted to get something nice for Helen for Christmas, and Loehmann's has perfectly *darling* designer-line clothes like Anne Klein, Beene Bag, Blassport . . .'
'Frannie.'
'I have to *explain* this, Edgar! Loehmann's has these marvelous clothes, see, only they cut the labels out because they're overruns, so you can get them for practically *nothing* . . . and since I'm crazy about Helen, but not *that* crazy, I thought I'd buy her this precious Calvin Klein cashmere cowl-neck sweater that I could *tell* was a Calvin Klein, even though they'd cut the label out, because it had GJG in it.'
Edgar gave up and let it wash over him. 'GJG?' he asked blandly.
'That's the *code*. Anyway, it's just plain tacky to give your best friend a sweater without a label in it, so I asked them at Loehmann's if they had any extra labels, and they said that they were all cut out by the manufacturers, so . . .'
'Macy's, Frannie.'
'I'm getting to that. I went to Macy's . . . well, not exactly Macy's, but that new place called the Shop on Union Square, and I picked out a couple of Calvin Klein sweaters . . . and when I was in the dressing room I noticed one of the labels was so loose it was practically *falling off*, so I took out a pair of nail scissors and . . .'
'Jesus Christ!'
'Oh, don't be sanctimonious, Edgar! They've got *hundreds* of labels, and I wasn't . . . Well, when that horrid little Chicano clerk barged in, you would have thought I was *stealing* or something!'

He was back on the phone two minutes after Frannie had hung up.
'Anna?'
'Hello?'
'I have to see you, Anna.'
'Edgar . . . I don't think that's . . .'
'No arguments. I want to show you something.'
'What?'

'You'll see. I'll pick you up tomorrow after breakfast.'
'What about Mr Williams?'
'He's not coming until six. We'll be back by then.'

Breaking and Entering

On the night before Christmas Eve, Michael phoned Mona in Pacific Heights.

'Hi, Babycakes!'

'Mouse!'

'Don't Mouse me! I thought you were becoming a dyke, not a nun! Where the hell have you been?'

'Mouse . . . I'm sorry . . . It's just that I've had so much adjusting . . .'

'*Tell* me. It's a strain being pissy. I tried it once for three days in Laguna Beach . . . and I nearly OD'd on kaftans.'

Mona managed a laugh. 'I've missed you, Mouse. I really have.'

'Prove it, then, and come to Mrs Madrigal's wingding.'

'When?'

'Tomorrow night.'

'I can't. Jesus . . . I don't even want to *think* about it.'

'What?'

'I'm having D'or's parents over for dinner.'

'Christ . . . in laws and everything! D'or must be a *lot* of fun!'

'She doesn't even know about it.'

'She . . . ? What are you up to, Babycakes!'

'It's a long story. Suffice it to say I'm freaked.'

'Mrs Madrigal will be disappointed.'

'I know. I'm sorry.'

'Maybe you should give her a call or something. I think she thinks you're . . . bummed out with her.'

'Why should she . . . ?'

'You haven't talked to her in weeks, Mona.'

'Thanks for the guilt trip.'

'It isn't a guilt trip. She asked me to call you. She really misses you.'
Silence.

'I'll explain about your dinner party. She'll understand. But give her a call, OK?'

243

'OK.' Her voice seemed unusually weak.

'You doin' all right, Babycakes?'

'Mouse . . . I think D'or has a drug problem.'

Michael couldn't help but laugh.

'I'm *serious*, Mouse!'

'What's the matter? She pinching your Quaaludes or something?'

'For your information, smartass, I found some totally *unidentifiable* pills in her dresser last night, and she started acting really spooky when I asked her about them.'

'Has she been acting spooky otherwise?'

'No. Not particularly.'

'Well, relax then.'

'I can't. I'm saving my last Quaalude for tomorrow.'

Mary Ann, meanwhile, was trying to decide what to do about Norman.

He had made himself unreachable for days, avoiding Barbary Lane during daylight hours, often returning to his house on the roof as late as 3 or 4 A.M., when Mary Ann could hear his labored footsteps on the stairs.

He was drinking heavily, she guessed, and it made her uncomfortable to think that *she* might be the reason.

Mrs Madrigal had left him two notes about the party, neither of which he had answered. He seemed to be a man of single purpose now, moody and slightly manic, lunging uncontrollably toward a Holy Grail that no one but himself could see.

Something *had* to be done.

It was dark in the foyer of the house when Mary Ann opened the door under the stairwell leading to the basement. Fumbling in the blackness for the light switch, she listened carefully for sounds on the stairs above her. She would *die* if anyone caught her doing this.

The key board was just beyond the fuse box, shrouded in cobwebs. She searched for half a minute until she found the key marked 'Roof House'. Then she closed the door as quietly as possible and crept up three flights of stairs to the door that was painted orange.

Although she was *certain* that Norman was gone, she rapped twice on the door. The sound reverberated in the stairwell. She froze. Had anyone heard it?

The house was completely still.

244

She slipped the key into the lock. A tight fit. She jiggled it until the door swung open and the darkness of the little house engulfed her.

It took her less than a minute to find the Nutri-Vim suitcase.

At the Grove

The forester who admitted them never once looked at Anna, curled up placidly on the front seat of Edgar's Mercedes.

She winked at the stony sentinel as they drove in.

'I hope he thinks I'm a hooker.'

'It wouldn't be the first time.'

Anna squeezed his knee. 'For him or you, sir?'

He wouldn't joke about it. 'You're the only woman I've ever brought here, Anna.'

They parked the car in a lot adjacent to the entrance and began their odyssey on foot.

'Well, well,' said Anna, as they moved through the towering redwoods. 'Anna Madrigal at the Bohemian Grove.'

'I think that's as it should be.'

'Just the same . . . thank you.'

'I wish I'd thought of it twenty years ago.'

'Twelve.'

Edgar grinned. 'Twelve,' he repeated.

Slipping her arm through his, Anna simply smiled and shook her head in amazement.

Edgar switched easily into the role of White Rabbit. His Alice blinked her wide blue eyes at him when he showed her the Grove Stage.

'You *performed* here?'

'I stopped the show once as a Valkyrie.'

'In *drag*, Edgar?'

'Hell . . . the Greeks did it.'

'The Greeks did a lot of things.'

He smiled. 'Get off my back, will you?'

'That's what the Greeks used to say.'

Edgar slapped her on the behind and chased her up the River Road, ignoring the tightness that had begun to grow in his chest.

*

The camps they passed had names like honeymoon suites at the Madonna Inn: Pink Onion, Toyland, Isle of Aves, Monastery, Last Chance . . .

Edgar's camp was *Hillbillies*.

A two-story chalet dominated the enclave, opening into a courtyard with a barbecue pit. Admitting himself with a key, Edgar led Anna to the second floor, where a couch and a stone fireplace awaited them.

Anna grinned slyly. 'Oh, I get it!'

He smiled like a satyr.

'Don't look so smug, Edgar Halcyon. I can match your decadence any day!'

She reached into the pocket of her peacoat and produced a thin tortoise-shell cigarette case. She extracted a joint.

'Anna . . .'

'It's good for what ails you.'

He arched an eyebrow. 'Wanna bet?'

'I'm sorry. I . . . Damn, I'm usually so *good* with words.'

His smile forgave her. She kept the joint held out for him.

'Anna . . . can't you just make do with the last of a breed?'

She tapped the joint against her lower lip, then returned it to the case. 'Damn right,' she said softly.

Wrapped in an Indian blanket, they sat in front of the fire.

'If this were the old days, we could run away together to the wilds.'

She rearranged his white mane with her fingers. 'We're already in the wilds, aren't we?'

'Then . . . wilder wilds.'

'That would be lovely.'

'We don't have to go back, Anna.'

'Yes we do.'

He turned and stared into the fire. 'Would you have told me, if Mr Williams hadn't come along?'

'No.'

'Why not?'

'It wasn't . . . necessary.'

'You're still beautiful, Anna.'

'Thank you.'

'What shall I tell him tonight?'

Anna shrugged. 'Tell him . . . his rent's due.'

Edgar laughed, hugging her. 'One more question.'

'What?'

'Why haven't you invited me to your party?'

'Now, how on earth . . .'

'I heard Mary Ann talking about it.'

She smiled at him in wonderment. 'You dear man.'

'That doesn't answer my question.'

'Is eight o'clock OK?'

He nodded. 'Right after I finish with Mr Williams.'

Art for Art's Sake

Mary Ann's morning was a hellish blur of remembered images. Petrified of meeting Norman in the hallway, she crept out of the house and ran down the lane to Leavenworth Street. She caught the first cab she saw.

'Where to?'

'Uh . . . what's a nice museum?'

'The Legion of Honor?'

'Out beyond the bridge?'

'Yep. Lotsa nice Rodin stuff.'

'Fine.' It was perfect, really. She *needed* Art now . . . and Beauty . . . and anything else with a capital letter that would pull her through the worst Christmas Eve of her life.

She wandered through the museum for almost an hour, then returned to the therapeutic sunlight of the colonnade courtyard. She sat at the base of *The Thinker* until the comic irony of the scene drove her back indoors to the Café Chanticleer.

After three cups of coffee, she made up her mind.

She found a phone booth near the entrance way on the ground floor, dug Norman's Nutri-Vim business card from her purse, and dialed the number scribbled in pencil on the back.

'Yeah?'

'Norman?'

'Yeah.'

'It's Mary Ann.'

'Hello.' He sounded drunk, *very* drunk.

'I have . . . sort of a problem. I was hoping you could come meet me.'

247

There was a pause, and then he said, 'Sure.' Even now, knowing what she did, she hated herself for the way she could govern his feelings.

'I'm out at the Palace of the Legion of Honor.'

'No problem. Half an hour, OK?'

'OK. Norman?'

'Huh?'

'Drive carefully, will you?'

She was waiting for him in the parking lot, under the statue of *The Shades*. Norman crawled out of the Falcon with exaggerated dignity. He was blitzed.

'How ya doin'?'

'Pretty good, pretty good.' Why did she *say* that? Why was she being nice to him?

'You wanna go in the museum?'

'No, thanks. I've been there all morning.'

'Oh.'

'Could we take a walk?'

Norman shrugged. 'Where?'

'Over there?' She pointed across the road to what appeared to be a golf course with a network of footpaths. She wanted to get away from people.

Norman extended his arm with drunken gallantry. Everything he did, in fact, seemed a hideous parody of the things she had once admired about him. She took his arm, suppressing a shudder. If nothing else, it would keep him from falling flat on his face.

They crossed the road and descended a path along the edge of the golf course. The fog had begun to roll in, blurring the Monterey cypresses on a distant rise. Somewhere beyond those trees lay the ocean.

Mary Ann let go of Norman's arm. 'I wanted to talk to you in private, Norman.'

'Yeah?' He smiled at her, apparently allowing his hopes to rise again.

'I know about the pictures.'

He stopped in his tracks and stared at her, slack-jawed. 'Huh?'

'I've seen the pictures, Norman.'

'What pictures?' Of *course* he wasn't going to make it easy for her.

'You know what I'm talking about.'

248

He stuck out his lower lip like a petulant child and began to walk again. Faster now. 'I *don't* know what you're talking about!'

'"Tender Tots"? "Buxom Babies"?'

'You must be . . .'

'I know about you and Lexy, Norman!'

Guess Who's Coming to Dinner?

Hovering over a table set for four, Mona hummed her mantra in a last-minute effort to calm her nerves.

D'orothea's parents were arriving in ten minutes.

And D'orothea still didn't know.

'I'm not kidding, Mona. I hate surprises. If you've invited those dreary backpacking dykes from Petaluma, you can count me out. I know all I need to know about skinning squirrels, thank you.'

Mona didn't look up. 'You'll like them. I promise, D'or.'

Shit, she thought. What if she *doesn't*? What if she feels more alienated than ever? What if the Wilsons' oddly bourgeois inter-racial marriage had left unimaginable scars on the psyche of their daughter?

'And another thing, Mona . . . the *minute* one of those garage-sale gurus of yours starts spouting off about The Third Eye or whose moon is in . . .'

'I'll split a Quaalude with you, OK?'

'You can't *drug* me into submission, Mona.'

Mona turned away and readjusted a fork. 'Forget it, then.'

'I'm sorry. That wasn't fair.'

'Will you *try* to act human, D'or?'

'Sure. What the hell.'

'I want this to be . . . well, I want it to be nice.'

'I know. And I'll try.'

The next fifteen minutes were the worst in Mona's memory.

She scurried around the house, pretending to busy herself with housekeeping, *certain* her terror would show if she stayed in one place.

The Wilsons were late.

D'orothea was upstairs, fixing her face in the bedroom.

249

Mona forsook her mantra and recited a childhood prayer. She was halfway through it when the doorbell rang. There was no way out now. No excuses. No postponements.

She opened the door just as D'or reached the landing on the stairs. 'I'm sorry we're late,' said Leroy Wilson quietly. 'This is Mrs . . .'

His eyes, climbing to the stairs, grew large and glassy. 'Dorothy?' My God! Dorothy, what in God's . . . ?'

D'orothea stood frozen on the landing. 'Mona . . . Jesus, Mona, what have you . . . ?' She spun around and dashed back up the stairs, weeping like a mad-woman.

Mona was wrecked, speechless before Leroy Wilson and the short, dumpy woman who had come in too late to witness the bizarre scenario.

The short, dumpy *white* woman.

With the Wilsons in limbo downstairs, D'or wept like a baby in Mona's arms.

'I swear, Mona . . . I swear to God . . . I never meant to lie to you. I wanted to work . . . I just wanted to work. When I moved to New York five years ago, nobody would hire me. Nobody! Then I did a couple of jobs in dark makeup . . . one of those Arab harem girl things . . . and all of a sudden people started asking for the foxy black chick . . . I didn't *plan* it. It just sort of . . .'

'D'or, I don't see what . . .'

'I'm a fraud, Mona!' Her sobs grew louder. 'I'm nothing but . . . a white girl from Oakland!'

'D'or . . . your skin . . . ?'

'Those pills. The ones you found in my drawer. They're for vitiligo.'

'I don't . . .'

'It's a disease that causes white spots to break out on your body. People with vitiligo take the pill to make their pigment darker. If you're white, and take enough of them over a two-month period . . . Didn't you ever read *Black Like Me*?'

'A long time ago.'

'Well, that's what I did. I found a dermatologist in New Orleans who would give me the pills, along with ultraviolet treatments, and I disappeared for three months and came back to New York as a black model. I made *money*, Mona . . . more money that I had ever seen in my life. Naturally, I dropped all contact with my parents, but I never intended . . .'

'But doesn't it wear off?'

'Of course. It's a constant strain. I had to sneak off every few months or so to get more ultraviolet treatments . . . and, of course, I kept taking the pills . . . and finally one day I just couldn't take the sham anymore, so I decided . . .'

'. . . to move to San Francisco and go white.'

D'or nodded, wiping her eyes. 'Naturally, I felt that you would be my refuge until . . . I had changed back . . . and I always planned to see my parents again, but not until . . .'

'Why didn't you *tell* me, D'or?'

'I *tried.* I tried lots of times. But every time I got close you would whip up a mess of chitlins or start talking about my beloved African heritage . . . and I felt like such a phony. I didn't want you to be . . . ashamed of me.'

Mona smiled. 'Do I look ashamed?'

'This really is my hair, Mona. I *do* have naturally curly hair.'

'Do you have any idea what I thought, D'or?'

D'or shook her head.

'I thought you were dying. I freaked. I thought you were taking those pills because you were dying.'

'Of what?'

'What else? Sickle cell anemia.'

The Confrontation

Norman was almost running now, lurching recklessly towards the cypresses on the edge of the rise.

'Jus' shuddup, OK? Jus' shuddup!'

'I'm not shutting up, Norman! I'm not standing by while you exploit that child in such a horrible, *disgusting* . . .'

'It's none o' your business!'

'I saw those magazines in your suitcase, Norman!'

'What were you doin' in my suitcase?'

'You're sick, Norman. You're . . .' She was breathing almost as heavily as he was. She pulled at his arm. 'Will you *stop*?'

He obeyed, jerking to a halt at the top of the rise. Swaying for a moment, he clutched at her to regain his balance. She gasped, not at him, but at the stomach-churning scene that confronted them in the fog.

'Norman . . . *get back!*'

'Wha . . . ?'

'It's a cliff! Get back! Please!'

He stared at her dumbly, then staggered several steps in her direction. She latched on to his arm, hooking her other arm around a tree.

Norman was indignant. 'Thass not what I do, ya know.'

'Norman, if you don't . . .'

'Those stupid pictures are nothin'! I got bigger things'n *that* going for me!'

'Norman . . .' She softened her tone somewhat, leading him away from the precipice. 'What you are doing is . . . against the law, for one thing.'

'Ha! You think I don't know that?'

'How *could* you, Norman? You've been so sweet to Lexy.'

'So?'

'I won't stand for it, Norman. I'm calling that child's parents.'

'You think they don't *know?*'

She clenched her teeth. 'Dear God!'

'How the hell you think they make a livin', huh? Lexy's a goddamn *star*! She's a goddamn famous little . . . Hell, I'm jus' . . . her agent!'

'But you're in the magazines!'

He nodded almost proudly. 'A few movies too.'

'Jesus.'

'I can't help it. She won't do it with anybody else.'

'Norman, stop . . .'

'You think I'm chickenshit, don't you? You think I'm a chicken-shit child pornographer!'

'Norman, stop . . .'

'I've got news for you, Miss Fancypants! I'm a goddamn private investigator and I'm jus' about to break the biggest goddamn case of my goddamn career!'

'Norman, get away from the . . .'

She couldn't look.

When she turned around again, he was lumbering down the path along the edge of the cliff. To her relief, he had moved beyond the precipitous portion to a place where the drop-off seemed less pronounced.

'Norman, come back!'

He snarled over his shoulder at her. 'Find your own goddamn way home!'

Then, suddenly, he lost his footing, sliding off the path into the loose rock and sand on the slope leading to the sea.

She ran to him, horror-stricken. He was spread-eagled on his back thrashing like an overturned cockroach. A dozen feet below him another cliff awaited. He whimpered pathetically.

'Please . . . jus' help me, please . . .'

Mary Ann dropped to the ground and reached as far as she could down the slope. 'Don't move, Norman. Just hold still, OK?'

He wasn't listening. His limbs flailed wildly until the ground beneath him began to shift and rumble like molten lava. She lunged desperately for his arm and missed.

His progress to the edge of the cliff was slow, steady and horrible.

He left behind his clip-on-tie, dangling limply from her hand.

She ran back to the museum in the swirling fog, his screams reverberating in her head.

In the phone booth, she checked her purse. Thirty-seven cents. She had counted on riding home with Norman.

She dialed 673-MUNI.

'Muni,' said a man on the other end.

'Please . . . how do I get to Barbary Lane from the Legion of Honor?'

'Barbary Lane? Let's see. OK . . . walk down to Clement and Thirty-fourth and take the Number 2 Clement to Post and Powell, then transfer to the Number 60 Hyde cable car.'

'The Number 2 Clement?'

'Yes.'

'Thank you.'

'Sure. And Merry Christmas.'

'Merry Christmas to you,' she said.

The Party

'Where's Mary Ann?' asked Connie Bradshaw, standing under Mrs Madrigal's red-tasseled archway. 'I thought you said she'd be here.'

Brian selected a joint from a Wedgwood plate. 'She's here. At least . . . I saw her upstairs.'

'Jeez, it's been a zillion years since I've seen her!'

'You two are good friends, huh?'

'Oh, the best! I mean . . . we haven't been too good about keeping in touch or anything, but . . . well, *you* know how it goes in this town.'

'Sure.'

'Uh . . . I think someone wants to talk to you, Brian.'

'Oh . . . Hi, Michael.'

'Hi. You haven't seen Gale Storm, have you?'

'Who?'

'Mary Ann.'

Brian took a toke off the joint, then passed it to Connie. 'We were just talking about that. What's with her, anyway? I thought she was orchestrating this orgy.'

'She was. I guess she's fixing her face or something. Hey, don't go 'way. I've got something for you.' He ducked into the kitchen and returned with a small package wrapped in silver foil.

Brian flushed. 'Hey, man . . . we said no presents, remember?'

'I know,' said Michael, 'but this isn't for Christmas, really. I just forgot to give it to you earlier.'

'That's nice,' Connie beamed.

Brian glanced at her, then back at Michael. There was something more impish than usual about Michael's grin. 'Hey, Michael, this isn't . . . ?'

'Go on,' squealed Connie. 'I can't stand the suspense!'

Brian looked directly into Michael's eyes. 'Shall I?' He smiled.

'What the hell. The sooner you open it, the sooner you can use it.'

'Right!' Connie agreed.

Brian tore into the package. He was fully prepared when the heavy brass ring emerged from the tissue paper. 'It's a nice one, Michael. Very handsome.'

'Are you sure? I can take it back if . . .'

'No. I'm . . . nuts about it.'

Michael stayed poker-faced. 'I hope it's your size.'

'What is it?' asked Connie.

Brian held it up so she could look at it. 'Nice, huh?'

'It's *gorgeous*. What's it for?'

Brian's eyes flashed towards Michael for a split second, then back at Connie. 'It's . . . an ornament,' he said appreciatively. 'You hang it on your tree.'

*

254

Michael picked up a tray of brownies in the kitchen. 'Are these loaded?' he asked.

Mrs Madrigal merely smiled at him.

'I thought so,' said Michael.

'Has Mary Ann come down yet?'

'Not yet.'

'What on earth could have . . .'

'I can check, if you want.'

'No. Thank you, dear . . . but I need you down here.'

'Are you expecting any others?'

She checked her watch. 'One,' she said vaguely, 'though I'm not sure . . . It's nothing definite, dear.'

'Is everything . . . all right, Mrs Madrigal?'

She smiled and kissed him on the cheek. 'I'm with my family, aren't I?'

When Michael returned to the living room, he almost dropped the brownies.

'Mona!'

'In the firm but pliant flesh.'

'Hot damn! What happened to D'orothea?'

'She's having a White Christmas with her parents in Oakland.'

'It's *snowing* in Oakland.'

'It's too long a story, Mouse.'

He set the tray down and flung his arms around her. 'Goddammit, I've missed you.'

'Yeah. Same here.'

'Well, you don't look any worse for wear.'

'Yeah,' she grinned. 'Same ol' Mona . . . smiling in the face of perversity.'

Saying Good-bye

When Mary Ann finally appeared, she made her apologies to Mrs Madrigal.

'I hope it hasn't been a hassle. I . . . well, I guess I just lost track of the time with Christmas shopping and all.'

'Don't be silly, dear. It's been no problem at all, and Michael's been the perfect . . . You haven't seen Mr Williams, have you, dear? If he's in the house, we should certainly invite him to . . .'

'No. No, I haven't. Not for a day or so, anyway.'

'Well, that's too bad.'

'He's been gone a lot recently. He hasn't seemed himself . . . to me, anyway.'

'No, he hasn't, has he?'

'It's nice to see my friend Connie again.'

'I know. Isn't that a *coincidence*? And Mona was able to make it, after all, and . . . well, God bless us, every one!' She kissed Mary Ann a bit too breezily on the cheek and rushed past her out of the room.

It seemed to Mary Ann that she was crying.

Fifteen minutes later, Mona looked for the landlady and found her on the stairway at the entrance to the lane.

'Waiting for somebody?' she asked, sitting down beside her.

'No, dear. Not anymore.'

'Anybody I know?'

'I wish you had.'

'Had?'

'I meant . . . It's hard to explain, dear.'

'I'm sorry I haven't kept in touch with you more.'

Mrs Madrigal turned and looked at her. There were tears in her eyes. 'Oh, thank you for saying that!' she cried. She held on to Mona for a moment, then straightened up again, regaining her composure.

'I'd like to move back in,' said Mona, 'if you can stand me.'

'*Stand* you? You simple child! I've missed you more than you'll ever know!'

Mona smiled. 'Thank you . . . and Merry Christmas.'

'Merry Christmas, dear.'

'Why don't you come back in? It's *cold* out here!'

'I will. In a minute. You run along.'

'Couldn't your friend meet you inside?'

'He's not coming, dear. He's already left us.'

He left at Halcyon Hill.

Dr Jack Kincaid administered a sedative to his wife, while his daughter and son-in-law said good-bye to him.

He was flat on his back in bed. His skin was so pale that it seemed translucent.

'Daddy?'

'Is that you, DeDe?'

'It's me and Beauchamp.'

'Oh.'

'We have a surprise for you, Daddy.'

Beauchamp flashed an uneasy glance at his wife. DeDe glared back at him, then turned and knelt at her father's bedside.

'Daddy . . . we're going to make you a grandfather.'

Silence.

'Did you hear me, Daddy?'

Edgar smiled. 'I heard.'

'Aren't you glad?'

He lifted his hand feebly. 'Could you . . . show me?'

'She's so small.' DeDe stood up, taking his hand, pressing it gently against her belly. 'I don't think you can feel . . .'

'No. I can feel her. You think it's a girl, huh?'

'Yes.'

'So do I. Have you picked out a name yet?'

'No. Not yet.'

'Name her Anna, will you?'

'Anna?'

'I've . . . always liked that name.'

Smiling again, he kept his hand pressed against the warm new life. 'Hello, Anna,' he said. 'How the hell are you?'

The Golden Gate

Bundled up against the wind, Mary Ann and Michael set out across the bridge on New Year's Day.

'I've never done this,' she said.

'I can't believe it,' he grinned. 'There's something *you've* never done?'

'Lay off, Michael!'

He squeezed her arm. 'You've had a busy year, Lucrezia.'

'Michael, look! You can joke about it with me, but we've got to be very, very careful about . . .'

257

'You think I don't know what being an accomplice means?'

'I'm still so freaked out about it I could die!'

Michael leaned against the rail. 'Show me where it happened.'

She looked faintly annoyed, then nodded toward the cliffs. 'Over there. See where that buoy is? Right behind it.'

He pointed at the buoy. '*That* one?'

'Don't *point*, Michael!'

'Why?'

'Somebody'll see you.'

'Oh, please! The body hasn't even turned up yet.'

'But it *could*. It could turn up at any time.'

'So?'

'Well, it's possible that the police could think it was . . . foul play. And it's possible that some witness somewhere could identify me as the person who was with him at the museum. And . . . there are *lots* of things that could implicate me in . . .'

'I still don't see why the hell you just didn't report the accident. It *was* an accident, wasn't it?'

'Yes!'

He grinned. 'Just checking.'

'Michael . . . if I tell you something, will you *swear* on a stack of Bibles that you'll never, *ever* tell another living soul?'

'You think I'd cross you, baby? I've *seen* what you do to your enemies!'

'Forget it.'

'No, please! I promise. C'mon, tell me.'

She studied him sternly, then said, 'Norman wasn't *just* a pornographer, Michael.'

'Huh?'

'He was a private eye.'

'Jesus! How do you know?'

'He told me. Right before he fell. He also told me he was working on a big case that was going to make him a lot of money. It made me start to wonder about why he came to Barbary Lane in the first place, and why he would question me about . . . certain things.'

'Wow! Go on!'

'Well . . . when I got back to the house after . . . you know . . . I got his spare room key out of the basement again and went through his room again. And this time the child porn didn't stop me!'

Michael whistled. 'Nancy Drew, eat your heart out!'

'He had a huge file, Michael. And do you know what he was investigating?'

'What?'

'Mrs Madrigal.'

'What?'

'I couldn't believe it, either.'

'Well, what did it *say*?'

'I don't know.'

'Now *wait* a minute!'

'I burned it, Michael. I took it back to my room and burned it in a trash can. Why do you think I was late for the party?'

Down the Peninsula at Cypress Lawn Cemetery, a woman in a paisley turban climbed out of a battered automobile and trudged up the hillside to a new grave.

She stood there for a moment, humming to herself, then removed a joint from a tortoise-shell cigarette case and laid it gently on the grave.

'Have fun,' she smiled. 'It's Columbian.'

THE END

More Tales of the City

For Ken Maley

As the poets have mournfully sung,
Death takes the innocent young,
The rolling in money,
The screamingly funny,
And those who are very well hung.

W.H. AUDEN

Hearts and Flowers

The valentine was a handsome pastiche of Victorian cherubs, pressed flowers and red glitter. Mary Ann Singleton took one look at it and squealed delightedly.

'Mouse! It's magnificent. Where in the world did you find those precious little . . .'

'Open it.' He grinned.

She turned to the inside of the magazine-size card, revealing a message in Art Nouveau script: MY VALENTINES RESOLU-TIONS. Underneath were ten numbered spaces.

'See,' said Michael, 'you're supposed to fill it in yourself.'

Mary Ann leaned over and pecked him on the cheek. 'I'm that screwed up, huh?'

'You bet. I don't waste time with well-adjusted people. Wanna see *my* list?'

'Aren't you mixing this up with New Year's?'

'Nah. That's nickel-dime stuff. Smoking-eating-drinking resolutions. These are the – you know – the hardcore, maybe-this-time, kiss-today-goodbye, some-enchanted-evening resolutions.'

He reached into the pocket of his Pendleton and handed her a sheet of paper:

MICHAEL TOLLIVER'S DIRTY THIRTY FOR '77

1. I will not call anyone nellie or butch, unless that is his name.
2. I will not assume that women who like me are fag hags.
3. I will stop expecting to meet Jan-Michael Vincent at the tubs.
4. I will inhale poppers only through the mouth.
5. I will not spend more than half an hour in the shower at the Y.
6. I will stop trying to figure out what color my handkerchief would be if I wore one.
7. I will buy a drink for a Fifties Queen sometime.

8. I will not persist in hoping that attractive men will turn out to be brainless and boring.
9. I will sign my real name at The Glory Holes.
10. I will ease back into religion by attending concerts at Grace Cathedral.
11. I will not cruise at Grace Cathedral.
12. I will not vote for *anyone* for Empress.
13. I will make friends with a straight man.
14. I will not make fun of the way he walks.
15. I will not tell him about Alexander the Great, Walt Whitman or Leonardo da Vinci.
16. I will not vote for politicians who use the term 'Gay Community.'
17. I will not cry when Mary Tyler Moore goes off the air.
18. I will not measure it, no matter who asks.
19. I will not hide the A-200.
20. I will not buy a Lacoste shirt, a Marimekko pillow, a secondhand letterman's jacket, an All-American Boy T-shirt, a razor blade necklace or a denim accessory of any kind.
21. I will learn to eat alone and like it.
22. I will not fantasize about firemen.
23. I will not tell anyone at home that I just haven't found the right girl yet.
24. I will wear a suit on Castro Street and feel comfortable about it.
25. I will not do impressions of Bette Davis, Tallulah Bankhead, Mae West or Paul Lynde.
26. I will not eat more than one It's-It in a single evening.
27. I will find myself acceptable.
28. I will meet somebody nice, away from a bar or the tubs or a roller-skating rink, and I will fall hopelessly but conventionally in love.
29. But I won't say I love you before he does.
30. The hell I won't.

Mary Ann put down the paper and looked at Michael. 'You've got thirty resolutions. How come you only gave me ten?'

He grinned. 'Things aren't so tough for you.'

'Is that right, Mr Gay Chauvinist Pig!'

She attacked the valentine with a Flair, filling in the first four blanks. 'Try *that* for starters!'

1. I will meet Mr Right this year.
2. He won't be married.
3. He won't be gay.
4. He won't be a child pornographer.

'I see,' said Michael, smiling slyly. 'Moving back to Cleveland, huh?'

Fresh Start

She was *not* moving back to Cleveland. She was not running home to Mommy and Daddy. She knew that much, anyway. For all her trials, she loved it here in San Francisco, and she loved her makeshift family at Mrs Madrigal's comfy old apartment house on Barbary Lane.

So what if she was still a secretary?

So what if she had not met Mr Right . . . or even Mr Adequate?

So what if Norman Neal Williams, the one semi-romance of her first six months in the city, had turned out to be a private eye moonlighting as a child pornographer who eventually fell to his death off a seaside cliff on Christmas Eve?

And so what if she had never worked up the nerve to tell anyone but Mouse about Norman's death?

As Mouse would say: 'Almost *anything* beats the fuck out of Cleveland!'

Mouse, she realized, had become her best friend. He and his spacy-but-sweet roommate, Mona Ramsey, had been Mary Ann's mentors and sidekicks throughout her sometimes glorious, sometimes harrowing initiation into the netherworld of San Francisco.

Even Brian Hawkins, an oversexed waiter whose advances had once annoyed Mary Ann, had lately begun to make clumsy yet endearing overtures of friendship.

This was *home* now – this crumbling, ivy-entwined relic called 28 Barbary Lane – and the only parental figure in Mary Ann's day-to-day existence was Anna Madrigal, a landlady whose fey charm and eccentric ways were legendary on Russian Hill.

Mrs Madrigal was the true mother of them all. She would counsel them, scold them and listen unflinchingly to their tales of amatory disaster. When all else failed (and even when it didn't), she would reward her 'children' by taping joints of home-grown grass to the doors of their apartments.

Mary Ann had learned to smoke grass like a seasoned head. Recently, in fact, she had given serious thought to the idea of smoking on her lunch hour at Halcyon Communications. Such was the agony she suffered under the new regime of Beauchamp Day, the brash young socialite who had assumed the presidency of the ad agency upon the death of his father-in-law, Edgar Halcyon.

Mary Ann had loved Mr Halcyon a great deal.

And two weeks after his untimely passing (on Christmas Eve), she learned how much he had loved *her*.

'You stay put,' she told Michael gleefully. 'I've got a valentine for *you*!'

She disappeared into the bedroom, emerging several seconds later with an envelope. Mary Ann's name was scrawled on the front in an assertive hand. The message inside was also hand written:

> Dear Mary Ann,
> By now, you must need a little
> fun. The enclosed is for you
> and a friend. Head for some
> place sunny. And don't let
> that little bastard give you any trouble.
>
> Always,
> EH

'I don't get it,' said Michael. 'Who's EH? And what was in the envelope?'

Mary Ann was about to burst. 'Five thousand dollars, Mouse! From my old boss, Mr Halcyon! His lawyer gave it to me last month.'

'And this "little bastard"?'

Mary Ann smiled. 'My *new* boss, Beauchamp Day. Mouse, look: I've got two tickets for a cruise to Mexico on the *Pacific Princess*. Would you like to go with me?'

Michael stared at her, slack-mouthed. 'You're shittin' me?'

'No.' She giggled.

'Goddamn!'

'You'll go?'

'Will I *go*? When? How long?'

268

'In a week – for eleven days. We'd have to share a cabin, Mouse.'

Michael leaped to his feet and flung his arms around her. 'Hell, we'll seduce people in *shifts*!'

'Or find a nice bisexual.'

'Mary Ann! I'm shocked!'

'Oh, *good*!'

Michael lifted her off the floor, 'We'll get brown as a goddamn berry, and find you a lover –'

'And one for you.'

He dropped her. 'One miracle at a time, please.'

'Now, Mouse, don't be negative.'

'Just realistic.' He was still stinging from a brief affairette with Dr Jon Fielding, a handsome blond gynecologist who had eliminated Michael as lover material when he discovered him participating in the jockey shorts dance contest at The Endup.

'Look,' said Mary Ann evenly, 'if *I* think you're really attractive, there must be plenty of men in *this* town who feel the same way.'

'Yeah,' said Michael ruefully. 'Size queens.'

'Oh, don't be silly!'

Sometimes Michael was sensitive about the dumbest things. He's at least five nine, thought Mary Ann. That's tall enough for anybody.

Widow's Weeds

Frannie Halcyon was an absolute wreck. Eight weeks after the death of her husband, she still dragged around their cavernous old house in Hillsborough, wondering bleakly if it was finally time to apply for her real estate license.

Oh, God, how life had changed!

She was rising later now, sometimes as late as noon, in the futile hope that a shorter day might somehow seem fuller. Her languorous morning coffees on the terrace were a thing of the past, a defunct ritual that had failed her as surely and swiftly as Edgar's diseased kidneys had failed her.

Now she made do with a languorous afternoon Mai Tai.

Sometimes, of course, she drew a glimmer of comfort from the knowledge that she was soon to be a grandmother. *Twice* a grandmother, actually. Her daughter DeDe – the wife of Halcyon

Communications' new president, Beauchamp Day – was about to give birth to twins.

That had been the latest report from Dr Jon Fielding, DeDe's charming young gynecologist.

DeDe, however, begrudged her mother the simple indulgence of even *discussing* her new heirs. She was downright sullen on the subject, Frannie observed. And that struck the matriarch as very strange indeed.

'And why *can't* I dote a little, DeDe?'

'Because you're *using* it, Mother.'

'Oh, piffle!'

'You're using it as an excuse to – I don't know – an excuse to keep from living your own life again.'

'I'm half a person, DeDe.'

'Daddy's *gone*, Mother. You've got to get it together.'

'Then let me start shopping for the babies. There's a *precious* place called Bebe Pierrot in Ghirardelli Square, and I'm sure I could –'

'We don't even know their sexes yet.'

'Yellow would be darling, then.'

DeDe frowned. 'I *loathe* yellow.'

'You love yellow. You've always loved yellow. DeDe, darling, what *is* the matter?'

'*Nothing.*'

'You can't lie to me, DeDe.'

'Mother, please . . . can't we just . . . ?'

'I have to feel needed, darling. Can't you see that? No one needs me anymore.' The matriarch began to sniffle.

DeDe reached out and took her hand. 'The deYoung needs you. The Legion of Honor needs you.'

Frannie smiled bitterly. 'So that's how it goes, then. When you're young, it's your family that needs you. When you're old, it's museums.'

DeDe rolled her eyes in exasperation. 'Look, if you're determined to wallow in self-pity, there's not a damn thing I can do about it. It's just such *waste*, that's all.'

Frannie's eyes were full of tears now. 'What in God's name do you expect me to do?'

'I expect you . . .' DeDe softened her tone to one of daughterly concern. 'I expect you to start being good to yourself again. Live it up a little. Join a backgammon club. Enroll in Janet Sassoon's exercise class. Get Kevin Matthews to take you to the symphony, for heaven's sake! His boyfriend is on Hydra until June.'

'I know you're right, but I —'

'Look at yourself, Mother! You've got the money . . . you ought to be taking tucks in everywhere!'

'DeDe!' Her daughter's impertinence overwhelmed her.

'Well, I mean it! Why not, for God's sake? Face, boobies, fanny — the full catastrophe! What in the world have you got to lose?'

'I simply don't think it's very dignified for a woman of my —'

'Dignified? Mother, have you seen Mabel Sussman lately? Her face is as smooth as a baby's fanny! Shugie says she found this marvelous man in Geneva who did it all with hypnosis!'

Frannie blinked in disbelief. 'There had to be *some* sort of surgery.'

'Nope. All hypnosis — or so Shugie *swears* on a stack of *Town and Countrys.*' DeDe giggled wickedly. 'Wouldn't you just *die* if one of these days somebody clapped their hands or said the secret word or something and the whole damn thing fell like a soufflé!'

Frannie couldn't help but laugh.

And later that afternoon, feeling curiously clandestine, she drove into town to wander through F.A.O. Schwarz in search of a Steiff creature for the twins.

She felt better now, so she toyed with the idea that maybe DeDe was right. Maybe she *had* moped too long, longer than was healthy, longer than Edgar himself would have wanted.

As she left the store, she caught her reflection in the window of Mark Cross. She stopped in her tracks long enough to grasp the flesh under her ears and pull it tight across her cheekbones.

'All right,' she said out loud. 'All *right!*'

Sisters with a Secret

Mona Ramsey's life was — in her own words — down to the seeds and stems.

Once a $25,000 a year copywriter for Halcyon Communications, she had been relieved of that position following a brief, but satisfying, feminist tirade against the president of Adorable Pantyhose, the ad agency's biggest client.

Her subsequent days of leisure as Michael Tolliver's roommate had been pleasant on a superficial level, but in the long run, emotionally unfulfilling. It was *permanence* she craved. Or so she had told herself when she moved out of 28 Barbary Lane to take up residence in D'orothea Wilson's elegant Victorian house in Pacific Heights.

D'orothea was a Halcyon model, perhaps the highest-paid black model on the West Coast. She and Mona had once been lovers in New York. Their San Francisco arrangement, however, had been devoid of passion, a bloodless pact designed to alleviate the loneliness that had begun to engulf both women.

It hadn't worked out.

For one thing, Mona never quite forgave D'orothea for not being black. (Her skin color, Mona learned eventually, had been artificially induced by pigment-altering pills and ultraviolet treatments, a ruse that had rescued the model from professional obscurity.) For another, she had come to grips, however grumpily, with the fact that she missed the company of men.

'I'm a shitty heterosexual,' she had told Michael when she returned to the nest at Barbary Lane, 'but I'm a shittier dyke.'

Michael had understood. 'I could have told you *that*, Babycakes!'

Her last Quaalude had begun to take effect as Mona climbed the rickety wooden stairway leading up to the lane. She had spent all evening at the Cosmic Light Fellowship, but her mood was blacker than ever. She simply wasn't *centered* anymore.

What had happened to her? Why was she losing her grip? When did she first peer up from the dark, wretched pit of her life and see that the walls were unscalable?

And *why* hadn't she bought more Quaaludes?

She moved groggily through the leafy canyon of the lane, then crossed the courtyard of number 28 and entered the brown-shingled building. She rang Mrs Madrigal's buzzer, hoping that a glass of sherry and a few mellow words from the landlady might somehow banish her bummer.

Mrs Madrigal, she realized, was a special ally. And Mona was not just one of the landlady's 'children.' Mona was the only person in the apartment house whom Mrs Madrigal had actively recruited as a tenant.

And she was — she believed — the only one who knew Mrs Madrigal's secret.

That knowledge, moreover, formed a mystical bond between the two women, an unspoken sisterhood that fed Mona's soul on the bleakest of days.

But Mrs Madrigal wasn't at home, so Mona trudged upstairs to her second-floor apartment.

Michael, as she had dreaded, was also gone. Upstairs, no doubt, planning his trip with Mary Ann. He spent a lot of time with Mary Ann these days.

The phone rang just as she flipped on the light. It was her mother, calling from Minneapolis. Mona slumped into a chair and made a major effort to sound together.

'Hi, Betty,' she said evenly. She had always called her mother Betty. Betty had insisted on it. Betty actually *resented* the fact that she was older than her daughter.

'Is this your . . . permanent number again?'

'Yeah.'

'I called the place in Pacific Heights. D'orothea said you'd moved back. I can't believe you'd leave that charming home in a nice neighborhood for that shabby –'

'You've never even seen it!' She's always in character, thought Mona. For Betty was a realtor, a hard-assed career woman whose husband had left her when Mona was still a baby. She didn't care much for buildings, without security guards and saunas.

'Yes I have,' snapped Betty. 'You sent me a picture last summer. Does that . . . woman still run it?'

'If you mean Mrs Madrigal, yes.'

'She gives me the absolute creeps.'

'Remind me not to send you any more pictures, will you?'

'What was wrong with D'orothea's place, anyway?' Betty, of course, didn't know about the shattered relationship. She seldom thought about relationships at all.

Mona hedged. 'I couldn't handle the rent.'

'Oh, well, if *that's* the problem, I can tide you over until you're able to –'

'No. I don't want your money.'

'Just until you're able to find a job, Mona.'

'Thank you, but no.'

'She's lured you in there, Mona!'

'*Who?*'

'That woman.'

Mona blew up. 'Mrs Madrigal *offered* me an apartment after we became good friends! And that was over three years ago! Why are you suddenly so goddamned concerned about my welfare?'

Betty hesitated. 'I . . . I didn't know what she *looked* like until you sent me –'

'Oh, come off it!'

'She's just so . . . extreme.'

If she only knew, thought Mona. If she only knew.

Down on the Roof

Brian Hawkins was thirty-three.

And *that*, he realized with a shudder as he shed his denim-and-corduroy Perry's uniform and flopped on the bed with an Oly, was as old as Jesus on Calvary.

Or the idiot in *The Sound and the Fury*.

He was treading water now. Nothing more. He was working to survive, to continue, to pay for his pork chops, and his beer and his goddamn Ivory Liquid. And no amount of laid-back, mellowed-out, half-assed Californian philosophizing could compensate for the emptiness he felt.

He was getting old. Alone.

Most of his mail still said 'Occupant.'

Once upon a time, of course, he had been a fiery young radical lawyer. Before that fire subsided (and relocated in his groin), he had fought the good fight for the cause of draft resisters in Toronto, blacks in Chicago, Indians in Arizona, and Mexican-Americans in Los Angeles.

Now he was waiting tables for WASPS in San Francisco.

And he loved 'chasing pussy' almost as much as he had once loved hating Nixon.

He pursued this tarnished grail through fern bars and coed bathhouses, laundromats and supermarkets and all-night junk-food restaurants, where the pickings were slim but the gratification was almost instant. There was little time to waste, he told himself. Menopause was just around the corner.

If he needed something lasting – and sometimes he felt that he did

– he never stayed with anyone long enough to let that need be visible. His logic was circular but invincible: The kind of woman he wanted could not possibly be interested in the kind of man he'd become.

His libido had taken charge of everything.

It had even governed the selection of this latest apartment, this drafty, cramped little house on the roof of 28 Barbary Lane. Women, he had reasoned, would get off on its panoramic view and nursery-tale dimensions. It would work for him as an architectural aphrodisiac.

'Are you *sure* you want it?' Mrs Madrigal had asked when he requested a change of apartments. (At the time, he was living on the third floor, just across the hall from the foxy but hopelessly uptight Mary Ann Singleton.)

He had told her yes without hestiation.

The landlady's spookiness, he presumed, had to do with the apartment's former occupant, a fortyish vitamin salesman named Norman Neal Williams.

But all he knew about Williams was that he had disappeared without a trace in December.

A stiff wind shook the little house, giving Brian a morbid sense of déjà vu.

Five on the Richter, he thought.

He knew what that meant now, for he'd felt his first earthquake only the week before. A deep, demonic growling had awakened him at 2 A.M., rattling his windows and reducing him instantly to a frightened, primeval creature.

But this was only the wind, and the crunch of the Big One would be just as horrendous on the third floor as it would be on the roof. Or so he had told himself as soon as the little house became his.

His door buzzer startled him. Pulling on a sweat shirt, he opened the door in his boxer shorts. It was Mary Ann Singleton.

'Brian, I . . . I'm really sorry to bother you this late.' The shorts had obviously flustered her.

'That's OK.'

'You're not dressed. I'll get somebody else.'

'No problem. I can throw on some pants.'

'Really, Brian, I don't need –'

'Look! I said I'd help, didn't I?'

275

His tone jarred her. She managed a faint smile. 'Michael and I are going to Mexico. There's a suitcase that I can't quite –'

'Hang on a second.'

He pulled on a pair of Levi's and led the way down the stairs to her apartment. He dislodged the suitcase she needed from the top shelf of her closet. 'Thanks,' she smiled. 'I can make it from here.'

His eyes locked on her. 'Can you?'

'Yes, Brian.' Her inflection was firm and faintly school teacherish. She knew what he had meant, and she was saying no. Again.

Back on the roof, he shucked the Levi's and picked up the binoculars he kept on the shelf by the bed. Facing the cottage's south window, he cursed the impenetrable Miss Singleton as he scanned the midnight cityscape.

First the green-black enigma of Lafayette Park, then the Maytag agitator of the ultramodern St Mary's Cathedral, then the Mark's obscenely oversized American flag, flailing against the inky sky like a Bircher's acid trip.

All of which was foreplay.

His real quarry was something he called the Superman Building.

Father of the Year

For the first time in weeks, DeDe rose before Beauchamp.

She greeted her husband with a kiss and a croissant when he stumbled into the kitchen at seven forty-five. She was chirpy for that time of the morning – excessively chirpy – so Beauchamp instinctively grew wary.

He leaned against the butcher-block countertop, rubbing his eyes. 'League meeting, or something?'

'Can I fix breakfast for my husband?'

'You can,' he said dryly, nibbling tentatively at the croissant, 'but you don't.'

DeDe thrust two shallots in the Cuisinart. 'We're having omelets. And some of those marvelous French sausages from Marcel & Henri.' She smiled faintly 'I . . . worry about things too much, Beauchamp, and today I . . . well, I heard those silly parrots in the eucalyptus tree outside the window, and I just thought . . . well, we're a lot luckier than most people.'

He massaged his temples, still trying to wake up. 'I *hate* those fucking parrots.'

DeDe simply stared at him.

He turned away and began to fiddle with the Mr Coffee machine. Her face was positively *suffused* with that idiotic, imploring look she used to make him feel guilty. He refused to deal with it this early in the morning.

'Beauchamp?'

He kept his back to her. 'This goddamn thing hasn't been cleaned in at least –'

'Beauchamp! Look at me!'

He turned very slowly, keeping a thin smile plastered on his face. 'Yes, my sweet?'

'Will you at least tell me . . . you're happy?'

'About what?'

She laid her hands on her swollen belly. 'About *this*, dammit!'

Silence.

She stood firm. 'Well?'

'I'm delirious.'

She moaned melodramatically and turned away from him.

'DeDe . . . there are grave responsibilities attached to parenthood.' He kept his voice calm. 'I've accepted the responsibility of raising *one* child, but with great reluctance. Forgive me, won't you, if I'm not exactly jumping for joy at the prospect of –'

'Oh, shut up!'

'There you go. Being witty again.'

'I don't need your goddamn thesis on parenthood. I need your *support*. I can't do this alone, Beauchamp. I just *can't*!'

He smirked and motioned toward her belly. 'You sure as hell didn't do *that* alone.'

'No,' she replied instantly, 'but I sure as hell didn't do it with *you*!'

They stood there over the Cuisinart, eyes locked and fangs bared. Beauchamp broke the silence with a short sardonic laugh, then slammed the counter with the flat of his hand and sank down into a Marcel Breuer chair.

'That wasn't bad, actually. For you.'

'Beauchamp . . .'

'There are *better* ways to get my attention, but all in all it wasn't half bad.'

'It's true, Beauchamp! You're *not* the father!'

Silence.

'Dammit, Beauchamp! Can't you even *add*? Look . . .' Her voice began to waver. She pulled a chair up next to him and sat down. 'I wanted to tell you a long time ago. I really did. I even considered –'

'*Who?*' he said coldly.

'I don't think we should –'

'Splinter Riley, maybe? Or how about the charming but terminally greasy Jorge Montoya-Corona?'

'You don't know him, Beauchamp.'

'How *interesting*. Do you?'

She burst into tears and ran from the kitchen. He knew she would lock herself in the bedroom and sulk until he had left the building. Then she would fill her quivering palm with dozens of multicolored tablets and down them in a single gulp.

In a time of crisis, she could never resist her M & M's.

When Beauchamp arrived at Jackson Square, Mary Ann Singleton handed him his messages.

'Also, D'orothea Wilson called about five minutes ago.'

That was all. Not Mr Day. Not even Beauchamp. He didn't have a goddamn name since this *fluffball* had become his secretary.

Beauchamp grunted. 'I don't suppose she bothered to tell you why she didn't show for that Adorable shooting at The Icehouse? She's canceled three shootings this month alone.'

'She says she doesn't . . . look right anymore.'

'What the hell does *that* mean?'

The secretary shrugged. 'Maybe she gained weight over the holidays or –'

'Or maybe she just doesn't give a good goddamn about Halcyon Communications! Maybe she wants to go to *Mexico*!' The barb stung his secretary exactly the way he hoped it would.

Her fingers began mangling a paper clip. 'Beauchamp . . . it was Mr Halcyon who wanted me to –'

'I don't need to hear this again.' He stormed into his office and slammed the door.

Then he raged in silence against the Halcyon family.

Letter from Mama

Dear Mikey,

Your Papa and I were so glad to hear about your trip to Mexico with Mary Ann. I know it will be a lot of fun for both of you. Please send us a postcard when you get a chance, and remember not to drink too much tequila. Ha ha.

Orlando has been real cold this winter, but I expect you heard all about that on Walter Cronkite. The grove down by the Bledsoes' new split-level was hurt the worst. Some of the oranges were frozen clear through. Papa says that's OK, though, because we can sell them for juice. I'm doing my best to help Papa, but you know how he is around harvest time. Just kidding.

Papa says not to worry because we're getting about $3.50 a box, and anyway overall production is up, even with the freeze and all. The only problem now is with the homosexuals.

I guess you don't know about that. It all started when the Dade County Commission passed a law in favor of homosexuals. It said you can't refuse to hire homosexuals or rent to them, and Anita Bryant spoke out against this, being a Christian mother of four and Miss America runner-up and all, and all the normal, God-fearing people in Miami backed her up 100 percent.

We didn't think too much about it, of course, because we don't have near as many homosexuals up here as they do in Miami. Papa says they like the ocean. Anyway, pretty soon this organized group of homosexuals tried to force the Citrus Commission to take Anita Bryant's commercials off TV. Can you imagine? Anita said go right ahead, if that was what she had to do to make it safe for her children to walk the streets of Miami. God bless her.

I wouldn't know so much about this, except that Etta Norris (Bubba's mother) stopped by Tuesday to watch Oral Roberts on our new color set, and she said she was signing up folks in Orlando to support Anita Bryant's group, Save Our Children, Inc. I signed right away, but Papa said he wouldn't sign because you were a grown man and no son of his needed saving from any homosexuals. I said it was the principle, and what if the homosexuals stopped drinking orange juice? He said most homosexuals didn't drink orange juice, but he signed anyway.

We had our first meeting last night in the VFW room at Fruitland Bowl-a-Rama. Etta said the important thing was to show Anita Bryant that we support her. She also said we should put in something about how we aren't prejudiced but we believe that homosexuals aren't good examples for children in school. Lolly Newton said she thought the teacher part was important too, because if the teacher is standing up there being sissy all day, the pupils are bound to turn out sissy too. Ralph Taggart seconded the motion.

Your father kept telling me to hush up and don't be a damn fool, but you know me, I had to put in my two cents worth. I stood up and said I thought we should all get down on our knees and thank the Lord that someone as famous as Anita Bryant had stepped forward to battle the forces of Sodom and Gomorrah. Etta said we should put that in the resolution, so I felt real proud.

Reverend Harker said maybe we shouldn't say anything about the rental part, because Lucy McNeil rents the room over her garage to that sissy man who sells carpets at Dixie Dell Mall. Lolly said that was OK because Lucy had done it of her own free will, and besides, it was easier when you could tell they were homosexual. That way you could warn your children.

I guess I sound like a real crusader, don't I? I hope you don't think your old Mama's being a foolish idealist. I just believe the Lord made us all to carry out His Holy Word.

I saw Bubba at Etta's this morning. He's such a nice young man. Goodness! I can hardly believe it's been over eight years since you and him used to go camping at Cedar Creek. He asked after you. He's teaching history at the high school now and still isn't married yet, but I guess it's mighty hard to find the right girl these days.

Blackie didn't like the freeze much and just lays around the house looking tired. I'm afraid we might have to put him to sleep. He's awful old.

Take care of yourself, Mikey. We love you very much.

Mama.

P.S. If you need reading for your trip, I recommend Anita Bryant's autobiography. It's called 'Mine Eyes Have Seen the Glory.'

The Getaway

On the eve of their Mexican cruise, Mary Ann and Michael huddled conspiratorially over their suitcases. 'Maybe,' grinned Michael, 'if we rolled it up in some Kleenex and stuffed it in your bra . . .'

'That's not funny, Mouse.'

'Well, look: we don't have to take it off the ship. It's not like we'll be smoking it on the street in Acapulco. Hell, we won't even see a customs agent until we get back to LA.'

Mary Ann sighed and sat down on the edge of the bed. 'I used to be a Future Homemaker of America, Mouse.'

'So?'

'So now I'm smuggling dope into Mexico.'

'And travelling with' – he lowered his voice to a sinister basso – 'a known homosexual.'

She smiled faintly. 'That too.'

He stared at her for a moment to determine exactly how seriously she had taken him. There were times, even now, when his irony came perilously close to describing the way she felt about things. She winked at him, however, so he continued packing.

'I love that expression,' he said, without looking up.

'What?'

'"Known homosexual." I mean, you *never* hear about known Southern Baptists, do you? Or known insurance salesmen. And when you're not a known homosexual, you're an *admitted* one. "Mr Farquar, an admitted stockbroker, was found stabbed to death in Golden Gate Park early this –'

'Mouse, you're giving me the creeps!'

'Sorry.'

She reached over and squeezed his hand. 'I didn't mean to bark at you. It's just . . . well, I'm still a little jumpy about dead people, that's all.'

He started to say, 'I can dig it,' but thought better of it. Instead, he held on to her hand and reassured her for the third or fourth time, that week. 'It'll get better, Babycakes. It's only been two months.'

Her eyes became moist. 'You don't think we're . . . escaping or anything?'

'From what?'

She brushed a tear from her eye, shrugged and suggested feebly: 'The law?'

'You haven't *broken* any law, Mary Ann.'

'I didn't report his death.'

He fought to be patient with her. They had hashed this out so many times before that the conversation had become ritual. 'That guy,' said Michael softly, 'was a certified prick. He was a child pornographer, for Christ's sake. You didn't *push* him off that cliff, Mary Ann. His death was an accident. Besides, if you had reported his death, you would have been obligated to tell the police that he was investigating Mrs Madrigal. And we *both* love Mrs Madrigal too much for that, no matter *what* was in that file.'

The very mention of the file made Mary Ann shudder. 'I never should have burned it, Mouse.'

So Michael ran through *that* again. Burning the file, he told her, had been Mary Ann's most intelligent move. By destroying the private eye's dossier on Mrs Madrigal, Mary Ann had scored a twofold triumph: She had kept herself from being privy to information she might have been obligated to pass along to the police. And she kept the file out of the hands of the police.

The police had turned up at 28 Barbary Lane as soon as Mrs Madrigal had reported her tenant missing. Their investigation appeared to have been routine and short-lived. Norman Neal Williams had been a transient, they learned, an itinerant vitamin salesman with no known relatives. His involvement in the child-porn racket surfaced immediately, though Mary Ann feigned ignorance of it.

She had 'gone out with him' several times, she told police. She hadn't known him well. He had seemed 'a little weird' to her at times. And yes, it seemed possible he had moved to another town.

When the police had gone, Mary Ann had summoned Michael to her apartment, where they pondered the real mysteries of this terrible chapter in her life.

Did the police know that Norman Neal Williams had been a private eye?

Did Mrs Madrigal know that she had been the subject of Williams' investigation?

Would Williams' body turn up in the bay?

And why would anyone want to investigate a woman as warm and compassionate and . . . harmless as Anna Madrigal?'

Mexico, of course, *was* an escape, but not the sort that Mary Ann had meant. Depression and morbidity had settled into her bones like mildew. She would *bake* it out, she decided, reverting to her adolescent solution for everything.

She tucked a bottle of Coppertone into a side pocket of her American Tourister. 'You know what?' she said, her voice ringing with pep-rally optimism.

'What?'

'This trip is gonna work for me. I'm gonna meet somebody, Mouse. I know it.'

'A man, you mean?'

'Not that you aren't the best company in the world, Mouse, but I really –'

'Look, you don't have to explain *that* one. I've got this dynamite plan, anyway. I spot a guy, right? Lounging out by the ship's pool, maybe, or . . . whatever, and I saunter up kind of casual like, with you on my arm all tanned and gorgeous, so that he's *bound* to be eating his heart out, and then I say in my very *butchest* Lee Majors voice, "Hi, guy, I'm Michael Tolliver and this is Mary Ann Singleton. Which one of us would you like?"'

Mary Ann giggled. 'What if he doesn't want either of us?'

'Then,' said Michael matter-of-factly, 'you push him off the first available cliff in Acapulco.'

Mona Flees

After Mona had driven Mary Ann and Michael to the airport, she returned to Barbary Lane and fell into a cosmic funk.

She felt grossly disorientated, partially because of her mother's weird phone call, and partially because two of her friends had managed to break the bonds of this incestuous backwater Babylon called San Francisco.

That was what she needed, really. Fresh territory. Blue skies. Communion with the Eternal. A chance to restructure her life into something that would bring her the inner tranquillity she so desperately wanted.

She mapped out a plan of action in less than ten minutes, leaving a terse note on Mrs Madrigal's door:

> Mrs M,
> I'll be gone for a while.
> Please don't worry. I
> need to breathe.
> Love,
> Mona

She made *her* escape by cable car, irked by the bitter irony of it all. Wouldn't Tony Bennett be tickled to know that Mona Ramsey, aging freak and transcendental cynic, had been forced to flee Everybody's Favorite City on one of these cloyingly cute tourist trolleys?

At Powell and Market she disembarked, separating herself from the double-knit masses as soon as possible. She strode up Market to Seventh, and stopped with a sigh in front of the Greyhound bus station.

After three minutes' consideration, she bought a ticket to Reno, deciding on the spot that sun and sky and desert might somehow offer new horizons. The bus, they told her, would leave shortly after midnight.

For the rest of the afternoon she sat in Union Square, where the drunks and derelicts and burned-out hippies could only reinforce her decision to leave. Then, as soon as night fell, she smoked a potent mixture of grass and angel dust and drifted back to the bus station.

She was eating a cheese sandwich, when a garishly painted crone – eighty if a day – tried to make conversation with her in the snack bar.

'Where ya headin', dolly?'

'Reno,' she said quietly.

'One stop after me. You takin' the midnight bus?'

Mona nodded, wondering if the angel dust had made this woman more grotesque than she really was.

'How 'bout sitting with me, then? I get real nervous on the bus, what with the perverts and all?'

'Well, I'm not sure I'd be much –'

'I won't bother you none. I won't say nothin' unless you want me to.'

Something about that touched Mona. 'Sure,' she said finally. 'It's a deal.'

The old woman grinned. 'What's your name, dolly?'

'Mo . . . Judy.'

'Mine's Mother Mucca.'

'Mother . . . ?'

'Mucca. It's a kind of nickname. I'm from Winnemucca, see?' She cackled gleefully. 'It's a long story, and I don't see no point in . . . Say, dolly, are you O K?'

'Yes.'

'You look kinda fucked up.'

'What?' A terrible sea roar was resounding in her head, as if someone had lashed a giant conch shell to her ear.

'I said you looked fucked up. Your eyes are all . . . You ain't been smokin' no reefers have you, dolly?'

Mona nodded. 'Sort of.'

'Meanin'?'

'I don't think you'd –'

'Somethin' in it?'

'Ever heard of angel dust?'

Mother Mucca's hand came down on the counter so hard that several sleepy diners looked up from their coffee. 'Holy shit! That stuff is for puttin' elephants to sleep, girl! If you don't know any better than to fuck yourself up with an animal tranquilizer, you ain't got no business ridin' –'

Mona lurched to her feet. 'I don't have to sit here and listen –'

A bangled talon of a hand clamped onto her wrist and pulled her back down.

'The fuck you don't!' shrieked Mother Mucca.

Animal Magnetism

'Some people drink to forget,' said Mrs Madrigal, basking in the sun of her courtyard. 'Personally, I smoke to remember.' She took a toke of her new Colombian and handed the joint to Brian.

'Like what?' he asked.

'Oh . . . old lovers, train rides, the taste of fountain Cokes when I was a kid. Grass is a lovely, sentimental . . . *Reader's Digest* kind of a thing. I can't understand why the bourgeoisie doesn't approve of it.'

Brian smiled, stretching his legs out on the beach towel. 'You've been smoking long?'

'Not by my standards. Oh, I think . . . since you were a teenager, probably.'

'That's not long.'

She smiled. 'I thought you might say that.'

'Do you remember the first time?'

'No. I remember the third time, though.'

'The first time didn't work?'

'No. It worked.' She chuckled. 'Don't you hate people who say that?' She mimicked the voice of a middle-aged matron. 'The children *insisted* I smoke pot, so I tried it, Madge, and it didn't do a *thing* for me, not one thing.'

Brian laughed. 'Sometimes it's true, though. My first time didn't work.'

'So?' The landlady shrugged. 'Your first time at sex doesn't *work*. It's still the first time, though. Isn't that enough?'

'I guess so.'

'There's nothing that beats the high of a first time. *Nothing.*'

'Something tells me you've had a lot of first times.'

'I try to. And you're changing the subject.'

'Sorry. I'm ripped.'

'I was going to tell you about my third time.'

'Oh, right.'

'The third time,' said Mrs Madrigal, adjusting the sleeves of her kimono, 'happened at the San Francisco Zoo just after Bobby Kennedy was killed.'

'Bummer, huh?'

'No . . . I mean, I didn't get stoned because of that. He had just been killed, that's all. Anyway, I knew this lovely little man at the zoo who was in charge of the monkeys. Actually, that's the wrong term. He was more like *one of* the monkeys. He had rather long arms and he was quite hairy and the monkeys simply *adored* him. I adored him too. He was a marvelous backgammon player.

'Well, on this particular day, we had a nice long chat in this funny causeway thing that led from the gorilla quarters to the cage where the gorillas go to diddle with themselves in public –'

Brian chuckled.

Mrs Madrigal raised an eyebrow. 'Well, isn't that what zoos are for? Why else do people watch gorillas?'

'I see what you mean.'

'So there we were, standing in this causeway, chatting pleasantly, when this rather formidable-looking lady gorilla strolled up and joined our little group. She stood next to my zookeeper friend and flung an arm across his shoulder, like an old school chum or something. They my friend said, "Oh, I almost forgot," and pulled a joint out of his shirt pocket. He lit the joint, took a toke off it and handed it to the gorilla –'

'C'mon!'

'So help me god! And *then*, if you please, the gorilla took a long hit and handed the joint to me!'

'Jesus. What did you do?'

'I am not *rude*, dear boy. I accepted it graciously, without Bogarting, and passed it back to my friend. The gorilla stayed for two more hits, then promenaded down the causeway to greet her public. She was a very mellow lady by then.'

'She did this all the time?'

'Everyday. It helped her cope, I suppose.'

'Is she still there?'

Mrs Madrigal tapped a forefinger against pursed lips. 'You know, I'm not really sure. I often wonder if she's still alive. Gorillas can live to be quite old, I understand. I'd rather like to see her again.'

'Why?'

'Oh . . . I guess, because we have a lot in common. She was a tough old cookie, and she had fun the best way she knew how. And . . . because she learned a lot late in life.'

'So what have you learned?'

She smiled at him reprovingly. 'I've learned how snoopy you get when you're loaded.'

'I wasn't asking for your life story.'

'What a pity. You should sometime. But not when *I'm* loaded.'

'Why?'

'Because, dear . . . I *might* tell you the truth.'

The Kindest Cut

Emma was getting old, Frannie noted wistfully, as the rail-thin black maid tottered into the master bedroom with a breakfast tray in her hands.

'Open the drapes, Miss Frances?'

Miss Frances! That was what made Emma an absolute gem, the last of her species. As long as she had worked at Halcyon Hill, it had been Miss Frances, Miss DeDe, Mr Edgar . . .

'No, thank you, Emma. Just leave the tray on the table, please.'

'Yes'm.'

'Emma?'

'Ma'am?'

'Do you think I'm . . . Sit down, will you, please, Emma?'

Emma complied, perching delicately on the edge of a button-tufted lady chair near the bed. 'You aren't . . . sick, Miss Frances?'

'No . . .'

'Mr Edgar's gone, Miss Frances. You gotta live with that now. He's passed on to the bosom of Jesus, and there's not a livin' thing in this whole blessed world that can bring him back until the final judgment of the Lord delivers His people from –'

Frannie cut her off with a jingle of the bedside bell. 'Emma, dear . . . you're giving me a headache.'

'Yes'm.'

'Now, what I'd like to know is . . . Emma, I trust your opinion a great deal. I think you know that, and . . . Do you think I need a face-lift, Emma?'

Silence.

'You *do* know what a face-lift is, Emma?'

The maid nodded sullenly. 'Cuttin'.'

'No . . . well, yes, that's part of it, but it's a complete cosmetic process that's really quite common these days. I mean, *lots* of ladies –'

'White ladies.'

'Don't be impertinent, Emma.'

A quarter century of faithful employment at Halcyon Hill entitled Emma to the scowl with which she now confronted her mistress.

'Miss Frances, the Lord gave you a perfectly fine face, and if the Lord had intended for –'

'Oh, poo, Emma! The Lord doesn't have to go to Opera Guild meetings!'

'Ma'am?'

'I'm so *old*, Emma. And everybody I know looks like . . . Nancy Kissinger! I'm nothing but an old turkey gobbler!' She pinched the flesh along her cheekbone. 'Look at that, Emma!'

Emma's expression was dour. 'Mr Edgar wouldn't like that kind of talk.'

Frannie rolled over in bed and pushed out her lower lip. 'Mr Edgar is dead,' she said dully.

When Emma was doing the laundry, Frannie locked the bedroom door and phoned Vita Keating. The furtiveness of this act made her realize that, even at fifty-nine, she was not an adult. She had always been answerable to *someone*.

Edgar, however, was gone now; Emma was all she had left.

Vita, thought Frannie, had never known that kind of emotional servitude. Vita was a trailblazer, a vigorous independent whose nineteen-fifty-something Miss Oklahoma title had spurred her on to runner-up stardom in Atlantic City and a Republican husband in San Francisco.

A hostess of impeccable credentials, Vita sometimes shocked her stuffier peers by shattering long-established social traditions in the city: She was, after all, the *first* socially registered localite to pair denim place mats with Waterford crystal. And she did the cutest things with bandannas.

Who else but Vita had the panache to show up at the Cerebral Palsy Ball wearing a gingham granny dress and twirling a lasso? She was *such* fun.

Naturally, she laughed heartily when Frannie blurted out her request.

'My face man? God, honey, for all I know, he's bottling sheep semen in Switzerland. His last patient was a *total* washout – some poor woman in Santa Barbara who ended up looking like the Phantom of the Opera.'

Frannie couldn't hide her disappointment. 'I see,' she said glumly.

'Have you thought about the shots,' chirped Vita.

'The shots?'

'The sheep semen, honey.'

'Vita!'

'Well, *I* couldn't agree with you more, but Kitty Cipriani says it's made her a new woman. Personally, I think someone's pulling the wool over her eyes!' Vita roared with laughter, and Frannie, despite her ever-blackening mood, joined in with her.

Finally, Vita said abruptly, 'How old are you, Frannie?'

The question stung more than it might normally have. Vita was Frannie's junior by at least fifteen years. 'I'm asking for a reason,' Vita added apologetically.

'Fifity-four,' said Frannie.

'Oh. Too bad.'

'Don't rub it in, Vita.'

'No, honey. I mean, it would help if you were sixty.'

'Why on God's green earth would that help?'

Vita chuckled throatily. 'I won't tell you unless you tell me your real age!'

Frannie hesitated for a moment and then told her.

'Ooh, boy,' said Vita. 'Ooooh, *boy*!'

'Vita, what in the world are . . . ?'

'Just you wait, Frannie Halcyon! Just you wait!'

The Cruise Begins

The agonies of last-minute packing, a lingering cold and a nerve-jangling PSA flight to Los Angeles all but disappeared when Mary caught her first glimpse of the *Pacific Princess*.

'Oh, Mouse! It's so *white*!'

Michael poked the flesh of his forearm. 'We'll blend right in, won't we?'

Mary Ann didn't answer, lost in the majesty of the huge, moonlit ship. There was something scary yet exhilarating about this moment. She felt like a skydiver, hurtling recklessly through space, knowing that *this* time would matter, this time was real, this time her chute had to open.

The cabdriver looked over his shoulder at the couple in the back seat. 'You folks married?'

'Shacked up,' said Michael, provoking the expected glare from Mary Ann.

'Well.' The driver chuckled. 'I guess you seen *The Love Boat*?'

Michael nodded. 'Movie for TV, right?'

'Yeah. Bert Convy. Lyle Waggoner. Celeste Holm . . .'

'All the biggies.'

The driver nodded. 'Filmed it right there. On the *Pacific Princess*. Pretty sexy stuff.'

'Mmm. I remember,' said Michael, smirking privately at Mary Ann. 'Celeste Holm was a plump but lovable matron who thought she was washed up with men, until she met Craig Stevens on the cruise. Craig had been her boyfriend years before, and Celeste . . . well, the poor thing was *petrified* that Craig would find out what a chubbette she'd become.'

'Did he?' asked Mary Ann.

'Nope. Happy ending. Craig turned out to be blind.'

'You made that up, Mouse.'

'Scout's honor! And they were *married* at the end. Isn't that right driver?'

'Yep.'

'Apparently,' shrugged Michael, 'ol' Craig couldn't *feel* either.'

The ship's photographer surprised them on the gangplank, shouting out a jovial, 'Smile, young lovers!'

Michael obliged and clamped his hand over Mary Ann's right breast.

'Christ!' he said, as they boarded the ship. 'Is this a cruise or a senior prom?'

'Mouse, would you try to be just a *little* respectable?'

'For eleven whole days?'

'It's a *British* ship, Mouse.'

'Ah, yes! But with *Italian* stewards.' He held his forefingers erect, several feet apart.

Mary Ann flushed, then giggled. '*Straight* Italian stewards,' she corrected him.

'You *wish*,' said Michael.

Their stateroom was on the Promenade Deck, deluxe accommodation with twin beds, wood-grain cabinetry, comfortable chairs, and a tub in the bathroom. A bottle of chilled champagne awaited them.

Mary Ann proposed the first toast. 'To Mr Halcyon. God bless Mr Halcyon.'

'Right on. God bless Mr Halcyon.'

'And' – she filled their glasses again – 'to . . . to adventure on the high seas!'

'And romance.'

'And romance!'

'To Mrs Madrigal . . . and marijuana . . . and the munchies . . . and to every goddamn person in Florida except Anita Bryant!'

'Yeah!'

'But most of all,' said Michael, turning mock-grave suddenly, 'to that well-bred, debonaire, but incredibly hunky number who gave the eye to *one* of us when we came on board tonight.'

'Where? Who?'

'How do I know who? I just got here, woman. You *saw* him, didn't you?'

'I don't think so.'

Michael rolled his eyes in exasperation. 'He never stopped staring at us!'

'A passenger?'

'Yep.'

'Looking at *us*?'

'You got it, girl.'

Mary Ann bit the tip of her forefinger. 'Do you think he was blind?'

Michael whooped and raised his glass. 'OK, then . . . to blindness!'

'To blindness,' echoed Mary Ann.

Mother Mucca's Proposition

Mona woke from an uneasy sleep when the Greyhound pulled into Truckee, California, just before dawn. She was sure her tongue had turned into a dead gopher. The bizarre old woman next to her patted her hand.

'This ain't it, dolly. Go back to sleep.'

It? What was It? Where was It?

'It's OK, dolly. Mother Mucca's here. I'm lookin' for ya.'

'Look, lady, I –'

'Mother Mucca.'

'OK. I appreciate your help, but –'

'That angel dust'll fuck you up every time. You shoulda heard yourself talkin' in your sleep, dolly!'

'I don't . . . what did I say?'

'I don't know. Crazy stuff. Somethin' about mice.'

'*Mice?*'

'Somethin' like that. Somethin' like: "Where did the mouse go? I can't find the mouse." Then you started hollerin' for your daddy. It was goddamn spooky, dolly.'

Mona rubbed her eyes and watched the zombie-faced passengers shuffle out for coffee in the Truckee station. They looked like haggard infantrymen bracing for a predawn assault.

What in the name of Buddha was she doing here?

When Mother Mucca insisted on buying breakfast, Mona was too weak to refuse. Besides, the old biddy seemed kind of together, even if she *did* look like a refugee from a Fellini movie.

'I had a girl named Judy once.'

'What?'

'You said your name was Judy, didn't you?'

Mona nodded, opting to remain as anonymous as possible. She'd had all she could take of Mona Ramsey.

'Judy was a peach,' continued Mother Mucca. 'I guess she stayed with me longer'n any of 'em.' She shook her head, smiling, lost in rosy recollection. 'Yessir, she was a peach!'

Mona found herself warming to her. 'You had lots of children?'

'*Children?*' She spat the word.

'You said . . .'

Mother Mucca began to cackle again. 'You're a lot dumber'n you look, dolly. I'm talkin' about the best damn whorehouse in Winnemucca!'

Mona was jarred, but instantly fascinated. Of course! A genuine Nevada madam! A rawboned relic of the West's first group encounter enterprise!

'You . . . ? How long have you . . . ?'

'Oh, Lord, dolly. Too fuckin' long!'

They both laughed exuberantly, sharing the same emotion for the first time since they'd met. Mona found herself riveted by the sheer, unembarrassed ballsiness of this extraordinarily ugly old woman.

'What brought you to San Francisco?' she asked.

'Hookers union meeting. Coyote.'

Mona nodded knowledgeably. One of the cardinal earmarks of North Beach Chic was an unflinching familiarity with Margo St James and her prostitutes' union.

'You know Margo?' asked Mother Mucca.

'Oh, yes,' lied Mona. She had, however, *seen* the woman several times, breakfasting on coffee and croissants at Malvina's.

Mother Mucca arched a painted eyebrow. 'She's a lot classier'n me, huh, dolly?'

'I think you're very classy.'

Mother Mucca ducked her head and blew into her coffee.

'I do,' Mona persisted. 'Really. You're a very . . . together person.'

'You're a damn liar, too.' She reached over suddenly and squeezed Mona's arm above the elbow. For a moment, it seemed that her crusty veneer might crack, but then she cleared her throat abruptly and continued in a tone that was tougher than ever.

'Well, dolly! You ain't told me why you're headin' to Reno with a head full o' angel dust!'

'There's nothing special about Reno.'

The old woman snorted. 'You're right about *that*!'

Mona laughed. 'I just wanted – I don't know – to get away for a while. I've never seen the desert.'

'We got plenty o' that in Winnemucca.'

Mona looked down at her hash browns, avoiding what seemed to be an invitation of sorts.

'It's a big place, dolly. I need some help with the phones. It's real clean and pretty too. I think you'd be kinda surprised.'

'I'm sure it's a nice –'

'Hell, dolly! I'm not white-slavin' ya or anything! You'll keep me company, that's all. You can leave whenever you want to.'

'I just don't think I'm –'

'What do you do, anyway?'

'What?'

'For a livin'.'

'I'm . . . I used to be an advertising copywriter.'

Mother Mucca roared. 'Well, don't be so fuckin' uppity, then!'

Mona grinned and dropped her napkin on her plate. 'The bus is leaving, Mother Mucca.'

'You won't do it, then?'

'Nope,' said Mona, chewing on the knuckle of her forefinger. 'Not unless I can have my own waterbed.'

294

Life Among the A-Gays

For the Hampton-Giddes, the mechanics of party-giving were as intricate as the workings of Arch Gidde's new Silver Shadow Rolls.

After careful scrutiny, prospective guests were divided into four lists:

The A List.

The B List.

The A-Gay List.

The B-Gay List.

The Hampton-Giddes knew no C people, gay or otherwise.

As a rule, the A List was comprised of the Beautiful and the Entrenched, the kind of people who might be asked about their favorite junk-food or slumming spot in Merla Zellerbach's column in the *Chronicle.*

There was, of course, a sprinkling of A-Gays on the A List, but they were expected to behave themselves. An A-Gay who turned campy during after-dinner A List charades would find himself banished, posthaste, to the purgatory of the B-Gays.

The B-Gays, poor wretches, didn't even get to *play* charades.

The range and intensity of cocktail chatter at the Hampton-Giddes' depended largely on the list being utilized.

A List people could talk about the arts, politics and the suede walls in the master bedroom.

B Listers could talk about the arts, politics, the suede walls in the master bedroom, and the people on the A List.

The A-Gays could talk about whoever was tooting coke in the bathroom.

The B-Gays, being largely decorative, were not expected to talk.

'Binky *swears* it's the truth,' said William Deveraux Hill III, on a night when the Hampton-Giddes' Seacliff mansion was virtually swarming with A-Gays.

'*Chinese?*' hissed Charles Hillary Lord.

'Twins!'

'A *litter!*' exclaimed Archibald Anson Gidde, butting in.

'I can't *stand* it!'

'*You* can't? Honey, Miss Gidde over there practically *ruined* her nails on the Princess phone this morning, just spreading the news.'

'I did *not*.' The host was indignant.

'You told *me*.'

'Well, that was all.'

'Stoker says you told him too.'

'She lies!'

Charles Hillary Lord needed more dish. 'Christ, Billy, an *Ornamental*? DeDe's been doing it with an *Ornamental*?'

'They have *teeny* pee-pees.' This from Archibald Anson Gidde.

'I think you're *all* disgustingly prejudiced,' said Anthony Latimer Hughes, joining the group.

'Oh, Mary! You're *not* having another *Chinoiserie* period, are you, darling?' Gidde again.

'There are two things one should know about San Francisco,' interjected Charles Hillary Lord. 'Never meet *anyone* at the Top of the Mark. And never walk through Chinatown in the rain.'

'Why?' chorused everyone.

'Because they're so *short*. Their umbrellas will blind a white man!'

Across the room huddling under the Claes Oldenburg, Edward Paxton Stoker, Jr, swapped pleasantries with his host, Richard Evan Hampton.

'I wish,' said the guest, 'that Jon Fielding were here.'

'Oh, pullease!' Rick Hampton had never fully recovered from the fall soiree at which Jon Fielding had suddenly exploded, exiting in a terrible huff. 'You won't find that bitch on any guest list of *mine*, Edward.'

'But he *is* DeDe's gynecologist, and I'm sure he –'

'*And* an Occasional Piece for Beauchamp.'

'Not any more he isn't.'

'*Really*?'

'The doctor, as we *all* know he is wont to do, got *very* sanctimonious all of a sudden and gave our Beauchamp the old heave-ho. Beauchamp was *livid*.'

'I'd love to hear Fielding's version of it!'

'You'll have to wait a while, I'm afraid. He's on the way to Acapulco.'

'What on earth for?'

'What else? A gynecologists' convention.'

The richer – and older – half of the Hampton-Giddes rolled his eyes laboriously. 'Acapulco has gotten *so* tacky these days.'

Fantasy on the Fantail

Somewhere off the coast of Mexico, a dazzling midday sun found dozens of willing worshippers on the fantail of the *Pacific Princess*. Mary Ann was on her stomach – her bikini top untied – when an unannounced hand glopped something gooey on her back.

'Mouse?'

Silence.

'Mouse!'

'I do not know thees Mouse, signorina. I am but a seemple Italian dining room steward who wants to make ze whoopee weez zee beyootiful, horny American girls!'

'You smoked that joint, didn't you?'

Michael sat down next to her and sighed dramatically. 'I *wish* you'd learn to fantasize.'

'What is that stuff, anyway?'

'What stuff? Oh . . . tortuga cream. The room steward gave it to me. He says they make it in Mazatlán.'

'It smells yummy.'

'Uh huh. Ground-up turtles.'

'Mouse!'

'Well, that's what he *said.*'

'Ick!'

'What the hell do you think Polly Bergen uses? Rose petals?'

Mary Ann sat up, blinking into the sun, holding her bikini top in place with her right arm.

'Tie me up, will you?'

'Bondage *already*? You haven't tried bingo yet. And there's a swell seniors mambo class this afternoon in the Carrousel Lounge, if you'd care to –'

'Mouse . . . don't look now, but he just dove into the pool.'

'Who?'

'Our Mystery Man. The guy you saw when we were boarding.'

'The one who was cruising us?'

Mary Ann corrected him. 'One of us.'

'Maybe he's into three-ways.'

'Mouse, do you think he's gay?'

'Well . . . his backstroke *is* a little nellie.'

'Mouse, I'm serious.'

'Then *ask* him, dummy! Invite him over for a Pina Colada!'

Mary Ann turned and studied the strong white body thrashing through the green water of the pool. He was a strawberry blond, she noticed, and he shook his head like a wet collie when he surfaced at the ladder.

She looked back at Michael. 'You don't think I'll do it, do you?'

Michael just grinned at her, maddeningly.

'OK. Just watch me!'

The wet collie was stretched out on a towel at the pool's edge. Mary Ann approached as casually as possible, her eyes fixed on the surface of the water. Her intent was to look vigorous and liberated, like Candice Bergen out for a swim after a rough day of photographing the African wilds.

The collie looked up and smiled. 'The only way to do it is to close your eyes and jump.'

'Is it cold?' Mary Ann asked.

Not too swift. Very un-Candy Bergen.

'Go ahead,' he urged. 'You can take it.'

She shrugged her shoulders and mugged, hoping it wasn't too late to try for a Marlo Thomas effect. A tolerant smile spread over the collie's face when she held her breath and jumped.

It was a funny little hatbox of a pool, not really wide enough for swimming laps. The cold ocean water was invigorating, but impossible to take for long. Shivering, she reached for the ladder.

The collie extended his hand. 'The goose bumps are very becoming.'

'Thanks,' she said, smiling.

'Will you join me for a drink? You and your husband, that is.'

'My . . . ? Oh, that's not my . . .' She turned and looked at Michael, who was smirking at her. He gave his imitation of Queen Elizabeth's royal wave. 'Michael's just a friend.'

'That's nice,' said the collie.

For whom? thought Mary Ann. Me or Michael?

*

The collie introduced himself to both of them. His name was Burke Andrew. He was traveling alone on the cruise. He shook Michael's hand firmly and excused himself to get the drinks.

'Well,' said Mary Ann. 'Is he?'

'How the hell should I know? There hasn't been a secret queer handshake since 1956.'

'He's gorgeous, isn't he?'

Michael shrugged. 'If you like big thighs.'

Staring out to sea, Mary Ann sighed. 'I think he likes me, Mouse. Help me figure out what's wrong with him.'

The Superman Building

The irony, thought Brian, as he dragged back to Barbary Lane at midnight, was that he could have gone home with her.

Easily.

She had practically *drooled* on him, for Christ's sake, jammed up against him there in the brutal, nuclear glare of Henry Africa's Tiffany lamps. He could've bagged her without batting an eye.

So why *hadn't* he? What perverse new quirk of his personality had prompted him to sabotage a sure thing and scuttle his butt back to his little house on the roof?

The scene in the bar had gone like this:

'I still can't get over Freddie Prinze.'

It figures, he thought. A Farrah Fawcett-Majors fright wig. A Bernadette Peters pout. She gets her material from the tube. In a minute, she'll be talking about *Roots*.

'I mean, he was so *young*, and . . . well, even if he *was* taking drugs and all, I don't see why that would depress him enough to . . . God, it's just such a *bummer* . . . and he was doing so much for the Chicano people.'

Brian didn't look up from his beer. 'He was Puerto Rican,' he pointed out.

'Besides, cocaine isn't supposed to . . . He was?'

'Yep.'

'I had a Puerto Rican roommate once. I got her through the Ethnic Studies Program at college.'

He sipped his Oly, poker-faced. 'She work out?'

'It was really educational.'

'Good.'

'Her name was Cecilia.'

'Nice name.'

'Cecilia Lopez.'

'Mmm. I sent off for a spider monkey once when I was eleven or twelve.'

'I'm sorry. I don't . . .'

'Those things in the back of comic books. Darling Pet Monkey. Fits in a Teacup . . .'

'But what does that . . . ?'

'Her name was Cecilia too.'

'Oh.'

'She was dead when I got her. All packed up in her little crate. It nearly killed me.'

'How awful! Was . . . whose fault was it?'

'Nobody's really.'

She nodded solemnly.

'It was . . . suicide!'

She looked at him morosely.

'Drugs,' he explained. 'And she was so *young*.'

She reached out to lay her hand on his, but he rose abruptly and slapped some money on the bar.

'I'm sorry,' he said. 'I'm too depressed to fuck tonight.'

The Superman Building was a towering Deco apartment house at the corner of Green and Leavenworth. Brian loved it because it reminded him of the Daily Planet building in the old television series.

Able to leap tall buildings in a single bound . . .

He also loved it because it afforded him a kind of power that sometimes bordered on the erotic.

Tonight, as he shucked his Levi's and rugby shirt, he noted that there were still six or eight lights burning in the Superman Building.

He lifted his binoculars and studied the sixth floor for several minutes, concentrating on a large corner apartment. A dumpy-looking woman with short hair and a red sweater moved sluggishly from room to room, plumping pillows.

At midnight?

A lover arriving? Not likely. An early departure in the morning?

Maybe, but what guest could be *that* important? It was probably a simple case of boredom. Boredom or nervousness . . . or insanity.

Bored himself, he shifted his gaze to the – what – eighth floor? There, against a well-lighted window, a thin, balding man was lifting his foot slowly to meet his outstretched arm.

The movement seemed too expressive for exercise, too erratic for dance. Some sort of martial art, maybe . . . or maybe the whole goddamn building was full of loonies.

If he wasn't careful, he'd start making up names for these people. Like Jimmy Stewart did in *Rear Window*.

A light came on.

He raised his binoculars again and zeroed in on an eleventh floor room that was suffused with a dim, rosy light. Seconds later, a woman appeared.

She stood near the window in a long gown of some sort, a dark form against the fleshy warmth of her room. She was motionless for a moment, then her hands went down to her waist and up again suddenly to her face.

She was wearing binoculars.

And she was looking at Brian.

The House

At dawn the desert around Winnemucca was gray and jagged-looking, as if built from shattered concrete, fragments perhaps of a pre-Columbian freeway.

Or so it seemed to Mona from the window of the battered Ford Ranchero that bore her swiftly and unceremoniously from the bus station to a place called the Blue Moon Lodge.

'Well, that's her,' bellowed Mother Mucca, nodding through the windshield to the one-storey stucco building squatting in the distance.

'Nice,' said Mona.

'Yep,' said Mother Mucca.

'You had it long?'

'Sixty years long enough for ya?'

Mona whistled.

The octogenarian emitted a gravelly chuckle. 'Mother Mucca is an *old* motherfucker!'

Before Mona could muster a comment about the Young in Heart, the Ranchero swung abruptly into a dusty parking lot adjacent to the brothel. Mother Mucca leaned on the horn.

'Now where the hell is Bobbi?'

An aluminum door banged open, revealing a nervous-looking blond woman in her mid-twenties. She was wearing cut-off Levi's and a pink Qiana blouse knotted at the waist. Hobbling slightly, she ran out to meet the car.

'Welcome back,' she beamed.

'What the hell happened to your feet?'

'Nothin'.'

Mother Mucca climbed out of the Ranchero, scowling like a cigar store Indian. 'Nothin', huh?'

'Mother Mucca, I didn't let him –'

'Now you listen to me, dolly! If you turn one more trick with the crazy-ass Elko shitkicker, I'll boot your ass outa here so fast you'll wish you never . . . You ain't broke nothin', have ya?'

Bobbi shook her head.

'Fetch the bags, then. This here's Judy.' She jerked her head toward Mona. 'Judy's gonna stay and work the phones for a few days.'

The two young women nodded to each other.

'Give her Tanya's room,' said Mother Mucca, mellowing a little now. 'But take out the swing first.'

Their first stop was the kitchen, where Mother Mucca swilled half a quart of milk and toasted Pop-Tarts for the two of them.

'She's a sweet little thing, ain't she?'

'Who?'

'Bobbi.'

'Oh . . . yes. She seems very nice.'

'Fucked up, though. Loco as they come. You gotta watch her like a mother hen. Hell, when I found that dolly she'd sunk plumb to the bottom. She couldn't go no lower.'

Mona shook her head sympathetically. 'Heavy drugs?'

'Nope. Worse. Key punch operator.'

Mona's room looked out on the desert, the last of a series of rooms opening, motel-style, on a common sidewalk.

Her furnishings consisted of a bed (neither water nor brass), a green vinyl butterfly chair, a Formica-topped night stand, and an Eisenhower-era vanity displaying, among other things, an Autograph Hound (Tanya's?), a plastic fern and an Avon cologne bottle shaped like a stage-coach.

Mona was face down on the bed – wondering whether a week in a whorehouse would seriously screw up your karma – when Bobbi entered the room.

'Knock, knock,' she said sweetly.

Mona rolled over, rubbing her eyes. 'Oh . . . hi.'

'I brought you some towels.'

'Thanks.'

'You settled in now?'

'Yeah. Thanks, Bobbi.'

She smiled. 'Sure, Judy.'

Mona returned the smile, feeling an odd sense of communion with this simple creature.

'You'll like Mother Mucca,' said Bobbi softly. 'She talks real mean, but she's not that way at all. She loves us all like daughters.'

'I guess she never had any of her own, huh?'

'No. No daughters. She had a son once.'

'What happened to him?'

'He ran away, they say. When he was a teenager. A long time ago.'

Land Ho!

Breakfast on the *Pacific Princess*. The Aloha Deck dining room was humming with sun-flushed passengers, eager for their first glimpse of Puerto Vallarta. Mary Ann made her entrance without Michael, who was still showering.

'Well,' boomed Arnold Littlefield, dousing his scrambled eggs with ketchup, 'the hubby stood you up, huh?'

Arnold and his wife, Melba, shared a table with Mary Ann and Michael. The Littlefields were fortyish and always wore matching clothes. Today, in deference to their destination, they were sporting identical Mexican flour sacks outfits. They were from Dublin. Dublin, California.

'He always takes longer than I do,' said Mary Ann breezily, as she sat down. It was easier, by far, to pass off Michael as her husband than to explain what Michael called 'our bizarre but weird relationship.'

'Right on,' said Melba, with a mouthful of bacon. 'Men are much fussier than girls.'

Mary Ann nodded, grateful that Michael wasn't around to comment on *that* one.

She ordered a huge breakfast, then remembered Burke Andrew and canceled the waffles. She was downing her orange juice when Michael appeared, looking spirited and squeaky clean.

He was wearing Adidas, Levi's and a white T-shirt emblazoned with a can of Crisco.

'Apologies, apologies.' He grinned, nodding toward the Littlefields as he sat down.

'No sweat,' said Arnold. 'You better keep an eye on the little lady, though.' He winked at Mary Ann. 'She's too pretty to be let out without a leash.'

'Arnold!' That was Melba.

'Well, Mike knows that. Don't you, Mike?'

'Can't let her out of my sight for a minute.'

Melba elbowed her husband. 'You don't ever say that about *me*, Arnold!'

'Well, these kids are younger than us and you remember how it was when . . . Say, Mike, how long you been with Crisco?'

'What?' Michael had been cruising a waiter at the next table.

'Your shirt. You affiliated with Crisco?'

Mary Ann thought of crawling into her oatmeal.

'Yeah,' Michael answered soberly. 'I've been . . . in Crisco – oh, I don't know – four, five years.'

'Sales?'

'No. Public relations.'

'Mouse . . .'

Michael winked at Arnold. 'The little woman doesn't like me to talk business at the table.'

'Right on,' said Melba, siding with Mary Ann. 'Arnold talks about aluminium honeycomb until he's blue in the face. And it's *so* boring!'

'It may be boring to you, Melba, but it's not boring to *some* people, not if that's the way they choose to make their living! You don't think Crisco is boring, do you, Mike?'

'Hell, no,' said Michael assertively.

*

From the Promenade Deck, the white sands and palm trees of Puerto Vallarta seemed almost within reach. Mary Ann leaned against the rail and watched the taxi drivers and serape salesmen who had already begun to swarm across the landing.

'Where shall we go, Mouse?'

'I don't know. Down the beach, I guess.'

'We don't have any Mexican money.'

'The purser said they'll take . . . Hang on. Here he comes!'

'Who?'

'The mysterious but hunky Mr Andrews.'

Mary Ann wheeled around to see the strawberry blond striding down the deck toward her. 'It's *Andrew*,' she corrected Michael quickly. 'No *s*.'

Michael shrugged. 'His *s* looks fine to me.'

Mary Ann missed the joke; Burke Andrew was beaming at her. 'I've been looking for you two,' he said.

Both of us? thought Mary Ann.

Baby Talk

Even three Scotches at the University Club couldn't take Beauchamp's mind off the letter he carried in the breast pocket of his Brioni.

'Well,' said Peter Cipriani, joining the young executive on the terrace, 'so life *isn't* a cabaret, old chum?'

Beauchamp scowled. 'Not even *half* the time.'

'It could be worse.'

'How?'

'You could be *me, mon petit*. You could be doomed to dinner tonight at Langston's house.'

Beauchamp glanced at him ruefully over the rim of his glass. 'What's on the menu tonight? Antique pheasant?'

'Worse – oh, worse!'

'Victorian venison?'

Peter shook his head soberly. 'The rumor – God help us – is Edwardian elk! Heaven *knows* how long that creature's been in his freezer. Miss Langston hasn't felled an elk since the late sixties!'

What a pisser, thought Beauchamp bitterly as he rode the elevator to his Telegraph Hill penthouse. Other people's problems were laughable next to his.

DeDe was in the library, curled up on the camel-back sofa with a copy of Rosemary Rogers' *Sweet Savage Love*. Her free hand was partially submerged in a cloisonné bowl of M & M's. Beauchamp glared at her from the doorway.

'Behold! The Total Woman!'

'I've had a long day, Beauchamp.'

He dropped his attaché case and headed for the bar. 'I'll bet you have.'

'What the hell's that supposed to mean?'

He kept his back to her as he filled a shot glass with J & B. 'It must be *murder* finding a super jumbo bag of M & M's. You drive all the way to Woolworth's?'

'Very funny.'

'If *fat* amuses you, go right ahead and yuck.'

'May I remind you I'm carrying *two* babies!'

'I know,' he said, downing his Scotch. 'Plain and Peanut.'

Dinner that evening was cold quiche and salad. They ate in glacial silence, avoiding each other's eyes, waiting petulantly for the moment they both knew would come.

'We have to talk,' Beauchamp said finally.

'About what?'

'You know goddamn well about what!'

'Beauchamp . . . I'm tired of talking about it. I don't blame you for being upset. I really don't. But I'm having these babies and I can't take this . . . harassment anymore.' She looked him squarely in the eyes. 'I've thought about this a long time. I've decided to move to Mother's.'

'Brilliant. Just brilliant.'

'I don't know whether it's brilliant or not, but at least I'll be –'

'Look, goddammit! You've got some explaining to do. You're not running home to Mommy until I get a few answers.' He fumbled in his pocket for the letter, thrusting it into her hands. 'This charming anonymous missive came to me at the office today!'

DeDe's hands shook as she removed a sheet of notebook paper from the envelope. The message, printed in yellow with a felt-tip pen, consisted of eight words:

WHY DON'T YOU NAME THEM YIN AND YANG?

'Now,' said Beauchamp ominously, 'will you please tell me what the hell that means?'

DeDe stared at the horrible note for several seconds, stalling for time, commanding herself to stay calm. The cycle, she realized, was complete. From her best friend Binky, to Carson Callas the gossip columnist, to the city at large, the ignominious truth had spread. She was bearing the children of a Telephone Hill grocery boy!

She laid the letter on the table, face down. 'That's disgusting,' she said quietly.

'Answer the question, DeDe.'

'Beauchamp, please . . .'

He was poised like a cobra.

'Oh, fuck it, Beauchamp! The babies' father is Chinese!'

The Landlady's Lesson

When he had finished his shift at Perry's, Brian went straight home to Barbary Lane. Mrs Madrigal was perched on a stepladder in the hallway, replacing a light bulb. Up there, in her sixty-watt aura, she shone like a B-movie madonna about to descend on an unsuspecting French village.

'Welcome to Manderley,' she mugged. 'I'm Mrs Danvers. I'm sure you'll be very happy here.'

Brian laughed. 'Feeling gothic tonight?'

'My dear! Aren't you? This place is a veritable *tomb*, what with Mary Ann and Michael in Mexico and Mona God knows *where* – and you out there terrorizing half the female population.'

'I was working.'

'Mmm. It *is* work, isn't it?'

He bridled at her teasing, but let it go. She had cast him as the aging Don Juan of her Barbary Lane family, and the label seemed as apt as any at this point. 'Well,' he sighed, 'I guess I'd better go confront my kitchen sink. It's beginning to grow penicillin, I think.'

'Brian?'

'Yeah?'

'Would you care to smoke a quick joint with an old lady?' Her huge blue eyes blinked at him unembarrassedly.

307

'Sure,' he smiled. 'I'll bring the joint, if you bring the old lady.'

Her apartment seemed fussier than ever, as if the doilies and tassels had taken to breeding in their unguarded moments. Still flanking the archway to the dining room were the two marble statues that had fascinated Brian on his very first visit to the landlady's home: a boy with a thorn in his foot and a woman with a water jug.

Mrs Madrigal sat on the ancient velvet sofa, curling her feet up under her kimono in a movement that seemed surprisingly girlish. She took a short toke off the joint and handed it to her tenant. 'So who is she, dear?'

'Who?'

'The creature who's driving my carefree boy to utter distraction.'

Brian held the smoke in his lungs for as long as possible. 'I think you've got the wrong carefree boy.'

'Have I?'

Her eyes were on him again, offering refuge.

'Mrs Madrigal, it's late and I don't feel like playing games.' His abruptness embarrassed him, so he laughed and added: 'Of course, if you *know* any . . . creatures, I could use another notch or two in my gun!'

'Brian, Brian . . . that isn't *you*, dear.'

He snapped at her. 'Would you just lay off with the –'

'I *worry* about you, dear. Hell, I know I'm a nosy old biddy, but look, I've got nothing better to do. I mean, if you ever want somebody just to *talk* to . . .' She leaned forward slightly and smiled like a stoned Mona Lisa. 'May I give you some unsolicited advice?'

He nodded, feeling more uncomfortable by the second.

'The next time you meet a girl – someone that you really like – pretend that you're a war hero and that all your basic plumbing got shot off in the war.'

Brian grinned incredulously. 'What?'

'I'm perfectly serious, dear. Don't tell a soul – especially *her*, for heaven's sake – but pretend to yourself that this dreadful thing has happened and the *only* way you can communicate your feelings is through your eyes, your heart.'

'And what if she wants to go home with me?'

'You *can't*, dear. You've lost your wee-wee, remember? All you can do is smile bravely and invite her to dinner the next night – or maybe a nice walk in the park. She'll accept, too. I promise she will.'

Brian took a long drag on the joint. 'So how long . . . ?' He exhaled in midsentence, making sure he maintained an expression of amused tolerance. 'How long am I supposed to keep pretending?'

'As long as possible. Until she asks you.'

'Asks me what?'

'If you were wounded in the war, of course.'

'And what do I tell her?'

'The truth, dear. That everything's intact. It'll be a *lovely* surprise for her.'

He folded his arms across his chest, and smiled at her.

'And,' she said, raising her forefinger, '*you'll* have a nice surprise too.'

'What?'

'You'll *know* the poor dear, Brian. And you might even *like* her by then.'

Minutes later, as he stood in the window of his little house on the roof, he marveled at how well Mrs Madrigal could read him, how swiftly she had detected 'the creature who's driving my carefree boy to utter distraction.'

Did it show on his face now? Did the pupils dilate from the sheer, loin-twitching force of the fantasy? What set of the jaw or tic of the eye betrayed the passion that had begun to consume him?

At two minutes before midnight he lifted his binoculars to his face and focused on the eleventh floor of the Superman Building.

She appeared, as he prayed she would, on the hour.

And he heard himself whimper when their binoculars locked in mid-air.

Bobbi

Exhausted by the drugs and the long bus ride, Mona crashed after breakfast at the Blue Moon Lodge. The broiling midday sun had already forced her to kick off the covers when Bobbi knocked on the door of her cinder-block cubicle.

'Knock-knock,' she said.

Mona groaned silently. How long would she be able to endure the puppy love of this sugar-coated tart?

'Hi Judy. Mother Mucca asked me to show you how the phones work.'

Arrggh. The phones. This was a job, wasn't it? She was paying her way on this acidless trip. Dragging herself into a semi-upright position, she leaned against the headboard and rubbed her eyes. 'Three minutes, OK?'

She staggered into the tiny bathroom and splashed water on her face. It would only be for a week, she reassured herself, and prostitution was legal in Nevada. Besides, if she ever decided to take up copywriting again, *this* gig would looking stunning on a résumé.

Two large metal hooks in the ceiling caught her eye as she left the bathroom.

'What's that for?' she asked Bobbi.

'What?'

'Those hooks.'

'Oh. This used to be Tanya's room.'

Gotcha. Thanks a helluva lot. 'Tanya did something with hooks?'

Bobbi giggled, as if Mona were a new kid on the block who didn't know the first thing about hopscotch. 'That's where she hung the swing.'

Should I ask about that? thought Mona. Yes. I'm a receptionist in a whorehouse. I should know about swings. 'The swing was part of . . . her routine?'

Bobbi nodded. 'Water sports. She was real famous for it.'

'You mean . . . ? I don't get it.'

'Oh, silly,' chirped Bobbi. 'She *tinkled* on them from up there. While she was swinging, see?'

'I think I saw her on *The Gong Show* once.'

'Huh?'

'Nothing. What happened to her, anyway?'

'Tanya? She switched to a house in Elko.'

'Was that good?'

Bobbi shrugged. 'For her, I guess. Mother Mucca was plenty pissed. But Tanya'll be back, probably. There aren't that many good houses in these parts. Elko, Winnemucca, Wells . . . that's about it.'

Mona suppressed a smirk. This dippy child who said tinkled when she meant pissed and pissed when she meant angry could still distinguish between a respectable and an unrespectable whorehouse. 'Where are the crummy ones?' Mona asked.

Bobbi pursed her lips thoughtfully, obviously delighted with her role as the Duncan Hines of whorehouses. 'Oh . . . Mina, I guess, and Eureka and Battle Mountain. Battle Mountain is definitely the pits. When a girl hits that circuit . . . well, she might as well hang it up.'

Bobbi's income, Mona learned, was about three hundred dollars a week. That was *after* Mother Mucca had taken her cut and Bobbi had paid her room and board.

All of the girls at the Blue Moon Lodge were required to work three weeks straight before taking a week off. The state saw to it that they were issued a work permit, fingerprinted, photographed and examined by a doctor prior to setting up shop – or swings.

The most profitable season, according to Bobbi, was summer, when transcontinental traffic on Interstate 80 was heavier, and a period between mid-September and mid-October, when deer hunters invaded the area.

In accordance with the Municipal Code of Winnemucca, the girls of the Blue Moon Lodge took turns in exercising their privilege to go into town for shopping, movies and medical attention.

There was also a law that forbade a woman from working in a Winnemucca brothel if a member of her family resided in the county.

'C'mon,' bubbled Bobbi, as soon as Mona pulled herself together.' I wanna show you something neat.'

Mona braced herself for the abomination. A rubber room, perhaps? A mirrored ceiling? A sex-crazed donkey? A crotchless Naugahyde wet suit by Frederick's of Hollywood?

Bobbi led the way out of the cubicle into the sunshine. The warm desert air made Mona acutely aware of the original purpose of her escape from Francisco. Communion with Nature. Harmony with the Elements.

But no . . . oh no. That was not Buddha's Design.

Buddha, for some goddamn reason, wanted her to have a room with hooks in the ceiling.

Their destination was Bobbi's cubicle, a space identical to Mona's, three doors closer to the main building. Bobbi swung open the door with a flourish.

'Over there,' she exclaimed, 'on the shelf above the bed.'

Mona's jaw went slack.

'Dolls of All Nations,' said Bobbi. 'I've been collecting since I was twelve.'

'They're . . . very nice,' said Mona.

The child-whore beamed proudly. 'Their faces are really all the same, but . . . well, I guess you can't have everything.'

'No.'

'You can touch 'em if you want.'

Mona went to the shelf and pretended to examine one of the dolls. 'Very pretty,' she said quietly.

'You picked my favorite. Norway.'

'Yeah?'

'Do you think girls in Norway really have dresses like . . . ? Is something the matter, Judy?'

'No, I . . . I was just distracted for a minute.'

Moments later, Mona excused herself and returned to her own cubicle, where she locked herself in the bathroom and cried for a while.

Angel dust did that to her sometimes.

Day of the Iguana

Underneath a thatched umbrella at the Posada Vallarta, the unlikely threesome sipped Coco Locos and gazed out at the bluest of oceans.

'This is nice,' said Burke, stretching his arms above his head. 'I'm glad you two let me join you. I don't exactly . . . relate to most of the people on the ship.'

Michael grinned over the top of his coconut. 'You don't get off on blue rinse?'

'Blue what?'

'Old ladies,' translated Mary Ann.

'Oh.' He laughed warmly, looking first at Mary Ann, then at Michael. 'I guess I'm a little out of it, huh?'

Mary Ann shook her head. 'Mouse talks in code, Burke. Half the time, I don't have the slightest idea what he's talking about.'

'How long have you two . . . known each other?'

Michael glanced at Mary Ann. 'How long ago was the Safeway? Nine months? A year?'

'Yeah. I guess.'

'We met in a grocery store,' explained Michael. 'Mary Ann was trying to pick up my boyfriend.'

Burke blinked. 'You . . .'

'Gay as a goose,' said Michael. He stood up, smiling, adjusting his blue satin Rocky shorts. 'I'm gonna take a hike. I'll give you two exactly an hour to get it on.'

Mary Ann turned and watched Michael sprint recklessly to the surf. Her smile to Burke was amused and apologetic. 'I can't do anything with him,' she said.

'Apparently,' laughed Burke.

She laughed with him. 'I didn't mean it like *that*.'

'He seems very nice, actually.'

'He is. I love him a lot.'

'But he's not your . . .'

She shook her head, then giggled. 'He says he thinks of himself as my pimp service.' Her smile faded when she saw Burke's expression. 'Did that sound gross?'

'Not at all. I must . . . well, I've never met anybody like you two.'

Mary Ann pored over his face for a moment, assessing the firm jaw and the full mouth and the baffling naïveté of those wide-spaced gray eyes. Was anybody *that* innocent anymore?

'Where are you from, Burke?'

He looked back at her for a moment, then traced the rim of his coconut with his forefinger. 'All over, really.'

'Oh. Well, then, most recently.'

'Uh . . . San Francisco.'

'Great! So am I! Where do you live?'

'Actually, I'm from Nantucket. I mean, my parents live there now, and I'm staying with them. I used to live in San Francisco for a while, but I don't anymore.'

'Where did you stay when you were –'

He pushed his chair back abruptly. 'Would you like a swim or something? I feel like we should use that hour.'

She smiled at him. 'You're right. Let's go.'

They strolled up the beach in the direction of town, stopping occasionally to romp in the surf or gasp at the billowing parasails soaring through a cloudless sky. Burke took it all in with unembarrassed wonder, as gleefully open as a child catching his first glimpse of the sea.

313

He was gentle, Mary Ann observed, gentle in a primitive, manly sort of way. And manly without being macho. It was impossible to imagine him hustling Kelly Girls at Thomas Lord's. When a peddler appeared, draped in a hideous necklace of stuffed iguanas, Burke reached immediately for his wallet.

'Which one do you want?'

'Ick! You're not serious?'

'One of those shirts, then? With the embroidery?'

'Burke . . . you don't have to buy me anything.'

He wrinkled his brow solemnly. 'How will you remember me if you don't have an iguana?'

Smiling, she laid her hand on his back at the spot where a patch of golden hair peeped over the top of his swim trunks.

'I'll remember,' she said. 'Don't you worry about that.'

Desperate Straights

When DeDe Halcyon Day was ten years old, her parents sent her to camp at Huntington Lake. For six excruciating weeks, she hurt as only a fat child can hurt when forced to paddle canoes, stitch wallets and sing songs to the tune of 'O Tannenbaum.'

The end came as a merciful release, an escape from the tyranny of children into the comfortable, protective sanctuary of Halcyon Hill.

She felt something of that now, something of that ancient longing for home, as she packed her Gucci luggage and prepared herself mentally for Hillsborough.

She wanted Beauchamp behind her.

She wanted him to be like poison-oak and short-sheeted beds and pretty preteens who made jokes about Kotex.

She wanted him gone.

But Beauchamp persisted.

'This isn't doing a goddamn bit of good, you know!'

She ignored him, continuing to pack.

'OK. So you run home to Mommy. Then what? What the hell do you think people are gonna say when those babies are born?'

'I don't care what they say.'

'How very *au courant* of you!'

DeDe's voice remained calm. 'I want them, Beauchamp.'

'Do you think their father wants them? What the fuck's he gonna do, anyway? Strap 'em to the back of his delivery bike?'

'Leave him out of this.'

'Oh, heavens, yes! For Christ's sake don't offend his delicate Asian sensibilities. All *he* ever did was take an innocent ethnic poke up my –'

'Shut up, Beauchamp!'

He was snarling now. 'Why don't you just drop the Pearl Buck routine, Miss Tightass! You couldn't give a flying fuck about those babies and you know it!'

'That's not true.'

'Half your friends have had abortions, DeDe.'

'Not in the sixth month.'

'It's a simple salt injection. It's no more complicated than –'

'I don't want to talk about this anymore.'

He mimicked her tone. '"I don't want to talk about this anymore." Shit! Do you even give a rat's ass about all the humiliation you're going to put me through? Do you give a good goddamn about Halcyon Communications – your *own father's* business?' His voice lowered dramatically, becoming almost plaintive. 'Jesus, DeDe, we're up for the PU club this year.'

'You, Beauchamp. Not me.'

'It's the same goddamn thing.'

Looking up from her suitcase, she mustered a faint smile. 'Not anymore it isn't,' she said.

He glared at her murderously for several seconds, then slammed the bedroom door and stormed out of the house.

Hunched over his desk at Halcyon Communications, Beauchamp spent the rest of that Saturday afternoon immersed in the new campaign for Tidy-Teen Tampettes. The work allowed his thoughts to solidify, so that by six o'clock he had settled on another approach to his problem.

He phoned a number in West Portal.

'Yeah?' growled a voice at the other end. Its fuzziness, Beauchamp knew from experience, was not caused by postnasal drip.

'Bruno?'

'Yeah, yeah.'

'It's Beauchamp Day.'

'Oh. Yeah. More snow already?'

'No. Well, maybe that too. I've got a kind of special request this time.'

315

'I got some Purple Haze now. And some dynamite Black Beauties.'

'No. This is different. Remember that friend of yours who . . . settles differences?'

Silence.

'It's not what you think. Nothing heavy. I just need . . . well, it's kind of special . . . I mean, a special situation.'

'It'll cost ya.'

'I know. When can we talk?'

'Tonight? Eight o'clock?'

'Where?'

'Uh . . . the Doggie Diner. On Van Ness.'

'Right. The Doggie Diner on Van Ness at eight o'clock.'

'No snow, huh?'

'No, Bruno. Not tonight.'

Lady Eleven

Against his better instincts, Brian Hawkins made up a name for the woman in the Superman Building.

Lady Eleven.

This wasn't some sort of sicko fantasy trip, he told himself. She was *there*, like Everest, a nightly reality as fixed and inevitable as the clang of the cable cars or the toot of the foghorns on the bay. It seemed only natural to give her a name.

She would appear, invariably, on the stroke (could a digital clock strike?) of midnight, assuming her stance against the dim pinkish glow of her bedroom. After that she would scarcely move, except to raise and lower her binoculars and to make an unceremonious exit less than twenty minutes later.

She would never acknowledge Brian's presence, nor would she shift her gaze from the window of his little rooftop house. Viewed with the naked eye, she was nothing more than a dark blemish against the distant rectangle of light. With the field glasses, however, it was possible to discern her features.

A long, full-lipped face framed by hair that was . . . dark brown? The color was impossible to determine, but Brian settled on auburn.

Her hair fell lower than her shoulders and appeared to be tied in the back. Her robe was light-colored and undramatic, terry cloth maybe, and it revealed little about the rest of her body.

There was something about Lady Eleven's look that suggested she had just stepped from a shower.

Brian always wondered if her hair was wet and smelled of Herbal Essence.

This was the sixth night.

When Brian returned from Perry's, he couldn't help but remind himself again how radically his behavior patterns had changed. It was eleven o'clock, for Christ's sake, and he was home!

Furthermore, he found that he was showering after work now. Tonight he spent even longer than usual in the bathroom, primping like a college freshman about to immerse himself in a sorority mixer.

After brushing his teeth and shaving (shaving?), he slipped into his terry cloth bathrobe and sat in an easy chair by the south window with a dogeared copy of *Oui*.

Only seven minutes to go.

The sky around the rooftop house was alive with Wagnerian tumult. Hoky white clouds, phony as angel's hair props, drifted past the ghostly monolith of the Superman Building. At 11.56 a light appeared on the eleventh floor.

The light.

Brian dropped the magazine and moved to the window. He picked up the binoculars and focused on the lair of Lady Eleven. She wasn't in sight yet; there was no movement in her bedroom.

Nor was she in sight at midnight.

She had stood him up.

Brian remained at the window, numbed by disappointment and betrayal, like a child who had been awakened suddenly from a summer dream about Christmas morning. Then, gradually, his face began to burn with rage as he leaned there immobile against the cold windowpane (a window he had Windexed just that morning) and cursed the secret siren who had made him shave at midnight.

It would always be like this, wouldn't it? The ones you wanted could sense it with cunning, primeval precision. Your lust, not its fulfillment, was all these women required. And as soon as they felt it, as soon as they experienced the first acrid waft of your musk in their nostrils, they were gone from your life forever.

317

But then – sweet Jesus! – she appeared.

Poised and majestic as a figurehead on the great white clipper ship of the Superman Building, Lady Eleven materialized in her window and lifted her binoculars to her face. Brian matched her pose.

And then he caught his breath.

For now she was holding the binoculars with her right hand . . . and using her left hand to unknot the cord of her bathrobe.

As the robe slipped to the floor, so did Brian's.

On that sixth enchanted evening, across a crowded city.

On-the-Job Training

Mona's first afternoon at the Blue Moon Lodge was disappointingly uneventful. The phone rang only twice. The first call was from a man who wanted to know if Monique still worked there. A quick aside with Mother Mucca revealed that she did not.

'She left last month,' the madam explained. 'She's a directory assistance operator in Reno.'

'What do I tell this guy, then?'

'Tell him Doreen knows that bit too.'

'What bit?'

'Don't be so goddamn nosy!'

Mona frowned and picked up the receiver again. 'Uh . . . Monique isn't here anymore, but Doreen . . . knows how to do that too.'

The customer hesitated. 'The whole thing?'

'Uh huh.'

'With the rabbit's foot and all?'

'Uh . . . one moment, please.'

Mother Mucca was looking irritated. 'Don't you know the first damn thing about –'

'He's asking about a goddamn rabbit's foot!'

The old woman's mouth puckered into a pout. 'Don't you talk nasty to your elders, dolly! I'll wash your fuckin' mouth out with soap!'

Mona softened her tone. 'What about the rabbit's foot?'

Mother Mucca shrugged. 'Doreen can do it.'

Mona returned to the customer. 'Yes, she can do the . . . rabbit's foot thing.'

'All the way?'

'Yes. Satisfaction guaranteed.'

'The girls in Battle Mountain fake it, ya know?'

'Maybe so,' snapped Mona, 'but this isn't Battle Mountain. This is the Blue Moon Lodge!'

Mother Mucca beamed, squeezing Mona's arm. 'Atta girl, Judy! Atta girl!'

And the glow Mona felt came from pure, unadulterated pride.

One by one, the girls of the Blue Moon Lodge began to straggle into the parlor. There were seven in all, including Bobbi. The oldest seemed to be in her mid-thirties. She had ratted hair and thin lips and looked like a gospel singer from the Billy Graham Crusade.

'You're Judy, ain't ya? I'm Charlene.'

Charlene, Bobbi, Doreen, Bonnie, Debby, Marnie and Sherry. Jesus, thought Mona. What the hell are they? Hookers or Mouseketeers?

Charlene was checking her out. 'Mother Mucca says you're workin' the phones this week?'

'Yeah, just – you know – for the experience.'

That was wrong, all wrong. Patronizing as hell. Charlene knew it, too. 'You ain't writin' one o' them – whatchacallit – college papers?'

'No.'

'Good.' She knelt, stretching her lime-sherbert Capri pants to the limit, and turned on a mammoth color television set. Mona noticed for the first time that the top of the set was adorned with a Plasticine bust of JFK.

Most of the girls were watching Merv Griffin when the second customer call came in.

'Who's this?' asked a well-modulated voice.

'I'm Mo . . . I'm working here this week.'

'Oh.'

'Mother Mucca has authorized me to –'

'I think I'd better talk to her, please.'

Mona was piqued. 'Sir, if you would like to make an appointment, I'll be glad –'

Sensing a problem, Mother Mucca moved to Mona's side. 'He givin' you trouble, Judy?'

'He insists on talking to you.'

The madam took the phone. 'Yeah, this is . . . Oh, yes, sir . . . No, she's a new girl. I've . . . Yes, sir, she can be trusted completely . . . Yes, sir . . . Of course, sir . . . No, that's not short notice at all . . . I'll take the usual precautions . . . Fine, sir . . . Goodbye and thank you very much.'

The old woman hung up the phone, curiously subdued. The gentility she had mustered for the conversation left Mona somewhat stunned.

'Charlene?' said Mother Mucca.

'Yeah?'

'Get rid o' the other johns tonight.'

'Huh?'

'You heard me. Get rid of 'em. Call 'em up or reschedule 'em or somethin', but get rid of 'em.'

'Was that . . . ?'

Mother Mucca nodded. 'He's flyin' in from Sacramento.'

Charlese whistled softly. 'Which girl did he ask for?'

'He didn't.'

'Huh?'

'He wants a new one.'

Cravings

Under way again, the *Pacific Princess* steamed south toward Manzanillo, washed in the light of a full moon. Shortly after eight o'clock Mary Ann emerged from her bath and anointed her body with turtle lotion.

In less than an hour she would be having her first real date with Burke.

'Am I getting brown yet, Mouse?'

'What? Oh, yeah . . . fine.'

'Watcha reading?'

'Holy shit!'

'It must be good.'

He whistled in disbelief, still hunched over his book. Mary Ann grew impatient. 'Mouse . . . show me!'

Michael held up the paperback. It was entitled *Cruise Ships – The Inside Story.* 'I bought this damn thing down in the gift shop. I mean, they were actually pushing it!'

He read to her: ' "There are two categories of aggressive women among cruise passengers. There are those who are after the medals and those who just like tramping around."'

'That's the most sexist thing I've ever –'

' "The former like to aim at officers. The latter like nothing better than to disappear into crew quarters and spend the rest of the voyage in a variety of arms." '

'Well, variety is the –'

'Wait. Here comes the good part: "Occasionally, wealthy and lonely male homosexuals –" '

'You're making that up!'

'Listen, will you? "Occasionally, wealthy and lonely male homosexuals will appear on a cruise, attempting to buy the favor of crew members. It is an easy task." '

'Let me see that!'

He held the book so she could see it and continued to read. ' "A generous tip will carry the request to a willing crew member. Sometime later, the cabin phone will ring and a deal will be struck." '

'Leave it to you to find that.'

'Well, don't get snotty, just because *you've* found Mr Right already.'

Like a long-married couple, they sensed a pun together and spoke it in unison. 'All right, already!'

She tried on three blouses, unable to settle on the best complement for her beige slacks.

'Stick with the blue,' said Michael. 'That orange thing makes you look like Ann-Margret.'

'Maybe I *want* to look like Ann-Margret.'

Michael sighed laboriously. 'All right. If you *seriously* think that nice Nantucket boy is hot for the kitten-with-a-whip type, go right ahead and –'

Mary Ann threw off the blouse and scowled at him. 'You're worse than Debbie Nelson!'

'Thank you. Who's Debbie Nelson?'

'My freshman roommate.'

'The blue is very wholesome.'

'Screw wholesome.'

Michael pretended to be aghast. 'Wash your mouth out, young lady!' He buttoned up the blue blouse. 'There. Look at yourself. Isn't that better?'

'My mother hired you, didn't she? You're a plant.'

'A pansy, to be specific.'

'Look, don't you think that cream blouse might –'

Michael ignored her. 'Blow,' he ordered.

'What?'

'Blow in my face. You had two slices of garlic bread tonight.'

'Mouse! I am perfectly capable –'

'Strong men have turned queer over two slices of garlic bread!'

She blew.

Leaving the stateroom, she turned and winked at him. 'Don't wait up for me Babycakes!'

He stuck his tongue out at her.

'Thank you, Mouse. I love you.'

'Save the schmaltz for Thunder Thighs.'

'What are you gonna do?'

'Right now it's a tossup between shuffleboard and self-abuse.'

She laughed. 'There's a Cole Porter revue in the Carrousel –'

'Will you get outa here!'

He read for an hour, then wandered out onto the Promenade Deck, where he leaned on the rail, watching the ocean. Up here, away from the white vinyl shoes and harlequin glasses, it was easier to visualize the kind of sea cruise that inhabited his dreams: Noel Coward and Gertie Lawrence. Eccentric dowagers and rakish gigolos and steamer trunks stuffed with stowaways . . .

Romantic self-delusion, all of it. Like his hope for a lover, really. A futile, if harmless, fantasy that did little more than distract him from the imperturbable, central fact of his life: He was alone in this world. And he would always be alone.

Some people – the happy ones, probably – could deal with that knowledge the way they dealt with the weather. They skimmed along the surface of life exulting in their self-sufficiency, and because of it, they were *never* alone. Michael knew about those people, for he had tried to mimic them.

The ruse, however, rarely worked. The hunger always showed in his eyes.

Back in the stateroom, he smoked a joint and worked up the nerve to push the steward's button on the telephone. The steward appeared five minutes later.

'Yes, sir?'

'Hi, George.'

'Good evening, Mr Tolliver. What can I do for you?'

'Yes. Well, I'd like . . . I mean, if you don't mind . . . ' He reached for his wallet. 'George, I'd like you to have this'. He handed the steward a ten-dollar bill.

'Very kind, sir.'

'George, would you . . . ? I understand it's possible for you to make arrangements . . . Do you think you could bring me some ice cream?'

'Certainly, sir. What flavor?'

'I don't . . . Chocolate, I guess.'

The steward smiled, pocketing the bill. 'One of those late-night cravings, eh?'

'Yeah,' said Michael. 'The worst.'

Vita Saves the Day

The artifacts of DeDe's maidenhood still haunted her old bedroom at Halcyon Hill. A tattered Beatles poster. A Steiff giraffe from F.A.O. Schwarz. A swizzle stick from the Tonga Room. A jar of dried rose petals from Cotillion days.

Nothing had been altered, nothing touched, as if the occupant of this artless little pink-and-green room had perished in a plane crash, and a grieving, obsessive survivor had preserved it as a shrine for posterity.

In a way, of course, she had died.

In Mother's eyes, at least.

'Darling, I'm sorry. None of it makes any sense to me.'

'It's between me and Beauchamp, Mother.'

'I could help, if you'd just let me.'

'No, you can't. Nobody can.'

'I'm your *mother*, darling. Surely there's –'

'Just drop it.'

'Have you told Binky?'

DeDe's anger rose. 'What the hell's that got to do with it?'

'I just wondered.'

'You just wondered if any of those leathery old bitches at the Francesca Club are gonna be gossiping about your precious, darling daughter!'

323

'DeDe!'

'You think the separation's gonna hit Carson Callas's column tomorrow, and you won't be able to hold your head up at the Cow Hollow Inn. Well, too bad, Mother! Too goddamn bad!'

Frannie Halcyon sat on the edge of her daughter's bed and stared numbly at the wall. 'I've never heard you talk this way, DeDe.'

'No. I guess not.'

'Is it the pregnancy? Sometimes that can –'

'No.'

'You ought to be radiant, darling. When I was expecting you, I felt so –'

'Mother, please don't start on this again.'

'But why *now*, darling? Why would you leave Beauchamp only *weeks* before –'

'Look, I can't help it. I can't help it if I don't feel radiant. I can't help a goddamn thing about Beauchamp. I'm having the babies. I want them. Isn't that enough, Mother?'

Frannie's brow wrinkled. 'Why on earth shouldn't you want them?'

Silence.

'DeDe?'

'I've got a headache, Mother.'

Frannie sighed, kissed her on the cheek and stood up. 'I love you, but you don't seem like my child anymore. I think I know . . . how Catherine Hearst must feel.'

The matriarch of Halcyon Hill was mixing a Mai Tai when the phone rang.

'Mrs Halcyon?'

'Yes.'

'My name is Helena Parrish. I was referred to you by Vita Keating.'

Frannie braced herself for another well-bred pitch to join the board of another museum. 'Oh . . . yes,' she said cautiously.

'I'll get straight to the point, Mrs Halcyon. I have been asked to approach you concerning your interest in affiliating with Pinus.'

Frannie wasn't sure she had heard right.

'You're not familiar with us, perhaps?'

'No, I . . . Well, of course, I've *heard* of . . . Excuse me, if this is one of Vita's jokes, I don't think it's . . .'

The caller chuckled throatily. 'It's no joke, Mrs Halcyon.'

'I . . . I see.'

324

'Do you suppose we could get together for a little chat sometime soon?'

'Yes. Well, of course.'

'How's tomorrow?'

'Fine. Uh . . . shall we meet somewhere for lunch?'

'Actually, we prefer to keep a lower profile. May I call on you at Halcyon Hill?'

'Certainly. When?'

'Oh . . . twoish?'

'Lovely.'

'Good. Ta-ta, then.'

'Ta-ta,' said Frannie, feeling her heart rise to her throat.

Looking for a Lady

Brian spent the morning in Washington Square, sunning his body for a person who would probably never know the difference. As he trudged back up Union Street to Barbary Lane, he suddenly decided that it was time to confront his fantasy face to face.

He turned off Union at Leavenworth and walked a block up the hill to Green Street, where the Superman Building shimmered magically in the sunshine.

Up close, its modern hieroglyphics seemed to take a kind of mystical significance, as if they themselves concealed the secret identity of Lady Eleven.

As Brian approached, a Luxor cab deposited a passenger on the sidewalk. An LOL. And she was headed for the door of the Superman Building.

'Excuse me, ma'am?'

'Yes?'

'I'm looking for a friend of mine who lives here. It's kind of embarrassing, actually. I've forgotten her name. She lives on the eleventh floor. She's about my age, with longish hair and –'

The old woman's face slammed shut on him. Brian was certain she carried Mace in her purse. 'The names are by the buzzers,' she snarled.

'Oh. Yes, I see.'

He walked to the buzzers, feeling the woman's eyes on him all the time. He stood there for a moment, pretending to survey the names. Then he turned around and faced his white-gloved accuser.

'I'm not a rapist, lady.'

The old woman glared at him, drew herself up and stormed into the building. She spoke several words to the security guard, who turned and studied Brian, then said something to the LOL.

Brian continued to scan the names, hoping his nonchalance didn't appear too hoky. He was burning with guilt and hated himself for it.

There were six names listed on the eleventh floor: Jenkins, Lee, Mosely, Patterson, Fuentes and Matsumoto. A big goddamn help.

Maybe if he left a note with the guard . . . No, the asshole was already giving him the evil eye. And there was no *way* he could lurk around the lobby until Lady Eleven showed up. On the other hand, if he . . .

'Can I help you?' The guard had moved in. Trying his damnedest to look like Karl Malden.

'Well, I'm looking for a young woman.'

The guard's expression said: I'll just *bet* you are, sonny boy.

'Forget it,' said Brian.

He would see her in twelve hours, anyway.

He reversed his course again and headed back down Union Street to La Contadina. He needed a glass of wine to steady his nerves. Sometimes a fascist in uniform could screw up your whole day.

When he reached the restaurant, an outlandish figure waved at him from a huge, thronelike chair by the window. It was Mrs Madrigal, decked out in a paisley turban, blue eye shadow and harem pyjamas. She beckoned him in.

'Will you join me?'

'Sure,' he said, sitting down across from her. He felt slightly out of sync in his gym shorts and sweat shirt. Mrs Madrigal herself seemed somewhat frayed around the edges.

'Brian . . . you haven't seen Mona, have you?'

'No. Not for a week or so.'

'I'm worried. She left me a note when Mary Ann and Michael left, saying she'd be gone for a while, but I haven't heard a word since. I thought maybe you . . . Nothing, huh?'

Brian shook his head. 'Sorry.'

The landlady fidgeted with her turban. 'She can be . . . quite foolish sometimes.'

'I don't know her that well. How long has she been at the house?'

'Oh . . . well over three years. Brian, has she ever . . . talked to you about me?'

He thought for a moment. 'Never. Why?'

'I'm afraid I've been a little foolish myself. I just hope it's not too late.'

'I don't . . .'

'Mona is my daughter, Brian.'

Her tenants, thought Brian, are always her 'children.' He smiled understandingly. 'You must be very close to her.'

'No, Brian. I mean she's my *real* daughter.'

His jaw went slack. 'Your . . . Does Mona know that?'

'No.'

'I thought she said her mother lived in –'

'I'm not her mother, Brian. I'm her father.'

Before he could utter a word, she pressed a finger against her lips, signaling him to remain silent. 'We can talk about it back at the house,' she whispered.

Company's Coming

There was something eerie about the sudden change of mood at the Blue Moon Lodge. Mona sensed it immediately, watching the tension mount as Mother Mucca mobilized her girls for the arrival of the big customer from Sacramento.

'Bobbi, you get the 409 outa the kitchen and clean the crapper in Charlene's room. It looks like a goddamn truck stop! Marnie, you straighten up the parlor. Get rid o' those movie magazines. Bonnie, you and Debby take the Ranchero into town and pick up that costume at the Chinaman's. Wouldn't ya know it! He shows up here the only goddamn week of the year we sent the costume to the cleaners!'

Mona kept clear of the eye of the storm, wanting to help but certain she'd only be in the way. Observing her discomfort, Charlene winked and handed her a dustcloth. 'Crazy, huh?'

Mona nodded. 'Who is this guy, anyway?'

'I . . . You better talk to Mother Mucca first.'

'Where do you want me to dust?' *Well, Mona, you stumped the panel!*

327

Arlene, Bennett, I think you'll be surprised to learn that the lovely Miss Ramsey . . . dusts whorehouses for a living!

'Over behind the bar. And that Kennedy statue on the TV.'

'OK. Charlene?'

'Yeah.'

'Mother Mucca said he wanted a new girl. Is she gonna trade with another house or something?'

Charlene continued to dust. 'Yeah. I guess she could.'

'You mean . . . she's never done that before?'

'He's never asked for a new girl before.'

'Oh. Well, then, how come she's not –'

'Don't talk so much. We're wastin' time.'

Moments later, Mother Mucca charged into the parlor, saw Mona at work, and snapped at the head girl. 'Charlene! What's Judy doin' cleanin' for?'

'Well, you said for everybody to –'

'Judy is my receptionist, Charlene! She ain't got no business dustin' –'

Mona interrupted. 'Really, Mother Mucca, I don't mind helping out a –'

'Course you don't, Judy. But it just ain't fittin' for you to be doin' housework, when I hired you as a receptionist.'

Mona shrugged at this breach of protocol and smiled her apologies to Charlene, who frowned and skulked off.

'C'mon,' said Mother Mucca, taking Mona's arm. 'We'll have a nice big glass of milk in the kitchen.'

The old woman's request hit like a sledge hammer.

'What?' gasped Mona, almost choking on her milk.

'He's a piece o' cake,' said Mother Mucca.

'Well, let *them* eat cake! I'm a receptionist, remember?'

'I'll pay you extra, Judy.'

'You've gotta be . . . Oh, no . . . Ohhh, no. Got that? *No!*'

Mother Mucca reached across the table and grasped Mona's hand. 'He wants somebody with class, Judy. Nobody in Winnemucca's got your kind of class.'

'Thanks a lot.'

'You don't have to fuck him.'

That threw her. 'Well, what the hell does he . . . ? Never mind. Spare me the gory details.'

'Judy, do ya think ol' Mother Mucca would . . .? Judy, you're like my own flesh and blood. I wouldn't do nothin' to make you think less o' yourself. I swear, it hurts me a heap to think . . .?'

The old woman let go of Mona's hand and fumbled in her grizzled cleavage for a hanky. Turning away, she dabbed at her eyes.

Mona was shaken. 'Mother Mucca, look . . .'

'You *hurt* me, child!'

'I didn't mean to.'

'I'll tell you the God's honest truth. I've been runnin' this place for sixty years, and you're the first girl I've ever felt was . . . Judy, I'd adopt you, if you'd let me.'

This time Mona reached for the madam's hand. 'You've been really good to me, Mother . . .'

'Did you know I used to have a little boy?'

'No.'

'I did. He was the sweetest little thing you ever laid eyes on. He used to sit right here on this floor and jus' laugh and giggle, and me and the girls, we'd do anything for that little tyke, and I never thought . . .'

'Please don't cry.'

'I never thought in a million years that little darlin' would run off an' leave his mama when he was sixteen. I never thought nothin' like that. I trusted him Judy, jus' like I trust . . .'

She silenced herself when Bonnie and Debby appeared with the important bundle from the laundry.

'Take it away,' ordered Mother Mucca.

Bonnie frowned. 'But didn't you say . . . ?'

'Take the goddamn thing away!'

'Wait a minute,' said Mona. 'I have to see if it fits OK.'

Mother Mucca stared at Mona for several seconds, dabbed her eyes, and grinned. 'You're an angel, dolly.'

'And you're full of shit,' said Mona.

This Year's Song

'This is nice,' said Mary Ann, sipping a Pina Colada in the Starlight Lounge of the *Pacific Princess*, while a pianist played 'I Write the Songs.' Burke answered with a nod, smiling at her.

'Michael says this song is this year's "What I Did for Love."'

'I don't get it.'

'Well, you know. Like every year there's a song that *everybody* records. Two years ago it was "Send in the Clowns" – or was it three? Anyway, last year it was "What I Did for Love," which I really like, even though they do play it to death. I mean . . . if a song is good, I don't see what's wrong with playing it a lot, do you?'

'No. I guess not.'

'I think "What I Did for Love" is probably my all-time favorite. At least . . . well, it's the only one on the album that you can hum. Not that that's all that important, but . . . well, I mean, who can hum "The Music and the Mirror"?'

'You've got me there. I don't even know what *album* you're talking about.'

'You know. *Chorus Line.*'

He shook his head. 'Sorry.'

'The musical, Burke. It came to San Francisco.'

'I told you I was out of it.'

Mary Ann shrugged, but she was inwardly relieved. He *couldn't* be gay if he'd never heard of *A Chorus Line.* She decided to change the subject. Burke seemed uncomfortable with popular music.

'How long did you live in San Francisco, Burke?'

'Not long, really. Actually, I consider Nantucket my home.'

'You work there?' She felt that was more tactful than 'What do you do?' Nine months in San Francisco had programmed that question out of her system forever.

'Sort of. My father's in publishing. I help him out sometimes.'

'Oh, what fun!' Was *that* ever gushy! Why was this conversation such a dud?

'Mary Ann, let's get some air, OK?'

Out on the fantail, they leaned against the rail and watched the moon rise above a calm sea. As usual, she was the one to break the silence.

'I talk too much, don't I?'

He slipped an arm around her shoulder. 'Not at all.'

'Yes, I do. I won the Optimist Oratory Contest in high school, and I haven't stopped talking since.'

He laughed. 'I'm afraid you're holding up both ends of the conversation.'

330

She let that go, turning to face the water again. 'Do you know what blew me away this morning?'

'What?'

'The lifeboat drill . . . what the captain said. I didn't know that women and children don't get to go first anymore.'

'Yeah. Things have changed, I guess.'

'I wish they wouldn't.'

He answered by squeezing her shoulder.

'I mean, it isn't a bit fair. The song says it's still the same old story, but it isn't, is it? Who the hell gets to be Ingrid Bergman anymore?'

'Now *that*'s one I know.' He chuckled.

'How old are you, Burke?'

'Twenty-seven.'

'You seem – I don't know – not *older* exactly, but more . . . It's hard to explain. You seem like you're twenty-seven, but someone who was twenty-seven a long time ago.'

'Out of it, in other words.'

'Why do you keep saying that? I *like* it, Burke. I really do.'

He leaned down and kissed her lightly on the mouth. 'I like *you*.'

'Do you?' she asked.

'Yes. Very much, Mary Ann.'

'Ingrid,' she said, and kissed him back.

Family Planning

Under the fluorescent lights of the Doggie Diner, the crags and craters of Bruno Koski's face assumed lunar proportions. The corners of his mouth, Beauchamp noticed, were hydrophobic with mayonnaise.

'Now, lemme get this straight, man. You don't want her greased, you just –'

'Keep your voice down, Bruno!'

Bruno shrugged and cast a contemptuous glance around the diner. 'They're all space cadets, man. They ain't listenin'.'

'You don't know that.'

'I know a fuckin' space cadet when I see one.'

This was true. Bruno did know his space cadets. Beauchamp

looked down at his hamburger. 'OK. I didn't mean to . . . Look, I'm just jumpy. I've never done this before.'

'So tell me what the fuck you want, man.'

Beauchamp kept his head down, laboriously removing the onions from his hamburger. 'I want you to . . . see to it that she doesn't have the baby – the babies.'

Bruno blinked at him ingenuously. 'You want me to kick her gut in?'

'I don't want you to hurt her, Bruno.'

'OK. You want me to kick her gut in without hurting her.'

'Your tone is shitty, Bruno.'

'Oh, kiss my ass!'

'Look: she's my wife, right? I don't want her – I don't want any permanent harm done. If you can't promise me that, we might as well forget the whole thing.'

'How the fuck do you expect me to guarantee . . . ? What about . . . I mean, there could be – whatchacallit? – complications.'

Beauchamp made his patient-but-piqued face, an expression that never failed to exasperate harried art directors at Halcyon Communications. 'Now, Bruno, she's seven months pregnant. It shouldn't be *that* hard to arrange for . . . an accident of some sort.'

The coke dealer stared at his client. 'Look, man –'

'On the other hand,' said Beauchamp dryly, 'this may be totally out of your league.'

'Says who?'

'You seem a little hesitant. Maybe I should check with someone . . . more professional.'

Bruno sulked momentarily, then looked up. 'How much?'

'What's it worth?'

That stopped him for a moment. 'Uh . . . five thousand. Considerin' the hassle.'

'I'll give you seven. But I want it done right.'

'You know I'll subcontract it.'

'I don't care.'

'I want cash. In advance.'

'You'll get it. How soon?'

'Soon as I get somebody.'

'It has to be soon, Bruno.'

'Fuck off!'

'Bruno?'

'Huh?'

'Wipe your mouth, will you?'

Fifteen minutes later, Beauchamp called DeDe at Halcyon Hill. Her voice was expressionless, a telltale defense against the uncertainties of their day-old separation.

'Just checking on you,' he said.

'Thanks.'

'Is your mother there?'

'Yes.'

'Good. If you need anything sent out, let me know, will you?'

Silence.

'OK, DeDe?'

She began to cry. 'Why are you being . . . so goddamned nice?'

'I don't know. I guess I miss you.'

'Beauchamp . . . I want these babies so much. I'm not trying to hurt you, I promise.'

'I know, darling. We'll give it some time, OK?'

'If I weren't so confused, I'd be a better wife. I just need . . . I want to be by myself for a while.'

'I understand.'

She sniffed, then blew her nose. 'There's a chicken pot pie in the freezer and some leftover quiche in –'

'I'll be OK.'

'Beauchamp . . . I do love you.'

'I know,' said her husband. 'I know.'

Mrs Madrigal's Confession

For the first time ever, Brian declined a joint.

He wanted to be straight when he heard this.

'Once upon a time,' said Mrs Madrigal, 'there was a little boy named Andy Ramsey. Andy was not a particularly extraordinary little boy, but he grew up under extraordinary circumstances: his mother was a madam. She ran a brothel called the Blue Moon Lodge, in Winnemucca, Nevada, and Andy's best friends and nursemaids were the whores who made that house their home. Perhaps for that reason – or perhaps not – Andy made a startling

333

discovery by the time he reached puberty: There was nothing about him that felt like a boy.

'Oh, he *looked* like a boy, all right. All the appropriate plumbing was there. But he never stopped feeling like a girl, a girl locked up inside a boy's body. To his horror, that feeling intensified as Andy grew older. By the time he was sixteen, he was so frightened that he ran away from the whorehouse and hitched a ride to California.

'For a while he held body and soul together by working as a migrant laborer. Then he worked as a soda jerk in a drugstore in Salinas, then as a laborer again, this time in Modesto. Shortly after his twentieth birthday, he left Modesto for Fort Ord, where he enlisted in the Army as a private. He was a good soldier, but he stayed at Ford Ord throughout the war – World War II, that is – mostly typing munitions reports for a drunken colonel. In the long run, however, Andy hated the all-male environment of the Army as much as he had hated the all-female environment of the whore-house. And the feeling that he was really a woman persisted through it all.

'One night, shortly after the end of the war, Andy met a pretty young woman at a dance in Monterey. She was *very* young, actually, about seventeen at the time; Andy was twenty-five. She was visiting Minneapolis, staying at her cousin's house in Carmel. Her name was Betty Borg, and Andy was quite taken with her, in his own way. She had a perky, independent spirit that he admired, and he was relieved to discover that he was attracted to her. Even sexually.

'Betty wanted to get married and move back to Minneapolis. It was she who proposed, in fact, and Andy decided that this might be the best cure for his problem. So . . . they did just that. Andy fulfilled his responsibilities as a husband by working in a bookstore in Minneapolis. A year later, a little girl was born to the couple. They named her Mona, after Andy's estranged mother back in Winnemucca.

'None of it worked. Not for Andy, anyway. He ended up leaving his wife and child – deserting them – when the child was two years old. For the next fifteen years, he virtually dropped out of sight, drifting from city to city, a miserable, self-pitying creature who had botched his own life and the lives of the people around him. All of that ended, however, when Andy was forty-four. That was when he picked up the pieces and traveled to Denmark and spent his life savings on a sex change.'

*

334

'And came back as Anna Madrigal.' It was Brian who supplied this information. More fascinated than shocked, he smiled at the landlady.

She smiled back. 'It's a nice name, don't you think? It's an anagram.'

'But if Mona is your daughter . . . ? Well, I thought you said she doesn't know.'

'She doesn't. She moved to San Francisco three or four years ago, and shortly thereafter I read an item in Herb Caen's column about a Mona Ramsey working at Halcyon Communications. I knew there couldn't be *that* many Mona Ramseys in the world, so I did a little checking and I cornered her one night at the Savoy-Tivoli.'

'And?'

'She *liked* me, if you please. So I invited her to come live at Barbary Lane. She fancies herself a bohemian, and I think she rather relished the idea of having a transsexual as a landlady.'

'She knew that, then?'

'Oh, yes. From the beginning.'

'Does your . . . your wife know where you are? Or your mother?'

Mrs Madrigal shook her head. 'They must think I'm dead.' She smiled faintly. 'Of course, Andy *is*.'

'And now you think Mona's found out you're her father and freaked out over it?'

'It's possible, don't you think?'

He smiled. 'I'm not thinking very clearly right now.'

'You poor boy!'

'I'm . . . I'm very flattered that you told me, Mrs Madrigal.'

'Good. *Now* can we smoke that joint?'

He laughed. 'The sooner the . . . Wait a minute. How can Anna Madrigal be an anagram for Andy Ramsey?'

'It's not.'

'But you said . . .'

'I said it was an anagram. I didn't say what for.'

'Then what is it?'

'My dear boy,' said the landlady, lighting a joint at last, 'you are talking to a Woman of Mystery!'

Once in a Blue Moon

Bobbi buzzed around Mona like a bridesmaid making last-minute adjustments to a bridal gown. 'I think you've got the headpiece on backward, Judy. Try it . . . no, the other way. There. Look how pretty that is!'

'For Christ's sake, Bobbi. It's not supposed to be *pretty*!'

'Well, you know. Anyway, you *are* pretty. You should be real proud.'

Mona managed a tiny smile. 'Stop trying to cheer me up.'

'You're gonna be the best yet, Judy. He's gonna *love* you!'

'He'd better *not*.'

Bobbi giggled. 'Don't worry. Lots of our customers are like him.'

'Like *this*?' Mona pointed to her costume.

'No, but they . . . well, they don't wanna screw you. They just want . . . like special services they can't get anywhere else. Like I had this one guy from Stockton who wanted me to wear black lace panties and sit on his knee while he dictated his will to me.'

'Sure.'

'I swear, Judy. And it took *forever*. I had to go see Dr Craig that week.'

'Why?'

Bobbi tittered. 'He said I had single-handedly turned writer's cramp into a veneral disease.'

Still wearing the costume, Mona wandered back to the parlor and took a beer out of the refrigerator behind the bar. She longed for a joint.

Charlene appeared and smirked at Mona's outfit. 'Mighty early, aren't you?'

'I don't like to be rushed.'

'He's not comin' for an hour.'

'It's OK.'

'You'll have BO.'

'Lay off, Charlene!'

'Nervous, ain't you?' Her tone was openly bitchy now. She resents me, thought Mona. It pisses her off that Mother Mucca likes me.

'I'm fine,' said Mona blandly.

'Maybe so,' said Charlene, 'but you're spillin' the beer.'

At fifteen minutes and counting, Mona sat alone in the parlor. Mother Mucca entered from the kitchen and took her place quietly at Mona's side.

'You OK?'

Mona nodded.

'It's something you can tell your grandchildren about.'

'Sure.'

The old woman put her arm gently around Mona's shoulders, taking care not to disturb the costume. 'You look . . . real fine.'

'Thanks.'

'The other girls are all in their rooms. They'll stay there till he's gone. You'll use Charlene's room, so I'll tell you when to come in. He'll be there already. You remember what to do?'

'I think so.'

Mother Mucca patted her hand. 'You'll do just fine.'

'Mother Mucca?'

'How can he . . . ? How's he getting here?'

'Oh, in a limousine.'

'A *limousine?*'

'Sure,' said Mother Mucca, tapping her head to signal a clever man. 'That way, nobody'll think it's him, see?'

The rap came on Mona's door.

'He's here,' whispered Mother Mucca.

Mona slipped out into the starry desert night. A warm breeze blew in from the north, flapping the sleeves of her habit. Mother Mucca took one last look at her new girl, readjusted her wimple and scurried back to the parlor. Then Mona opened the door of Charlene's cubicle.

The customer was seated cross-legged on the floor next to the bed. He was wearing the saffron robes of a Buddhist monk.

'Sister . . . I have sinned.'

Mona cleared her throat. 'I know, my child.'

The whip, as arranged, was lying on the bed.

Interrupted Idyll

The taxi ride from Manzanillo offered little more than crumbling hamburger stands, palm-thatched shanties, and occasional burros rummaging in the roadside garbage.

Mary Ann's and Burke's destination, however, was not to be believed.

Perched airily above an azure bay, the resort of Las Hadas gleamed like an opium dream from the *Arabian Nights*. Bougainvillaea blazed electrically against whitewashed walls, gargoyles peered from minarets into sun-drenched courtyards, birds sang and palms swayed.

And Mary Ann's heart took flight.

'Oh, Burke, just *look* at it!'

She didn't mean that, of course. What she meant was: Look at us.

The beach was a crescent of silvery sand with water so clear that Mary Ann could watch tiny fish darting between her legs. Burke dunked her with infantile glee, holding fast to her waist as they surfaced into the sunshine.

How long had it been since someone had done that?

How long had she waited for this smile, these eyes, this strong, simple spirit that had come to her in a world marred by greed and anxiety and computer dating? And how long, dear God, would it last?

They sunned together on their backs, fingertips touching.

'Where's Michael today?' asked Burke.

'On the ship.'

'He could have come with us, you know.'

'I think he wanted to take it easy.'

'I see.'

'Burke?'

'Yeah?'

'Why did you leave California?'

There was a pause, and then: 'I don't know. I guess . . . my father and all.'

'Your father?'

'The publishing business. He needed help.'

'Were you . . . in the publishing business in San Francisco?'

'No. I was just . . . bumming around.'

'For three years?'

He rolled onto his side, facing her, smiling slightly. 'Are you asking me how rich I am?'

It *did* sound that way, and she was horrified by her gaffe. 'No, Burke! Really. I was just . . . Never mind. I'm flustered, I guess.'

'Why?'

'Oh, it's just so damn typical!'

'What is?'

'You know. You meet somebody nice, and you get along with them fabulously, so *of course* they live three thousand miles away! It's a gyp, that's all.'

He slid closer to her and cupped his hand against her cheek. 'Was last night a gyp?'

'No. You know that.'

He kissed the tip of her nose. 'We've got a week, Mary Ann. Let's make the best of it, huh?'

They ate lunch overlooking the water in a garden of manicured tropical foliage. An artificial waterfall made lush sounds in the swimming pool behind them.

A child approached wearing a sandwich board that announced the resort's coming events. 'How precious!' said Mary Ann, noticing his blue clown's costume and pointy-toed court jester shoes.

But as he came closer, she made the discovery that he wasn't a child at all.

He was a dwarf.

Embarrassed, she turned away, hoping the little man would pass up their table for a group of boisterous tourists seated near the pool. He didn't, though. He approached the young lovers with a toothy, imploring smile, holding a red rose in his outstretched hand.

Now it was unavoidable. 'Burke, have you got a peso or something for him?'

Her companion didn't answer. He was chalk white, and still as a corpse.

'Burke, is something . . . ?'

His voice was scarcely more than a whimper, a pathetic trapped-animal sound. 'Make him go,' he said.

'Burke, he's only a –'

339

'Please, please . . . make him go!'

The dwarf needed no encouragement. He was three tables away by the time Burke stumbled into the shrubbery and fell to his knees, vomiting. Mary Ann moved to his side and gently stroked the strawberry curls on the back of his neck.

'It's OK,' she said. 'It's OK.'

Seconds later, he straightened up and tried to regain his dignity. 'Forgive me, please. I'm really sorry. I should have . . .'

'It's OK,' she said softly. 'I can see how he might make you . . .'

Burke shook his head. 'It wasn't him, Mary Ann.'

'What?'

'It was the rose.'

Douchebag

Once a Philippine nightclub specializing in bosomy chanteuses, the Mabuhay Gardens had mutated almost overnight into San Francisco's only punk rock showplace. There, amid the dying palms and tattered rattan, Bruno Koski came off like a bona-fide heavy from an early Bogart film.

The punks and punkettes eyed him with ill-disguised envy, lusting silently after his pitted complexion, his garbanzo-bean eyes, his casual air of native degeneracy.

Bruno Koski was the real thing.

Jimmy, the stage manager, recognized him immediately. 'Hey, Bruno, what's . . . ?'

'I'm lookin' for Douchebag.'

'You know *her?*'

'Just tell me where she is, kid.'

'Over there. Next to the amplifier. The one in the garbage bag.'

Bruno glanced sullenly toward the sound equipment, avoiding the eyes of the assembled punks. Three of the punkettes were wearing Hefty bags, modified as ponchos with safety pins.

'Oh,' amended Jimmy, seeing Bruno's irritation. 'The one with the green hair.'

Bruno approached her.

'You Douchebag?'

'Yeah.' She was chewing gum viciously. Her hair, several shades lighter than the Hefty bag, was chopped off close to her scalp. She was wearing a button that said PUNK POWER.

'My name's Bruno.'

She chewed even harder. 'So?'

'So I wanna talk to you.'

'Nope. Crime is comin' on.' She nodded toward the stage, where a gang of black-leather musicians was slithering into position for its next assault on the audience.

Bruno glowered at Douchebag, but decided to humor her. He *needed* the little bitch, after all. He could put up with her for a few minutes longer.

Crime was so loud he felt his brain was bleeding. The punks and punkettes turned spastic under the spell of the music, quivering like convicts in a hundred different electric chairs. The song was called 'You're So Repulsive.'

At the first break, she turned back to him. 'Outasight, huh?'

'Yeah,' he lied.

'You shoulda seen it when they had Mary Monday and the Bitches.'

'Yeah?'

'Shit, man. They trashed the microphones and tore up the tables and the stage manager freaked out . . . and, man, it was just deee-praved!'

'Sounds like it.'

'Course, that's nothin' – I mean *nothin'* – compared to The Damned or The Nuns. I mean, that's heavy metal . . . really scuzzy stuff. Some o' that stuff makes you wanna really *puke*!'

The cud-chewing mouth became too much for him. 'Hey . . . get rid o' that stuff, will ya?'

She stared at him, unblinking for several seconds, then removed the gum from her mouth, rolled it into a neat little ball and stuffed it up her nostril.

She didn't flinch when he outlined his proposal.

'I just . . . trash her a little bit, huh?'

'Yeah. She don't live far from here.'

'You'll gimme her schedule and all? I mean, I don't have to bust in, do I?'

'Nope. We'll arrange a time. You leave that to me, punk.'

341

She beamed at that. She *was* punk now. She was earning her punk credentials for real. 'Hey, Bruno . . . like what do I get out of this?'

'What d'ya want?'

She thought for a moment. 'I wanna start my own group. We need three hundred bucks.'

'It's yours.'

'You know The Scorpions?'

'Sure.'

'It's gonna be a group like that. Only it's gonna be all chicks, and we're only gonna sing during our periods, so that we can *really* gross people out when we –'

'Hey, punk . . . OK, OK!'

Douchebag's mouth curled. 'Shit, man! I can't *wait* till I'm thirteen!'

A Changed Man

Brian was on his way out the door when the phone rang in the little house on the roof.

'Yeah?'

'Hey! What's happenin'?'

It had to be Chip Hardesty. Chip Hardesty would ask 'What's happenin'?' at his grandmother's funeral. He lived in Larkspur, but his home was barely distinguishable from his Northpoint office. Both had Boston ferns, Watney's Ale mirrors and basket chairs suspended from chains. He didn't particularly get off on being a dentist.

'Not much,' answered Brian. For the first time in years, he was lying through his teeth.

'Bitchin'! I've got a plan.'

'Yeah,' said Brian noncommittally. Chip's last plan had involved a case of Cold Duck, a rental cabin at Tahoe and two sure-thing dental receptionist students from the Bryman School. One of these women – Chip's, of course – had been a dead ringer for Olivia Newton-John.

Brian's date had been uncomfortably suggestive of Amy Carter and had loped along at a strange angle in an effort to compensate for a left breast she felt to be smaller than her right.

'Are you working tonight?' asked Chip.

'Afraid so.'

342

'What time you get off?'

'Eleven.'

'OK. Listen. You remember Jennifer Rabinowitz?'

'Nope.'

'OK. Huge knockers, right? Works at The Cannery. Pierced nose–'

'Barfed at the Tarr and Feathers sing-along.'

'Says who?'

'Says me. The barfee.'

'You never told me that.'

'Sorry. I should have mentioned it on my Christmas card.'

A hurt silence followed. Then: 'I'm doin' you a favor, man. You can take it or leave it.'

'Go ahead. I'm listening.'

'OK. Jennifer's got this friend –'

'Makes her own clothes. Great personality. All the girls in the dorm just love –'

'What the hell's wrong with you, man?'

'I'll be out of it, Chip. Better count me out.'

'What's that mean? Out of it.'

'Beat. Exhausted. Eleven o'clock's a little late for –'

'Christ! You haven't crashed before two in five years!'

'Well, maybe I'm getting old, then.'

'Yeah. Maybe you are.'

'Chip?'

'Yeah?'

'Go spray your hair, will ya?'

As a matter of fact, he wasn't a bit tired when he finished with his last customer at Perry's. He felt vigorous, exhilarated, as spirited as a fourteen-year-old about to lock himself in the bathroom with a copy of *Fanny Hill*. Lady Eleven was the best thing that had happened to him in years.

Later, as he climbed out of the shower, he acknowledged the fact that he felt a strong sense of fidelity toward the siren in the Superman Building. She *belonged* to him, in the purest, most satisfying sense of the word. And he belonged to her. If only for half an hour.

He had met an equal, at last.

Love on a Rooftop

The Hampton-Giddes were the first to arrive from the ballet. 'Fabulous latticework,' gushed Archibald Anson Gidde, appraising his host's new rooftop deck.

Peter Cipriani nodded. 'I found this *gorgeous* twink carpenter in the Mission. Dirt cheap and pecs that won't quit. Jason something-or-other.'

'They're *all* called Jason, aren't they?'

Peter snickered. 'Or Jonathan.'

'Was his ear pierced?'

'Nope. But he wore cut-offs to *die*. And knee socks with Lands End come-fuck-me boots. He was hot.'

'How is he with kitchens?'

'Who knows? I can only speak for bedrooms, my dear.'

'Ooooh,' said Archibald Anson Gidde.

Minutes before midnight, the deck was crowded with A-Gays, tastefully atwitter over glissades and pirouettes. Charles Hillary Lord lifted a spade of cocaine to Archibald Anson Gidde's nostril.

'I talked to Nicky today.'

Arch inhaled the powder noisily. 'And?'

'I think he's going in on it.'

'Good,' said Arch indifferently. 'That should help you a lot.'

'We don't need *help*, Arch. It's a sure thing. I just want you in on the ground floor.'

'Then you won't be hurt if I say no.'

Chuck Lord sighed dramatically and swept his arm over the rooftops of Russian Hill. 'Arch . . . do you have any idea at all how many faggots are out there?'

'Just a sec. I'll check my address book.'

'There are – and this is conservatively speaking – one hundred and twenty thousand practicing homosexuals within the city limits of San Francisco.'

'And practice *does* make perfect.'

'Those one hundred and twenty thousand homosexuals are going to grow old together, Arch. Some of them may go back to Kansas or wherever the hell they ran away from, but most of them are gonna stay right here in Shangri-la, cruising each other until it's pacemaker time.'

'I need a Valium.'

'Goddammit, Arch, don't you see? *We're* OK. We've got houses and cars and trust funds and enough ... assets to pay for Dial-a-Model until we're a hundred and two, if we want to. It's those fuckers on food stamps and ATD, selling crap at the flea market and painting houses in the Haight, who're gonna need this when the time comes.'

Arch's face grew serious. 'Doesn't that smack of exploitation to you, Chuck?'

'Oh, for God's sake! *Somebody's* gonna do it! You know that, Arch. Why shouldn't we be the first?'

'I don't know. It just seems . . . risky.'

'Risky? Arch, it's social history! It's *Wall Street Journal* stuff! Think of it! The first gay nursing home in the history of the world!'

Arch Gidde turned and looked at the city. 'Gimme some time, OK?'

Chuck flung an arm over his shoulder and adopted a more affectionate tone. 'Nicky's even thought of a name.'

'What?'

'The Last Roundup.'

'Oh, for God's . . .'

'Don't you see? A tasteful butch Western motif, with barn siding in the rooms and little chuckwagons for the food –'

'Let's not forget the denim colostomy bags.'

Chuck glared at him. 'You joke, but I *know* you see the profit in this!'

Silence.

'Look, Arch: it's very civilized, in a way. I mean, we could have a steam room and everything. The orderlies could be Colt Models!'

'That's always nice to know when they're carrying you to the toilet. Look, Chuck, everybody's different. This is *your* fantasy. What are you gonna do with, like, the drag queens?'

'We could – I don't know – we could have a separate wing.'

'And Helen Hayes look-alike contests?'

'Well, I don't see any reason why –'

He was cut short by Peter Cipriani, shouting excitedly to his guests.

'OK, don't crowd. One at a time, gentlemen, one at a time.' He handed a pair of binoculars to Rick Hampton, who aimed them in a northerly direction.

'Which building?' asked Rick.

'The shingled one. On Barbary Lane. That little house on the roof, see?'

'Yeah, but I don't –'

'The right window.'

'Jesus Christ!'

'What?' asked Arch, as the others crowded around.

'Oh, Jesus, look what he's –'

'What's he doing?' shrieked Arch.

'Wait your turn, Mary. Oh, Jesus, I can't *buhleeve* . . . How long has this been going on, Peter?'

'A couple of weeks, at least. There's a woman he's watching in that white building.'

'He's *straight?*'

'Apparently.'

'He *can't* be! Straight people don't have bodies like that!'

'Lemme see!' said Arch.

The Slumber Party

Back in her own cubicle, Mona sat perfectly still on the bed and performed the only rite of exorcism she knew:

She recited her mantra.

It wasn't that she felt guilty, really. Or even embarrassed. She had kept her agreement and she could live with that. She had pleased the client. She had pleased Mother Mucca. She had been flawlessly seventies about the whole fucking thing.

It wasn't shame, then, that consumed her. It was . . . nothing. She felt nothing at all, and it scared the hell out of her. The yawning Black Hole of her existence had reached seismic proportions, and she was perilously near the abyss. If she did not keep running, if she did not keep changing, the random and monstrous irrationality of the universe would swallow her alive.

'Knock, knock.'

Silence.

'Knock, knock.'

'Yeah, Bobbi?'

The child-whore peered in, cautiously. She waved a cellophane package through the door, like a vampire-killer brandishing a crucifix. 'I've got some Oreos. Wanna help me eat 'em?'

'I don't think so, Bobbi.'

A pause, and then: 'You feelin' OK, Judy?'

'Why shouldn't I? *He's* the one who's smarting.'

Bobbi giggled and shook her package again. 'Don't you want just a *few*?'

'You don't lick the centers, do you?'

'No. I hate that.'

'Me too.'

'My mother wouldn't let me have 'em if I licked the centers.'

Mona smiled. Mothers were good for something, anyway. So what if we ended up turning S & M tricks in a Winnemucca whorehouse? We *always* remembered not to lick the centers out of Oreos, not to sit with our legs apart, not to point at people or scratch ourselves when we itched.

'How 'bout it?' Bobbi persisted.

'Sure,' said Mona. 'Why not?'

Hopping onto the bed with unsuppressed glee, Bobbi tore into the package of cookies. 'So,' she said, offering one to Mona, 'what did you think of him?'

Mona deadpanned. 'Beats me.'

Bobbi missed it. 'I think he's real handsome.'

'Bobbi . . . I don't wanna talk about it, OK?'

'Sure. Sorry.'

Bobbi drew her knees up under her chin hugging them. She munched meditatively on an Oreo as if she were checking its vintage. Then she studied Mona soulfully.

'You know what, Judy?'

'What?'

'You're my best friend.'

Silence.

'Cross my heart, Judy.'

'Well, that's . . . Thank you.'

'Could I stay tonight?'

'Here?'

Bobbi nodded. 'It would be like a slumber party or something.'

'Bobbi, I don't think . . .'

'I'm not a lesbo, Judy.'

Mona smiled. 'What if *I* am?'

Bobbi looked startled at first, then amused. 'No way,' she laughed. 'Not you.'

Mona laughed with her, despite the implicit deception involved. D'orothea, after all, was long gone from her life. In Mona's eyes, lesbianism had simply been the logical follow-up to macrobiotics and primal screaming. She had gotten into it, but seldom off on it, and *never* behind it.

She took an Oreo from Bobbi and split it apart. 'How can we have a slumber party without a stack of 45's and a record player?'

'I know some ghost stories.'

Mona grinned. 'We could do our toenails.'

'I did mine yesterday.'

'Oh, well, then we could –'

'Lick the centers out of Oreos!' They squealed in unison as Mona held up a cookie with the creamy filling exposed. Bobbi held her tongue out expectantly. 'We need milk,' Mona blurted, dropping the Oreo in Bobbi's hand and springing from the bed.

She avoided the parlor, where she could hear Mother Mucca lining up four of the girls for a pair of drunken truckers. She entered the kitchen from the back door, fumbled for the light switch and made her way to the refrigerator. There was half a quart of milk on the top shelf.

A pitcher would be nice, she decided. They could pour each other milk from a pitcher. Bobbi would like that.

She found one on the shelf over the stove, a pale green Depression-ware piece that would fetch a small fortune in a San Francisco antique shop.

As she reached for it, her hand brushed past a row of tattered cook-books, knocking one to the floor. She bent over to pick it up. The name on the flyleaf filled her with instant terror.

Mona Ramsey.

Temper, Temper

Two days before the *Pacific Princess* was scheduled to arrive in Acapulco, Michael awoke to find himself alone in his stateroom. Mary Ann's bed was still made. Eager for a play-by-play, he showered hurriedly and raced down to breakfast on the Aloha Deck.

Mary Ann was already seated, as were Arnold and Melba Littlefield, resplendent in matching denim pantsuits. Arnold's outfit was embroidered with rainbows; Melba's had butterflies. God help us, thought Michael. The Summer of Love is alive and well in Dublin.

' 'Well,' thundered Arnold, as Michael sat down, 'don't you two *ever* make it to chow at the same time?'

Mary Ann flushed, casting a nervous glance at her lapsed roommate.

Michael turned elfin. 'The little woman's probably worked up one hell of an appetite.'

Mary Ann kicked him under the table.

Arnold chuckled knowingly and winked at Michael.

Melba, as usual, looked puzzled. 'Out boogying all night?' Melba was abnormally fond of words like 'boogy', 'rap' and 'ripoff,' a vocabulary Michael was certain she had picked up from *People* magazine.

'Boogying?' He might as well have fun with it.

'You know. Dancing. Didn't they set up a disco in the Skaal Bar?'

'Oh, yeah. I forgot. I hit the sack early. With Christopher Isherwood.'

Mary Ann was squirming. 'Mouse, you haven't ordered yet.'

'Wait a minute,' said Arnold, addressing Michael. 'Run that one by me again.'

'It's a book,' said Mary Ann.

Michael nodded. '*Christopher and His Kind.*'

'Mouse . . . I think the steward . . .'

'What's it about?' asked Arnold.

'He wrote *Cabaret*,' said Mary Ann.

'About krauts, huh?'

'You bet,' said Michael.

'They have blueberry pancakes today, Mouse.'

Melba sighed. 'Isn't Liza Minnelli just *darling*!'

*

'OK,' said Michael, as soon as they had left the dining room. 'Gimme the dirt.'

Mary Ann sulked.

'C'mon. Did he ravish you on the poop deck?'

Silence.

'Brutalize you in the bilge? Suck your toes? Buy you a cup of coffee?'

'Mouse, you *ruined* breakfast for me!'

'You could have asked Burke to join you.'

'Right. And play footsy with him while you're telling Arnold and Melba snappy stories about the little woman?'

'Hey, look: the young marrieds routine was your idea, remember?'

'Lower your voice.'

'Lower your own goddamn voice! What the hell do you think I am, anyway? Rent-a-Hubby?'

Mary Ann glared at him for a split second, groaned in exasperation, and strode past him down the passageway. Michael cooled off on the Promenade Deck, walking laps under the lifeboats until his thoughts were clear. Fifteen minutes later he returned to the stateroom.

Mary Ann was seated at the desk, writing postcards. She didn't turn around.

'Guess what?' said Michael.

'What?' She had drained her voice of expression.

'I'm jealous.'

'Mouse, don't –'

'I am. I'm one jealous little queen. I'm jealous of Burke because he's taken away my playmate, and I'm jealous of you because you've found a lover.'

Mary Ann turned around with tears in her eyes.

'You'll find somebody, Mouse. I know you will. Maybe even in Acapulco.'

'Maybe this time, huh?'

She smiled and hugged him, holding him tight. 'I love you for that, Michael Mouse.'

'What?'

'Turning everything into song lyrics.'

'Yeah,' said Michael. 'Isn't Liza Minnelli just *darling*?'

Later, it was her turn to apologize. 'I've been crabby too, Mouse. I mean . . . well, I'm a little edgy, I guess.'

'About what?'

She hesitated, then said: 'Burke.'

'He wasn't . . . ?'

'He's perfect, Mouse. He's sensitive, strong, considerate. We're – you know – sexually whatever. He's protective, yet he treats me like an equal. He doesn't crack his knuckles. He's perfect.'

'But not perfect?'

'He's afraid of roses, Mouse.'

'Uh . . . pardon me?'

'This dwarf at Las Hadas tried to give us a rose and Burke took one look at it, turned white and threw up in the bushes.'

'Maybe he's from Pasadena.'

'It worries me, Mouse. That's not normal, is it?'

'You're asking *me*?'

'I tried to talk to him about it, and he changed the subject. I don't think he has the slightest idea why he reacted that way.'

The Mysteries of Pinus

Everything about Helena Parrish was smart but safe. She wore a navy blue fedora, a navy blue Mollie Parnis suit, and navy blue, medium height, T-strap calf shoes from Magnin's. She looked, to Frannie, like the kind of woman who would *never* miss a Wednesday night travelogue at the Century Club.

'More tea?' asked Frannie, wondering where her guest had her hair streaked so beautifully.

'No thanks,' smiled Helena Parrish, dabbing her lips with a linen napkin.

'Bourbon balls?'

'No. They're lovely, though. May I call you Frannie, by the way?'

'Of course.'

'How much do you know about Pinus, Frannie?'

The hostess flushed, startled by this abrupt approach to the subject. 'Oh . . . well, most of it's just hearsay, I suppose.' Discretion seemed wise at this point. Helena could do the talking.

The visitor nodded solemnly. 'Word-of-mouth, we find, is our best safeguard.' She smiled thinly. 'Discrimination seems to be a nasty word these days, doesn't it?'

'Isn't it dreadful?'

'We prefer to think of it as quality control. And of course, the less publicity we receive, the more we're able to . . . cater to the needs of our members.'

'I understand.'

'Aside from the social criteria, the only other requirement for membership is the attainment of one's sixtieth birthday.' She spoke the last two words in a stage whisper, as if to apologize for an embarrassing, if necessary, invasion of privacy.

Frannie's smile was sheepish. 'Your timing is close to perfect.'

'I know,' said Helena.

'Vita?'

Helena nodded and continued. 'Our philosophy is that women of our mature station in life are entitled to carve out any lifestyle we can afford. We have, after all, played the rules for forty years. Raising children, tolerating husbands, joining the right clubs, supporting the correct charities.' She leaned forward and looked Frannie straight in the eye. 'We have paid our dues, Frannie, and we will *not* piddle away the rest of our days as long-suffering Mary Worths!'

Frannie was mesmerized. Helena Parrish had begun to assume the aura of a guru.

'There *are* alternatives, of course. Pinus is not the only solution. It's simply the only *fulfilling* one. And if we have the money for it, why on earth should we squander it on face-lifts and body tucks and youth injections?

'Fortunately,' continued Helena, 'people like us can afford to indulge in this sort of . . . luxury. And what's wrong with that? What's wrong with demanding our piece of the pleasure pie?'

She handed Frannie a brochure. It was printed in brown ink on heavy cream stock with hand-torn edges. There were, of course, no pictures.

PINUS

For gentlewomen who are 60. And Ready.

Nestled snugly in the rolling hills of
Sonoma, Pinus is unquestionably the most
remarkable resort of its kind in the
world. Resort, perhaps, is an ill-
chosen word, for Pinus is a Way of Life.

Pinus is a Flight of Fancy, a mature
woman's idyll, a Dream of Wild Abandon.
Once you have experienced Pinus, nothing
is quite the same again.

'I'll leave it with you,' Helena said quietly. 'I'm sure you'd like to
mull over it alone.'

'Yes. Thank you.'

'As you may know, Frannie, admission depends ultimately on our
board of directors. In your case, however, I'm sure there won't be
any . . .' She finished the sentence with a little wave of her hand.
Frannie's social acceptability had never been at issue.

'The decision is yours to make, Frannie. If you feel you're ready,
please give me a call at Pinus. The number's on the brochure.'

'Thank you. Uh . . . Helena, when would I . . . how soon?'

'On your birthday, if you like.' The visitor smiled cordially. 'We
even provide a *very* interesting cake.'

'What fun.'

'Yes,' said Helena. 'It's about time, isn't it?'

Mona Times Two

In a house with ten bedrooms, Mona had never expected to encounter
the biggest shocker in the kitchen. But there she stood – immobilized
by fear – *reading her own name in the flyleaf of a cookbook.*

Her own name! Why? Why?

She dropped the book and lunged at the others, already certain of
what she would find. *Mona Ramsey . . . Mona Ramsey . . . Mona
Ramsey!* All of them the same, all of them inscribed in the halting,
primitive hand of a child – or perhaps a semi-literate adult.

A flashback. That was it. This was the LSD flashback they had
warned her about. She sank into a chair, moaning softly, waiting with
patient resignation for large purple caterpillars to crawl up out of the
sink drains.

Minutes passed. No caterpillars. Only the distant, pervasive whine
of the desert wind and the insistent drip of the faucet. Out in the
parlor, a trucker was laughing raucously with Marni, who kept saying,
'Gross me out! Gross me out!' in her tinny Modesto accent.

353

Rising on wobbly legs, Mona went to the sink and doused herself with water. Then she blotted her face with a JFK-Bobby Kennedy-Martin Luther King dish towel and lurched through the back door into the blackness.

She counted the doors from the end of the building until she found the one that was hers.

The light was still on.

Bobbi looked up with a smile. 'No milk, huh?'

'No.'

'I think there's some Dr Peppers in the bar, if you . . . Judy, what's the matter?'

'I don't know.' Mona sank to the edge of the bed and stared glassily at the Autograph Hound the room's former occupant had left on the vanity.

'Bobbi . . . what's my name?'

'Huh?'

'What's my name?'

'Are you . . . ?'

'Please answer.'

'It's Judy.'

'Judy what?'

'I don't know. You never told me.'

'If I . . . if I had another name, and you knew about it, would you tell me so? Or would you tease me about it, Bobbi? Do you think Charlene would . . . ?' She couldn't finish. It was all so paranoid. If Charlene wanted to torment her about her real name, why the hell would she write it in a goddamn cookbook?

Bobbi smiled forgivingly. 'Lots of us have fake names, Judy. Marni's real name is Esther. I don't give a hoot if your name isn't –'

'How long have you worked here, Bobbi?'

'Off and on?'

Was there any other way to work at a whorehouse? 'Yeah.'

'Oh, I guess . . . three years.'

'You've known a lot of the girls who've been through here, then?'

'Sure.' Bobbi popped a stick of Dentyne into her mouth and chewed it soberly, suddenly aware that she was being interrogated.

'Do you remember one called Mona?'

The chewing continued. If the name had jolted Bobbi, the expression on her face didn't betray it. 'Mona, huh?'

354

'Yeah.'

Bobbi shook her head languidly. 'No. Not right offhand.'

'Think, Bobbi, please.'

'You know her last name?'

'Ramsey. Mona Ramsey.'

The light dawned. Bobbi giggled at her own stupidity. 'Oh, gee,' she said. 'We *never* call her that!'

'*Who*, Bobbi?'

'Mother Mucca.'

'*Mother Mucca?*'

'Sure. Mona Ramsey is Mother Mucca's real name.'

Minutes later, when Bobbi had left, Mona sat alone and pondered her mounting paranoia. She hadn't felt so confused and frightened – so utterly abandoned – since Rennie Davis, the foremost deity of her youth, had been discovered selling John Hancock insurance in Colorado.

Why was Buddha doing this to her?

Two Mona Ramseys in the same whorehouse! One grizzled and ancient and weathered by debauchery. The other jaded but youngish and teetering on the brink of lunacy.

Past and future? Yin and Yang? Donny and Marie?

Mother Mucca had been right from the beginning: 'That angel dust'll fuck you up every time!'

It will and it did, thought Mona. It will and it did.

I am twisted beyond recognition, beyond redemption. There are no longer laws that apply to me. Only a miracle could save me now.

She walked back to the empty parlor in a glazed stupor and placed a phone call to 28 Barbary Lane.

'Madrigal.'

'Thank God!'

'Who is this, please?'

'It's me, Mrs Madrigal. Mona.'

'Child! Where are you?'

'Oh, God! Winnemucca!'

Silence.

'Mrs Madrigal?'

'Are you all right, dear?'

'Well, I'm . . . No, I feel like shit.'

355

'Are you . . . are you at the Blue Moon?'

Mona began to whimper. 'How did you know?'

'Mona, I –'

'*How did you know?*'

'The question, dear, is how did *you* know?'

'How did I know *what*?'

'About . . . Winnemucca?'

'I'm cracking up, Mrs Madrigal.'

'Please, Mona. I would have told you earlier –'

'Told me *what*?'

'I was *so* afraid you'd hate me for it, for running off and leaving –'

'I didn't *run off*! I needed space. I told you that in the –'

'Not *you*, dear. Me.'

'What? You haven't run off. What in the world are you talking about?'

Silence.

'Mrs Madrigal?'

'It looks like we'd better take this from the top, dear. Are you alone?'

'Yes.'

'Well, sit down, then. I've got a little story to tell you.'

Acapulco Blues

It was dusk on board the *Pacific Princess*. Michael sat in a deck chair, smoking a joint and watching the gentle, seductive curve of the beach at Acapulco. The air was warm, and the sky was exactly the color it should have been.

Even before he got stoned.

'Mouse?' It was Mary Ann. Dressed for a date.

'Hi,' said Michael.

'I've looked all over for you.'

'I'se heah, Miz Scahlett.'

She pulled up a deck chair and sat on the edge of it. 'Are you all right, Mouse?'

He nodded. 'I'm always all right.'

'You weren't at dinner.'

He patted his stomach. 'Chubbette.'

356

'Burke and I thought you might . . . We'd really like it if you came into town with us tonight. Somebody told us about this place called BabyO's.'

'Thanks. I don't think I'm up for that tonight.'

'It's a disco.'

'Maybe tomorrow, OK?'

She brushed a lock of hair off his forehead. 'Are you sure?'

He nodded as her hand slid down the side of his face. His cheek was wet. She sat with him for almost a minute, holding his hand, saying nothing.

'You better go,' he said finally. 'I'm OK.'

'You're too hard on yourself, Mouse.'

He shrugged. 'If I don't do it, who will?'

'Mouse, you're the most wonderful –'

'I know, Mary Ann. I know I'm a nice guy. I really do. I know that you love me. I know that old ladies love me and my mother and dogs and cats . . . and every goddamn person I meet except someone who'll commit himself to . . . Please don't get me started.'

'Mouse, I wish you could –'

'The hell of it is, I know the answer. The answer is that you never, ever, rely on another person for your peace of mind. If you do, you're screwed but good. Not right away, maybe, but sooner or later. You have to – I don't know – you have to learn to live with yourself. You have to learn to turn back your own sheets and set a table for one without feeling pathetic. You have to be strong and confident and pleased with yourself and never give the slightest impression that you can't hack it without that certain goddamn someone. You have to fake the hell out of it.'

'You aren't faking it, Mouse. You *are* strong.'

'I'm tired of it. I'm sick of picking up the pieces and marching bravely onward. I want things to work out just *once*.' He rubbed the corner of his eye, smiled suddenly, and shrugged. 'I wanna do a Salem commercial with a Marlboro Man.'

Mary Ann squeezed his hand. 'We're all that way, Mouse.'

'I know, but it works out for some people.'

'It'll work out for you.'

'No it won't.'

'Mouse . . .'

'I want it too badly, Mary Ann. Any idiot can see that. When you want it too badly, no one wants you. No one is attracted to that . . . desperation.'

357

He turned away from her, wiping his eyes.

'Christ!' he said softly, reaching for her hand again. 'Look at that sky, will you?'

After Mary Ann and Burke had left, Michael spent half an hour in his stateroom reading another chapter of the Isherwood book, then wandered out onto the deck again.

The lights of the city blinked at him beguilingly.

But why should I? he wondered. Why should I put my heart through the wringer again? Who could I find that would possibly matter on a two-day stay in an unfamiliar foreign city?

And should I wear the pink or the green Lacoste?

The taxi driver had a huge white mustache and a jovial, grandfatherly face. Michael hated to ask him.

'Uh . . . do you know any gay places?'

The driver blinked, puzzled. 'Red light?'

'No, not red light. Men.'

'Men?'

'*Sí.*'

'Ah, homosex!'

'*Sí.*'

The driver peered over the seat and studied his passenger for several seconds. 'Homosex,' he repeated, then turned his eyes back to the road.

The Man in White

The road up the mountain was poorly lit. Michael caught only rough impressions of dusty foliage and black palms, shabby stucco houses that cowered under the headlights like illicit lovers trapped in the flash of a detective's camera.

The cab stopped at a blocky white building with a central archway. Iron grillwork over the entrance spelled out SANS SOUCI.

Without care, Michael translated. Without care in Acapulco in a gay bar with a French name on a night when nothing in the world made any goddamn sense at all. He realized now, with some embarrassment, that he had laid the heaviest of trips on Mary Ann.

She had glimpsed his soul at its blackest, devoid of humor, poisonous with self-pity. She had seen beyond the brave Disney elf, and the sight couldn't have been pretty.

He paid the driver and walked through the archway, nodding to an old woman sweeping the floor. She returned the greeting without expression. Michael wondered if she had a word for gringo fag.

The archway led to a rear terrace overlooking another hillside and a chunk of the bay. There was a thatched bar at one end of the terrace where an old man seemed to serve as both sentinel and bartender. The whole scene was so shadowy that Michael tripped on a chair while making his entrance.

Recovering his cool, he looked around the terrace for witnesses to his clumsiness. There were none. The place was empty. The only sounds were the skeletal rattle of palms along the hillside and the sepulchral wail of Donna Summer singing 'Winter Melody.'

Something was gravely wrong.

Or maybe not. Maybe this was *exactly* the way a gay bar in Mexico was supposed to look. Or there might have been a language problem with the cabby? No. What else could 'homosex' mean? A joke, then? A macho prank on a simple American pervert?

It was half-past nine when Michael ordered a Dos Equis from the old man and sat down at a table on the edge of the terrace. He lost himself for several minutes in the onyx shine of the bay, the huge illuminated cross at the Capilla de la Paz. A neon Pepsi sign glowed obscenely on a distant hillside.

Several people straggled onto the terrace. Women. Lesbians? A man appeared. He was decked out in spray-on white pants, several dozen gold chains and a patent-leather Latin Lover hairdo right out of *GQ*. In LA, he would have been straight. But here . . . ?'

The man began to boogie by himself, rolling his eyes back like a corpse that had died in copulation. His movements were the tip-off for Michael. He didn't stop at limp wrists; he had limp *ankles*.

By eleven o'clock the dance floor was packed. The crowd, for the most part, was nellie, though Michael spotted a coterie of pseudo-lumberjack numbers watching the proceedings with ill-concealed amusement. He made a point of avoiding them. If they were San Franciscans, he didn't want to know about it. He didn't want to meet

359

on a mountainside in Mexico someone he might have gone down on in the back room of the Jaguar Book Store.

A man asked him to dance. Michael accepted, feeling awkward and insincere. He didn't want to dance, really; he wanted to be held.

'First time?' asked his partner, shimmying half-heartedly. He was Mexican.

'Yes,' said Michael, making a conscious effort not to speak in broken English. He usually did that when confronted with foreigners.

'You unhappy, I think?'

Michael tried to smile. 'I'm sorry. I –'

'It's O K. Sometimes . . . me too.'

Damn, thought Michael. Don't be nice. If you're nice, I'll cry all over you. 'I'm happy most of the time, really, but sometimes . . .' He gave up trying to explain it and fell back on a bar cliché he never would have used in California. 'Do you come here often?'

When the answer came, Michael was only half listening.

His eyes were glued to the archway, where a tall blond man in a white linen suit was watching the dance floor. Out of ancient habit, Michael cruised him for a fraction of a second, then he stopped with all the abruptness of a dog that had caught its own tail.

It was Jon Fielding.

Playing Games

There were times when Brian was sure she was following him.

His imagination conjured her up in the oddest of places: in laundro-mats on Saturday mornings, on crowded cable cars and empty escala-tors, in darkened movie houses when he was ripped on Colombian.

It usually started with a look. A heavy-lidded glance. A private wink. A slow, sardonic smile that devoured him from head to foot. He was used to that, of course, but before, it had meant something different.

Before, it had meant a conquest, *his* conquest, a simple, uncompli-cated adventure that remained under his control from beginning to end.

But now . . .

Now it could be someone who knew full well his dependence on her.

Now it could be Lady Eleven.

And *she* could be the one in control.

The question that plagued him remained the same: If she knew who he was, if she knew where to find him . . . why wouldn't she want to get it on with him?

Maybe, of course, she had tried to do exactly that. Maybe she had checked out 28 Barbary Lane in the same way he had searched for her at the Superman Building. His name, he reminded himself, had never been displayed on the mailbox.

Even so, she could have *asked*. Mrs Madrigal would have told her, for Christ's sake! Maybe Mrs Madrigal *had* told her and had forgotten to tell *him* that . . .

On the other hand, there could be something terribly wrong with her. Maybe she was afraid for him to meet her and thereby discover that she was . . . what? Crippled? Insane? Blind? Right, Brian. Blind people always keep a pair of binoculars handy.

Then again, she *could* be somebody famous, a local celebrity who couldn't afford the notoriety of an overt sexual liaison. Or a Hite Report volunteer doing free-lance research? Or a lesbian trying to reform, one step at a time? Or a porno star practicing for her big scene?

Or an All-American cunt trying to drive Brian Hawkins right up the wall.

That night, as they undressed in front of their windows, Brian decided to try a new approach. He stripped to his boxer shorts, but kept his cock out of sight. Leaving the binoculars on the window sill, he folded his arms across his chest and waited.

Lady Eleven watched him through the binoculars, then mimicked his stance.

Brian counted to twenty and lifted his binoculars.

Lady Eleven did the same.

It's a chickenshit *game*, he thought. We're a couple of bratty kids playing copycat. All right, bitch! Let's see if you can handle this one!

He left the window and ran to the kitchen, returning with a large brown paper bag. He tore open the bag and flattened it. Using a Magic Marker, he wrote seven digits on the poster-size banner.

928–3117

Then he held it up to the window, watching Lady Eleven's reaction through the binoculars. She stood frozen for several seconds, finally

361

lifting the binoculars to study the inscription. She held that position for a long time.

Suddenly – God almighty! – she walked away from the window, and came back moments later holding a telephone. Brian lunged for his own phone, instantly grateful he had ordered the model with an extension cord.

They were both in position now, once again duplicates of each other.

Brian watched her through the binoculars. In the conch-shell pinkness of her room, her robed body seemed to pulse with warmth. He *knew* what she smelled like – the sweet, grassy scent of her wet hair, the smoldering musk of her breasts . . .

Oh, Jesus, she was dialing!

One . . . two . . . three . . . four . . . five . . . six . . . seven.

Brian's phone rang.

He lifted the receiver gently, fearful of frightening her. 'Hello,' he said, in a calm, well-modulated voice.

Silence.

'Look, if you'd just give me your phone number, we could . . . I could call you sometime . . . that's all.' He could hear her breathing now. He could watch her standing mute by the phone.

'Hey . . . tell me your name, then . . . just your first name, if you want. I'm a nice guy . . . I swear. Christ! Don't you think this is a little weird?'

The breathing grew louder. At first, he thought she was toying with him, taunting him with sexy noises. Then he realized she was crying.

'Hey . . . I'm sorry, really. I didn't mean it to sound like –'

She hung up on him. He watched her sink into a chair and crumple into a tight little knot of despair. Half a minute later she stood and closed the curtains.

Brian pulled up a chair and sat watching her window until he fell asleep.

Kinfolks

Mona's conversation with Mrs Madrigal took forty-five minutes. When it was over, she left her cubicle and wandered out into the desert. About a hundred yards from the house a discarded truck seat offered her a sheltered refuge.

She sat down and watched the midnight sky for several minutes, halfway believing that a flying saucer would appear there to take her away from this hideous, surreal landscape.

In San Francisco now the hills would be green – a delicate shade of celadon – and soft as the fuzz on a deer's antlers. There would be daffodils in Washington Square and purple pleroma trees on Barbary Lane and dozens and dozens of calla lilies stoically bracing themselves for Michael's annual impression of Katharine Hepburn.

And her *father* would be there! Her father, her mother, her best friend and her landlady, all rolled into one joyful and loving human being!

She sprang from the truck seat and ran back to the lodge, her heart pounding with anticipation, her brain almost short-circuiting on hope. Who needed a flying saucer? Like Dorothy of Oz, she had only to click her heels three times to find her way back to Auntie Em.

Without a moment's pause, she flung open the door of Mother Mucca's room, completely unintimidated by the old woman's crabbiness.

The madam was brushing her hair. 'Can't you knock'?

'Mother Mucca . . . Oh, I'm sorry, but I . . .' She leaned against the wall, trying to catch her breath. 'There's something I . . .'

A look of concern furrowed the old woman's brow. 'Are you OK, Judy?'

'No. Not Judy. Mona.'

'Don't you call me that, dolly.'

'I'm *not*, Mother Mucca. I'm saying my name's not Judy. It's Mona. Mona Ramsey . . . the same as yours.'

Mother Mucca glared at her briefly, then turned her gaze back to the mirror and resumed brushing. 'I told you about that angel dust, dolly.'

'Mother Mucca, I haven't –'

'If I catch you smokin' in the house, you're out on your ass, Judy!'

Mona regained her composure and tried to reason with her. 'Look, I *know* you can't believe it. I can hardly believe it myself. It's like a . . . well, it's like a miracle, Mother Mucca. Some invisible cosmic force brought us together because we need each other, because we –'

'Look, dolly, if ya don't mind –'

'I'll get my bag! I'll show you my . . . well, I can't show you any ID's, come to think of it. I *promise* you that's my name. I told you my name was Judy because I . . . I was a little embarrassed about working here and all . . . Please, just answer one question for me.'

'Go on . . . git!'

'Not until you answer this.'

'I *said* –'

'What was your little boy's name?'

'What the hell do you think you're . . . ?'

'*What was his name?*'

Mother Mucca picked up the house phone on her vanity. 'I'm callin' Charlene, Judy.'

'Mona!'

'You're so plumb pitiful I don't even –'

Mona jerked the phone out of her hand. 'Listen to me! I love you, goddammit! It was Andy wasn't it? Your son's name was Andy!'

A stunned silence, then: 'Who told you that?'

'Who do you think? Charlene? Marnie? Bobbi, maybe? You never told *anyone*, did you? It must've hurt too much to talk about him.' Mona caught her breath, then sank to her knees, taking the old lady's hands in hers. 'Mother Mucca . . . *he* told me. *Andy* told me. I live with him in San Francisco . . . and he's my father.'

The madam's eyes were full of tears. 'I'm an old lady, dolly. A lie can hurt mighty bad.'

'I would never hurt you, Mother Mucca.'

'Why . . . why did you come here?'

Mona smiled at her. 'You picked *me* up, remember?'

'It don't make no sense.'

'I *told* you. It's a miracle! I'm your granddaughter, Mother Mucca. I've found my goddamn roots!'

The old woman's eyes narrowed. 'Who taught you to talk like that, Mona?'

Falling in Love Again

The man dancing with Michael could tell that something was wrong. 'Excuse, please . . . you know that man?'

Michael's condition was almost trancelike. 'I . . . yes. I hope you don't mind. He's somebody I used to . . . I'm sorry, OK?'

The man nodded, apparently more puzzled than offended, and boogied off the dance floor toward the bar. Michael stood frozen in his tracks, composing opening lines. Jon hadn't seen him yet.

A scratchy phonograph blared out 'Cherchez la Femme.' The same tune they had played at The Endup when Michael won the jockey shorts dance contest . . . and Dr Jon Fielding walked out of his life forever.

Michael's forevers never lasted for long.

'Hey, greengo! You wan buy my seester? She virgin!'

'Michael! Christ!'

'Please, just Michael.'

Jon hugged him heartily. The kind of hug, Michael noted, that Danny Thomas might have given George Burns on Johnny Carson. 'What the hell are you doing here?'

Michael shrugged. 'It's the only queer joint in Acapulco.'

Jon laughed. 'I mean, in Acapulco?'

'I'm on a cruise. Ship-type, that is.'

'The *Pacific Princess*?'

'Yep. What brings *you* here?'

'Oh . . . vaginal infections.'

'You don't *look* sick.'

The gynecologist grinned. 'A convention, turkey.'

'A million laughs, huh?'

'It is, actually. We get a lot of free time.'

That bothered Michael. People he'd been hot for were not supposed to enjoy themselves in his absence. But the doctor was having a ball, so why torture himself? 'It's good seeing you, Jon.'

'You're leaving?'

'Yeah. This place looks like The Kokpit on a bad night. I've had enough.'

Jon gave the terrace another once-over. 'I see what you mean.'

'Yeah. Well, I'm sure you'll find something.'

'I thought I had.'

Michael ignored that. 'I guess it gets better as the evening wears on.'

'I've got a car, Michael. We could go for a ride or something.'

Michael looked at him for a moment, then shook his head. 'I don't think so, Jon. Thanks, though.'

The doctor smiled faintly. 'You're punishing me, aren't you?'

'For what?'

'For . . . that night at The Endup.'

Michael managed a blithe shrug. 'It was a tacky scene. I don't blame you for –'

'No. I was the tacky one. I was . . . embarrassed, Michael. I was out

365

with some pissy queens from Seacliff, and I couldn't handle it. That was my failing, not yours.'

Michael smiled. 'I won, you know.'

'You should have.'

'*Gracias.*'

They drove to the Capilla de la Paz in Jon's rented Volkswagen Thing. Like strangers in a foreign city, they chatted breezily about night spots in Acapulco, the boredom of sea cruises and the perils of smoking grass in Mexico.

The mountaintop chapel was deserted. Above it loomed the leviathan cross, white as bleached bones against the starry sky. They walked to its base in silence.

'Somebody told me,' said Jon, 'that this is a shrine to two brothers who were killed in a plane crash.'

'That's nice. I mean . . . a nice story.'

'I may have it wrong.'

'I like the story anyway.'

'You can see the ship, see?' Jon pointed to the toy boat twinkling below in the harbor. Michael could feel the doctor's breath against his cheek.

'And over there,' continued Jon, 'behind that row of hotels . . . Michael?'

'Sorry. I was thinking.'

'About what?'

'Shrines. Funerals, actually.'

'Charming.'

Michael looked at him. 'Don't tell me you've never planned your own funeral?'

Jon shook his head, smiling.

'Well, take this down, please. I'd like a big party at the Paramount theater in Oakland, with lots of dope and munchies and all my friends ripped to the tits in the midst of all that Deco decadence. And when it's over I'd like them to prop me up in a front-row seat, leave the theater . . . and bury the whole goddamn thing.'

Jon laughed and squeezed the back of his head. 'Couldn't you do that without dying?'

'Mmm. I often do.'

Jon laughed, then cupped Michael's face in his hands and kissed him. 'Don't die, OK? Not until I'm through with you.'

366

The Trouble with Burke

Seated in a pink-and-orange booth at the Acapulco Denny's, Mary Ann inspected her french fries and found them suspiciously grayish. 'Ick,' she said, holding one up for Burke's examination.

He smiled uncomplainingly. 'Ditto on the milk shake.'

'I'm sorry, Burke.'

'Why?'

'I shouldn't have dragged you here. I just felt like a hamburger, I guess.'

'That's OK. So did I.'

'We should have eaten at Colonel Sanders.'

He shrugged. 'We can eat on the ship tonight.'

'I'm not . . . being a drag, am I?'

'I can't tell,' he grinned. 'I'm too much in love with you.'

They rented a horse-drawn carriage and clopped through the city, trailing balloons behind them. It's a Harlequin Romance, thought Mary Ann. Too corny, too perfect to be true. If I think about it too long or plan on *anything*, it'll go away forever. So she nestled against Burke's shoulder and slipped her mind into neutral.

'How's Michael?' asked Burke, as they passed the Ritz.

'Much better. He had company last night. This morning too. I found out the hard way.'

'What d'ya mean?'

'I walked in on them.'

Burke smiled. 'That blond guy he had breakfast with?'

'Uh huh. God, I can't *imagine* what Melba and Arnold thought about that.'

'Who's Melba and Arnold?'

'Mr and Mrs Matching. The couple at our table. They think Michael and I are married.'

'How did that happen?'

'Well . . . I told them. I mean, I didn't want it to look like we were . . . shacked up or something. Plus, if I'd told them he was gay, they'd have freaked out and thought I was a fag hag.'

'A *what*?'

Mary Ann kissed him on the ear. 'I love you. You don't know *anything*.'

Back on the beach, they basted themselves in turtle lotion and stretched out on the sand. The simple, unspoiled beauty of the scene made Mary Ann painfully conscious of her dwindling days with Burke.

But you mustn't push, she ordered herself. You mustn't frighten him.

'Burke?'

'Mmmm?'

'This is really nice.'

'You bet.'

'I mean . . . I never thought I'd meet anybody like you on this trip.'

'C'mon! With *your* looks?'

'That's sweet, but I mean it. Most of the guys I meet in San Francisco wanna talk about their dumb Porsches or their tape decks or getting their head together or something. I don't hang around with Michael because I'm . . . desperate or anything. It's just that . . . well, Michael makes me feel like I'm worth something. I was beginning to think that a straight man couldn't do that for me.'

Silence.

She reddened instantly. 'I embarrassed you, didn't I?'

'No, really . . .' He reached over and squeezed her hand. 'I haven't felt very communicative, Mary Ann.'

'It isn't what you *say*, Burke. It's – I don't know – how you look at me, how you react to things. I know that you see me as a person. I'll always be grateful for that. I want you to know that.'

He rolled over on his side and pulled her against his chest, prompting giggles from two passing urchins. Mary Ann couldn't have cared less. For one single, delirious moment she was *certain* they looked like Burt Lancaster and Deborah Kerr in *From Here to Eternity*.

'Burke?'

'Yeah?'

'Have you ever thought about moving back to San Francisco?'

Silence.

You blew it, you dink. He's on to you now. 'I'm sorry, Burke. I shouldn't have said that.'

'That's OK.'

'No, it's not. We'll change the subject. I won't get heavy, I promise.'

'No. We should talk. There's something I should have told you a long time ago.'

Somehow, she had known this moment would come. Her whole body tensed as she waited for the truth to fall like an executioner's axe. 'Please,' she said feebly. 'I'd rather not hear it.'

'Mary Ann, I lived in San Francisco for three years . . . three whole years out of my life!'

Oh, God! Had Michael been right all along?

'Do you know why I'm out of it, Mary Ann? Do you know where my goddamn boyish naïveté comes from?'

Please no! Please don't let him be . . .

'I can't remember *anything*, Mary Ann. Not a single goddamn thing about those three years in San Francisco.'

She pulled away from him. 'You've got . . . *amnesia?*'

· He nodded.

Thank God, she thought, hugging him. Thank God!

Try to Remember

'I'm sorry,' said Burke, sitting up in the sand and rubbing his forehead with his fingertips. 'I should have told you a long time ago.'

Mary Ann flailed for the right words. 'You . . . can't remember anything at all?'

He shook his head. 'Nothing about my time in San Francisco. I'm clear on the rest. I mean everything up to 1973. When I was in Nantucket. There are some . . . images or whatever that come to me from time to time. They don't mean anything, really.'

'Like what?'

'Mary Ann, there's no point –'

'I want to help, Burke.'

He traced a line in the sand. 'Everybody wants to help.' Then, seeing her expression, he added, 'I didn't mean it like that. You're not everyone. It's just that . . . well, everything's been done that can be done. My parents even sent me on this cruise, so I could – you know –'

'It doesn't matter to me, Burke.'

'It's a form of insanity.'

'I don't believe that.'

'I can't be honest in a relationship, Mary Ann. I don't know what there is to be honest about. I don't even know *why* I –'

Mary Ann gasped, anticipating him. 'God, Burke! The thing about the roses!'

He nodded. 'That's part of it. Cute, huh? I also freak out on walkways with railings.'

'Where?'

'Anywhere. Any walkways with railings. Haven't you noticed me on the ship? That's why I hang around the fantail all day long. I'm scared shitless, Mary Ann.'

Mary Ann moved closer to him, placing a reassuring hand on his knee. 'Well, look: if you can't remember what happened to you in San Francisco . . . I mean, how did you get back to Nantucket?'

'I didn't, exactly . . . Are you sure you want to hear all this?'

'Positive.'

'Well. They found me.'

'Who?'

'Some cops in Golden Gate Park. Mounted policemen. I had . . . passed out or whatever in the woods. It took them three days to figure out who I was.'

'And then you went home?'

He nodded. 'I was lucky, I guess. The Nantucket part came back almost immediately – along with my name and all that. I just don't know what I was doing in San Francisco.'

Mary Ann smiled ruefully. 'Welcome to the club,' she said.

They walked for a long time on the beach, watching the sky turn the color of a ripe nectarine. Mary Ann continued to probe gently, certain he would shut her out completely if she ever stopped talking.

'You haven't told me why you went to San Francisco in the first place.'

'Oh, I was a reporter. For the AP.'

'Grocery stores have reporters?'

He touched the tip of her nose. 'The Associated Press.'

She flushed. 'I just did that to make you feel good.'

'Of course.'

'So, what did you do before that? Before the AP.'

'I didn't. I left my father's publishing house and interviewed with the head AP bureau in New York. They stuck me in a little glass booth with a lot of disjointed facts about Lucille Ball's wedding in ... whenever, and I wrote a typical AP story and ... they assigned me to the San Francisco bureau.'

'And you don't remember anything after that.'

He chuckled. 'Oh, yeah. That part's gruesomely clear. The boredom, the shitwork, perpetual deadlines. I quit five weeks later. That's where the blackout comes.'

'What about your parents? You couldn't just disappear for three years. You must've written them or something?'

'Not enough to really let them know what was going on. Just I-am-fine-don't-worry-about-me stuff. I lived on Nob Hill for a while, I know that. I did temporary shiftwork – clerical stuff. Sometimes I attended services at Grace Cathedral.'

'Well, at least you remember *that* much.'

He shook his head. 'I told them that in the letters. I don't remember a bit of it.'

'You mean there's no record whatsoever ... no evidence of where you were or what you were doing for –'

'Wait!' He stopped suddenly and dug in his pockets. 'Hold out your hand,' he instructed her. Somewhat reluctantly, she complied. He pressed something small and metal into her palm.

'A key,' she said flatly. 'What's that mean?'

'You tell me. It's all that's left of me.'

'What?'

'It was in my pocket, my shirt pocket, when they found me in the park.'

She examined it more closely. 'It's ... smaller than a door key, or a car key. I guess it could ...' Finally, she shrugged, giving up.

He shrugged back at her, smiling. It was his collie look again. Gentle and golden and vulnerable beyond her wildest dreams. She knew instantly why she had loved him from the beginning. He was a clean slate, a virgin ...

And she could show him the way.

Back to Babylon

There they were again, back where they had met, back at the seedy old Greyhound bus station on Seventh Street in San Francisco.

Mona surveyed the snack bar, feeling an unexpected flash of nostalgia, while Mother Mucca slurped coffee noisily out of her spoon. The old lady was still being ornery, but at least she had consented to this visit.

Mona had told her everything about Andy/Anna only three days before.

And the mother-and-child reunion was only an hour away.

Mother Mucca belched. 'I don't feel so good,' she grumbled.

'Now don't start on that again.'

'I *don't*, Mona. My stomach feels a tetch –'

'Your stomach's perfectly fine. You're just nervous, Mother Mucca. That's OK. It's OK to experience a –'

'It ain't OK with *me* girl. This just ain't the right time to –'

'Please, Mother Mucca! I *know* you can handle this. We've been through this before, and we both agreed that . . . well, it's the best thing, that's all.'

The old lady ducked her head moodily. 'Maybe for *you*.'

'For *all* of us.'

'I ain't seen my son for forty goddamn years!'

Mona winced. 'Daughter.'

'Huh?'

'She's your *daughter* now. I know that's hard to deal with, but it would mean so much to Mrs Madrigal . . . I mean, to Anna. Try to remember that, will you?'

Mother Mucca wouldn't look up. 'Whatever.'

'No. Not whatever. Your daughter. Anna.'

'I called him Andy for sixteen years!'

'I know, but a lot's changed. You must've changed yourself.'

'Says who?'

'Please don't be difficult.'

'What does he look like?'

'I *told* you that already.'

'Well, tell me another goddamn time!'

Mona sought for another description. 'She's very . . . majestic.'

Her grandmother snorted. 'Sounds like a fuckin' race horse.'

'See for yourself, then.'

'Does he . . . look like me?'

'You'll just have to wait.'

Mother Mucca glared at her granddaughter, then at a pimply teenager in glitter wedgies eating a doughnut at the next table. 'Nothin' but weirdos in this town,' she growled.

Mona's first glimpse of Barbary Lane brought her heart into her throat. Nothing had changed in the sylvan city canyon. The cats were still there, the miniature cottages and the eucalyptus trees and Mrs Madrigal's courtyard beckoning in the moonlight.

'You tell him we're comin'?' asked Mother Mucca, surveying the cozy old house.

'No. She knows we're coming, of course, but I didn't tell her exactly when.'

'Stupid!'

Mona snapped back, 'I didn't want to put her in a negative space before we got here.'

The old lady blinked uncomprehendingly.

Mona smiled and translated. 'I didn't want her to feel uncomfortable about our arrival.'

'You didn't mind makin' *me* pretty damn uncomfortable.'

'C'mon now. Behave yourself.'

Mona stepped into the alcove next to the door buzzers. Mother Mucca lagged behind, pacing nervously in the courtyard. 'C'mon,' coaxed Mona. 'It's gonna be just fine.'

'I can't, Mona.'

Mona turned and saw the piteous expression on the old woman's face. Mother Mucca took several steps toward her. 'Mona, darlin' . . . I don't look like an ol' witch, do I?'

'Oh, Mother Mucca . . . you're beautiful! Don't worry, please. Anna's gonna love you.'

'We ain't brought her nothin'.'

Mona hugged her. 'We're all she needs.'

'Yeah?'

Mona smiled. 'Yeah.'

'Well, ring the doorbell, girl!'

Key to Her Heart

Up in the Starlight Lounge, Mary Ann and Burke hoisted Pina Coladas and proposed a toast. 'To new memories,' said Burke.

'Right, and to –' She frowned suddenly, realizing with a little shiver that the pianist had begun to belt out 'Everything's Coming Up Roses.'

'Burke . . . if that bothers you, I don't mind asking him to stop.'

He smiled weakly. 'I hadn't noticed it.'

'Until I mentioned it, huh?'

'It's OK.'

'I'm sorry, Burke.'

He downed his drink. 'I can't bury my head in the sand, Mary Ann.'

'I wish there was something I could –'

'It's just something I have to deal with, that's all. I mean, you can't avoid roses, can you?' His mouth curled in a rueful smile. 'Try it sometime.'

'I know. It must be . . . Burke, couldn't a psychiatrist do something? It seems like . . . well, if you could cure your amnesia, wouldn't that take care of your fear of roses and . . . walkways with railings or whatever?'

'I've seen a shrink already.'

'Oh.'

'He hypnotized me and interrogated me and did everything but stick pins in a voodoo doll . . . and not a goddamn thing happened. Except his bill at the end of the month.'

Mary Ann stared down at her drink for a moment, wondering if she could phrase the next question. 'Burke, what if you . . . ?'

'Yeah?'

'Oh . . . nothing.'

'It didn't sound like nothing.'

'Well, I was wondering if . . . Wouldn't it jog your memory or something if you . . . came back to San Francisco?'

An interminable silence followed. She had risked this question not once but twice. Her face flushed instantly, and Burke seemed to sense her embarrassment. 'It would almost be worth it,' he said at last, 'to be around you.'

Mary Ann tore the edge off her cocktail napkin. 'It just seems like . . . well, if you were exposed to some of the old places and . . . experiences and all, your memory might come back and you could sort of . . . exorcise your phobias.' She looked up at him imploringly. Her eyes were full of tears. 'Oh, who the hell am I fooling!'

He dabbed at her eyes with a cocktail napkin. 'Not me,' he smiled.

'I *hate* goodbyes. I always lose it. *Always.*'

'I know. Me too.'

'Nothing's ever been quite as nice as this.'

'I know. I agree.'

'You do?'

He nodded.

'Well, then, why don't we . . . ? Oh, God, do I look like I'm begging?'

He held both her hands in his. 'Do I look like I'm saying no, dummy?'

They snuggled under a blanket on the fantail, watching the lights along the shore.

'You won't be sorry,' she said.

'You don't have to promise that. You *can't.*'

'What about your parents?'

'I'll phone them and tell them. They'll understand.'

'Won't they be a little . . . freaked. I mean, about San Francisco?'

'No more than I am.'

'Don't be. I'll be there this time.' She paused, then said as offhandedly as possible: 'In fact, if you'd like, I think there's a vacancy in my building.'

'Good. Where's that?'

'Russian Hill. Barbary Lane. It's a darling little walkway, like something out of a fairy tale, and the landlady's so neat. Michael lives downstairs.'

'Where's the vacancy, then?'

'Just across the hall.'

'Handy.'

She giggled. 'The guy who lived there moved up to this little house on the roof.' Never mind what had happened to the guy who'd lived *there*.

Sitting up, Burke reached in the pocket of his windbreaker and handed Mary Ann a small package wrapped in tissue paper. She peeled it away, layer by layer, scarcely taking her eyes off Burke's embarrassed face.

Inside, suspended from a twenty-four-karat gold necklace, was the curious little key he had shown her on the beach.

'For what it's worth,' he said almost apologetically, 'I love you.'

DeDe on the Town

DeDe knew she made a ludicrous sight. An eight-months pregnant woman dining alone at the counter at Vanessi's, her battered Gucci tote bag propped against the stool.

Well, screw it, she thought. North Beach had seen weirder things. A lot *weirder*. Like that freaky teeny-bopper hanging out in front of Enrico's. Green hair and a garbage bag. Yecch!

Besides, she loved this restaurant. She delighted in its unaffected sophistication and burly Italian chefs who wielded skillets with all the grace and precision of tennis players.

Beauchamp, she realized, was probably home at the penthouse, and that was only four blocks up the hill. While she dreaded the prospect of a confrontation with her husband, she also drew a kind of perverse pleasure from the knowledge that she was stalking the old neighborhood on her own.

What puzzled her now was why her mother hadn't protested this unorthodox trek into town. She had barely looked up from the suitcase she was packing for the trip to Napa. She had seemed curiously distracted.

But by what?

'Wouldn't you be more comfortable in one of the booths?'

DeDe looked up from her sweetbreads at the kind brown eyes that had posed the question. The woman was very pretty, with dark curly hair and cheekbones that Veruschka would have killed for.

'Thanks. I like watching the show,' she replied, motioning to the chefs behind the counter.

'Oh, God, isn't it *marvelous*? I think it's the best therapy there is, watching them fling that zucchini in the air. You expect all hell to break loose, but it never does.'

'Unlike life.'

The woman laughed. 'Unlike life.'

A waiter set a huge plate of pasta in front of the woman. 'Well,' she sighed, with a grin, 'oink, oink oink.'

'You look fine,' said DeDe. 'I'm the one who ought to be watching it.'

'Well, you're eating for *two*, honey!'

'Three.'

The woman whistled. 'You get dessert, then.'

They both laughed. The woman was quite fair-skinned, DeDe observed, but there was something almost negroid about the warmth and earthiness of her mannerisms. DeDe liked her immediately.

Setting her fork down, the woman smiled at her. 'You're not married, are you?'

Silence.

'Oh, God,' said the woman. 'If you're a tourist, forgive me. We're a little too liberated for our own good in this town.'

'No . . . I mean, yes, I'm married, but I'm separated . . . I mean, *we're* separated. I live here, though. I'm a native.'

'Mmm. Me too. If you count Oakland, that is.'

'I have lots of friends in Piedmont.'

'That's *not* what I meant.' She appeared to understand the East Bay caste system all too well.

'Why did you think I wasn't married?'

The woman turned and scrutinized DeDe's face, as if to reconfirm something. 'I don't know. You just look . . . independent.'

'I do?'

The woman smiled. 'No. But I thought you'd like to hear it.'

DeDe looked down at her food, fascinated by this stranger's insight, and a little afraid of it. 'Do you think it's too late for me to . . . do something about it?'

An elfin grin spread over the woman's face. 'What would you *like* to do – I mean, right this very minute – if you could do anything you wanted and . . . you didn't have friends in Piedmont who might not approve of it?'

DeDe smiled uneasily. 'Oh . . . you mean, in the neighborhood?'

'If you like.'

'I'd like to see that topless dancer across the street who turns into a gorilla.'

'Why?'

'Just to see how they do it. With mirrors, I guess.'

377

The woman shook her head soberly. 'It's actually a gorilla in a girl mask with a flesh-colored body stocking.'

'You mean they . . . ?' When the light dawned, DeDe laughed. 'You *see* how gullible I am?'

'There's only one way to find out for sure.'

'You're joking!'

'There's *nothing* I'd rather do than take a pregnant friend to a topless lady gorilla act.'

DeDe thought for a moment, then extended her hand. 'It's a deal. I'm DeDe Day . . . or DeDe Halcyon. Take your pick.'

A flicker of recognition seemed to pass over the woman's face. 'Have we met before?' asked DeDe.

'I . . . read the social columns.'

'Oh, God!'

'It's OK. I like you anyway. I'm D'orothea.'

'That's a pretty name,' said DeDe.

Mama's Boy

When she opened the door, Mrs Madrigal was wearing a red satin cloche with her plum-colored kimono. Her makeup was better than Mona had ever seen it.

The landlady smiled at her daughter. 'Do I get a hug or don't I?'

Mona flushed. 'Oh, yes . . . oh, yes, you do!' She stepped gracelessly into the apartment, dropped her Persian saddlebag on the floor and threw herself into Mrs Madrigal's arms. The landlady patted Mona's head for a moment, then gently removed herself.

'Isn't there someone you'd like me to meet, dear?'

'Oh . . . God, I'm sorry.' She turned and confronted Mother Mucca, still standing in the doorway. The old woman glowered, shook her head at Mona, and addressed Mrs Madrigal.

'She ain't got the manners God gave a mule!'

Mrs Madrigal smiled evenly, holding out her hand to Mother Mucca. 'I'm so glad you came.'

The madam took her hand and grunted. 'It was *her* idea.'

'Well, then I should thank you, Mona. It's good to see you both.'

'I can't stay long,' said Mother Mucca.

'I know,' said the landlady, taking Mona's arm. 'We'll have a little sherry and a nice chat.' Her eyes linked only briefly with Mother Mucca. It was the same cordial, but distant, expression Mrs Madrigal used on Jehovah's Witnesses.

The hostess ducked into the kitchen, leaving Mona and her grandmother in the living room. Mother Mucca was rouged granite, sullen and unreadable.

'Well,' said Mona, 'isn't she nice?'

'It ain't natural.'

'I thought we'd gotten past that.'

'Speak for yourself. That's my son out there.'

'Well, she's *my* father!'

'That's different.'

'Oh, please!'

'I raised that child, girl! That's my own flesh and blood!'

'You raised her in a goddamn whorehouse! What did you expect, anyway? John Wayne?'

'I'm gonna slap you right –'

The old woman stiffened again as Mrs Madrigal reentered the room. She was carrying a tray containing three glasses of sherry and a bowl of chocolate-covered cherries.

'I thought I had some butter cookies, but I think Brian or one of the other children may have polished them off.'

Mother Mucca frowned. 'You got children?'

'He's a tenant,' snapped Mona.

'Yes,' said Mrs Madrigal calmly. 'I call them my children. It's a little silly, I suppose, but they don't seem to mind.' She smiled at Mona. 'At least, if they do, they don't tell me.'

Mother Mucca reached for a chocolate and popped it into her mouth. She wouldn't look at her hostess. Mona sensed that disaster was imminent.

'So,' said Mrs Madrigal, curling her legs up under her on the sofa, 'you've had *lots* of adventures, I suppose?'

Mona nodded. 'Winnemucca's a trip.'

'I can imagine.' The landlady turned to Mother Mucca, who had just finished sucking the chocolate off her teeth. 'I hope this young lady didn't get in the way.'

The old woman snorted, forgoing comment by swilling her glass of sherry in one motion. Mrs Madrigal held her ground, keeping her eyes on Mother Mucca. 'Mona's a lot like both of us, isn't she?'

Silence.

'She's got your looks, though,' added Mrs Madrigal.

Mother Mucca stared into her glass. 'Ain't no wonder,' she said finally.

'What?'

'You call that a hat?'

'I don't see what that –'

'Damnation, girl! Ain't ya got no hair?'

'Of course I've got –'

'Well, why the hell do ya keep it all crammed up under that bonnet like you was bald or somethin'? Look, girl . . . you and me gotta talk!'

'I *assumed* that was the purpose of this little –'

'Where's your bedroom?'

'What does that have to do –'

'*Where's your goddamn bedroom?*'

The two women had been gone for at least ten minutes. Mona sat terror-stricken in the living room, listening to their muffled voices. Then she heard Mrs Madrigal say, 'Mama, Mama,' and begin to cry.

She waited until the sound died down again, then moved quietly to the bedroom door and opened it. Mrs Madrigal was seated at her vanity. Her back was to the door. Mother Mucca was standing beside her, brushing her daughter's shoulder-length hair. She looked up and saw Mona.

'Git,' she said softly.

Table for Five

As the *Pacific Princess* pulled out of Acapulco, Michael's eyes stayed glued on the ever-diminishing figure on the dock. 'Look at him,' he said. 'That asshole would look gorgeous in an aerial photograph!'

Mary Ann slipped her arm around his waisst. 'Didn't I tell you things would work out?'

'Yeah. I guess you did.'

'When's he flying back to San Francisco?'

'Friday. I'm meeting him at the airport.'

'He's awfully nice, Mouse.'

'I know. It scares the hell out of me.'

'Why?'

'Don't make me analyze it. When I analyze things they . . . stop happening.' He turned and looked in her eyes. 'You know what I mean, don't you?'

She nodded grimly. 'God, yes.'

'It seems like every time I start up with somebody new . . . I don't know . . . I see the beginning and the end all at once. I *know* how it'll die. I can play those scenes in my sleep. This time, though . . . well, I don't wanna know the end. Not for a while, anyway.'

'Maybe there won't be an end.'

He smiled at her indulgently. 'Everything ends, Babycakes.'

'Now, Mouse, that's not . . . What about us, then? You and I haven't ended.'

He laughed. 'We'll be cruising the old folks' home together.'

'Then what's the difference?'

'The difference, dearheart, is that you don't need me and I don't need you. It's these *other* turkeys we need . . . these one-and-onlys. Or at least, we *think* we do. Our poor little psyches have been marred forever by Rock Hudson and Doris Day.'

Mary Ann was composing a retort when Burke suddenly appeared behind her. 'Well, we're off, huh?'

She turned and took his hand. 'We wondered where you were. We were just waving goodbye to Jon.'

'I did a little dickering with the maître d'.'

'About what?'

'I'm at your table now. That's OK, I hope?'

'Of course! That's wonderful!'

Michael grinned wickedly. 'Arnold and Melba will just adore you.'

'Oh, hell,' said Mary Ann. 'What in the world are we gonna tell them?'

'Well . . .' Michael tapped his forefinger on his chin. 'I think we should say that you and I are mature, freethinking adults. Our marriage simply isn't working, so . . . we're planning an amicable divorce, after which Burke and I will have a simple Episcopal wedding at Grace Cathedral.'

'Very funny.'

Burke laughed, winked at Michael. Then, turning to Mary Ann: 'He's got a point, you know. I *could* be gay. I mean, if I don't remember . . .'

'You are *not* gay. That's an order.'

'I don't know,' said Michael ominously. 'I'm sure I've seen him wearing green on Thursdays. And look at that body, girl. Straight dudes don't have washboard stomachs.'

Mary Ann patted Burke's waist. 'This one does.'

Burke reddened visibly.

Michael took both their hands. 'C'mon, you sickos. I'm so hungry I could eat a steward.'

The trio shared a joint in Mary Ann and Michael's stateroom before heading to the dining room. When they sat down at the table, the matched pair from Dublin was conspicuously absent.

'What?' mugged Michael. 'How can I eat without Arnold and Melba?'

Mary Ann giggled. 'Maybe they ran out of clothes.'

'Or,' suggested Burke, 'the maître d' tipped them off, and they're busy reporting us to the –'

He cut himself short when the couple appeared, pink as cooked shrimp and obviously delighted with their latest ensemble: matching Mexican cotton shirts, each embroidered with a single red rose.

Melba's voice was pure white sugar. 'Hi, Young Marrieds! Who's your friend?'

Mary Ann began to stammer, seeing the Littlefields, seeing the rose, seeing Burke.

'Oh, hi. This is . . . Oh, Burke, why don't you . . . ?' She jerked to her feet, knocking over her water glass. Burke had his head between his knees, gagging. She snatched a linen napkin off the table and pressed it to his mouth.

'Burke . . . here, I'll help you. Melba, I'm sorry. Give me your arm, Burke. It's O K . . . There, it's O K.' She led him away from the table without further explanation. Michael and the Littlefields watched their exit in silence.

'*Goddamn*!' thundered Arnold. 'What the hell was that about?'

'Seasick,' said Michael quietly, still watching his friends.

Arnold grunted. 'He sure doesn't seem like that kind of a fellow.'

'No,' said Michael under his breath. 'Great legs, though.'

'Huh?'

'Uh . . . it's great to have sea legs.'

'Right on!' concurred Melba.

Eccentric Old Bachelors

Somewhere in the nighttime sky above the Monterey peninsula, Michael loosened his seat belt and turned to check on his traveling companions.

Burke was asleep, sprawled obliviously against the window like a Raggedy Andy doll.

Mary Ann was still awake, trying her damnedest to get engrossed in P S A's in-flight magazine. When she saw Michael watching her, she managed a tired smile.

'I'm reading about Swinging Singles in San Francisco.'

'Arrgh.'

'It's so depressing. Do you think I'm a Swinging Single?'

Michael shook his head. 'Not a bit.'

'Thank God!' She leaned closer, whispering. 'I don't think you're a faggot, either.'

'Much obliged.'

'I've come a long way on that, Michael.'

'I know. I've noticed.'

'No. You don't know how bad I was about it.'

'It doesn't matter.' He paused, massaging his brow with his fingertips. 'I just hope my parents can hack it.'

'You've told them.'

'No. but I think I'm going to.'

'Mouse . . . do you think they're ready?'

'No, they'll never be ready. They're past changing now. They just get more the same.'

'Then why?'

'I love them, Mary Ann. They don't even know who I am.'

'Yes they do. They know that you're kind and gentle and . . . funny. They know that you love them. Why is it necessary for you to . . . ?'

'They know a twelve-year old.'

'Mouse . . . lots of men never marry. Your parents are three thousand miles away. Why shouldn't they just keep assuming that you're . . .' She sought for a word, making a little circle with her hand.

'An Eccentric Old Bachelor,' smiled Michael. 'That's what they used to call them in Orlando. My Uncle Roger was an Eccentric Old

Bachelor. He taught English and raised day lilies, and we never saw much of him, except at weddings and funerals. My cousins and I liked him because he could make puppets out of knotted handkerchiefs. Most of the time, though, he kept to himself, because he knew what the rules were: Shut up about it, if you want us to love you. Don't make us think about the disgusting thing you are.

'He did what they said, too. I don't know . . . maybe he'd never *heard* about the queers in New Orleans and San Francisco. Maybe he didn't even know what queer was. Maybe he thought he was the only one . . . or maybe he just loved living in Orlando. At any rate, he stayed, and when he died – I was a junior in high school – they gave him a decent eunuch's funeral. Mary Ann . . . I had never seen him touch another human being. Not one.'

Michael hesitated, then shook his head. 'I hope to God he got laid.'

Mary Ann reached over and put her hand on his arm. 'Things have changed, Mouse. The world has grown up a lot.'

'Has it?' He handed her the third section of the *Chronicle* and pointed to Charles McCabe's column. 'This enlightened liberal says there's gonna be a big backlash against homosexuals, because the decent folks out there are sick and tired of the "abnormal."'

'Maybe he –'

'I've got news for him. Guess who else is sick of it? Guess who else has tried like hell *not* to be abnormal, by joking and apologizing and camping our way through a hell of a lot of crap?'

'*Abnormal?* Anita Bryant would be a nonentity today if she hadn't put on a bathing suit and strutted her stuff in that cattle call in Atlantic City. If you know how that differs from a jockey shorts dance contest, I wish the hell you'd tell me.'

His voice had grown strident. Mary Ann glanced nervously at the other passengers, then said in a placating tone: 'Mouse, it's not *me* you have to convince.'

He smiled and kissed her on the cheek. 'I'm sorry. I sound like Carrie Nation, don't I?'

They slept for the rest of the flight. Michael woke during the descent into San Francisco, feeling the comforting hand of the city on his shoulder again.

'Well,' quipped Mary Ann as the trio deplaned, 'it's all over but the Hare Krishna in the airport.'

Michael winked at Burke. 'No sweat. If they try to sell us a rose, we've got the perfect secret weapon.'

The pilot emerged from the cockpit. As Michael disembarked, the ancient, unwritten but unmistakable eye signal passed between the two men.

'Welcome home,' said the pilot.

'Really!' said Michael.

Mary Ann ribbed him in the terminal. 'I saw that, you know.'

'You're right about one thing,' grinned Michael. 'They don't make Eccentric Old Bachelors like they used to.'

Reunion on Barbary Lane

Tonight, because it was a special occasion, Mrs Madrigal had piled her hair into a Gibson Girl do and adorned it with a large silk iris.

Thank God it wasn't a rose, thought Mary Ann instantly, watching the landlady turn almost coquettish in the company of her newest tenant.

'Well, Burke, I asked Mary Ann to pick up something nice for me in Mexico, but I didn't expect it to be *this* nice.' She appraised the young man long enough to see his embarrassment, then shifted her focus to Michael. 'What about you, child? Didn't you bring me anything?'

Mary Ann giggled. 'He's arriving on Friday.' Michael shot her a reproving glance, so she covered her mouth in mock penitence.

'What's that all about?' asked Mrs Madrigal.

'Mouse doesn't like to talk about it.'

The landlady's eyes widened. 'Ah hah!'

'C'mon,' said Michael. 'Lay off.'

Mrs Madrigal passed a joint to him. 'I understand, dear. You're . . . superstitious about him.' She touched his arm suddenly. 'It *is* a him, isn't it?'

Michael took a toke off the joint and nodded.

'Thank heavens,' sighed Mrs Madrigal 'There are *so* few things you can count on these days.'

Michael laughed. 'Speaking of which . . . where's Mona? I haven't seen her since we got back.'

'She's down at the Searchlight, picking up some munchies for us.'

'No, I mean . . . the apartment's just like I left it. It doesn't look like she's even been home.'

The landlady patted her hair nervously. 'No. She's been away. And lately she's been staying here, in my spare room.'

Michael hesitated, certain now that something was amiss. 'Where . . . where did she go?'

'Nevada.'

'Tahoe?'

Mrs Madrigal shook her head. 'Winnemucca.'

'Winnemucca?' Michael frowned. 'Why in the world did she pick that tacky place?'

The landlady shrugged. 'To get it together. In her words.'

'Did she?'

'She says she did.'

Michael smiled. 'She's lying.'

'Maybe,' said Mrs Madrigal, clearly relishing the enigma she had begun to spin, 'but she brought me a present.'

Baffled silence.

'She's down at the store with Mona now, so I've got some quick explaining to do, if we're going to be one big happy family again.' Mrs Madrigal excused herself and hurried to the phone. Mary Ann heard her ask Brian to come down.

He appeared minutes later, barefoot, in Levi's and a shrimp-colored T-shirt. He nodded greetings to Mary Ann and Michael ('Hey, long time no see!') and shook hands with Burke. Mrs Madrigal took his arm in a gesture that struck Mary Ann as surprisingly intimate.

'Brian's heard all this before,' said the landlady calmly, 'but I want the whole family here while I clear the air.'

It took her fifteen minutes to do just that.

She told her story without stopping. When she had come to the end, she fussed distractedly with her hair again and glanced apologetically at Burke. 'So, dear boy . . . it's not too late to back out.'

Dazed and touched, Mary Ann looked first at Mrs Madrigal, then at a red-faced Burke, then back at Mrs Madrigal again. Brian stood by awkwardly, hands in pockets. Michael's eye caught Mary Ann's briefly, just as Mary Ann stepped forward.

'Mrs Madrigal, please don't . . .' She took the landlady's hand and squeezed it. 'I'm so . . . proud of you. I think Mona's the luckiest

386

person in town.' She flung her arms around the landlady's neck and held on tight.

When she let go, Michael was standing there, smiling at Mrs Madrigal. 'I don't believe you,' he said admiringly.

She smiled back at him, cupping her hand against his cheek. 'You'll manage,' she said softly.

When Mona arrived with Mother Mucca, there were more introductions and hugs, more hasty explanations and heartfelt apologies and clumsy declarations of love.

Burke found a natural ally in Brian, Mary Ann noted.

Brian, however, excused himself from the gathering just before midnight.

'Late date?' Burke asked discreetly.

Brian nodded.

Mary Ann couldn't resist kidding him. 'Look what can happen in two weeks,' she said coyly. 'Are you seeing somebody now, Brian?'

'Yeah,' he replied. 'You could say that.'

The Road to Ruin

Pinus-bound at last, Frannie Halcyon made herself comfortable in Helena Parrish's Fawn Mist Mercedes and smiled out at the golden Sonoma countryside.

Helena took a long drag on her Du Maurier. 'What did you tell your daughter?' she asked.

'The truth. At least, part of it. I said I was going to the house in Napa. She wasn't really listening. She's been so *distracted* lately.'

'Didn't I read somewhere that she's pregnant?'

'Uh huh. Eight months. Eight and a half, actually.'

'You aren't nervous about leaving her?'

Frannie looked at Helena. 'How long will this *take*?'

'It depends.'

'On what?'

Helena smiled. 'On how much you like it.'

Frannie giggled. 'A few days can't hurt. DeDe's been – you know – irritable lately, and I think she'd probably like a little time to herself. Besides, she's got a divine young gynecologist, and I'm a little tired of playing doting grandmother before the fact.'

387

Helena chuckled. 'You won't have to worry about that at Pinus. Most of us are grandmothers, but you're shot at dawn if you talk about it.'

They rode in silence for several minutes. It was almost as if Helena knew instinctively not to disrupt the fantasies that had begun to shape in Frannie's mind.

'Well,' said Helena finally, 'it's almost time to go like sixty!'

'I'm not sure if this road is safe enough to –'

Helena smiled. 'I meant your birthday.'

'Oh, yes.' Frannie looked at her watch. 'In only one day, four hours, twenty-three minutes and thirteen *wonderful* little seconds.'

'You're a new woman already!'

'I can hardly believe it. Do you realize that a month ago I was seriously considering face-lifts and rejuvenation shots!'

'Oh, Frrrannie . . . no! You *must* have known that Pinus was just around the corner.'

Frannie thought for a moment. 'I'm not sure I actually believed in it. I'd heard stories, of course, but that was all hearsay. Oh, Helena . . . I feel so privileged!'

The Pinus hostess beamed proudly. 'We are *all* privileged, Frannie.' Keeping one hand on the wheel, she pointed to the glove compartment. 'Open it, darling.'

'Why?'

'Go on, open it.'

Frannie did as she was told. 'And . . .'

'The little silver pillbox.'

'This?'

'Mmmm. Now . . . there's a thermos on the back seat. Pour yourself a nice cup of apple juice and take a vitamin Q tablet.'

'Vitamin Q?'

'Don't ask questions. It's good for what ails you. You're in our hands now, Frannie.' Her smile was warm but authoritative.

The initiate removed a tablet and studied its inscription. It said: Rorer 714.

'Down the hatch,' said Helena.

And down it went.

Driving through Glen Ellen, Helena motioned toward a sign marking the mental hospital. 'If Pinus gets too much for you,' she smiled, 'we can shift you with no problem at all.'

Frannie giggled, feeling sort of comfy-groggy. 'This is such a sleepy little town. I used to think this was all there was to it.'

'You'd never guess, would you?'

'Is it near here?'

'The turnoff's just up the road. You'll see.' Helena sucked on her cigarette, then winked. 'We haven't blindfolded initiates since the early forties.'

Frannie grew reflective. 'There's something about all this that reminds me of Edgar.'

'We're *all* widows, Frannie. The past is behind us.'

'I didn't mean it ... sentimentally. Edgar was so damned mysterious about his two weeks at the Bohemian Grove. All that hocus-pocus about owls and goblins and muses in the forest. He *used* it, Helena. He used it to keep me at arm's length.'

Helena sniffed. 'Compared to Pinus, darling, the Bohemian Grove is a Boy Scout jamboree.'

After leaving the highway, they bumped down a dirt road for several minutes, passing the grove of towering pines that presumably gave the resort its name. When the Mercedes rounded the last bend, Frannie drew in her breath and clutched the dashboard.

'My *God*, Helena!'

'Yes,' beamed the hostess. 'Isn't it grand?'

Before them, marking the entrance, loomed a sixty-foot fieldstone tower, rounded at the top. As they passed it, Frannie peered out the window at the discreet brass plaque affixed at eye level.

PINUS
Established August 23, 1912
Too Much of a Good Thing is Wonderful

Mona's Law

Jon had no trouble spotting Michael in the crowd at the American Airlines terminal. He was wearing Levi's, a clean white T-shirt, and a black and silver satin Jefferson Starship baseball jacket.

And roller skates.

The doctor brushed past him, striding toward the baggage claim area in his blue Brioni blazer. 'I don't know you,' he muttered.

'Aw, c'mon, big boy . . . you remember. We bumped into each other at the roller rink in South City. Nineteen forty-eight I believe it was.'

'You're an asshole, you know that?'

'How was your flight?'

'Michael, that gray-haired man over there is the most distinguished gynecologist on the West Coast.'

The skater slowed down and shifted his gaze. 'He has dandruff,' he said.

'He knows me,' said Jon.

'I would *never* hire a gynecologist with dandruff.'

'Would you at least slow down?'

'Why? You wanna smooch?'

'I'll punch you out. So help me.'

'I love it when you're butch.'

'Somebody's gotta do it.'

'You're a stuffy bastard, you know that?'

Jon glared daggers at Michael and grabbed the back of his belt, bringing him to a standstill. Then, in full view of the most distinguished gynecologist on the West Coast, he spun him around and kissed him on the mouth.

'Satisfied?'

'Satiated,' beamed Michael.

They picked up Jon's car in the airport garage and drove to his apartment in Pacific Heights. On the way, Michael rattled on about Barbary Lane and Mrs Madrigal's recent revelation to her 'family.'

Jon shook his head incredulously. 'That is . . . a mind-fucker.'

'Don't you love it?'

'You mean Mona didn't *know*?'

Michael shook his head. 'She knew that Mrs Madrigal was a transsexual – she was the *only* one who knew that – but she didn't know that Mrs Madrigal was her father.'

'What about Mona's mother?'

'What about her?'

'Does *she* know?'

Michael shrugged. 'She called Mona just before Mona left for Winnemucca. She was acting pretty freaky, Mona said – about Mrs Madrigal, that is – but Mona isn't sure how much she knows.'

Jon whistled. 'Bizarre!'

'And I haven't even gotten to Mary Ann yet. She's turned into Nancy Drew under our very noses.'

'Jesus. How's Burke taking all this?'

'Not badly, everything considered. He and Mary Ann are too obsessed with that damn key to notice much of anything else.'

'Any leads?'

'Zilch. I think it's a locker key myself.'

'Like a bus station or something?'

'Or a bathhouse.'

Jon scolded him. 'The whole world isn't gay, Michael.'

'I know, I know.'

'Well, is that it?'

'What d'ya mean?'

'That's *all* the news? No earthquakes to report? No Mongolian hordes barricading the bridge?'

Michael smiled mysteriously. 'You're close.'

'What?'

'I got a job today.'

'Great! Where?'

'Halcyon Communications. Mary Ann got me the interview. The mailboy Xeroxed his cock one too many times, and Beauchamp Whatshisname canned him. I take his place starting Monday.'

'That's wonderful, Michael.'

'Yeah, I guess.'

'Sure it is. You can advance from there, Michael.'

'I know. I know it's not a good job. That's the problem. It got me to thinking about Mona's Law.'

'Huh?'

'Mona's Law. That's what she calls it. She says you can have a hot job, a hot lover and a hot apartment, but you can't have all three at the same time.'

Jon laughed, then winked at Michael. 'What makes you think you've got a lover?'

Heroic Couplets

Burke's first week back in San Francisco offered no new clues to the cause of his amnesia. One night, after a particularly nasty red rose scene at the Washington Square Bar & Grill, Mary Ann made up her mind to propose a new plan of attack.

'You know,' she said casually, as she crawled into bed with Burke, 'maybe we've been handling this whole business in the wrong way.'

He grinned at her. 'You wanna start carrying barf bags?'

'Burke, be serious!'

'Right.'

'The thing is, we've been *avoiding* roses and walkways – at least, we've been *trying* to – and as long as we do that, we're gonna keep avoiding the cause of your amnesia.'

'That's fine with me.'

She frowned. 'You don't mean that. I know you don't.'

He shrugged. 'Go on. Finish.'

'Well, I just think we should be . . . dealing with it, that's all.'

'What shall I do? Camp out in a rose garden?'

'Well, yes . . . something like that.'

'Forget it.'

'Look, Burke: there's a place down south of Market called the San Francisco Flower Mart. It's where the retailers get their flowers.'

'At five o'clock in the morning, no doubt.'

'Three.'

'Ouch.'

'We could stay up all night and find a place with onion soup, like they used to do at that flower market in Paris. We could make it into a real adven –'

'Now *you've* flipped out.'

'Don't you see, Burke? If we exposed you to a *lot* of roses, thousands of them, we might be able to – I don't know – short-circuit whatever it is that's freaking you.'

'Terrific.'

'It wouldn't be like a surprise or anything. You'd know about it in advance. You could prepare yourself. And I'd be with you the whole time. Doesn't that sound reasonable?'

He stared at her in disbelief. 'And just when do you propose we pull off this caper?'

'Well . . .'

'Tonight, right?'

She nodded.

He flung back the covers and leaped out of bed.

'Where are you going?'

'Back to my apartment.'

'Burke, I didn't mean –'

'I have to change, don't I? Will jeans do . . . or do I need a tuxedo for Les Halles?'

'Come back here.'

'Why?'

'Because,' she grinned, 'if I'm going to deflower *you*, you can at least return the favor.'

It was midnight now. Downstairs, on the second floor of 28 Barbary Lane, Michael and Jon were in bed watching a rerun of *The Honeymooners*.

'I love the tube,' sighed Michael, passing Jon their communal dish of Rocky Road ice cream. 'I loved this program almost as much as I loved *Little Lulu* comics.'

Jon smiled. 'Remember Little Itch?'

'Sure. And Tubby! My father built me a playhouse just like Tubby's, complete with a No Girls Allowed sign.'

'Maybe *that's* what turned you queer.'

'Nah. I know who did that. That guy on ice in LA.'

'*Who?*'

'Walt Disney. The Mickey Mouse Club.'

'The Mickey Mouse Club turned you queer?'

'Well . . .' Michael took a long drag on the hash pipe and handed it to Jon. 'You either got off on Annette's tits or you didn't. If you did, you were straight. If you didn't, you had only one alternative.'

'I'm waiting.'

'*Spin and Marty*. God, I used to agonize over that show!'

Jon smiled wistfully. 'I'd almost forgotten about that.'

'That's because you identified with Spin. Those of us who identified with Marty will never, ever, forget it.'

'What makes you think I identified with Spin?'

'Because you were cool even when you were eight years old. You've *never* known what it feels like to be a wimp. You won all the prizes at summer camp, and the other kids were electing you to some-fucking-thing-or-another every time you turned around. Am I right?'

Jon ignored the question. 'You ate all the ice cream,' he said.

'I *knew* I was right.'

The doctor simply smiled at him.

To Market, to Market

A blue and yellow armada of *Chronicle* delivery trucks was the only sign of life on Fifth Street when Mary Ann checked her wristwatch just after 3 A.M.

'It's eerie,' she said, settling back in the cab again, 'but kind of glamorous at the same time. I feel like Audrey Hepburn in *Charade*.'

Burke nodded in silence.

'You aren't nervous, are you?'

'I think the word is numb.'

'We can turn back, Burke, if you really think –'

'No. I wanna do it.' His eyes were glazed with steely determination, but Mary Ann could sense the terror beneath. 'Burke, you have nothing to fear but –'

He put his hand to her lips. 'Don't say it.'

Just then, the cab stopped at Brannan Street, where a row of pastel florist vans marked the entrance to the San Francisco Flower Mart. Burke paid the driver, while Mary Ann waited anxiously on the curb.

The market was a series of interlocking buildings, fragrant white caverns ablaze with fluorescent light. The pungent odor of cut stems tingled in Mary Ann's nose even before they entered the largest building.

'Burke . . . do you want me to go in first?'

'No. I'm ready.'

'Remember, we can leave whenever –'

'I know. Let's go.'

The mammoth floral hangar was bustling with tired-eyed retailers. Nodding to each other in the intimate language of night people, they pawed through mountains of blooms to find exactly the right gladiola, the right cyclamen, the right tinted daisy or potted palm.

Mary Ann felt awkward and conspicuous, like a space traveler on another planet. She took Burke's arm. 'Do you think they can tell the Flower People from the Non-Flower People?'

'Beats me.'

'I haven't seen any roses yet.'

'Who's looking?'

They moved from table to table, chatting briefly with the pleasant, Norman Rockwell-looking people who stood wrapping flowers in newspapers.

'Do you have roses?' Mary Ann asked at last.

'Over there,' smiled a dumpling-shaped woman in a green smock. 'The table against the wall. This is wholesale, though.'

Burke grinned uneasily as they walked away. 'They *can* tell, can't they?'

'Burke . . . I want you to let me know if –'

'It's OK, sweetheart. I promise.'

The roses were crammed by the thousands into large green metal cans. Seeing them, Mary Ann unconsciously tightened her grip on Burke's arm.

Burke seemed to grow paler. 'It's all right,' he assured her. 'Let's go closer.'

Next to the table, half a dozen retailers were surveying the selection of roses. Mary Ann tried to concentrate on the people, suddenly realizing that Burke's discomfort had brought her to the brink of sympathetic nausea.

The customer closest to them was a hawk-faced man in his early forties. He was wearing a pale blue leisure suit, and the flesh above his brow was covered with neat rows of tufted scabs. Mary Ann flinched and turned away.

Burke, she suddenly realized, was white as chalk.

'C'mon,' she said forcefully. 'This isn't fair to you.'

'No . . . wait . . .'

'We can't, Burke!'

'But . . .'

'C'mon!'

Out in the parking lot, he threw up behind a coral-colored van that said ROSE-O-RAMA. Mary Ann stood by silently in the shadows, racked with guilt.

When Burke returned, he managed a smile. 'Well, it seemed like a good idea at the time.'

'It was a *crummy* idea. And we should have left earlier.'

395

'I would have, but . . . Did you see that guy next to us?'

'With the hair transplant?'

He nodded. 'Maybe I'm wrong, but I could have sworn he recognized me.'

'Burke, are you *sure*?'

'No, but . . . it was like I startled him, like he knew me from somewhere. I thought if I waited around long enough, he might –'

'Wait here!'

Her heart pounding, Mary Ann ignored the puzzled gazes of he flower sellers and raced back into the building, back to the table with the roses.

But the man with the transplant was gone.

It was 3.35 when they left the market. At that moment, back at Barbary Lane, Jon stirred in his sleep, then woke to the sound of Michael's voice.

'Jon . . . help me . . . something's wrong.'

'You're dreaming, sport. It's OK.'

'No . . . it's not. I can't move, Jon.'

The doctor propped himself up on his elbow and looked into Michael's face. His eyes were open, blinking. 'Sure you can,' said Jon. 'You just reached for me.'

'No . . . it's my legs. I can't move my goddamn legs!'

The Emergency Room

When Mary Ann and Burke returned to 28 Barbary Lane, Jon heard their footsteps on the stairway and motioned them into Michael's apartment.

'Michael's sick,' he explained tersely, leading them into the bedroom, where an illuminated plastic goose cast a yellow glow on the motionless figure in bed. Then the doctor knelt down next to his patient.

'Mary Ann and Burke are here.'

'They're . . . you woke them up?'

Mary Ann took a step forward from the doorway. 'We've been out at the . . . Mouse, what's the matter?'

Michael hiked himself up on his elbows. 'We're working on that. My leg's . . . gone to sleep.'

Jon tapped on his leg with a hemostat – the hemostat that Michael used as a roach clip. 'Feel that?'

'Nope,' said Michael, as the clamp moved up his calf. 'Nope . . . nope . . .' Finally, when it reached midthigh, he said, 'There.'

'Good.'

'Good, my ass! What's the matter with me?'

'I think it's only temporary, Michael. I'm gonna take you to the hospital.'

'I'm in labor, right? C'mon, you can tell me.'

Jon smiled. 'Don't talk, babe. We'll have you out of here soon.'

'Will you stop playing Chad Everett and tell me what the fuck –'

'I don't know, Michael. I don't know what it is.'

Jon arranged for an ambulance, which arrived fifteen minutes later. He and Burke and Mary Ann rode in the back with Michael, making small talk most of the way to St Sebastian's Hospital. It was anything but natural, and Mary Ann felt painfully inadequate in the crisis.

'Mouse,' she said softly as they passed Lafayette Park, 'if you give me your parents' number, I'll call them when we get to the hospital.'

He hesitated before replying. 'No . . . I'd rather you didn't.'

'Mouse, don't you think they should . . . ?'

'No, I don't.'

Jon leaned over and stroked Michael's hair. 'Michael, I think your family deserves to –'

'This is my family,' said Michael.

Mary Ann and Burke sat mute in the waiting room while Jon accompanied Michael into the emergency room. Twenty minutes later, he reported back to them.

'They're going to do a spinal,' he said.

Mary Ann fidgeted with the *McCall's* in her lap. 'Jon . . . I don't know what that means.'

'A lumbar puncture. They check for elevation of the protein level and . . . diminishment of the white cells in the . . .' The doctor was barely looking at his friends. 'They think it's Guillain-Barré.'

This time Burke stepped in. 'Jon . . . a translation?'

'Sorry. Remember those people who were paralyzed by the swine flu shots?'

Burke shook his head.

397

'I do,' said Mary Ann.

'Well, that was the Guillain-Barré syndrome. I mean, the syndrome caused the paralysis.'

Mary Ann frowned. 'But . . . I don't think Michael ever had a swine flu shot.'

'That's just one cause. They don't know what causes it, really.'

'But . . . what does it do?'

'It's an ascending paralysis. It starts in the feet and legs usually, and it . . . well, it climbs.' He looked down at his hands, tapping his fingertips gently against each other. 'Lots of times it goes away completely.'

'Jon, he's not . . . ?'

'The only real danger is to the respiratory system. If the paralysis becomes advanced enough to impede breathing, they have to perform a tracheotomy in order to . . .' He brought his hands up to his face and pressed his fingertips against his eyes. For a moment, Mary Ann thought he might cry, but his face retained the same masklike expression. 'That poor little fucker,' he said softly.

Mary Ann resisted the urge to touch him, to stroke him. He looked like a man about to explode. 'Jon, he won't . . . ? Did the doctors . . . ?'

'Fucking doctors!'

'What . . . did they tell you?'

'Nothing! Not a goddamn thing!' The rage in his voice made Mary Ann flinch, so he reached out and squeezed her shoulder apologetically. 'I think he could die, Mary Ann. We've gotta get ready for that.'

Inside Pinus

The long drive up to Pinus came to an abrupt end at an imposing steel security gate. Helena Parrish stopped the Mercedes and spoke into an intercom. 'A cheeseburger, an order of fries and a chocolate shake – and step on it.'

Laughter. A young man's laughter. 'Mrs Parrish . . . you're back!'

'Six whole hours. You miss me, Bluegrass?'

'The Pope Catholic?'

'You're sweet. Open up, Blue. We've got the new girl with us.'

'You bet!'

The gate swung open. Helena smiled at Frannie as she maneuvered the car along yet another tree-lined road. 'You're gonna like Bluegrass,' she winked. 'Under normal circumstances, he's assigned to me, but . . . well, I like you, Frannie. I'd like you to have him.'

'Helena! I couldn't!'

'No . . . please. I'd like you to. Really.'

'You're a dear.'

'Pish.'

'Goodness, I feel just . . . I feel so marvelous.'

The hostess smiled. 'We're inside now. You can jane, if you like.'

'What?'

'Scream. We call it janing here – as in "Me Tarzan, you Jane." It's sort of a Tarzan yell for women – like primal screaming, but a *lot* more fun. Go ahead, give it a whirl.'

Frannie felt inhibited. 'Oh, Helena!'

'Go on! You're at Pinus now.'

'Now? In the car?'

'Now and any other time you please, darling.'

Frannie grinned sheepishly, then stuck her head out the window and made a noise that sounded like: 'Eeeeeiiiiii!'

'Nice,' said Helen unexcitedly, 'but you're not janing, darling.'

'Well, how do you . . . ?'

'Like this.'

The hostess extended her swanlike neck and opened her mouth to the fullest. 'Aaaahhhhaaaahhhheeeeaaaahhhh!'

Somewhere in the depths of the pine forest an identical sound reverberated.

'An echo!' exclaimed Frannie.

'No,' smiled Helena. 'Sybil Manigault. She's into nature.'

The hostess parked the car next to the reception building, a rambling, chalet-like structure with leaded glass windows. Lady Banksia roses trailed along the dark wooden eaves.

Frannie clucked her tongue admiringly. 'Lovely . . . absolutely lovely.'

'The cottages are of the same design. They're all Julia Morgan – perhaps her greatest triumph.'

'Incredible! Edgar was intrigued by Julia Morgan's architecture, but I never heard a *word* about this.'

'Naturally. There was a clause in Morgan's contract with Pinus that forbade publicity. Originally, the founders had hired Bernard

Maybeck as architect, but he backed out when he discovered . . . well, you know.'

Helena led Frannie into the spacious lodge, allowing the newcomer to soak up the atmosphere in silence: the parchment-shaded lamps, the dusty-rose velvet upholstery, the copper pots brimming with wild-flowers.

'I feel funny without luggage,' said Frannie.

'Why? Everything you need is here. Two days from now it'll kill you to part with your kaftan.'

'Where is everybody?'

Helena chuckled. 'Hiding, probably.'

'Why?'

'Oh, it's silly, really. Technically, you're not sixty until tomorrow at – what? Seven-thirty or so? The other girls are a little wary of talking to initiates until after you're . . . one of us.'

'Then . . . what do I do until then?'

Helena slid a willowy arm across her shoulder. 'First of all, darling, I think you should take another vitamin Q. Then I suggest you ask Birdsong.'

'Who?'

Helena winked. 'Follow me.'

Three minutes later, the hostess flung open the door of Frannie's cottage. A young man sitting on the edge of the bed jumped to his feet. He was about twenty-four, Frannie guessed, with a lean body, curly black hair and astoundingly blue eyes. He was wearing a dusty-rose terry cloth jumpsuit, unzipped to the waist.

And he was clearly flustered. 'Mrs Parrish, I'm sorry. I didn't mean to –'

'That's all right, Birdsong. You didn't know we were coming. This is Mrs Halcyon.'

Birdsong nodded shyly. 'Hullo.'

'How do you do?'

'Birdsong is your houseboy,' explained Helena. 'He can fill you in on everything. Meanwhile, I must get ready for your little do tomorrow, so . . . ta-ta!' She made a lightning-quick exit. Frannie was left standing there, smiling nervously at Birdsong.

'Well,' said the houseboy, suddenly more sure of himself. 'It's time for our bath, I suppose.'

Outside in the toasty Sonoma sunshine, Helena Parrish was janing at the top of her lungs.

Bedside Manner

When Michael woke at St Sebastian's Hospital, Jon was at his side, armed with a pot of mums, three back issues of *Playgirl* and something in a brown paper bag.

'Look at you,' smiled Michael. 'A queen's wet dream.'

Jon winked at him. 'How ya feeling?'

'Less and less. But that's normal, isn't it?'

'Sure. It usually . . . ascends. Michael . . . it gets worse before it gets better.'

'Gotcha.'

'Are you . . . can you feel it moving?'

'Yeah, I guess. Kind of a tingling, right?' He placed his hand on his leg just below the groin. 'Won't be long now, kiddo. Better get it while the gettin' is good!'

Jon laughed. 'Speaking of which, I just checked out the orderly. I'm a lot more worried about *him* than I am about . . . this.'

'Right. So what's in the bag, liar?'

Jon dropped the bag in his lap. 'Guess.'

'My very own Accu-Jac?'

'Open it, turkey.'

Michael picked up the bag. A *Little Lulu* comic book fell out. 'God Jon! It's . . . vintage! It must be late fifties at least! Where did you find it?'

'That comics store on Columbus.'

'Christ!' he flipped excitedly through the comic book. 'Look! There's that clubhouse with the No Girls Allowed sign! And the ads must be . . . Oh, god I *gotta* see the ads!'

'Whatdya mean?'

'You know . . . joy buzzers and whoopee cushions and that goddamn little metal thing that was supposed to turn you into a ventriloquist when you stuck it under your tongue. Christ! Didn't you ever send off for one of those?'

The doctor shook his head, smiling.

'No,' sighed Michael, 'of course you didn't. And you never read the Charles Atlas ads either. You were *never* a ninety-eight-pound weakling. Or was it ninety-seven?'

'You got me. And listen, asshole, if you were ever a whatever-pound weakling, you got over it pretty quick.' He reached over and felt Michael's bicep, then kept his hand cupped gently against the muscle.

Michael looked down at his arm. 'That'll go.'

'Michael . . .'

'*And* the pecs. The pecs'll go down like a preacher's daughter.'

Jon chuckled. 'Where the hell did you pick *that* one up?'

'Where else? Florida. Land of the Free and Home of the Butch. When will this be over, Jon?'

Jon let go of his arm. 'Well . . . sometimes the syndrome can run its course in a matter of weeks.'

'Sometimes.'

'A high percentage of cases have –'

'Jon, what the fuck. I'm gonna be paralyzed, aren't I? Completely.'

The doctor nodded. 'I think so.'

'How am I gonna breathe?'

'It may not spread that far.'

'What if it does?'

'If it does, a tracheotomy may be necessary. It's not as awful as it sounds, Michael. In most cases, the condition is only –'

'You poor bastard!' Michael laughed sardonically.

'What?'

'You thought you had a fruit, but you ended up with a vegetable!'

'Just shut up, will you?'

'I thought that was pretty good.'

'Well, don't think, then.'

'Hold my hand, will you?'

Jon took his hand. 'That better?'

'It's tingling.'

'Your hand?'

'Uh huh. Act Two, right?'

Silence.

'I don't wanna die, Jon.'

'Michael, shut up!'

'I'm sorry. That was terribly Jane Wyman of me.'

'There's nothing to worry about. I'm gonna be with you the whole time.'

'You won't let me get zits, will you? I'm twenty-six years old . . . I don't need zits.'

402

'Such vanity.'

'I love you, Dr Fielding.'

The answer was a squeeze of his hand.

The Last Straw

Mary Ann's anxiety over Michael severely hampered her efficiency at Halcyon Communications. Beauchamp Day found three typos in his letter to the chairman of the Board of Adorable Pantyhose.

'Mary Ann, for God's sake!'

'What?'

'Look at this shit! I know the Old Man didn't put up with this kind of sloppiness! Christ! I could do better with a Kelly Girl!'

'I'm sorry. I . . . Beauchamp, I can't seem to concentrate on –' She spun her chair away from him, buried her face in her hands and began to sob.

Beauchamp watched her, unflinching. 'Cheap shot, Mary Ann. Cheap shot.'

Her sobs grew louder. 'I'm not . . . Oh, God, I . . .'

'All right. Do your little Gidget number or whatever. I'll get Mildred's secretary to retype it.'

She straightened up. 'No, I'll do it.'

'You aren't being very professional, you know that?'

'I'm sorry. I have a friend who's sick. He . . . may die.'

'A boyfriend?'

'No. I mean, he's a good friend.' She had decided earlier not to tell Beauchamp about Michael in the faint hope that Michael would recover in time to take over the mailboy job.

Beauchamp studied her for several seconds, then said, 'I'm sorry about that, but you'll just have to cope with it, Mary Ann. I can't afford to give you any time off right now.'

'I didn't ask for that.'

'You were crying. I've seen that routine before.'

'It's not a *routine.*'

He shrugged blithely. 'Whatever. I've seen you do it before, that's all.'

'Gimme the letter.'

'Look, I said I was sorry about your friend. You don't need to get sullen with me.'

'Gimme the letter, goddammit!'

Beauchamp glared at her murderously, then held out the letter and dropped it, allowing it to float to her desktop. Mary Ann looked at the letter, then back to Beauchamp again. She picked up the letter and crumpled it into a ball.

Beauchamp shook his head and smiled. 'You're pushing it, girl.'

'No. You are.'

'Tsk tsk. Is that right?'

'Leave me alone.'

Beauchamp folded his arms, staying put. 'You think you're a fucking *fixture* around here, don't you? You think I won't shitcan you because you worked for the Old Man. Or better yet, because I screwed you a couple of times!'

Mary Ann pushed back her chair and stood up. 'Actually I think about you as little as possible.'

'Oh, that's clever! Farrah Fawcett-Dumbshit made a funny! Yuck yuck!'

Mary Ann looked him in the eye. 'Get out of my way.'

Beauchamp didn't budge. 'God, you're a laugh!'

'I'm leaving.'

'You're goddamn right you're leaving! Jesus H. Christ! How long did you really think I could stomach you and your cutesy-pie *Snoopy* cartoons on the filing cabinets? And that precious goddamn bug-eyed frog planter with the –'

'Decorate it yourself, then. Maybe one of your chic closet-case friends can help out.'

Beauchamp's eyes were ice blue. 'You're as common as they come.'

'Maybe.'

'*Maybe?* Hah! Why the hell do you think you're a secretary, sweetie pie? You're a dumb little bourgeois bitch! Christ, look at you! You're the same bland little thing you were at fifteen, and you'll stay that way until somebody gives you a set of Tupperware for twenty years of faithful service – only it won't be me, thank God!'

She stared at him, blinking back the tears. 'I've never met anyone as . . . horrible . . .' She pushed past him and headed for the door.

'By the way,' Beauchamp added, 'if you plan to keep pushing paper, you might as well forget about the other agencies. There won't be any glowing references from Halcyon.'

Mary Ann stopped in the doorway, composed herself as much as possible, then turned and raised her middle finger to the president of Halcyon Communications.

'Go fuck yourself,' she said.

Bruno Comes Through

Five minutes after Mary Ann stormed out of his office, Beauchamp used his private line to call Bruno Koski.

'It's me, Bruno.'

'I know a lotta me's.'

'Yeah. Well . . . the one at Jackson Square. Look, I haven't heard from you.'

'The first move is yours, remember?'

'OK, OK. You got the man?'

'Yeah. I got the . . . person.'

'Is he reliable, and discreet?'

'Nah. He's a fucked-up junkie, man. Don't know his ass from a hole in the ground. What the fuck you think, man? My ass is on the line more than yours is!'

'Does he know about me? Does he know I'm the one who . . . ?'

'Look, numbnuts! If you don't trust me, why don't you get another patsy to do you –'

'All right. OK. When is he . . . available?'

'I told ya. Soon as ya get me the money.'

'How do I know you won't –'

'Ya don't. Tough shit.'

'OK. Look. She's going to a League fashion show tomorrow night –'

'League?'

Beauchamp sighed. 'Junior League, Bruno. That doesn't matter. It's out at the Palace of the Legion of Honor. It starts around eight, so you can tell your man . . . well, you can figure out when it'll be over. She'll be driving her mother's Mercedes, I'm sure. The license plate says FRANNI.'

'Her old lady's gonna be with her?'

'Nope. She's in Napa, I think. I'm sure she'll be alone.'

'I thought you two was separated.'

'We *are*, Bruno.' Beauchamp's patience was growing short.

'Well, if you guys are separated, how the fuck do you know all this, anyway?'

'I read it.'

'You *read* it?'

'In the social columns, Bruno.'

'Oh.'

'Don't worry. She'll be there. If there's a photographer around, she'll be there.' His tone became more businesslike. 'How do you want the money?'

'Tens and twenties.'

'Just like the movies, huh?'

'This ain't no fuckin' movie.'

'You want to meet the same place we did before?'

'Yeah. Eight o'clock. Tomorrow night.'

'Isn't that pushing it?'

'You gimme the money. I'll call the contact. Ain't no big deal.'

'You sure he knows how to . . . ?'

'It'll happen. You gimme the money and it'll happen.'

'I don't want her . . .'

'I know.'

'I won't accept responsibility if she's . . . if it's permanent. I want to make that perfectly clear.'

'Right. Gotcha. You're a fuckin' prince.'

After an hour-long conference with the copywriter for Tidy-Teen Tampettes, Beauchamp paced his office for ten minutes, then telephoned an office at 450 Sutter.

'Dr Fielding's office.'

'Is he in?'

'One moment, please.'

A thirty-second wait, and then: 'Yes?'

'What's up, Blondie?'

Silence.'

'Well,' said Beauchamp, 'I didn't expect a trumpet fanfare, but after all this time . . . well, the least you could do is muster a cheery hello.'

'Are you calling about your wife's pregnancy?'

'Actually, I thought you and I might get together and make a few babies. Just for old time's sake, mind you.'

406

'I'm going to hang up.'

'Oh, come off it!'

'I think I made it clear to you before that I don't want you calling this office – or anywhere else, for that matter.'

'Whatsamatter? You goin' steady or something?'

'You're a slug, Beauchamp.'

'I'll bet you say that to all the boys.'

The doctor hung up. Beauchamp sat at his desk for half a minute, spinning himself around in his chair. Then he got up, went to the refrigerator and made himself a Negroni, downing it in a single gulp.

Life, sometimes, was a pain in the ass.

The Girl with Green Hair

Manuel the gardener was grumpy, so DeDe didn't have the nerve to ask him to clean the yucky things out of the swimming pool at Halcyon Hill. Instead, she sat on the terrace, munching M & M's and reading the copy of *Fear of Flying* she had bought the previous summer.

With mother in Napa and Beauchamp in the city and Daddy only a memory, she felt like an orphan princess in the great house. As usual, her loneliness drove her to the telephone.

Only *this* time it wasn't to call Binky, Muffy, Oona, BoBo or Shugie.

'Hello,' said the honeyed voice on the other end.

'Hi. It's DeDe Day.'

'Ape Woman.'

DeDe laughed. 'I promise *never* to drag you to something like that again!'

'As I recall, I dragged *you*, hon.'

'You were right, though. An ape in a girl mask would have been cuter.'

'Whatever. Hey . . . how's the tummy?'

'Bigger.'

'But not better?'

'I don't know, really. I worry a lot.'

'About what?'

'Nothing in particular. I know it's morbid, but sometimes I get the creepiest feeling that something is wrong. My gynecologist says that's typical for a first-timer, so I guess I just shouldn't *think* about it so much.'

'You need to get out more.'

'I don't think I could handle any more Ape Women.'

'Well, don't feel like the Lone Ranger, honey!'

'Actually, I was wondering if you could handle going to a Junior League fashion show tonight?'

Silence.

'I know it's late notice . . .'

D'orothea chuckled throatily. 'You don't know how funny that is.'

'I know it's kind of a bore, but I thought we might get a giggle or two out of –'

'I used to be a model, DeDe. At your father's agency. At Halcyon Communications.'

'What?'

'I was one of the Adorable Pantyhose girls.'

'Why didn't you tell me?'

'For one thing, your husband fired me . . . and I wasn't sure if you find him as big an asshole as I do.'

DeDe laughed, reservedly at first, then with happy abandon. 'Oh, God, D'orothea. We separated, remember?'

'Yeah, but things are so goddamn mellow these days. I mean, you two could be taking est together or going to Incompatibility Rap Sessions or something.'

'How well did you know Beauchamp, anyway?'

'Long enough to merit one of his infamous tirades.'

'Why did he fire you?'

'Oh . . . I didn't show up for a couple of jobs. My skin was . . . I had a skin condition, and I looked like hell. It's a long story.'

'My *precise* words about me and Beauchamp!'

'You still want me to go with you to that fashion show?'

'Of course! Even more now.'

'Sure they won't check my pedigree at the door?'

'Positive. We're on, then?'

'We're on, honey!'

Back in the city, something else was on. Douchebag had made final arrangements with Bruno Koski.

'You got it straight now?' he asked on the phone.

'Yeah, yeah. I got it.'

'You don't move until I call you. When I call, you run like hell up the hill to the Legion of Honor. You sure you know where . . . ?'

'I *told* you, man!'

'It'll be sometime after eight o'clock. I promise, punk – you screw this up and you won't get the dough!'

'OK, OK.'

Bruno hung up.

Fifteen minutes later, the punkette made preparations to leave. Her mother appeared in the bedroom door.

'Do you *have* to wear that garbage bag?'

'What's wrong with it?'

'Heidi, for God's sake, it's disgusting! It's all torn and . . . disgusting.'

'I *told* you to buy some new ones.'

'I'm not going to argue with you. Where are you going, anyway?'

'I . . . to the Mab.'

'The what?'

'The Mabuhay!'

'You'll miss *The Brady Bunch*.'

'Big deal.'

'Heidi . . . promise you won't stick gum up your nose tonight.'

'OK.'

Douchebag smiled at her mother, then retrieved a wad of Dentyne from her left nostril, popped it in her mouth and began to chew rhythmically.

'See ya,' she said, heading for the door.

Thinking out Loud

In less than twenty-four hours Michael's paralysis was complete. He could blink his eyes and move his lips, but the rest of him was horribly still. He looked at his visitor using a mirror angled over his bed.

'Hi lover,' he said.

'Hi.'

'Shouldn't you be at the office?'

'It's OK. Slow day.'

Michael grinned. 'Me too.'

'I talked to Mary Ann. She and Burke are coming over later.'

'God, I'm popular today! Miss Congeniality. Brian and the Three Graces just left.'

'Who?'

'That's what I call 'em now. Mona and Mrs Madrigal and Mother Mucca.'

Jon laughed. 'They're quite a trio.'

'Yeah. And it's good for Mona, too. I'm glad.'

'Are you . . . doin' OK, Michael?'

'Well . . . I remembered something funny today.'

'Yeah?'

'When I was a kid, fourteen or so, I used to worry about what would happen when I didn't get married. My father was married when he was twenty-three, so I figured I had nine or ten years before people would figure out that I was gay. After that . . . well, there weren't a whole lot of good excuses. So you know what I used to hope for?'

Jon shook his head.

'That I'd be paralyzed.'

'Michael, for Christ's sake!'

'Not like this. Just from the waist down. That way, I could be in a wheelchair, and people would like me, and I wouldn't have to worry about what they'd say when I didn't get married. It seemed like a pretty good solution at the time. I was a *dumb* little kid.'

'You're also a maudlin grownup. You can't dwell on this stuff, Michael. It's not healthy for you to . . . Hey, I almost forgot. *Chorus Line* is coming back. I sent for our tickets today.'

'Nice fake.'

'Goddammit, Michael! Will you stop being so . . . melodramatic! I hate to disappoint you, but you're not gonna . . .'

'The word is die, Babycakes.'

'You're *not*, Michael. I'm a doctor. I know.'

'You're a gynecologist, turkey.'

'You *like* playing this scene, don't you? You're getting off on this whole goddamn Camille –'

'Hey, hey.' Michael's voice was gentle, consoling. The flippancy was gone. 'Don't take me seriously, Jon. I've just gotta talk, that's all. Don't listen to what I'm saying. OK?'

'You got a deal.'

'You know what? They've got me on The Pill. I mean, they call it steroids or something, but it's still The Pill. I've been tripping on that all morning. I'm on The Pill, and my gynecologist spends more time with me than my doctor does. Isn't that a hoot?'

Jon smiled. 'That's pretty good, all right.'

'Maybe there's a lot to be said for all this. I mean, for one thing, I can go for hours at a time without looking nellie. If they could prop me up or something, I'd be *dynamite* in a dark corner at The Bolt!'

Mary Ann arrived half an hour later. Michael winked at her in the mirror.

'Hi, gorgeous. Where'd ya get that Acapulco tan?'

'Hi, Mouse. Burke's here too.'

'I see. Hello, Hunky.'

'Hi, Michael.'

'The coast is clear, kiddo. Not a rose in sight.'

The couple laughed nervously. 'Mouse,' said Mary Ann. 'I picked up your mail for you. Do you . . . want me to read it to you?'

'What is it? A pink slip from the Clap Clinic?'

Mary Ann giggled. 'I think it's from your parents.'

Michael said nothing. Jon cast a warning glance at Mary Ann, who instantly tried to backtrack. 'I can leave it, Mouse . . . and maybe later Jon can –'

'No. Go ahead.'

Mary Ann looked at Jon, then back to Michael. 'Are you sure?'

'What the hell.'

So she opened the letter.

Saving the Children

Mary Ann began to read:

Dear Mikey,

How are you? I guess you're back from Mexico by now. Please write us. Your Papa and I are real anxious to hear all about it. Also, how is Mary Ann and when will we get a chance to meet her?

Everything is fine in Orlando. It looks like we'll do fine with this year's crop, even with the frost and all. The homosexual boycott may make orange juice sales drop off a little, but Papa says it won't make any difference in the long run, and besides it won't . . .

Mary Ann looked up, 'Mouse . . . I think we should save this for some other time.'

'No. It's OK. Go on.'

Mary Ann looked at Jon, who shrugged.

'I've handled it for half my life,' said Michael. 'Another day won't make a difference.'

So Mary Ann continued:

. . . besides it won't do anything but show Jesus whose side we're on.

You remember in my last letter I said we didn't say anything in our resolution about renting to homosexuals, because Lucy McNeil rents her garage to that sissy man who sells carpets at Dixie Dell Mall? I thought that was OK, because Lucy is a quiet sort who has stomach trouble, and I didn't think it would be Christian to upset her unduly.

I guess the man was right when he said the road to Hell is paved with good intentions, because Lucy has all of a sudden become real militant about the homosexuals. She said she wouldn't sign our Save Our Children resolution, and she called us all heathens and hypocrites and said that Jesus wouldn't even let us kiss His feet if He came back to earth today. Can you imagine such a thing?

I was real upset about it after the meeting until your Papa cleared it up for me. You know, I never thought about it much, but Lucy never *did* marry, and she was really pretty when her and me used to go to Orlando High. She could of gotten a real good husband, if she had set her mind to it. Anyway, your Papa pointed out that Lucy takes modern art classes at the YWCA now and wears Indian blouses and hippie clothes, so I guess it's possible that the lesbians have recruited her. It's mighty hard to believe, though. She was always so pretty.

Etta Norris had a Save Our Children get-together at her house last Saturday night. It was real nice. Lolly Newton even bought a Red Devil's Food Cake she made using Mrs Oral Roberts' recipe from Anita Bryant's cookbook. That gave us the idea of making lots of food from the cookbook and selling it at the VFW bazaar to raise money for Save Our Children.

We are all praying that the referendum in Miami will pass. If the homosexuals are allowed to teach in Miami, then it might happen in Orlando. Reverend Harker says that things have gotten so bad in

Miami that the homosexuals are kissing each other in public. Your Papa doesn't believe that, but I say that the devil is a lot more powerful than we think he is.

Mikey, we had to put Blackie to sleep. I hate to tell you that, but he was mightily old. I know the Lord will look after him, like he does with all His creatures. Bubba says hi.

Love,
Mama

Mary Ann moved to Michael's bedside, addressing him directly without using the mirror. 'Mouse . . . I'm really sorry.'

'Forget it. I think it's a riot.'

'No. It's awful. She doesn't know what she's saying, Mouse.'

Michael smiled. 'Yes she does. She's a capital-C Christian. They *always* know what they're saying.'

'But she wouldn't say that, Mouse. Not if she knew. Not her own son.'

'She'd say it about somebody else's son. What the hell's the difference?'

Mary Ann looked back at Jon and Burke, tears streaming down her face. Then she reached out and touched the immobile figure in the bed.

'Mouse . . . if I could change your life for you, so help me I'd –'

'You can, Babycakes.'

'What? How?'

'Got your Bic handy?'

'Sure.'

'Then take a letter, Miss Singleton.'

Letter to Mama

Dear Mama,

I'm sorry it's taken me so long to write. Every time I try to write to you and Papa I realize I'm not saying the things that are in my heart. That would be OK, if I loved you any less than I do, but you are still my parents and I am still your child.

I have friends who think I'm foolish to write this letter. I hope they're wrong. I hope their doubts are based on parents who loved and

413

trusted them less than mine do. I hope especially that you'll see this as an act of love on my part, a sign of my continuing need to share my life with you.

I wouldn't have written, I guess, if you hadn't told me about your involvement in the Save Our Children campaign. That, more than anything, made it clear that my responsibility was to tell you the truth, that your own child is homosexual, and that I never needed saving from anything except the cruel and ignorant piety of people like Anita Bryant.

I'm sorry, Mama. Not for what I am, but for how you must feel at this moment. I know what that feeling is, for I felt it for most of my life. Revulsion, shame, disbelief – rejection through fear of something I knew, even as a child, was as basic to my nature as the color of my eyes.

No, Mama, I wasn't 'recruited.' No seasoned homosexual ever served as my mentor. But you know what? I wish someone had. I wish someone older than me and wiser than the people in Orlando had taken me aside and said, 'You're all right, kid. You can grow up to be a doctor or a teacher just like anyone else. You're not crazy or sick or evil. You can succeed and be happy and find peace with friends – all kinds of friends – who don't give a damn *who* you go to bed with. Most of all, though, you can love and be loved, without hating yourself for it.'

But no one ever said that to me, Mama. I had to find it out on my own, with the help of the city that has become my home. I know this may be hard for you to believe, but San Francisco is full of men and women, both straight and gay, who don't consider sexuality in measuring the worth of another human being.

These aren't radicals or weirdos, Mama. They are shop clerks and bankers and little old ladies and people who nod and smile to you when you met them on the bus. Their attitude is neither patronizing nor pitying. And their message is so simple: Yes, you are a person. Yes, I like you. Yes, it's all right for you to like me too.

I know what you are thinking now. You're asking yourself: What did we do wrong? How did we let this happen? Which one of us made him that way?

I can't answer that, Mama. In the long run, I guess I really don't care. All I know is this: If you and Papa are responsible for the way I am, then I thank you with all my heart, for it's the light and the joy of my life.

I know I can't tell you what it is to be gay. But I can tell you what it's not.

It's not hiding behind words, Mama. Like family and decency and Christianity. It's not fearing your body, or the pleasures that God made for it. It's not judging your neighbor, except when he's crass or unkind.

Being gay has taught me tolerance, compassion and humility. It has shown me the limitless possibilities of living. It has given me people whose passion and kindness and sensitivity have provided a constant source of strength.

It has brought me into the family of man, Mama, and I like it here. I *like* it.

There's not much else I can say, except that I'm the same Michael you've always known. You just know me better now. I have never consciously done anything to hurt you. I never will.

Please don't feel you have to answer this right away. It's enough for me to know that I no longer have to lie to the people who taught me to value the truth.

Mary Ann sends her love.

Everything is fine at 28 Barbary Lane.

Your loving son,
Michael

The End

Mary Ann was severely shaken when she and Burke left St Sebastian's. She had planned on staying most of the evening, but her tears had proved uncontrollable. Jon had promised, however, he would call her 'if anything changes.'

Back on Barbary Lane, she tried to thaw a strip steak under the hot-water tap.

'Don't do that on my account,' said Burke.

'I thought you liked steak.'

'I'm not hungry. Really.'

She sighed and tossed the meat onto her Rubbermaid dish rack. 'Neither am I.' She turned to face Burke, forcing a smile. 'Do you know how I met Michael?'

'In a supermarket, right?'

'I told you already?'

Burke nodded. 'In Puerto Vallarta.'

415

Mary Ann dried her hands with a dish towel and sat down opposite Burke at the kitchen table. 'He was so cute, Burke . . . but I was *furious* with him, because he was with this guy I really liked, and all night long I just kept saying to myself, "What a waste . . . what a waste." I believed that, too. I really believed he was wasted, that he had gone wrong somehow. Of course, I *told* myself I felt sorry for him, but I was really just feeling sorry for myself. I found out all the Mr Rights weren't made for me, and I couldn't handle it.'

'That's OK. People change.'

'I didn't. Not for a long time. I used to feel . . . I don't know. I guess I thought I could change him, become his friend and make him relax around women or something. I didn't count on finding out that *I* was the one who needed to relax.'

'Don't be so hard on yourself.'

'It's the truth, Burke.'

'Michael loves you, Mary Ann. You must've done *something* right.'

'I hope.'

'Hope? Dammit, Mary Ann, there were times in Mexico when I was almost eaten up with jealousy.'

'Jealousy? Of Michael?'

'Michael and you together. Michael and you laughing and conspiring together. Michael and you playing tricks on Arnold and Melba. Michael and you pretending – hell, you weren't pretending – you *were* married. You were as married as two people could ever be.'

She blinked at him in amazement, unconsciously fingering the funny little key around her neck. 'Burke . . . I love you. I never meant to –'

'I'm not accusing you. I just don't want you to chastise yourself. Not about Michael. You two have had something great together.'

She let go of the key and reached for his hand. 'Could we go to the bedroom?' she asked.

There, on the bed, she lay in his arms and cried.

Later, they watched television, each pretending for the sake of the other to be interested. Then Burke rose and switched off the set.

'Do you want to call the hospital?'

'No . . . I . . . no.'

'You might feel better.'

'Jon's there. I don't think I should . . .'

'I think Michael would like it.'

416

'Well, what could I . . . ?'

The phone rang. They both jumped.

'Do you want me to get it?' asked Burke.

She hesitated. 'No . . . I'll get it.'

She turned her back as she spoke. She didn't want Burke to see her face.

'Hi, Jon . . . All right, I guess . . . Yes . . . God! Oh, my God! . . . No, I'm all right. What time did he . . . ? Thanks . . . Yeah, I will . . . I will, Jon. I love you, Jon.'

She hung up.

Burke put his arm around her.

'Thank God,' she said softly. 'It wasn't Michael, Burke. It was Beauchamp Day. Jon and Michael just heard it on the radio. Beauchamp's car hit the side of the Broadway tunnel and blew up. They couldn't get to him, Burke. He burned alive.'

Sixty at Last

The delectable herbal scent of Vitabath tingled in Frannie's nose as she lay back in the huge marble tub and enjoyed the effects of vitamin Q.

'Oooh, goodness! This thing is big enough for two.'

Birdsong stopped massaging her feet. 'Do you want me to come in, Mrs Halcyon?'

'Oh, no.' She giggled. 'No, that wasn't a hint, Birdsong.'

'It's no problem.'

'No. I'm sure it isn't . . . Birdsong?'

'Yes, ma'am?'

'How long have you worked at Pinus?'

'About two years.'

'Since you were how old?'

'Uh . . . twenty.'

'You like it here, then?'

'Yes, ma'am.'

'All these old ladies. You like . . . waiting on them?'

'I don't think of them as old.'

Frannie smiled forgivingly. 'I know they tell you to say that, but

417

surely . . . well, I mean, we're all over sixty, aren't we? A young man like you must feel a little . . . strange . . . you know.'

'No, ma'am. I like mature women.'

She grinned at him under heavy-lidded eyes. 'You're a diplomat, young man.'

Birdsong winked and wiggled her big toe.

'What's your real name?' she asked.

'We're not allowed to tell that.'

'You're not, huh?'

'No, ma'am.'

'Are you going to rub my back?'

'If you like.'

'I like,' smiled Frannie, rolling over in the suds.

The matriarch slept soundly until 6 P.M., when Helena Parrish rapped on her door. 'The hour is nigh,' she said cheerily, peering into the cottage. She had changed from her street clothes into the dusty-pink kaftan of the resort. Her hair was down now, flowing triumphantly into a single reckless braid.

Frannie rubbed her eyes and swung her feet off the bed. 'I'm not especially nervous. Should I be?'

'Darling . . . this is going to be the most extraordinary night of your life.'

'*Now* I'm nervous.'

'You'll do fine.'

'I'm beginning to feel like a silly old fool.'

'Nonsense. You'll be the youngest girl there.'

Frannie giggled. 'I hadn't thought of it that way.'

'Don't *think*, darling . . . *feel*. That's the secret to Pinus. Let yourself feel.'

'I'll try.'

'Good. Now . . . one more vitamin Q and we'll be on our way.'

The amphitheater took Frannie's breath away. Against the darkening hillside a hundred women lounged in dusty-pink deck chairs, gazing languidly at the open-air stage before them.

In the center of the stage, a bonfire was blazing, casting a mystical light on the giant golden P that dangled overhead. When Helena made her entrance, the audience began janing.

'Aaaahhhhaaaahhhheeeeaaaahhhh!'

The sound was thunderous, almost deafening. It sent little shivers down Frannie's spine. She readjusted her kaftan and fidgeted with her hair, awaiting the signal from Helena.

'Ladies,' boomed Helena, without a microphone, 'we all know why we're here tonight, so let's get on with it. Without further ado, may I present to you . . . the newest recipient of the mysteries of Pinus . . . Frannie Halcyon!'

This time the janing nearly shook the trees. Frannie walked onto the stage with her head held high, taking her place beside Helena at the bonfire. Then simultaneously, the women rose to their feet and a gargantuan cake was wheeled onto the stage. The women janed again and broke into a jubilant chorus of 'Happy Birthday'.

The top of the cake exploded in a flurry of flesh and firelight.

The naked figure that emerged sent gasps of delight and recognition through the audience. 'Bluegrass,' squealed a woman near the stage. '*She got Bluegrass!*'

Frannie looked up to see an enormous golden-haired man who looked for all the world like Joe Palooka. He smiled down at the Birthday Girl and leaped enthusiastically out of the cake.

In a single effortless motion, he scooped Frannie into his arms and ran off with her into the forest.

And the janing began again.

The Last of Beauchamp

When Bruno finally phoned, Douchebag was livid.

'Jesus Christ, man! You said eight o'clock!'

'Yeah? Well, I lied. Go home, punk.'

'Watcha mean, go home? I been freezin' my ass off out here for —'

'I said go home!'

'What about the money?'

'There ain't gonna be no money, 'cause there ain't gonna be no job. The client just got barbecued in the Broadway tunnel.'

'Huh?'

'I'll explain it to you when you grow up.'

'Wait just a fuckin' —'

'Look, kid, if you want a blue face to go with that green hair, just keep messin' with me, hear?'

Douchebag composed a hardass reply, then decided against it and hung up. Readjusting the safety pin on her garbage bag, she slammed out of the phone booth and set off in the direction of home.

There might be a cat she could kick on the way.

Leaving the Palace of the Legion of Honor, DeDe paused for a moment to watch the Golden Gate Bridge twinkling in the darkness.

'It never fails, does it?'

'What?' asked D'orothea.

'That. I mean . . . it never gets old. I was born here, and I've never stopped catching my breath whenever I see it. Sometimes I think there's a huge magnet in it that keeps me from leaving.'

'Do you want to leave?'

'I think about it. *Everybody* thinks about leaving home, don't they? The problem is, when you're born at the end of the rainbow, there's no place to go.' She turned and smiled at her new friend.

'It's not really fair, is it?'

'Maybe there's a city you haven't seen.'

'There are lots of cities I haven't seen. Athens . . . Vienna . . .'

'No. I mean here.' D'orothea smiled, arching an eyebrow. 'Those Junior Leaguers back there are as alien to me as . . . Mars. DeDe, there are a surprising number of people in this town whose shoes don't match their handbags.'

DeDe thought about that in silence all the way back to D'orothea's house in Pacific Heights. When they reached the cinnamon-and-buff Victorian, D'orothea thanked her for 'an edifying evening.'

DeDe smiled apologetically. 'Pretty dull, huh?'

'Not with you, hon.' She leaned over suddenly and kissed DeDe on the cheek. 'Where are we having the babies, by the way?'

'St Sebastian's,' said DeDe. 'And thanks for that *we*.'

D'orothea shrugged. 'You can't do it alone, can you?'

'I thought I might have to.'

'Bullshit.' She bounded out of the car, slammed the door authoritatively and blew a kiss to DeDe from her front steps. 'I'll call you soon,' she yelled.

Forty minutes later, DeDe arrived at Halcyon Hill alone. A police car was parked in the circular driveway. As she locked the Mercedes, she spotted a chunky officer standing next to the cast-iron negro lawn jockey that Mother had painted white after the Watts riots.

'Mrs Day?' The officer approached her.

'God! Not another burglary?'

'No, ma'am. I'm sorry. We couldn't find any other members of your family, so they asked me to . . . There's been an accident, Mrs Day.'

'Mother! Is it Mother?'

The officer took her arm. 'No, ma'am. It's gonna be OK. Why don't we go sit down?'

Inside, she took the news more stoically than the officer might have expected.

'When did it happen?' she asked.

'Several hours ago. His car apparently skidded in the Broadway tunnel. There was . . . a fire.'

'God.'

'Mrs Day . . . I'm really sorry. If there's somewhere you'd like to go, I'd be more than happy to take you.'

'No. Thank you. I'm OK.'

'Would you like me to stay for a while?'

'I don't think that'll be necessary, thank you.'

With obvious discomfort, the officer handed her an envelope. 'I'm supposed to give you this. It's his – your husband's – personal effects.'

Two Scotches and several hundred M & M's later, DeDe retreated to her bedroom and worked up the nerve to open the envelope.

All that was left of her husband landed with an ugly clatter on her mirror-topped vanity.

A golden belt buckle, composed of interlocking G's.

Burke's Bad Dream

For different reasons, Mary Ann and Burke both slept fitfully on the night of Beauchamp's death. When she awoke, Mary Ann called St Sebastian's and checked on Michael's condition. Nothing had changed, Jon told her. Mona and Mrs Madrigal were expected at the hospital later that morning.

Then the secretary called Halcyon Communications and asked for Mildred in Production. It was not yet eight-thirty; the spinster's voice sounded tired and far away.

'When did you hear?' she asked.

'Last night,' said Mary Ann, consciously injecting a funereal note in her voice. 'A friend called me.'

'It's awful. The media is eating it up. I'm *dreading* Van Amburg and his Happy Talk news tonight.'

'Should I come in, Mildred?' The *real* question, of course, was whether Beauchamp had told Mildred – or anyone else in power – that he had fired Mary Ann.

'No,' replied Mildred. 'We've shut down, actually. I'm just handling the calls . . . and the press. Oh, one thing?'

'Uh huh?'

'I talked to DeDe Day this morning. She's holding up just fine, all things considered. It must be *terrible* for her, with the babies due any day now, and – worst of all – her mother is missing.'

'Mrs Halcyon is missing?'

'Well, not exactly missing. They just haven't been able to locate her. She told DeDe she was going up to their house in Napa, but so far she hasn't turned up there. I suspect – this is just *my* theory, mind you – you know, she's a deeply religious woman, and she may just be touring the missions like Angelina Alioto.'

'Does the press know she's –'

'Heavens, no! DeDe told me in strictest confidence! She's making a few discreet inquiries with her mother's friends. I think she expects her to turn up any minute now. Keep it under your hat, will you, Mary Ann?'

'Of course. Mildred . . . have there been any arrangements made about the funeral?'

'Oh . . .' Mildred's voice faltered. 'That's the sad part, I'm afraid. Beauchamp had a provision in his will for cremation. But considering the . . . nature of the accident, the family felt that cremation might be in bad taste.'

'I see.'

'I think there'll be a memorial service of some kind. DeDe talked to Beauchamp's parents in Boston this morning.'

'Thanks, Mildred. I won't keep you.'

'I know you must be wondering about your job at this point . . . so don't worry about that, dear. I'm sure there'll be a place for you when the dust settles. In the meantime, why don't you take a little time off?'

'Thank you, Mildred.'

'Not at all, Mary Ann. I'm sure that's the way Beauchamp would have wanted it.'

*

422

If Mary Ann had so much as a moment's speculation about what to do with her leisure time, the question was settled in the middle of breakfast.

'I dreamed about our friend last night,' said Burke.

Mary Ann set down her mug of Orange Cappuccino. 'Michael?'

'No. The man with the transplant . . . at the flower market.'

'Ick.'

'You're right. I shouldn't have brought it up.'

'No. You should talk about it, Burke.'

'It was only a dream.'

'It could have been a *memory*, Burke. Tell me about it.'

He looked at her skeptically. 'I don't want to be . . . your favorite hobby, Mary Ann.'

'Is that what you think?'

He hesitated. 'No. Not really.'

'Then *tell* me.'

'Well, there was a walkway in it, the kind that I've told you about. There was a metal railing on it, and I think I was walking on concrete – only it was really high up.'

'From what?'

'I don't know. People, maybe – but I couldn't see anybody down below. There were people with me on the walkway – people I knew.'

'Who?'

'I don't know. I just know that I knew them.'

'Great.'

'Then the man with the transplant came up – I mean, walked up beside me – and suddenly there was this rose, this *horrible* rose.'

'Why was it horrible?'

'I . . . don't know.'

'Did he give you the rose? The man with the transplant.'

'No, not exactly. It was just there. And then he leaned over and said, "Go ahead, Burke, it's organic" . . . and then I started to run.'

'And?'

'That's it. I woke up.'

Mary Ann took a sip from her mug. 'Well, I suppose we shouldn't make too much of the guy with the transplant. I mean, we've both been talking about him, and you could've, like, superimposed him on your existing memories.'

'Mmm. Except for one thing.'

'What?'

'He didn't have a transplant in my dream. He was bald as an egg.'

The Proposal

Michael's night nurse was a fellow Floridian named Thelma. Sometimes she would sit and talk to him after giving him his eight o'clock injection of pentazocine.

'Thelma?'

'What, hon?'

'Is this my fourth day here?'

'Uh . . . your fifth, I think.'

'If I'm completely paralyzed, how come it hurts? I mean . . . I can *feel* it hurt.'

'Where?'

'My legs . . . my thighs . . . and my arms a little bit. It's freaky. I can see my leg lying still down there, but it feels exactly like somebody's bending it toward the ceiling. I almost asked you to push it down for me.'

She stroked his brow. 'It'll go away, hon.'

'Last night I woke up and I was positive I was propped between two pews.'

'Like in a church?'

'Uh huh. I could feel the edge of – you know – the plank behind my ankles and up behind my neck. God, I could almost *see* it.'

'That's normal, believe it or not. Dr Beery says there's almost always some sensory disturbance with Guillain-Barré.'

'Can't I be wacko, Thelma? I'd love to be wacko.'

'Go on!'

'I would. Just a little bit. A mild schizoid, maybe, with traces of melancholia and occasional drooling.'

Thelma smiled. 'You're not crazy, hon. You might as well face it. You're normal.'

'Not in Florida I ain't.'

Thelma reddened. 'I wouldn't know about that.'

'You know what?' said Michael.

'What, hon?'

'You're cute as pie.'

She tucked in his sheet with nervous efficiency. 'I wasn't even cute in Florida.'

'I'll bet you were, Thel. I'll bet you made those good ol' boys horny as hell.'

'You hush up!'

'I'll bet they used to wait outside in their Chevy pickups and bay at the moon like hound dogs and . . . take you downtown for an R C and a Moon Pie . . . and I'll bet you loved every minute of it.'

'I bet you're gonna get another shot in about two seconds.'

'I don't care if you give me a lobotomy. I know cute when I see it.'

'Get some sleep.'

'You won't leave, will you, Thel?'

'No, hon. Not until your friend comes.'

His friend came shortly after nine. Thelma excused herself as soon as she saw Jon in the doorway.

'Hi,' said Michael sleepily.

'Hi. I won't stay long. You sound tired.'

'No, please. I need the company.'

'Good.' Jon pulled up a chair next to the bed. 'I had a great idea today.'

'What?'

'We're gonna paint your apartment!'

'Swell. I'll be the stepladder.'

Jon smiled. 'Look: I brought you some paint samples from Hoot Judkins.' He held out one of the cardboard strips in front of Michael's eyes. 'I kind of like this putty color.'

'Mmm. Faggot fawn.'

'Cut it out.'

'Well it *is* the color of the year. Three years ago it was chocolate brown, then forest green. It was handy, anyway. If you woke up in a strange bedroom, at least you knew what year it was . . . Look, Dr Kildare, painting my apartment is definitely above and beyond the –'

'Bullshit. If I'm gonna live there, that cosmic orange of Mona's has gotta go!'

The impact of Jon's words registered in Michael's face instantly. 'Uh . . . isn't this a little premature, Jon?'

'Haven't you always wanted to shack up with a doctor?'

'Jon. I'm so fuckin' flattered I could –'

425

'I'm not flattering you, asshole. I'm asking you to marry me.'

Silence.

'So?'

'Jon, you can't . . . haul me to the toilet.'

'Says who?'

'This isn't *Magnificent Obsession.* It doesn't work like that. You're gonna take all the mystery out of our unnatural relationship.'

'I'll risk it. What about it?'

Michael hesitated. 'When will . . . I get out of here?'

'I . . . I don't know. It depends on a lot of things, Michael.'

'Ahh.'

'Michael, look . . .'

'You know how to cheer a person up, anyway. I'll give you credit for that, Babycakes.'

Ashes to Ashes

The memorial service for Beauchamp Talbot Day was held on a Tuesday at 11 A.M. in St Matthew's Episcopal Church, San Mateo.

The front pew was occupied by members of the immediate family, including Mr and Mrs Richard Hamilton Day of Boston, Massachusetts; Miss Allison Dinsmore Day of New York City; Mrs Edgar Warfield Halcyon (nee Frances Alicia Ligon) and the widow, Mrs Beauchamp Talbot Day (nee Deirdre Ligon Halcyon).

Accompanying the widow and her mother were the family maid, Miss Emma Ravenel; Miss D'orothea Wilson of San Francisco; and a young man of unidentifiable origin who answered to the name of Bluegrass.

Seated four rows behind the family were Miss Mary Ann Singleton, secretary to the deceased; her escort, Mr Burke Christopher Andrew; and Dr Jon Philip Fielding, the widow's gynecologist.

Friends of the deceased in attendance included Mr Archibald Anson Gidde, Mr Richard Evan Hampton and Mr Peter Prescott Cipriani.

The Reverend Lindsey R. McAllister of Boston conducted the service.

At the request of the deceased's family, there were no floral offerings at the ceremony, with the exception of the single red rose that adorned the processional cross.

Shortly after the commencement of the service, Mr Burke Christopher Andrew clutched his stomach suddenly, dropped his hymnal, and vomited onto the pew in front of him.

There was no eulogy.

Voice from the Past

After the memorial service, Jon drove Mary Ann and Burke back to 28 Barbary Lane. The couple were unusually quiet, he noticed, presumably because of the mishap involving the rose on the processional cross.

'I wouldn't worry about that,' the doctor said at last.

'I should have brought more Wash'n Dris,' said Mary Ann.

Jon shook his head. 'He was a horse's ass. I thought it was entirely appropriate.'

'Who?' asked Burke.

'Beauchamp. He was a gaper from way back.'

Mary Ann looked puzzled. 'I thought you just knew DeDe.'

'Yeah. Mostly. But I met him once or twice.'

There was no point in telling them about his brief affair with Beauchamp. He had never even told Michael, because he had never been proud of that interlude in his life.

Back at Michael's apartment, he checked the bedroom for closet space. As soon as Mona's stuff could be shifted downstairs – she had already expressed her intention of moving in with Mrs Madrigal – there would be plenty of room for his clothes and furniture. Michael's possessions were minimal.

He stood at Michael's dresser for a moment and examined the items decorating the perimeter of the mirror.

Polaroids of Mona mugging in the nude at Devil's Slide. Others of Mary Ann posing demurely in the courtyard. A gold pendant charm shaped like a pair of jockey shorts – obviously Michael's prize from The Endup's dance contest. A photo, torn from a magazine, of a shirtless Jan-Michael Vincent.

There was nothing of Jon, nothing of the two of them. They had not been together long enough. The only evidence of their relationship was a cocktail napkin from the Sans Souci, tucked jauntily at an angle behind Jan-Michael Vincent.

Suddenly, sinking to the edge of Michael's bed, Jon began to cry.

Michael, as usual, had been right. The fuss over the paint chips *had* been premature. There was no indication – none whatsoever – that Michael's condition was improving. And that flip little romantic perched on the brink of death could not be bullshitted when it came down to the end.

Jon rose, rubbing his eyes, just as the phone rang.

'Hello,' he said, answering the phone in the kitchen.

'Who is this?' A woman's voice. Brassy.

'Jon Fielding. A friend of Michael's.'

'Isn't this Mona Ramsey's apartment?'

'Oh . . . well, sort of. She's –'

'Sort of?' Not brassy, actually. Bronze.

Jon gave up any effort of cordiality. 'She's in the process of moving right now. You can reach her downstairs at her . . . at the landlady's apartment.'

The caller muttered under her breath. 'Bloody idiot.'

'Would you like the number?'

'Yes. Please.'

Jon gave it to her.

The call came while Mrs Madrigal and Mother Mucca were shopping in North Beach. Mona was alone in the apartment.

'Yeah?'

'Mona?'

'Hello, Betty.'

'I thought you were dead.'

'Oh, yeah? Well . . . surprise!'

'That's no bloody way to talk to your mother!'

'I sent you a postcard from Nevada.'

'I was worried sick. What were you doing in Nevada?'

'Just . . . stuff.' Mona thought it best to change the subject. 'How's the weather in Minneapolis?'

'The winter was horrid.'

'Too bad. Hope it didn't hurt your property values. Hey . . . how did you get this number?'

'I called your apartment. A young man there told me.'

'That must've been Jon.'

428

'Mona, listen to me . . . I have to talk to you.'

'Fine. Go ahead.'

'No. In person. You're making a serious mistake, Mona.'

'About what?'

'I can't talk about it over the phone. I'm coming to see you.'

Silence.

'Did you hear me, Mona?'

'It won't work, Betty. There's not enough room.'

'I can stay at a friend's apartment. I've already . . . worked that out. You can give me two hours of your time, Mona. I'm not asking your permission . . . I'm coming. You owe me that, at least.'

'Yeah,' said Mona resignedly. 'I guess I do.'

Minor Miracles

Jon returned to St Sebastian's with Michael's mail in hand: a postcard from a friend on Maui, a newsletter from his congressman and a notice from the Reader's Digest Sweepstakes informing him happily that he might already be a winner.

Michael was asleep, so the doctor sat quietly in a chair by the window.

Five minutes later, the night nurse entered.

'Just get here?'

'Yeah.'

The nurse nodded toward her patient. 'He's a nice boy.'

Jon nodded.

'Him and you are . . . good friends, aren't you?'

'Uh huh.'

'He talks about you a lot.'

'I know.'

'Him and me spent a long time talking today. We're both from Florida, ya know. I'm from Clearwater. I mean, my folks used to live there when I was a teenager, and I met my husband there and all, but then we moved to Fort Bragg, North Carolina, when he joined the Army.'

'I see.'

'I don't mind admittin' it one bit: we're both real conservative, Dr Fielding. We voted for Goldwater in '64 and Earl always says that socialism is gonna ruin this country, and I guess I agree with him. I don't think that's reactionary, no matter what people say. I was raised to believe in the Constitution and the Bible and Free Enterprise, and I guess I always will.'

The nurse moved closer to Michael's bed. Jon felt vaguely uneasy. What was she getting at?

'Sometimes,' she continued, 'I think things are just moving too fast. The world is goin' crazy, and people don't have . . . they just don't have standards of *decency*. You can't *depend* on things the way you used to. Families and marriages are falling apart, and the liberals are just destroying everything that ever mattered to folks.'

Now she was standing by the head of the bed. She looked down at Michael for a moment. When she looked up again, there were tears in her eyes.

'I know all that's true. I *know* it, Dr Fielding. There's lots of things I'd change about this world, but . . . I don't . . .' She wiped her eyes, then looked down at Michael again. 'I'd be proud . . . I'd be *proud* for this boy to teach my children. I swear to God I would!'

Jon blocked his emotions with a smile. 'Thank you,' he said quietly.

The nurse turned away, blowing her nose. She busied herself with straightening Michael's covers, avoiding Jon's eyes. She didn't confront him again until she was ready to leave.

'Doctor, I hope you didn't . . . take offense?'

'No. Of course not. That was a very nice thing to say.'

'Aren't you mighty tired?'

'A little.'

'Why don't you go home. I'll look after him.'

'I know. I'll go soon.'

'Doctor?'

'Yes?'

'When this is over . . . when he's better . . . I'd be glad to have you . . . I mean, the two of you . . . over for dinner sometime. I make good red beans and rice.' She smiled, nodding toward Michael. 'He says he likes that.'

'Thank you. We'd be happy to.'

'Earl's real nice. You'll like him.'

'I'm sure. Thank you.'

'Good night, Doctor.'

'Good night. God bless you.'

*

430

He sat there for another hour, finally dozing off in the chair. An insistent voice awakened him.

'Pssst, turkey.'

'Wha . . . ? Michael?'

'No. Marie Antoinette.'

'What's the matter?'

'Come here.'

Jon went to his bedside. 'Yeah?'

'Look.'

'At what?'

'Down there, dummy. My hand.'

Jon saw Michael's index finger moving ever so slightly.

'Don't just stand there,' grinned Michael. 'Clap your hands if you believe in fairies!'

The Shop at St Sebastian's

A sudden hint of spring in the air caught Mrs Madrigal off guard as she swept the courtyard at 28 Barbary Lane.

Spring again on the lane! Vagrant daffodils loitering among the garbage cans, the smell of cat fur and lilacs and sun-warmed eucalyptus bark . . . and dear sweet Brian sunning himself on the bricks.

For the first time in weeks, her family seemed intact again. Michael was greatly improved, according to Jon, and would be coming home in a matter of days. Mary Ann and Burke were nesting comfortably in their respective apartments, though they appeared to need only one.

Brian, of course, was still in the little house on the roof.

And Mona – her own precious daughter – had moved in permanently downstairs as soon as Mother Mucca had returned to Winnemucca.

It was springtime, and all was well.

Except for . . . something about Mona's behavior that disturbed her.

'Brian, dear?'

He arched his neck, smiling up at her, greased and graceful in his green Speedo trunks. This boy, thought Anna, is a curious mixture of menace and vulnerability. A coyote begging for scraps. 'Yeah?' he said. 'I'm in your way?'

'No, no. I can sweep around you. I wanted to ask you something.'

'Sure. Shoot.'

'Do you and Mona . . . communicate very often?'

Brian laughed cynically. 'I think "relate" is the word she'd use.'

'Oh, dear. There's been friction?'

He nodded. 'Nothing drastic. I invited her to dinner and she told me that the *energy* was wrong. She couldn't relate to someone who – in her words – spent his Wonder Bread years learning to unhook bra straps.'

'Oh, my! I hope you didn't let her get away with that.'

Brian smiled wickedly. 'I told her she wasn't putting off enough energy to power a dime-store vibrator. Just your basic small talk. She told you about it, huh?'

'No. I just thought you might have some clue as to why . . . She isn't herself, Brian. Something's bothering her a great deal, but I can't get her to talk to me about it, and I thought that maybe you . . . I guess it'll pass.'

Brian sensed her distress. 'She's happy with you – her new home, I mean. I know that much.'

'Oh . . . she told you that?'

'She's told *everybody* that.'

The landlady smiled. 'She's a good person most of the time. Please don't give up on her for dinner.'

So Brian tried again. He called Mona as soon as he got back to the little house on the roof.

'Why do you hate me?'

'Who is this?'

'Is it because I work at Perry's? Or that I'm straight?'

'Brian, I'm in no mood –'

'I'm not a pig, Mona. I'm promiscuous as hell, but I'm *not* a Male Chauvinist Pig. For Christ's sake! I was at Wounded Knee, Mona!'

'Don't expect me to validate your . . . You were?'

'Uh huh.'

'I don't believe you.'

'I cooked a meat loaf.'

'At Wounded Knee?'

'*Yesterday*, you heartless woman! I cooked a goddamn meat loaf for the first time in my life, and you won't even eat it with me!'

432

She laughed in spite of herself. 'You didn't tell me that.'

'I'm telling you now. Come to dinner, Mona. Tonight.'

She accepted more readily than he expected.

He spent the rest of the afternoon cooking his first meat loaf.

Mona and Mary Ann passed on the stairway at four-thirty. Mona was making a last-minute dash to the laundry. Mary Ann was heading out to meet Jon for a trip to St Sebastian's.

Mona, Mary Ann noted, seemed far less laid back than usual. And she was *smiling*.

'Give Mouse a sloppy kiss for me, OK?'

'I will,' said Mary Ann.

When she and Jon reached St Sebastian's, Mary Ann realized with some guilt that kisses were *all* she had given Michael during his time of crisis. Burke's phobia had ruled out even the quickest visit to the hospital florist.

But Burke was in Jackson Square now, getting a haircut at Alexandre's, so why shouldn't she pick up a nice azalea or something?

She told Jon she would meet him upstairs and headed for the glass-fronted shop in the hospital lobby. When she entered, there was no one in sight, so she rang the bell on the counter.

Presently a man emerged from the refrigerated chamber in the rear of the shop. 'Brrr,' he said merrily, 'I like it better out here.' If he recognized his customer, he gave no indication of it.

But she knew who he was. Instantly.

The man with the transplant.

Meat Loaf at Wounded Knee

Brian's dinner was a qualified success. Mona remarked on the tastiness of his meat loaf, but chastened him for being scornful of vegetarian principles.

'Wait a minute,' he countered. 'If you're such a vegetarian, why didn't you tell me so in the . . . ?'

'You said you'd already cooked it, Brian. Besides, I'm not as . . . strict with myself as I used to be.'

'I see.'

433

'Ground beef isn't nearly as personal as a solid hunk of steak. I mean, it seems much less of a violation of the sanctity of the animal. You don't know which part of the cow it came from.' She grinned suddenly, recognizing the inanity of the remark.

Brian grinned back at her, dropping another chunk of meat loaf onto her plate. 'This isn't *cow*, I'll have you know!'

'Well, steer or whatever.'

He shook his head. 'Dog. Cocker Spaniel, to be specific. Do you think a waiter from Perry's can afford *beef*?'

After dinner, they sat on the edge of his bed and perused a scrapbook opened across their knees. A MAKE LOVE, NOT WAR bumper sticker was plastered to the cover.

'Look,' said Brian uneasily, 'if this gets to be a big drag . . .'

'It was my idea, wasn't it?'

'OK. Well . . .' He flipped past the first few pages. 'This is just boring stuff.'

'No. Stop. What's that?'

'Law School. The *Law Review* at George Washington.'

'Which one is you?'

'The dip with the David Harris glasses.'

'You wear glasses?'

'Not any more. Contacts.'

'Green-tinted, huh?' She smiled teasingly. He pretended to be mildly affronted, but inwardly he was pleased. She had noticed his eyes. That was a start, anyway.

He pointed to a newspaper clipping. 'This one made the AP wires. That's me in Chicago, 1968, on the left.'

'How can you tell? Your head is down.'

'I was going limp for the police.'

'Really? Where else did you go limp?'

'Oh . . . Selma, Washington . . . Are you making fun of me?'

She smiled. 'I went limp in Minneapolis.'

'No shit?'

She nodded, beaming.

'The War?'

'Yeah. Did you know Jerry Rubin?'

'I met him once in Chicago. We talked for about half an hour, I guess.'

'I just read his book. *Growing Up at 37*. I was really blown away.'

'Good, huh?'

She made a face, shaking her head. 'He said he got on this big power trip – militancy and all that – because he was uptight about the size of his penis. I mean, that's a really heavy thing to say.'

He nodded solemnly. She wasn't joking.

'Christ,' she said angrily. 'Is *that* what we did it for? Is that what the sixties were all about? The size of Jerry Rubin's goddamn *dick*?'

There was simply no profound reply for that. Brian ended up laughing. 'It's enough to make you go limp,' he said.

Later, they stood together by the window facing the bay. Brian lit a joint of Maui Zowie and handed it to Mona. She took a short toke and handed it back. 'That's all I want,' she said. 'I might get bummed out.'

'What's the matter?'

She sighed and stared out at the beacon on Alcatraz. 'My mother's coming to town,' she said finally.

The implication took a while to sink in. Then Brian whistled. 'Does Mrs Madrigal know?'

Mona shook her head glumly. 'I want to try and handle it myself. My mother said something really weird on the phone. She said I was making a terrible mistake.'

'Do you think she knows about Mrs Madrigal?'

'I'm not sure. But if she does know, she must assume that I know and that I know she knows. So what could she possibly tell me? What's all this "terrible mistake" shit?'

Her voice was trembling. Brian slipped his arm around her waist.

'I don't need any more surprises, Brian. I'm frightened.' She was crying now. Pulling away from him, she crossed the room to the other window, where she stood wiping her eyes.

'Mona . . .'

'I'm all right now.' She looked around for a clock. 'It's late. I should go.'

He moved to her side, risking it all. 'You can stay . . . if you'd like.'

'No. But ask me again.' She hugged him awkwardly, laying her head against his chest. 'I like you, Brian. You're a closet Tom Hayden.'

He kissed her forehead. 'Where's my Jane Fonda?' he asked.

They held each other tight, framed against the window like a cliché out of Rod McKuen.

Lady Eleven watched them for less than a minute, then took off her binoculars and closed the curtains.

A Poem to Ponder

It may have been the palm trees or the oddly tropical night or the swarthy man sipping Campari at the next table, but *something* about the terrace at the Savoy-Tivoli gave Mary Ann a shivery flashback to Mexico.

Burke felt it too. 'Remind you of Las Hadas?'

'I didn't plan it that way, I promise.' She had called him excitedly from the hospital, choosing this as the spot for their rendezvous. She had refused to reveal her discovery over the phone.

'So what's up?' asked Burke, as soon as their coffee and desserts had arrived.

Mary Ann smiled mysteriously and plunged a spoon into her butterscotch trifle. 'I've found our friend,' she replied at last.

'Who?'

'The man at the flower mart. With the hair transplant.'

'Jesus. *Where?*'

'At the hospital. He runs the flower shop there. I went by there this afternoon to pick up an azalea or something for Michael, and there he was behind the –'

'Did you talk to him? Did you ask him about me? Did he recognize you?'

She was surprised at the urgency in his voice. 'I didn't ask him, Burke. I was afraid to.'

'*Why?*'

'Because I think he *did* recognize me. He acted like he didn't, but I just couldn't shake the feeling that he knew who I was.'

'What if he did? Look, Mary Ann, *I* don't mind approaching him, if you're squeamish about it. Anything is better than this constant speculation and anxiety. This man could be the key to it all.'

'I know that, Burke. I'm sure of it. I just don't think we should risk the . . .' She reached across the table and took his hand. 'Something horrible may have been the cause of your amnesia, Burke. This man may have been a part of it.'

'You've seen too many movies. Maybe I worked for him or something.'

She shook her head. 'I asked Jon to check the hospital records for

436

me. You were never on the payroll at St Sebastian's, and you were never a patient there. There's no evidence that you ever set foot in the place before this month.'

He smiled at her affectionately. 'You have been the little sleuth, haven't you?'

'I want to help,' she said quietly.

'Good.' He reached in the breast pocket of his corduroy jacket and produced an index card which he placed in front of her. 'Tell me what *that* means, then.'

She picked up the card. On it Burke had written a verse of four lines:

High upon the Sacred rock
The Rose Incarnate shines,
Upon the Mountain of the Flood
At the Meeting of the Lines.

'What is it?' she asked.

'I dreamed it. Pretty nifty, huh?' His tone was much too flip, a defense mechanism that Mary Ann had learned to recognize. He was more frightened now than ever.

'Did you *hear* it in your dream, Burke?'

'Yep. Up on that damned walkway thing with the railing. The rest of the dream is the same. It's dark and the transplant man is there and there are people just beyond me in the darkness and the transplant man says, "Go ahead . . . it's organic."'

'So how did you hear it? The poem.'

'They were chanting it. Over and over again.'

'How many people?'

'I don't know. They were whispering, sort of . . . as if someone nearby could hear.'

Mary Ann looked down at the index card, then fingered the little key around her neck. Did any of this fit together? Was she exorcising Burke's demons or simply helping to create new ones?

'You dreamed this last night?'

He nodded. 'So what now, my love?'

'I'm . . . not sure.'

'I think we should talk to the man with the transplant.'

'No. Please. Not yet. Let's give it a little longer, Burke.'

437

He agreed to that begrudgingly. Mary Ann was about to restate her argument, when a familiar figure moved into her line of vision.

'Burke, we've gotta go.'

'I haven't finished my coffee yet.'

'Please, Burke, leave some money!'

He complied, looking peeved. He pushed his chair back noisily and stood up.

Mary Ann took his arm and propelled him down Grant Avenue, only seconds before Millie the Flower Lady descended upon the regular customers with a basketful of roses.

Penance

On the day after his dinner date with Mona, Brian sailed smoothly through his shift at Perry's. He felt *comfortable* about Mona now, confident he had stumbled onto something more real, more fulfilling – and infinitely more sensual – than he had ever known before.

He also felt guilty as hell about Lady Eleven.

How could he have forgotten her so easily? He had seen her – yes, that *was* the only word for it – for almost a month now. Every night for a month. She had blessed their relationship with predictability, if nothing else. Surely that counted for something?

He had planned, of course, on phasing her out eventually. The fantasy aspects of their liaison had all but vanished, and he had recently found it impossible to achieve orgasm with her without thinking of someone else. Still, he had treated her shabbily; he had broken their unwritten pact on the strength of a little Maui Zowie and a simpatico bird in the hand.

So that night at midnight he sat penitently in his chair by the window and watched the eleventh floor of the Superman Building.

Her window, however, remained dark.

She's punishing me, he thought. She's making me suffer for my transgressions. Or perhaps – just perhaps – she's in torment herself, torturing herself needlessly over her failure to hold my interest.

But then, at 12.07, her light came on, and Brian detected a slight stirring of her curtains. He stood up excitedly, lifting his binoculars to his eyes. The curtains opened.

It was Lady Eleven, all right, but her appearance had changed

438

radically. She was no longer wearing the floppy terry cloth robe. She was dressed in what appeared to be a gray wool suit. Her hair was bound up in a tight little bun, and her features – even at that distance – seemed severe and judgmental.

She raised her own binoculars and studied Brian for a moment.

He suddenly felt silly, wearing only his bathrobe. He wondered if she had planned it that way.

She left her window for several minutes, returning with a large piece of poster paper. She laid it on a table by the window and scribbled something on it. Then she held it up to the window.

It said: DROP HER.

Brian felt the blood rising to his face. Anger, confusion and guilt warred within him. He stared out across the moonlit city at the sign that accused him, then skulked into the kitchen in search of a large paper bag.

He found one, tore it open and scrawled on it with a Magic Marker. His reply was: SHE'S JUST A FRIEND.

He held the paper up to the window for half a minute while she studied it with her binoculars. When he finally put it down, Lady Eleven was standing with her arms folded, shaking her head.

Brian muttered 'Goddammit' under his breath and retaliated by writing I SWEAR on the paper bag. He held it up again, shaking the paper for emphasis. Lady Eleven kept her stance for several more seconds, then bent over her poster paper again.

This time she wrote: TAKE OFF YOUR CLOTHES.

Enraged, Brian shook his head emphatically.

Lady Eleven shook the poster.

Brian shook his head.

Lady Eleven scribbled on the poster again and held it up. To TAKE OFF YOUR CLOTHES she had added, IF YOU LOVE ME.

For one angry moment, Brian considered closing the curtains and curling up in bed with his scratch 'n sniff *Hustler* centerfold. He didn't need this kind of bullshit. There were *loads* of girls who loved his ass without such degrading demands.

Why *this* one, then? Why should he demean himself before this anonymous, neurotic, compulsive weirdo?

He knew the answer, of course:

Because she needed him. Because there was something more pathetically humbling about writing 'If you love me' to a stranger than stripping naked before a stranger. Because she was desperate and no one else could save her.

439

So he unknotted the cord of his bathrobe.

Lady Eleven lifted her binoculars again as Brian let the bathrobe drop. She watched him – smiling? – until his hard-on was visible. Then she began to unbutton her suit.

When they were both naked, the ritual began again, more feverish and committed than ever.

From the purple haze of his passion, Brian heard someone knocking on his door.

Then a voice: 'Brian, it's Mona. I just scored some you-know-what. What say we share a few lines?'

Frozen like a satyr on a Pompeian frieze, he waited in silence until the intruder had gone.

Then he turned back to his lover again.

Riddle at Dawn

For the third time that week, Mary Ann slept at Burke's apartment. Something – a noise, a bad dream, or the last cry of the trout she'd cooked for dinner – woke her just before dawn. She propped her head on her elbow and willed Burke awake.

He blinked at her. 'What's the matter, sweetheart?'

'It *must* be in the country somewhere.'

'What?'

'The Sacred Rock.'

'For God's sake! Get some sleep, will you?'

'In five minutes. Just say it one more time.'

Burke groaned. Then he recited the verse like a sixth-grader spitting out the Gettysburg Address under duress:

> High upon the Sacred rock
> The Rose Incarnate shines,
> Upon the Mountain of the Flood
> At the Meeting of the Lines

'See?' said Mary Ann. 'The terrain is hilly.'

'Clever girl.'

She dug her fingers in his side. 'What's the name of that mountain in the Bible?'

'Calvary.'

'No, silly. The one that Noah's ark landed on. The Mountain of the Flood, get it?'

'Ararat.'

She chewed meditatively on her forefinger. 'I wonder if anything is named that. Around here, I mean.'

'You got me.'

Mary Ann threw back the covers and scrambled out of bed.

'What the hell are you doing?' asked Burke.

'Checking the phone book.'

'Come to bed, goddammit!'

'It won't take a second.' She found the directory on the floor and leafed through it hurriedly. 'Arante . . . Araquistain . . . Ararat! Ararat Armenian Restaurant, 1000 Clement Street! Look, Burke!'

'So?'

'There could be some connection.' She wrinkled her nose, piqued by his total lack of enthusiasm. 'Don't you *want* to figure this out, Burke?'

His smile was meant to goad her. 'All right, Angie Dickinson. What's Rose Incarnate, then? A belly dancer at the restaurant?'

'It *could* be, smartass.'

'And the Meeting of the Lines?'

'I don't like your attitude.'

'Then you don't wanna hear *my* theory, I guess?'

'You've got one?'

'Yep.'

'Then let's hear it.'

'It'll cost ya.'

'No *way*.'

He pressed his fingertips to his forehead histrionically. 'Ohhh . . . it's going. I'm afraid I'm losing it. It's only dim, dim . . .'

'Oh, all riiight!' She grinned at him and crawled back into bed. There was an air of urgency and intrigue to their love-making that made it the best in weeks.

Afterward, Burke heated some milk in the kitchen. They drank from the same steaming mug, sitting up in bed.

'So, what's your theory?' asked Mary Ann.

Burke took a sip before answering. 'I think it could have something to do with cocaine.'

'*Cocaine?*' She was still very Cleveland about *that* drug.

'Yeah. A line of coke, see? The Meeting of the Lines.'

'Oh.'

'You don't like that one, huh?'

'But why would anyone be chanting about that?'

He shrugged. 'People chant about *everything* in Northern California. Some cult might have –'

'You think it was a cult?' The thought had already occurred to her, but she'd been terrified of broaching the subject. Burke had grown increasingly sensitive about his veiled past.

'I don't know,' he replied.

'Yes, you do. You think it was a cult.'

'I don't *think* anything,' he snapped. 'I'm guessing. I'm guessing about my own goddamn life, which is not the easiest thing in the world to do.'

'I know. I'm sorry.'

He pulled her closer. 'I didn't mean to growl.'

'I know.'

'Let's get some sleep, OK?'

'OK. Burke?'

'Yeah?'

'In the dream . . . do you remember if you . . . Never mind, it doesn't matter.'

'C'mon. What is it?'

'I was wondering . . . do you remember if you were chanting?'

'No.'

'You weren't?'

'No, I mean, I don't remember.'

For the first time ever, she wasn't sure that she believed him.

Michael's Theory

Mary Ann left Burke's apartment after breakfast. She was uneasy, she told him, about her status at Halcyon Communications. She had to make a few phone calls to remind the hierarchy of her need for a new position. This unexpected vacation couldn't last forever.

She was telling only half the truth.

After a quick call to Mildred (who assured her that the board would elect a new president next week), she dialed the number of the Ararat Armenian Restaurant and asked if a Burke Andrew had ever worked there.

They had never heard of him, the manager told her.

It had been a dumb idea, of course, but that stupid poem and the man with the transplant and the messy ordeal with Burke and the roses had begun to make her genuinely nervous.

Burke himself seemed on edge these days. His irritability, moreover, seemed to increase as Mary Ann delved deeper into the riddle of his past. Had he remembered enough, she wondered, to be frightened of the final revelation?

Was he telling her all he knew?

She needed an ally, she realized, an impartial third party who could help her sort out the pieces of the puzzle.

'Anybody home?'

Michael grinned at her from his hospital bed. 'Just me and Merv.'

'Oh . . . yeah.' She went to the bed, kissed Michael on the cheek and feigned interest in the television. 'Eva Gabor still looks so *young*,' she said lamely.

'That's because of the clothespins.'

'What?'

'She's got clothespins.' Using both hands, he pinched the scalp behind his temples. 'Here . . . and here. They fit under her Eva Gabor wigs.'

Mary Ann giggled. 'Oh, Mouse . . . I've *missed* you.' She sat on the edge of the bed and fussed with his hair. 'You're getting all shaggy,' she said.

He turned off the television with a remote switch. 'How's ol' Mystery Meat?' he asked.

Mary Ann groaned softly. 'It's getting more bizarre every day.' She told him about the dream poem, about the subtle shift in Burke's behavior, about her growing fear that Burke had begun to resent her amateur sleuthing.

Michael's eyes were dancing. 'Tell me the poem again.'

She repeated it. 'What do you think?'

'It sure smacks of a cult.'

'I was afraid you'd say that.'

'Well, it would explain a lot. The amnesia, for instance. Maybe they

443

had him deprogrammed or something. Maybe his *parents* had him deprogrammed. Like a Moonie.'

'Oh, Mouse!' *That* possibility had never even occurred to her.

'It's possible.'

'Do you think they would *do* that? Without telling him, I mean?'

He shrugged, smiling. 'My parents would *love* to deprogram me. Hmmm . . . I wonder what that entails? Maybe they lock you in a padded cell full of Muzak and zap your genitals with an electric shock every time you respond positively to a Bette Davis movie.'

'Mouse, have you *heard* from your parents?'

'I guess you could call it that. My mother wrote to say that my "sin against the Lord" was killing my father, and my father wrote to say that it was killing my mother.' He smiled wanly. 'They're terribly worried about each other.'

Later that afternoon, Jon showed up at St Sebastian's.

'Guess who's gonna be checking into the maternity ward pretty soon?'

'Who?' asked Mary Ann and Michael in unison.

'DeDe Day. She's almost a week overdue. With twins, no less.'

Mary Ann frowned. 'That's kind of sad.'

'How so?'

'Well, with no father, I mean.'

Jon shrugged it off. Beauchamp Day had been no loss to the institution of fatherhood. 'I saw that guy in the parking lot,' he said, changing the subject.

'Who?'

'The guy who runs the flower shop. I don't blame you for being spooked.'

'*Why?*' Mary Ann felt the hair on her forearm prickling.

'Well, he looked at me like I'd just caught him raping a nun or something.'

'What was he doing?'

Jon shrugged. 'Nothing that I could see. He was loading a cooler into the trunk of his car.'

'A cooler?'

'You know . . . Styrofoam. Like for beer.'

'Speaking of which,' said Michael, 'didn't my gynecologist promise to get me loaded today?'

Jon laughed, then made sure the door was closed. He handed

Michael a joint of Mrs Madrigal's finest Home Grown. 'You two can smoke it,' he said, 'but keep the door shut, and wait till I'm out of the building.'

Mary Ann didn't even hear him.

A Styrofoam cooler?

Father Knows Best

Mona was washing dishes with a vengeance when Mrs Madrigal walked into the kitchen.

'Are you upset with me, dear?'

Mona frowned. 'No. Of course not.'

'You're upset with *somebody*. Is it Brian?'

Silence.

'I thought you said you had a lovely dinner with him.'

'He is totally fucked up,' Mona said flatly.

Mrs Madrigal picked up a towel and began drying dishes next to her daughter. 'I know,' she deadpanned. 'I thought he'd make a splendid son-in-law – with or without the sacrament of marriage. You need a friend, Mona.'

'I don't need this one.'

'What did he *do*, for heaven's sake?'

Mona turned off the tap, dried her hands and slumped into a chair. 'We did have a nice dinner. It was wonderful, OK? So I went back to see him the next night. It was late, I guess, but not *that* late, and he could've at least shouted through the door or something, if –' She cut herself off.

'If what?' asked Mrs Madrigal.

'If he had somebody with him.'

'Ah.'

Mona turned away, fuming.

'How do you know he was even there?' asked Mrs Madrigal.

'He was there. I saw him going up the stairs less than ten minutes before.'

'Was he with someone then?'

'No, but he could've . . . I don't know. Let's drop it, OK?'

Mrs Madrigal smiled benignly at her daughter, then pulled up a chair and sat down next to her. She laid her hand gently on Mona's

445

knee. 'You know that sign you hate so much, the one outside Abbey Rents?'

'Yeah,' said Mona sullenly. '"Sickroom and Party Supplies."'

'Well, that's it, isn't it?'

'What?'

'*Life*, dear.' She gave Mona's knee a squeeze. 'We have to put up with the sickrooms if we want the parties.'

Mona rolled her eyes. 'That's so simplistic.'

'No, dear,' smiled Mrs Madrigal. 'Just simple.'

Mona's snit subsided. Later that afternoon, she and Mrs Madrigal strolled arm in arm to Molinari's Delicatessen, where they bought salami and cheese and a carton of pickled mushrooms. They picnicked in Washington Square, watching Chinese grandmothers perform martial arts exercises on the grass.

Finally, Mona took the plunge. 'I have something to tell you,' she said blandly.

'Yes, dear?'

'It's kind of . . . sickroom.'

Mrs Madrigal smiled. 'Go ahead.'

'My mother's coming to town.'

Mrs Madrigal's smile faded.

'The lovely Betty Ramsey,' explained Mona. 'I believe you've met her.'

'Mona . . . why?'

'I don't know exactly.' She reached out and took Mrs Madrigal's hand. 'I'm sorry. Really. I begged her not to come. She said I owed it to her and told me I was making a terrible mistake. I did everything I could to stop her.'

'Did you tell her about me, Mona?'

'No! I swear!'

'Well, what's this "terrible mistake" business?'

'I was hoping you could tell me. I mean, is there anything I should know, besides your operation and all?'

'I can't imagine what . . .' Mrs Madrigal's voice faltered. She fussed distractedly with the loose wisps of hair that framed her angular face. 'Mona, if she doesn't know that you and I are together, I don't see how I could possibly know anything that would be pertinent to her remark.'

'But she *does* know. I mean, I *think* she knows. Oh, Christ – the moon is in ca-ca!'

446

Mrs Madrigal managed a chuckle. 'So what do we do, daughter?'

Mona smiled weakly. 'Invite her to dinner?'

'Oh, sickroom, sickroom!'

Mona laughed. 'Maybe I should talk to her first. If she doesn't know about you, there's no point in blowing our cover.'

'Splendid idea.'

But less and less splendid as the day wore on. That night, while Mona was visiting Michael at the hospital, Mrs Madrigal broke one of her own rules of life by sitting in her room and agonizing over the future.

She knew that was silly. If a confrontation with Betty was inevitable, what point was there in fretting over it? The important thing now was to direct all her energy toward Mona's happiness.

So she marched upstairs and had a little talk with Brian.

He told her more than she had expected to hear.

Burke Explodes

A low-hanging spring fog slid under the bridge toward the city as Mary Ann filled her lungs with air and read the instructions for an isometric squat.

'Ick. This one is the pits.'

Burke grinned and placed his back firmly against an oak piling, easing himself down slowly. 'This was *your* idea, remember.'

She stuck out her tongue at him. He was right, of course. For weeks she'd been promoting this trip to the Marina Green exercise course, spurred on by a semi-flabby tummy and a sexy *Apartment Life* article about couples who work out together.

Burke reveled in her agony. 'It's not too late to quit before you rupture something.'

'Ha! Who beat you at the hop kick *and* the log hop?' She chose the piling facing Burke and lowered herself defiantly into position.

Burke's face was bright red as he held the squatting position. 'That's because you're doing Intermediate stuff. I'm going for Championship.'

'And you'll poop out at the end. Don't you know anything about endurance?'

Burke completed his count of thirty, springing into an upright position again. 'Healthy body, healthy mind!' he exclaimed.

Mary Ann couldn't manage a snappy comeback. They were both thinking the same thing.

'Well,' shrugged Burke, 'some of us can't have both.'

When they had finished their run, they strolled back to a bench on the edge of the bay. Mary Ann smiled into the wind, feeling the blood tingle in her limbs. She slipped her arm through Burke's and leaned her head on his shoulder.

'Do I smell as gross as you do?'

He kissed her damp temple. 'Every bit.'

'Swell.'

'We won't shower when we get back. I wanna screw you on the living room floor.'

'Burke!'

'I *like* musky women.' He kissed her again and began to sing a chorus of 'I Remember You.'

Mary Ann ignored the irony. 'I don't think I've ever heard you sing. You have a gorgeous voice.'

'I do, don't I?' He continued singing.

'Did you ever sing . . . like professionally?'

He turned and looked at her, hesitating. 'Not professionally. Only in church, back in Nantucket. The Good Shepherd choir. What are you up to, anyway?'

Her tone was defensive. 'Nothing. Can't I be curious about you?'

'That's what my mother said on the phone last night.'

'She called you?'

He nodded grimly.

'They're freaking, aren't they?'

'What do you expect? They hate this town. Their only child ended up in a bush in Golden Gate Park with amnesia. Now he's back, chasing ghosts.'

'Do you remember that, Burke?'

'What?'

'Waking up under that bush in the park.'

'Not really. I remember being in a hospital for a while, then –'

'*What* hospital, Burke?'

'Presbyterian.' He smiled sympathetically.

'Well, then how do you know it happened? The stuff about the park and all.'

He stared at her uncomprehendingly. 'What?'

448

'How do you know your parents are telling the truth?'

'What in hell are you . . . ?'

'They could've deprogrammed you, Burke.' Mary Ann drew back slightly, bracing herself for the repercussions. Burke blinked at her momentarily, then exploded with a derisive laugh.

'I may be loony, lady, but I'm not *dumb*! Christ, don't you think I know when people are jacking me around? Don't you think I have enough sense to . . . Christ!'

There was nothing to do but placate him. 'Burke, don't take it so personally. I'm sorry, OK?'

He brooded in silence, gazing out at the fog-blurred bay. 'I'm no baby,' he said at last. '*I was in the AP, Mary Ann.*'

That night, at her suggestion, they slept apart for the first time since his arrival in San Francisco.

Mary Ann dreamed about roses.

She was walking along a catwalk with a dozen roses, cradled in her arms. Behind her was the man with the transplant, leading an entourage of rose-bearers.

They were all there: the dwarf from Las Hadas, the rose vendor from the flower market, Millie the Flower Lady, and Arnold and Melba Littlefield, brandishing the processional cross from Beauchamp's funeral.

Suddenly, Burke appeared at the end of the catwalk. He grabbed Mary Ann by the shoulders and shook her beseechingly. '*I was in the AP, Mary Ann. I was in the AP.*'

When she woke up, she knew what she had to do next.

The Freak Beat

The Associated Press, Mary Ann learned, was located on the third floor of the Fox Plaza high-rise, a cold concrete tombstone of a building that marked the grave of the old Fox Theater.

The theater had been demolished about five years before Mary Ann's arrival in San Francisco, but Michael had told her of its loveliness, its rococo majesty which conformed so gracefully to the needs of human beings.

She thought about that now as she stood in the fluorescent-lit

449

office, waiting for a man named Jack to look up from his computer-screen typewriter long enough to acknowledge her presence.

'Uh . . . excuse me. The bureau chief said you might . . .'

His eyes didn't stray from the symbols on the screen in front of him. 'Fuck, shit, piss!'

'I'm sorry, if this is a bad time.'

'Not *you*.' He turned off the machine and spun around to face her, offering a tired smile. 'How many goddamn words can you write about Patty Hearst, anyway?'

Mary Ann smiled back. 'I've never tried.'

'Well, *don't*. For sheer column-inches, that broad's a bigger pain than Angela Davis, Charlie Manson and Zodiac put together!'

'It must be kind of exciting, though.'

The reporter snorted. 'I put in for Buffalo. I *begged* 'em for Buffalo. But oh, no! Those assholes in New York thought ol' Jack Lederer would be fuckin' *perfect* for San Francisco.' He fumbled for a More, lit it and tossed the match on the floor. 'So what can I do for you?'

'The bureau chief said you used to work with –'

'Pull up a chair.'

She obeyed, wedging herself uncomfortably between his desk and a filing cabinet marked 'Mass Murders, Etc.'

'The bureau chief said you used to work with a guy named Burke Andrew.'

He thought for a moment. 'Yeah. Two – no – at *least* three years ago. But not that long. Four or five months at the most. He couldn't hack it for shit.'

'They fired him?'

'Nah, he quit. He was slow, that's all. Spent *hours* workin' on goddamn grabby leads when the world was fallin' apart around him. He was nice enough, I guess. Friend of yours?'

'Yeah.'

'Disappear or something?'

'No, why?'

He shrugged. 'This is the place, right? For droppin' off the face of the earth?'

Mary Ann smiled, inwardly shuddering. She hadn't thought of Norman Neal Williams in ages. 'Burke has amnesia, Mr Lederer. He can't remember anything after the AP. I thought maybe you might –'

The reporter whistled. 'It's a friggin' soap opera!'

'Tell *me*.'

'You want me to fill in the pieces, right?'

She nodded. 'Did he tell you anything about where he was going after the AP? Did he talk about his plans?'

'Are you makin' this up?'

'No! Why in the world should I? Look, the bureau chief says you and Burke worked together a lot.'

'Yeah. We worked nights together. But he never talked about personal stuff.'

'When he was here did he ever do stories about cults?'

Jack Lederer shook his head. 'The freak beat is mine, sweetheart.' He grinned annoyingly. 'You think the Moonies got him, huh?'

She ignored it. 'Do you think there's any possibility he might have –'

'When did this amnesia zap him, anyway?'

'About three months ago the police found him in Golden Gate Park. He was passed out or something.'

The reporter jerked open a desk drawer and removed a spiral notebook. 'I think it must've been – no, earlier than that – right about . . .' He began to slip through the notebook. 'I saw your boyfriend just briefly about five months ago at Lefty O'Doul's one night. He told me he was free-lancing and that I could eat my heart out because he was onto something really bizarre.'

Mary Ann's mind raced wildly. 'You mean he was still a *reporter?*'

The AP man smirked. 'A *free-lancer.* There's a difference. They always talk crazy.' He looked down at the notebook again. 'Yep. There it is. "Transubstantiation."'

'What? I'm afraid I don't . . .'

'Yeah. Well, neither did I. I asked your boyfriend if he had any substantiation for his so-called bizarre story and he laughed and said, "*Trans*ubstantiation is more like it." So I asked him what the hell that was supposed to mean, and he polished off his drink and told me to look it up.'

'And?'

'He walked out of the joint.'

'But what *does* it mean?'

Jack Lederer stubbed out his More, then pointed to a dictionary on top of the 'Mass Murders, Etc.' filing cabinet. 'Look it up, sweetheart.'

Homecoming

With Michael in his arms, Jon took a deep breath and confronted the precipitous wooden stairway leading up to Barbary Lane. 'Are you ready?' he asked.

'Am *I* ready? *You're* the one I'm worried about. What happened to our Sherpa guide, anyway?'

'He died of exposure at eight thousand feet.'

'Well, shit! You just can't get good Sherpas anymore.'

Jon staggered under his weight. 'Don't make me laugh. I'll drop you.'

'The hell you say. If I go, you're goin' too.'

Jon took long, steady strides up the steps. 'I think we'd better pack in provisions. Something tells me we won't be going out too often.' He stopped, panting, on the landing at the entrance to the lane.

'For God's sake,' Michael said melodramatically. 'Whatever you do, *don't look down.* Pretend you're Karen Black in *Airport.*' He smiled bravely up at Jon, crossing his eyes.

'So help me, Michael, if you don't . . .'

'Sorry.'

The doctor lumbered down the leafy walkway, cursing angrily when Boris, the resident cat, emerged from the shrubbery to rub his back ecstatically against Jon's leg. 'Aw,' said Michael. 'A little pussy never hurt anyone.'

Mona was waiting for them in the courtyard. 'Can I run get your wheelchair or something?'

Jon shook his head. 'It's easier to carry him.'

'Across the threshold, please note.' Michael winked at Mona.

'You could've at least thrown me the garter belt,' she said.

'Since when did *you* wanna get married?'

'A *joke*, Mouse.'

Mrs Madrigal scurried into the courtyard and held the door for them. 'Welcome home, dear. It just hasn't been the same.'

Michael blew her a kiss. 'This place never is, is it?'

Jon fixed pot roast for dinner. Afterward, he moved Michael's wheelchair to the window and pulled up a chair next to him.

'I've missed that fish,' said Michael.

'What fish?'

'Down there. The neon one on the wharf. It's always seemed kind of cheerful to me.'

Jon lit a joint and handed it to Michael. 'The fish was an early Christian symbol for hope. They carved it on the walls of the catacombs when they were hiding out.'

'You don't say?' Michael grinned and took a toke. 'I could learn a lot from you.'

Jon kept his eyes fixed on the bay. 'I can stay, then?'

Silence.

'Well . . . say *something*.'

'I love you, Jon –'

'That's good for starters.'

'I don't want it to be a doctor-patient thing, that's all.'

Jon turned and stared at him. 'Is that what you think?'

'You're a doctor, Jon. It would only be natural for you to get off on nursing someone back –'

'I *hate* wiping your butt!'

'Look. I didn't mean to . . . You do?'

'Goddamn right!'

Michael smiled. 'You don't know how much that means to me.'

They laughed until the tears streamed down their faces. Michael lost control of the smoldering roach, letting it fall to the floor. Jon snuffed it with his foot, then leaned over to look directly into Michael's eyes.

'I want you well, sport. I don't care who does it.'

'I know.'

'On the other hand, I *do* get off on sex with paraplegics.'

They sat up in bed together, poring over back issues of *Architectural Digest*.

'Hey,' said Jon, 'you wanna have Mona up for brunch tomorrow?'

'She may be in no mood. She's seeing her mother tonight.'

'Her mother's a bitch?'

'According to Mona, it's "hair by L'Oreal, jewels by Cartier and heart by Frigidaire." But who knows?'

'Yeah.' Jon got lost in his magazine.

Michael stopped reading and savored for a moment this rare new form of inactivity. All his adult life he had searched for someone to do

453

nothing with in bed. And now he had found him, this bright, generous person, whose love was so strong that sex was in perspective again.

Jon held up his magazine. 'Isn't that magnificent?' It was an early photograph of the Pacific Union Club, the palatial stone edifice that still adorned the top of Nob Hill.

Michael shook his head in appreciation. 'Imagine a club with that kind of money!'

'The club didn't build it. The Floods did.'

'The Floods?'

'The Flood family. *Big* bucks in the old days.'

Michael's brow wrinkled. 'You don't suppose . . . ?'

'What?'

'Christ!' yelped Michael. 'That could be it, Jon. *That could be it.*'

The Mountain of the Flood

It was late, but Michael was too excited to wait until morning before calling Mary Ann.

'Ajax Detective Service here.'

'Mouse?'

'You thought you'd screw me up with that damn poem, didn't you?'

'You've got something?'

'*Mais naturellement*! Can you come down?'

'*Can* I!' She hung up without another word.

Jon laid his *Architectural Digest* on the nightstand. 'Shall I get up?'

'Why?' asked Michael.

'Isn't she coming down?'

Michael looked mildly miffed. 'I think she knows we sleep together, Jon.'

'I know, but . . .' The doctor smiled at himself. 'I'll feel like Nora Charles or something.'

Michael tugged at the lapel of Jon's pajamas. 'It's OK. You're wearing your peignoir.'

Seconds later, they heard Mary Ann in the hallway, rapping demurely on the door. 'It's open,' Michael shouted.

When Mary Ann peered cautiously into the bedroom, Michael made sure there would be no embarrassed silences. 'It's OK,' he grinned. 'Just pretend we're Starsky and Hutch.'

Mary Ann giggled. 'You *do* sorta look like them.' She pulled up a chair next to the bed. 'I hope you don't mind this intrusion, Jon.'

Jon smiled. 'I can't wait to hear what this is about myself.'

'In fact,' added Michael, 'he's the one who gave me the clue.'

Mary Ann was practically bounding in the chair. 'Tell me, tell me!'

Michael smiled mysteriously, heightening the suspense. 'I think Burke's little dream poem is about the P U Club.'

'The what?'

'The P U Club, you poor cornfed thing! The Pacific Union Club, up on Nob Hill.'

'That big red brick thing?'

Michael nodded. 'It was built by a man named Flood, which makes Nob Hill the Mountain of the Flood! And the P U Club is not only a *cult*, it's our *oldest* cult. All those overstuffed old banker farts, sitting around in their overstuffed chairs!'

Mary Ann was slack-jawed. 'Mouse do you think they recite that poem in one of their rituals or something?'

'Doesn't it make a lot of sense?'

Mary Ann thought for a moment. 'Well, *that* part makes sense. But what about the rest of it? What about the Meeting of the Lines, for instance?'

Jon, who had been listening intently, couldn't resist asking, 'What's the Meeting of the Lines?'

'It's part of the poem,' Michael explained. ' "High upon the Sacred Rock/The Rose Incarnate shines,/Upon the Mountain of the Flood/At the Meeting of the Lines." '

Jon grinned. 'Maybe they snort coke at the P U Club.'

'That's what Burke thinks it means,' said Mary Ann.

Michael demurred. 'They just snort, period, at the P U Club.'

'Wait!' exclaimed Jon. 'What about the cable cars?'

'What about them?' asked Mary Ann.

'The cable car lines. They cross at California and Powell, just a block away from the P U Club!'

Mary Ann and Michael yelped in unison. 'That's brilliant,' blurted Michael. 'That's positively brilliant!' Mary Ann beamed in agreement. 'That *must* be it.'

Jon bowed grandly. 'Now all we have to do is figure out what any of this has to do with a florist from St Sebastian's Hospital, right?'

Mary Ann nodded, deep in thought. '*And* what any of this has to do with transubstantiation.'

455

Michael did a double take. 'Come again, ma'am.'

'Have you got a dictionary?'

'On the shelf by the door,' said Michael. 'Next to *The Persian Boy*.'

Mary Ann found the dictionary and began to thumb through it. 'I went down to the A P today. Where Burke used to work. A man there told me he ran into Burke about five months ago, and he said Burke told him he was working on . . . Here it is. Transubstantiation.' She handed the book to Jon.

The doctor read aloud. '"The changing of one substance into another."'

'Read the second definition,' said Mary Ann.

'"In the mass of the Roman Catholic Church, the conversion of the whole substance of the bread and wine into the body and blood of Christ, only the external appearance of bread and wine remaining." So what does that have to do with Burke?'

'This guy at the A P says he was working on a really bizarre story connected with transubstantiation.'

Michael frowned quizzically. 'Have you tried this out on Burke yet?'

Mary Ann shook her head soberly. 'I think he's beginning to resent my curiosity, Mouse. I'm not sure what that means, but I'm trying to be discreet about all this, until I've got something solid to go on.'

'Do you know what I think?' said Jon.

'What?' asked Mary Ann.

'I think you've got *too many* clues.'

Mary Ann sighed. 'I think you're right.'

Betty

The first thing Mona noticed about Betty Ramsey was her clothes. She was decked out in Kelly green and white, the recognizable racing colors of women realtors everywhere.

And Mona's clothing was the first thing Betty noticed.

'Where *did* you get that frock? Goodwill?'

Mona's smile was smug. 'As a matter of fact, yes.'

'Well, it's grossly unflattering.'

'Thank you.'

'The hippie thing is over, Mona. The pendulum is swinging.'

Mona ignored her, heading for the window.

'What are you doing?' asked Betty.

'Checking out your view.' She turned and smiled at her mother. 'The first thing *every* San Franciscan does when visiting somebody else's apartment.' She parted the curtains and gazed down upon the nighttime splendor of the city. 'Mmm. Very nice. Whose place is this, anyway?'

Betty began dropping ice cubes into a glass. 'Susan Patterson's. Someone I knew *years* ago in Carmel. She's in Switzerland for the spring.'

Mona surveyed the room. 'It looks like you've been here since *last* spring.' The floor was cluttered with Gump's boxes and shopping bags from Saks; Betty's yoga mat and an assortment of French body creams were visible through the bedroom door.

Betty held up a gin bottle. 'This or bourbon?'

'Neither, thanks.'

'I don't have any Perrier.'

'That's fine. I took a Quaalude a little while ago.'

'For God's sake!'

Mona sat down on the sofa. 'Would you rather I'd taken one of your Valiums?'

'A *doctor* prescribed those.'

'Don't they always.'

'You shouldn't have to rely on . . . Mona, let's not argue. We haven't seen each other for a long time, darling. The least we can do is –'

'Why are you here, Betty?'

Betty didn't answer immediately. She finished fixing her gin-and-tonic, then joined her daughter on the sofa. 'Why do you think?'

Mona locked eyes with her mother. 'I don't think it has a damned thing to do with me.'

'That's not fair, Mona.'

'It's the truth.'

Betty looked down at her drink. 'You know about Andy, don't you?'

Mona made her face into a mask. 'I know that he left you. That's old news.'

'Don't play games, Mona. I know he's your landlord. I know about the sex change, and I know that you know about it.'

Mona held firm. 'I repeat. Why are you here?'

457

'Because I have a bloody *right* to be! He deserted me, Mona! He left me with a child to support! He walked out of my life without leaving so much as a note, and now he thinks he can waltz right back and lay claim to the child he never even –'

'I am not a child and nobody's *laid claim* to me, Betty. I didn't even know that he – that she was my father until two weeks ago.'

Betty glared at her in disgust. 'And now you're living with him!'

'Her.'

'Did he tell you – oh, pardon me, *she* – did *she*, by any chance, tell you what she did with the private detective I hired?'

'The *what?*'

'Mona, darling, this is so much more complicated than you could ever –'

'Just tell me what you're talking about.'

Betty held her daughter's hand. 'Last summer, when you sent me that photograph of your landlady, I saw the similarities immediately, so I hired a private detective to help me find out if it was true.'

Mona stared in amazement.

'And,' continued Betty, 'he never reported back.'

'What?'

'I never heard another word from him. He was living in your house, Mona. At 28 Barbary Lane.'

'Mr Williams? That guy on the roof?'

Betty nodded, holding tight to Mona's hand. 'We stayed in touch by telephone. He called me at least once a week. He said he thought Andy had become . . . Anna Madrigal, and he told me that Anna Madrigal was an anagram for something. Then he just disappeared.' She let go of Mona's hand and took a sip of her drink. 'Did you *know* him, Mona?'

Stunned, Mona shook her head. 'Not at all. He was . . . weird.'

'I know. He was the best I could round up on short notice. The point is, what *happened* to him?'

Mona took a sip of Betty's gin. 'We wondered that too.'

'We?'

'*Everybody.* Including Mrs Madrigal. She even called the police about it.'

'I want to see her, Mona. Will you arrange it?'

A look of wretched resignation came over Mona's face. 'You'll do it anyway,' she sighed.

'You're right,' said Betty. 'I will.'

The Rose Incarnate

In keeping up with her new strategy, Mary Ann said nothing to Burke about the Pacific Union Club. Or about her transubstantiation findings. She kept quiet all through breakfast and all through a leisurely morning walk across Russian Hill.

Finally, at noon, she excused herself.

'Jon's at his office,' she explained. 'I promised him I'd keep Mouse company for a while.'

When she entered Michael's apartment, the invalid was pacing the room in his wheelchair, his eyes flickering with excitement. 'You know what?' he said without preliminaries. 'We didn't even consider the red rose business in our discussion last night.'

'I got the feeling you guys were O D'ing.'

Michael smiled. 'Not me, Babycakes. I'm *hooked*. Look, it all comes back to the man with the transplant, doesn't it?'

'Maybe. Burke only *thinks* that the transplant man recognized him.'

'Assuming he did, then what do we have?'

'He could be a member of the P U Club, I guess.'

Michael shook his head. 'I suggested that to Jon. He says the P U Club would *never* admit a hospital florist. Maybe Burke worked as a waiter or something at the P U Club.'

'It's hard to picture,' said Mary Ann.

'O K, then maybe we're on the wrong track altogether. You know, the Mountain of the Flood could mean just Nob Hill in general.'

'So what else is *there*?'

'Plenty. The Mark, the Huntington, the Fairmont.'

'Great. A hotel cult.'

Michael grinned. 'You're stuck in that cult rut, aren't you?'

'I don't know,' groaned Mary Ann. 'Sometimes I feel like I made the whole thing up.'

Michael laughed. 'It's possible. I was looking through some of my old school lit books this morning – you know, *Silas Marner* and *The Great Gatsby* and all that – and I just about cracked up because I had written 'symbolism' in the margin on every other page. Christ! In *The Great Gatsby* I had underlined the word 'yellow' every time it appeared.'

'God!' smiled Mary Ann. 'I remember those awful papers, but I don't get it, Mouse. What does that have to do with all this?'

'Well, maybe *we're* looking for too much symbolism. *Everything* doesn't have to mean something.'

'Yeah, but it sure would be nice if *something* did.'

'What about the transub . . . whatchamacallit?'

'What about it?'

'Well, for starters, is Burke Catholic?'

Mary Ann shook her head. 'Episcopalian.'

'That's close.'

'Is it?'

Michael nodded. 'The High Church ones are more Catholic than the Catholics. Believe me, I know. I used to have a boyfriend who was a High Church Episcopal seminarian. He practically *shaved* in holy water. I'm sure *he* believed that the bread and wine turn into the body and blood of Christ.'

Mary Ann shuddered a little. 'Is that what they believe? Literally?'

'Literally. You saw the definition, Babycakes.'

'I know, but that's kind of creepy, isn't it?'

Michael shrugged. 'Christians are the only people on earth who kneel before an instrument of torture. If Christ had been martyred in this century, I guess we'd all be wearing little electric chairs around our necks.'

Mary Ann was shocked. 'Mouse, that's sacrilegious!'

'No, it's not. It's just an observation about the nature of –'

Suddenly, Michael's hands clamped onto the arms of his wheelchair, his face screwed into an expression of intense concentration. 'Jesus Christ!' he shouted. '*Jesus Christ!*'

'Mouse, for heaven's sake, what's the matter?'

'The Sacred Rock! The goddamn Sacred Rock! It's Grace Cathedral, it's gotta be Grace Cathedral!'

'Grace Cathedral?'

'What else? Right next door to the P U Club, Mary Ann! On the Mountain of the Flood at the Meeting of the Lines! And guess what the Rose Incarnate is?'

'What?'

'The biggest rose in the whole friggin' city! The rose window at Grace Cathedral!'

Labor of Love

D'orothea Wilson paused briefly in the lobby of St Sebastian's Hospital to study an antique portrait of the institution's namesake.

The holy man was tied to a tree, wearing only a loincloth and a beatific smile. His bloodied body was prickly with arrows. Half a dozen of them, at least.

D'orothea made a face that attracted the attention of a passing nurse. 'I know,' winced the nurse. 'Isn't it awful?'

'Why do they even hang it? In a hospital, for God's sake!'

The nurse smiled wearily. 'The board fights over it every year. I think it came with a big endowment or something. Nobody wants to offend the old bat who donated it. They've moved it two or three times. This is the least conspicuous it's ever been.'

'Someone should come in here some night with a can of spray paint,' suggested D'orothea.

'Right on!' said the nurse.

After checking at the desk on the location of DeDe's room, D'orothea made a quick stop at the hospital florist, where she picked up a dozen roses. Then she hurried to the second floor to see her friend.

'You can't stay long,' grinned DeDe. 'They just chased my mother out.'

'I won't.' D'orothea set the roses on the bedside table, then leaned over and kissed DeDe on the cheek. 'You look *fabulous*, hon.'

'Thanks. And thanks for the roses.'

'How's the tum-tum?'

DeDe rolled her eyes. 'Thumpety-thump. Thumpety-thump.'

'You mean . . . ?'

'The pains are fifteen minutes apart.'

'Holy shit! When you called, you sounded so casual about it. I thought . . . Oh, hon, aren't you excited?'

DeDe smiled thinly. 'Sure.'

'*Course* you are! Hey, you haven't even told me about names.'

'Names?'

'For the babies. You picked 'em yet?'

DeDe smoothed the bedsheet over her mountainous belly. 'Oh,

Edgar, I guess, if one is a boy. After my father. And if one is a girl, I'll name her Anna.'

'That's pretty. Any particular reason?'

'Daddy asked me to. Just before he died.'

'A family name, huh?'

DeDe shook her head. 'Not that I know of. Daddy just said he liked the name.' She fidgeted with the sheet again, looking away. It took D'orothea a moment to realize that she was crying.

'Hon? Hey, hon. What's the trouble?'

'I'm so frightened, D'or.'

D'orothea sat on the edge of the bed and stroked DeDe's hair gently. 'Why?' she asked.

'I feel like I'm going to be punished or something.'

'Punished? What for?'

DeDe's face was shiny with tears. She reached for a Kleenex, blew her nose, then dropped the tissue on the bedside table. Finally, she looked up at D'orothea and sighed. 'The twins are gonna be Chinese, D'or.'

D'orothea stared at her expressionlessly. Then she said, 'Big fucking deal.'

A smile fought its way through the desolation of DeDe's face. 'That's easy for you to say.'

'Fine,' said D'or. 'Then I'll say it again. Biiiiig fucking deal!'

DeDe laughed at last. 'Oh, D'or, thank you!'

'Don't mention it. Eurasians are *always* gorgeous, by the way.'

'They are, aren't they?'

'Does Big Mama know?'

DeDe winced, then shook her head.

'Thought so,' said D'or. '*That's* what you're bawling about, isn't it?'

'In part, I guess.'

'What's the other part?'

'I don't know. D'or . . . none of my friends have even called.'

'Why, your luck is changing, hon.'

'Why?'

''Cause I'm the first of your *new* friends, DeDe. And we're not that easy to get rid of.' She leaned over and kissed DeDe again. ''Cept when you're dropping babies. Then I get squeamish as hell. I'll be here, though. Right outside the door.'

'You don't have to.'

'I want to.'

'Thanks, D'or.'

'Do you want me to tell your mother about the babies, by the way?'

'No, I'll do it. I love you, D'or.'

'Ditto, Kiddo.'

Back to Nantucket?

Burke, of course, was the hardest one to convince.

'It's just plain goofball, Mary Ann. Why would a *cathedral* make anybody have amnesia? You seem to forget I get violently ill whenever I –'

'You threw up at Beauchamp's funeral, didn't you? That was a church.'

Burke gestured impatiently. 'That was the rose, for God's sake.'

'But don't you see? Maybe it isn't the *image* of the rose that nauseates you. Maybe it's just the word, the association with the rose window.'

Looking bleaker than ever, he sat down on the edge of his bed. 'It isn't a window I see in my dream. It's a red rose. Not a pink one or a yellow one – a *red* one, Mary Ann.' He peered up at her through eyes that had changed from vibrant gray to dull pewter. 'I think it's time for me to go home.'

Her first thought was that they were already *in* his apartment. Then his meaning struck her like a bundle of briars across the face. 'Burke, you don't mean that!'

The kindness of his tone was devastating. 'Yes, I do,' he said softly. 'I have to put this behind me, Mary Ann.'

'But, Burke . . .' She sat next to him and slipped her arm across his hunched shoulders. 'You'll *never* put it behind until you find the cause of your amnesia. You can't go on being terrified forever.'

'I'm not terrified.'

She squeezed his shoulder gently. 'I know, but what about the roses?'

'I can handle that. I just have to . . . I have to start getting on with life.'

'What will you do back East?'

'My father's offered me a position in his publishing firm.'

She looked at him soulfully. 'Couldn't you do something like that here?'

He smiled, stroking her hair. 'I *will* miss you. I should have said that first thing.'

She felt tears welling in her eyes. 'Dammit,' she said quietly. 'I'm so pissed at myself.'

'Why?'

'I shouldn't have pushed it. I shouldn't have freaked you out.'

His face turned the color of an American Beauty. '*You didn't freak me out, Mary Ann!*'

She looked at him in silence, reading the anguish in his face. Then she stood up and walked across the room. If this was it, if they had passed the point of no return, she had nothing to lose by telling the whole truth.

She turned to face him. 'Burke, the man with the transplant sings in the choir at Grace Cathedral.'

'*What?*'

'I checked on it this morning. And I think you used to sing with him.'

'Wait a minute! How did you find that out?'

She averted his eyes. She didn't want to seem too proud of herself. 'I . . . well, first I asked Jon to call the hospital and find out his name. Then I called Grace Cathedral and talked to some guy they call the verger, and he told me that the transplant man – his name is Tyrone, by the way – he said that Tyrone sings in the choir at Grace.'

Something like hope glimmered in Burke's eyes. 'And you think . . . you think I sang with him?'

'You *could* have,' she said warily. 'You told me you sang in the choir back in Nantucket. You also told me, when we were in Mexico, that you had sent letters to your parents about attending services at Grace Cathedral.'

Mary Ann must have looked like a frightened rabbit, for Burke smiled suddenly and patted the bed next to him. She came to him and sat down, peering at him balefully. 'Am I a pain in the ass?' she asked.

He kissed the tip of her nose. 'So you think that Burke Andrew, boy reporter, stumbled onto some sinister goings-on at Grace Cathedral?'

She smiled sheepishly. 'It's only *today's* theory.'

'An *Episcopal* cult, huh?'

She goosed him. 'Don't rub it in.'

'Actually,' he smiled. 'I kinda like it.'

Scurrying back to her own apartment, Mary Ann encountered Mrs Madrigal, who was vacuuming the hallway. The landlady's hair was up in curlers.

'Trying out a new do?' asked Mary Ann.

'We'll see. I may end up looking like Medusa. Where are *you* off to in such a hurry?'

'Burke's taking me to church.'

'How very sweet,' said Mrs Madrigal earnestly.

'I'm expecting lightning bolts. This is the first time I've been to church since I came to San Francisco ten months ago.'

The landlady smiled. 'Well, say one for me.'

'You don't need it.'

'I do *tonight*.'

'Why?'

Mrs Madrigal leaned forward furtively. 'Tonight, my dear child, I have a heavy date with my ex-wife.'

Questions and Answers

'Hello, Betty.'

Mrs Madrigal spoke the words with a warmth and self-assurance that astounded Mona. Furthermore, the landlady had never looked more beautiful. Smooth, glowing skin. Shining eyes. A pale green kimono fluttered about her like butterfly wings.

And tonight she wasn't wearing her usual cloche. Her hair fell about her face in soft, romantic ringlets. Betty was visibly stunned.

'Hello. I hope this isn't . . . How are you?'

Mrs Madrigal smiled like a benign Hindu goddess. 'Call me Andy, if you like. I know Anna must be a little hard to get out.'

'No, that's perfectly . . . This is a *darling* neighborhood. I see why Mona's so mad for it.'

Mrs Madrigal took her guest's coat. 'I understand you're just a few blocks away.'

'Yes. Well, that's a high-rise. This is just . . . precious. Those steps up from the street are straight out of . . . I don't know where.'

She stepped into the living room, nervously appraising everything in sight. Except, of course, the person who had once been her husband.

Mrs Madrigal brought sherry from the kitchen. 'There's not one for you, Mona, dear. I think your mother and I should have a little talk.'

Mona rose like a shot. 'OK. Fine. I'll take a walk or something.'

465

'We won't be long,' said Mrs Madrigal. 'Why don't you go to the Tivoli. Perhaps we can join you later.'

'Fine,' said Mona lamely, heading out the door.

Mrs Madrigal sat sipping her sherry in silence, her eyes glued on Betty Ramsey's rapidly wilting smile. 'My goodness,' she said at last, 'you've certainly held up well. Your figure's as good as it was thirty years ago.'

Betty tugged at her skirt, assuring that her knees were covered. 'Yoga helps,' she said flatly.

'Mmm. And a few snips here and there.'

Betty stiffened. 'I don't see what that –'

'I'm not being bitchy, Betty.' She laughed heartily. 'I'm the *last* person to denigrate the value of surgery!' Her merriment vanished as rapidly as it had come. 'So what can I do for you?'

The realtor looked down at her glass. 'I have a right to see my daughter,' she said quietly, measuring her words, as if on the verge of exploding. 'I have a right to know what you're doing with her.'

A faint smile rippled across the landlady's face. 'It's monstrously perverse. I'm giving her a home. And love.'

'And I didn't. Is that what you're saying?'

'This is silly, Betty. Mona's over thirty.'

A large vein began to pulse in Betty's sinewy neck. 'I know what you're doing. You're deliberately poisoning her against me. You're using her to satisfy some sick maternal urge that will make you feel like a *real* woman! God! That's so bloody twisted I can't even . . .'

'I'm sorry you resent me so much. It may help you to know that I think there's some justification for the way you feel.'

'*Some* justification! Listen to me, Andy! I want more than a bloody glass of sherry and a few weak-kneed apologies. I want some answers, goddammit!'

Mrs Madrigal set down her glass and folded her hands in her lap.

'Fine,' she said quietly. 'I'll do my best.'

Her composure rattled Betty. 'For one thing, I want to know what happened to Norman Williams.'

Mrs Madrigal's Wedgwood eyes turned into saucers. 'You *knew* him?'

'Don't give me that!' snarled Betty.

'Betty, honestly, what *are* you talking about?'

'I hired him, and you know it! What did you do? Buy him off?'

'He disappeared several months ago. He just never came back, Betty. My God, was he a *detective?*'

'How *demurely* you lie.' Betty sprang to her feet. 'I should have known better than to expect the truth from you. And I think it's about time that Mona learned the truth about her *real* father!'

'Betty, please . . .'

'Unless, of course, you've already told her, in all your liberated candor.'

Silence.

Betty smiled savagely. 'I didn't think you had.'

'How can you be so vindictive? You'll only hurt her.'

'You said it yourself. Mona's over thirty. She can take it. She's a big girl now.'

The Sacred Rock

It was dusk when they reached Nob Hill. In front of the Mark and the Fairmont, pastel-colored tourists scrambled in every direction. They reminded Mary Ann of baby chicks that had been dyed for Easter and were looking for their mothers.

But these people, more likely, were looking for their children.

Like Mona's mother. Like Michael's parents and Burke's and her own. And even like Mother Mucca. Stunned and scandalized, yet secretely titillated, they had flocked to this latter-day Sodom to observe firsthand the fate of their long-flown offspring.

There was fear in their eyes. And confusion. And a kind of mute despair that made Mary Ann want to reach out and hug them. Some of them were nearing the end of their lives, yet, in many ways, they *were* the chicks. They were the children of their children.

The traffic light changed. Burke and Mary Ann pressed through the mob at the crosswalk and strode west up California Street. To their right, the mud-brown fortress called the Pacific Union Club squatted disapprovingly in the midst of this middle-American chaos. Silent, foreboding, impenetrable.

Mary Ann ran her fingers along the massive bronze fence that protected the building, examining its ornamentation for some sort of rose motif. Nothing. Only Nancy Drew found clues that easily.

When they reached Huntington Park, they sat on a bench near the fountain, their backs to the PU Club, their eyes fixed on the mammoth rose window of Grace Cathedral.

'Did you call them?' asked Burke.

Mary Ann nodded. 'A woman in the cathedral office says there's a Holy Communion service tonight.'

'What time?'

She looked at her watch. 'Forty-five minutes.'

'We should go in now, then. I don't want to be there with a lot of people around.'

'Why?'

He smiled and pointed to his mouth. 'I've had enough scenes for one week.'

'You don't think you'll . . . ?'

'How do *I* know?' he shrugged. 'I think we should stay long enough to see if it triggers anything, then get the hell out.' He smiled at his own phraseology, apologizing to the huge window. 'Sorry about that.'

'Burke, before we go in . . .'

'Yeah?'

'I was just wondering. Back in Nantucket, when you went to church there, did you believe that the wine turned into blood and the bread turned into flesh?'

He smiled. 'Didn't everybody?'

She shook her head. 'We were Presbyterian. It was all grape juice to me.'

'I guess we were pretty High Church,' he grinned.

'Don't you find that a little grotesque?'

'Maybe. If you stop to think about it long enough. But not grotesque enough to make a hot news story, if that's what you're thinking. Look, Mary Ann, for most Episcopalians, it's just a bunch of words. If you actually backed a High Churcher into the corner, he might *say* he believed he was drinking the blood of Christ, or eating His flesh, but I think most people regard it in a kind of mundane, symbolic way.'

'Have you thought about why you might have been writing a story on it then?'

He chuckled. 'You're more literal than the High Churchers. Look, you said Jack Lederer told you I had *mentioned* the word 'transubstanti-ation' in connection with the story I was writing. In a broad sense, that word can simply mean transformation. Hell, maybe I was talking about my career . . . or *anything*. The only reason Lederer wrote the word down was because he himself didn't know what it meant.'

468

A chill evening wind whipped through the little park. Mary Ann turned up her coat collar and gazed again at the great cathedral. She slipped her arm through Burke's.

'It's beautiful,' she said reverently. 'It's almost blue in this light.'

He nodded, pulling her closer.

'Why do I feel so creepy, Burke?'

He turned and smiled at her. 'Because *your* heritage is the Little Brown Church in the Dell.' He rose suddenly, taking her with him. 'C'mon, you heathen. Let's go get religion.'

The irony of the turnabout did not escape her.

Now she was the one who wanted to back out.

Showdown

Mrs Madrigal sat down on the edge of her red velvet sofa, momentarily stunned. The horrid part, the part that made her knees weak and her throat dry, was that Betty was clearly enjoying herself.

'She wouldn't even *be* here,' snarled the realtor, 'if she didn't think your blood was flowing in her veins.'

'That's not true,' said Mrs Madrigal ineffectually. 'Anybody can tell you that's not true.'

Betty's eyes narrowed. 'Why don't we ask Mona? Hmmm?'

'What point is there in doing that? What would you gain, Betty?'

Betty's lip curled. 'Not as much as you'd lose, I suppose.'

'No. You're wrong. Mona would be the loser, Betty. She needs a family now. She needs to feel kinship. The *last* thing she needs is to hear about your long-dead little escapade with an oversexed plumber.'

'He was a *contractor*. And I find it *very* odd, Andy, that you don't think the identity of Mona's *real* father might be of some interest to her.'

'It was of no interest to *him*. Then or now. It was a one-night stand, for heaven's sake!'

'And *you* have more claim on her, I suppose? You who left her *completely* fatherless!'

Mrs Madrigal's eyes grew moist. 'I've tried to make good on that, Betty. Can't you *see*?' She gestured feebly around the room, as if 28

469

Barbary Lane might somehow testify to the purity of her intentions. 'Can't you see what I've tried to do for her?'

'It's too late for that, Andy. Thirty years is too late.'

'Do you want me to beg you, is that it?'

'I'm telling you, Andy. You're not going to stop me.'

'She won't come back to Minneapolis. I can promise you that.'

'I don't care.'

'Then what can you *gain*, other than hurting Mona? In the long run, it won't make any difference to her. She'll love you less, Betty, not more.'

The realtor's features were rigid. 'We'll see.'

'No,' said Mrs Madrigal firmly. 'No, we won't.'

'*What*?' The landlady's tone had jolted her.

'You will leave town, Betty. You will leave town tomorrow or I will tell all parties concerned about what you've been doing in that building at Leavenworth and Green.'

Betty sensed the shift in power. It hung in the air like ozone after a thunderstorm. 'What,' she said testily, 'are you talking about?'

'I mean,' said Mrs Madrigal, sipping her sherry, 'that you've been in town a lot longer than you told Mona.'

'And what if I have?'

'More like a month than a few days,' smiled the landlady.

'Look, Andy. I *knew* something was wrong. Norman Williams had disappeared, for God's sake!' She paced the room frantically, casting angry sideways glances at her ex-husband. 'I had to do *something*.'

'Mmm. So you thought you'd do a little poking around on your own.'

'What else could I do?'

'Indeed,' said Mrs Madrigal calmly. 'So how's the view from the eleventh floor?'

Silence.

'I did get the floor right, didn't I? I believe Mona said it was the eleventh.'

'Andy, I haven't the slightest idea what –'

'There must be a *lovely* view of this place from the eleventh floor.'

Mrs Madrigal's eyes locked on her prey. '*Particularly* at midnight.'

Betty stopped pacing. Her determinedly pursed mouth went slack. 'Did Mona tell you that?'

The landlady smiled. 'I have many more children than Mona.'

Betty stood there staring. Finally, she said, 'Jesus.' It came out like the hiss of a snake.

'So,' said Mrs Madrigal cheerily, 'I think you will agree with me that there are *lots* of things that Mona would be better off not knowing. Besides, Betty, she *needs* that boy, almost as much as he needs her.'

'She . . . doesn't know about . . . me?'

Mrs Madrigal shook her head. 'Nor does he. He thinks you're a veritable Salome, a siren on the rocks!' She winked at the realtor. 'I won't tell him, if you won't.'

Betty glared at her in silence.

'I won't tell *anyone*, Betty. Not if you leave. Tomorrow.'

'I can't trust you.'

'Yes, you can. I was a weasel of a man, but I'm one helluva nice woman.'

'You're a *bastard* is what you are!'

'Please,' smiled Mrs Madrigal. 'Call me a bitch.'

The Man Who Wasn't There

As Burke and Mary Ann entered the cathedral, their shoes clattered angrily on the floor, betraying their presence to the handful of worshipers scattered throughout the great room.

'I feel like such a tourist,' Mary Ann whispered.

Burke smiled, squeezing her hand. 'It's all right. No one would ever take you for a Presbyterian.'

'Shouldn't we sit down or something?'

He shrugged. 'If you want.'

They ducked into a pew next to an awesome stone pillar. Above them to the left, the Technicolor grandeur of a stained-glass window was fading into black. Mary Ann sat down and fumbled in her purse for a Dynamint.

'Want one?' she asked.

Burke shook his head. 'Let's just sit quiet for a while.'

Complying, Mary Ann scanned the room, wondering uneasily if

she and Burke were registering the same impressions. Two pews in front of them, an old woman was saying her prayers, a pink floral hanky pinned to the back of her gray bun. Across the aisle, a man wearing a T-shirt that said 'the pines 75' was crossing himself with great aplomb.

These people weren't Catholics, Mary Ann reminded herself. They were Episcopalians, High Church presumably, but ordinary Protestants who had come to this echoing chamber so that wine could turn to blood in their mouths.

She shuddered and popped another Dynamint. Then she caught Burke's eye.

'Anything?' she said.

He shook his head.

'Do you remember this space?'

'Not really. It's a lot like St John the Divine's in New York.'

'It's so huge,' Mary Ann observed vacantly.

Burke peered around the pillar. 'I guess the choir sits up by the altar. Maybe we should go up there.'

'Uh . . . why?'

He smiled at her. 'Are you scared, Mary Ann?'

'No. I just . . . Well, we'll be so . . . obtrusive, won't we?'

He took her hand. 'C'mon. Just for a minute. Maybe I'll recognize the choir loft or something.'

So they walked down the aisle together. Mary Ann forgot her anxiety for a moment, secretly amused at the symbolism of this action. Was this how a wedding rehearsal felt?

As they passed the communion rail, he slowed down to read the message inscribed in needlepoint on the kneeling pads: IF ANY MAN EAT OF THIS BREAD HE SHALL LIVE FOREVER. She tugged at Burke's elbow. 'Look,' she whispered. 'Transubstantiation.'

He couldn't hide his amusement. 'You act like you're visiting an Incan ruin or something.'

The organist was positioned just beyond the communion rail near the enclosure for the choir. He was the only person in that part of the cathedral. He adjusted his sheet music gravely, without looking up. Then he began to play.

Mary Ann flinched as the music rolled thunderously through the cathedral. 'Burke, maybe they're starting.'

'He's just practicing,' explained Burke. 'Let's go. I don't need to see the choir loft.'

'If you'd *really* like to –'

He shook his head. 'None of this is familiar. I'd know by now if it was.'

They turned in their tracks and made a dignified exit down the aisle. The old lady in the pink hanky looked up as they passed her pew. Mary Ann smiled at her apologetically, then gazed heavenward at the great rose window. Its brilliance was gone now; it was black as the night outside.

'Burke?'

'Mmm?'

'Let's do something mindless and cheerful tonight. Like a Burt Reynolds movie, or maybe that country-western sing-along place in the – Oh, God, stop! Don't look, Burke!' She grabbed his hand and jerked him unceremoniously into a pew, pulling him down to the prayer bench. 'Don't move,' she whispered. 'Don't turn around.'

'What in the hell are . . .'

She kept her head bowed in pseudo piety. 'Shhh! Mr Tyrone is here.'

'*Who?*'

'*The man with the transplant.*'

'Where?'

'By the door. *He was standing by the door, Burke.*'

Burke's tone accused her of overdramatizing. 'If he sings in the choir, Mary Ann, he has every reason in the world to –'

'Burke, he had something with him.'

Burke peered over his shoulder.

'*Don't*, he'll see you.'

'He's doing better than I am, then.'

'What?'

'There's no one there, Mary Ann.'

She turned slowly and looked toward the door again.

Burke was right. *There was no one there.*

Tears at the Tivoli

Mona was beginning her second half liter of red wine when Mrs Madrigal arrived at the Savoy-Tivoli.

Alone.

'Are you all right, Mrs Madrigal?'

The landlady nodded 'It could have been nastier, I suppose.' She slipped into a chair and grasped Mona's hand across the table. 'I did my best, dear.'

'Did she make a scene?'

'She tried to.'

Mona hesitated, then blurted out the question that had been plaguing her all evening. 'Did she talk to you about Mr Williams?'

'Yes.'

'Well?'

'I was flabbergasted. I had no idea he was a detective, much less *hers*. And of course, I can't imagine what happened to him.'

Mona was gazing down at her wineglass.

'Look at me, dear. That's the truth.'

'I believe you.'

'You must, Mona. You *must*.'

'I do,' smiled her daughter. 'Where is she, anyway? Was she bent out of shape?'

'Totally. May I have a sip of your wine, dear?'

Mona pushed her glass across the table. 'I'm sorry you had to go through all this.'

'She's leaving tomorrow. You should give her a call.'

'All right.'

'Don't forget, she loves you, Mona. She made a lot of sacrifices for you in her time.'

'I know.' Mona retrieved the wineglass and took a sip. 'Do you mind if I ask you about one more thing?'

'Go ahead.'

'Betty said that Mr Williams told her your name was an anagram.'

'How interesting.'

'Well?'

'Well what?'

'Is it true?'

Mrs Madrigal smiled enigmatically. 'Haven't you tried to work it out yet?'

'Then it is?'

The landlady picked up a bread stick and nibbled on it. 'I'll make a very shady deal with you, young lady. I'll tell you the anagram if you'll invite a friend of mine to dinner.'

'Who?'

'Brian Hawkins.'

'Forget it.'

Mrs Madrigal set the bread stick down demurely. 'Very well.'

'I'm your daughter,' countered Mona. 'I have a right to know that anagram.'

'Indeed. And as your parent, I have a right to discuss grand-children.'

'Bullshit.'

Mrs Madrigal wagged her finger. 'Mother Mucca will wash your mouth out with soap.'

'Brian Hawkins is not even *vaguely* interested in me.'

'I think he *will* be.'

'Huh?'

'Trust me, Mona.'

Mona looked away. 'He made me feel like such a damned fool.'

'Oh, Mona, we're all damned fools! Some of us just have more fun with it than others. Loosen up, dear! Don't be so afraid to cry . . . or laugh, for that matter. Laugh all you want and cry all you want and whistle at pretty men in the street, and to *hell* with anybody who thinks you're a damned fool!' She lifted the wineglass in a toast to the younger woman. 'I love you, dear. And that makes you free to do anything.'

Mona didn't answer. There were tears streaming down her face. Mrs Madrigal reached across the table and dabbed her eyes with a napkin.

'Wet enough for you?' asked Mona.

Suddenly, the waiter loomed over them.

'Oh, Luciano,' exclaimed Mrs Madrigal. 'Have you met my daughter?'

The waiter made a courtly bow. Mona flushed and extended her hand. The waiter kissed it, saying, '*Bella.*'

475

Mrs Madrigal smiled proudly. 'Of course she's *bella*! She takes after her . . . whatever.'

Mona smiled at her through bleary eyes. 'You're so weird.'

'*Grazie*,' said her landlady.

Descent into Nowhere

Mary Ann's eyes grew as big as communion wafers as she stared at the spot where the man with the transplant had been. 'I swear, Burke. He was right there next to the door.'

'Maybe,' shrugged Burke. 'But he ain't there now.'

'I guess he went back outside.'

'Do you want to look?'

She hesitated. 'I think we should. But we can't look like we are.'

'Right. And what did you mean, he had something with him?'

She shifted from a kneeling position to a sitting position, following Burke's cue. 'I'm not sure,' she said uneasily. 'It looked like a Styrofoam cooler.'

He blinked at her. 'Am I supposed to know what that means?'

She shook her head. 'I never mentioned it. Jon saw him leaving the hospital with a Styrofoam cooler last week.'

'So?'

'So nothing. That's just what he saw. Out in the parking lot.'

Burke raised his eyebrows. 'Do you think,' he asked dramatically, 'that he prefers beer to wine at communion?'

'I'm not making a big deal out of it, Burke.' She knew his flippancy was a defense, but it still irritated her.

He stood up and led her out of the pew. As they headed toward the doorway, three or four more worshipers entered the building. 'How much time have we got?' asked Burke.

'Fifteen minutes,' came the reply.

They reached the doorway. 'I'll go first,' said Mary Ann. 'We'll just stroll out naturally, like we're getting some fresh air or something.'

Burke winked and gave her a thumbs-up sign.

Mary Ann tugged at the heavy door and led the way into the dark. As casually as possible, she checked out the people chatting in the courtyard in front of the cathedral. The man with the transplant was not there.

She took Burke's arm and reentered the cathedral. 'It doesn't make sense,' she whispered. 'There's nowhere else he could've gone.'

'Unless . . .' Burke turned and pointed to the elevator just to the right of the entrance. Set back in the shadows, it had totally escaped their notice. 'It must go up to the bell tower or something.'

'To *what*?'

'Beats me. Quasimodo, maybe?' He reached out and pushed the button.

'Burke! *What are you doing*?'

'We can't stop now, can we?'

The elevator door slid open suddenly, spilling profane fluorescent light into that inky corner of the cathedral. Burke gripped Mary Ann's arm and pulled her into the elevator. The door closed immediately.

'Burke, we could get in trouble.'

He didn't answer. He was examining the control buttons. 'There's 2 and 3 and LL.' he said. 'LL must be Lower Level. Let's try 2 for starters. It's more celestial to go up, don't you think?' He pushed the 2 button. Nothing happened.

'C'mon, Burke. Open the door.'

'Wait a minute.' He tried the 3 button. The elevator didn't budge.

'Burke!'

'One more.' This time the LL button got them moving. Down. The ride took less than ten seconds. The door opened onto a lighted hallway. Burke stepped out, taking Mary Ann with him. The elevator abandoned them.

'It's just the gift shop,' whispered Mary Ann. A series of windows along the hallway offered a glimpse of the religious emporium. Mostly St Francis statuary and felt wall hangings with hippie peace-and-love mottoes.

The shop was in semi-darkness, but Burke tried the door. It was locked. So were the other two doors in the hallway. The elevator was the only way out. Burke grinned sheepishly at Mary Ann, then pushed the Up button. Nothing happened.

'Aha!' said Burke. 'Mr Tyrone Transplant must be on the way down.'

Mary Ann's blood froze. 'Down *here*?'

477

Burke smiled. 'Down from 2 or 3. Obviously, he went up instead of down. He's probably getting off on the ground floor right now. That is, unless someone else is using it.'

'But how could he have gone up, when we could only go down?'

The answer came to her in a single dizzying flash, just as the door of the elevator opened.

They boarded the elevator in silence and rode to the main floor. When the door opened, Mary Ann moved to the control panel and pushed the Close Door button. Burke stared at her in bewilderment.

'Push the 2 button again,' she said.

He did. Nothing happened.

Her hands moved to the nape of her neck and unfastened the latch on the gold chain he had given her in Mexico. She handed him the key, then pointed to a slot on the control panel.

'See if it fits,' she said.

The Way Out

'Edgar and Anna, huh?'

D'orothea's smile seemed almost maternal as she sat by DeDe's bed and held the new mother's hand.

DeDe beamed. 'You saw them, huh?'

'You betcha. They're magnificent, hon. And one of each. How perfect can you get?'

'Would you tell my mother that?'

D'orothea frowned. 'She couldn't handle it, huh?'

'You might say that. She told me I should have had an abortion.'

'I thought she was Catholic.'

'She is,' muttered DeDe. 'She's also from Hillsborough and a member of the Francesca Club. Those things have a dogma all their own. One of their most well-known tenets is that you don't have a baby with slant eyes.'

D'orothea squeezed her hand. 'Don't even think about it, hon.'

'I have to. I have to live with it.'

'Do you?' D'orothea's eyes challenged her.

'I can't run away, D'or.'

'Maybe not. But you could run *toward* something.'

'Like what?'

D'orothea shrugged. 'A new life. A life where you don't have to deal with the kind of people you're dealing with.'

'I think it's a little late for me.'

D'orothea shook her head. 'Wrong, hon. It wasn't too late for me.'

'I don't get it.'

D'orothea smiled understandingly. 'We're not that far apart, you know. I may be from the wrong part of Oakland, but I got very grand *very* early. I was worshiping false idols before I was out of a training bra. Hell, I was *worse* than you, hon. With me, it was a conscious choice. With you, it's just a question of family tradition.'

'Never underestimate the power of family tradition,' said DeDe ruefully.

'*Or* the power of the Almighty Dollar. Listen, I wanted money so bad I dyed my skin black to get it.'

'*What?*'

'It's a long and sordid story. I'll tell it to you someday when you . . . DeDe, look: do you remember that night we went to the fashion show at the Legion of Honor, when you said it was tough living at the end of the rainbow?'

'Sure.'

'Well, maybe your premise was wrong.'

'How's that?'

'Maybe this isn't it, hon. Maybe San Francisco isn't the end of the rainbow.'

DeDe absorbed this radical suggestion slowly. 'D'or, do you mean *leave?*'

'Why not?'

'I *can't*, D'or. My family is here. My mother, at least. And all my friends are here.'

'What good have they done you so far?'

DeDe studied her friend's face for a moment. 'Why do I get the feeling you're trying to convert a sinner?'

D'orothea laughed. 'I *have* been going to church a lot lately. And that's part of it, I guess. We don't get that much time on this planet, DeDe, and unless a few of us make an effort to change ourselves and the corruption around us . . . well, it just won't happen, that's all.'

'I see that, D'or. I *agree* with it, but I don't see how running away can –'

'Not *away*, hon. To. *To* something.'

'What are you driving at?'

D'orothea smiled. 'I guess I should come right out and say it, huh?'

It took her fifteen minutes to outline her proposal. When she had finished, DeDe stared at her with a mixture of doubt and fascination.

'You mean I could take the babies?' she asked.

'Of course! That's the really wonderful part of it. A brand-new life for them, free from the bigotry and small-mindedness of your mother's friends! A brand-new life for all of us, DeDe!'

DeDe flushed excitedly. 'In a crazy way, it makes a lot of sense.'

'Damn straight!'

'Mother will have a fit.'

'No she won't. Well, maybe at first. But in the long run, this saves her from all that embarrassment. You can get the hell out of town before the Hillsborough crowd has a chance to prey on your children. Your mother will be *grateful* for that, DeDe.'

'I have to think about it,' said DeDe.

'I know. Of course. There's time.'

'It *is* exciting!'

'You betcha!' said D'orothea.

The Cooler

Burke's hands were trembling when he slipped the key into the slot on the control panel of the elevator. Mary Ann hovered over him. 'Burke, jiggle it or something.'

'I did. That's it.' The key was only halfway in.

'Try it the other way, then.'

Burke removed the key and inserted it again. This time, it slid in effortlessly. Mary Ann let out a little yelp. Burke turned and beamed at her admiringly. 'We can turn it to 2 or 3 now. What'll it be?'

Without knowing why, Mary Ann chose 3.

Burke pushed the 3 button and the elevator began its slow ascent.

Mary Ann's exhilaration gave way to gnawing fear again. 'What if he's up here, Burke? The transplant man.'

'We'll play dumb,' shrugged Burke.

'Yeah. And we don't know for sure that he even *took* the elevator.'

'He took it.' His grim certainty terrified Mary Ann.

'But why would someone who just sings in the choir have a key to this elevator?'

'Obviously,' said Burke flatly, 'the same reason I had one.'

The elevator shook them when it stopped. The door opened. They stepped out into a space about the size of Mary Ann's living room. There were no windows. A flickering fluorescent tube mounted on the wall next to the elevator cast a greenish light on the stacks of hymnals and the prayerbooks lining the room.

The only way out was a cast-iron spiral staircase.

Going up.

Mary Ann shuddered and stepped back into the elevator. 'Burke . . . let's try 2.'

Burke shook his head. 'This is it.'

'This is *what*?'

'I don't know. It just feels right somehow.'

'This room?'

'No.' He nodded toward the spiral staircase. 'Up there.'

'Oh, God, Burke! Are you sure we ought to?'

His jaw was set, but his voice sounded thin and unsure. 'I have to.'

'Maybe we could come back later or something.'

'No. I might lose my nerve.'

'But what if the transplant man is up there?'

Burke looked away from her. 'He had time to come back down.'

'But what if . . . ?'

'I'm going up, Mary Ann. You can do what you want. You've helped me enough already.'

She took his hand, silencing him. 'I'll come,' she said softly.

Burke went first. Mary Ann followed so closely that the back of his corduroy jacket kept grazing her face. They passed through the ceiling into a darker place. A much darker place. Mary Ann tugged on Burke's coattail.

'We can't even *see*, Burke.'

481

'It's OK,' he whispered. 'Our eyes'll get used to it.'

The staircase continued to wind upwards. Some fifteen feet above the room with the prayerbooks they arrived at a kind of landing.

'We can't go any higher,' said Burke.

'Burke, for God's sake, let's –'

'Wait.' She heard him fumbling with something. 'I think there's a door somewhere.'

Suddenly, there *was* a door. It swung outward, blinding them momentarily with light. Both of them shrank from the sight that confronted them: a metal catwalk, stretching towards the altar. *At least a hundred feet above the floor of the cathedral.*

'I *can't*,' said Mary Ann, without being asked.

'If I can, you can. Look, there's a railing. There's no way you can fall.'

'It isn't a matter of –' The word 'railing' was what silenced her. 'Burke! "*A walkway with a railing!*" This is the place in your dream!'

'I repeat,' he said somberly. 'If I can, you can.'

He took her hand and led her onto the catwalk. Mary Ann checked her watch. The mass would begin in twelve minutes. Eight stories beneath them, the congregation materialized in splotches of red and blue and yellow, reduced at this height to their primary colors. A human rose window.

They walked at least fifty yards, until they were directly above the transept of the cathedral. There, conforming to the cross-shaped structure of the building itself, another catwalk intersected the one they were on.

And there sat a Styrofoam cooler.

Mary Ann looked behind her, then left and right on the other catwalk. The man with the transplant was nowhere in sight. Burke stood stone still, eyes locked on the cooler. The sickly, grayish cast to his face compelled Mary Ann to be strong.

'Burke, is this the Meeting of the Lines?'

He nodded.

She reached for the cooler. 'Do you want me to open it?'

'Please,' he said feebly.

She lifted the lid. A thick cloud of white smoke billowed over the edges of the cooler. No. Not smoke; dry ice. She knelt by the cooler and blew on the surface of the cloud. It parted.

482

What she saw was pale purple, mauve, almost. A thin ridge of hair ran along the top of it. It was black on one end, where it had been severed, and the toenails were a horrid shade of yellow.

But it was undeniably a human foot.

Dropping the lid, Mary Ann lurched to her feet and fell into Burke's arms. She tried to scream, but gagged instead, pulling away from him just in time to lean over the railing.

The people below hardly knew what hit them.

The Cult

When Mary Ann straightened up again, Burke's distorted features filled her with fresh terror.

'Burke . . . God, did you see it?'

He nodded mechanically, his eyes fixed on the lid of the cooler.

'It was a foot, Burke. *It was somebody's foot.*'

He blinked dumbly, never shifting his gaze.

'We have to get out of here, Burke!'

He gripped her wrist. 'No . . . wait . . .'

'Burke, for God's sake! We have to tell someone. We can't just –'

'It wasn't a foot.'

'What?'

'It wasn't a foot.' His eyes widened as he spoke the words, as if some rare spiritual revelation were sweeping over him. 'It was . . . something else.'

Mary Ann's voice grew shrill. 'I *saw* it, Burke. There's nothing else it *could* be.' She tried to break free from his hold, but his hand was like a vise. 'Burke, what are you doing? *Let go of me, Burke!*'

His hand went slack. Huge beads of sweat erupted like blisters along his hairline. He turned and looked at her. 'It wasn't a foot,' he said pathetically. 'It was an arm.'

'Burke, for God's . . . !'

'It *was*, Mary Ann. When I was here before . . . it was an arm.'

'You were . . . ? Burke, you *remember*?'

'They wanted me to . . . They told me I had to . . .'

'*Who*, Burke?'

'Them. *Him.*'

'The man with the transplant?'

Burke nodded.

'What did he want you to do?'

Silence.

'Burke?'

'We have to get out of here.'

'Wait, Burke. *What did they want you to do?*'

Now Burke was moving down the catwalk, away from the cooler, back to the spiral staircase. Reaching out to take Mary Ann's hand, he quickened his pace until they were almost running.

'Burke, what if the man with the transplant . . . ?'

'What time is it?' He pulled her wrist into view and looked at her watch. 'Christ! We have three minutes!'

'*For what?*'

'They'll be here in three minutes! The mass starts in three minutes!'

They were back at the door now, plunging once more into darkness. Burke led the way down the staircase, holding tight to Mary Ann's hand. When they reached the room with the prayerbooks, he lunged at the button by the elevator, then leaped back as if it had shocked him.

'Shit!'

'What's the matter?' whispered Mary Ann.

'Listen . . . the elevator! They're coming!'

'Dear God.'

Burke looked about him frantically, pulled Mary Ann into the darkest corner of the room, behind the towering pillar of prayerbooks. They were crouching in the shadows when the elevator door clattered open.

There seemed to be five or six of them, at least two of whom were women. Their voices were jovial and matter-of-fact until the man with the transplant began the incantation that Mary Ann now knew by heart.

High upon the Sacred Rock
The Rose Incarnate shines,
Upon the Mountain of the Flood
At the Meeting of the Lines.

484

The coppery taste of her own vomit made Mary Ann nauseous again. She tried to think of daisy-strewn fields, of raindrops on roses and whiskers on kittens, but the image of that grisly purple foot flashed in her brain like a strobe light.

Instinctively, Burke reached for her hand and gave it a reassuring squeeze. In doing so, he grazed the pillar of prayerbooks, causing it to wobble menacingly. Mary Ann sucked in her breath and did her best to steady the trembling monolith.

They waited for an eternity.

Finally, the faceless celebrants began to ascend the staircase to the catwalk. When their footsteps had died out, Burke dashed to the elevator and leaned on the button.

The door opened immediately.

'Where's the key?' asked Burke.

Mary Ann clutched at her neck. 'I must've left it –'

'Christ!'

'Check the floor, Burke! Maybe it –'

'Hold it! We might not need it!' He pushed the button for the first floor. The elevator made an eerie sighing noise and the door rumbled shut again. They began their descent.

When they were back on the main floor of the cathedral, a growl from the great organ signaled the start of the mass. Never stopping to look back, they fled through the mammoth doors and ran all the way to Huntington Park.

Now they were huddled together on a bench, catching their breath.

'It's come back, hasn't it?'

'Yeah.'

'All of it?'

'Most of it.'

'Why are you crying?'

'I'm . . . relieved, that's all.'

'Did you know those people?'

'Yeah.'

'Should we talk about it now?'

'I guess. That is, if you don't mind.'

'I don't mind.'

'That foot, Mary Ann . . . Those people.'

'Uh huh?'

'They're eating it. They're up there now eating it.'

Walking Alone

One week later.

Leaning on Jon, Michael took faltering steps to the bathroom.

'Look at you!' Jon beamed. 'You're fabulous!'

'I am, aren't I?'

'I think you can do it on your own.'

'Oh, no.'

'C'mon, turkey. Try.'

'Don't be so goddamn B-movie! I'm not ready yet!'

'I'm gonna let go.'

'You do and I'll tell your father you sleep with boys!'

'Get ready!'

'Jon!'

'You've been copping feels long enough. You're on your own now.'

The doctor slipped out from under Michael's arm and withdrew several feet. Michael's arm flailed as he fought to maintain his balance. His knees were jelly, but he managed to remain in a static, upright position.

'Now, walk,' said Jon calmly.

'This is really corny. I hope you know that.'

'Go ahead.'

'You could have picked a better room for this touching human drama. I'll fall and hit the toilet. I'll die with a Johnny Mop in my hand.'

'Shut up and walk.'

Michael sighed and lifted his left foot, placing it about six inches in front of him. Then he dragged his right foot forward. 'Godzilla approaching Tokyo,' he groaned.

He repeated the process until he was in front of the toilet. Using a towel rack for support, he turned himself around. He made a face and let go.

He landed on target.

Jon was leaning cavalierly against the doorway, smiling at him. 'You see?'

'Can't a lady have a little privacy?' said Michael.

486

'Just a sec.' Jon dashed into the living room and came back with the *Chronicle*. He dropped it in Michael's lap. 'A little light reading for you.'

The front page was dominated by a picture of Burke and Mary Ann, looking flustered at a press conference.

The banner headline read:

EPISCOPAL CANNIBAL CULT EXPOSED

Later, Jon and Michael discussed the week's events over coffee and raisin toast in the kitchen. Michael held up the newspaper.

'What's with this, anyway? I thought Burke was gonna break the story in *New West*.'

'He was, but the police jumped the gun on him. The chief apparently called a press conference yesterday and scarfed up on a little publicity of his own. Burke was livid, because the chief had promised to keep quiet about it until the *New West* piece broke. Anyway, the end result was roughly the same. Pandemonium. Burke called his own press conference at *New West* late yesterday afternoon.'

Michael smiled. 'Mary Ann must be wrecked.'

'She's holding up OK, actually. She says she's coming by to see you this afternoon.'

'Good.'

'But *no* wisecracks, Michael. She's still a little shaken over the whole thing.'

'OK. I promise not to put my foot in my mouth.' Michael grinned. 'So to speak.'

'That's *exactly* the sort of thing I'm talking about.'

'OK. OK. Look, in one way, I'm just as involved as Mary Ann was.'

'How's that?'

'Well, what if I had died at St Sebastian's? Those cultists would have been munching on *me* up there on the catwalk.'

Jon shook his head and smiled. 'They didn't eat whole people, my love. Just parts. Amputated parts.'

'Well, they *could* have.'

'Nope. The parts were easier to hide. And to transport. They had no problem at all moving them from surgery to the refrigerated room in Tyrone's flower shop. And they could also fit nicely into the cooler for the trip to the cathedral.'

Michael made a face. 'How many times did they *do* that, anyway?'

'Who knows?' shrugged the doctor. 'Maybe as often as twice a week for four or five months. Burke apparently stumbled onto the cult in its early stages, when he was still singing in the choir.'

Michael rolled his eyes. 'That's when I would have moved back to Nantucket.'

'No way. Burke's a journalist, remember? He wanted the story badly. Bad enough to sweet-talk his way into the cult and sneak a peek at the goings-on up on the catwalk at Grace. He expected something freaky, of course, but not *that* freaky. He couldn't handle it.'

'Then he never went to the flower shop at St Sebastian's?'

'Apparently not. He says he knew nothing at all about the contacts at the hospital until Mary Ann pointed it out to him.'

Michael frowned. 'That doesn't make any sense.'

'Why?'

'Because of the rose phobia. What about the goddamn red rose?'

'Good question,' said the doctor.

A Rose is a Rose

Michael was using his walker when he greeted Mary Ann at the door. 'Hi,' he said breezily. 'Welcome to the Barbary Lane Home for the Disabled.'

She kissed him on the cheek. 'You look pretty fabulous to me.'

'Guess what I did this morning?'

'What?'

'I *walked*, Babycakes. Without *this* damn thing.'

'Mouse!'

'Ain't that the cat's ass?'

'Do it now, Mouse. Do it for me.'

He grinned at her. 'Sorry, I never perform without my organ grinder. What about *you*, anyway? How does it feel to be a Media Star?'

She moaned and sat down on the sofa. 'I'm exhausted. I've talked to all three networks, *People* magazine, *Time*, *Newsweek*, the *New York Times*, the *National Enquirer* and my parents. My parents were the toughest of all.'

'Of course.'

'They are totally *hysterical*, Mouse. You'd think the town was *teeming* with Episcopal cannibals. I tried to explain that the press was blowing it all out of proportion, but they won't even listen to me. They want me on the next flight back to Cleveland.'

'Are you going?'

She shook her head, smiling. 'Sit down, Mouse. I need a hug.'

He abandoned the walker and dropped to the sofa. They held on to each other for a long time.

'How's my girl?' asked Michael.

'All right.'

'It'll get better. I promise.'

'I shouldn't gripe, I guess. I've got it easy compared to Burke. He's been with the police all morning, trying to remember stuff.'

'Naming names?'

Mary Ann nodded. 'He's come up with fourteen so far, including three members of the cathedral choir, two surgeons at St Sebastian's, and even a couple of businessmen.'

'His memory must be completely back, then?'

'Just about. He regained most of it the night we found the . . . that night. Though he still can't remember how he ended up in Golden Gate Park. My guess is they drugged him after they realized he had amnesia.'

'It seems funny that they wouldn't have been a little more thorough about getting rid of him.'

'Not really. For one thing, they weren't really committing a crime. That part's driving the police crazy right now. The doctors can be nailed on some sort of ethical-practices violation, of course, but the law isn't very clear about the rest of it. Those body parts were just medical garbage, really. There's no law against eating garbage.'

Michael frowned. 'Is that *actually* what they were doing?'

She nodded. 'Apparently, they sort of . . . tasted it. It was supposed to be symbolic or something. One step beyond transubstantiation. Burke says they did it at the very moment the people below were eating the bread and the wine. The transplant man's job was to see that the stuff was delivered to the catwalk at each of the designated masses.'

'What's gonna happen to that guy, anyway?'

'Who knows? Burke says he'll probably make a fortune. He's already hired a literary agent.'

'You're kidding!'

'Nope. It's disgusting, isn't it?' She shivered a little, turning away. 'I just want it to be over with as soon as possible.'

Michael looked at her a moment, hesitating. 'Do you mind if I ask you one more thing?'

'Sure. Go ahead.'

'What was all this red rose business? Was that just the rose window – the Rose Incarnate they chanted about?'

Mary Ann smiled faintly. 'That's what I thought at first. Or that it had something to do with the flower shop at St Sebastian's. It turned out to be neither. It was a tattoo.'

'A *tattoo?*'

She nodded. 'The night Burke lost his memory was the first night the cult trusted him enough to let him join them on the catwalk. The thing he hadn't counted on was that they expected him to participate in the ceremony. He knew they were High Church, of course –'

Michael chuckled, interrupting her. 'You can't get much higher than that,' he said.

She managed a laugh. 'Anyway, he didn't *really* know what was going to happen until they started chanting and Tyrone opened the Styrofoam cooler and pulled out an arm.'

'Arrggh!'

'I know,' winced Mary Ann. 'Who *wouldn't* try to block that one out?'

'My God! Then the red rose was . . .'

Mary Ann nodded. 'Tattooed on the arm.'

'Did Burke . . . I mean, did he . . .'

Mary Ann shrugged. 'I guess he must've *tried*, poor baby.'

The Anagram

'Well,' said Mrs Madrigal, smiling.

'Well, what?' asked Mona.

'How did your date go?'

'None of your business. That wasn't part of the deal.'

The landlady arched an eyebrow mischievously and looked down at the tray of dope she was cleaning. 'It was that good, was it?'

Mona flushed. 'You're avoiding the subject.'

'Which is?'

'The anagram. *The anagram.*'

'Ah.'

Mrs Madrigal looked up. 'Goodness gracious! Does love make you testy?'

'You're not gonna tell me, are you?'

'I didn't say that.'

'Do I have to *guess*, then?'

Mrs Madrigal craned her neck to examine the piece of paper in her daughter's hands. 'We have a list, do we? What fun! I feel like Rumpelstiltskin.'

Mona groaned and slumped down onto the sofa next to her. 'You are *truly* perverse!'

Mrs Madrigal directed her attention to the dope tray again. 'What's your first guess?'

Sighing noisily, Mona read from the paper: DARLING AMANA.'

'DARLING AMANA? What does *that* mean?'

Mona frowned peevishly. 'It means you're a cute refrigerator.'

'Indeed. Next?'

'A GRANDMA IN LA.'

'A GRANDMA IN LA,' repeated the landlady. 'My, my. Now *that's* a dark secret!' She looked up briefly at Mona, who was scowling exactly like a certain madam from Winnemucca. 'Go on, dear. This is wonderful!'

'A GRAND ANIMAL.'

Mrs Madrigal roared, nearly spilling the dope. 'I *adore* that one! A GRAND ANIMAL! I am indeed!'

'*That's it?*'

'Nope.'

Mona rolled her eyes. 'I hate this game.'

'Go on. What's next?'

'That's it, goddammit.'

'What about LAD IN ANAGRAM?'

Mona dropped the paper and stared at her father. 'LAD IN ANAGRAM? You're kidding!'

Mrs Madrigal smiled faintly. 'Yes. But I rather like it just the same.'

'You're sick,' said Mona.

'Give me that pencil,' said the landlady.

Mona obeyed her. The landlady scrawled five words at the bottom of her daughter's list: A MAN AND A GIRL.

Mona blinked at it in disbelief. 'This . . . this is it?'

Mrs Madrigal nodded.

'God . . . it's so . . . sexist.'

'I beg your pardon, young lady.'

'Girl?' gasped Mona. 'You're a woman!'

Mrs Madrigal shook her head. '*You're* a woman, dear. I'm a *girl*. And proud of it.'

Mona smiled. 'My own goddamn father . . . a sexist!'

'My darling daughter,' said Mrs Madrigal, 'transsexuals can *never* be sexists!'

'Then . . . you're a transsexist!'

The landlady leaned over and kissed Mona on the cheek. 'Forgive me, won't you? I'm terribly old-fashioned.'

Happy Ending

Mother's Day, 1977.

The mistress of Halcyon Hill sat in her late husband's study, listening to a Bobby Short album and sipping a Mai Tai. Her maid, Emma, entered the room, carrying a stack of mail.

'There's a card from Miss DeDe, Miss Frances.'

The matriarch set down her drink. 'Thank heavens!'

'I knew she'd write her mama,' said Emma. 'She's a good child.' She handed the mail to Frannie and remained standing by the side of the wingback chair. Emma's lonely too, thought Frannie. She wants to talk about DeDe.

Making a face, Frannie set aside the latest issue of *New West*. The cover story was 'Inside the Cannibal Cult' by Burke Andrew. 'I won't even *look* at that,' said the matriarch. 'I simply can't believe what's happening to this city.'

Emma grunted her agreement. 'Some folks get mighty serious about religion.' The remark, Frannie knew, was more an indictment of Episcopalians than anything else. She declined to defend the church, however. She had too many crosses to bear already.

'Where's the card, Emma?'

'There, next to the phone bill, Miss Frances.'

To Frannie's disappointment, it wasn't a picture postcard; it was one of DeDe's own Florentine gilt-and-green things, and the message was thoughtlessly terse:

Mother,
     Happily settled in now. Babies are
just fine, and I feel all tan and
healthy. I've met *so* many nice
people here. This is my first
job ever, and I love it.
Miss you much, but think this is
for the best. D'or sends hugs.

All my love,
DeDe

Frannie sighed noisily and laid the card down. Emma reached out and touched her shoulder consolingly. 'Don't you fret, Miss Frances. She'll grow out o' that. She's a smart child. She'll come to her senses.'

The matriarch shook her head, then dabbed her eyes with a cocktail napkin. 'It's too much, Emma.'

'What do you mean?'

'It's *Mother's Day*, Emma. Edgar usually brought me some Godiva chocolates or something. Sometimes I just forget that he's gone and it's like losing him all over again. And now Beauchamp's gone . . . and DeDe . . . and my only grandchildren.'

Emma squeezed her mistress' shoulder. 'You gotta be strong, Miss Frances.'

Frannie was silent for a moment, then smiled wanly at her maid.

'You're so *wise*, Emma.'

'Just don't you fret.'

Frannie nodded decisively and picked up the postcard again. Squinting slightly, she examined the stamp and postmark. 'I don't even know where Guyana *is*,' she said.

Back in the courtyard of 28 Barbary Lane, Michael Tolliver was testing his legs like a newborn colt. Mary Ann emerged from the house. 'I just talked to Mildred,' she yelled.

'Yeah?'

'It's OK, Mouse. They can start you as mailboy in two weeks, if you're up to it.'

He let out a cheer. 'A working girl at last!'

'You'll like the new boss, I think. He used to be the creative director.'

'Uh oh,' mugged Michael.

Mary Ann nodded. 'Gay as a goose.'

'Oh, happy ending! Happy ending!'

'In part, at least.'

'*In part*? The world has never been so good! Mona and Brian have been shacked up for almost a week. Mrs Madrigal is grinning like the Cheshire Cat. You may get rich selling your confessions . . . and Burke even *richer*. I'm a healthy, strapping boy again, and Jon and I can . . . well, never mind that part. *Plus* – oh, miracle of miracles! – my mother sent me a pound cake yesterday.'

Mary Ann smiled. 'I know. Jon gave me some. I'm glad she's coming round, Mouse.'

'We don't know that yet. There wasn't a message. Just the pound cake.'

'She's *trying*, Mouse.'

He smiled. 'A fruit cake would've made me a little nervous.'

Mary laughed half-heartedly.

'What is it?' asked Michael. 'Something's the matter.'

Silence.

'Oh, God! Not Mr Williams? His body hasn't shown up, has it?'

'No! For God's sake, Mouse, don't bring that up again! It's Burke, Mouse. He's moving to New York. He's been offered a job with *New York* magazine.'

'Oh, no!'

'I *should* be happy for him, Mouse. It's a fabulous opportunity. Most journalists would kill to have a chance to work there.'

'Has he asked you to go with him?'

She nodded. 'It was the *first* thing he asked.'

'And . . . ?'

'I *can't*, Mouse.' She looked despairingly around the courtyard. 'It's too pretty here.'

'Good girl.'

'No. Dumb girl. *Dumb* girl.'

He shook his head.

'What's the matter with me, Mouse?'

'*Nothing*, Babycakes. You're just tired of running away from home.'
He took her arm and steered her slowly toward the house.

'Where are we going?' asked Mary Ann.

'Back to Tara,' he grinned. 'We'll figure out a way to get him back.
After all, my dear, tomorrow *is* another day!'

THE END

Further Tales of the City

For Steve Beery

Surely there are in everyone's life certain connections, twists and turns which pass awhile under the category of Chance, but at the last, well examined, prove to be the very Hand of God.

Sir Thomas Browne
RELIGIO MEDICI

Home and Hearth

There were outlanders, of course, who continued to insist that San Francisco was a city without seasons, but Mrs Madrigal paid no heed to them.

Why, the signs of spring were everywhere!

Those Chinese schoolboys, for instance, sporting brand new green-and-yellow baseball caps as they careened down Russian Hill on their skateboards.

And what about old Mr Citarelli? Only a seasoned San Franciscan could know that this was *exactly* the time of year he dragged his armchair into his garage and opened the doors to the sunshine. Mr Citarelli was infinitely more reliable than any groundhog.

Here on Barbary Lane, the vernal equinox was heralded by an ancient scarlet azalea that blazed like a bonfire next to the garbage cans. 'My goodness,' said Mrs Madrigal, stopping to adjust her grocery bag. 'It's you again, is it?' It had also bloomed in August and December, but nature was always forgiven for offering too much of a good thing.

When Mrs Madrigal reached the lych gate at Number 28, she paused under its peaked roof to survey her domain – the mossy brick plain of the courtyard, the illegal lushness of her 'herb garden,' the ivy-and-brown-shingle face of her beloved old house. It was a sight that never failed to thrill her.

Dropping the groceries in the kitchen – three new cheeses from Molinari's, light bulbs, focaccia bread, Tender Vittles for Boris – she hurried into the parlor to build a fire. And why not? In San Francisco, a fire felt good at any time of year.

The firewood had been a Christmas gift from her tenants – a whole cord of it – and Mrs Madrigal handled it as if she were arranging ingots at Fort Knox. She had suffered too long under the indignity of those dreadful pressed sawdust things they sold at the Searchlight Market. Now, thanks, to her children, she had a fire that would *crackle*.

They weren't really her children, of course, but she treated them as such. And they appeared to accept her as a parent of sorts. Her own daughter, Mona, had lived with her for a while in the late seventies, but had moved to Seattle the previous year. Her reason had been characteristically cryptic: 'Because . . . well, because it's The Eighties, that's why.'

Poor Mona. Like a lot of her contemporaries, she had capitalized The Eighties, deified the new decade in the hope that it would somehow bring her salvation, deliver her from her own bleak vision of existence. The Eighties, for Mona, would be the same in Seattle as in San Francisco . . . or Sheboygan, for that matter. But no one could tell her that. Mona had never recovered from The Sixties.

The landlady's ersatz children – Mary Ann, Michael and Brian – had somehow kept their innocence, she realized.

And she loved them dearly for that.

Minutes later, Michael showed up at her door with his rent check in one hand and Boris in the other.

'I found him on the ledge,' he said, 'looking faintly suicidal.'

The landlady scowled at the tabby. 'More like homicidal. He's been after the birds again. Set him down, will you, dear? I can't bear it if he has bluejay on his breath.'

Michael relinquished the cat and presented the check to Mrs Madrigal. 'I'm sorry it's so late. Again.'

She waved it away with her hand, hastily tucking the check into a half-read volume of Eudora Welty stories. She found it excruciating to discuss money with her children. 'Well,' she said, 'what shall we do about Mary Ann's birthday?'

'God,' winced Michael. 'Is it that time already?'

Mrs Madrigal smiled. 'Next Tuesday, by my calculations.'

'She'll be thirty, won't she?' Michael's eyes danced diabolically.

'I don't think that should be our emphasis, dear.'

'Well, don't expect any mercy from me,' said Michael. 'She put me through hell last year on *my* thirtieth. Besides, she's the last one in the house to cross The Great Divide. It's only proper that we mark the event.'

Mrs Madrigal shot him her Naughty Boy look and sank into the armchair by the hearth. Sensing another chance to be picturesque, Boris dove into her lap and blinked languidly at the fire. 'Can I interest you in a joint?' asked the landlady.

Michael shook his head, smiling. 'Thanks. I'm late for work as it is.'

She returned his smile. 'Give my love to Ned, then. Your new haircut looks stunning, by the way.'

'Thanks,' beamed Michael, reddening slightly.

'I like seeing your ears, actually. It makes you look quite boyish. Not at all like you've crossed The Great Divide.'

Michael showed his appreciation with a courtly little bow.

'Run along now,' said the landlady. 'Make little things grow.'

After he had left, she permitted herself a private grin over this Great Divide business. She was sixty now, for heaven's sake. Did that mean she had crossed it twice?

Sixty. Up close, the number was not nearly so foreboding as it had once been from afar. It had a kind of plump symmetry to it in fact, like a ripe Gouda or a comfy old hassock.

She chuckled at her own similes. Is that what she had come to? An old cheese? A piece of furniture?

She didn't care, really. She was Anna Madrigal, a self-made woman, and there was no one else in the world exactly like her.

As that comforting litany danced in her head, she rolled a joint of her finest sensemilla and settled back with Boris to enjoy the fire.

Michael

For almost three years now Michael Tolliver had been manager of a nursery in the Richmond District called God's Green Earth. The proprieter of this enterprise was Michael's best friend, Ned Lockwood, a brawny forty-two-year-old who was practically the working model for the Green-collar Gay.

Green-collar Gays, in Michael's lexicon, included everyone who dealt with beautiful living things in a manly, outdoorsy fashion: nurserymen, gardeners, forest rangers and some landscape architects. Florists, of course, didn't qualify.

Michael loved working in the soil. The fruits of his labors were aesthetic, spiritual, physical and even sexual – since a number of men in the city found nothing quite so erotic as the sight of someone's first name stitched crudely across the front of a pair of faded green coveralls.

Like Michael, Ned hadn't always been a Green-collar Gay. Back in the early sixties, when he was still a student at U C L A, he had paid his tuition by pumping gas at a Chevron station in Beverly Hills. Then one day a famous movie star, fifteen years Ned's senior, stopped in for an oil change and became hopelessly smitten with the lean, well-muscled youth.

After that, Ned's life changed radically. The movie star wasted no time in setting up house with his newfound protégé. He paid for the remainder of Ned's education and incorporated him – as much as propriety and his press agent allowed – into his life in Hollywood.

Ned held his own quite well. Blessed with a sexual aura that bordered on mysticism, he proceeded to win the heart of every man, woman and animal that crossed his path. It was not so much his beauty that captivated them but his innate and almost childlike gift for attentiveness. He listened to them in a town where no one ever listened at all.

The love affair lasted almost five years. When it was over, the two men parted as friends. The movie star even helped subsidize Ned's move to San Francisco.

Today, in his middle years, Ned Lockwood was handsomer than ever, but balding – no, bald. What remained of his hair he kept clipped short, wearing his naked scalp proudly in the long-haul trucker tradition of Wakefield Poole porno movies. 'If I ever start raking my hair over from the back and sides,' he once told Michael earnestly, 'I want you to take me out and have me shot.'

Ned and Michael had gone to bed together twice – in 1977. Since then, they had been friends, co-conspirators, brothers. Michael loved Ned; he shared his romantic exploits with the older man like a small dog who drags a dead thing home and lays it adoringly on the doorstep of his master.

And Ned always listened.

'You wanna go to Devil's Herd tomorrow night?' asked Ned. 'They've got a live band.'

Michael looked up from the task at hand. He was boxing primroses for a Pacific Heights realtor who had fretted far too long over a choice of the pink or the yellow. The realtor eyed Ned bitchily, then resumed his fussing:

'Of course, there *are* some potted fuchsias on the deck and those are sort of purplish. I mean, the purple might not even *go* with the yellow. What do you think?'

Michael shot Ned an apologetic glance and tried to remain patient with his customer. 'All flowers go together,' he said evenly. 'God isn't a decorator.'

The realtor frowned for a split second, perhaps determining if the remark had been impertinent. Then he laughed drily. 'But some decorators are God, right?'

'Not around my house,' smiled Michael.

The realtor leaned closer. 'You used to know Jon Fielding, didn't you?'

Michael rang up the purchase. 'Something like that,' he replied.

'Oh . . . if I hit a nerve, I'm sorry.'

'Not a bit.' He smiled nonchalantly, hoping he didn't sound as feisty as he felt. 'It's been a long time, that's all.' He slid the box of primroses in the direction of his inquisitor. 'You know him, huh?'

The realtor nodded. 'We did a fly-in together once. Gamma Mu.' He tossed out the name like bait, Michael noticed, as if *everyone* had heard of the national gay millionaires' fraternity.

Michael didn't bite. 'Give him my best when you see him,' he said.

'Right.' The realtor simply stared for a moment, then reached over and stuffed his business card into the pocket of Michael's coveralls. 'This is who I am,' he said *sotto voce*. 'You should come over one night. I have a Betamax.'

He left without waiting for a reply, passing Ned in the doorway.

'What about it?' asked Ned.

Michael looked at the realtor's card long enough to read the name, Archibald Anson Gidde, then dropped it into the trash can. 'Sorry, Ned, what did you say?'

'Devil's Herd,' said Ned. 'Tomorrow night?'

'Oh . . . yeah. Sure. I'd love to.'

Ned checked him out for a moment, then tousled his hair. 'You O.K., Bubba?'

'Sure,' said Michael.

'Did that guy . . . ?'

'He knew Jon,' said Michael. 'That's all.'

The A-Gays Gather

Arch Gidde was a mess. Twenty minutes before his dinner guests were scheduled to arrive the yellow primroses were still in their tacky little plastic pots. And Cleavon – damn his lazy, jiveass soul – was still in the kitchen, dicking around with the sushi.

Arch bellowed from the bedroom. 'Cleavon . . . *Cleavon!*'

'Yo,' replied Cleavon.

The realtor winced at himself in the mirror. *Yo*, for Christ's sake. Harold had never said yo. Harold had been campy, to be sure, but never, ever disrespectful. Arch had lost Harold in the divorce, however, and Rick was too selfish (and far too shrewd) to part with a competent servant who was both black *and* gay.

'Cleavon,' yelled Arch. 'I cannot stress too strongly that the primroses *must* be potted before the guests arrive. I want four of them in that elephant planter and four in the box on the end of the deck.'

A pause. Then another yo.

Arch Gidde groaned out loud, then pushed up the sleeves of his new Kansai Yamamoto sweater from Wilkes. It was embroidered with a huge multihued hyena that draped itself asymmetrically across his left shoulder. Is it too much? he wondered.

No, he decided. Not with the sushi.

The guests arrived almost simultaneously, all having attended a cocktail party thrown by Vita Keating, wife of the Presto Pudding heir.

They included: Edward Paxton Stoker Jr. and Charles Hillary Lord (the Stoker-Lords), William Devereux Hill III and Anthony Ball Hughes (the Hill-Hugheses), John Morrison Stonecypher (sometimes referred to as The Prune Prince) and Peter Prescott Cipriani.

Conspicuously absent was Richard Evan Hampton, Arch Gidde's ex; the Hampton-Giddes were no more.

'Well,' cooed Chuck Lord as he swept into the living room, 'I must say I approve of the help.'

Arch smiled reservedly. 'Somehow I thought you might.'

'He's not from Oakland, is he?' asked Ed Stoker, Chuck's Other Half.

'San Bruno,' said Arch.

'Pity. Chuckie only likes the ones from Oakland.'

Chuck Lord cast a withering glance at his lover, then turned back to his host. 'Don't mind *her*,' he said. 'She's been having hot flushes all week.'

Arch did his best not to smirk. Chuck Lord's addiction to Negroes from the East Bay was a matter of common knowledge among the A-Gays in San Francisco. While Ed Stoker stayed home, popping Valiums and reading Diana Vreeland's *Allure*, his multi-millionaire husband was out stalking the streets of Oakland in search of black auto mechanics.

And whenever Ed asked Chuck for a divorce (or so the story went), Chuck would recoil in genuine horror. 'But darling,' he would gasp, 'what about the baby?'

The baby was an eight-unit apartment house in the Haight that the two men owned jointly.

'Guess who I saw at the nursery today,' said Arch over dessert.

'Who?' asked The Prune Prince.

'Michael Tolliver.'

'Who?'

'You know. The twink who used to be Fielding's lover.'

'The cripple?'

'Not anymore. Jesus, where have *you* been?'

'Well, pardon me, Liz Smith.'

'He practically groped me in the greenhouse.'

'Where *is* Fielding, anyway?'

'On a ship or something. Handing out Dramamine. Too awful for words.'

Peter Cipriani passed by and dropped a magazine into Arch's lap. 'Speaking of too awful for words, have you checked out Madame Giroux this month?' The magazine was *Western Gentry*, and the object of Peter's disdain was one Prue Giroux, the society columnist. Arch turned to the inside back page and began to read aloud to his guests:

'"This morning, while talking to the charming and delightful black man who parks cars in the garage next to L'Etoile, it occurred to me how truly blessed we are to live in a town that's just chock full of so many interesting races, creeds and colors."'

Tony Hughes moaned and rolled his eyes. 'The stupid twat thinks she's Eleanor Roosevelt now.'

Arch continued: '"As a simple country girl from Grass Valley . . ."'

More groans from everyone.

'"As a simple country girl from Grass Valley, it gives me such joy and fulfillment to count myself among the friends of such well-known black people as Kathleen Cleaver, wife of the noted militant, and such distinguished Jewish persons as Dr Heinrich Viertel (author of *Probing the Id*) and Ethel Merman, whom I met when she came through The City plugging her fabulous new disco album."'

This time there were shrieks. Tony jerked the magazine out of Arch's hands. 'She didn't say that! You made that up!' Arch yielded the floor to Tony, who obviously wanted to continue the reading.

Almost unnoticed, Arch slipped away from the table to deal with a situation which may have reached crisis proportions: Cleavon had not shown up with the coffee. *And Chuck Lord had not returned from the bathroom.*

Purple with rage, Arch listened outside the bathroom door, then flung it open ingloriously.

Cleavon was seated on the black onyx sink, holding one nostril shut while Chuck Lord spaded cocaine into the other. Showing not the slightest trace of remorse, Chuck smirked and returned the paraphernalia to the pocket of his Alexander Julian jacket.

Arch eyed his guest murderously. 'Come back to de raft, Huck honey. You are missed.'

When Chuck was gone, Cleavon climbed down from the sink and sucked the crystals noisily into his sinuses. His employer was livid but controlled. 'We are ready for coffee now, Cleavon.'

'Yo,' said the servant.

Out in the dining room, Peter Cipriani brayed a drunken riddle to the returning Chuck Lord: 'Hey, Chuckie! What's twelve inches and white?'

'What?' came the wary reply.

'Nothing,' shrieked Peter. 'Absolutely nothing!'

Arch Gidde could have died.

True Prue

People said the meanest things about Prue Giroux.

Her willowy good looks, they said, had gotten her everything she had ever wanted but respect. When people spoke of her divorce from Reg Giroux, it was Reg who had always been 'the nice one.' He had also, by the strangest coincidence, been the one with the forty million dollars.

Prue had some of that now, thank God. Plus a Tony Hail town-house on Nob Hill. Plus enough Galanos gowns to last her through all of the Nancy Reagan Administration, even if – knock on wood – it lasted eight years.

The real secret of her power, however, lay in her column in *Western Gentry* magazine. It didn't matter, Prue had discovered, if your blood wasn't blue and your wealth was all alimony. So what if you slipped up and pronouced *Thaïs* 'Thayz' or applauded after the first movement or held a black tie function in midafternoon? If you wrote a social column, the bastards would always let you in.

Not all of them, of course. Some of the old-line San Mateo types (she had taught herself not to say Hillsborough) still regarded Prue from a chilly distance. The young lionesses, however, seemed grimly aware that their niches would never be secure without at least nominal recognition by the society press.

So they invited her to lunch.

Not to dinner usually, just to lunch. When, for instance, Ann Getty threw her February soiree for Baryshnikov at Bali's, it wasn't really necessary to include Prue in the proceedings; the guests simply phoned her the juicy particulars the morning after.

Prue didn't mind, really. She'd come a long way, and she knew it. Her penchant for dubbing herself 'a simple country girl from Grass Valley' was no affectation. She *was* a simple country girl from Grass Valley – one of seven children raised by a tractor salesman and his Seventh Day Adventist wife.

When she met Reg Giroux, then president of a medium-sized aeronautical engineering firm, Prue was still a fledgling dental hygienist; she was, in fact, flossing his teeth at the time. Reg's friends were horrified when he announced their engagement at the Bohemian Grove summer encampment.

Still, the marriage seemed to work for a while. Prue and Reg built a sprawling vacation home in the Mother Lode country which became the site of many lavish, theme-oriented costume galas. At her Pink-and-Green Ball Prue played hostess to Erica Jong, Tony Orlando and Joan Baez, all in the same afternoon. She could scarcely contain herself.

That, eventually, became the problem. Complacent in his aristocracy, Reg Giroux did not share or comprehend his wife's seemingly insatiable appetite for celebrities. Prue's weekly Nob Hill star luncheon, which she had grandly labeled 'The Forum', was so universally scorned by the old-liners that even her husband had begun to feel the sting.

So he had bailed out.

Luckily for Prue, the divorce coincided conveniently with the arrest and conviction (on indecent exposure charges) of *Western Gentry* society columnist Carson Callas. So Prue invited the magazine's editor to lunch and made her pitch. The editor, a country boy himself, mistook Prue's studied elegance for patrician grace and hired her on the spot.

She was her own woman now.

Prue's three-year-old Russian wolfhound, Vuitton, had been missing for nearly a week. Prue was frantic. To make matters worse, the man at Park & Rec was being annoyingly vague about the crisis.

'Yes ma'am, I seem to remember that report. Where did you say you lost him again?'

Prue heaved a weary sigh. 'In the tree ferns. Across from the conservatory. He was with me one moment, and the next he was . . .'

'Last week?'

'Yes. Saturday.'

'One moment, please.' She heard him riffling through files. The jerk was whistling 'Oh Where Oh Where Has My Little Dog Gone.' Several minutes passed before he returned to the phone. 'No ma'am. Zilch. I checked twice. Nobody's reported a Russian wolfhound in the last . . .'

'You haven't seen any suspicious Cambodians?'

'Ma'am?'

'Cambodians. Refugees. You know.'

'Yes ma'am, but I don't see what . . .'

'Do I have to spell it out? They eat dogs, you know. *They've been eating people's dogs!*'

Silence.

'I read it in the *Chronicle*,' Prue added.

Another pause, and then: 'Look, ma'am. How 'bout I ask the mounted patrol to keep their eyes open, O.K.? With a dog like that, though, the chances of dognapping are pretty high. I wish I could be more helpful, but I can't.'

Prue thanked him and hung up. Poor Vuitton. His fate lay in the hands of incompetents. Somewhere in the Tenderloin the Boat People could be eating sweet-and-sour wolfhound, and Prue was helpless. Helpless.

She took a ten minute walk in Huntington Park to calm her nerves before writing the column. When she returned, her secretary reported that Frannie Halcyon had called to invite Prue to lunch tomorrow 'to discuss a matter of utmost urgency.'

Frannie Halcyon was the reigning Grande Dame of Hillsborough. She had never even communicated with the likes of Prue Giroux, much less summoned her to the family estate for lunch.

'A matter of utmost urgency.'

What on earth could that be?

The Matriarch

Sometimes Frannie couldn't help wondering whether there was a curse on Halcyon Hill.

It made as much sense as anything when she stopped to consider the horrid consequences that had befallen the members of her family. At sixty-four, she was the sole surviving Halcyon, the last frayed remnant of a dynasty that had all but capitulated to death, disease and destruction.

Edgar, her husband, succumbed to 'bum kidneys' (his term) on Christmas Eve, 1976.

Beauchamp, her son-in-law, perished the following year in a fiery crash in the Broadway tunnel.

Faust, her beloved Great Dane, passed away shortly thereafter.

DeDe, her daughter and Beauchamp's estranged wife, gave birth to half-Chinese twins in late 1977 and fled to Guyana with a woman friend of questionable origin.

The Jonestown Massacre. Even now, three years after the event, those words could pounce on Frannie from a page of newsprint, prickly and poisonous as the fangs of a viper.

Edgar, Beauchamp, Faust and DeDe. Horror upon horror. Indignity upon indignity.

And now, the ultimate humiliation.

She had finally been forced to invite Prue Giroux to lunch.

Emma appeared on the sunporch with a tray of Mai Tais.

'A little refreshment?' asked Frannie.

The columnist flashed her syrupy little-girl smile. 'It's a teensy bit early for me, thanks.'

Frannie wanted to kick her. Instead, she accepted a drink from Emma with a gracious nod, sipped it daintily, and smiled right back at this hopelessly common woman. 'By the way,' she said. 'I find your column . . . most amusing.'

Prue beamed. 'I'm so glad, Frannie. I do my best to keep it light.'

'Yes. It's very light.' Inside, Frannie was raging. How dare this creature address her by her first name!

'As far as I'm concerned,' Prue continued, obviously developing a familiar theme, 'there is far too much ugliness in this world, and if each of us lit just one little candle . . . well, you know.'

Frannie saw the opening she needed. 'I suppose you know about my daughter.'

'Yes.' The columnist's face became a mask of tragedy. 'It must have been awful for you.'

'It was. It is.'

'I can't even imagine what it must have been like.'

'Most people can't.' Frannie took another sip of her Mai Tai. 'Except maybe Catherine Hearst. She comes to visit sometimes. She's been terribly sweet. Uh . . . do you mind if I show you something?'

'Of course not.'

The matriarch excused herself, returning moments later with the evidence, now tattered almost beyond recognition. 'These used to be DeDe's,' she said.

The columnist smiled. 'Pompons. I was a cheerleader, too.'

'DeDe sent for them.' Frannie continued, 'when she was in Jonestown. She used them when she was at Sacred Heart, and she thought it would be cute if she had them in Guyana for the basketball games.' She fidgeted with her cocktail napkin. 'They found them with her things . . . afterwards.'

'She . . . uh . . . led cheers in Guyana?'

The matriarch nodded. 'Just as a lark. They had a basketball team, you know.'

'No,' said Prue carefully. 'Actually, I didn't.'

'DeDe was a *doer*, Prue. She loved life more than anything. I have verified for certain that she and the children weren't among the dead in Jonestown . . . and in my heart, my most basic instincts tell me that they made it out of there alive.'

'When?'

'I don't know. Earlier. Whenever.'

'But didn't the authorities presume . . . ?'

'They presumed a lot of things, the fools! They told me she was dead, before they even checked to see if her body was there.' Frannie leaned forward and looked at Prue imploringly. 'I know you've probably heard all this before. I called you here, because I need you to help me publicize a new development.'

'Please,' said the columnist, 'go ahead.'

'I spoke to a psychic this week. A very reliable one. She says that DeDe and her friend and the twins are alive and living in a small village in South America.'

Silence.

'I'm not a hysterical woman, Prue. I don't normally subscribe to that sort of thing. It's just that this woman was so *sure*. She saw everything: the hut, the mats they sleep on, the villagers in the marketplace, those precious little twins running naked in the . . .' Frannie's voice broke; she felt herself coming apart. 'Please help me,' she pleaded. 'I don't know who else to turn to.'

Prue reached over and squeezed her hand. 'You know I would, Frannie, if there was any way to . . . well, surely the newspapers or the TV stations would be better equipped to handle this sort of thing.'

The matriarch stiffened. 'I've talked to them already. You don't think I would call you *first*?'

What was the use? This ridiculous woman was like all the rest, humoring her as if she were some sort of senile old biddy. Frannie dropped the matter altogether, hastening her guest through lunch and out of her house without further ado.

By three o'clock, she was back in bed, drinking Mai Tais and watching the little 'belly telly' that DeDe and Beauchamp had given her after Edgar's death. The afternoon movie was *Summertime* with Katharine Hepburn, one of Frannie's favorites.

During the 'intermission', a pretty young woman offered shopping tips to viewers: where to find good factory seconds in the Walnut Creek-Lafayette area. Frannie turned off the sound and poured another Mai Tai.

When her gaze returned to the television, she nearly dropped her drink.

That face! Of course! It was Edgar's old secretary. Frannie hadn't laid eyes on her for at least four years. Since Beauchamp's funeral, probably.

What *was* her name, anyway? Mary Jane something. No . . . Mary Lou?

The matriarch turned the sound up again. 'This is Mary Ann Singleton,' chirped the young woman, 'wishing you bargains galore!'

Mary Ann Singleton.

Maybe, thought Frannie. Just maybe . . .

A Daytime Face

After almost two years of being a woman in television, Mary Ann Singleton was finally a woman *on* television.

Her show, *Bargain Matinee*, attempted to update the old *Dialing for Dollars* afternoon movie format by offering inflation-fighting consumer tips to Bay Area viewers. This was, after all, The Eighties.

The movies, on the other hand, were firmly grounded in The Fifties: comfy old chestnuts like *Splendor in the Grass* and *The Secret of Santa Vittoria* and today's feature, *Summertime*. Movies that used to be called women's movies in the days before E R A.

Mary Ann's shining hour was a five minute spot interrupting the movie at midpoint.

The formula was fairly consistent: dented cans, factory seconds, Chinese umbrellas that made nifty lampshades, perfume you could brew at home, places you could shop for pasta, new uses for old coffee cans. Stuff that Michael persisted in calling 'Hints from Heloise.'

Mary Ann was faintly embarrassed by the homebody image this format compelled her to project, but she couldn't deny the delicious exhilaration of the stardom it brought her. Strangers stared at her on the Muni; neighbors asked her to autograph their grocery bags at the Searchlight Market.

Still, something was wrong, something that hadn't been cured by becoming a Woman on Television.

A real Woman on Television, Mary Ann felt, was a glamorous hellraiser, a feminine feminist like Jane Fonda in *The China Syndrome* or Sigourney Weaver in *Eyewitness*. A real Woman on Television was invariably an investigative reporter.

And Mary Ann would settle for nothing less.

Immediately after the sign-off she left Studio B and hurried back to her cubbyhole without stopping in the dressing room to remove her makeup.

It was five o'clock. She could still catch the news director before he mobilized for the evening newscast.

There was a note on her desk: MRS HARRISON CALLED.

'Did you take this?' she asked an associate producer at the next desk.

'Denny did. He's in the snack bar.'

Denny, another associate producer, was eating a microwaved patty melt. 'Who's Mrs Harrison?' asked Mary Ann.

'She said you knew her.'

'*Harrison?*'

'That's what it sounded like. She was shitfaced.'

'Great.'

'She called right after your show-and-tell. Said it was "mosht urgent."'

'It's *Summertime* is what it is. The drunks always call during the tear-jerkers. No number, huh?'

Denny shrugged. 'She said you knew her.'

Larry Kenan, the news director, lounged back in his swivel chair, locked his fingers behind his blow-dried head, and smirked wearily at the Bo Derek poster he had pasted on the ceiling above his desk. Its inscription, also his doing, was burned indelibly on Mary Ann's consciousness: FOR LARRY WITH LUST — NOBODY DOES IT BETTER. BO.

'You wanna know the honest-to-God truth?' he said.

515

Mary Ann waited. He was always disguising his goddamned opinion as the honest-to-God truth.

'The honest-to-God truth is you're a daytime face and the public doesn't wanna see a daytime face on the six o'clock news. Period, end of sentence. I mean, *hey*, what can I say, lady? It ain't pretty, but it's the honest-to-God truth.' He tore his gaze from Bo Derek long enough to flash her his 'that's the breaks, kid' grin.

'What about Bambi Kanetaka?'

'What about her?'

Mary Ann knew she had to tread softly here. 'Well . . . she had a daytime show, and you let *her* do the . . .'

'Bambi's different,' glared Larry.

I know, thought Mary Ann. She gives head on command.

'Her GSR's were dynamite,' added Larry, almost daring Mary Ann to continue.

'Then test *me*,' said Mary Ann. 'I don't mind being . . .'

'We *have* tested you, O.K.? We tested you two months ago and your GSR's sucked. All right?'

It stung more than she wanted it to. She had never really *believed* in Galvanic Skin Response. What could you prove for certain, anyway, by attaching electrodes to a guinea pig audience? Just that some performers made some viewers sweat more than others. Big fucking deal.

She tried another tack. 'But I wouldn't have to be on camera all the time. I could research things, investigate. There are lots of subjects that the regular reporters don't have the time or the inclination to cover.'

Larry's lip curled. 'Like what?'

'Well, like . . .' Think, she commanded herself, think! 'Well, the gay community, for instance.'

'Oh really?' he said, arching an eyebrow. 'You know all about that, huh?'

Mary Ann puzzled at his inflection. Did he think she was a lesbian? Or was he just toying with her again? 'I have lots of . . . contacts there,' she said. A lie, but what-the-hell. Michael had lots of contacts there; it was practically the same thing.

He smiled at her as a policeman would smile at a runaway child.

'I'll tell you the honest-to-God truth,' he said. 'The public is sick of hearing about faggots.'

The Man in Her Life

If Larry Kenan was an asshole – for there was no longer any doubt about that – Mary Ann's paycheck at least provided certain amenities that made life in the city considerably more graceful:

She ate at Ciao now.

She drove a Le Car.

She wore velvet blazers and button-down shirts over her Calvins – a look which Michael persisted in labeling as 'Ivy Lesbian.'

She had stripped her apartment of all furnishings that were either yellow or wicker and installed gun-metal gray industrial carpeting and high-tech steel factory shelving.

She had canceled her subscription to *San Francisco* magazine and started reading *Interview*.

She had abandoned Cost Plus forever.

Still, she couldn't help but feel a certain frustration over the progress of her career.

That frustration was only heightened later that night when she watched a particularly compelling episode of *Lou Grant*, one featuring a scrappy woman journalist in her struggle to uncover the truth.

It was almost too painful to endure, so Mary Ann turned off the set and marched into the bedroom to Sassoon her hair. Sometimes a shower was the best of all possible sedatives.

Her hair was shorter now than it had been in years. Waifish and sort of Leslie Caron-like with just the vaguest hint of New Wave. Anything more pronounced would have been pressing her luck with the management of the station.

As she towel-dried her new do into place, she found it extraordinary that she had ever endured the rigors of long hair in the first place. ('You kept trying for a French twist,' Michael was fond of recalling, 'but it kept going Connie Stevens on you.')

After searching in vain for her rabbit slippers, Mary Ann knotted herself into an oversized white terrycloth robe and climbed the stairs to the little house on the roof of 28 Barbary Lane.

She paused for a moment outside the familiar orange door, peering out through an ivy-choked window at a night full of stars. An ocean liner slid past aglitter with lights, like a huge chandelier being dragged out to sea.

Mary Ann heard herself sigh. Partly for the view. Partly for the man who waited inside.

She entered without knocking, knowing he was already asleep. He had worked a double shift that day, and the crowd at Perry's had been more boisterous and demanding than usual. As she expected, he was sprawled face down on the bed in his boxer shorts.

She sat on the edge of the bed and laid her hand gently on the small of his back.

The most beautiful part of a man, she thought. That warm little valley just before the butt begins. Well, maybe the *second* most beautiful.

Brian stirred, then rolled over and rubbed his eyes with his fists the way that little boys do. 'Hey,' he said throatily.

'Hey,' she replied.

She leaned over and lay against his chest, enjoying the heat of his body. When her mouth sought his, Brian turned his head away and mumbled a warning: 'Moose breath, sweetheart.'

She took his chin in her hand and kissed him anyway. 'So?' she said. 'What if the moose is cute?'

Chuckling, he wrapped his arms around her. 'So how was your day?'

'Shitty,' she said, speaking directly into his ear.

'You spoke to Larry Kenan?'

'Uh-huh.'

'And?'

'He still wants nookie before he'll negotiate.'

Brian jerked away from her. 'He *said* that?'

'No.' Mary Ann smiled at his alarm. 'Not in so many words. I just know how he operates. Bambi Kanetaka is living proof of *that*.'

Brian pretended not to understand. 'I find her most incisive myself.'

Mary Ann goosed him.

'Incisive and perky. A winning combination.'

'I'll do it again,' warned Mary Ann.

'I was hoping you'd say that,' grinned Brian. 'Only slower this time, O.K.?'

Remembering Lennon

The beauty of being a waiter, Brian used to think, was that you could dump the whole damn thing tomorrow.

There were no pension plans to haunt you, no digital watches after fifty years of service, no soul-robbing demands for corporate loyalty and long-term commitment. It was a living, in short, but never, ever a career.

He used to think.

Now, after six years of working at Perry's, he'd begun to wonder about that. If it wasn't a career now, when would it be? After ten years? Fifteen? Is that what he wanted? Is that what *she* wanted?

He rolled away from her and stared at the ceiling in silence.

'O.K.,' said Mary Ann. 'Out with it.'

'*Again?*'

She laughed at his joke, then snuggled up against his shoulder. 'I know pensive when I see it. So what are you pensing about?'

'Oh . . . the bar, I guess. I think it may be time for that.'

'I thought you hated tending bar.'

He winced. 'The *state* bar, Mary Ann. As in lawyer?'

'Oh.' She glanced over at him. 'I thought you hated that, too.'

There was no quick answer for that one. He *had* hated it, in fact, hated every boring, nerve-grinding minute he had ever been Brian Hawkins, Attorney-at-Law. He had sublimated his hatred in the pursuit of causes – blacks, Native Americans, oil slicks – but the 'old ennui', as he had come to call it, proved as persistent and deep-rooted as the law itself.

He still cringed at the thought of the singing fluorescent bulb that had tormented him for hours on end in the grass-cloth-and-walnut conference room of his last law firm. That fixture came to symbolize all that was petty and poisonous about life – if you could call it that – in the Financial District.

So he had fled his profession and become a waiter.

He had also become a rogue, terrorizing singles bars and laundromats in a frenzied and relentless search for 'foxes'. He had simplified his life, stream-lined his body and subjugated the 'old ennui'.

But now something different was happening. The woman he had once described as 'that uptight airhead from Cleveland' was easily the love of his life.

And she was the one with the career.

'I have to do *something*,' he told Mary Ann.

'About what?'

'Work,' said Brian. 'My job.'

'You mean your tips aren't . . . ?'

'It isn't the money.' His voice had an edge to it. His flagging pride was making him cranky. *Don't take it out on her*, he warned himself. 'I just can't go on like this,' he added in a gentler tone.

'Like what?' she asked cautiously.

'Like your dependant or something. I can't hack it, Mary Ann.'

She studied him soberly. 'It *is* the money, then.'

'It's one thing to go dutch. It's another to be . . . I don't know . . . kept or something.' His face was aflame with self-contempt and embarrassment.

Mary Ann laughed openly. '*Kept?* Gimme a break, Brian! I paid for a weekend shack-up in Sierra City, I *wanted* to do that, you turkey. It was as much for me as it was . . . oh, Brian.' She reached over and took his hand. 'I thought we'd gotten over all that macho stuff.'

He aped her mincingly. 'I thought we'd gotten over all that macho stuff.' It was so petty and cruel that he was instantly sorry. Examining her face for signs of hurt, he made the maddening discovery that she had already forgiven him.

'What about John?' she asked.

'John who?'

'Lennon. I thought you admired him for becoming a house-husband when Yoko . . .'

Brian snorted. 'It was John's money, for Christ's sake! You can do anything you goddamn want when you're the richest man in New York!'

Mary Ann stared at him incredulously. Now she really was wounded. 'How could you do that?' she asked quietly. 'How could you cheapen the thing that we shared?'

She was talking about the Memorial Vigil on the Marina Green. She and Brian had spent six hours there mourning Lennon's death. They had cried themselves dry, clutching strawberry-scented candles, singing 'Hey Jude' and smoking a new crop of Hawaiian grass that Mrs Madrigal had named in honor of the deceased.

Brian had never before – and never since – made himself so vulnerable in Mary Ann's presence.

Afterwards, he had tacked this note to her door: HELP ME, IF YOU CAN, I'M FEELING DOWN, AND I DO APPRECIATE YOUR BEING 'ROUND. I LOVE YOU – BRIAN.

He was feeling down all right, but it had more to do with mid-life crisis than the passing of a Beatle.

For, on the day that John Lennon died, everyone in Brian Hawkins' generation instantly and irrevocably turned forty.

'I'm sorry,' he said at last.

'It doesn't matter,' she said, leaning over to kiss his shoulder.

'I'm just . . . edgy right now.'

'I could sleep at my place tonight, if you need the . . .'

'No. Stay. Please.'

She answered with another peck on the shoulder. 'Do me a favor,' she said.

'What?'

'Don't become a lawyer on my account. I'm a big girl now. I don't need any dragons slain on my behalf.'

He looked into her radiant face. Sometimes she understood him better than anyone. 'Right,' he murmured. 'I'll get by with a little help from my friends.'

And sometimes she made him say the corniest things.

Cowpokes

Across town on Valencia Street, Michael and Ned were sharing a Calistoga at Devil's Herd, the city's most popular gay country-western bar.

What Michael liked most about the saloon was its authenticity: the twangy down-home band (Western Electric), the horse collars dangling from the ceiling, the folksy Annie Oakley dykes shouting 'yahoo' from the bar.

If he squinted his eyes just so, the dudes doing cowboy dancing could be grizzled buckeroos, horny claim-jumpers who were simply making do until the next shipment of saloon girls came in from the East.

True, the beefcake cowboy murals struck a somewhat citified note in the overall scheme of things, but Michael didn't mind. Someday, he believed, the homoerotic cave drawings in San Francisco's gay bars would be afforded the same sort of reverence that is currently heaped upon WPA murals and deco apartment house lobbies.

'Oh look!' a sophisticated but hunky workman would cry peeling back a piece of rotting wallboard. 'There seems to be a painting back here! My God, it's from the school of Tom of Finland!'

The band was playing 'Stand By Your Man.' As soon as they recognized the tune, Michael and Ned smiled in unison. 'Jon was big on that one,' said Michael. 'Just as a song, though. Not as a way of life.'

Ned took a swig of the Calistoga. 'I thought it was you that left him.'

'Well, *technically*, maybe. We left each other, actually. It was a big relief to both of us. We were damn lucky, really. Sometimes it's not that easy to pull out of an S & M relationship.'

'Wait a minute. Since when were you guys . . . ?'

'S & M,' Michael repeated. 'Streisand and Midler. He was into Streisand. I was into Midler. It was pure, unadulterated hell.'

Ned laughed. 'I guess I bit on that one.'

'I'm serious,' said Michael. 'We fought about it all the time. One Sunday afternoon when Jon was listening to "Evergreen" for about the three millionth time, I suddenly found myself asking him what exactly he saw in . . . I believe I referred to her as "that tone-deaf, big-nosed bitch."'

'Jesus. What did he say?'

'He was quite adult about it, actually. He pointed out calmly that Bette's nose is bigger than Barbra's. I almost brained him with his goddamned Baccarat paperweight.'

This time Ned guffawed, a sound that told Michael he had struck paydirt. Ned was the only person he knew who actually guffawed. 'It's the truth,' grinned Michael. 'Every single word of it.'

'Yeah,' said Ned, 'but people don't really break up over stuff like that.'

'Well . . .' Michael thought for a moment. 'I guess we just made each other do things we didn't want to do. He made me alphabetize the classical albums by composer. I made him eat crunchy peanut butter instead of plain. He made me sleep in a room with eggplant walls. I made him eat off Fiesta Ware. We didn't agree on much of anything, come to think of it, except Al Parker and Rocky Road ice cream.'

'You ever mess around?'

'You betcha. None o' that nasty heterosexual role-playing for *us*. Lots of buddy nights at the baths. I can't even count the number of times I rolled over in bed and told some hot stranger: "You'd like my lover".'

'What about rematches?'

'Once,' said Michael grimly, 'but never again. Jon sulked for a week. I saw his point, actually: once is recreation; twice is courtship. You learn these nifty little nuances when you're married. That's why I'm not married anymore.'

'But you could be, huh?'

Michael shook his head. 'Not now. Not for a while. I don't know . . . maybe never. It's a knack, isn't it? Some of us just don't have the knack.'

'You gotta want it bad,' said Ned.

'Then, maybe I don't want it bad enough. That's a possibility. That's a distinct possibility.' Michael took a sip of the mineral water, then drummed his fingers on the bar in time to the music. The band had stopped playing now; someone at the jukebox had paid Hank Williams Jr. to sing 'Women I Never Had.'

Michael handed the Calistoga back to Ned. 'Remember Mona?' he asked.

Ned nodded. 'Your old roommate.'

'Yeah. Well, Mona used to say that she could get by just fine without a lover as long as she had five good friends. That about sums it up for me right now.'

'I hope I'm one of 'em,' said Ned.

Michael's brow wrinkled while he counted hastily on his fingers. 'Jesus,' he said at last. 'I think you're three of them.'

House of Wax

Prue Giroux and Victoria Lynch were kindred spirits.

For one thing, they were both handsome women. For another, Victoria was engaged to Prue's ex-husband. Bonds like that were not easily broken.

Today, Victoria had called to share a secret with her spiritual sister.

'Now listen, Prudy Sue, this is cross-your-heart stuff, definitely not for publication, understand?' (Prue's closest friends always addressed her by her childhood name.)

'Of course,' said Prue.

'I mean, eventually of course I would adore for you to give it a little publicity in your column, which is part of the reason I called, but right now it's just in the embryonic stage, and we don't want to kill the baby, do we?'

'Of course not,' said Prue.

'Well,' announced Victoria, sucking in breath as if she were about to blow a trumpet fanfare, 'yours truly is in the process of organizing the world's first society wax museum!'

'The . . . come again?'

'Now, shut up a sec, Prudy Sue, and hear me out. I met this absolutely divine little man at the Keatings' house in Santa Barbara, and it seems he's fallen on rather hard times lately, which is too tragic, because it turns out he's descended from the Hapsburgs or something. I mean, he's got the prominent lower lip and everything. Anyway, Vita told me he used to work at Madame Tussaud's, where he was their principal designer . . .'

'Ah, yes. I have one of his gowns.'

A pause, and then: 'You do *not* have one of his gowns, Prudy Sue.'

'But that mauve cocktail dress I wore to . . .'

'That's a Madame *Gres*, Prudy Sue. You do not own a Madame Tussaud. Madame Tussaud's is a wax museum in London.'

'I knew that,' sulked Prue. 'I thought you said . . .'

'Of course you did, darling. Those French names all sound alike, don't they? Now . . . where was I?'

'He used to work at Madame Tufo's.'

'Uh . . . right. He worked . . . there, and he's terribly aristocratic and all, and he thinks that it's just a damn shame there's never been a wax museum for society figures. Think about that, Prudy Sue! We have wax museums for historical people and show business people and sports people, but nary a thing for the movers and shakers of society. It's shocking really, when you stop and think about it.'

'That's a good point,' said Prue. 'I never really . . .'

'And if *we* don't take the initiative on this, who will? I mean, that's what this little man said to me, and I was absolutely *floored* by his insight. Our children can see for themselves how short Napoleon really was, for instance, but where can they go to look at a replica of, say, Nan Kempner. Or Sao Schlumberger. Or Marie Hélène de Rothschild. These people are *legends*, Prudy Sue, but they'll be lost to prosperity forever, if we don't take decisive action now. At least, that's what Wolfgang says, and I think he's dead right.'

'Wolfgang?'

'The little man. He's such a dear, really. The wax figures usually run about fifteen thousand apiece, but he's offered to do them for ten as a sort of public service. He wants me to scout locations for the museum, which is a damn good thing, since he was leaning towards Santa Barbara when I talked to him, but I think I convinced him to move it here. That way, see, we can have a San Francisco wing as well as an international wing.'

'I see.'

'I thought you might, darling.' Victoria giggled conspiratorially. 'God, isn't it fabulous? We'll get to donate our old gowns and everything. Plus Wolfgang can make marvelous paste imitations of your emeralds, and . . . well, I'm just positive we can raise the money in no time.'

'Have you talked to Denise yet?'

Victoria chuckled. 'I'm way ahead of you, Prudy Sue. I think she's good for fifty thousand, *if* we put her in the international wing. Ditto Ann Getty. That one may be a little tougher to pull off unless we stack the board of directors, but what-the-hell, we'll stack the board of directors.'

Prue finally managed to laugh. 'You haven't told Shugie Sussman, have you?'

'God no! We hadn't planned on a Chamber of Horrors, darling! On second thought, let's do – have you seen Kitty Cipriani's latest facelift?'

Prue laughed even louder this time. Then she said: 'Oh Vicky, thank you! I've needed to laugh more than anything. I've been so depressed over Vuitton.'

'Over . . . ? Oh, your dog.'

'It's been almost two weeks now. The Park & Rec people haven't seen him anywhere. I don't know what to do except . . .' Prue's voice trailed off as the melancholy swept over her again.

'Except what, Prudy Sue?'

'Well . . . I thought I might go back to the park and . . . wait for him.'

'That's an awfully long shot, isn't it? I mean, *two weeks*, Prudy Sue. It's not very likely that he's still . . .'

'I *know* he's there, Vicky. I can feel it in my bones. I know he'll come back to me, if I give him the chance.'

Even as she spoke, Prue knew how she sounded. She sounded like poor old Frannie Halcyon, still believing against preposterous odds that her long-lost daughter would return from the jungles of Guyana.

But stranger things had happened.

No Big Deal

On his way home from Perry's, Brian stopped at a garage sale on Union Street and bought an antique Peter, Paul & Mary album for a quarter.

Also available: two Shelley Berman albums, an early Limelighters album featuring Glenn Yarborough, and the soundtracks of *Breakfast at Tiffany's*, *Mondo Cane* and *To Kill a Mockingbird*.

Somebody's youth, in other words.

There was nothing like a stack of dog-eared albums to remind you that the past was just so much dead weight, excess baggage to be cast overboard when the sailing got tougher. Or so Brian told himself.

Nevertheless, he lit a joint upon returning to Barbary Lane and crooned along euphorically while PP&M sang 'If I Had a Hammer,' 'Five Hundred Miles' and 'Puff the Magic Dragon.'

Had it really been eighteen years – Christ, half his life! – since Nelson Schwab had cornered him during Hell Week at the Deke House to impart the privileged information that 'Puff' was really an underground parable about – no shit! – smoking marijuana?

Yep, it really had.

He fell into a black funk, then snatched the record off the turntable and shattered it with the hammer he kept in the tool box under the kitchen sink. Inexcusable symbolism, but somehow richly satisfying.

So much for the iron grip of the past.

Now, what about the present?

The *Chronicle* 'help wanted' ads were so dismal that Brian postponed any immediate career decisions and trekked downstairs to help Mrs Madrigal plan Mary Ann's birthday party. He found the landlady installing a Roach Motel in a dark corner of her pantry.

Looking up, she smiled defeatedly. 'I told myself I would never buy one of these dreadful things. Those TV commercials seem so sadistic. Still, we can't love absolutely all of God's creatures, can we? They haven't found their way up to your place, I hope?'

Brian shook his head. 'The altitude's too much for 'em.'

Mrs Madrigal stood up, wiping her hands against each other as if they were sticky with blood. She cast a final glance at the grisly Motel, shuddered, and took Brian's arm. 'Let's go and sit in the sunshine, dear. I feel like Anthony Perkins waiting for Janet Leigh to check in.'

Out in the courtyard, she ticked off a list of prospective delights for Mary Ann's upcoming celebration: 'A nice roast of some sort with those baby carrots that she likes . . . and some ice cream from Gelato, of course, to go with the birthday cake. And . . . well, I guess it's about time for Barbara Stanwyck, isn't it?'

'A movie?' asked Brian.

Mrs Madrigal clucked her tongue at him. 'Miss Stanwyck, my dear boy, is my heartiest specimen yet.' She pointed to the edge of the courtyard where a sensemilla plant as big as a Christmas tree was undulating softly in the warm spring breeze.

Brian whistled in appreciation. 'That stuff knocks your socks off.'

The landlady smiled modestly. 'I didn't name her Barbara Stanwyck for nothing.'

They previewed Miss Stanwyck. Then they wandered down the hill to Washington Square and sat on a bench in the sunshine, docile and groggy as a couple of aging house cats.

After a long silence, Brian said: 'Does she ever talk to you about me?'

'Who? Mrs Onassis?'

Brian smiled languidly. 'You know.'

'Well . . .' Mrs Madrigal chewed her lower lip. 'Only about your extraordinary sexual prowess, that sort of thing . . . nothing really personal.'

Brian laughed. 'That's a relief.'

The landlady's Wedgwood saucer eyes fixed on him lovingly. 'She cares about you a great deal, young man.'

Brian tore up a tuft of grass and began to shred it. 'She told you that, huh?'

'Well . . . not in so many words . . .'

'It only takes three.' His voice was tinged with doubt, more than he wanted to show. 'I don't know,' he added hastily, 'maybe it's just her work or something. She's so obsessed with becoming a reporter that nothing else seems to matter. I don't know. Screw it. It's no big deal.'

Mrs Madrigal smiled wistfully and brushed the hair off his forehead. 'But it is, isn't it? It's an awfully big deal.'

'It wasn't before,' said Brian.

The landlady's eyes widened. 'Oh, I know how that can be.'

'I want this to work out, Mrs Madrigal. I never wanted anything so bad.'

'Then you shall have it,' said the landlady. 'My children always get what they want.' She gave Brian's knee a friendly shake.

'But *she's* one of your children,' said Brian. 'What if it's not what *she* wants?'

'I expect it will be,' said Mrs Madrigal, 'but you must be patient with her. She's just now learning how to fly.'

Ah, Wilderness

At least twice a year the San Francisco Gay Men's Chorus made a point of retreating to the wilds of Northern California for a weekend of intensive rehearsals and camping-around-the-campfire camaraderie.

The 'wilds' were always the same: Camp Eisenblatt, a summer camp for Jewish teenagers which leased its sylvan facilities to the one-hundred-fifty-member homosexual choir during the off-seasons. And *this* season was about as off as it could get.

'What a pisser!' groaned Michael as he stared out at the driving rain. 'I was gonna start on my tan line this weekend.'

Ned laughed and clipped an olive drab jockstrap to the clothes-line strung across one end of the baritones' bunkhouse. 'Cowboys don't have tan lines,' he said.

Since the theme of this year's retreat was 'Spring Roundup,' the western motif was in evidence everywhere. Even their name tags were affixed with swatches of cowboy bandannas; red for the first tenors, tan for the second tenors, dark blue for the baritones, dark brown for the basses and royal blue for the nonmusical 'chorus widows' who had come along to make sure that their lovers didn't have too much fun in the redwoods.

'Just the same,' said Michael. 'I liked it better last fall when we had the luau and the eighty-degree weather.'

'And the sarongs,' added Ned. 'I thought we'd never get you out of that damn thing.'

Michael inspected his fingernails blithely. 'As I recall, there was a first tenor who succeeded.'

'Well, shift fantasies,' suggested Ned. 'Pretend you're in a real bunk-house. You've just come in from a long, hot cattle drive and the rain is cooling off the livestock.'

'Right. And my ol' sidekick Lonesome Ned is about to dry his jockstrap with a blowdryer. Listen, pardner, I don't know how to break this to you gently, but *real* bunkhouses don't have REBECCA IS A FAT SLOB written in pink nailpolish on the bathroom wall.'

Ned smiled lazily. 'Jehovah moves in mysterious ways.'

After a long morning of wrestling with Liszt's Requiem and Brahms' Alto Rhapsody, the chorus converged on the Camp Eisenblatt dining hall for a lunch of bologna sandwiches and Kool-Aid.

Later, Michael and Ned and a dozen of their compatriots gossiped jovially around the fireplace. There were so many different plaids in the great room that it looked like a gathering of the clans.

'Hey,' said Ned, as he warmed his butt in front of the gas-jet embers. 'I almost forgot. I got a call from ⸺ this week.'

'No kidding,' said Michael, his voice ringing with unabashed fandom. It was almost inconceivable that someone he knew got personal phone calls from movie stars. Even if Ned *had* been this movie star's lover.

'He's royally bummed out,' said Ned. 'They canceled the musical he was gonna tour with this summer.'

'He sings?'

Ned shrugged. 'When you look like that, no one notices.'

'Tell him to come with us,' offered Michael, meaning the chorus's own nine-city summer tour. 'God, wouldn't that knock 'em dead in Nebraska?'

'I think he'll survive,' said Ned. 'He still gets two million a picture.'

Michael whistled. 'Where does he spend it?'

'On his friends mostly. And the house. Wanna see it?'

'Uh . . . pardon me?'

'He invited me down for a weekend. Said to bring a friend. How about it?'

Michael almost yelped. '*Me*? Are you serious? Lordy mercy, man! Me at _____ _____'s house? Is this for real?'

Ned nodded, beaming like a father who had just offered his eight-year-old a shot at Disneyland.

They rode back to the city in Ned's pickup, carrying six buddies and their bedrolls as cargo.

The illusion presented was almost redneck – except for the telltale chartreuse crinolines from last night's Andrews Sisters sketch. And, of course, the three identical auburn wigs on styrofoam stands.

At a stop sign near the K-Mart in Saratoga, Ned pulled alongside a bronze Barracuda that was draped in pink toilet paper and spray-painted with this legend: JUST MARRIED – SHE GOT HIM TODAY – HE'LL GET HER TONIGHT.

A whoop went up from the back of the truck.

The bridegroom, resplendent in a powder blue tuxedo with matching ruffled shirt, cast a nervous glance in their direction, frowned and turned back to his bride. Michael saw the word 'fags' form on his lips.

Rolling the window down, he shouted across at the couple: 'Hey!' They were moving again now, but Ned kept the truck even with the car.

'Yeah?' said the bridegroom.

'Congratulations!' yelled Michael.

'Thanks!' shouted the bride, still holding tight to her husband's free arm.

'What's your song?'

'Huh?'

'Your *song*. What is it?'

The bride beamed. '"We've Only Just Begun".'

Michael hollered to the guys in the back of the truck. 'HIT IT, GIRLS!'

The Andrews Sisters were never lovelier.

Idol Chatter

Michael waited until the family was assembled for Mary Ann's birthday dinner before breaking the news.

Mary Ann was the most flabbergasted.

'Now wait just a minute!'

530

Michael held up his hand. 'Scout's honor, Babycakes. Ned invited me yesterday.'

'I'm not questioning that,' said Mary Ann, 'but, you mean _____ _____ is *gay*?'

'As the proverbial goose,' said Michael.

'Hell,' said Brian, sawing off a chunk of pot roast. 'Even I knew that. Remember that story about his gay wedding to _____ _____ back about . . . ?'

'Well, of course I *heard* that, but . . .' Mary Ann was almost sputtering; she hated it when her Cleveland naiveté popped up like an overnight zit. 'Well, I always thought it was just some sort of . . . bad joke.'

'It *was* a bad joke,' said Michael. 'A couple of tired queens in Hermosa Beach or some place sent out party invitations announcing a mock wedding and . . . the rumor just got started. _____ and _____ were never even lovers. Just friends. They couldn't be seen in public together after that. It would only confirm the rumor.'

'Do you always refer to him by his first name?' teased Mary Ann.

Michael grinned. 'Just practicing.'

Mrs Madrigal heaped more carrots onto Michael's plate. 'That's a rather sad story, isn't it?'

Michael nodded. 'It must've been a bitch, staying closeted all these years.'

'Yeah,' said Brian, his mouth full of pot roast, 'but two mil a movie must soften the blow.'

Mary Ann giggled. 'So to speak.'

Michael's eyes widened in pseudo-horror. 'Well, look who's getting smutty in her senior years.' Mary Ann stuck her tongue out daintily.

Mrs Madrigal stirred her coffee as she stared off into space. '_____ _____,' she murmured, intoning the matinee idol's name as if it were one of Mona's mantras. 'Well, it makes perfect sense. He's always been a stunning creature. Remember when he took off his shirt in _____?' The landlady heaved a prolonged sigh. 'I was quite taken with him when I was a young . . . whatever.'

Mrs Madrigal's tenants laughed at this playful reference to her veiled past. Then Michael lifted his glass: 'Well, here's to our birthday girl . . . who's about to become an *old* whatever like the rest of us.'

Mary Ann leaned over and kissed him on the cheek. 'Prick,' she whispered.

Then she turned to her other side and kissed Brian lightly on the mouth.

Michael completed the circle by blowing a kiss to Brian.

Smiling contentedly, Mrs Madrigal watched the ritual like a doting match-maker, hands clasped under her chin. 'You know,' she said. 'You three are my favorite couple.'

After dinner, the landlady produced a Wedgwood plate of Barbara Stanwyck joints. Then came cake and ice cream and Mary Ann's presents: a bottle of 'Opium' from Brian, a cat-shaped deco pin from Michael, an antique teapot from Mrs Madrigal.

'And now,' announced the landlady, 'if you gentlemen will kindly excuse us, I would like to do a Tarot reading for Mary Ann.'

Mary Ann's eyes danced. 'I didn't know you knew how to do that!'

'I don't,' replied Mrs Madrigal, 'but I make up *wonderful* things.'

So Brian and Michael retired to the roof, where they watched the bay through the eyes of Miss Stanwyck.

'You know what?' said Brian.

'What?' said Michael.

'She's right. Mrs Madrigal, I mean. The three of us do so much stuff together that we're kinda like a couple.'

'Yeah. I guess so. That bother you?'

Brian thought for a moment. 'Nah. You're my friend, Michael. And she's your friend, and . . . hell, I don't know.'

Michael handed the joint back to Brian. 'Lots of people do things in threes here. Check out the audience the next time we go to a play.'

Brian laughed. 'Trisexuals. Isn't that what you called them?'

'For want of a better term.'

Brian laid his arm across Michael's shoulder. 'You know what's bugging me, Michael?'

Michael waited.

'It just bugs the hell out of me that I'll never be everything she needs.'

Michael smiled feebly. 'I know that one.'

'Yeah?'

'You betcha. I busted my butt trying to be everything to one person. Finally, I had to settle for being one thing to every person.'

'What's the one thing?'

Michael hesitated. 'Hell, I was hoping you could tell me.'

Brian laughed and squeezed his shoulder. 'You're crazy, man.'

'Maybe *that's* it.'

'I tell you what,' said Brian, looking directly at his friend. 'I love you, Michael. I love you like my brother.'

'No shit?'

'No shit.'

There was a moment, a very brief moment, when their eyes met with unembarrassed affection. Then Michael retrieved the joint and took a hit. 'Is your brother cute?' he asked.

Father Paddy

Having made up her mind to search the park for her missing wolf-hound, Prue Giroux spent the morning at Eddie Bauer choosing just the right safari jacket for the job. To her surprise, she encountered one of her Forum regulars in the camping supplies department.

'Father Paddy!'

Swinging sharply – so sharply, in fact, that his crucifix grazed Prue's chest – Father Paddy Starr turned to face his public, flashing the fluorescent grin that had endeared him to thousands of local late-night television viewers.

'Prue daaarrrllling!' He pecked her once on each cheek, then held her at arm's length as if to check the merchandise for damage. 'What on earth are you doing in this he-man, roughneck place?'

'I'm looking for a safari jacket. What about you, Father? They don't make cassocks in khaki, do they?'

Father Paddy shrieked, then sighed dramatically. 'And more's the pity, my child, more's the pity! Wouldn't that be divine? This tired old basic black . . . year in, year out. It's truly loathsome. I *long* for a new dress.'

Prue tittered appreciatively. She loved the cute way Father Paddy joked about his 'dress' and used the word 'divine' in the civilian sense. It made him seem accessible somehow. Not like a priest at all, more like a . . . spiritual decorator.

'Actually,' the cleric added breathlessly. 'I'm desperate for a good, no-nonsense picnic basket. I promised Frannie Halcyon I'd take her to Santa Barbara to see the Shroud of Turin.'

'Ah,' said Prue cheerily. 'Who's in that?'

Father Paddy seemed to ponder for a moment, then explained: 'It's not actually an opera, my child. It's a . . . well, a shroud. The cloth that Christ was buried in. At least, that's what they *think* it is. Quite fascinating, really, and all the rage in ecclesiastical circles.'

'How marvelous,' said Prue.

Father Paddy leaned closer, as if to disclose confidential information. 'Hotter than the Tut and Tiffany exhibits combined. You should write about it in your column.'

Prue retrieved her Elsa Peretti pen from her Bottega bag and made a brief notation in a tiny Florentine notebook. 'So,' she chirped when everything was in place again, 'I'd say you deserve a little vacation . . . after all that awful business with the . . . militants trying to sing at St. Ignatius.'

Father Paddy nodded grimly. 'The Gay Chorus. Yes. That was most unfortunate. Dreadful. The Archbishop, bless his heart, had his back against the wall. In a manner of speaking.'

Prue shook her head sympathetically. 'Some people just don't know where to stop, I'm afraid.'

Another nod, even graver.

'They can hire a hall,' Prue added.

'Of course they can. We're *liberals*, you and I. It isn't that we aren't in favor of . . . well, human rights and that sort of thing. We are. We *feel*. We care. We reach out and touch those in need of our caring. But a chorus of admitted homosexuals singing in a church? Well, *please* . . . I haven't lived this long not to know tacky when I see it!'

Prue's driver dropped her off at the conservatory in Golden Gate Park shortly before noon.

His instructions were to return in two hours.

If her efforts proved fruitless, she could mount the search from another corner of the park, systematically combing every acre of the terrain until the dog was found. Or not found. Prue was braced for the latter, but she knew she would never forgive herself if she didn't at least try.

She had lost Vuitton in the tree ferns, so that was where her search began, there amidst the lush and lacy extravagance of those otherworldly plants.

Momentarily moved by the beauty of her surroundings, she stopped and jotted a reminder in her notebook: 'If *W* calls, ask to be

534

shot in the tree ferns.' She expected to be included in the magazine's summer spread. And why be photographed at home, looking stiff and matronly like the rest, when they could shoot her here, framed in exotica, wild and free as a white-plumed cockatiel?

She set off along an asphalt path that wound through the tree ferns then dramatically ascended to a densely wooded ridge lined with eucalyptus trees.

'Vuitton,' she called. 'Vuitton.'

An aging hippie woman, dressed in Birkenstocks and a fringed poncho, passed Prue on the pathway and frowned at her.

But Prue was lost in the singlemindedness of her search.
'*Vuitton . . . Vuiiiiitton . . .*'

Chain Reaction

It was noon when Emma brought in the Mai Tai with the morning mail. Frannie Halcyon was still propped up in bed, her peach satin sleep mask askew across her forehead, like the goggles on an aviator who had died in a dogfight.

'Mornin', Miss Frannie.'

'Set it on the dresser, please, Emma dear.'

'Yes'm.'

'Miss Singleton didn't call back, did she?'

'No'm.'

'What about Miss Moonmeadow?'

Emma scowled. 'No'm.'

'You needn't look at me like that. I am fully aware of your feelings about Miss Moonmeadow.'

Emma fluffed her mistress' quilt almost violently. 'Mr Edgar would turn over in his grave if he knew you was seeing that witch woman.'

Frannie sighed wearily and removed the sleep mask. 'Emma, she is a *psychic*. Please don't call her a witch woman. It distresses me so.'

'She takin' yo' money. I know that.'

'She keeps me in touch . . .'

'Oh Lord, Miss Frannie . . .'

'She keeps me in touch with my only child, Emma, and I don't want to hear another word about it. Is that understood, Emma?'

Emma, pouted, unrepentant, then skulked to the window and jerked open the Roman shades. She kept her back turned to her mistress.

'Don't you see?' Frannie asked in a gentler tone. 'Miss DeDe was all I had left. Miss Moonmeadow gives me hope that . . . that Miss DeDe is still alive.'

Emma walked for the door, rigid as a poker. 'It was them kinda folks that killed her.'

The mail offered little in the way of refreshment: a bill from Magnin's, an invitation to Vita Keating's Italian Earthquake Relief concert, a thank-you note from that Giroux woman, and a chain letter from Dodie Rosekrans.

This is the Socialite Chain Letter. Break it and you invite risk to life, limb, and personal or inherited wealth. Chrissie Goulandris broke the chain, and a week later broke not one but two nails on the evening of Helene Rochas' Red Ball in Geneva. Ariel de Ravenel broke the chain, and broke a collarbone at Gstaad the same day. Betty Catroux broke the chain, and three weeks later her two-year-old Asti had to be quarantined in a tiny kennel in Managua for eight months without cohabitation privileges. DON'T LET THIS HAPPEN TO YOU!!!!
Mail six copies of this letter to friends whom you KNOW to be serious minded when it comes to fun. Add your name to the bottom of the list and place your return address on the envelope. In six weeks you will have 1,280 new addresses. Ideal for planning international get-togethers. P.S. Husbands who try to interfere with the chain will also be hit by bad luck. Paquita Paquin's husband threw her copy into the wastebasket and a week later his foundation lost its tax exempt status in Argentina. THE FORTUNE YOU SAVE MAY BE YOUR OWN!!!!

D.D. Ryan
Marina Cicogna
Delfina Ratazzi
Dominique Schlumberger de Menil
Nan Kempner
Paloma Picasso
Loulou Klossowski
Marina Schiano
Apollonia von Ravenstein

Countess Carimati de Carimate
C.Z. Guest
Douchka Cizmek
Betsy Bloomingdale
Nancy Reagan
Jerry Zipkin
Adolfo
Dodie Rosekrans

It was cute of Dodie to send the chain letter, but Frannie knew she was beyond the cheering-up stage. That list of names, furthermore, depressed the matriarch more than all her other tribulations combined.

This desolation took tangible shape when she watched the afternoon movie on television: Susan Hayward in *Back Street*. Even Mary Ann Singleton's perky mid-movie commentary on homemade refrigerator magnets failed to revive her sagging spirits.

She seemed like such a nice girl, that Mary Ann.

Couldn't she at least have called back?

Or had she simply deduced the reason for Frannie's call and chosen to ignore it?

Emma, of course, had been dead right. *Dead right*. An uncannily accurate choice of words. *DeDe was dead*. The first person to receive that news had been the last to accept it as the truth.

Now she accepted it.

DeDe was dead and Edgar was dead and Beauchamp was dead and Faust was dead and Frances Alicia Ligon Halcyon was utterly and inexorably alone in the world.

It was time to join her family.

Où est Vuitton?

It looked, to Prue, like a scene from a dinosaur movie.

She was standing on a U-shaped ridge, peering down into the dark green center of the U – a primeval lake-swamp ringed with tree ferns so large that she half expected a sixty-foot Gila monster to come lumbering into view.

Her Maud Frizons were killing her.

Still, she pressed on, following the path that led her deeper and deeper into the unpopulated regions of the park. 'Vuitton,' she called. 'Vuiiiiton.' If the wolfhound was there, she would know; he had never failed to respond to his name.

The swamp, she decided, was a bad idea. Most of the terrain around it was too open to be able to conceal her beloved dog. She chose instead a westerly route – at least, she *thought* it was west – and skirted the Paleolithic bowl until the landscape fanned out around her to form the rhododendron dell.

The flowers were almost gone. They lay against their dusty green-black foliage like a thousand cast-off corsages on the morning after the prom. Prue thought about that for a moment: *Like a thousand cast-off corsages on the morning after the prom.*

That was really good. She dug her little notebook from her purse and made another notation. She was getting so much better at this writing business.

The asphalt eventually petered out. The path became whatever route she could weave for herself through the mammoth rhododendrons. Some of them were as big as small carousels. Hmm. *The rhododendrons were as big as small carousels as I continued my relentless search for my beloved . . .*

The notebook came out again.

Then Prue plunged onward. 'Vuitton . . . Vuitton.' Her ankle straps were almost more than she could take now, but she tried not to think about them. What a foolish mistake. She would just have to leave out the Maud Frizons when she wrote the story.

One of the rhododendrons repeated itself. Or maybe there were two rhododendrons with the same arrangement of dead blossoms. Wasn't she still heading west? Had she veered off her course after taking the last note?

She looked for the sun. The sun would be west. She remembered that much from Camp Fire Girls. *I struggled to remember the training I had received as a Camp Fire Girl in Grass Valley.* Did they still have Camp Fire Girls? It made her sound awfully old, she realized.

Anyway, the sun wasn't even visible; a thick summer fog had already settled over the park.

It was all too hopeless for words.

Vuitton had been missing for well over two weeks now. Even if he had managed to remain in the park, where would he have lived all that time? What would he have eaten? Where would he be safe from dognappers . . . or average citizens showing kindness to a lost dog . . . *or Cambodians*?

If only she could find a clue, some tiny shred of evidence affirming Vuitton's presence in this wilderness. She needed more than determination now: she needed a *sign*.

And then she stepped in it.

She knew from experience how difficult it was to clean wolfhound poop off a pair of pumps. And *this* was wolfhound poop, pure and simple; this was Vuitton's poop. Her heart surged with joy.

Looking about her in the dell, she tried to whistle but failed. 'Vuitton,' she cried. 'Mommy's here, darling!'

She heard the rustle of dry leaves, subtle as a zephyr in the underbush. Twenty feet away a carousel of dead corsages quivered ominously, then parted. Something pale appeared. *Like a newborn chick pecking out of a painted shell.*

It was Vuitton!

'Vuitton, baby! Precious! Darling!'

But the wolfhound merely stood there, appraising her.

'Come on, sweetheart. Come to Mommy.'

The dog withdrew into the dying blossoms; the carousel slammed shut.

What on earth . . . ?

Prue pushed her way into the shrub, ducking under its huge black branches until she emerged in a kind of clearing, bounded on the opposite side by a tangle of ivy and eucalyptus trees. Cream-colored fur flickered in the shadows.

'Vuitton, for God's sake!'

The terrain dropped sharply. Vuitton was shimmying clumsily down a steep, sandy slope which ended in a cul-de-sac on an ivy-strangled ledge. There on the ledge stood a curious-looking shack.

And next to the shack stood a man.

He smiled up at the society columnist for *Western Gentry* magazine. 'Got time for coffee?' he asked.

Downers

Frannie Halcyon heaved a long sigh of surrender and reached for the pills on her bedside table.

They had been a birthday present, oddly enough, a sixtieth birthday present from Helena Parrish, the elegant proprietress of Pinus, a resort in the hills of Sonoma County where Frannie had spent several languorous weeks making a graceful passage into her senior years.

'They're Vitamin Q,' Helena had explained, 'and they're good for what ails you.'

Even now, Frannie managed a thin smile at the thought of her earlier innocence. Vitamin Q, indeed. They were Quaaludes, what the young people called 'downers'. She had taken maybe half-a-dozen of them during her days at Pinus, giving them up when she discovered they didn't mix well with Mai Tais.

Well, now it didn't matter.

She popped two of them into her mouth, washing them down with her Mai Tai. There were at least a dozen pills in the bottle, surely enough to put her out of her misery. She was about to swallow two more when she remembered an important detail.

'Emma!' she called.

She waited for the sound of the maid's footsteps.

Nothing.

'EMMA!'

Finally, there was a shuffling noise in the hallway. Emma appeared at the door, holding a dust mop. 'Yes'm?'

'Have you seen my rosary beads, dear?'

'No'm. Not lately.'

'I think they're in the desk in the library. Would you check for me please?'

'Yes'm.'

She was gone for several minutes, long enough for the matriarch to down two more Quaaludes and tidy up the bedclothes. Taking the beads from the old black woman, Frannie felt a great sadness sweep over her. She fought back the tears. 'What would I do without you, Emma?'

And what would Emma do without her?

It was too late for that now, too late for turning back. Emma was handsomely provided for in Frannie's will. That would just have to do. Still . . .

'You feelin' poorly, Miss Frannie?'

Frannie refused to meet her companion's eyes. The rosary beads had betrayed her. No one knew better than Emma that Frannie's commitment to the church was minimal. 'I'm fine, dear. Really. I just want to say a little prayer for Miss DeDe.'

Emma didn't budge. 'You sure?'

'Yes, dear. Now leave me alone for a while, will you?'

Emma looked around the room, as if searching for evidence to refute the matriarch's statement. (The Quaaludes were hidden under Frannie's pillow.) Then the maid sighed, shook her head, and trudged out of the room.

As Frannie reached for the pills, the phone rang.

She thought for a moment. If she didn't answer it, Emma would take the call and return to the bedroom with the message. So she reached for the phone, hoping to eliminate this final obstacle to her departure.

'Hello.' Her voice sounded sluggish to her. She felt as if she were speaking in a dream.

'Who is this, please?' asked the voice on the other end.

'This is . . . who is *this*?'

'Mother? Oh God, Mother!'

'Wha . . . ?'

'It's DeDe, Mother! Thank God I got . . .'

'DeDe?' It *was* a dream . . . or a hallucination . . . or a wicked prank perpetuated by one of those sick minds that . . . but that voice, *that voice*. 'DeDe, baby . . . is it you?'

She heard loud sobs on the other end. 'Oh Mother, I'm sorry! Please forgive me! I'm safe! The children are safe! We're O.K., understand? We're coming home just as soon as we can!'

Now Frannie had begun to wail, so loudly in fact that Emma rushed into the room.

'Miss Frannie, what on earth . . . ?'

'It's Miss DeDe, Emma! Our baby's coming home. Precious baby's coming home! DeDe . . . *DeDe, are you there?*'

'I'm here, Mother.'

'Thank God! But *where*, darling?'

'Uh . . . Arkansas.'

'*Arkansas?* What on earth are you doing there?'

541

'They're holding me here. At Fort Chaffee. Can you mail me a credit card or something?'

'*Who's* holding you? Not . . . oh God, not those Jonestown people?'

'No, Mother. The government. The American government. I'm at the settlement camp for gay Cuban refugees.'

'*What?*'

'It's a long story, Mother.'

'Well, tell them to let you out, for heaven's sake! Tell them who you are! Tell them there's been a mistake, DeDe!'

A long pause, and then:

'You don't understand, Mother. I *am* a gay Cuban refugee.'

The Breastworks

Michael had seen it a dozen times, but the sign on the pathway to Lands End never failed to give him a delicious shudder: CAUTION – CLIFF AND SURF AREA EXTREMELY DANGEROUS – *People have been swept from the rocks and drowned.*

'I love that thing,' he told Mary Ann and Brian as the trio passed the signpost. 'It's so . . . Daphne Du Maurier. "People have been swept from the rocks and drowned." It's almost lyrical. Where else but here could you find a government sign painter with poetry in his soul?'

Mary Ann studied the sign for a moment, then continued the trek down the railroad tie stairs. 'I don't know why,' she said, 'but I agree with you.'

'So do I,' added Brian, 'and I'm not as loaded as you guys.'

'It's because we're all Jeanettes,' explained Michael. 'Jeanettes always notice that sort of thing.'

Mary Ann shot him a wary glance. 'I'm afraid to ask.'

Michael grinned. 'Just a new theory of mine. I've come to the conclusion that there are really only two types of people in San Francisco, regardless of race, creed, color or . . . what's the other one?'

'Sexual orientation,' said Brian.

'Thank you,' said Michael.

Mary Ann rolled her eyes. 'So what are they?'

'Jeanettes,' answered Michael, 'and Tonys. Jeanettes are people who think that the city's theme song is "San Francisco" as sung by Jeanette MacDonald. Tonys think it's Tony Bennett singing "I Left

My Heart in San Francisco." Everyone falls into one camp or another . . . in a manner of speaking.'

Brian's brow wrinkled in thought. 'That makes sense, but it's always subject to change. Mary Ann used to be a Tony, for instance. Some people don't know . . .'

'I was *never* a Tony.' Mary Ann was quietly indignant.

'Sure you were,' said Brian breezily. 'I remember. You had a Pet Rock, for God's sake.'

'Brian, that was Connie Bradshaw and you know it.'

'Well, it's the same thing. You lived with her. The Pet Rock was on your premises.'

Mary Ann sought Michael's support. '*He's* the one who picked her up in a laundromat, and I get the lecture on taste.' She turned back to Brian. 'If I remember correctly, you were still calling women "chicks" when I met you.'

'You remember correctly,' said Brian.

'Well?'

Brian shrugged. 'Women still *were* chicks when you met me.'

'Which reminds me,' said Mary Ann, ignoring his deliberate piggery. 'Would you watch it with the naked ladies this time?'

'Hey,' Brian protested. 'All I did was *talk* to them. How was I supposed to know they were dykes?'

'You weren't,' said Mary Ann.

'Hell,' added Brian. 'It all evens out, anyway. Most of the guys down there must think I'm gay.'

Michael smiled. 'Or wish you were.'

For San Francisco, it was a scorcher, a day when half the population called in sick to the other half. Some of them came here to recover, here to a secret, sun-drenched cove where they stripped off their clothes and offered up their cocoa-buttered bodies to The Goddess.

The beach would have been an odd sight from the air. It was checkerboarded with dozens of tiny stone forts, makeshift windbreaks accommodating anywhere from two to ten sun-worshipers in varying stages of undress.

Michael called it The Breastworks.

Today, the three of them had a fort all to themselves. Mary Ann and Brian sunbathed bare-chested but with bottoms; Michael took off everything, having finally decided that tan lines went out with The Seventies.

The celebrants lay in silence for several minutes. Mary Ann was the first to speak.

'Maybe this would do.'

'That's putting it mildly,' said Brian.

'I mean, as a story. I need a really hot feature idea if I'm ever gonna get liberated from *Bargain Matinee*.'

'You need more than that,' said Brian.

'Besides,' added Michael, 'nude beaches are old stuff. They've been done to death.'

'You're right,' sighed Mary Ann. 'What about S & M?'

'Not right now,' said Brian. 'I just put the Coppertone on.'

'That's even more tired,' said Michael. 'Whenever these local stations see their ratings flagging they do another exposé on S & M. It's like earthquake stories or Zodiac letters. Anything to keep the public spooked.'

'The problem,' remarked Mary Ann, 'is that you can't really plan it. The really big San Francisco stories just drop out of nowhere without warning.'

'Like Guyana,' added Brian.

'Or Burke and those cannibals at Grace Cathedral.' This interjection was Michael's, and he regretted it instantly. Mary Ann's old boyfriend, Burke Andrew, was now an associate editor at *New York* magazine. Brian appeared to be jealous of the long-dead relationship, so Mary Ann and Michael usually avoided mentioning it in his presence.

Mary Ann changed the subject by interrogating Michael. 'So you're off to ＿＿＿'s house on Memorial Day weekend?'

Michael nodded. 'I'll never be tan enough.'

'Maybe he'll come out,' mused Mary Ann, 'and offer me an exclusive on the story.'

'Uh-huh,' said Michael. 'And maybe the sky will fall.'

Luke

The man on the ledge was still smiling up at Prue, waiting for an answer to his question.

'Uh . . . what?' she mumbled. Her right hand, meanwhile, burrowed deep into her bag until it closed around her tiny Tiffany rape whistle. If he made so much as a move, she would . . .

'I said . . . you got time for coffee?'

He gestured behind him towards the shack, a makeshift wooden structure straight out of Zane Grey. A thin curl of smoke rose from a rusty stovepipe that protruded from the building like an exclamation point.

There was coffee inside?

Prue cleared her throat. 'That dog is mine,' she said evenly. 'The one that ran into your . . . into that place.' Her face was crimson now; her throat was dry as chalk.

The man continued to smile, hands thrust deep into the pockets of his baggy woolen trousers. 'That so?' he replied, using a tone that seemed to taunt more than inquire. 'S'nice dog, ol' Whitey.'

Whitey? Had this derelict tried to stake a claim on Vuitton by giving him a new name? His proper name and owner were clearly engraved on his dog tags. Even his collar – a Christmas present from Father Paddy Starr – had been crafted out of Louis Vuitton vinyl.

'I was here several weeks ago,' Prue exclaimed feebly. 'He ran away from me down in the tree ferns. I'm so relieved that he's safe.'

The man nodded, still smiling.

'If you've been . . . taking care of him,' Prue continued, 'I'll be happy to reimburse you for any expenses you might have incurred.'

The man laughed. 'But no coffee, huh?'

Prue's hand tightened on the whistle. 'Really, I'm . . . that's awfully kind . . . but, um . . . my driver . . . that is, I have a friend waiting for me down at the conservatory. Thank you, though. That's very nice.'

The man shrugged, then turned and entered the shack, closing the door behind him.

Prue waited.

And waited.

This was really *too* annoying. What did he think he was doing, anyway? It would be easy enough to prove ownership of the dog, to have this tramp arrested for holding Vuitton against his will.

Prue considered her options: She could walk back to the conservatory and wait for her driver to return; he was imposing enough to intimidate this man into releasing Vuitton. Or, of course, she could simply call the police.

On the other hand, why compound the nuisance by official intervention? Surely this was something she could handle on her own.

Clutching at shrubbery for support, she made her way down the sandy slope until she reached the ledge where the shack stood. It was amazing really, this secret cul-de-sac, virtually invisible to the casual passerby, yet still within hearing distance of the traffic down below on Kennedy Drive.

Prue strode purposefully towards the door of the shack – so purposefully, in fact, that she snagged a heel on a root and tumbled to the ground, scattering the contents of her purse. Mortified, she scooped up her belongings as quickly as possible and staggered to her feet.

She rapped on the door.

The first thing she heard was Vuitton's off-key bark. Then came the sound of wood scraping wood as a homemade latch was undone.

The door swung open, revealing the same smiling face, a face made almost handsome by high cheekbones, a strong jawline and unusual amber-colored skin. The stranger's longish dark hair was combed neatly into place. (Had it been before?) He appeared to be in his late forties.

'That's better,' he said.

Prue tried to placate him. 'I'm sorry if I offended you in some way. I've been so anxious about my dog. I'm sure you understand.'

Vuitton poked his long, pale muzzle through the crack in the door. Prue reached down to stroke him. 'Baby,' she cooed. 'It's O.K., Mommy's here.'

'You got proof?' asked the man.

'Look at him,' said Prue. 'He knows me. Don't you, baby? His name is Vuitton. It's on the collar. For that matter, *my* name is on the collar.'

'What's your name?'

'Giroux. Prue Giroux.'

The man extended his hand. 'Mine's Luke. Come on in.'

Inside

When Prue entered the shack, her mind raced back to Grass Valley . . . and to the tree house her brother Ben had built on the hill behind the barn.

Ben's tree house had been a holy place, a monk's cell for a thirteen-year-old that was incontestably off limits to his little sister and her friends.

One day, however, when Ben was at the picture show, Prudy Sue had climbed into the forbidden aerie and perused, with pounding heart, the secret icons of her brother's adolescence: dirty dime novels, joy buzzers, a Lucky Strikes magazine ad featuring Maureen O'Hara.

Today, forty years later, Prue couldn't help remembering the surprising *order* of Ben's lair. There had been something almost touching about the neat rows of Tom Swift books, the hand-sewn burlap curtains on the tiny windows, the quartz rocks displayed on orange crates as if they were diamonds in a vault . . .

'I wasn't expecting company,' said Luke. 'You'll have to excuse this.'

'This' was a single room, about six-by-ten-feet, furnished with wooden packing crates, an Army surplus cot, and a large chunk of foam rubber which appeared to function as a couch. A rock-lined pit in the packed earth floor was filled with graying embers. On the grate above the fire sat a blue enamel coffee pot.

The man picked up the pot and poured coffee into a styrofoam cup. 'You take cream? I only have the fake stuff, I'm afraid.'

'Uh . . . what? . . . oh, no thank you.' Prue was still absorbing the room. How long had he been here, anyway? Did the park people know about this?

The man read her mind and winked. 'You'll get used to it,' he said. 'Sweet 'n Low?'

'Yes, please.'

He cracked open the pink packet like an egg, shook it into the coffee and handed her the cup. 'I thought you might like to see where your dog's been living, that's all.'

Vuitton, in fact, having greeted his mistress at the door, had returned to a bed of rags in a corner near the fire. He looked up and wagged his tail at her appeasingly, apologizing perhaps for such an effortless abandonment of his Nob Hill lifestyle.

Prue blew on her coffee, then looked about her. 'This is . . . just fascinating,' she said. She meant it, too.

The man chuckled. 'Every kid loves a playhouse,' he said.

Then he *is* like Ben, thought Prue.

A further examination of the room revealed additional touches of boyish whimsy. Ball fringe over the bed, forming a faux-canopy. A can of sharpened pencils on a shelf above the 'sofa'. A soot-streaked map of the city tacked to the wall above the fire.

Over the doorway hung a plywood plaque, its lettering laboriously crafted in bent twigs:

Prue smiled when she read it. 'That's nice,' she said.

'Santayana,' replied the man. '*Life of Reason.*'

'Excuse me?'

The man seemed to study her for a moment, then said quietly: 'Why don't you take your dog now?'

'Oh . . . of course. I didn't mean to keep you.'

The man went to the bed of rags and roused the wolfhound. 'C'mon, Whitey. Time to go, boy.' Vuitton rose awkwardly to his feet and licked the man's hand excitedly. 'He thinks we're going exploring,' explained his keeper. 'I made a leash for him, if you want it.'

He opened a box next to Vuitton's bed. It contained canned dog food, a battered grooming brush, and a length of rope with a handmade leather tag reading WHITEY. The top of the box said WHITEY in bent twigs.

Earlier, Prue had felt real resentment about his alien name; now, for some reason, she thought she might cry.

She fumbled in her bag. 'Please . . . I insist on reimbursing you for your . . .'

'No,' said the man sharply. Then, in a softer tone: 'The pleasure was mine.'

'Well . . .' She looked about her, suddenly at a loss for words. The man clipped the rope on Vuitton's collar and handed it to Prue.

'Thank you,' she said as earnestly as possible. 'Thank you so much . . . Luke, isn't it?'

The man nodded. 'If you're ever back in these parts, I wouldn't mind a visit from him.'

'Of course, of course . . .' She had nothing further to say as she led Vuitton away from the shack and up the steep, sandy slope. The wolfhound went willingly, barking his goodbye when they reached the top of the rise.

But the door of the shack was closed again.

Off to Hollywood

Ned Lockwood's pickup was parked on Leavenworth when Mary Ann came down the rickety wooden stairway from Barbary Lane. He offered her a jaunty salute, cupping his huge hand against his forehead. His bald pate was tanned the color of saddle leather.

'He'll be down in a minute,' she said. 'He's trying to choose between fifteen different shades of Lacostes.'

Ned grinned and threw up his hands, bringing them to rest on the steering wheel. 'So where are you off to?'

Mary Ann mugged. 'Work. Not all of us get to spend the weekend with a movie star.' She held up a large Hefty Bag. 'Care for a darling bow-wow?'

Ned looked into the bag. 'Stuffed animals? What for?'

'My show. What else?'

'They're some sort of bargain, huh?'

'Factory seconds. God, it's so depressing, Ned. Get me out of here, will you? Abduct me or something. Hasn't _____ got an extra cabana he could hide me in?'

Ned smiled. 'I'm afraid it's one of his all-boy weekends.'

'How dumb,' said Mary Ann.

'I think so, too. But he's sort of an old-world fag.'

'Big deal. Couldn't I be an old-world fag hag?'

Ned threw back his head and laughed. 'I wish he could be that comfortable about it.'

Mary Ann managed a smile herself. 'So you're leaving me to my misery, huh?'

'You're a star,' said Ned. 'Stars aren't supposed to be miserable.'

'Who's a star?' A cheap ploy to fish for praise, but right now she'd take anything she could get.

The nurseryman shrugged. 'My aunt in the East Bay says you're a star. She watches your show all the time.'

'Harlequin glasses, right?'

Ned grinned.

'Not to mention Harlequin *books*. And a bedroom full of yarn poodles that she made on her doodle-loom. Am I right?'

'Actually,' said Ned, 'she makes braided rugs out of old neckties.'

549

'Right,' nodded Mary Ann.

Michael appeared at the top of the stairway, decked out in an apricot Polo shirt, white linen trousers and emerald green Topsiders. 'Get him,' said Ned. 'Is that L.A. or what?'

Michael presented himself to Mary Ann for inspection.

'Very nice,' she remarked, 'but you'll be pitted out by the time you reach the pea soup place.'

'Then I'll *change* at the pea soup place.' He pecked her on the mouth and sprang into the truck. 'If I'm not back in three days, send in the Mounties.'

'Make him wear a bathing suit,' Mary Ann instructed Ned.

'That's a tall order,' said the nurseryman.

'I know,' replied Mary Ann. 'He almost burned his butt off last week at Lands End.'

As usual, there wasn't a legal parking space within five blocks of the station. She finally settled on a commercial zone in an alley off Van Ness, leaving an outdated press pass on the dashboard of the car.

She hurried past the security guard, eating Cheetos at the front desk, and boarded the elevator where she stabbed the button for the third floor.

She checked her Casio. Two-thirty-eight. God, she was pushing it these days. Time was when she would show up two hours early for the three o'clock broadcast. Time was she had actually found this crap *exciting*.

Bambi Kanetaka was leaving the dressing room when Mary Ann arrived.

'Hi,' said Mary Ann. 'Why so early?'

'We're shooting on location,' the anchorperson replied breathlessly. 'Larry's found some woman who used to date the Trailside Killer. What's in the bag?'

It was almost uncanny, Mary Ann decided, how Bambi could find her way straight to the soft spot. 'Just some seconds,' she muttered.

'Awww,' said Bambi, peeking into the bag. 'They're *precious*. Honestly, you get to do the most fun things, Mary Ann. I get so tired of all the . . .' She sighed world-wearily. 'You know, the heavy stuff.'

The makeup man, who had just returned from his grandmother's funeral in Portland, was done up in gold chains and black Spandex – his idea of mourning garb.

'. . . and so I went to the funeral home and I *insisted* . . . look up, would you, hon . . . good . . . I insisted that they open the casket . . . a little to the left now . . . so they opened it for me, and *what* do you think they had on Grandma's lips? TITTY PINK! I mean, *really* . . . head up, hon . . . so I said just let me handle this because *my* grandma is getting nothing less than Cocksucker Red when they put her in the ground. . . .'

Denny spied Mary Ann and stuck his head through the doorway. 'There you are.'

She hated 'There you are' when it meant 'Where have you been?'

'That woman's on the line again,' said the associate producer.

'What woman?'

'The drunk. She spelled her name this time. It's *Halcyon*, not Harrison.'

'God,' said Mary Ann.

'Ring a bell?'

'I think I used to work for her husband.' She checked the wall clock: six minutes to air time. 'Tell her I'll call her back after the intro.'

We Must Have Lunch

Mary Ann delivered her spiel on stuffed animals in less than three minutes, which meant that she had to spend the same amount of time getting gushy about *Say One for Me*.

It wasn't easy. She had never been able to buy Bing Crosby as a priest. Or Rosalind Russell as a Mother Superior. Or Helen Reddy as a nun. Hollywood had some pretty funny ideas about what Catholics were supposed to look like.

'Mary Ann, you were too yummy for words. I watched you on the monitor.'

It was Father Paddy Starr, San Francisco's idea of a priest, hell-bent for Studio B as Mary Ann beat a hasty retreat.

'Thanks, Father. Break a leg.' It sounded weird, saying that to a priest, but this one was in show business, after all. Father Paddy's late-night show, *Honest to God*, was taped every afternoon following Mary Ann's show.

*

551

Back at her cubbyhole, she checked to see if Denny had left a number for Mrs Halcyon. He hadn't, of course, but she finally got it out of Directory Assistance after two overlapping recorded voices – one male, one female – chastised her for doing so.

She dialed the number.

'Halycon Hill.'

Mary Ann recognized the voice from her days at Halcyon Communications when she had spent a fair amount of time relaying messages between Edgar Halcyon and his wife. 'Emma?'

'Yes'm?'

'This is Mary Ann Singleton. Remember me?'

''Course I remember you! It's mighty good to hear you, *mighty* good! Oh Lord, I could fairly bust, Mary Ann. Jesus looks out for his children, if we only just . . .' There was a scuffling noise in the background. 'Give me that!' snapped a voice that Mary Ann recognized as Frannie Halcyon's.

'Mary Ann?' Now the voice had softened to a matronly purr.

'Yes, Mrs Halcyon. What a nice surprise.'

'Well . . . I'm just a *big* fan of yours.'

'How sweet.'

'I am. Truly. You're a very talented young lady.'

'That's so nice. Thank you so much.'

A long pause, and then: 'I . . . uh . . . I called because I hoped you'd be able to have lunch with us . . . with me, that is, on Sunday. The weather's just lovely down here now and the pool is . . . well, you could bring your bathing suit if you like and . . .'

'I'd be delighted, Mrs Halcyon.' Mary Ann almost giggled. Michael's getaway to L.A. had made her yearn for escape, and she and Brian hadn't had a good, cheap mini-vacation in a long time. This was practically a Godsend. 'Would it be O.K. if I brought a friend?'

'Oh . . . I . . . actually, I'd rather you didn't, Mary Ann.'

'Of course . . .'

'I'm really not prepared to entertain more than one.'

'Fine. I understand.' She didn't, actually, but now her curiosity was aroused.

'Just a little . . . girl talk. You and I have got so much to catch up on.'

Mary Ann was thrown. She and Frannie Halcyon had absolutely *nothing* to catch up on. Why was this sweet, but rummy, society dowager talking to her like an equal?

Well, she thought, the poor woman lost a daughter in Guyana. That was reason enough to be a little indulgent. Besides, she had a pool. That was an offer no San Franciscan could refuse.

'What time shall I be there?' asked Mary Ann.

Larry and Bambi were returning to the station when Mary Ann left the building. It was all they could do to keep their hands off one another, she observed.

'Great tie,' said Mary Ann, breezing past them in the lobby. He was wearing the one with the Porsche emblem in a repetitive pattern.

'Hey,' said Larry, 'thanks.'

The only fun thing about assholes, Mary Ann decided, was that they almost never noticed when you were calling them assholes. 'How was the Trailside Killer's girlfriend?' she asked Bambi.

'Shaken,' said the anchorperson.

'Mmm. I'd imagine.'

Ever so subtly, Larry steered Bambi towards the elevator. 'Stay out of this business,' he told Mary Ann. 'It ain't a bit pretty.'

'Mmm.'

'Really,' he added. 'You're better off out of it.'

She cursed him all the way back to Barbary Lane.

Tinseltown

Ned Lockwood checked the clock on the dashboard as his pickup rattled through the corridor of palms flanking Hollywood High.

'Ten-twenty. We did O.K. Hail to thee, Alma Mater.'

'You went to Hollywood High?' asked Michael.

Ned's jaw squared off in a grin. 'Didn't everybody?'

'Then you were *trained* to live with a movie star. It didn't come natural to you.'

'I suppose you could say that,' laughed Ned.

Michael shook his head in wonderment. 'Hollywood High,' he murmured, as the pale building slid by in the darkness. 'I always wanted to go to school with Alan Ladd's son when I was a little boy.'

'Why?'

Michael shrugged. 'The quickest way to Alan Ladd, I guess. I had the biggest crush on him.'

553

Ned laughed. 'When you were *how* old?'

'Eight,' said Michael defensively. 'But a kid can dream.'

'Horny little bugger.'

'Well,' retorted Michael, 'if I remember correctly, you had some sort of thing for Roy Rogers, didn't you?'

'I was at least ten,' said Ned.

Michael laughed and looked out the window again. There weren't many libidos that hadn't been stirred, one way or another, by the kingdom which stretched out luxuriantly before him.

Like a lot of his friends, he made a ritual of bad-mouthing Los Angeles behind her back – her tacky sprawl, her clotted freeways, her wretched refuse yearning to breathe free. . . .

But at times like this, on nights like this, when everyone in town seemed to own a convertible and the warm, thick jasmine-scented air made itself felt like a hand creeping up his thigh, Michael could abandon the obvious and believe again.

'It's amazing,' he said. 'Every time I come here I feel like Lucy and Ricky hitting the town. This place must get more second chances than any place on earth.'

Suddenly, Ned swerved the truck, narrowly missing a bottle blond teenager on a skateboard. His 69 football jersey had been hacked off just below his nipples to reveal a foot of tanned midriff. Passing him, Ned exhaled with relief: 'Nobody *walks* the streets anymore!'

Michael looked back to see the kid leaning into a silver Mercedes parked at the curb in front of the Famous Amos chocolate chip cookie headquarters. 'Bingo,' he said. 'He's got one.'

'A star is born,' said Ned.

The truck turned off Sunset and climbed into Beverly Hills, a land of shadowy lawns and deathly silence.

The streets grew steeper and narrower. Most of them appeared to be named Something-crest, though it was next to impossible to tell where one left off and another began. Michael found it unimaginable that anyone who lived in this neighborhood could find his way home at night.

'Will he be there when we get there?' he asked Ned. 'I must look like shit.'

Ned reached over and squeezed his knee. 'There's a roach in the ashtray. Why don't you smoke it?'

'If you think that'll relax me, you're crazy. I'll meet him and run screaming into the night.'

'He may not be back from Palm Springs yet. Don't sweat it.'

Michael looked out the window. The lights of the city were spread out beneath them like computer circuitry. 'If he's not there,' he asked, 'who'll let us in?'

'The houseman, probably.'

'Is he the whole staff?'

Ned shook his head. 'There's a cook, most of the time. And a secretary and a gardener. Probably just the houseman tonight, though.'

Michael tried to picture such an existence, falling silent for a moment. 'You know what?' he said at last.

'What?'

'My mother thought _____ _____ was the hottest thing going. She'd shit a brick if she knew I was doing this.'

Ned turned and smiled at him. 'Take careful notes, then.'

'Right . . . how big was his dick again?'

The nurseryman chuckled. 'Big enough to make some people suspicious about his Oscar nomination.'

'Bigger than a breadbox?' Michael laughed nervously at his own bad joke, then leaned over and kissed Ned on the neck, 'I can't believe this is happening. Thanks, pal.'

Ned shrugged it off. 'I think you'll both enjoy each other. He's a real nice guy.' He pulled the truck off the road, stopping in front of a huge metal gate. Then he pushed a button on a squawk box partially concealed in the bushes.

'Yes?' came a voice.

'It's Ned.'

'Lions and tigers and bears,' said Michael.

'That was the houseman. Relax.'

There was nothing much to see from this vantage point. Just a bougainvillea-covered wall and an archway, apparently leading into a courtyard. 'Ned?'

'Yeah, Bubba?'

'This isn't like a date, is it?'

'Why?'

'I don't know. Suddenly I feel like a mail-order bride or something.'

'Just take it easy, Michael. There are no expectations, if that's what you mean.' Ned turned and grinned slyly at his friend. 'Not on *his* part, at least.'

555

Prayers for the People

Back in the city, Father Paddy Starr was discussing the state of his flock over a late supper at L'Etoile. 'Poor Bitsy,' he sighed, nibbling on an asparagus tip, 'I'm afraid she needs our prayers again.'

Prue knew there was only one Bitsy: Bitsy Liggett, Society Kleptomaniac. Her infamy had been an embarrassment to the social set for almost a decade now.

'Oh dear,' said Prue, trying to sound prayerful in spite of the fact that she herself had lost a Lalique vase, several crystal dogs and an antique tortoise shell brush set to the pathological compulsion of the woman being prayed for.

'The problem is,' the cleric lamented, 'you can't *not* invite her, can you? It wouldn't do. The Liggetts are good stock. Bitsy's a charming woman. You just have to be ready for her, that's all.'

'Who wasn't ready for her this time?'

The priest's mouth curled slightly. 'Vita.'

'No!'

'Bitsy's on her Italian Earthquake board. When she left Vita's house after the meeting yesterday, a Fabergé box fell out of her pantyhose.'

'No!'

'Right there in the foyer. Could you die?'

Prue pressed both hands against her mouth and giggled.

'Could you die?' repeated Father Paddy, arching an eyebrow for maximum comic effect. Then, suddenly, the lines of his face turned down, as if he were made of wax and melting. 'Really, though, it's quite dreadful. It's a disease, like alcoholism. She needs our prayers, Prudy Sue.'

Then he told her three more people who needed their prayers.

Prue got to *her* news over dessert.

'I've been meaning to tell you,' she said. 'I found Vuitton.'

'Ah.' Father Paddy reached across the table and fondled her hand. 'I'm so happy, my child! Where was he? The poor thing must have been famished!'

Prue shook her head. 'That's the amazing part. He was living with this man in the park.'

'A park official, you mean?'

'No. A man in a funny little shack. Up on the ridge above the tree ferns. He had a bed and a fireplace and everything. Vuitton seemed to adore him, so I couldn't really get upset about it. Him keeping Vuitton, I mean.'

'He didn't call you?'

'No. I found him. Or rather, I found Vuitton and Vuitton led me to him. He seemed a little sad when I took Vuitton away. He'd made a leash for him, and he had a grooming brush and everything.'

Father Paddy poured cream on his raspberries. 'How endearing.'

'It was. I was truly *touched*, Father. He told me to bring Vuitton for a visit sometime. I think I may do it.'

The priest's smile hovered, but his brow furrowed. 'Well, I don't know about *that*, Prudy Sue.'

'Why?'

'Well, you really have no way of knowing who he . . .'

'I'm trusting my instincts, Father. This man is a gentle spirit. Life hasn't treated him well, but he's still smiling back at it. He even has a quote from one of the saints on his wall.'

'Really,' smiled Father Paddy, 'who?' Now they were back on *his* turf again.

Prue thought for a moment. 'Santa somebody. I forget. It's something about remembering the past. He made it out of twigs.' She took a bite of her trifle. 'Besides, characters like him are a San Francisco tradition. Like Emperor Norton, and . . . remember Olin Cobb, that man who built the little lean-to on Telegraph Hill?'

Father Paddy grinned at her sideways. 'You're going to write about this, aren't you?'

'Maybe,' said Prue coyly.

'Uh-huh.'

'Anyway, I *have* to go back at least one more time.'

'Now, Prue . . .'

'I left my rape whistle there.'

'Oh, *please*.'

'It's from Tiffany's,' explained the columnist.

The priest corrected her. 'Tiffany, darling. No apostrophe *s*.'

'Tiffany,' repeated Prue. 'Reg gave it to me. I'm sort of sentimental

557

about it. I dropped my purse on the ridge. The whistle must've fallen out. Don't look at me like that, Father.'

The priest simply shook his head, a gently chastising smile on his lips.

'You're so sweet,' said Prue, picking up the check. 'It's nice having somebody worry about me.'

The Castle

The silence was shattered by the sound of yapping dogs. They seemed a motley group, judging by their barks – young and old, big and small. Michael smiled, remembering a hot summer night in Palm Springs when he and Ned had eaten mushrooms and tried to climb Liberace's fence.

'Oh no,' he whispered, 'does *he* have attack poodles, too?'

Ned chuckled, his teeth flashing like foxfire in the darkness. 'These aren't guard dogs. These are family.'

The big neo-Spanish door swung open. The houseman, a diminutive, jockey-like man in his mid sixties, held the door ajar with one arm and fended off the dogs with the other. 'Hurry,' he said, 'before one of these retards makes a run for it.'

Ned led the way, with Michael heavy on his heels. The dogs – an ancient, rheumy-eyed shepherd; a pair of hysterical Irish setters; a squat, three-legged mongrel – cavorted deliriously around the feet of the man who had once shared the house with them.

Ned knelt in their midst and greeted them individually. 'Honey, ol' Honey, how ya doin', girl? Yeah, Lance . . . *good* Lance! Heeey, Guinevere . . .'

Michael was impressed. It was one thing to know _____ _____. It was quite another to be on a first name basis with his dogs.

Ned cuddled the three-legged runt in his lap. 'How's this one been doing?'

The houseman rolled his eyes. 'He got out last week. The little pissant made it all the way down to Schuyler Road. Lucy found him, of all people. Called _____. He was practically in mourning by then, wouldn't eat, wouldn't take calls . . . well, you know.'

Still kneeling, Ned held the dog up for Michael's inspection. 'Noble beast. Named after yours truly.'

Michael didn't get it at first. He was still wondering if it had been *the* Lucy who'd found the dog. 'Uh . . . you mean his name is Ned?'

The mutt yipped asthmatically, confirming the claim. Ned let him down and stood up. 'We go back a long ways, him and me. Guido, this is my friend, Michael Tolliver.'

Michael shook hands with the houseman, who offered a half-smile, then turned back to Ned. 'He's not back till tomorrow. You've got the place to yourself tonight. I left the heat on in the Jacuzzi.'

Michael breathed a secret sigh of relief. At least there would be time to collect himself.

Guido led them down a tiled walkway under an arbor that framed the courtyard. Fuchsia blossoms the color of bruises bumped against their heads as they walked. Across the courtyard, floating above the rectilinear lights of Los Angeles, a swimming pool, gigantic and glowing, provided the only illumination. It might have been a landing strip for UFO's.

Guido opened another door – the *real* front door, Michael presumed. He caught a fleeting impression of oversized Spanish furniture, suits of armor, crimson carpets (Early Butch, Ned once had dubbed it) as they climbed the grand staircase to the second floor.

'I put you both in the trophy room tonight,' said Guido drily, 'if that's all right.'

'Fine,' said Ned.

'The red room's a mess. Two kids from Laguna stayed over last night. Lube on the sheets, poppers on the carpet. Honestly.'

Ned and Michael exchanged grins. 'We won't be nearly as much trouble,' said Ned.

The trophy room was almost too much for Michael to absorb: a whole row of plaques from *Photoplay* magazine (mostly from the fifties); keys to a dozen cities; telegrams from Hitchcock, Billy Wilder, DeMille; silver-framed photos of _____ _____ with JFK, _____ _____ with Marilyn Monroe, _____ _____ with Ronald Reagan; a needlepoint pillow from Mary Tyler Moore.

After Guido had left Michael just stood there, shaking his head. 'Is this *his* room?'

'Across the hall,' said Ned. 'Wanna see it?'

'Should we?'

Ned smiled sleepily. 'It used to be my room, too, remember?'

They passed through double doors, massive and oaken, into a space that looked like a set for a movie star's bedroom. The windows opened onto the pool and the world. The bed was enormous, exactly the sort of bed Michael expected _____ _____ to sleep in.

He approached it in earnest, like a pilgrim, and sat down tentatively on the edge. Smiling sheepishly at Ned, he admitted, 'I feel like such a tourist.'

'You'll get used to it soon enough.'

'The *bed?*' laughed Michael.

'There's coffee in the morning if you want it.'

Michael sprang to his feet, feverish with guilt. Guido stood in the doorway, eyeing them.

'Thanks,' said Ned, apparently unruffled. 'I'm just giving Michael the house tour.'

Guido grunted. 'Don't trip any alarms,' he said as he left the room.

Michael listened until his footsteps had died out, then gave a nervous little whistle.

'He's just doing his job,' Ned explained.

'Yeah,' said Michael, 'like Mrs Danvers in *Rebecca*.'

Halcyon Hill

Memorial Day dawned bright and clear. Mary Ann left for Hillsborough just before noon, only to get caught in a traffic snarl at the intersection of DuBoce and Market. She puzzled over this turn of events until she saw the throng gathered on the pavement at the 76 station.

About five hundred people were cheering hysterically while a statuesque man in nurse drag – boobies, bouffant, the works – thrashed about violently on the back of a mechanical bull. In other words, thought Mary Ann, just another Memorial Day.

A battered Volvo pulled alongside the Le Car. 'What the fuck *is* this?' asked a frizzy-haired woman with an infant child and a back seat full of No Nukes posters.

'The Great Tricycle Race,' said Mary Ann. She had learned that much from Michael.

'What's that?' asked the woman.

'Uh, well . . . gay guys on tricycles. It's a benefit for the SPCA.'

The woman beamed. 'Wonderful!' she shouted, as the cars began to move again. 'How goddamn wonderful!'

Curiously enough, Mary Ann knew exactly what she meant. How could anyone feel threatened by this kind of whimsy? If she ever had a child, she would want him to grow up in San Francisco, where Mardi Gras was celebrated at least five times a year.

She hadn't always felt that way, of course. Once she had harbored deep resentment at the sight of dozens of near-naked men gamboling in the streets, their cute little butts winking unavailably in the sunshine.

But some straight men, thank God, took care of their bodies as well as gay men did.

Besides, a cute butt was a cute butt, so what-the-hell?

She almost jumped the curb looking at one.

She was sorry that Brian wasn't with her. He had been such a sport about it when she told him of Mrs Halcyon's luncheon invitation. 'Go ahead,' he had said. 'She might do you some good. I'll catch some rays in the courtyard. We'll do a flick or something when you get back.'

God, she did love him. He was so easy, so uncomplicated, so willing to understand, whatever the circumstances. They were friends now, she and Brian. Friends who had terrific sex together. If that wasn't love, what was?

By the time she hit the freeway, she was buzzing along merrily on one of Mrs Madrigal's Barbara Stanwyck joints. She turned on the radio and sang along as Terri Gibbs sang 'Somebody's Knockin'.'

Once more, she couldn't help wondering about this summons to Hillsborough. She knew that some society people liked to court celebrities, but surely her own limited fame was far removed from Frannie Halcyon's league.

Was she just being nice, then?'

Maybe.

But *why*, after all these years?

As a secretary, Mary Ann had worked for the Halcyon family for almost two years – first for Edgar Halcyon, the founder of Halcyon Communications; later for Beauchamp Day, Mr Halcyon's slimy son-in-law.

Today, however, was the first time she had ever laid eyes on the family estate.

561

Halcyon Hill was a mammoth mock-Tudor mansion, probably built in the twenties, set back from the road in a grove of towering oaks. A black Mercedes, with a license plate reading FRANNI, was parked in the circular driveway.

An old black woman, very thin, opened the door.

'You must be Emma,' said the visitor, 'I'm Mary Ann.'

'Yes'm, I feel like I . . .' Before the maid could finish the sentence, Frannie Halcyon came scurrying into the foyer. 'Mary Ann, I am delighted, just *delighted* you could come. Now, you brought your bathing suit, I hope?'

'Uh . . . in the car. I wasn't sure if . . .'

'Emma, get it for her, will you?'

'Really, I can . . .' Mary Ann abandoned the protest; the maid was already tottering towards the car.

'Now,' said Mrs Halcyon, 'we'll have a nice lunch on the terrace . . . I hope you like salmon?'

'Yum,' replied Mary Ann.

'And then we can chat.'

'Fine.'

The matriarch took her arm protectively. 'You know, young lady, Edgar would be so *proud* of you.'

Dames

High atop Beverly Hills, Michael and Ned were lolling by _____ _____'s pool, breakfasting on the eggs Benedict that Guido had brought them.

'He's O.K.,' Michael commented, after the houseman had left. 'He had me sorta spooked last night.'

Ned popped a triangle of toast into his mouth. 'He didn't know you last night. It's his job to be careful. The *National Enquirer* tries to scale the wall here about once a week. _____'s lucky to have Guido.'

The three-legged mongrel named Ned hobbled up to Michael's chaise longue and presented his muzzle for scratching. Michael obliged him. 'These old dogs,' he said. 'You expect something sleek, like greyhounds or something. Or ferocious, maybe. It makes me feel so much better about him to know that he keeps these mangy mutts.'

'That one's fourteen,' said Ned. 'We found him when he was a

562

puppy, scrounging in a garbage can behind Tiny Naylor's. _____adores him. He got hit by a car about five years ago, so the leg had to go.' Ned smiled lovingly at his namesake. '*He's* the one who should write the book.'

Guido appeared on the terrace with a tray of bullshots. 'I thought you gentlemen could use a little refreshment before the twinkies invade.'

'Thanks,' said Ned, taking a drink. 'What twinkies?'

Guido's pupils ascended. '_____ called a little while ago, still in P.S. Won't get here till two. Meanwhile, God help us, one of his buddies from West Hollywood decides to throw a little spur-of-the-moment Welcome Home. *Here*, thank you very much.'

Michael looked at Ned, suddenly feeling anxious again. 'Should we be getting dressed or something?'

'Forget it,' Guido reassured him. 'The last time this happened the party lasted two days. There were so many Speedos hung out to dry that the Danny Thomases called to ask why we were flying signal flags.'

Guido's forecast proved uncannily accurate. One by one, the young men began arriving, long-limbed and Lacosted to near perfection.

'What is this?' asked Michael, hovering near the kitchen. 'The summer spread of G Q?'

'They *wish*,' said Guido, frantically fluffing the parsley on a tray of deviled eggs. 'They're anybody's spread, at this point . . . and honey, when you've been in this business as long as I have, you see them come and you see them go. Mostly come . . . ya know?'

'They're so gorgeous,' said Michael. 'Are they actors or what?'

'What, mostly. Starlets. Harry Cohn knew all about it, only he did it with girls. Same difference. Same dumb dames standing around the pool.' The houseman wolfed down a deviled egg and scurried out the door with the tray.

Michael found Ned by the swimming pool.

'I need a joint,' Michael whispered, surveying the crowd. 'If I'm going to be paranoid, I want there to be a good reason for it.'

'I wouldn't do it here,' Ned warned him.

'Huh?'

'_____'s kind of old fashioned.'

'Right,' said Michael, looking around him. 'Gotcha.'

The movie star's arrival was heralded by joyful barking at the front gate. The dogs, in fact, provided the only official greeting that Michael could observe. While most of the men around the pool exuded airs of easy familiarity with their surroundings, none stepped forward to welcome the host.

They don't know him either, Michael realized.

The idol was grayer than he had expected – a little paunchy, too – but he was truly magnificent, a lumbering titan in this garden of younger, prettier men. When he knelt and scooped the three-legged dog into his arms, he won Michael's heart completely.

'C'mon,' said Ned. 'I'll introduce you.'

'Couldn't we save it?'

'Why?'

'Well, won't he be swamped for a while?'

Ned smiled at him indulgently, rising from his chaise. 'Come on over when you feel like it, O.K.?'

Michael stayed by the pool, watching silently as the chatter resumed.

'He must be on great drugs,' said a voice behind him.

'Who?' said another.

'The Pope.'

'Huh?'

'Well, they've had him on painkillers since the shooting, right? And he's the Pope, right? He must be getting great stuff.'

'Yeah, I never thought of that. Did I tell you that Allan Carr wants me for *Grease II*?'

Michael rose and headed for the buffet table, where Guido was emptying ashtrays and grumbling. He was no longer Mrs Danvers at Manderley; he was Mammy at Tara, entertaining the resident Yankees against her better instincts.

'Where's Ned?' asked Michael.

'In the screening room,' said Guido, 'with ____.'

So Michael took a deep breath and went in to join them.

Buying Silence

As promised, Mary Ann enjoyed a lunch of cold salmon and Grey Riesling on the flagstone terrace overlooking the swimming pool at Halcyon Hill.

Mrs Halcyon was extraordinarily solicitous, oohing and aahing melodramatically over Mary Ann's brief, but snappy, repertoire of true-life TV horror stories.

'It certainly is,' she agreed, when Mary Ann had finished. 'It's *just* like the *Mary Tyler Moore Show*. They didn't exaggerate one bit, did they?'

'I love it, though,' Mary Ann hastened to add. 'I'll just love it more when they let me do some nighttime work.' She smiled a little ruefully. 'They will sooner or later. They just don't know it yet.'

'That's the spirit!' Mrs Halcyon clamped her plump, bejeweled hands together, then appraised her guest, smiling. 'Edgar always said you were ambitious. He told me that many times.'

'He was a great boss,' Mary Ann replied, returning a dead man's compliment. She felt increasingly uncomfortable under the matriarch's steady gaze.

'He also said you were tactful,' continued Mrs Halcyon, 'and extremely discreet.'

'Well, I always *tried* to be.' *What the hell was going on here?*

'He trusted you, Mary Ann. And *I* trust you. You're a young woman with character.' A kindly twinkle came into her eyes. 'I wasn't trained for much in this life – outside of opera guilds and museum boards – but I'm a pretty good judge of character, Mary Ann, and I don't think you'll let me down.'

Mary Ann hesitated. 'Is there something . . . uh, specific you had . . .'

'I need a PR person. The Halcyon family needs a PR person. On a short-term basis, of course.'

'Oh . . . I see.' She didn't, of course.

'It shouldn't interfere with your job at the station. I need you as a consultant, more or less. I'm prepared to pay you a thousand dollars a week for a period of roughly four weeks.'

Mary Ann made no attempt at playing it cool. 'That's wonderfully generous, but I don't . . . well, I'm not *trained* at PR, Mrs Halcyon. My duties at Halcyon Communications were strictly . . .'

'There's a story in this, Mary Ann. A big one. And it's yours when the right time comes. This will get you on nighttime television, young lady – I can promise you that.'

Mary Ann shrugged helplessly. 'Then . . . what do you want me to do?'

The matriarch rose and began pacing the terrace. When she clasped her hands behind her back, the pose was so suggestive of Patton briefing the troops that Mary Ann was forced to suppress a giggle.

'I want you to give me your utter allegiance for a month,' said Frannie Halcyon. 'After that, you are free to act as you see fit. The Halcyon family has a story to tell, but I want it told on our own terms.'

She stopped dead in her tracks; her tiny fist clenched determinedly. 'I will not . . . I will *not* be chewed up and spit out by the press the way the Hearsts were!'

She was obviously rolling now, so Mary Ann waited, reinforcing her hostess with sympathetic little nods. Mrs Halcyon continued, shaking her head somberly as she stared at the light dancing on the surface of the swimming pool.

'Poor Catherine,' she intoned softly. 'Her family knew everything about journalism, but nothing about PR.'

Mary Ann smiled in agreement. This dowager was no dummy.

Mrs Halcyon continued: 'The really *good* PR people, as my husband must have taught you, are the ones who keep people's names *out* of the newspapers. That's what I want from you, Mary Ann – for a month, anyway.'

'Why a month?'

'That will be explained later. The point is this: if you take this job, I don't want Barbara Walters crawling through my shrubbery a week from now. I'm too old to take on the networks alone, Mary Ann.'

'I can understand that,' said Mary Ann. 'It's just that I can't *guarantee* . . .'

'You don't have to guarantee anything . . . except your silence for a month.'

'I see.'

'That's four thousand dollars for your ability to keep a secret for a month. After that, we'll give you . . . an exclusive. That's the word, isn't it?'

Mary Ann smiled. 'That's the word.'

'It's agreed, then?'

Mary Ann didn't hesitate. 'Agreed.'

Mrs Halcyon beamed.

'So what's the story?' asked Mary Ann.

The matriarch signaled Emma, who was standing just inside the double doors on the edge of the terrace. The maid scurried away, returning moments later with a young blond woman, very lean and tanned.

'*That's* the story,' said Frannie Halcyon. 'Mary Ann, may I present my daughter DeDe. I believe you two have already met.'

566

The Bermuda Triangle

The bars where Michael hung out, when he did that sort of thing, often featured a big black Harley-Davidson bike, reverentially pinspotted and suspended from the ceiling on shiny chrome chains.

Mary Ann, on the other hand, haunted a place called Ciao, a white-tile, toilet-tech bistro on Jackson Street where a pristine wall-mounted moped – a Vespa Ciao, of course – reigned supreme as the house icon.

Today, Memorial Day, while Mary Ann was poolside in Hillsborough and Michael was poolside in Hollywood, Brian was worshiping the motorcycle of *his* choice, a glossy wine-red Indian Warrior from the fifties, dangling overhead at the Dartmouth Social Club, a watering hole on Fillmore Street for the terminally collegiate.

Jennifer Rabinowitz had appeared out of nowhere.

'God, what are *you* doing back in The Bermuda Triangle?'

Brian smiled. Regulars to the Cow Hollow singles scene often referred to the intersection of Fillmore and Greenwich as The Bermuda Triangle. Nubile computer programmers and other innocents had been known to pass through this mystical nexus and never be heard from again.

It was stretching it, however, to regard Jennifer as nubile. Brian had been freshening her coffee at Perry's for over half a decade now. They were veterans of the bar wars, he and Jennifer, and Jennifer, like her incredible breasts, was still hanging in there.

'Gotta eat somewhere,' grinned Brian, holding up his hot roast beef sandwich. 'Grab a seat. Sit down.'

She did just that, smiling ferociously. 'You look great, Brian. Really.'

'Thanks.'

'You *went* to Dartmouth, didn't you? This must be like old home week or something.' She pointed to a plate glass window emblazoned with a gold leaf Dartmouth Indian. Once upon a time, Brian realized with a twinge of nostalgia, he would have insisted on calling it the Dartmouth Native American.

'Yeah,' he admitted, 'but that's not it. I just like the sandwiches.' He was damned if he'd let her peg him as an old preppie finding his roots.

'Yeah,' she said, 'they are primo.' Her smile was relentless. *This is a pick-up*, he told himself. Why did the peaches always fall when you weren't shaking the tree?

'Look,' she added, 'do you have plans for the day or what?'

He shrugged. 'Just this.'

'I've got some great weed,' she said. 'My new place is just around the corner. What say? Old times' sake?'

He was already suffering for her. He liked this cheerful, good-hearted woman. He'd felt a curious kinship with her for five or six years now, ever since she'd barfed on him at the Tarr & Feathers sing-along. He knew what drove her, he thought – the same thing that had driven him before Mary Ann came into his life.

'I've got a better idea,' he said. 'How 'bout I buy you a drink?'

The smile wavered for a moment, then she salvaged it. 'Sure. Whatever. No big deal.'

He reached across the table and took her hand. 'You look great yourself. Better than ever.'

'Thanks.' She smiled at him quite genuinely for a moment, then fumbled in her purse for a cigaret, lighting it herself. 'I've watched your friend all week,' she said.

'Who?'

'The afternoon movie girl. Isn't she your girlfriend now?'

Brian flushed. 'Sort of,' he said. 'Not exactly.'

'She's very good, I think. Natural. It's hard to find that on television.'

'I'll tell her you said so.'

'You do that.' Jennifer took a long drag on her cigaret, appraising him with an air of faint amusement. 'You've been domesticated, haven't you?'

'Jennifer, I . . .'

'It's all right if you have, Brian. It happens to the best of us. I'm still relentlessly single myself.'

'Oh?'

Jennifer nodded very slowly. 'Relentlessly.'

'Whatever,' said Brian.

'Exactly.' She blinked at him for a moment, then chucked him affectionately under the chin. 'Some guys don't recognize a friendly fuck when it's staring 'em right in the face.'

Give a Little Whistle

Vuitton bounded down the familiar slope and barked joyously at the door of the shack. Luke emerged almost immediately and greeted his former companion.

'Whitey, ol' boy . . . well, look who's back!'

He glanced up at Prue, who found herself vaguely embarrassed about invading the intimacy of this reunion. 'I've missed this ol' boy,' he said.

She smiled a little awkwardly. 'It looks like he missed you, too.'

'Happy Memorial Day,' grinned Luke.

'Same to you.'

'The coffee's on, if . . .'

'I'd be delighted,' said Prue. Now, she realized, she felt almost *privileged* to be asked, like a little girl from a fairy tale who had earned the confidence of the troll who lived under the village bridge.

Luke was no troll, however. If you discounted his seedy clothes and his rustic surroundings, he was quite a striking man, really. His amber skin and high cheekbones suggested . . . what? . . . Indian blood?

She followed him into the shack and sat down on the big chunk of foam rubber. Vuitton remained outside, chasing small animals through the underbrush. When Prue called to him, Luke advised her: 'He knows his way around. Don't worry about him. He'll be back when you want him.' He handed the columnist a mug of steaming coffee, catching her eye as he did so. 'He's home now.'

Prue faltered for a moment, then looked down at her coffee. 'This smells marvelous.'

'Good. Glad you like it.'

'By the way, Luke . . . uh, you haven't run across a little silver whistle, have you?'

Smiling, he opened a cigar box on the shelf above the fire. He handed her the Tiffany trinket.

Prue glowed. 'Thank heavens. I'm so sentimental about this silly thing. My husband gave it to me when we were divorced.'

'You dropped it on the ledge. I was saving it for you.'

'I'm so glad. Thank you so much.'

There was something gentle and boyish in his eyes when he looked at her. 'It's good protection for a woman. I was worried about you not having it. There's a lot of crazy folk running around these days.' He smiled, revealing teeth that were surprisingly even and white. 'I guess a lot of people would take me for crazy, huh?'

'I wouldn't,' said Prue.

'You did,' Luke replied, without malice. 'It's natural. People judge people by the houses they live in, the clothes they wear. It takes a little longer to look into the heart, doesn't it?'

'Yes,' said Prue, 'I guess it does.' She looked down, then blew on her coffee, touched and embarrassed by such an accurate assessment of their first encounter.

'Do you know who trusts me?' asked Luke.

Prue flushed. 'Luke, I'm sorry. I trust you. I was just . . .' She threw up her hands, unable to finish.

Luke's smile was forgiving. 'Besides you, I mean?'

She shook her head.

'Watch,' said Luke, sitting down on the edge of his bed. He drummed his fingers on the packed earth floor. 'Chipper, Jack, Dusty . . .'

Right on cue, three chipmunks scampered from under the bed and climbed onto Luke's hand. He lifted them to his face and nuzzled them. 'These fellows trust me. The buffalo down the road trust me. So do the raccoons over by Rainbow Falls.' He let the tiny creatures down again. 'I'm nice to humans, too, but I don't do so well with them. It's just a question of knowing where your talent lies, I guess.'

Prue was captivated. She reached down to touch the chipmunks, but they scurried under the bed again. 'I see what you mean,' she said.

'I used to have a whole flock of humans,' said Luke.

'What do you mean?'

'A congregation,' smiled Luke.

'You were a preacher?'

Luke nodded. 'People are the hardest way to find God, though. It's easier out here with the animals . . . and the beauty. Sometimes there's so much beauty it makes me want to cry.' His white teeth shone at her again. 'See what I mean? Crazy as all get-out.'

'I don't think that's crazy,' Prue replied. 'What happened to your congregation?'

Luke shrugged. 'They left me . . . lost the faith. No one wants to find God anymore.'

570

Prue stared at him, tears in her eyes. 'Luke . . . if I . . . would you mind if I . . . helped you tell your story?'

'Tell who?'

'The people . . . the public.'

'You're a reporter?'

'No. Not exactly. Just a writer. You can trust me, Luke, I promise.'

He looked at her for a long time, then lifted his big calloused finger and brushed the tear from her eye. 'You are filled with God,' he said.

Meeting——

Michael stood in the doorway of the screening room and studied the two giants kneeling over film cans in the corner. They looked like Vikings ransacking a wine cellar, but their laughter was so intense and so intimate that an outsider might have come to the erroneous conclusion that they were still lovers.

—— held up a film can so Ned could read the label. 'What about this one?'

'I dunno,' answered the nurseryman. 'I kinda doubt it.'

The movie star smiled ruefully. 'Me too. I screened it for some teenyboppers the other day and they were all in hysterics by the time we got to the hayfork scene.'

'You were great in the hayfork scene.'

'My *lats* were great in the hayfork scene.'

'Fuckin' A! And they'll appreciate that. Play to your audience, man!' Ned rapped ——'s chest with the back of his hand.

'Well,' said ——, 'maybe it'll keep 'em outa the bushes. Mr Shigeda will have my ass if his begonias get crushed. Where did they come from anyway?'

Ned shrugged. 'Santa Monica Boulevard, for all I know. Guido said that Charles told him that Les thought it would be a hot idea.'

'And God knows,' laughed ——, 'Les can round 'em up quicker than Selective Service.'

Ned laughed with him. 'My friend Michael is out there somewhere.'

Michael saw an entrance and raised his hand. 'Uh . . . present and accounted for.'

Two heads turned instantly in Michael's direction. Both of them smiled at him. Michael stepped forward hastily and extended his hand. 'I'm Michael Tolliver,' he said. 'This is a great party.'

'Yeah?'

'Well, I don't know anybody, of course, but . . .'

'Here's a handy guideline,' grinned ――――. 'The blonds are all named Scott. The brunettes are all named Grant. Now you know everybody. Except me. I'm ――――.'

Michael nodded. 'The suspense wasn't killing me.'

―――― looked at Ned. 'You two aren't married, huh?'

'No way,' said the nurseryman, winking at Michael.

'He needs a lover,' ―――― told Michael. 'Find a lover for him, will you?'

'He turns them away every week,' said Michael.

'Is that right?' asked ――――.

Ned shrugged. 'I like being single. Lots of people like being single. *Michael* likes being single.' He looked at his friend for confirmation of this fact.

'He likes being a slut,' said Michael.

―――― roared, then crooked his arm around Ned's head and kissed his naked scalp. 'I love this slut,' he said. 'Hey . . . how 'bout a house tour, you guys?'

'I think I'll pass,' said Ned.

'Hot date?' asked ――――.

Ned nodded smiling. 'Somebody named Scott.'

The matinee idol turned to Michael. 'What about you?'

'Sure,' said Michael. 'I'm game.'

The house tour included an extensive film library, the pool and cabanas, a terraced garden under the deck off the pool, and the upstairs bedrooms. In *the* bedroom, ―――― flung open the French windows overlooking the guests. 'The movie should start in a minute. That'll quiet things down.'

'What's the movie?' asked Michael.

The actor made a face. '――――. Pure crapola, if you ask me.'

'I've never seen it,' Michael admitted.

'There's a reason for that,' grinned ――――.

Michael looked at him directly for the first time. 'I think you put yourself down too much. Those guys must be down there for something.'

'Who?'

'All those . . . Scotts and Grants. That must tell you something. If you're fooling people about your talent, at least you're fooling a lot of them.' Michael smiled suddenly, embarrassed by his own audacity. 'If you ask me, that is.'

The movie star appraised him jovially. 'You work with Ned at the nursery, huh?'

'Right.'

'And you guys sing together in some sort of group?'

'Uh-huh.' Michael couldn't hide his pride. 'The Gay Men's Chorus. We're touring nine cities beginning next week.'

The movie star frowned. 'I'm afraid I don't understand that.'

'What?'

'Why some people make such a big deal out of being gay.'

Michael hesitated. He'd heard this line countless times before, usually from older gay men like ＿＿ who had suffered silently for years while *other* people made a big deal out of their homosexuality. 'We just want to make it easier for people,' he said at last. 'Easier for straight people to like us. Easier for gay people to be proud of their heritage.'

＿＿ chuckled ruefully. 'Their heritage, huh?'

Michael felt himself bristling. 'That's a good enough word, I think.' He looked at the movie star and smiled. 'You're part of it, incidentally.'

DeDe

The woman who stood there was almost a stranger, not at all the marshmallow-plump post-debutante that Mary Ann remembered from days gone by.

This woman was wiry and brown, with long, sun-bleached hair that flowed down her back in a ponytail. Dressed up in one of her old shirtwaists – vintage 1975 or so – she seemed as awkward as a desert island castaway attempting to walk in shoes again.

Mary Ann was speechless. She stared at DeDe, then turned back to Mrs Halcyon, slackmouthed. 'I can't . . . I never *dreamed* . . .'

Mrs Halcyon beamed, obviously delighted with the impact she had made. 'You two need to get acquainted again. I'll leave you alone for a while. If you need anything, Emma can help you.' The matriarch squeezed her daughter's arm, pecked her on the cheek, and entered the house through the double doors on the terrace.

Mary Ann fumbled for words again, advancing clumsily to embrace the apparition that confronted her. 'I'm so glad,' she murmured, almost on the verge of tears. 'I'm so glad, DeDe.'

She was glad mostly that *someone* could have a happy ending to the Jonestown tragedy. She had never known DeDe very well; she had simply been the boss's daughter. And Beauchamp's wife. The two women, in fact, had seen each other last at Beauchamp's funeral, where neither had made a particularly visible display of grief.

Mary Ann let go of DeDe, suddenly remembering: 'Oh . . . the twins?'

DeDe smiled. 'Upstairs. Sleeping.'

'Thank God.'

'Yes.'

'And . . . D'orothea?'

'She's in Havana,' said DeDe.

They sipped wine by the pool while DeDe told her story.

'D'orothea and I joined the Temple in Guyana in 1977. The twins were just babies, but I wanted them to grow up in a place without prejudice. Their father was Chinese. I suppose you know that.'

Mary Ann nodded. The whole town knew it.

'I don't expect you to believe this, but I actually felt a sense of purpose in Jonestown that I had never felt before. For a while, anyway. On my third day there Jones held a catharsis session and made me stand up and explain . . .'

'A catharsis session?'

'That was his term. They were nights when he called us together and made us confess our sins. When I stood up, he said: "O.K., Miss Rich Bitch, what is it that you think *you* can do for the revolution?" I knew I couldn't lie to him, so I told him I had no skills, and he said: "You buy things, don't you?" So that's what I ended up doing. I became a kind of procurement officer for Jonestown.'

'What was your schedule like?'

'Well, twice a week I took the *Cudjoe*, this little shrimp boat that belonged to the Temple. I caught it in Port Kaituma . . .'

'I'm afraid I don't know . . .'

'The nearest village. On the Barima River. The airstrip is there. Where they killed the congressman.'

Mary Ann nodded gravely.

'It was six hours from Port Kaituma to Kumaka, where I did most of my shopping. I supervised the loading of the *Cudjoe*, foodstuffs mostly. That took about three hours, and we always headed back the same day. The captain was a man named William Duke, who didn't work for the Temple but was . . . uh, sympathetic. He was a Communist, the PPP representative in Port Kaituma, and he liked me and adored the twins. Several days before . . . it happened, Captain Duke took me into his cabin and told me about the hundred-pound drum he had on the fantail. It was full of potassium cyanide.'

Mary Ann winced. 'Jesus.'

'Thank God for that little guy,' said DeDe. 'Thank God for that crummy job. I never would've known otherwise.' A hunted look came into her eyes.

'Well,' said Mary Ann, trying to help, 'it's over now. You're home and you're safe.'

DeDe finished off the last of the wine, then set the bottle down with a frown that suggested anything but safe at home. 'I'm sorry,' she said. 'I need some more of this before we continue.'

Meanwhile . . .

Jennifer Rabinowitz sat up in bed and put her bra back on. 'Was that great weed or what?'

'Mmm.'

'My friend Scooter gets it directly from Jamaica. He says Bob Marley used to smoke the stuff. It's like . . . official reggae grass or something.'

'Rastafarian grass.'

'Right. That's the word. I think I could get into that, couldn't you?' She was on her hands and knees now, feeling under the covers for her pantyhose.

'What? The religion?'

'Yeah. I mean, it's a pretty terrific religion. They smoke enormous joints and dance their asses off and support equal opportunity and all that.'

'They also think Haile Selassie was God. *Is* God.'

575

'Yeah. I know. I'd have a problem with that, I guess.' She considered the issue as she wriggled into her pantyhose. 'Still . . . it might be worth it for the grass. Do you see my skirt on your side?'

He shook his head slowly. 'The other room.'

'Riiight. I am such a space case.' She bounded out of bed, stopping suddenly when she reached the door. 'Look,' she said earnestly, cocking her head, 'if it looks like I'm tossing you out, I guess I am. I've got Dancercise at four, and this wasn't exactly an official date.'

'No problem,' he said.

'You're a great guy. I've had a swell time.' She was hopping on one foot now, pulling on a pump. 'And I know how whory this looks, believe me.'

He laughed. 'I've had a great time, too.'

'Can I drop you off somewhere?'

'No thanks. I live in the neighbourhood.'

'What's your last name, by the way?'

'Smith.'

'John Smith. For real?'

He nodded rather dolefully. 'I'm afraid so.'

'That's a riot. We should check into a hotel sometime.'

He let her joke slide by. 'Maybe we'll bump into each other again at the Balboa.'

'Sure,' she said cheerfully. 'Maybe so. It's been great. Really. I was feeling kind of bummed out when you met me.'

The Saga Continues

A robin was trilling in a treetop at Halcyon Hill – an odd accompaniment, indeed, for a story as grisly as this one.

'Wait a minute,' said Mary Ann. 'How could you be sure that the cyanide was intended for . . . for what he used it for?'

'I knew,' DeDe replied grimly. 'If you were there, you knew. Captain Duke was even more certain than I was. He also knew about Dad's fixation with the twins, and he knew that . . .'

'Your *father* was . . . ?'

'My father?'

'You said Dad.'

DeDe grimaced. 'I meant *him*. Jones. We called him Dad, some of us.' She shuddered, sitting there in the sunshine, then smiled wanly at Mary Ann. 'If that doesn't give you the creeps, nothing will.'

The flesh on Mary Ann's arm had already pebbled. She held it up so DeDe could see.

DeDe continued: 'The point is . . . Jones was obsessed with my children. He called them his little third world wonders. He saw them as the hope of the future, the living embodiment of the revolution. Sometimes he would single them out at the day-care center and sing little songs to them. I knew he wouldn't leave without taking them.' She looked directly into Mary Ann's eyes. 'I knew he wouldn't kill himself without killing them.'

Mary Ann nodded, mesmerized.

'So I discussed it with D'orothea and we planned the escape . . . with Captain Duke's help. We left on a regular morning run to Kumaka. Sometimes D'orothea would go along with me, so nobody was particularly suspicious. The twins, of course, had to be sneaked on board when nobody was looking. When we got to Kumaka we took on supplies, then we just kept on going down the river to a village called Morawhanna, where Captain Duke bribed the captain of the *Pomeroon*, a freighter that made regular trips between Mora-whanna and Georgetown . . . usually with fish on board.'

'Uh . . . dead fish, you mean?'

DeDe shook her head. 'Tropical fish. It's a big export item in Guyana. They had these big tin drums on board for the fish, and some of them were empty, so we hid out in two of them until we reached Georgetown. Twenty-four hours later.'

'Jesus,' said Mary Ann.

'I fed a sedative to the children. That helped some. But most of the trip was at sea. Ghastly. The worst experience of my life. It was a little easier when we reached Georgetown. Captain Duke arranged for us to be met by another PPP official . . .'

'You mentioned that before. What's PPP?'

'People's Progressive Party. Jungle Communists. They had us on a flight to Havana within twenty-four hours. D'orothea and I were already working in a cannery when the news of the slaughter broke.'

'How long did you live in Havana, then?'

'Two-and-a-half years. Up until last month.'

'They wouldn't let you come home?'

577

'If you mean, here, I didn't *want* to go home. D'orothea and I were happy. The children were happy. There were principles involved, things that mattered to us.' DeDe smiled forlornly. 'Mattered. Past tense. One of our beloved comrades found out.'

'Found out?'

'That D'orothea and I were lovers.'

Mary Ann flushed, in spite of herself. 'So they . . . uh . . . deported you?'

DeDe nodded. 'They gave us a choice, sort of. D'orothea decided to stay. She felt that being a socialist was more important than being a lesbian.' She smiled almost demurely. 'I didn't agree with that, so I ended up at Fort Chaffee, Arkansas, where I did what I always do when the shit gets deep.'

'What?'

'I called Mother,' grinned DeDe.

Later, they tiptoed into an upstairs bedroom where DeDe's four-year-olds lay sleeping. Seeing them there, sprawled blissfully against the bedclothes, Mary Ann was reminded of the little silk dolls sold on the street in Chinatown.

'Beautiful,' she whispered.

DeDe beamed. 'Edgar and Anna.'

'Named for your father and . . . who?'

'I don't know,' said DeDe. 'Daddy just liked the name. He asked me to name her that on the night he died.'

'What they've seen,' said Mary Ann, looking down at the children. 'They don't remember anything, do they?'

'Not from Guyana, if that's what you mean.'

'Thank God.'

After a moment of silence, Mary Ann said: 'I can't help telling you . . . this is just the most . . . amazing story, DeDe. I'm so flattered you chose me for this.'

DeDe smiled. 'I hope it'll do you some good.'

'There's one thing I don't understand, though.'

'Yeah?'

'Why do you want to wait before releasing the story? It ought to be told now, it seems to me. You'll only have to hide out, and sooner or later someone will . . .'

'There are things I have to do,' DeDe said sternly.

'Like . . . what?'

'I can't tell you yet,' DeDe replied.

When she leaned down to kiss her children, there was something indefinable in her eyes.

Wishing Upon a Star

____ ____ sat up in bed and lit a cigaret. 'Maybe we'd better take a break, huh?'

'Yeah,' said Michael, 'I'm sorry.' *God, was he sorry.*

'It's O.K., pal.'

'Maybe with you.'

'Nah. It's fine. Happens all the time.'

'It does?' Michael sat up, so that now they were both propped against the regal headboard.

The movie star gave his thigh a friendly shake. 'Sure. All the time.'

'That must be kind of a drag,' said Michael.

The same sleepy, half-lidded smile that seemed to work so well on ____ ____'s leading ladies flickered across the actor's face. 'I'm just another guy like you, you know.'

Michael smiled back at him. 'Not yet, you aren't.'

'No sweat,' said ____, taking another drag on his cigaret. 'We're not in any hurry. I'm not, anyway.'

'Won't the movie be over soon?'

The movie star shrugged. 'You didn't miss anything. I can promise you that.'

'Not *downstairs*, maybe.'

'Hey, ease up, pal . . . if I don't turn you on, there's no harm done.'

'Are you kidding? You've turned me on since I was eleven.'

'Hey,' grinned ____, 'thanks a helluva lot.'

Michael laughed apologetically. 'I'm not doing very well, am I?'

____ looked at him with affection, then tousled his hair. 'All right. Pretty damn all right.'

'It's such a waste,' Michael lamented. 'Your dick is so beautiful.'

The actor nodded his thanks.

'I can't believe what a fuck-up I am. I mean, Jesus God . . . how many cracks do you get at ____ ____?'

'Two or three,' said the movie star, tweaking Michael's nipple. 'And possibly lasagna. Guido's dishing it out to the hordes downstairs. Why don't I bring us a plate?'

Fifteen minutes later, when _____ came back with the food, Michael had some good news for him: 'I found the popper case. It was wedged between the mattress and the headboard.'

'Great,' said _____, easing into bed holding two forks and a plate of lasagna.

Michael examined the black leather pouch. 'Jees. Your initials and everything. And *real* poppers inside. Lord, it's so grand here at the Harmonia Gardens.'

_____ speared a chunk of lasagna and handed the fork to his guest. 'That was a present from Ned. Christmas before last. He knows how to buy for me.'

Michael took a healthy bite out of the lasagna. 'That was what did it, you know. Those goddamn initials on that little leather case. All I could think of was: "Hey, that's right. That must make me _____."'

'She's a little tougher than you,' said the actor, 'but I like your body better.'

Michael smiled with a mouthful of lasagna. 'Something tells me you've said that before.'

_____ spoke to the tip of his fork. 'Well, you're not exactly the first guy to say he feels like _____.'

'Good point.'

'It'll pass. It just takes a while sometimes.'

'I think it already has.'

'Huh?'

'Do you mind if we ditch the lasagna and have another go at it?'

'You're on,' grinned _____.

Somewhere in Arizona, Michael is hitchhiking on a stretch of desert highway. The trucker who picks him up is older than he is – gray and a little grizzled – but his body is massive and hard. Without a word, he lays a thickveined hand on Michael's thigh and takes him to a sleazy motel on the edge of the desert. It is there that it finally happens, there that Michael tastes diesel fuel on a sunburned neck and commits himself totally to the appetites of a stranger.

'Uh . . . Michael?'

'Mmm?'

'You O.K.?'

'Does Nancy have a red dress?'

'What?'

'Sorry. Just a little post-coital campy.'

'Oh.'

'I'm great. How are you?'

'Great. All things are possible, huh?'

'Uh-huh,' said Michael dreamily, wondering if somewhere in Arizona a lonely hitchhiker was sleeping with a truck driver, but fantasizing about ____ ____.

It seemed only fair.

Womb for One More

The Samadhi Centre on Van Ness was across the street from a Midas muffler shop and next door to Hippo Hamburgers. Brian pointed this out to Mary Ann, adding wickedly: 'It kinda makes me feel mystical already.'

Rolling her eyes, Mary Ann pushed the button for the third floor. 'This isn't like *Altered States*, you know. It isn't a psychedelic number. It's whatever you want it to be. Brian, promise me you won't be a wiseass with the attendant. They take this place seriously.'

'Right.' Brian assumed an appropriately sober expression. 'Are you actually a member here now?'

'I signed up for ten floats,' said Mary Ann. 'I can take them anytime.'

'How much was that?'

'A hundred and twenty-five dollars.'

Brian whistled.

'That's not so much,' said Mary Ann. 'Not for what it does for me. Besides, it's close to work and I . . .'

'Where are you getting this kind of money?'

'What kind of money?'

'We've been living like lords for the past *week*, Mary Ann. Ever since you got back from Hillsborough.'

'We may have splurged a bit now and then.'

581

'Yeah.' Brian counted on his fingers. 'Dinner at L'Orangerie. Uh . . . scalper's tickets for Liza Minnelli. That big motherfucker floral horseshoe you sent Michael when he left on the tour. Have I left anything out?'

Mary Ann wouldn't look at him.

'It's that old lady,' persisted Brian. 'She's giving you money, isn't she?'

'Brian . . .'

'Just tell me that much, O.K.?'

'All right!' said Mary Ann. 'She's giving me money. Are you satisfied now?'

'I knew it! She's buying hot consumer tips from you!'

The elevator door opened. 'Very funny,' said Mary Ann, striding briskly across gray industrial carpeting. 'Will you behave yourself now?'

The room assigned to Brian contained a Samadhi tank and a private shower. The tank stood chest high, roughly as long and wide as a twin bed. According to the attendant, it contained ten inches of water in which 800 pounds of Epsom salts had been dissolved.

'Is it dark in there?' asked Brian.

The attendant nodded. 'Completely. We also have earplugs, if you like.'

'How do I know when my hour is up?'

'They play music,' said Mary Ann.

'*In the tank?*'

The attendant smiled euphorically. 'Pachelbel.'

'My favorite,' said Brian.

Mary Ann shot daggers at him. 'I'll be in the tank across the hall.'

Brian winked at her. 'Last one to Nirvana is a rotten egg.'

It took him several minutes to get used to it, to accept the fact that he could relax, even sleep, lying flat on his back in the pitch darkness, suspended like a fetus in this vat of warm, viscous water.

The earplugs, furthermore, obliterated everything but the sound of his own breathing.

It was not what he wanted.

He crawled out of the tank, showered off the salty slime, and stole across the hallway to Mary Ann's room. Still naked, he knocked on the door of her tank.

582

The vinyl-covered hatch opened slowly, revealing the whites of her eyes.

'Brian! You scared me to death!'

'Sorry,' he said.

'Did they see you come over here'

Brian shook his head. 'Cohabitation is against the rules?'

'It's supposed to be a *womb*, Brian.'

'And I should go back to mine, huh?'

Finally she smiled at him. 'You're just the worst.'

'Anyway,' said Brian, 'we can tell them we're twins.'

They were floating in space, fingertips touching.

'I'll make a deal with you,' whispered Brian.

'What?'

'If you'll tell me about your secret mission to Hillsborough, I'll tell you about Jennifer Rabinowitz.'

'No deal.'

'I'll tell you anyway.'

'I figured you would,' said Mary Ann. 'Who is she?'

'Just a Good Time Charlene I used to know.'

'And?'

'And . . . I didn't fuck her while you were in Hillsborough.'

Mary Ann laughed. 'Terrific.'

'I *could* have. Easy as pie. She knew about you and didn't mind . . .'

'Brian, *I* don't mind.'

'I knew *that*, too. She didn't mind and you didn't mind, and she *knew* that I knew that you didn't mind. I had the whole god-damn world's permission to fuck Jennifer Rabinowitz, and I didn't do it.'

She squeezed his hand affectionately. 'I don't think there's a medal for that, sport.'

'I don't want a medal,' he murmured. 'I want you to know what it means.'

'I know what it means,' she said softly.

A Man Like Saint Francis

Behind the wheel of his red 1957 Cadillac El Dorado Biarritz, Father Paddy took on a disturbingly secular aspect. Prue could see why the car was a continuing embarrassment to the archdiocese, but she also felt that a bona fide television personality should be entitled to a few idiosyncrasies.

'Well,' said Father Paddy, grinning at the society columnist, 'what's the latest on Nature Boy?'

Prue chastised him with a little frown. 'He's a very good man, Father.'

'Did I imply otherwise?'

'He used to be a man of the cloth, in fact.'

The cleric's eyebrow arched. 'A Catholic?'

'No . . . some sort of Protestant, I think. He was an investment broker before that.'

'*What?*'

'I have no reason to doubt him,' she said defensively. 'He doesn't talk much, but he's quite literate when he does. He's amazing, Father. He's done everything. He even taught English once at a private school in Rio. He's done it all, and now he's . . . doing this.'

'Doing *what?*'

'Living. Being. Existing with God.'

'Has he hit you up for cash yet?'

Prue was shocked. 'No! As a matter of fact, I *offered* to help him out and he turned me down.'

'I see.'

'He's been living there for almost a year-and-a-half, he says. The park police know about him, but they let him stay because he respects the environment. He's marvelous with animals, in fact. He has three little chipmunks that live under the bed.'

Father Paddy frowned. 'This is all very charming, my child. But how does he *eat?*'

'I don't know. He scrounges, I guess.' Prue turned and looked out the window as the Biarritz climbed into Pacific Heights. 'Your skepticism distresses me, Father. He's no different from Saint Francis, really.'

The priest smiled indulgently. 'I'm only concerned for your safety, darling.'

She took his hand appreciatively. 'I know that. But it's *such* a marvelous story, isn't it?'

'How many times have you been there, anyway?'

'Uh . . . I'm not sure.'

'Give us a guess.'

She searched in her bag for her lipstick. 'Maybe five or six times.'

Father Paddy's eyes flickered mischievously. 'My, my . . . such a *long* story, too.'

That Word

For almost a week now, Frannie Halcyon had been giddy as a schoolgirl. She believed in life again, in children, in sunshine, in motherhood, in miracles. And she longed, more than ever, to share her joy with the world.

'Viola called today,' she announced at lunch. 'It was all I could do to keep from blabbing.'

DeDe frowned. 'Don't even joke about that, Mother.'

'I know, I know.'

'I need time, Mother. Viola would be on the phone to the *Chronicle* in two seconds flat. Please help me out on this, O.K.?'

'I got Mary Ann for you, didn't I?'

'I know, Mother, and I appreciate . . .'

'I just don't understand why you need a whole month, DeDe. Surely a week or so would . . .'

'Mother!'

'Never mind, then,' Frannie looked down at her spinach salad. 'Have you talked to her today?'

'Who?'

'Mary Ann.'

DeDe nodded. 'She's coming by tomorrow.'

'She's such a sweet girl,' said Frannie.

'She wants to tape me,' said DeDe.

'Oh . . . I see.' The matriarch contemplated her salad again. 'About . . . your experiences, I suppose?'

DeDe looked faintly annoyed. 'That *was* our arrangement, Mother.'
'Of course.'

'She's promised not to release anything until the month's up. I trust her.'

'So do I. Uh . . . DeDe?'

'Yeah?'

'You won't be talking about the . . . business with D'orothea, will you?'

DeDe's fork stopped in mid-air. She looked up, smoldering. 'Mother, the *whole* business was with D'orothea. I lived with her for four years, remember?'

'You know what I mean,' said Frannie.

'Yes,' DeDe replied flatly. 'I know what you mean.' She dug into her salad as if she were trying to kill something in it. 'You've made your feelings quite clear about that.'

Frannie hesitated, dabbing the corners of her mouth with her napkin. 'DeDe . . . I think I've been a lot more . . . accepting than most mothers might have been. I accepted those precious children long ago, didn't I? I don't quite . . . *understand* your friendship with D'orothea, but I would never presume to pass judgment on you for it. I just don't think it's something that warrants public discussion.'

'Why?' asked DeDe. She didn't look up.

'It's in poor taste, darling.'

DeDe set her fork down and looked at her mother for a long time before speaking. 'So,' she said at last, her lip curling slightly, 'I should restrict my reminiscences to *tasteful* things like cyanide and public torture. Super, Mother. Thanks for the advice.'

'You needn't be snide, DeDe.'

'D'orothea Wilson helped save your grandchildren's lives. You owe her a *lot*, Mother.'

'I know that. And I'm grateful.'

'Besides, I ended up with the gay Cuban refugees. I'm a dyke on *paper*, Mother. It's a matter of public record, for God's sake!'

'Don't use that word around me, DeDe!' Frannie fumbled for her napkin. 'Anyway, the refugee people could have made a mistake, a clerical error or something.'

'I loved her,' DeDe said coolly. 'That was no clerical error.'

There was harmony again after supper when Frannie, DeDe, Emma and the twins romped together on the lawn. Frannie took new delight

586

in her grandchildren, these precious almond-eyed sprites who called her 'Gangie' and frolicked on American soil as if it had always been theirs.

When DeDe and the children had retired, Frannie repaired to her bed with a Barbara Cartland novel.

Shortly after midnight, she heard a moan from DeDe's room.

The matriarch clambered out of bed, made her way down the hall, and listened outside her daughter's door.

'No, Dad. PLEASE, DAD . . . NO, PLEASE DON'T . . . OH, GOD HELP ME! DAD! DAD!'

Frannie flung open the door and rushed to DeDe's bedside. 'Darling, it's all right. Mother's here, Mother's here.' She rocked her daughter in her arms.

DeDe woke up and whimpered pathetically.

In the next room, the twins were sobbing in unison.

Letter From the Road

Dear Mary Ann and Brian,

Greetings from Motown! The tour is going great so far, though I have failed to meet anyone even remotely resembling ____ ____. Yesterday morning, on the flight from Lincoln, we had a whole 737 to ourselves, so all hell broke loose. Mark Hermes, a fellow baritone, put on a wig, scarf and apron – and two teacups for earrings – and impersonated the stewardess while she did her oxygen mask instructions. She loved it. The flight people have all been fabulous, as a matter of fact – especially the two hot Northwest stewards we had (not literally, alas) on the flight between Chicago and Minneapolis. One was gay, the other questionable. Naturally, I fell for the questionable one.

Lincoln, believe it or not, has been the high point so far. The local homos threw a lovely little potluck brunch for us in Antelope Park. (In fact, I've been to so many potluck functions that I'm beginning to feel like a lesbian.) The main gay bar in Lincoln is called – is this discreet enough? – The Alternative. It is the scene of much bad drag. White boys impersonating Aretha Franklin, etc. Most of us opted for the alternative to The Alternative – a joint called the Office Lounge. It was stifling in there, so we took off our shirts after we'd been boogying for a while. A major no-no. Apparently there's a law that says you can't take your shirt off in Nebraska.

The chamber singers were supposed to appear on Channel 10 in Lincoln, but the station manager canceled at the last minute because he didn't want to 'rub people's faces in it' – whatever 'it' is. By and large, though, people have been pretty wonderful. The audience at First Plymouth Church was about fifty percent old ladies. Old ladies can always tell 'nice young men' when they see them.

The audience was skimpy in Dallas – possibly because the Dallas morning *News* refused to print our ads. Our consolation was a private swim party thrown at the fashionable Highland Park home of a gay doctor named – I'm not making this up – Ben Casey. Some of the boys did an impressive nude water ballet to the music of 'Tea for Two'.

We stayed at the Ramada Inn in Mesquite, Texas – the town that gave hairspray to the world – and we were a smash hit at the Denny's there, where a waitress named Loyette (pronounced Low-ette) thinks we're the biggest thing since the death of Elvis. Oh yes – we ran out of hot water at the Ramada Inn. One-hundred-and- thirty-five faggots without hot water. Not a pretty scene. As luck would have it, the friendliest place in town was the steam room at the First Baptist Church – an enormous complex that covers about four square blocks of downtown Dallas. A lot of organists hang out there, if you catch my drift.

After the Minneapolis concert, a bunch of us went to a bar called The Gay Nineties. Apparently it's been called that for years, even when it was the city's oldest strip joint. It has three separate rooms – one for leather types, one for disco queens, one for preppies. I wandered around aimlessly, having my usual identity crisis. Ned, of course, sauntered into the leather section and racked up so many phone numbers that he looked like the bathroom wall at the Greyhound station.

David Norton, one of our tenors, had twenty members of his family show up for the concert in Minneapolis. That's been happening a lot, all over. Lots of hugs and boo-hoos backstage. Also in Minneapolis, I met an old couple – both in their eighties – who came up and thanked me in the lobby after the concert. They were brother and sister, both gay, and they'd driven all the way from their farm in Wisconsin to hear us sing. They had thick white hair and incredible blue eyes and all I could think of was the 'eccentric old bachelor and his spinster sister' who used to live down the road from us in

Orlando. We talked for about fifteen minutes, and we hugged when we said goodbye as if we had known each other forever. The old lady said: 'You know, when we were your age, we didn't know there was a word for what we were.'

As the song says – 'Other places only make me love you best.' Next comes New York, Boston, Washington and Seattle. A big hug for Mrs M. Tell her the brownies were perfect.

In haste,
Michael

P.S. I have it on the best authority that the chorus will be returning to the city in the vicinity of 18th and Castro at 5 P.M. on Father's Day. If you can make it, I'd love to see your shining faces in the crowd. Make Brian wear something tight.

P.P.S. Dallas men wear their muscles like feather boas.

Her Wilderness Like Eden

Luke's favorite Biblical quotation came from Isaiah:

For the Lord will comfort you; he will comfort you; he will comfort all her waste places, and make her wilderness like Eden, her desert like the garden of the Lord.

Prue entered the passage in her notebook, then read it aloud again. 'That makes such perfect sense, now that I think of it.'

'What?' asked Luke, looking up from his cot. He was stroking one of the chipmunks with his forefinger.

'That quote. This place. You've made this spot your garden of the Lord. You've made this wilderness like Eden.' True, the rhododendron dell wasn't exactly a wilderness by most people's standards, but the metaphor worked for Prue.

Luke smiled benignly. 'You could do it, too.'

'Do what?'

'Change your wilderness into a garden.'

Prue's brow furrowed. 'Do you think I'm living in a wilderness?'

He let the chipmunk down and laid his hands to rest on his knees. 'That's for you to decide, Prue.'

The sound of her own name stunned her. She was sure he had never used it before. 'You don't know that much about me,' she said

589

quietly, trying not to sound defensive. Why did she suddenly feel like a butterfly on the end of a pin?

'I know things,' he said. 'More than you know about me. I've read your column, Prue. I know about the thing you call a life.'

She didn't know whether to feel flattered or indignant. '*Where?*' she exclaimed. 'How in the world did you . . . ?'

'How in the world did a hermit get a copy of *Western Gentry* magazine?'

'I didn't mean it like that, Luke.'

He seemed amused by her disclaimer. 'Yes you did. You can't help it. You're a woman who worships material things. I don't mind, Prue. Jesus found room in his heart for people like that. There's no reason why I can't too.'

She reddened horribly. 'Luke, I'm sorry if . . .'

'Sit down,' he said, patting a place on the cot next to him. Prue obeyed, responding instantly to a tone of voice that conjured up images of her father back in Grass Valley.

'It hurts me to see people in need,' said Luke.

Prue thought his was just plain unfair. Her Forum discussions often focussed on the needy. 'Luke, just because I have money doesn't mean I don't feel compassion for the poor.'

'I'm not talking about the poor. I'm talking about you.'

Silence.

'I've never seen such need, Prue.'

'Luke . . .'

'You need someone who doesn't see the fancy dresses and the house on Nob Hill. Someone who refuses to be distracted by the myth you've spent such a long time creating . . .'

'Now, wait a minute!'

'Someone who *really* sees Prudy Sue Blalock, not the party girl, not the pathetic creature who spends her time bragging about how far she's come. Someone who would have loved her if she had never left Grass Valley at all.'

'Luke, I appreciate your . . .'

'You don't appreciate a damn thing yet, but you will. I'll teach you to love God again, to love yourself as God made you, to love the little girl who's deep down inside of you, aching to cast off those stupid, god-damn Alice-in-Wonderland clothes and tell the world what's really in her heart. Look at me, Prue. Don't you see it? *Don't you see it in my eyes?*'

When she finally looked at him, all she felt was an uncanny

familiarity, as if she had known this man all her life – or in a past life. She *knew* these features: the extraordinary cheekbones, the amber skin, the full lips, the strong hands that now cradled one of hers as though it were a wounded bird.

Tears spilled out of Prue's eyes. 'Please don't do this,' she said.

'You can change,' he offered gently. 'It doesn't have to stay this way.'

'But . . . *how?*' Her heart was pounding wildly. Through the teary blur, she could see the chipmunks gamboling on the dirt floor. She felt as if she were in a Disney cartoon.

'You can start by trusting me,' he said. 'You can trust me to love you unconditionally. On your terms. At your pleasure. As often or as little as you want. Forever.'

She knew in her heart that he meant it.

So she took his hand and put it where she needed him.

Adam and Eve

'Prue?'

'Mmm?'

'You like some coffee?'

'Huh-uh. Don't get up yet. I'm fine.'

'You look fine. Beautiful.'

'Thank you.'

'What about your driver?'

'What about him?'

'You've been gone three hours. Won't he worry about you?'

'He's used to waiting. That's what he's paid for.'

'But . . . if he calls the police . . .'

'He won't call the police. Why should he call the police?'

'No reason. It's getting dark, that's all. I thought he might worry about you.'

'It's dark already?'

'Uh-huh.'

'If you want me to leave, I . . .'

'I don't want you to leave.'

'Good.'

'If I had my way, you would never leave. We would lock ourselves away from that madness out there and . . . Jesus, that feels good.'

591

'Mmm.'

'Your hair is so soft. Like a baby's.'

'Mmm.'

'I meant what I said, Prue.'

'Mmm.'

'Will you come back?'

'Mmm.'

'You wouldn't lie to me?'

'No.'

'Good. Do that some more.'

'Mmm.'

'I know you can't be seen with me. I know that.'

'Luke . . .'

'No. Listen to me. I know you. I know this isn't easy for you. Just promise me you won't torture yourself later.'

'Torture myself?'

'Feeling guilty. Punishing yourself for loving a man who could never fit into your world.'

Silence.

'That's the truth, isn't it? You know it, and I know it. What we have can only happen here. And never often enough. I know all that, Prue, and I accept it. I want you to do the same.'

'Luke, I would never . . .'

'Forget about never. Forget about forever. All I want, Prue, is a little now from time to time. Promise me that, and I'll be happy.'

'I promise.'

'I can show you wonderful things.'

'You already have.'

'I think you should go now.'

'All right.'

'Don't be afraid, Prue. Please.'

'Of what?'

'Us.'

'I'll never be afraid of that.'

'Don't be so sure.'

'I don't understand.'

'Just come back, O.K.?'

'Soon.'

'I'll be here.'

D'or

Mary Ann's Le Car barreled along Skyline Drive on a June evening at sunset.

'God,' said DeDe, glimpsing the sea. 'It's so infernally beautiful, isn't it?'

'It sure is,' said Mary Ann.

'It never goes away, you know.'

'What?'

'That. Or the memory of that. Even in the jungle . . . even in *that* jungle, there were things about California that never left me. Even when I wanted them to.'

Mary Ann hesitated, then asked: 'Why would you want them to?'

'You didn't grow up here,' said DeDe. 'Almost anything can be oppressive given the right circumstances.' She smiled almost wistfully. 'And salvation comes when you least expect it.'

Mary Ann turned and looked at her. 'Surely you don't consider Guyana your salvation?'

DeDe shook her head. 'I was talking about D'orothea.'

'Oh.'

'I'd like to now, if you don't mind. Does it make you uncomfortable?'

'Not at all,' said Mary Ann, lying only slightly.

'It makes Mother climb the walls.'

'Different generation,' said Mary Ann.

'Did you know her at Daddy's agency?'

'Who?' asked Mary Ann.

'D'orothea.'

'Oh . . . not very well, actually. She just came in and out sometimes. She was our biggest client's top model. Frankly, she intimidated the hell out of me.'

DeDe smiled. 'She had a way with her. Has, that is.'

'She used to be friends with a friend of mine. A copywriter named Mona Ramsey.'

'They were lovers,' said DeDe.

'Yeah.' Mary Ann grinned sheepishly. 'That's what I meant, actually. Sometimes the Cleveland in me takes over.'

DeDe chuckled, eyes glued to the sunset. 'You're doing better than I ever did. I never learned about a goddamn thing until it actually happened to me.'

Mary Ann pondered that for a moment. 'Yeah,' she said drily, 'but what hasn't happened to you?'

DeDe shot her a wry glance. 'Good point,' she said.

'It's a journalist's dream,' observed Mary Ann, adding hastily: 'I hope that doesn't sound callous.'

'No. I'm aware of its potential.'

'There's a book in it for sure. Maybe even a movie-for-TV.'

DeDe laughed ironically at the prospect. 'Won't Mother love the hell out of that? "Starring Sally Struthers as the Society Lesbo." Jesus.'

Mary Ann giggled. 'We should be able to do better than that.'

'Maybe . . . but I'm prepared for the worst.'

Mary Ann looked earnestly at her passenger. 'I'll do everything I can to help.'

'I know,' said DeDe. 'I believe that. But not until the month is out, O.K.?'

Mary Ann nodded. 'I wish I understood why.'

'If I tell you, will you promise me that Mother won't hear about it?'

'Of course.'

'She thinks I need the time to rest up, to get my bearings before the publicity begins. That's true enough, but not the whole truth. The whole truth has always been a bit too much for Mother.'

Mary Ann smiled. 'I've noticed that.'

'I need to talk to some people. People who might know . . . what I need to know.'

'Who? Can you say?'

'Temple members,' answered DeDe. 'And people who knew him.'

'Jones?'

DeDe nodded.

'You could start with the governor,' said Mary Ann. 'And half the politicians in town. He was quite a popular fellow around here.'

DeDe smiled faintly. 'I know. At any rate, I'm stalling right now, because I haven't got all the facts. And I certainly don't relish the thought of being branded as a nut case.'

'That would never happen.'

'In two weeks,' said DeDe, 'you may have changed your mind.'

*

594

They parked to watch the sun go down in flames.

'I guess I changed the subject,' said Mary Ann.

'When?'

'You wanted to talk about D'orothea.'

'Yeah, well . . . there wasn't much to say really. Just that she cared for me. And made me laugh a lot. And the twins worshiped her. And she made love like an angel. And I wish she'd get her silly socialist ass out of Cuba and come home to me and the children. The usual stuff. Not much.'

'Until you lose it,' said Mary Ann.

'Until you lose it,' said DeDe. She watched the sea in silence for a moment, then turned to her companion. 'I'm glad you're here. You're a generous listener. You take things in stride.'

Mary Ann smiled. 'Billie Jean King helped.'

'Huh?'

'I guess you haven't heard about that.'

'She's a dyke, too?'

'Well,' said Mary Ann. 'She had an affair with a woman. Does that make her a dyke?'

'It does if she did it right,' DeDe replied.

Gaying Out

The weather had been relentlessly sunny for almost a week, so Michael and Ned had their hands full at God's Green Earth. Business was so brisk at the nursery that it was three o'clock before they sat down amidst the other living things requiring partial shade and contemplated their Yoplait.

'What do you think I should do?' asked Michael.

'About what?'

'The parade.'

Ned shrugged. 'You're going, aren't you?'

'Sure. But what do I *wear*? There's a big demand for the All-American look, and I pull that off pretty well. On the other hand, the Sisters of Perpetual Indulgence have asked me to be a nun this year.'

Ned spooned yogurt into his mouth. 'Go for the nun,' he said.

Michael thought for a moment. 'Have you ever tried getting laid when you're dressed as a nun?'

'Why not? There must be nuns who have.'

'Climb every mountain, huh?'

Ned laughed. 'I suppose you could be an All-American nun.'

'What's that? A denim habit?'

'Denim *under* your habit,' smiled Ned.

'Right. So I can swing into action at a moment's notice. Like Superman. I like it, Ned – style *and* content. You got an answer for everything.'

The nurseryman gave him a once-over, then smiled. 'Sister Mary Mouse, huh?'

They remained there in the dappled light, finishing their lunches in silence.

Then Michael said: 'Do you ever get tired of all this?'

'The nursery, you mean?'

'No. Being gay.'

Ned smiled. 'What do you think?'

'I don't mean being homosexual,' said Michael. 'I wouldn't change that for anything. I love men.'

'I've noticed.'

'I guess I'm talking about the culture,' Michael continued. 'The Galleria parties. The T-shirts with the come-fuck-me slogans. The fourteen different shades of jockstraps and those goddamn mirrored sunglasses that toss your own face back at you when you walk into a bar. Phony soldiers and phony policemen and phony jocks. Hot this, hot that. I'm sick of it, Ned. There's gotta be another way to be queer.'

Ned grinned, tossing his yogurt cup into the trash. 'You could become a lesbian.'

'I might,' Michael replied. 'They do a lot of things that I'd like to do. They *date*, for Christ's sake. They write each other bad poetry. Look . . . we give them so much grief about trying to be butch, but what the hell are *we* doing, anyway? When I was a teenager, I used to walk down the street in Orlando and worry about whether or not I looked like . . . well, less than a man. Now I walk down Castro Street and worry about the same thing. What's the difference?'

Ned shrugged. 'They don't beat you up for it here.'

'Good point.'

'And nobody's *making* you go to the gym, Mouse. Nobody's making you act butch. If you wanna be an effete poet and pine away in a garret or something, you're free to do it.'

'Those are my choices, huh?'

'Those are everybody's choices.' said Ned.

'Then why aren't they exercising them?'

'They?' asked Ned.

'Well, I meant . . .'

'You meant "they". You meant everybody else but you. You're the only sensitive one, right, the only full-fledged human being.'

Michael scowled. 'That isn't fair.'

'Look,' said Ned, sliding his arm across Michael's shoulders, 'don't shut yourself off like that. There are two hundred thousand faggots in this town. If you generalize about them, you're no better than the Moral Majority.'

Michael looked at him. 'Yeah, but I know you know what I mean.'

'Yeah. I know.'

'It's just so fucking packaged,' said Michael. 'A kid comes here from Sioux Falls or wherever, and he buys his uniform at All-American Boy, and he teaches himself how to stand just so in a dark corner at Badlands, and his life is all posturing and attitude and fast-food sex. It's too easy. The mystery is gone.'

'Is it gone for you?'

Michael smiled. 'Never.'

'Then maybe it isn't for that kid. Maybe it's just what he needs to get Sioux Falls out of his system.'

A long silence, and then: 'I'm sounding awfully old, aren't I?'

Ned shook his head. 'You're just a little gayed out after the tour. I feel that way sometimes. Everybody does. Nobody ever said it would be easy, Michael.' He tightened his grip on his friend's shoulders. 'You want me to help you make your habit?'

Michael's eyes widened. 'You sew?'

'Sure,' said Ned, 'when I'm not standing in a dark corner at Badlands.'

Unoriginal Sin

Prue rummaged furiously for the right words. 'He's just . . . different, Father. He's different from any man I've ever known.'

'Somehow,' replied the priest, 'I have no trouble believing that.'

'He's decent and he's kind and intuitive . . . and he has such respect for nature, and he understands God better than anyone I've ever known.'

'And he's a helluva lot of fun in the sack.'

'Father!'

'Well, let's get the cards on the table, girl. This isn't the dressing room at Saks, you know.'

Prue didn't answer for a moment. She sat there rigidly in the darkness, hearing the scuffle of feet outside the confessional. 'Father,' she said at last, 'I think somebody's waiting.'

A sigh came back through the hole in the wall. 'Somebody's *always* waiting,' bemoaned the cleric. 'It's just that time of the month. Can't this wait till lunch on Tuesday?'

'No. It can't.'

'Very well.'

'You're so sweet to . . .'

'Get on with it, darling.'

'All right . . .' Prue hesitated, then began again. 'We *have* slept together.'

'Go on.'

'And . . . it was good.'

The priest cleared his throat. 'Is he . . . clean?'

Stony silence.

'You do understand me, don't you, my child? I'm talking hygiene, not morals. I mean, you don't know where he's been, do you?'

Prue lowered her voice to an angry whisper. 'He's perfectly clean!'

'Good. You can't be too careful.'

'I don't need you to tell me how . . . different he is, Father. I know that better than anyone. I also know that I need him in my life very badly. I can't eat . . . I can't write . . . I can't go back and make things the way they were before I met them. I can't, Father. Do you understand what I'm saying?'

'Of course, my child.' His voice was much gentler this time. 'How are his teeth, by the way?'

'For God's sake!'

'Prue, lower your voice. Mrs Greeley is out there, remember?'

A long silence, and then: 'How can I share this with you, if you won't be serious with me.'

'I'm being *deadly* serious, darling. I asked about his teeth for a reason. It would help to know how . . . uh, presentable he is. Does he look O.K., aside from his clothes? I mean, would we have to fix him up?'

'I cannot believe this!'

'Just answer the question, my child.'

'He's . . . magnificent,' Prue sputtered. 'He's a handsome middle-aged man with nice skin, nice teeth. His vocabulary is better than mine.'

'So all he needs is Wilkes?'

'For *what*?'

'To pass. What else? The man needs a new suit, darling. We all had to pass at one point or another. Henry Higgins did it for Eliza; you can do it for Luke. Simple, *n'est-ce pas*?'

Prue was horrified. 'Luke will not be . . . fixed up, Father.'

'Have you asked him?'

'I wouldn't dream of that. He's such a proud man.'

'Ask him.'

'I couldn't.'

The cleric sighed. 'Very well.'

'Anyway, where would I do it?'

'Do what?'

'This . . . makeover. He won't come to my place. I know that. What would I do? Make him hide in the closet when my secretary's there? It's perfectly ridiculous.'

Father Paddy seemed to ponder for a moment. 'Let me work on it, darling. I have an idea.'

'What?'

'It'll take a bit of arranging. I'll get back to you. Run along now. Father knows best.'

So Prue collected her things and left the confessional.

Glowering, Mrs Greeley watched her walk out of the cathedral.

White Night

It had been five days since their last taping.

'It's wonderful to see you,' said DeDe. 'I was going a little stir crazy at home.'

They were eating dinner at a seafood place in Half Moon Bay. DeDe was wearing a Hermès scarf on her head and oversized sunglasses. Mary Ann was reminded of Jackie O's old shopping get-up for Greece.

599

'I'd think you'd be used to it by now,' said Mary Ann.

'What?'

'Being confined. First Jonestown, then the gay Cuban refugee center.'

'You'll never know true confinement,' mugged DeDe, 'until you've lived with a hundred Latin drag queens.'

Mary Ann grinned. 'Grim, huh?'

'*Noisy*. Castanets day and night. Aye-yi-yi till it's coming out your ass.'

Mary Ann laughed, then concentrated on her scallops. Was this the time to ask? Could she ease into the subject delicately? 'Uh . . . DeDe?'

'Yeah?'

'Are you doing all right? I mean . . . is something the matter?'

DeDe set her fork down. 'Why do you ask?'

'Well . . . your mother says you've been having nightmares.'

Silence.

'If I'm prying, tell me. I thought it might help you to talk about it.'

DeDe looked down at the Sony Micro Cassette-Corder that Mary Ann had bought with her first paycheck from Mrs Halcyon. 'It wouldn't make bad copy, either.'

Mary Ann was devastated. She turned off her machine instantly.

'DeDe, I would never . . .'

'Please. I didn't mean that. I'm sorry.' DeDe's hand rose shakily to her brow. 'Turn it back on. Please.'

Mary Ann did so.

'I'm edgy,' said DeDe, massaging her temples. 'I'm sorry . . . I shouldn't take it out on you . . . of all people. Yeah, I'm having nightmares.'

'About . . . him?'

DeDe nodded.

'How well did you know him, anyway?'

DeDe hesitated. 'I wasn't in the inner circle, if that's what you mean.'

'Who was?'

'Well . . . mostly the ones who slept with him. He had a sort of coterie of young white women who were always getting screwed for the revolution. Sometimes he had sex as often as ten or twelve times a day. He used to brag about it. It was how he took control.'

'But he never . . . ?'

'He knew about me and D'orothea, and he hated it. Not because we were lesbians, because he couldn't have us.'

'It was that important to him?'

DeDe shrugged. 'His track record's available. He took two wives from Larry Layton, and he fathered a child by one of them. He fucked anything he could get his hands on, including some of the men.'

'I see.'

'He was . . . with me only once. At Jane Pittman Gardens.'

Mary Ann looked puzzled.

'Our dorm,' explained DeDe. 'A lot of them were named after famous black women. I was sick that night, with a fever. D'orothea and most of the others were at a white night . . .'

'Uh . . . ?'

'Suicide practice. Somebody else must've run the show, because Jones came to the dorm and climbed into bed with me.'

'Jesus.'

'He told me quite calmly that he thought it was about time the twins saw who their father was.'

Mary Ann shook her head in disbelief.

'And then . . . he raped me. The twins were in the crib next to us, screaming through the whole thing. When he finally left, he leaned over and kissed both of them rather sweetly and said: "Now you're mine forever."'

'Awful.'

'He means it, too.'

Mary Ann reached across the table and took her hand. 'Meant,' she said quietly.

DeDe looked away from her. 'Let's go get a drink somewhere.'

Man and Walkman

It was late afternoon, the time of day when sunshine streamed through the green celluloid shades at the Twin Peaks and made the patrons look like fish in an overpopulated aquarium.

Michael sat on a window seat, against the glass – like the snail in the aquarium, he decided, passive, voyeuristic, moving at his own pace. He was still wearing his God's Green Earth overalls.

The man next to him was wearing a Walkman. When he saw Michael watching him, he took off the tiny earphones and held them out to him. 'Wanna listen?'

Michael smiled appreciatively. 'Who is it?'

'Abba.'

Abba? This guy was built like a brick shithouse, with an elephantine mustache and smoldering brown eyes. What was he doing hooked up to *that* sort of smarmy Euro-pop? On the other hand, he was also wearing a Qiana shirt. Maybe he just didn't know any better.

Michael avoided the confrontation. 'Actually,' he said, 'I'm not big on Walkmans. They make me kind of claustrophobic. I like to be able to get away from my music.'

'I use them at work mostly,' said the man, 'when there's a lot of paperwork. I smoke a doobie at lunch, come back, put these babies on and go with the flow.'

'Yeah. I can see how that might help.'

The man laid the Walkman on the table. 'You're in the chorus, aren't you?'

'Uh-huh.'

'I came to your welcome home,' said the man. 'What a scene!'

'Wasn't it great?' grinned Michael. Five days later, he was still tingling with the exhilaration of that moment. Several thousand people had mobbed their buses at the corner of 18th and Castro.

'I saw you kiss the ground,' said the man.

Michael shrugged sheepishly. 'I like it here, I guess.'

'Yeah . . . me too.' He fiddled with the Walkman, obviously searching for something to say. 'You don't like Abba, huh?'

Michael shook his head. 'Sorry,' he replied, as pleasantly as possible.

'What sort of stuff do you like?'

'Well . . . lately I've been getting into country-western.' Michael laughed. 'I don't know what came over me.'

'Redneck music,' said the man.

'I know. I used to hate the crap when I was a kid in Orlando. Maybe it's just the old bit about gay people imitating their oppressors. Like those guys who spend their days fighting police brutality and their nights dressing up like cops.'

The man smiled faintly. 'Never done that, huh?'

'Never,' said Michael. 'Was that strike two?'

The man shook his head. 'I've never done it either.'

'Well, then . . . see how much we have in common?' Michael extended his hand. 'I'm Michael Tolliver.'

'Bill Rivera.' *Latin*, thought Michael. This was getting better all the time.

'I have a friend,' Michael continued, 'who used to go to The Trench on uniform night, because he loved having sex with people who looked like cops or Nazis or soldiers. One night he went home with a guy in cop drag, and the guy had this incredible loft south of Market, with neon tubing over the bed and high-tech everything . . . to die, right? Only my friend didn't say a word, because he was supposed to be a prisoner, and the other guy was supposed to be a cop, and a prisoner doesn't say "What a fabulous apartment" to a cop. He said he could hardly wait for the sex to be over so he could ask the guy where he got his pin spots from. I don't have that kind of self-discipline, I suppose. I wanna be able to say "What a fabulous apartment" first thing. Is that too much to ask?'

The big mustache bristled as he smiled. 'It is at *my* house.'

Michael laughed. 'It doesn't have to be fabulous.'

'Good.'

'It doesn't even have to be *your* apartment. Mine's available.'

'Where do you live?'

'Russian Hill.'

'C'mon,' said the man, downing his drink, 'mine's closer.'

He lived on 17th Street in the Mission. His tiny studio was blandly furnished, with occasional endearing lapses into kitsch (a Mike Mentzer poster, a Lava Lite, a plastic cable car planter containing a half-dead philodendron).

Michael was enormously relieved. Bill Rivera wasn't tasteless – he was taste free. Gay men with *no* taste were often the hottest ones of all. Besides, thought Michael, if we ever kept house together, he'd probably let me do the decorating.

Then he spotted the handcuffs on the dresser.

'Uh . . . pardon me?'

Bill looked up. He was sitting on the edge of the bed, removing his Hush Puppies. 'Yeah?'

Michael held out the handcuffs, as if presenting Exhibit A. 'Aren't into this, huh?'

Bill shook his head. 'It's just a living.'

'Uh . . . ?'

'I'm a cop. Does that mean you wanna leave?'

'Now wait a minute . . .' Michael was dumbfounded.

Bill stood up and removed something from a dresser drawer, holding it out to his accuser.

'My badge, O.K.?'

Michael looked at it, then back at Bill, then back at the badge again.

'O.K.?' asked Bill.

'O.K.,' said Michael.

Almost numb, he sat down on the bed next to the policeman and began unlacing his shoes. 'What a fabulous apartment,' he said.

The Pygmalion Plot

Prue had already ripped three sheets of paper from her typewriter when her secretary stepped into the study.

'It's Father Paddy,' she said. 'He says it won't take long.'

Prue groaned softly and picked up the phone. 'Yes, Father?'

'I know you're on deadline, darling, but I need you to answer a few questions.'

'Shoot.'

'How does your schedule look? The next three weeks or so.'

Prue hesitated. 'What are you up to?'

'Tut-tut. Aren't we snippy this morning. Just answer the question, my child.'

Prue checked her appointment book. 'O.K.,' she said. 'Fairly slow, actually.'

'Good. Keep it that way.'

'Father . . .'

'And tell your Mountain Man not to fill up his dance card either. I've plans for the two of you.'

'What?'

'Never you mind. In good time, my child, in good time.'

'Father, I don't know what you're cooking up, but you might as well know that Luke is not . . . well, he's not the sort of man who'll take orders from other people.'

'Even you?'

'Of course not!'

'But, surely, if he *really* cares about you, Prue . . . if he wants to be

604

part of your life, then he should be willing to meet you on some . . . middle ground.'

'We've already talked about that. There is no middle ground.'

'Ah, but I think there is! Something that will appeal to his love of nature and to your sense of propriety. For God's sake, girl . . . are you happy?'

A long silence, and then: 'No.'

'No,' repeated Father Paddy. 'You are not. And *why* are you not happy? Because you're in love with that creature, and you want to be with him night and day.' The cleric paused dramatically, then lowered his voice for emphasis. 'I'm going to give you that, darling. I'm going to give you exactly what you want.'

Prue sighed audibly. 'If you won't tell me what it is, how in the world can I . . .'

'All right, all right . . .'

So he told her.

Countdown

The line for *Raiders of the Lost Ark* was so hopelessly serpentine that Mary Ann and Brian decided to forgo their movie plans and watch television together at home.

'I like this better, anyway,' said Mary Ann, lifting her McChicken sandwich from its styrofoam coffin. 'I haven't had a good TV-and-junk-food pig-out in ages.'

Brian swallowed a mouthful of Big Mac, then mopped up with the back of his hand. 'It fits the budget, anyway.' He cast an impish glance at Mary Ann. 'But you don't have to worry about that now, do you?'

Mary Ann frowned. 'Why do you keep riding me about that?'

Brian shrugged. 'Why do you have to be so secretive about it? Who am I gonna tell, huh? Some gin-soaked old society dame puts you on her payroll, and you run around acting like I need a National Security Clearance just to talk to you.'

'C'mon, Brian. You're the one who keeps bringing it up.'

'Gimme a hint, then, and I'll shut up.'

Mary Ann hesitated. 'If I tell you . . .'

Brian beamed triumphantly.

'*If* I tell you, Brian, you've got to promise me it won't go any further than this. I mean it, Brian. This is deadly serious.'

Brian made a poker face and held up his hand. 'My solemn oath. A lovers' pact.'

'I haven't even told Michael.'

Brian bowed. 'I'm deeply honored.'

'DeDe Day is back in town,' said Mary Ann.

'Wait a minute . . .'

Mary Ann nodded. 'Mrs Halcyon's daughter. The one who disappeared from Guyana.'

Brian whistled. 'Holy shit.'

'She's been living in Cuba for the past two-and-a-half years.'

'What about . . . whatshername . . . Mona's old girlfriend?'

'D'orothea. They were living together . . . along with the twins that DeDe had by the delivery boy at Jiffy's. D'orothea's still in Cuba. DeDe's hiding out in Hillsborough now. Her mother hired me to handle the press when DeDe breaks the story.'

Brian's brow furrowed. '*When* she breaks it? You went to Hillsborough weeks ago. Why hasn't she broken it already? What's she hiding out for?'

'That's the part I'm fuzzy on. She claims she wants to talk to some Temple members about something. She won't tell me what it is yet.'

Brian smiled sardonically. 'She's probably looking for a good publisher. Half of those Jonestown people are writing books.'

Mary Ann shook her head. 'It's much more serious than that. Besides, *I'm* writing the book when the time comes.'

'Good.'

'I just don't know *what* I'll be writing.'

'Not so good.'

'You're telling me! Something big is missing, Brian . . . something she lives with night and day. I can almost feel it in the room with us when we're talking.'

'Like what?'

'I don't know.' Mary Ann shivered suddenly. 'God, it gives me the creeps. I agreed to keep quiet about everything until next week. Then I'm free to negotiate with the station. She's promised to fill me in as soon as she finds out . . . whatever she's trying to find out.'

'It sounds like she's afraid of recriminations.'

'I've thought of that,' said Mary Ann, 'but it doesn't really make any sense. If the other survivors are working the talk show circuit, as you pointed out, what has *DeDe* got to be afraid of?'

'She could be just plain wacko.'

'I don't think so,' said Mary Ann. 'She's a pretty solid person.'

'That airhead debutante . . . ?'

'She's changed a lot, Brian. I guess the children did it. She *lives* for them now. She may be a little paranoid about their safety, but that seems perfectly normal after what she's been through.'

'I think you're the one who should be paranoid,' said Brian.

'Why?'

'What's to stop another reporter from stumbling on this one before you break it?'

Mary Ann winced. 'I know, but she's being as careful as possible. She hides in the guest wing whenever visitors come. And she doesn't leave the house that much.'

'Just to visit Temple members, huh?'

She saw his point all too well.

They were in bed watching Tom Snyder when the phone rang.

Mary Ann answered it. 'Hello.'

'Mary Ann . . . it's DeDe.' Her voice sounded small and terrified. Mary Ann glanced at the digital clock on the dresser. It said 1:23.

'Hi,' said Mary Ann. 'Are you O.K.?' She assumed that DeDe was having those bad dreams again.

'I need to see you,' said DeDe.

'Sure. Of course. When?'

'Tomorrow morning?'

'Could we make it the afternoon? Brian and I had planned on . . .'

'*Please.*' The word reverberated like a scream in a tomb. It was all Mary Ann needed to hear.

'Where?' she asked.

'Here. Halcyon Hill. I don't want to leave the house.'

'DeDe, what on earth has . . . ?'

'Just come, O.K.? Bring your tape recorder. We can eat breakfast here. I'm really sorry about this. I'll explain everything in the morning.'

When Mary Ann set the receiver down, Brian smiled at her sweetly. 'Scratch the roller-skating, huh?'

'I'm afraid so,' she said.

'What's up?'

'I wish I knew,' said Mary Ann.

Nothing to Lose

It took Prue Giroux exactly twelve hours to succumb completely to the wild romanticism of Father Paddy's scheme. The following morning she hurried out to the park and made her own pitch, snuggled cozily in Luke's arms.

He gazed at the ceiling in stony silence.

'Well?' asked Prue.

'You would do that?' he said finally.

'I would if I thought it would bring us closer together.'

'Is that what you think?'

'It might.'

Another long silence.

'Besides, if it doesn't work out, what harm has been done? We've got nothing to lose, Luke.'

'I hate the bourgeoisie,' he replied sternly. 'I've spent most of my life subverting it . . . or running from it.'

The columnist bristled. 'Am *I* the bourgeoisie? Is that what you're telling me?'

He leaned down and kissed her forehead. 'Unlike a lot of good things, you're best when taken out of context.'

'But . . . this *would* be out of context. Just us, if that's the way we want it. Two weeks that belong to *us*, Luke.'

'And then what?'

'I don't know. Does it matter? Aren't you the one who said to forget about forever?'

She had him there. He smiled at her in concession, then shook his head slowly. 'Prue, I have no clothes for that sort of thing, none of the . . .'

'I can take care of that.'

'I don't want your charity.'

'It's a loan, then. It all reverts to me after two weeks. For God's sake, you're not selling your *soul*, Luke.'

'That remains to be seen.'

'Look,' she snapped, 'you keep telling me that I'd be ashamed to be seen with you. Well then . . . *prove* it, if you can!'

'Prue . . .'

'The truth is . . . you're ashamed to be seen with *me*. You're such a snob, Luke. You're the biggest snob I ever met!'

'If it helps you to think that, then go ahead.'

'What have you got to lose, Luke?'

He rolled away from her.

'Do you remember what you said that first night? You said you would love me unconditionally, at my pleasure . . . as little or as much as I wanted. Well . . . this is what I want. Do this for me, Luke.'

'I meant *here*,' he said quietly, speaking to the wall.

But she knew she had won.

DeDe's Tale

Mary Ann turned on the Sony. 'I'm afraid I'm a little muddled. I'm not exactly sure where to begin.'

'It isn't your fault,' said DeDe. 'I haven't let you play with a full deck.' The flesh around her eyes was so dark, Mary Ann observed, that she could have been recovering from a nose job. *What on earth had happened?*

'Where are the children?' asked Mary Ann.

'Upstairs with Mother and Emma. I don't want them here while this is happening. Any of them.'

'I see.'

'Frankly, I don't know *what* you think of me at this point. I suppose you have every reason to regard me as a certified nut case.'

'No way.'

DeDe smiled feebly. 'Well, it doesn't get better, I can promise you. I suppose you already know that Jim Jones wasn't a healthy man?'

'To put it mildly.'

'I mean physically, as well. He had diabetes and hypertension. One of the women who slept with him told me he was supposed to have seventeen hundred calories a day, but he was hooked on soda pop and sweet rolls. He also had a chronic coughing condition.'

'I've read about that,' said Mary Ann.

'He coughed all the time. A lot of Temple members thought he was just taking on their diseases.'

'I don't understand.'

'Well, he cured people, you know. Or he went through the motions, anyway. A lot of people looked on him as a healer. He would hold healing sessions where he'd pray for somebody who had, say, cancer . . . and he'd leave the room and come back a few minutes later with a handful of chicken gizzards which he said was the cancer.'

'You mean . . .'

'He had yanked the cancer right out of their body.'

'They believed that?'

'Some of them did. Others humored him, because they approved of his goals.'

'Like a lot of people here.'

'Yes. And a lot of those poor souls believed that he took on their disease as soon as he cured them of it. It was his way of going to Calvary. His illness was all the more pitiful – we were told – because it was really *our* illness, and he was bearing it for us.'

'How awful.'

DeDe shrugged. 'You have no idea how noble it made him look at the time.'

'You weren't buying it, were you?'

'The point is,' said DeDe, almost irritably, 'the man was sick. Anybody could see that. It's easy to look back *now* and see that a lot of it may have been psychosomatic or something . . . but it looked pretty damn real at the time. So did the arthritis. The swelling in his wrists and hands was quite noticeable. I was shocked the first time I saw it. I came into the nursery one day and found him with the twins . . .'

'There was a nursery?'

DeDe thought for a moment. 'The Cuffy Memorial Baby Nursery, to be precise.'

'Cuffy,' repeated Mary Ann. 'That's sort of sweet, actually.'

'He was a black liberation leader in Guyana.'

'Right.'

'At any rate, Dad was . . . Jones was standing there in the nursery, holding little Edgar, singing something to him . . . with those huge swollen hands. It was pathetic and horrible all at the same time. I should've felt complete revulsion, I guess, but all I could feel was an odd sort of pity . . . and panic, of course. I moved closer to hear what he was singing, but it wasn't his usual revolutionary anthem; it was "Bye Baby Bunting".'

Mary Ann almost said 'Aww', but caught herself in the nick of time.

'There must have been *something* decent about him or you wouldn't have stayed so long. You didn't even plan your escape, did you, until you heard about the cyanide?'

DeDe nodded. 'Partly because of his illness, I guess. It made him seem less threatening, more vulnerable. And partly because I was . . . used to things. It was a shitty little world, but at least I knew how it worked. You know what I mean?'

Mary Ann nodded, flashing instantly on Halcyon Communications.

'The truth is,' DeDe continued, 'I was an idiot. I actually cried when he called us together and announced that he had cancer.'

'When was that?'

'August, I guess. Early August. Later in the month, a doctor named Goodlett came in from San Francisco. He examined Jones and said he couldn't find any cancer. He said it was probably some sort of fungus eating at his lungs. Anyway, he tried to get Jones to leave the jungle for proper tests to diagnose his illness, but Jones was terrified of leaving Jonestown even for a day. Charles Garry made special arrangements for him to have a medical examination in Georgetown – without getting arrested, that is – but Jones was afraid of a rebellion in his absence.'

'So he was still *thinking* clearly.'

'Always,' said DeDe, 'when it came to keeping control. Of course, later that summer the addiction started. Quaaludes mixed with cognac, Elavil, Placidyl . . . Valium, Nembutal, you name it. Marceline saw him falling apart before her very eyes and realized that something had to be done.'

'Who was Marceline?'

'His wife.'

'Right,' said Mary Ann hastily, feeling stupider by the minute. 'I'd almost forgotten he was married.'

Chums

Brian and Michael spent Saturday morning roller-skating in Golden Gate Park – a precarious undertaking at best, despite the sleek, professional-looking skates Mrs Madrigal had given them the previous Christmas.

'You've been practicing,' Brian shouted accusingly as they wobbled past the de Young Museum. 'That's against the rules, you know?'

'Says who?'

'Mary Ann said you went skating on Tuesday. With your cop friend.'

'That was *indoors*. That doesn't count.'

'Where'd you go?'

'The rink in El Sobrante. It's loaded with Farrah Fawcett minors, blow-dried for days . . .'

'*Girls?*'

'You wish. Twinkies. It's an amazing sight. I should take you and Mary Ann sometime. We can take the bus.'

'There's a special bus?'

Michael nodded. 'It makes the rounds of half-a-dozen gay bars, then drops everybody off at the rink. It's a lot of fun. You get to make out on the bus on the way home.'

Brian smiled nostalgically. 'I remember that.'

'So do I. Only I never did it in high school. I never did it at all until last Tuesday. I remember, though . . . all those kids listening to Bread and making out in the dark in the back of the bus on the way home from out-of-town ball games.'

Brian held out his hand to stop Michael at the intersection. 'Watch it,' he said. 'Don't get lost in your memories. This place is lethal on weekends.'

'Think of that, though. I was thirty-one before I ever kissed anybody on public transportation. I consider it a major milestone.'

'It was more than that,' teased Brian. 'Some people *never* get around to kissing a cop, much less doing it on a bus. It *was* the cop, wasn't it?'

Michael feigned indignation. 'Of course!'

'Hey . . . what does a breeder know?'

Michael grinned. 'Where did you learn that word?'

The light changed. They proceeded with graceless caution across the pebbly asphalt. 'One of the guys at Perry's,' replied Brian. 'He said that's what the faggots call us.'

'Not this faggot,' said Michael.

'I know.' Brian turned to look at him, almost losing his balance.

Michael grabbed his arm. 'Easy . . . easy . . .'

'Anyway,' said Brian, regaining his composure, 'it's not even applicable to me. I'm thirty-six years old and I've never bred so much as a goldfish.'

When they reached the other side, Michael aimed for a bench and sat down. Brian collapsed beside him, expelling air noisily.

'Do you want to?' asked Michael.

'What?'

'Have children.'

Brian shrugged. 'Sure. But Mary Ann doesn't. Not right now, anyway. She's got a career going.' He smiled benignly. 'In case you haven't noticed.'

Michael began unlacing his skates. 'Where is she today, anyway?'

'Having lunch. On the peninsula.'

'What on earth for?'

'Just . . . business.'

They sat together in silence for several minutes, watching the passing scene in their bare feet. Finally, Michael said: 'I think you two should get married.'

'You do, huh?'

'Uh-huh.'

'Have you told her that?'

'Not in so many words,' replied Michael.

Brian grinned. 'Neither have I.'

'Why not?'

Brian reached down and yanked up a handful of grass. 'Oh . . . because I think I know what the answer would be . . . and I don't need to hear that right now. Besides, there are lots of advantages to living alone.'

'Name one.'

Brian thought for a moment. 'You can pee in the sink.'

Michael laughed. 'You do that, too, huh?' Suddenly, he clamped his hand on Brian's leg and exclaimed: 'Well, get a load of *that*, would you?'

'What?'

'Over there . . . by the conservatory. That overdressed blonde climbing into the limo.'

'Yeah?'

'That's Prue Giroux.'

'Who?'

'You know . . . the dizzy socialite who writes for *Western Gentry* magazine.'

'Never heard of her.'

'She's grinning like a Cheshire cat,' said Michael. 'Where do you suppose she's going?'

The Trouble With Dad

'Anyway,' DeDe continued, 'Marceline *knew* how sick he was. She was worried about it all the time.'

'You knew her?'

DeDe nodded. 'We were friends, of sorts. She was a pretty savvy woman.'

'Yet she didn't . . . ?'

'Hang on, O.K.? I wanna get through this. A Russian doctor named . . . Fedorovsky, I think . . . I'll have to check my diary . . . this doctor came to Jonestown in the fall and said that Jones had emphysema. Marceline made a special trip to San Francisco to tell Dr Goodlett that Jones' fever was getting worse. He told her he couldn't be responsible for treating him, if Jones wouldn't leave the jungle for proper treatment. He washed his hands of it, in other words.

'At this point, apparently, Marceline decided to approach a former Temple member who lived in San Francisco. This man was one of Jones' most devoted disciples, but he was also a serious mental case . . . so serious, in fact, that Jones had refused him permission to participate in Jonestown.'

'What was his name?' asked Mary Ann.

'I don't know. Marceline never told me. The point is . . . this guy bore a really freaky resemblance to Jones . . . the same body type and coloration, the same angularity to his face. He even capitalized on it by wearing sideburns and mirrored sunglasses.'

'But . . . why?'

DeDe shrugged. 'All of the others wanted to follow Jones. This one wanted to *be* him.'

'Did Marceline tell you this?'

'Uh-huh. I also saw it with my own eyes.'

'*In Jonestown?*'

DeDe nodded. 'I saw them meeting together one night. Jones and this guy. I could barely tell them apart. The plan – according to

Marceline – was for the imposter to run the operation until Jones could get to Moscow for medical treatment. A week at the most, she said. He would do most of his work on the loudspeaker system, with occasional walk-throughs to keep people in line. The man was briefed on *everything*, including the suicide drills. Jones was so sick, of course, that no one expected him to sound like himself . . . or even to actively participate in the day-to-day life of the camp. He just had to *be* there, a figurehead to prevent an insurrection.'

'Then . . . this happened? *Jones left?*'

'I don't know. Two days after the imposter arrived in camp, Captain Duke told me about the cyanide. I didn't stick around to find out. For once in my life, I missed out on the action and was damn glad of it.'

'So you left . . . when?'

'Two days before the congressman and the others were murdered at the airstrip.'

'Meaning that this man . . . the imposter . . . may have been the one who ordered the mass suicide?'

'Yes.'

'And may have been the one who . . .'

When Mary Ann faltered, DeDe finished the sentence. 'The one who died.'

'*My God!*'

DeDe simply blinked at her.

'That's . . . DeDe, that's *grotesque.*'

'Isn't it, though?'

'But . . . surely . . . the government must've checked those bodies at the time. Somebody must've . . . I don't know . . . what do they do? A blood test or something?'

DeDe smiled patiently. 'There were nine hundred bodies, remember?'

'I know, but . . .'

'One of those bodies was lying in front of the throne with its head on a pillow. Bloated as it was, it *looked* like Jones . . . and it was probably carrying his identification. Do you think they stopped to check his fingerprints?'

'Wasn't there an autopsy?'

'There was,' said DeDe, 'and I've been trying like hell to find the report. That's why I needed *time*, don't you see? If someone could prove to me conclusively that he was really dead . . .'

'What about those Temple members?'

DeDe grimaced. 'They were useless. They wanted no part of it. They treated me like I was crazy or something.'

Mary Ann said nothing.

'Mary Ann . . . please . . . don't write me off just yet.' DeDe looked at her imploringly as her eyes filled with tears. 'I haven't even gotten to the crazy part.'

Mary Ann took her hand. 'Go ahead,' she said. 'I'm listening.'

'I don't know what to do,' sobbed DeDe. 'I'm so damn tired of running . . .'

'DeDe, please don't. It can't be as bad as you . . .'

'I've *seen* him, Mary Ann!'

'*What?*'

'Yesterday. At Steinhart Aquarium. Mother was driving me crazy, so I drove to the city . . . just to walk around. I went to a concert in the park . . . and later I went to the aquarium . . . and I saw him there in the crowd.'

'You saw . . . Jones?' Mary Ann was thunderstruck.

DeDe nodded, her face contorted with fear.

'What was he doing?'

'Looking . . .' She was almost incoherent now. Feeling her own lip begin to quiver, Mary Ann squeezed DeDe's hand even tighter.

'Looking?' she asked guardedly.

De De nodded, wiping her eyes with her free hand. 'At the fish. The same as me.'

'It's awfully dark in there. Are you sure you . . . ?'

'*Yes!* He was thinner looking, and much healthier, but it was him. I knew the minute I looked into his eyes.'

'He *saw* you?'

'He smiled at me. It was awful.'

'What did you do?'

'I ran all the way back to the car and drove home. I haven't left the house since. I know how this sounds, believe me. You have every right to . . .'

'I believe you.'

'You do?'

'I believe it's real to you. That's enough for me.'

DeDe's sobs stopped. She glared at Mary Ann for a moment, then jerked her hand away angrily. 'You think I'm hysterical, don't you?'

'DeDe, I think you've been incredibly brave . . .'

'*Brave?* Look at me, goddamnit! I am scared shitless! Do you think I don't know what the police would say about this . . . what the whole goddamn world would say about that poor little rich girl who went off the deep end in Jonestown? Look how *you're* acting, and you're supposed to be my friend!'

'I am your friend,' Mary Ann said feebly.

'Then what am I gonna do? *What am I gonna do about my goddamn children?*'

Gangie

Little Edgar and his sister Anna ran across the brown lawn at Halcyon Hill and accosted their grandmother on the terrace, each tugging joyfully at a leg.

'Gangie, Gangie . . . look!'

Frannie set her teacup down on the glass-topped table and smiled at the four-year-olds. 'What is it, darlings? What do you want to show Gangie?'

Little Anna thrust out her tiny fist and uncurled it. A small gray toad, pulsing like a heart, was offered for examination. Frannie's nose wrinkled, but she did her best to sound appreciative. 'Well, now . . . just look at him, would you? Do you know what that is, Edgar?'

Edgar shook his head.

'It's a fwog,' said Anna, somewhat smugly.

Edgar cast a disdainful look at his twin. 'I found it,' he declared defiantly, as if to compensate for his vocabulary failure.

'Well, it's just wonderful,' said Frannie sweetly, 'but I think you should take it back where you found it.'

'Why?' they asked together.

'Well . . . because it's one of God's little creatures, and it looks like a baby to me. It probably misses its mommy. You wouldn't like it if someone took you away from *your* mommy, now would you?'

Four almond eyes grew larger; two little heads shook simultaneously.

'Well, then . . . you run along and put him right back where you found him and Gangie will have a big surprise for you when you get back.'

Frannie watched as they scurried back to the edge of the rose garden, delighting in the classic simplicity of the scenario. She was sure she had spoken the same words – in the same place, moreover – when DeDe had been that age.

'Could I have a word with you, Mother?'

The matriarch turned around to confront the grown-up DeDe, looking lean and beautiful and unusually . . . purposeful. 'Hello, darling. Will Mary Ann join us for tea?'

'She just left,' said DeDe.

Frannie pecked her daughter on the cheek, then glanced lovingly in the direction of the twins. 'They're such a joy. I can't tell you.'

DeDe's smile was weary. 'They seem to have taken to you, all right. Mother . . . could we talk for a moment?'

'Of course, darling. Is something the matter?'

DeDe shook her head. 'I think you'll like it. I *hope* you'll like it.'

Emma kept the children amused with ice cream in the kitchen, while DeDe sat with her mother on the sunporch and explained what was on her mind.

'Mary Ann is going to release the story,' she said. 'Not yet, though . . . maybe a week or so from now. We haven't quite worked that part out yet. The point is . . . I think you and the twins should be out of town when it happens.'

'*What?*'

'Think about it, Mother. The publicity will be excruciating no matter what we do. I just don't want you or the children subjected to that kind of pressure.'

'That's very sweet, darling, but sooner or later that's bound to happen, isn't it?'

DeDe nodded. 'To some extent . . . but things will have cooled down somewhat, and I think you'll be better equipped to handle it.' DeDe handed her mother a page from the travel section of the *Chronicle*. 'I think this looks marvelous myself. They say it's the most spacious ship afloat, and it sails for . . .'

'DeDe, what on earth . . . ?'

'Hear me out, Mother. It sails for Alaska next week for a two-week cruise. You see the glaciers and lovely old Russian buildings in Sitka . . .'

'DeDe, I'm touched by your thoughtfulness, but . . . well, I like it here, darling. And I really don't think the publicity will be too much for me to . . .'

'Mother, I want the children out of town!'

Frannie was taken aback by the ferocity of DeDe's declaration. 'Darling, I'll do anything you want. I just don't understand why it's so . . . well, so *important* to you.'

DeDe composed herself. 'Just help me on this, Mother. Please. It's a marvelous trip. The twins will adore it, and you'll get to know them so much better. It's perfect, really.' She looked at Frannie almost plaintively. 'Don't you think?'

The matriarch hesitated, then gave her daughter a hug. 'I think it sounds lovely,' she said.

A Starr is Born

The clothes from Wilkes Bashford arrived at Prue's house about half-an-hour before Father Paddy did.

'What do you think?' the cleric asked breathlessly. 'Daniel Detorie helped me pick them out. I *know* I went overboard on the Polo shirts, but the colors were so yummy I couldn't resist.'

'They're fine,' Prue replied, almost blandly. She was in shock, she realized, for now she *knew* it was going to happen. *It was really going to happen.* She conjured up a smile for the priest. 'I can't believe how sweet you're being.'

'Pish,' said Father Paddy. 'The pleasure was all mine, darling. I've never been turned loose in Wilkes before.' He lifted a blue blazer from its box. 'This is Brioni,' he said. 'I debated getting the Polo blazer, which was four hundred, but not nearly so *shaped* as the Brioni. And since we're going for effect here, eight hundred seemed reasonable enough. Has he gotten a haircut yet?'

'I don't think so,' said Prue.

Father Paddy rolled his eyes. 'He can't get on the ship looking like the Wild Man of Borneo, darling!'

'I know,' said Prue, 'but if we slick his hair back . . .'

'Forget that. I'll send over a hairdresser with the manicurist on Sunday.' He sighed exuberantly. 'God, this is fun, isn't it?'

'I'm still so nervous,' said Prue.

'Well, don't be. It's a piece of cake.' The priest removed a packet from his breast pocket. 'Now, here are the tickets, my child. You'll board between three o'clock and four-thirty on Sunday. Luke's stateroom is two doors down from yours on the same deck. You can board half-an-hour apart, if you like, so nobody'll be the wiser. Now . . . is he spending the night here on Saturday, I hope?'

Prue nodded. 'I've given my secretary the weekend off.'

'Good. Smart girl.'

Prue perused the tickets, her brow wrinkling. 'Wait a minute . . . this ticket says Sean P. Starr.'

'Right,' grinned Father Paddy. 'Yours truly.'

'But . . . Luke can't impersonate you, Father.'

'Why not?'

'Well, it's just too risky. What if he needs to show an ID or something?'

The priest shrugged. 'He'll show mine. That's included in the tour package, my child.'

'That's very sweet, but . . . well, Luke just wouldn't do that, I know it.'

'Do what?'

'Pretend to be a priest.'

Father Paddy held out the ID card for her examination. 'Show me where it says priest. He'll just be Sean Starr, *bon vivant* and world traveller, a charming middle-aged bachelor who just happens to meet a certain charming middle-aged society columnist on a cruise to Alaska. What could be more natural? Or more *romantic*, for that matter? Your readers will eat it up with a spoon!'

Prue laughed for the first time all day. 'You're absolutely insidious, Father.'

The cleric accepted the compliment with a demure little bow. 'The rest is up to you, my child. The church can only go so far in secular matters. If I were you, though, I'd lean very heavily on his investment broker background. Didn't you say he used to do that?'

Prue nodded. 'A long time ago. Before he was a preacher.'

'Marvelous. Then it's the truth. That's always handy.' He leaned over and pecked Prue impetuously on the cheek. 'Oh Prue . . . you've got such an adventure ahead of you, *such* an adventure.'

The columnist heard herself giggle. 'I do, don't I?'

'And you're giving that poor man a new start in life. That's something to be proud of . . . *and*, incidentally, something to write home about. I want *vivid* details, darling. That's my fee for this service. By the way, do you love him?'

'Oh, yes!'

'Then, he'll see that for two solid weeks, darling. He'll see it, and he'll never go back to what he was before. Some people *are* made for each other, my child, and when that happens, almost anything is possible. *Now* . . . what sort of hairdresser would you like?'

In Hillsborough, it was DeDe who gave the last-minute briefing.

'Just relax, Mother, that's the main thing. Relax and enjoy your grandchildren . . . but for God's sake don't tell people that's who they are or you'll defeat our whole purpose.'

'Then, what exactly am I supposed to tell them?'

'Simple. They're your *foster* grandchildren. Vietnamese orphans in your charge for the summer.'

The matriarch was indignant. 'No one will believe that!'

'Why not? It makes more sense than the truth, doesn't it?'

Silence.

'I know it'll be tempting to brag, Mother. But you mustn't. Not to anyone. There'll be time enough to celebrate with your friends after we break the story.'

'What if I see someone I know?'

'You won't, probably. Cruise ships have been middle class for years. But if you do, the story's still the same. Say "foster" every time you say "grandchild" and you've got it licked. O.K.?'

Frannie nodded begrudgingly. 'It seems awfully silly, somehow.'

'Mother,' DeDe's voice was all business now. 'It may seem silly to you, but it's of vital importance. Do you understand me? The most well-meaning person could leak the story to the press before we know what hit us. Remember what Daddy used to say: "Loose lips sink ships."'

Frannie wrinkled her nose at her daughter, 'I can do without the leaking and the sinking, thank you.'

DeDe laughed nervously. 'Bad choice. Sorry. Oh Mother, I hope you have the time of your life!'

'I will,' smiled Frannie. 'We will.'

Now, Voyagers

The gangplank to the *Sagafjord* was aswarm with passengers, but Prue could see only one. 'Look at him,' she purred. 'Have you ever beheld anything more beautiful?'

Father Paddy crossed himself, an altogether suitable reply considering the object of their scrutiny. For the creature in the Brioni blazer *was* beautiful, a sleek, chiseled racehorse of a man who might easily be mistaken for a diplomat or an international financier.

'I want to run up there and hug him,' said Prue.

'Easy,' muttered the cleric. 'Clothes might make the man, but *you* can't do it until the ship's under way.'

Prue giggled nervously. 'You're terrible, Father.'

'Does Luke have his ticket?'

Prue nodded. 'I gave him the Olaf Trygvasson Suite. I wanted the Henrik Ibsen for myself. It seemed more literary.'

'Entirely appropriate,' said Father Paddy. 'Do you want me to come on board, by the way?'

'That's sweet. I'll be able to manage, I think.'

The priest arched an eyebrow. 'I should certainly hope so.'

'*Stop* it, Father.'

Father Paddy chuckled and hugged his friend. 'Have a wonderful time, darling. I hope you meet someone *marvelous* on board.'

'Something tells me I will,' smiled Prue.

'But *don't* meet him until the proper occasion arises.'

Prue nodded. 'I understand.'

'And remember to call him Sean when other people are around.'

'I will.'

'And, for God's sake, don't fret over the fact that Frannie Halcyon is on board.'

'*What?*'

'I just spotted her on the pier. She may be seeing someone off of course. At any rate, you have a perfect right to any romance that may happen to . . . come up, once you're on board. Luke is certainly *more* than presentable at this point, and I doubt if Frannie . . .'

'Where is she?' asked Prue. 'God, that makes me nervous!'

'Oh, Prue . . . lighten up. This is a vacation, remember?'

Prue smiled gamely. 'I'll try to.'

'God bless,' said Father Paddy.

'Ta-ta,' said Prue.

Down on the pier, three women clustered around two small children and made uneasy chatter.

'Now promise me,' said DeDe, squatting to confront the twins, 'you'll do everything that Gangie says.'

Little Anna attached herself to DeDe's neck like a koala bear. 'Why don't you come, Mommy?'

'I can't sweetheart. Mommy's got some things to do. But I'll be right here to meet you when you get back, I promise.'

'Will D'orothea be here then?'

'She might, sweetheart. Mommy doesn't know yet.'

Mary Ann knelt next to DeDe and addressed the children: 'It's going to be so much fun. They have movies on the ship, you know. And you'll see wonderful animals up in Alaska.'

'What kind?' asked little Edgar.

Mary Ann's face went blank. 'What kind?' she murmured to DeDe.

'Uh . . . moose, I guess. Mooses?'

'*Big* animals,' explained Mary Ann. 'With big horns.' Then she saw the look on the little girl's face, and added hastily: 'But they're very sweet . . . like a big ol' dog or something.'

DeDe rose to her feet and embraced her mother. 'Thank you for doing this. I love you dearly. I hope that much is clear, at least.'

'It is,' said Frannie, beginning to weep. 'It always was, darling.'

DeDe found a Kleenex in her purse and blotted the matriarch's eyes. 'It's better this way,' she said. 'I know they'll be safe with their Gangie.'

'But what could be safer than home?'

'Now, now . . . you know the publicity would . . .'

'It isn't just the publicity, is it?' Frannie fixed her daughter with a gaze that demanded the truth.

DeDe turned away, discarding the Kleenex.

'Is it?' Frannie persisted.

A bone-rattling blast from the *Sagafjord* announced its impending departure.

'There we go,' said DeDe, a trifle too cheerily.

'DeDe, I want you to . . .'

623

DeDe silenced her with another hug. 'Everything will be fine. Mother . . . just fine.'

Keeping up with the Joneses

Larry Kenan didn't laugh – he *brayed* – when Mary Ann made her request. 'That's rich, lady! That is really rich!'

'Well, I'm sorry if it . . .'

'*Reserve* air time?'

'You don't have to repeat it, Larry. I get the message.'

'Air time is not something you reserve, like a room at the Hilton or something . . .'

'Right. Gotcha.'

'Air time is something you *create* . . . and we have to know what we're creating, right?'

'Right.' Mary Ann rose and headed for the door.

The news director kept his face tilted heavenward towards Bo Derek. 'Hold it,' he said.

Mary Ann stopped at the door. 'Yeah?'

'If you've got a story, you should let us know about it. You have a *responsibility* to let us know about it. As a journalist.'

'I'm not a journalist,' said Mary Ann crisply. 'You just said so yourself.'

'I said you were not a journalist *yet*. And, even if you were, I couldn't sign you up for free air time without knowing what the fuck you're gonna talk about!'

'I already told you,' said Mary Ann calmly. 'I can talk about it a week from today.'

'Then why don't you do that, huh?'

'Fine.'

'Only don't expect to talk about it on the air.'

'Larry . . .'

'Do you read me, lady? We have professionals we pay for that. That's not what we pay you for. I think we could work out a credit line on the crawl. *Maybe*. I don't know what rabbit you've got treed, but don't expect it to turn you into Bambi Kanetaka overnight.'

She squelched a 'God forbid' and walked out the door. So much for Plan A.

Plan B, she expected, would be a lot more fun.

DeDe seemed amenable to the idea. 'I don't care how we do it,' she said. 'I'm more concerned about when.'

'Would Tuesday be O.K.?' asked Mary Ann.

'A week from today?'

Mary Ann nodded. 'That'll give us a week to mop things up before your mother and the children get back. The trip was a good idea, really . . . if only for logistical purposes.'

DeDe's face clouded over. 'But you think I'm a little paranoid, just the same.'

'I think you're being conscientious.'

'Don't mince words, Mary Ann.'

'DeDe, I . . .'

'Jim Jones is dead, right? He must be. You saw it on the goddamn news!'

The outburst miffed Mary Ann. 'All I care about,' she said firmly, 'is that you get a fair chance to tell your story . . . in as safe a fashion as possible. This is a mind-boggling scoop, DeDe. Period. My opinion doesn't make a good goddamn at this point. The point is . . . to raise the questions. The answers will sort themselves out later.'

'You're right,' said DeDe resignedly.

'It won't be easy. I know that. If you like, you can confine your remarks to a written statement, and I'll handle the questions from the press. Then you and the twins can disappear, take another vacation, start life afresh.'

DeDe's smile was rueful. 'It'll be anything but that.'

'I know it'll be tough for a while, but . . .'

'It'll tough until I know for sure. I saw that guy, Mary Ann. I've never been so sure about something.'

Mary Ann appraised her for a moment. 'All right, then . . . let's say that you did.'

DeDe waited.

'Let's say that he made it to Moscow, and his double died in his place. The whole world thinks he's dead, but he's really alive and well and living in Moscow. Why on earth, then, would he come back to San Francisco and be seen working around Steinhart Aquarium?'

Silence.

Mary Ann was gentle. 'These are the things they're going to ask you, DeDe. I want you to be ready.'

'I'll never be ready,' she said grimly.

Mary Ann rose and moved to DeDe's side, hugging her clumsily. 'I'm so sorry. God, I . . . look, we can leave out the stuff about the double, if you want. We can just announce that you're back and leave out the rest . . .'

'No!' DeDe's head shook adamantly. 'I want to nail that asshole. I want this over once and for all. I don't want to creep around the rest of my life, wondering if he's waiting for me . . . wondering if . . . if the children . . .'

'What if it was the double you saw?'

Another decisive shake of DeDe's head. 'It wasn't.'

'How can you be so sure?'

'I just am, that's all.'

'He hasn't changed at all? Surely people would recognize him.'

'Would you?' asked DeDe. 'Who the hell expects to bump into *him* on the street?'

'Yeah. I see your point.'

'Besides . . . there *was* something different about him. His nose, maybe . . . I don't know. They could've given him plastic surgery in Moscow. God, I wish you believed me! I remember the past, Mary Ann. I *won't* be condemned to repeat it!' DeDe flinched as if she'd been slapped. '*Jesus!*'

'What's the matter?' asked Mary Ann.

'Nothing,' said DeDe. 'I'm still spouting his jargon, that's all.'

'What jargon?'

DeDe shrugged it off. 'Just a stupid quotation he hung over his throne.'

Taste Test

'Sorry I'm late,' said Bill Rivera, joining Michael at a table in Welcome Home. 'My ex-lover's brother's lover just left town.'

'Hang on. Your . . . ?'

The policeman smiled. 'Ex-lover's brother's lover. He came out about a week ago.'

'Out here, or out of the closet?'

'*Both*, more or less . . . and the sonofabitch picked my apartment to

626

do it in. He showed up on my doorstep with fourteen different fantasy costumes.'

'Like . . . leather?'

'Leather, cowboy stuff, bandannas out the ass, tit clamps, three-piece suits . . . you name it.'

Michael smiled. 'And guess who's supposed to show him around.'

Bill shook his head. 'I hardly saw the guy. He'd stop by long enough to crash or change costumes or swipe my poppers, and then he'd take off again. He trashed his way from Alta Plaza to Badlands to The Caldron and back again, while I stayed home and watched TV. This morning, when he left, he got real serious all of a sudden and said: "You know, Bill. This place is just too decadent. I could never live here." I felt like strangling the prick with his harness.'

Michael laughed and handed Bill a menu. 'The people from L.A. are the worst.'

'This guy's from Milwaukee. Even the faggots there think we've gone too far.'

Michael smiled suddenly, remembering something. 'Did you hear about the fire in the Castro Muni Metro station last week?'

The policeman shook his head.

'It wasn't much of one,' Michael continued. 'But a whole hook-and-ladder showed up, complete with half-a-dozen hot firemen. They parked across from the Castro Theatre, but couldn't get into the Metro station without passing through a hoedown being held by The Foggy City Squares.'

'Translate,' said Bill.

'A gay square dance group. They were doing this big do-si-do number in front of the Bank of America. Clapping and yee-hawing and singing "The Trail of the Lonesome Pine." All men. It was great. What struck me about it, actually, was the look on the firemen's faces: blasé as all get-out. They nodded to everybody kind of pleasantly and went right about their work . . . as if they *always* passed through a crowd of square dancing men before putting out a fire. That wouldn't happen anywhere else on earth. That's why I live here, I guess. That and the fact that some of the cops are a little funny.'

Bill grinned. 'More than a little.'

'Just enough,' said Michael. 'You're not real big on country-western, are you?' He'd deduced as much from Bill's reaction to his square dancing yarn.

The cop made a noncommittal grunt.

627

'I ask because . . . well, I was wondering if you'd like to go to the rodeo with me.'

Bill looked up from the menu. 'The gay one.'

Michael nodded.

Bill frowned. 'More faggots pretending to be cowboys, huh?'

'Not all of them,' Michael replied. 'Some are pretending to be Tammy Wynette.'

Mary Ann didn't hide her surprise when Michael showed up on her doorstep just before midnight. 'I thought you were seeing your Boy in Blue tonight.'

'I was. I did.'

'I see.'

'He doesn't like to sleep with people,' said Michael. 'All night, that is.'

Mary Ann made a face. 'He sounds like a lot of fun.'

Michael shrugged. 'I think we're both in it for the sex. It's just as well. He has sleepsleepsleep sheets.'

'He has *what*?'

'You know . . . those sheets that say sleepsleepsleep. They go with the towels that say drydrydry. It's awful, Babycakes. His taste is not to be believed.'

'Wait a minute! *I* had some of those sheets.'

'You did?'

'Yes, I did! What's wrong with those sheets?'

'That isn't the point,' said Michael. 'The point is . . . we have very little in common.'

'Except sex.'

Michael nodded. 'Except *great* sex. And that has a curious way of canceling out the tacky sheets. Not to mention a belt buckle that says BILL and a shower curtain with a naked man on it.'

'I think you're an awful snob,' frowned Mary Ann.

'Maybe so,' said Michael, 'but at least it keeps me from over-reacting to the great sex. If he had any style at all, I'd probably be in love with him by now.'

'And you don't want that?'

'No.'

'Why not?'

Michael thought for a moment. 'It's like this sweater. Have you seen this sweater, by the way?'

'It's nice,' said Mary Ann. 'The color's good on you. Is it cashmere?'

Michael nodded. 'Fifteen bucks at the Town School's second hand shop.'

'A steal!' She fingered a sleeve. 'It's almost new, Mouse.'

'Not so fast.' Michael lifted his arm to reveal a dime-sized hole in the sweater's elbow.

'You could patch it,' Mary Ann suggested.

'Not on your life. That's what I'm talking about. I *like* that hole, Babycakes. It keeps me from worrying about my new cashmere sweater. I can have the style, the feel, the luxury of cashmere without any fussing and fretting. It's *already* flawed, see, so I can relax and enjoy it. That's exactly the way I feel about Bill.'

'And how does he feel about you?'

'He thinks of me as a fuck buddy. Period.'

'How romantic.'

'Exactly. So I take refuge in his atrocious taste and tell myself that it would never work out, anyway. Even if he *wasn't* so crushingly unsentimental. Even if he *didn't* keep *Meat* on top of his toilet tank.'

'I don't think I'll ask about that,' said Mary Ann.

'It's a book,' said Michael.

'Thank God. Tell me something sweet. What have you heard from Jon lately?'

Michael managed a look of faint irritation. 'You can squeeze him into any conversation, can't you?'

'I don't care,' said Mary Ann. 'He was my friend, too. He was generous and gorgeous and . . . he thought you were the greatest thing going. He was cashmere without the hole, Mouse. That wasn't so terrible, was it?'

Michael sighed wearily. 'I don't hear from Jon, O.K.?'

'O.K. Sorry.'

He didn't bother to hide the wistfulness in his eyes. 'You haven't, have you?'

North to Alaska

Prue Giroux was wearing heels, Frannie noted. *Stiletto* heels on which she tottered precariously as she made her way along the rain-slick Promenade Deck of the *Sagafjord*. Her gown, as usual, was totally inappropriate, flouncy and cream-colored and dreadful.

Her escort, on the other hand, was as debonair as the Duke of Windsor in his elegant blue blazer, crisp white collar and gray silk tie. Good heavens, thought Frannie, how does she manage to do it?

Prue seemed to waver for a moment when she caught sight of Frannie in the deck chair. Then she smiled a little too extravagantly and clamped a hand on her companion's arm, as if he were a trophy she was about to present.

'Isn't this marvelous?' she cooed, meaning the scenery.

'Mmm,' replied Frannie. 'Magical.'

'Wasn't Alert Bay the most precious place? One's reminded of those little ceramic villages one buys at Shreve's at Christmastime!'

And sometimes, thought Frannie, one is much too common to get away with using 'one' all the time.

'Have you met Mr Starr?' asked the columnist.

The matriarch smiled as regally as possible and extended her hand, still recumbent and blanket-swathed. 'How do you do?' she said.

'Mr Starr is a stockbroker from London,' beamed Prue.

The woman is impossible, thought Frannie. Who else would volunteer her consort's credentials so eagerly. 'I adore London,' she said vaguely.

The poor man seemed horribly uncomfortable. 'I'm not a . . .'

'He's not British,' Prue interrupted, squeezing the man's arm even tighter. 'I mean . . . he's not a native. He's an American working in London.'

'I see,' said Frannie.

The man nodded to confirm Prue's statement, clearly humiliated by her incorrigible pushiness. Well, thought Frannie, here's one shipboard romance that won't last the duration of the cruise.

'Where are those precious little orphans?' asked Prue.

Frannie did her best not to scowl. This 'orphan' business, like melancholia and mild seasickness, was part of her vacation package.

'They're in the movie theatre,' she said casually, 'watching Bugs Bunny.'

The warmest smile imaginable stole across Mr Starr's aristocratic features. 'They are beautiful children,' he said. 'You must be very proud of them.'

'Oh, *yes*,' exclaimed Frannie, adding quickly: 'They aren't really *mine*, of course . . . but I'm alone in the world, and they're such splendid company, and . . . well, what else am I going to do with my time?'

Mr Starr's response was almost intimate, as if he had known Frannie for years. 'I think that's extraordinarily generous of you,' he said.

The matriarch flushed. 'Well, I . . . thank you, but . . . well, I get a lot of satisfaction out of it . . .' Her voice trailed off ineffectually. Mr Starr was all but caressing her with his eyes. Already, Frannie sensed a rapport with him that she was certain he didn't share with Prue Giroux.

'We should chat about that sometime,' said Prue.

'Uh . . . what?' Frannie was still mesmerized by Mr Starr's extra-ordinary gaze.

'The foster grandparent program,' said Prue. 'I'm sure my readers would love to hear your comments about that.'

'Oh, yes,' Frannie murmured absently. 'That might be . . . very nice.'

'I can tell you love them,' Mr Starr said to Frannie, all but ignoring Prue's presence. 'It shows in your face. And where there is love . . . there is a bond, regardless of blood.'

Prue grimaced. 'Blood?'

Frannie smiled indulgently. *What an idiot.* 'I think Mr Starr is referring to kinship, Prue.' She turned back to her new admirer. 'I love them as if they were my own, Mr Starr.'

He winked almost imperceptibly. 'I know,' he said. What a sweet thing to say, thought Frannie, trying to discern what it was that seemed so *familiar* about this stranger's face.

'Do you, by any chance, know a Father Paddy Starr in San Francisco?' asked Frannie.

'I asked him that already,' blurted Prue. 'I wondered the same thing myself.'

Frannie smiled. 'The name is the same, I just thought . . . there might be . . .'

'No,' said Mr Starr. 'There are lots of us, I guess.'

'Mmm,' said Frannie.

'By the way,' added Mr Starr, 'if you ever need help with the baby-sitting, I'd be glad to oblige.'

'How kind,' beamed Frannie. 'I think I can manage, though.'

'I'm good with children,' he said.

Frannie nodded. She was sure he was.

Aurora Borealis

That evening, while most of the passengers congregated in the ballroom for the rhumba contest, Prue and Luke snuggled under wooly Norwegian blankets on the Lido Deck and watched the miracle of the northern lights.

'My Daddy was right,' said Prue, her eyes riveted on the baby blue ribbon that trimmed the black velvet sky along the horizon. 'Now I know exactly what he meant.'

'About what?' asked Luke.

'Oh . . . beauty, I guess. He told me never to get bored with life, because there are some types of beauty you won't even understand until you see them for yourself. I've heard about the northern lights all my life, but I never really . . . believed in them . . . until now.'

Luke answered by tightening his grip on her shoulder.

'I guess,' Prue added, 'I never really believed in *us* until now. I wanted to, God knows, but I never allowed myself to surrender completely. It seemed too unreal, too much of a pipe dream somehow.'

Luke cupped her face in his hands. 'It's real, Prue. Every bit of it.' His smile flashed like whitecaps against a dark sea. 'Except maybe these damn clothes.'

'You look *magnificent*,' Prue gushed. 'I'm so proud of you, Luke. Have you *seen* the way those old biddies look at you when we walk into the dining room? They're eating you alive! I'd get a little nervous, if I didn't know better.'

Luke almost snapped at her. 'Can't you forget about appearances for once?'

Prue was hurt. 'Luke . . . I'm telling you what's in my heart.'

'I know, I know.' His tone was placating.

'I'm *happy*, Luke. That's a little miracle in itself. I didn't even know what the word meant until I met you. Now . . . I feel like singing at the top of my lungs.' She smiled at her own impetuousness. 'I've always gone to a lot of trouble to make people think of me as madcap. For the first time in my life, Luke, I *feel* madcap. I want this to go on forever.'

He turned and looked at the lights again. 'Two weeks isn't forever.'

Prue's brow furrowed. 'Luke . . .'

'Don't plan things, Prue. Or you'll lose the moment.'

'What if I want more than the moment?'

'You can't. We can't.'

'Why? There's no reason in the world why this can't keep going when we get back to San . . .'

'There are lots of reasons.'

'What? Why can't we just . . . ?'

'Hush, darling . . . hush.' He drew her closer, stroking her hair as if she were a child. 'You want so much, my love . . . so much.'

She pulled away from him, suddenly disoriented, flailing for absolutes. 'Is it too much to want to build on what we have? My God, Luke . . . have I been reading this wrong? Haven't I seen love in your eyes?'

'Yes,' he nodded, 'yes, you have.'

'Then what is it?'

He regarded her for a moment, then shook his head slowly. 'Who are we kidding, Prue? Your friends will never buy this act.'

'Luke . . . you would *charm* my friends.'

'Like that old bat with the Vietnamese orphans? No, thank you. I'm not interested in charming the bourgeoisie . . . and they'd *see* that in about ten minutes.'

Prue didn't hide her pique. 'If it really matters to you, that old bat – as you call her – lost a daughter and two grandchildren in Guyana. Those orphans are obviously her means of compensating for the loss of . . .'

'*What's her name?*'

The ferocity of his query startled her. 'Frannie Halcyon. I introduced you, didn't I?'

'No. The daughter's name.'

'Oh. DeDe Day. DeDe Halcyon Day. The papers made a big fuss about it at the time. You must've read . . . Luke, is something the matter?'

He was standing there, ramrod-straight, his hands clamped on the railing. A vein was throbbing in his neck, and his breathing seemed curiously erratic.

Prue struggled to undo the damage. 'Luke, I know you're not insensitive. I didn't mean to accuse you of . . .'

633

He wheeled around to face her. 'It's all right . . . it's all right. I'm sorry I yelled at you. Forgive me, will you? Will you do that?'

'Oh, Luke!' She scooped him into her arms and wept against his shoulder. 'I love you, darling. I'd forgive you for anything.'

'I pray you don't have to,' he said.

Telepathy

These days, Mary Ann did her banking at the Columbus Avenue branch of the Bank of America. She frequented this graceful old North Beach landmark because (a) it had starred in a Woody Allen movie (*Take the Money and Run*) and (b) its tellers were cheerful, Italian and gossipy.

Today's was no exception.

'My husband and I have never fit in,' announced a particularly aggressive teller in her late thirties. She delivered this information so earnestly, that it almost seemed as if Mary Ann had requested it.

'Really?' said Mary Ann.

'Never. *Never.* Years ago when nice girls didn't live with nice boys without benefit of matrimony, Joe and I were shacked up big as life. Then suddenly *everybody* was shacking up. What do we do? We get married. O.K., so along comes Z P G, and *nobody's* having babies, right? Wrong. Joe and I had babies like crazy. Now suddenly it's terribly fashionable to have babies again, so a lot of people my age are experiencing motherhood and mid-life crisis at the same time. Joe and me, our children are teenagers now, fairly independent. We've got the leisure to *plan* our mid-life crisis. He's decided to buy a Porsche and have an affair with a nineteen-year-old. My plans are roughly the same. I tell you . . . you can't help but gloat a little.'

This charming chronology (and the check from Frannie Halcyon she had just deposited) kept Mary Ann smiling all the way home from the bank.

Then she stopped to consider her own options.

Of course she would have children. She had always planned on that. But when? She was thirty now. *When?* After her career had taken hold? When would that be? Did babies mean marriage? She wasn't *that* modern, was she? What about Brian? Would marriage merely

634

heighten his insecurities about her upward career mobility? Did he even *want* to get married at this point? Was it fair to ask him to wait? Would he wait?

Who should be the first to ask?

They slept at her place that night, teaspoon nestled in tablespoon. Just before dawn, she felt him slip away from her. She rolled over, slept some more, and awoke half-an-hour later to find him sitting naked in the wingback chair facing the bed.

'Let's do it,' he said quietly.

She rubbed her eyes. 'What?'

'Get married.'

She blinked several times, then smiled sleepily. 'Telepathy,' she said.

'Yeah?'

'I've been thinking about it all day. I figured it was just Taurus meets Venus. What's your excuse?'

He shrugged. 'I thought I'd better make an offer *before* you're on the cover of *People*.'

She grinned. 'Take your time.'

'No. I'm proud of you. I want you to know that. Great things are about to happen to you, Mary Ann, and you deserve every bit of it. I think you're an amazing person.'

She looked at him lovingly for a long time, then patted the empty spot next to her. 'Why aren't you in bed?'

'Don't change the subject. I can adore you just as well from over here.'

'As you wish, sire.' It was true, anyway; she could almost feel it.

'When is the press conference?' he asked.

'Tuesday.'

Brian whistled. 'Close.'

'It's not actually a press conference. The station won't give me air time without knowing what I want it for, and I'm not about to tell them at this point.'

'Then how will you do it?'

'I've got my own show, remember?'

When the light dawned, Brian shook his head in wonderment. 'Jesus, that's brilliant!'

Mary Ann accepted the compliment with a gracious nod. 'How many escapes from Jonestown get to resurface on the afternoon movie show? I figure we can drop the bomb, then wait for somebody *else* to organize the press conference.'

'What sort of bomb is it?'

'What do you mean?'

'I mean . . . give us a preview.'

'Well . . .' Mary Ann pondered the request for a moment. She didn't want to talk about DeDe's double theory yet. It was still too shaky in her own mind. 'For one thing, she escaped down the river in a tin drum that was intended for tropical fish. And Jones raped her one time when she was bedridden.'

'Jesus,' murmured Brian. 'I guess that oughta hold 'em.'

'It's a story, all right.'

'Do you think you can tell it all in five minutes?'

Mary Ann shook her head. 'We won't even try. We'll sketch out the basics and give the rest to the highest bidder. I like doing things on my own terms. Speaking of which, come to bed.'

'You still haven't answered my question.'

'I know.'

'You don't have to answer it, actually. I just wanted to ask you before the commotion began. I wanted you to know.'

'I'm glad to know.' She smiled at him tenderly. 'You'll never know how glad.'

Claire

'Where, Gangie, *where?*'

Little Edgar was leaping ecstatically, trying to spot the whales that had been sighted off the starboard side of the *Sagafjord*. His sister, Anna, stood calmly at his side, somewhat less impressed.

Frannie knelt beside the four-year-olds and pointed. 'See? Over there . . . that big spout of water. That's the whale. He's blowing all that water through a hole in his back.'

Edgar frowned. 'Did somebody shoot him?'

'No, darling . . . why would . . . ? Oh, the hole. Well, you see . . . all whales have a hole like that, so they can . . . so they can blow water through it.' Frannie moaned softly and cast an imploring glance at Claire McAllister. 'Get me out of this.'

Claire chuckled throatily. 'Why does a whale have a hole? That's a dangerous question to ask *me*, honey!'

Frannie giggled. Claire was an ex-chorine of indeterminate age, with a chronic weakness for *double entendres* and racy jokes. Her very-red lips and very-black hair were oddly suggestive of Ann Miller, though Claire had long ago bid farewell to show business. She was currently married to the third richest man in Oklahoma.

'All right,' smiled Frannie. 'Forget I asked.'

Claire smiled expansively at the twins. 'They're just cute as a button, Frannie. What's that name they call you?'

Frannie reddened. 'Uh . . . Gangie. It's just a pet name. Frannie's a little too personal . . . and Mrs Halcyon seemed too . . . formal.'

'Gangie,' repeated Claire, her dark eyes twinkling with a hint ot playfulness. 'Sounds an awful lot like Grannie to me.'

Frannie fidgeted with a wisp of hair over her ear. 'Well . . . I . . . uh . . . wouldn't mind that one bit. They *seem* like my own grandchildren.'

'Uh-huh,' said Claire. The twinkle remained.

'*Well*,' exclaimed Frannie, turning to confront the twins again, 'we've seen the whales, so it's about time for a little nappie, don't you think?'

The children groaned in protest.

As Frannie took their hands and led them away, Claire winked at her conspiratorially. 'Meet you in The Garden, honey.'

'The Garden' was the Garden Lounge, an elegant bar on the Veranda Deck that featured chamber music by a group called the San José Trio. Frannie and Claire retreated there daily to bask in lovely, old-fashioned renditions of tunes like 'Over the Rainbow' and 'Londonderry Air.'

'Where's Jimbo?' asked Frannie, as soon as the Mai Tais arrived. Claire's husband was almost always with them. His loving attentiveness to Claire made Frannie quite lonesome sometimes.

Claire's eyelids fluttered histrionically. 'In the goddamn casino, wouldn't ya know it? I figured the bug would bite him sooner or later. I told him to go right ahead and gamble to his heart's content . . . I'd just find myself a nice gigolo.'

Frannie smiled. 'They don't actually have . . . ?'

'Of course they do, honey! They don't call them that, of course, but those boys on the cruise staff are all . . . shall we say *expected* to dance with the old ladies . . . and the last time I checked I *qualified*, goddamnit!'

Frannie laughed. 'But that's where it stops, isn't it?'

'You want more?' roared Claire. 'Forget it, honey. Most of 'em are gay. The boy that does the exercise class is shacked up with the tap dancer, and that magician only has eyes for the cute wine steward. And that's just the staff! Don't get me started on the passengers, honey. That Mrs Clinton, for instance . . . the one with diabetes who has to travel with a companion to make sure she doesn't eat too much sugar? Hah! Companion, my ass. Oh, I tell you, it is *rich*. The gossip on this tub is almost better than the food. I love it! I'm addicted to cruise ships. It's not like it used to be in the old days, though. Some of the glamor is gone. The truly rich don't ride these babies anymore. But there's nothing like being at sea, honey . . . nothing! Lord, look at the mist on that mountain!'

Frannie, in fact, was already looking. Edgar would have loved this, she thought. He was always such a grump on tropical vacations – and such a lovable creature when the air was brisk and the sky was gray.

Frannie set her Mai Tai down and smiled apologetically. 'I'm sorry, Claire. As usual, my timing is dreadful.'

'Honey, is something the . . . ?'

The matriarch laid her hand delicately on her waist. 'Just a little . . . queasiness.'

'Lord, you *do* look a little green. And me running off my goddamn mouth like that.' Claire checked her watch. 'You're in luck. The doctor's still in. You should stock up on Dramamine, honey. He's down on B-Deck near the elevator.'

Frannie rose and thanked her. 'Do you know his name?'

'Fielding,' replied Claire. 'You can't miss him. He's one gorgeous hunk of man.'

I See By Your Outfit . . .

If Remo was any indication, the number 6 had finally become synonymous with cheap motel. Besides the original Motel 6 (which actually *had* charged six dollars a night, long ago), Michael and Bill could choose from the Western 6 Motel (attached to a Denny's) and the 6 Gun Motel (near the Nevada State Fairgrounds).

They settled on the 6 Gun, because Michael felt that the weekend's cowboy motif should be carried out to the fullest. He wasn't disappointed. The motel's nightstands featured an upturned pistol surmounted by a lampshade. There was also an enormous foam rubber ten-gallon hat on the wall in the lobby.

'Ah, the West!' exclaimed Michael, as he flung open the curtains to let in the sunshine.

Bill continued unpacking. 'You live in the West.'

'Yeah,' said Michael, 'but sometimes you have to go east to be Western.'

'How's the view?'

'Awe inspiring. The Exxon station and the hills beyond.'

Bill chuckled. 'Great.'

'There are also seven – count 'em – seven homosexuals sunning on the ten square feet of grass between us and the Exxon station. God, is this town ready?'

Bill shrugged. 'Slot machines can't tell the difference between queer money and the other kind.'

'I don't know,' said Michael. 'According to the papers, the lieutenant-governor didn't seem any too thrilled. Besides, after that *Examiner* headline, they must be a little nervous about fags coming to Nevada.'

'What *Examiner* headline?'

'You know . . . the MGM Grand story: GAY SEX ACT SPARKS HOTEL FIRE.'

'Oh, yeah.'

'Think of it,' said Michael. 'The whole damn town could go up in flames tonight.'

A back-lighted plastic sign proclaimed the event to passersby on the highway: RENO NATIONAL GAY RODEO. As Bill swung his Trans Am into the dusty parking lot, Michael began to speculate out loud.

'Now, how many of these dudes do you think are real cowboys?' He related to this issue personally. His week-old Danner boots felt leaden on his feet; his teal-and-cream cowboy shirt seemed as fraudulent as a sport shirt worn by a sailor on leave.

'For starters,' said Bill, 'that one isn't.' He pointed to a wiry brunette wearing a T-shirt that said: MUSTACHE RIDES – 5¢.

639

There were similar signs of clone encroachment, Michael noted. Too many sherbet-colored tank tops. Too many straw hats that looked suspiciously like the ones at All-American Boy. Too many Nautilus-shaped bodies poured into too many T-shirts brazenly announcing: IF YOU CAN ROPE ME, YOU CAN RIDE ME.

One obvious city slicker, in deference to the occasion, had traded his nipple ring for a tiny silver spur, but Michael found the gesture unconvincing.

'God almighty!' he gasped, catching sight of the heroic pectorals on display at the entrance to the rodeo arena. 'Where do they all come from?'

'It ain't the ranch,' said Bill. 'Real cowboys have big bellies.'

'Don't be so jaded. One of them's got to be real.'

'Sure,' replied Bill, 'there's a real waiter from The Neon Chicken.'

Bill's defective imaginative powers were beginning to get on Michael's nerves. Inside the arena, he concentrated on the event itself – a raucous display of calf-roping, bull-riding and 'wild cow-milking.' The latter competition involved a cooperative effort between a lesbian, a drag queen and a 'macho man' – an impressive achievement in itself.

By mid-afternoon, most of the shirts had come off, turning the stands to a rich shade of mahogany. The beer flowed so freely that almost no one could resist the urge to clap along with the Texas Mustangs, billed as 'the only gay country-western band in the Lone Star State.'

'I like this,' Michael told Bill. 'Everybody's off guard. It's harder to give attitude.'

'Yeah,' said Bill, 'but wait till tonight.'

'The dance, you mean?'

Bill nodded a little too smugly. 'As soon as this dust gets washed off, all the little disco bunnies will emerge. Just watch.'

Michael didn't want to agree with him.

Physician, Heal Thyself

Frannie's utter disbelief was reflected in the face of the handsome, blond doctor who awaited her in his office on the *Sagafjord*'s B-Deck.

'Mrs Halcyon! My God!'

Frannie smiled and extended her hand. 'Dr Fielding.'

'How wonderful to see you,' said the doctor. 'I had no idea you were on board. I didn't check the passenger manifest this time, and . . . well, it's been a long time, hasn't it?'

Frannie nodded, already sensing the extreme awkwardness of the situation. This, after all, was the man who had brought the twins into the world. Would she be forced to lie to *him* about the 'orphans' in her care? And would he believe her?

'I feel so silly about this,' said Frannie feebly.

The doctor's smile was as white and crisp as his uniform. 'About what?' he asked.

Frannie touched her mid-section. 'Tummy problems. Mature women aren't supposed to get seasick, are they?'

The doctor shrugged. 'I'm afraid it strikes indiscriminately. I'm not exactly immune myself, and I've been sailing for a year now. How far topside are you?'

'Excuse me?'

'Your stateroom. Are you in one of the suites?'

Frannie nodded. 'On the Terrace Sun Deck.'

'I thought so,' grinned the doctor.

'Why?'

'Well . . . the motion's more noticeable up there. Usually it doesn't matter, but when the sea gets a little choppy, the luxury suites are the first to feel it.' He winked at her winningly. 'We peasants down here in the bilges have it a little easier.'

Frannie felt greener by the minute. 'There's not much I can do, I suppose?'

The doctor opened a white metal cabinet. 'We'll get you prone with a little Dramamine.' He handed Frannie a pill and a paper cup full of water. 'Can you keep me company for a while? It's a slow day. We'll have the place to ourselves, probably.'

Frannie accepted readily. No wonder DeDe had adored this man.

He sat in a chair near the bed, while she stretched out. After days at sea with the twins, it was nice to have someone fussing over *her*.

They shared a long moment of silence, and then he said: 'I'm sorry about DeDe and the children, Mrs Halcyon. I didn't hear about it until . . . somewhat after the fact.'

She thought her heart would break. She longed to share her good news with this gentle, compassionate man. Instead, she replied: 'Thank you, Dr Fielding. DeDe was terribly fond of you.'

641

After another pause, he said: 'I was working in Santa Fe when I read about it.'

'Oh, yes?' She jumped at the chance to talk about something else.

'I had a gynecological practice there for a while, before I went back to general practice and landed this job. My life got a little . . . confusing . . . and this was as close as I could get to joining the merchant marines.'

'You must've seen the world by now,' said Frannie. 'I envy you that.'

'It's . . . not bad,' replied the doctor. There was something bittersweet in his tone that puzzled Frannie.

'Alaska's extraordinary,' she offered. 'There's so *much* of it . . . and those fjords! They're like something out of Wagner . . . so grand, so heartbreaking. I'm just sorry . . .' She cut herself off.

'Sorry about what?'

Frannie smiled dimly, staring at the overhead. 'I forgot you never knew him.'

'Who?'

'My husband, Edgar. I miss having him with me. When you're a widow, doctor, the main thing that hurts is that you've lost your playmate. You've lost someone who can look at a mountain with you and know what you're thinking . . . someone to share the silences with. It takes a long time to build that . . . and it's hard to give it up.'

'I know,' he replied.

'You aren't married, are you?'

'No.'

'Have you ever had anybody who . . .?'

'Once,' he answered. 'Once I had that.'

'Then you know.'

'Yes.'

Frannie hesitated, suddenly wary of becoming too personal. Then she asked: 'How did you . . . lose her?'

Silence.

'I'm sorry,' said the matriarch. 'I didn't mean to . . .'

'It's O.K.,' said the doctor. 'I know exactly what you mean about those mountains. They don't look the same anymore.'

642

The Hoedown

A five-foot mirror boot, complete with spurs, spun slowly over the dance floor at the Nevada State Fairgrounds, casting its glittery benediction on the assembled multitudes. The event was called 'Stand By Your Man' and most of the dancers were doing just that.

Michael looked up at the shimmering icon and sighed. 'Isn't that inspired?' he asked Bill.

The cop regarded the boot for a split second, then frowned. 'Goddamnit!'

'What's the matter?' asked Michael.

'I forgot to get poppers.'

Michael smiled. 'This is country music, remember? Not disco.'

'No,' said Bill. 'I mean . . . for later.'

'Oh.'

'Maybe they sell them at The Chute.'

'It doesn't really . . .'

'Somebody there will know how to get them.'

'I don't need them,' said Michael. 'If you'd like some, then . . .'

'I don't *need* them,' barked Bill. 'I'd like some, that's all.'

Michael didn't want an argument. 'Fine,' he said evenly. 'What shall we do?'

'I'll drive into town,' answered Bill, sounding less hostile now. 'You can hold down the fort here. I shouldn't be long, O.K.?'

Michael nodded, soothed by his friend's inadvertent rusticism. *Drive into town. Hold down the fort.* They might have been hitching up the buckboard for a trip into Dodge City. 'O.K.,' he smiled. 'I'll be here.'

Bill nuzzled him for a moment, whispering 'Hot man' in his ear, then disappeared into the crowd.

It was an escape of sorts, Michael realized. Bill detested this music. He had managed to endure the rodeo with the aid of his Walkman and an Air Supply cassette. He was clearly not prepared to commit himself to an entire evening of country songs by Ed Bruce and Stella Parton and Sharon McNight.

Michael was relieved. He felt fragile and sentimental tonight –

643

achingly romantic – and he knew that those sensations could not long coexist with Bill's horrifying literalness. It wasn't poppers *per se* that had put Michael off – he got off on them himself – it was the soul-deadening way they sometimes reduced sex to a track event, requiring timing, agility and far too much advance planning.

How many man-hours had been wasted, he wondered, searching for that stupid brown bottle amid the bedclothes?

It wasn't Bill's fault, really. He *enjoyed* sex with Michael. He enjoyed it the way he enjoyed movies with Michael or bull sessions with Michael or late-night pizza pig-outs with Michael. He had never, apparently, felt the need to embellish it with romance. That wasn't Bill's problem; it was Michael's.

Michael moved to the edge of the dance floor and watched couples shuffling along shoulder to shoulder as they did the Cotton-Eyed Joe. There was genuine joy in this room, he realized – an exhilaration born of the unexpected. Queers doing cowboy dancing. Who would've thunk it? Kids who grew up in Galveston and Tucson and Modesto, performing the folk dances of their homeland finally, *finally* with the partner of their choice.

It doesn't matter, somehow, that teenagers out on the highway were screaming 'faggot' at the new arrivals. Here inside, there was easily enough brotherhood to ward off the devil.

Ed Bruce shambled onto the stage. He was a big, fortyish Marlboro Man type who spoke of golf and the Little Woman as if he were singing to a V F W convention in Oklahoma City. His big hit, 'Mamas, Don't Let Your Babies Grow Up to Be Cowboys,' took on a delectable irony in this unlikely setting.

Twenty years ago, thought Michael, gay men were content to shriek for Judy at Carnegie Hall. Now they could dance in each other's arms, while a Nashville cowboy serenaded them. He couldn't help smiling at the thought.

Like magic, across the crowded dance hall, someone smiled back. He was big and bear-like with a grin that seemed disarmingly shy for a man his size. He raised his beer can in a genial salute to Michael.

Michael returned the gesture, heart in throat.

The man moved towards him.

'Pretty nice, huh?' He meant the music.

'Wonderful,' said Michael.

'Do you slow dance?' asked the man.

'Sure,' lied Michael.

Learning to Follow

At five-nine, Michael was dwarfed by the man who had asked him to dance.

To complicate matters further, this lumbering hunk clearly expected him to *follow* – a concept that hadn't crossed Michael's mind since the 1968 Senior Prom at Orlando High. And then, of course, Betsy Ann Phifer had done the following.

There was a secret to this, he remembered. Ned had learned it at Trinity Place's Thursday evening hoedowns: *Extend your right arm slightly and straddle his right leg – tastefully, of course – so that you can pick up on the motion of his body.*

Check. So far, so good.

It felt a little funny doing things backwards like this, but it felt sort of wonderful, too. Michael laid his head on the great brown doormat of his partner's chest and fell into the music.

Ed Bruce was still on stage. The song was 'Everything's a Waltz.'

The man stepped on Michael's foot. 'I'm sorry,' he said.

'That's O.K.,' said Michael.

'I'm kinda new at this.'

'Who isn't?' grinned Michael.

Not so long ago, he realized, men *had* slow danced in San Francisco. He recalled the tail-end of that era, circa 1973. The very sight of it had revolted him: grown men cheek to cheek, sweaty palm to sweaty palm, while Streisand agonized over 'People' at The Rendezvous.

Then came disco, a decade of simulated humping, faceless bodies writhing in a mystic tribal rite that had simultaneously delighted and intimidated Michael. What that epoch had lacked some people were now finding in country music. The word was romance.

'Where are you from?' asked Michael.

'Arizona,' replied the man.

'Any place I know?'

'I doubt it. A place called Salome. Five hundred people.'

So he *was* a real cowboy. That explained the hands. They felt like elephant hide. Bill could just go fuck himself. 'Salome,' repeated Michael, copying the man's pronunciation (Sa-loam). 'As in Oscar Wilde?'

'Who?'

Michael's heart beat faster. *He's never heard of Oscar Wilde.* Dear God, was this the real thing? 'Nobody important,' he explained. 'It doesn't really matter.'

It really didn't. He felt so profoundly *comfortable* in this man's arms. Even his gracelessness was endearing. It wasn't the man, he reminded himself, but the circumstances. Two prevailing cultures – one very straight, one very gay – had successively denied him this simple pleasure. He felt like crying for joy.

'Did you . . . uh . . . ride in the rodeo?' he asked.

''Fraid not. I'm just a construction worker.'

Just a construction worker! Jesus God, had he died and gone to heaven? Why hadn't someone told him there was a place he could go to slow dance with a construction worker?

'What do you do for . . . this . . . in Salome?' Michael asked.

The man pulled away from him just enough for his smile to show. 'I go to Phoenix.' He leaned down and kissed Michael clumsily on the edge of his mouth. 'You're a nice guy,' he said.

'You too,' said Michael.

They danced for another minute in silence. Then the man spoke huskily into Michael's ear. 'Look . . . would you like to make love tonight?'

Make love. Not have sex. Not get it on. Michael's voice caught in his throat. 'I'm actually . . . here with a friend. He's just . . . off right now.'

'Oh.' The disappointment in his voice warmed Michael to the marrow.

'I could give you my phone number. Maybe, if you're ever in San Francisco . . .'

'That's O.K.'

'Never go there, huh?'

'Not yet,' said the man.

'I think you'd like it. I could show you around.'

'I don't travel much,' said the man.

Michael decided against suggesting a trip to Salome. 'Look,' he said, 'would you believe me if I told you that this is better than all the sex I've had this year?'

The man grinned. 'Yeah?'

'Infinitely,' said Michael.

'I'm stepping all over your . . .'

'I don't care. I love it.'

The man's chest rumbled as he laughed.

'You're doin' just great,' said Michael. 'Just keep holding me, O.K.?'

'Sure.'

So Michael settled in again, lost in a sweet stranger's arms until Bill came back with the poppers.

Over the Glacier

When the *Sagafjord* reached Juneau, Prue and Luke went ashore with the other passengers and explored the tiny frontier town – a place heralded by the local chamber of commerce as 'America's largest capital city.'

'It must be a joke,' said Prue, puzzling over the brochure in her hands.

Luke shook his head. 'They mean land mass.'

'But how . . . ?'

'It covers more square miles than any other capital city. Everything's out of whack up here. It's further from here to the Aleutians, at the other end of the state, than it is from San Francisco to New York.'

Prue thought for a moment. 'That's a little scary, somehow.'

'Why?'

'I don't know. It makes you seem so much smaller, I guess. Like the landscape could . . . swallow you up. You could just disappear without a trace.'

Luke smiled at her. 'People do. That's the point.'

Prue shivered. 'Not to me, it isn't.'

'Wait till you see the glacier.'

'What glacier?'

Luke slipped his arm around her waist. 'I thought we'd rent a float plane and fly over the ice fields. They say it's as close to God as you'll ever get.'

Prue looked troubled. 'Can't He just come to us?'

Luke touched the tip of her nose. 'What's the matter, my love?'

'Nothing . . . I just . . . well, those tiny planes and my tummy don't always get along.'

'It's just forty-five minutes.'

He pulled her closer until Prue relented. In many ways, she realized, he had aleady become her talisman against harm.

The float plane skimmed the surface of the water like a low-flying dragonfly, then lifted them into the slate-gray sky above Juneau. Besides Prue and Luke, there were four other passengers: a youngish couple from Buenos Aires and two lady librarians, traveling together.

Luke sat directly behind the pilot and conversed with him inaudibly, while Prue watched the alien world beneath her turn from dark blue to dark green to white. No, *gray*. A pale gray plateau as far as the eye could see – a living entity, sinuous as lava at the edges, brutal and beautiful and unexplainably terrifying.

It relieved her somewhat to see that the glacier had boundaries. Splintering and hissing, it tumbled into a dark sea where the water crackled like electricity. As the float plane dipped lower, Prue peered into fissures so brilliantly blue that they seemed unnatural, blue as the lethal heart of a nuclear power plant.

'Look, Luke . . . that color!'

But her lover was deep in conversation with the pilot, their voices drowned out by the engine sounds.

Prue leaned closer. 'Luke . . .'

He didn't hear her. He continued to interrogate the pilot, a rapt expression on his face. Prue could make out only two words. Oddly enough, the pilot repeated them.

She fell back into the seat, frowning. This moment should have been theirs: hers and Luke's. This buddy-buddy business with the cockpit was inexcusably selfish, thoughtless. When Luke finally sat back and squeezed her hand, she let him know she was pouting.

'You O.K.?' he asked.

She waited a beat. 'Well, what was all *that* about?'

'All what?'

'My God! You haven't stopped talking.'

He pumped her hand again. 'Sorry. Just . . . plane talk. I guess I got carried away.'

'What was that about dire needs?'

Luke blinked at her. 'Huh?'

'You said something about dire needs.'

'No, I didn't.' His face was resolute.

'Luke, I heard you. You said something, something . . . dire needs. And the pilot said it back. Just a minute ago.'

He studied her for a moment, then smiled and shook his head. 'You misunderstood me, darling. We were talking about geography.' He held up his hand like a Boy Scout. 'Honest injun. You didn't miss a thing.'

Prue let it drop. For one thing, the other passengers had begun to take an interest in her vexation. For another, she wanted this moment to be special, free from earthbound anxieties. Luke did, too, it seemed. He gave her his undivided attention for the rest of the tour, turning away only long enough to make a brief notation on the inside of a matchbook.

'What was that?' she smiled. 'A reminder?'

Luke looked up, distracted.

'I do that myself,' she added, not wanting to appear nosey. 'My mind's like a sieve.'

He smiled faintly and returned the matchbook to his breast pocket.

'Let's go dancing tonight,' he said.

The First to Know

Back at work at God's Green Earth, Michael unloaded his rodeo experiences on an ever-indulgent Ned. The saga suffered in the retelling. Michael's brief interlude with the slow-dancing construction worker emerged somehow as a hackneyed masturbatory fantasy, no longer the rare and wonderful thing it had seemed at the time.

That night, he tried invoking the spirit of the weekend by listening to country music on KSAN, but Willie Nelson took on an oddly hollow note in a room full of bamboo furniture and deco kitsch. Cowboys didn't collect Fiesta Ware.

So he wandered downstairs and smoked a roach on the bench in the courtyard. The dope and the silence and the tiny sliver of a moon hanging in the trees all conspired to make him more contemplative than usual.

Contemplative, hell – he was simply depressed.

Nothing grand, of course. This was a garden-variety depression, born of boredom and loneliness and a pervasive sense of the immense triviality of life. It would pass, he knew. He would make it pass.

But what would he put in its place?

*

649

The clock said 3:47 when the phone woke him.

He stumbled out of bed and lunged for the receiver. 'This better be good,' he told the caller.

'It is,' came the reply. Mary Ann's giggle was unmistakable. Michael settled himself in a chair. 'What's up, Babycakes?'

'Brian and I are getting married!'

'*Now?*'

Another giggle. 'Next month. You aren't pissed, are you?'

'Pissed?'

'About waking you up. We wanted to make it official. Calling you was the only thing we could think of.'

Michael was so touched he wanted to cry. What followed, though, was total silence.

'Mouse? Are you there? You *are* pissed, aren't you? Look, we'll talk to you in the . . .'

'Are you kidding? This is *fabulous*, Babycakes!'

'Isn't it, though?'

'It's about time,' said Michael. 'Are you pregnant?'

Mary Ann roared. 'No! Can you believe it?'

'Is Brian?'

He heard her speak to Brian. They were obviously in bed. 'He wants to know if you're pregnant.'

Brian came on the line. 'The bitch knocked me up.'

Michael laughed. 'Somebody had to do it.'

'Are you alone?' asked Brian.

'Hell, no,' answered Michael. 'Say hello to Raoul.'

'Hey, that's O.K. . . .'

'Calm down,' laughed Michael. 'I made that up.'

'You shithead.'

'I know. Sorry.'

'I was picturing some French Canadian with five o'clock shadow.'

'That's funny,' said Michael. 'So was I. God, Brian . . . this is so damn wonderful.'

'Yeah . . . well, we just wanted you to be the first to know.'

'Goddamn right,' said Michael.

'We love you, man. Here's Mary Ann again. She's got some more news for you.'

'Mouse?'

'Yeah?'

'Have you got a TV set at work?'

Michael thought for a moment. 'Ned's got a portable that he brings from home sometimes.'

'Good. Get him to bring it on Tuesday. I want you to watch the show.'

'*Bargain Matinee?*'

'Is there any other? You don't need to watch the movie . . . just my little halftime bit. I think you'll be mildly amused.'

'Don't tell me. You've found a new use for empty Clorox bottles.'

'Just watch the show, smartass.'

'Roger.'

'And get some sleep. We love you.'

'I know that,' said Michael.

But he slept much better knowing it.

That Nice Man

Claire McAllister's husband was in the casino again, so the raven-haired ex-chorine sought out Frannie's company on the Promenade Deck of the *Sagafjord*. Frannie was thrilled to see her.

'Pull up a chair,' she smiled, laying down her Danielle Steel novel. 'I haven't talked to a grown-up in ages.'

Claire mugged amiably. 'Who you callin' a grown-up?'

'You'll do,' said Frannie. 'Believe me.'

Claire lowered her formidable frame into an aluminum deck chair and sighed dramatically. 'So where *are* the little darlings?'

Frannie shushed her with a forefinger to the lips. 'Don't even mention it, Claire. It's almost too good to be true.'

'What?'

Frannie made a sweeping gesture with her arm. 'This. Solitude. Blessed relief. I *adore* the children, as you know, but . . .'

'You've found a baby-sitter!'

The matriarch nodded triumphantly. 'It was his idea, poor man. I hope he hasn't bitten off more than he can chew.'

'Do I know him?' asked Claire, pulling a blanket across her lap.

'I think so,' said Frannie. 'Mr Starr.'

Claire drew a blank.

'You know,' added Frannie. 'That American stockbroker from London.'

'That good-looking thing traveling with the hoity-toity blonde?'

Frannie smiled demurely. 'They aren't exactly traveling together.'

'Horseshit.'

'They met on the ship,' the matriarch explained, her face burning from the profanity. 'I know her . . . somewhat remotely. She's a gossip columnist in San Francisco. I'm afraid she's a little common.'

Claire snorted. 'You'd think she was the Queen of Sheba. She puts on airs something fierce. What the hell does that elegant man see in her?'

Frannie shrugged. 'She's rather pretty, don't you think? I understand she listens well, too. At any rate, I can't complain; she introduced me to *him*. I think I'm relaxed for the first time since we left San Francisco.'

'Did the children take to him?'

'Like a house on fire! He's full of wonderful stories and jokes.' Frannie thought for a moment. 'You know, he's rather moody around adults . . . not sullen or rude, really . . . just introspective. Around the children, though, he's a bundle of energy! He never stops trying to impress them. He's like a child competing for a grown-up's attention, instead of the other way around.'

'He sounds perfect,' said Claire.

Frannie nodded. 'I think it's important for the children to have a masculine presence.' She didn't elaborate on this thesis, but it gave her pleasure to articulate it to a woman as sensible and down-to-earth as Claire. The twins had never had a father, after all . . . only that woman who had kept DeDe company in Guyana and Cuba. It wasn't natural, Frannie reminded herself. Thank God for Mr Starr!

'Say,' said Claire, after an interlude of silence, 'Jimbo has a little business to do when we dock this afternoon. Howsabout you and me exploring Sitka together? There's a darling little Russian church and some marvelous scrimshaw shops. A couple of girls on the town . . . whatdya say?'

Frannie hesitated. 'Well . . . I . . .'

'I *know* it's a thrilling offer, honey, but try not to bust a gut!'

Franie smiled apologetically. 'I was just thinking . . . well, the children.'

'Can't your Mr Starr take them off your hands for a while?'

Frannie's brow wrinkled. 'He *did* offer, as a matter of fact.'

'Wonderful! Then, it's settled!'

'It seems such an imposition, though.'

'Look, honey, if that man is cuckoo for kids, that's *his* problem, not yours. You've gotta learn to recognize a gift from God when you see one!'

Frannie conceded with a grin. 'You're right. This is supposed to be a vacation.'

'Exactly,' said Claire.

Half-an-hour later, when Frannie went to pick up the twins, she found them giggling under a 'fort' that Mr Starr had constructed from two deck chairs and a blanket. Edgar had done that often – for DeDe – long, long ago.

Without announcing herself, Frannie stood outside the woolen shelter and reveled in the mirthful music of her grandchildren's voices.

Then Mr Starr began to sing to them:

'Bye baby bunting, Daddy's gone a-hunting, gone to get a rabbit skin to wrap the baby bunting in . . .'

The sheer familiarity of that ancient nursery rhyme was all the reassurance the matriarch needed.

It was comforting to know that some things never changed.

The Uncut Version

Mrs Madrigal's angular face seemed even more radiant than usual as she reached for the heavy iron skillet that meant breakfast at 28 Barbary Lane.

'I still can't take it in,' she said. 'Two eggs or three, dear?'

'Three,' said Michael. 'Neither can I. I've been promoting it for months, but I didn't think either one of them could handle the commitment right now. Mary Ann more so than Brian, I guess.'

Mrs Madrigal cracked three eggs into the skillet, discarded the shells, and wiped her long fingers on her paisley apron. 'I was the one who introduced them. Did you know that?'

'No.'

'I did,' beamed the landlady. 'Just after Mary Ann moved in. I had a little dinner one night, and Mary Ann told me she was afraid there weren't enough straight men in San Francisco.' Mrs Madrigal smiled nostalgically. 'That was before she knew about me, of course. If she *had*, I suppose we would've lost her to Cleveland for good.'

Michael smiled. 'So you introduced her to Brian?'

653

'Not exactly. I told Brian she needed help moving the furniture. I let them take care of the rest. Wheat toast or rye, dear?'

'Wheat, please.'

'It was an unmitigated disaster, of course. Brian was a shameless womanizer, and Mary Ann was madly in love with Beauchamp Day at the time – God help her.' The landlady shook her head with rueful amusement. '*Then* she started dating the detective that Mona's mother hired to check up on me.'

Michael nodded soberly.

'I was always rather glad he disappeared, weren't you?' Her grin was as mischievous as it could get. 'I do wonder what happened to him, though.'

Michael felt himself squirming. He avoided this subject as much as possible. Mary Ann alone had witnessed the detective's fall from a cliff at Lands End, and she had shared that secret with no one but Michael. There were some things that even Mrs Madrigal should never be allowed to know.

'Then came Burke Andrew,' said Michael, moving right along, 'and those cannibals at Grace Cathedral.'

Mrs Madrigal's Wedgwood eyes rolled extravagantly. 'She knows how to pick 'em, doesn't she?'

'Yep. But I think she's finally got it right.'

'So do I,' said the landlady. 'I'm a little surprised, frankly.'

'Why?'

'I don't know, exactly. I just have this gut feeling she's up to something. She seems so preoccupied lately. I would have guessed marriage to be the last thing on her mind.'

'So,' asked the landlady as they sat down to eat, 'what has our wandering boy been up to lately?'

Michael pretended to be engrossed in the marmalade jar. 'Oh . . . nothing much.' He knew she was inquiring into his love life, and he didn't feel like talking about it. 'I'm having a celibacy attack, I think, I stay home and watch TV a lot.'

'How *is* that?'

'How is what?'

The landlady flicked a crumb off the corner of her mouth. 'TV.'

Michael laughed. 'My favorite thing this week was a special report on circumcision.'

'Indeed?' Mrs Madrigal buttered another piece of toast.

'It was a hoot,' said Michael. 'They interviewed a circumcision expert named Don Wong.'

'No!'

Michael crossed his heart. 'Swear to God.'

'And what did he have to say?'

Michael shrugged. 'Just that there's no valid reason anymore for mutilating little boys at birth. Jesus. How long does it take people to figure things out? My mother isn't exactly a modern thinker, but she knew *that* thirty years ago.'

Mrs Madrigal smiled. 'You should write her a thank you note.'

'The funny thing is . . . I hated it when I was a kid. I was always the only kid in the shower room who wasn't circumcised, and it bugged the hell out of me. Mama said: "You just keep yourself clean, Mikey, and you'll thank me for this later. There's not a thing wrong with what God gave you."'

'Smart lady,' said Mrs Madrigal.

Michael nodded enthusiastically. 'I was invited to an orgy this week.'

The landlady set her teacup down.

'It was for uncut guys only.'

She blinked at him twice.

'It's O.K.,' said Michael. 'It was a benefit.'

'Oh, really?'

'For the chorus.'

'Ah.' Mrs Madrigal's deadpan was ruthless. 'A foreskin festival. Do they check you at the door or what?'

Michael laughed. 'I know. It's pretty silly. Still . . . I'm glad that attitudes have changed. There's no reason in the world to be snipping at your genitalia.'

The landlady looked down at her teacup, suppressing a smile until Michael added hastily: 'Unless, of course, you're prepared to go all the way.'

Mrs Madrigal looked up again and winked.

'More coffee, dear?'

Daddy's Gone

A vigorous fur-trading monopoly in the last century had given Sitka a distinctively Russian cast: a Russian blockhouse, Russian grave markers everywhere, Cossack dancers performing for tourists, even a pretty Russian Orthodox cathedral in the center of town.

Prue adored every inch of it.

'Isn't it incredible, Luke? To think that this is America!'

Luke, however, was occupied with the orphans. He was kneeling next to them on the street, adjusting the miniature fur-trimmed parkas he had bought for them half-an-hour earlier. With the hoods up, the children looked like little Eskimos, almost too adorable to be true.

'Isn't it a little warm for that?' asked Prue. 'The weather's practically like San Francisco.'

He looked up distractedly. 'Be with you in a second.'

He hadn't even heard her. Ordinarily, she might have been annoyed, or faintly jealous. Prue resented people – like Frannie Halcyon and her friend Claire, for instance – who demanded so much attention from Luke that they diminished her share of his love.

But the children were different. Seeing them with Luke, Prue remembered what it was that had captivated her about the scruffy, ill-dressed phantom who had cared for her wolfhound in Golden Gate Park. Luke related to children the way he related to animals – as a peer who respected their feelings.

The little girl knew that already. 'Mr Starr,' she chirped, tugging on his arm. 'Take us on a flying boat, *please*. Take us on a flying boat.'

Prue smiled. 'You told them about our float plane trip.'

Luke didn't look up. 'They pick up on things fast.'

'They speak English so well,' Prue observed. 'For Vietnamese, I mean.'

Luke zipped up the little boy's parka. 'They're refugees. They may have been raised by Americans . . . I don't know.' There was a slightly caustic edge to his voice, implying that Prue should mind her own business. Suddenly, she felt as if she had walked in on a private conversation.

The little boy took up the cry. 'Flying boat! Yeah! Take us on a flying boat!'

Luke confronted him sternly. 'Edgar . . . not now!'

A tiny lower lip pushed out. 'You promised.'

'His name is Edgar?' asked Prue.

Luke ignored her.

'Edgar was Frannie's husband's name. Do you think she named him?'

'Prue, would you shut up, please! I'm having enough trouble with *these* children!' The vehemence of the attack stunned her momentarily, until she realized that the children *were* genuinely upset. They were sniffling softly, not in a bratty way, but as if a trust had been violated.

'Luke,' she said warily, 'if you promised them a float plane trip, I wouldn't mind doing it again. Really.'

Luke stood up. He was rigid with anger. The big vein in his neck had begun to throb. 'I didn't promise them anything,' he muttered. 'C'mon, we haven't eaten since breakfast.'

Prue assumed a placatory tone of voice. 'A little food would do us all some good.' She smiled down at the orphans. 'I'll bet they have yummy ice cream in Alaska. Shall we go see?'

They peered up at her wet-eyed – sad, round faces encircled in fur – then reached out for her hands.

Luke walked ahead of them, sulking.

His mood had improved considerably by the time they reached the restaurant, a knotty-pine-and-Formica greasy spoon near the cathedral.

'The meatloaf isn't bad,' he said. 'How's your salad?' A feeble attempt at apologizing, but an effort nonetheless.

She decided to smile at him. 'Awful. It serves me right for ordering salad in Alaska.' She turned to the children. 'Those hot dogs went down awfully fast.'

The orphans flashed mustardy grins at her. She marveled at how soon children could forget a hurtful situation. Then she reached across the table and stroked Luke's hand. 'Do I dare risk the little girl's room?'

'Go ahead,' he winked. 'The experience will do you good.'

The bathroom proved to be pungent with disinfectant, but surprisingly clean. She was there for five minutes, taking care of business and thanking the powers-that-be that her first significant conflict with Luke had fizzled out before it exploded.

657

When she returned to the dining room, their table was empty. Luke and the orphans were gone.

'Excuse me,' she asked the man behind the counter. 'My friend and the children, did they . . .'

'They paid up and left,' said the man.

'*What?* Left? Where did they go? Did they say?'

The man shrugged. 'I figured you'd know.'

Panic in Sitka

The man behind the counter saw the confusion in Prue's face and managed a kindly smile. 'Maybe he just expects you to . . . catch up with him.'

'He didn't say *anything?*'

'No ma'am. Just paid the bill and took off.'

Prue stared at him, mortified, then glanced at the empty table again. Luke had left a tip, she noticed. What in God's name was happening? Was this his way of punishing her? That little tussle over the float plane trip certainly didn't justify this kind of childish stunt.

And what right had he to involve the orphans in this . . . this . . . whatever it was? Prue was livid now, scarlet with humiliation. There had better be a damn good explanation.

She left the restaurant and looked both ways down the street. They were nowhere in sight. To her right, the little gray-and-white frame Russian cathedral offered refuge to a steady stream of tourists. Maybe *that* was it. Maybe the children had grown restless while she was in the rest room, and Luke had taken them to the next logical stop on their tour of Sitka.

Maybe he had expected her to know that.

She entered the cathedral, paid a two-dollar donation, and stood in the back, scanning the room. She recognized several people from the *Sagafjord*, including the loud brunette who hung out with Frannie Halcyon, but Luke and the orphans were not there.

Out in the sunlight again, she considered her alternatives. If Luke was, in fact, trying to teach her some sort of lesson, then he could just got to hell. She could see the town on her own, if need be. On the other hand, what if some unforeseen emergency had arisen which had *demanded* that Luke leave the restaurant?

But what could have happened in five minutes?

She strode back to the restaurant, surveying it once more through a grease-streaked window.

Nothing.

Keep calm, she ordered herself. *There's an explanation for this.* If he had planned on upsetting her, he had succeeded completely. She would never let him know that, though. She would not let him see her cry.

Reversing her course, she walked in the direction of the ship, casting anxious sideways glances down the cross streets. When she was three blocks from the cathedral, she passed a narrow alleyway where a small furry figure caught her eye.

It was one of the orphans. The little girl.

She was standing at the end of the alleyway, framed prettily against a weathered wooden building.

'Hey!' shouted Prue.

The little girl remained immobile for a moment, looking confused, then waved tentatively.

Her name, thought Prue. *What was it?*

Remembering, she yelled again. 'Anna! It's me! Is Mr Starr down there?'

Her answer came in the form of a looming shadow . . . and then Luke himself, lunging in from the left to snatch up the startled child.

'Luke! For God's sake, what are you doing?'

His head pivoted jerkily, like the head of a robot, as he turned to look into her terrified face. The alien rage in his eyes made her blood run cold. Who was this man? *Who in the world was he?*

She ran towards him, screaming: 'What have I done, Luke? Just tell me what I've done!'

But he was gone again, sprinting down another alleyway with Anna under his arm.

Prue kept running, her heart pounding savagely in her chest. She watched Luke cross a vacant lot, then disappear into a thicket of weeds and wildflowers. Where was the other orphan, anyway? *What had he done with Edgar?*

When she tried to follow, her heel caught on a rusty bedspring, wrenching her violently to the ground. She lay there, disbelieving, choking on her sobs while blood gushed from her ankle.

'LUKE,' she screamed. 'PLEASE LUKE, I'M BLEED-ING . . . PLEASE . . . PLEASE . . .'

But there wasn't a sound.

659

Still on her stomach, Prue jerked an oily rag from beneath a discarded refrigerator and clamped it frantically against her ankle, scattering the flies that had already begun to gather.

She eased herself into a sitting position, leaning against the refrigerator as her eyes glazed over with the full horror of the thing that had happened.

A man with no last name, a man she had loved, a man carrying the identification of Father Paddy Starr, had kidnapped the foster grandchildren of Frannie Halcyon in a small town in Southeast Alaska. And the *Sagafjord* would sail in less than two hours.

It was time to pay the piper.

Atrocity

Remembering an ancient teaching of the Camp Fire Girls, Prue made a tourniquet from another oily rag and applied it hastily to her ankle.

Three minutes later, she loosened the device enough to see that the bleeding had stopped, then raised herself cautiously to her feet. A pearl-sized drop of blood, dark as a ruby, bubbled to the surface as soon as she placed weight on the ankle. She blotted it warily, whimpering as she did so, until she felt secure enough to walk.

Then she set off in the direction of the ship.

As she left the litter-strewn lot, an angry voice called out to her. 'Hey, lady!'

She flinched at the sound, turning to see a heavy-set, redheaded man in his late forties. He was wearing overalls and carrying a hoe upright, like a spear.

'*Was that son of a bitch with you?*'

Prue struggled to find her voice. 'I . . . if you mean . . . uh . . .'

'Look, lady . . . I'll kill the bastard if I have to! I'll find out who he is and I'll . . .' He stopped, seeing the blood on Prue's ankle. 'What's that?' he asked, using a tone that was only slightly less hysterical.

'I fell,' she said feebly. 'I cut myself on that bedspring. Please don't yell at me.' She began to sniffle. 'I can't take it anymore. *I can't.*'

The man dropped his hoe and walked towards her. 'Did he do this to you?'

'A man in a blue blazer?'

'Yep. You know him?'

Prue nodded defeatedly. 'I was . . . chasing him. Did you see which way he went?'

'Through there,' said the man, pointing to a dilapidated wooden fence with two missing planks. 'Through my goddamn garden, the son of a bitch!'

For about five seconds, Prue considered pursuing him, but her spirit was broken now, and she knew that Luke and the orphans would be long gone. She thanked the man and resumed walking, adding lamely: 'I'm sorry if he damaged your garden.'

The man exploded. 'Garden, hell!' He seized her wrist and pulled her towards the hole in the fence. 'You're gonna see this, lady!'

See *what*, for God's sake? What on earth had Luke done?

Passing through the opening, they came into a small backyard – virtually indistinguishable from the junk-scattered lot it adjoined. A row of tractor tires, painted white and planted with petunias, was the sole concession to aesthetics. Along the back fence stood a shed of some sort, compartmentalized for . . . what? . . . cages?

The man led her to the shed.

'All right now, you tell me what the hell that means!'

What she saw made her scream, then gag, then vomit in the weeds behind the shed.

The man stood by awkwardly, finally offering her his handkerchief.

'Your friend is crazy, lady. What else can I say?'

Half-an-hour later, Frannie Halcyon was nervously pacing the Promenade Deck of the *Sagafjord*. Since two other cruise liners were already docked in Sitka, the ship was moored in the harbor, with launches making shuttle runs to the pier. The matriarch's eyes were glued on those launches.

'If something's happened, I'll never forgive . . .'

'Nothing's happened,' said Claire. 'Relax, honey. You're worse than a new mother.'

'But we sail in an *hour*.'

'They know that,' said Claire.

'And I know that Giroux woman. She's nothing if not flighty. She's probably dragged that man off to a shop somewhere, with total disregard for . . .'

'Look!' cried Claire, pointing to the dock, 'there's another launch heading this way!'

Frannie's tension eased instantly. 'Thank God!'

Claire scolded her with a grin. 'You're the *worst* worrywart!'

'What deck's the gangplank on?'

'A-Deck, I think.'

'I'm going to meet them,' said Frannie.

'Want company?'

Frannie smiled. 'I know you think I'm silly. I get these feelings sometimes. There's no rational explanation for them.'

Her fears disintegrated as soon as she saw the gossip columnist's blonde tresses emerge from the launch.

'You see?' said Claire.

But then they saw that Prue was alone.

DeDe Day's D-Day

Mrs Madrigal was trimming the ivy in the courtyard when Mary Ann left for work.

'Off to the station, dear?'

Mary Ann nodded. 'A big day. A *big* day.'

The landlady set down her shears and stood up. 'Your little surprise, you mean?'

'You know about it?'

Mrs Madrigal smiled. 'Michael told me. He didn't say what, actually . . . just when. I can't imagine what it is.'

'It's a wonderful surprise, actually. Not to mention a great story, if I do say so myself.'

'A marriage proposal *and* a great story. How many milestones can you squeeze into one week?' The landlady grasped Mary Ann's shoulders, planting a kiss firmly on her cheek. 'Congratulations, in advance, dear. I always knew you could do it.'

Mary Ann beamed. 'Thanks.'

'And I want to plan a little do for you. For you and Brian.'

'As a matter of fact,' said Mary Ann, 'I was hoping you'd plan the wedding.'

The landlady's face lit up. 'I'd be *thrilled*. Here, you mean?'

Mary Ann nodded.

Mrs Madrigal looked about her in the courtyard. 'Let's see. You can say your vows under the lych gate. A coat of paint will fix it up just fine. And we can bring in a cellist, maybe . . . or a harpist . . . a harpist would be heavenly.' She clapped her hands together almost girlishly. 'This is so wonderful . . . my little family . . . God's been so grand to us, Mary Ann.'

'I know,' she replied.

And she meant it, too, for the first time in years.

Her revenge, she had just begun to realize, would be sweeter than she had ever dared to dream. Larry Kenan saw to that by being an even bigger bastard than usual.

'Well, how's our little fighting journalist today?'

Mary Ann didn't look up from her desk. She was organizing her note cards on DeDe, pruning and reshuffling to keep within her five minute format. It wasn't easy.

The news director remained in the doorway, thumbs hooked in his Gentlemen's Jeans. She could feel his smirk burning into the top of her head. 'Look,' he said, 'Denny needs to see your props for today's show.'

'Right,' muttered Mary Ann, continuing to smile.

'*Now*, lady.'

Mary Ann gazed up at him, steely-eyed. 'It's just a goddamn sea sponge, Larry.'

He snorted noisily. 'For *what?*'

Mary Ann looked down again. 'An alternative to tampons.'

There was silence for a moment, then Larry began chortling like an idiot.

Mary Ann picked up a pencil and made a meaningless note on her calendar. 'Toxic shock your idea of a big yuck, Larry?'

'Not at all,' said the news director, turning to leave, 'Just glad to hear you're doing a little *in depth* reporting. Break a leg, O.K.?'

The movie for today's show was *Move Over, Darling* and the irony wasn't lost on Mary Ann. Doris Day has been marooned on a desert island for seven years and comes home unexpectedly to find her husband, James Garner, on the verge of marrying Polly Bergen. Meanwhile, DeDe Day shows up at intermission. It was too delicious for words.

Mary Ann's phone rang at 2:15.

'Mary Ann Singleton.'

'It's DeDe, Mary Ann. Listen to me carefully. Have you told them anything yet?'

'Where are you? I need you here before the . . .'

'*Have you told them anything?*'

Mary Ann was thrown by the urgency in DeDe's voice. 'Of course not,' she replied. 'We won't say anything until we're on the air.'

'I can't do that, Mary Ann. We can't.'

'Now wait just a minute!'

'Mother just called! The children have been kidnapped!'

'What? *In Alaska?*'

'He's got them, Mary Ann, I'm almost positive.'

'Jesus . . . are you . . . ? How is that possible?'

'There isn't time to talk. I'm flying to Sitka in an hour. Will you come with me?'

'DeDe, I . . .'

'I'll pay for everything.'

'It isn't that. I'm supposed to be on the air in . . .'

'I need you, Mary Ann. *Please.*'

'O.K. of course. Where shall we meet?'

'At the airport – catch a cab. And don't say a word to anyone, Mary Ann . . . *not a word!*'

A Sucker for Romance

There was a rumor rampant that the hottest bodies from the City Athletic Club had graduated to the Muscle System farther down Market Street, but Michael found it hard to believe.

Today, for instance, the club was wall-to-wall horse flesh – sleek, river-tanned torsos straining heroically against the high-tech tyranny of the Nautilus machines. All in all, a profoundly discouraging sight.

For Michael's own body needed work. Badly.

After forty-five minutes of torturous leg lifts, decline presses, overhead presses, and super tricep exercises, he repaired to the Hollywood-size Jacuzzi where Ned was languishing like an aging gladiator.

Michael eased himself into the bubbling water. 'It's practically an unwritten law,' he said.

'What?' asked Ned.

'If I'm in shape, I'm not in love. If I'm in love, I'm not in shape.'

Ned laughed and squeezed the back of his neck. 'Who's the lucky guy?'

'Thanks a lot,' said Michael.

'Well, I assume you meant . . .'

'I know, I know. And there is no lucky guy, either. I'm just ready for . . . something nice.'

Ned extended his legs and floated on his back. 'What about your cop friend? I thought he was making the earth move.'

Michael shook his head. 'It was only the bed.'

The nurseryman laughed.

'Besides,' added Michael. 'I've had it with falling in love with love. I'm a lot more cautious than I used to be.'

'Right.' Still on his back, Ned turned his head and smirked at him.

'I *am*,' Michael insisted. 'You have to be cautious. Some guys have given up on love altogether, settling for a list of ten people they can have terrific sex with. You can think you're falling in love, when really you're just auditioning for the list. Does that make any sense?'

'Did you make his Top Ten?' grinned Ned.

'I didn't mean Bill specifically,' said Michael.

'Oh.'

'Anyway, I think I'm more of a Golden Oldie now. It doesn't matter. I'm kind of a washout at buddy sex. Why am I telling *you* this, anyway? You've got your own list.'

Ned let his legs drop and sat up again. 'It beats cruising the bars and fast-food sex. There's a lot to be said for sex with friends, Michael.'

'Maybe. But a little romance would be nice. A little sentiment.'

'Fine. Go get it, Bubba.'

Michael smiled. 'I'm trying, God knows.'

'Is that what you were doing at The Glory Holes last week?'

'In my own way. Hell, I don't know. I run in cycles, I guess. Sometimes I think I'm the horniest guy alive . . . and I don't need a damn thing in the world but some hot stranger tweaking my tits and calling me 'buddy' in the dark. I mean . . . some anonymous sex is so wonderful that it almost seems to prove the existence of God.'

Ned splashed water on him. 'That's because you're on your *knees*, kiddo.'

Michael laughed. 'But that's just part of the time. As soon as the moon changes or something, I want to be married again. I want to sit in a bathrobe and watch *Masterpiece Theatre* with my boyfriend. I want to *plan* things – trips to the mountains, dinners in Chinatown, season tickets to whatever. I want order and dependability and somebody to bring me NyQuil when I feel like shit.

'And yet . . . I know that'll pass too. At least, for a while. I *know* there'll be times when I want to prowl again. I'm too much in love with adventure. I panic at the thought of being with only one person for the rest of my life. So what the hell is the answer?'

Ned shrugged. 'You find somebody who understands all that. And loves you for it.'

Michael looked at his friend for a moment, then ducked beneath the surface of the water. When he reemerged, he said: 'Why am I getting heavy in the Jacuzzi? It must be that damn wedding.'

'Mary Ann and Brian's?'

Michael shook his head. 'Chuck and Di's.'

'Is that today?'

'Tomorrow morning. At three o'clock our time.'

'I think I'll miss that,' said Ned.'

'Not me. I think she's great. He's kind of a nerd, I guess, but she's a doll. And I'm such a sucker for romance.'

Ned regarded Michael affectionately, then gave his knee a playful shake. 'God save the Queen,' he said.

'C'mon,' grinned Michael, climbing out of the water, 'it's almost time for Mary Ann's show.'

The Search Begins

The Air Alaska flight to Seattle took almost two hours – the one to Sitka, about three, with a brief stopover in Ketchikan, just inside the Alaskan border. By the time they reached Sitka, Mary Ann was drained.

DeDe, however, showed amazing resilience.

'How do you do it?' asked Mary Ann, as the duo boarded a cab at Sitka Airport.

DeDe smiled wearily. 'Do what?'

'Well . . . I'd have fallen apart by now. Just thinking about it.'

DeDe searched for a mint in her tote bag. 'I did my falling apart earlier. I screamed for five solid minutes after Mother called. No more . . . that's it.' She popped a mint into her mouth. 'It would only get in the way of what I have to do.'

666

The faintly John Wayne-ish undertone of this remark unsettled Mary Ann.

'Are you sure we shouldn't notify someone. I mean . . . if not the police, then someone who'll at least know . . .'

'No. No one. If it's him, then media coverage is the last thing we need. The man doesn't take to being cornered. We would only freak him out.'

'But surely some sort of protection would be . . .'

'When we find him,' said DeDe. 'When we know we can nail him without harming the children . . . and not before.'

When, observed Mary Ann, not *if*. They had no proof whatsoever that the twins were still in Sitka, but DeDe kept the faith. It was hard to imagine a more courageous display of positive thinking.

The cab driver asked: 'Where to in town?'

'The Potlatch House.' DeDe turned to Mary Ann. 'The ship left this afternoon, I gather. Mother and Prue Giroux took rooms at this place.' She smiled sardonically. 'If there was ever an odd couple . . .'

'What did they tell the ship people?'

'Nothing,' said DeDe, 'at my instruction. They just disembarked, saying they had decided to spend more time in Sitka. Pretty flimsy-sounding, I guess, but we had no choice. *Any* report of the kidnapping would be deadly at this point.'

Mary Ann felt her flesh pebbling. She had never heard 'deadly' used quite so literally. 'I'm surprised your mother didn't call the police.'

'So am I,' said DeDe. 'Fortunately, she called me first. I'm sure that Prue encouraged it. He was *her* boyfriend, after all. The last thing she wanted was to tangle with the police. It's not really the sort of thing she can use in her column.'

'She met him on the ship, though. We can't exactly hold her responsible for . . .'

'She *says* she met him on the ship.'

Mary Ann frowned. 'I'm sorry. You're losing me again.'

'I think she knows more than she's telling Mother,' explained DeDe. 'And I think Mother knows more than she's telling us.'

'About what?'

DeDe sighed. 'I don't know . . . just . . . well, something about her beloved Mr Starr finally convinced her he was off the deep end.'

'I would certainly think so,' said Mary Ann.

'Something besides the kidnapping.'

'Oh.'

'She started to tell me, and then just shut up. I guess she's protecting me. We'll find out soon enough, won't we?' DeDe's smile was ironic and heartbreakingly brave.

Mary Ann took her hand to ward off her own tears. 'Don't make it any worse than it is,' she said.

'Is that possible?' asked DeDe.

The cab crossed a streamlined white bridge, while the driver drew their attention to an extinct volcano that presided majestically over an archipelago of tiny islands. The town lay ahead of them, clean and compact as Disneyland. As a setting for indescribable menace, it was not very convincing.

Mary Ann checked her watch. It was 9:13. Twilight.

DeDe peered out at Sitka harbor. 'It's kind of pretty, isn't it?'

'Yeah . . . I suppose.'

'I'm scared shitless,' said DeDe.

'So am I,' said Mary Ann.

The Interrogation

At Mary Ann's suggestion, DeDe's initial meeting with her mother was private. Mary Ann spent the time catnapping in her room at the Potlatch House, secretly relieved that she had escaped the anguish of the confrontation.

An hour later, DeDe returned to the room and collapsed into a chair next to Mary Ann's bed.

Mary Ann rubbed her eyes as she sat up. 'Rough, huh?'

DeDe nodded.

'Is she O.K.?'

'Better,' sighed DeDe. 'I gave her a Quaalude.'

'Poor thing,' said Mary Ann.

DeDe rubbed her forehead with her fingertips. 'She knows less than we do. I can't believe how out of it she is sometimes.'

'What about Prue?'

DeDe picked distractedly at the arm of the chair. 'She's next. I didn't want to question her with Mother around. I figured she'd be intimidated. It's gonna be hard enough as it is to get the truth.'

'How well do you know her?' asked Mary Ann.

'Not very.' DeDe laughed bitterly. 'I made a confession to her once, but that's about it.'

'What do you mean?'

'She has these luncheons,' explained DeDe. 'She calls it The Forum – very grand. Everyone sits around with a visiting celebrity and bares their souls. Consciousness-raising for social climbers. Pretentious and awful. I went to the one she did on rape. "A rap about rape," she called it.' DeDe shook her head in disgust. 'Jesus.'

'But . . . you said you confessed.'

'I told her I'd been raped.'

'When was this?'

'Oh . . . five years ago.'

'I didn't know you'd been raped *before* Jonestown.'

'I hadn't been,' said DeDe. 'I just told her that.'

'Why?'

DeDe shrugged. 'Social pressure, I guess. I'd also just been to bed with Lionel, and I needed someone to blame it on. Pretty revolting, huh?'

'Was Lionel . . . ?'

'You got it. The twins' father.'

'The grocery boy,' said Mary Ann.

'Not anymore. He *owns* the store now, according to Mother. In the meantime, I got raped for real in Guyana by Prue Giroux's goddamn boyfriend.'

'We don't know that for sure,' said Mary Ann. She had already decided that somebody had to play devil's advocate in this crisis.

'C'mon,' said DeDe, 'I need your help on this one.'

They found out less than they had hoped.

'I told you,' insisted Prue, 'all he said was that he was an American stockbroker living in London. We were on a cruise, for heaven's sake. You don't really ask much more than that.'

'Sean Starr,' repeated DeDe.

The columnist nodded but avoided DeDe's eyes. 'He appeared to be crazy about the children, and *everyone* liked him, and I think it was perfectly natural for your mother to entrust the children to him. He was quite polished . . . good-looking . . . an *elegant* man.' She shook her head woefully, her eyes still red from crying. 'It just doesn't make any sense.'

Mary Ann sat down next to Prue. 'Look,' she said gently, 'it isn't that we don't believe you.' (Not entirely true, of course; DeDe appeared extremely distrusting.) 'It's just that it would help us a lot if you could remember details . . . *any* details.'

'Well . . . he was in his late forties, I guess. He dressed nicely.'

'How nicely?' asked DeDe.

'You know. Blazers, silk ties . . . that sort of thing. Understated.'

'Do you have any pictures of him?' asked Mary Ann.

'The ship's photographer took one or two.'

Mary Ann glanced excitedly at DeDe, then turned back to Prue. 'Can we see them?'

'I didn't buy any,' said Prue. 'They're on the ship.'

DeDe looked as if she might slap the columnist at any moment. 'And you noticed nothing unusual in his behavior? Nothing at all.'

Preu shook her head. 'He didn't start acting funny, really, until we reached Juneau.'

'Funny how?'

'I don't know . . . moody, distracted. We took a float plane trip over the glaciers, and he didn't talk to me once. He spent the whole time mumbling to the pilot.'

'About what?' asked DeDe, almost ferociously.

'He kept saying dire needs,' said Prue.

Mary Ann's eyes widened. 'Maybe they left by plane!'

'Dire needs,' repeated DeDe, ignoring her colleague's brainstorm. 'Plural?'

Prue frowned. 'What?'

'He said dire needs, not dire *need*? That's the usual expression. In dire need.'

Prue looked confused. 'I think so. I heard the pilot repeat it. There was lots of plane noise, though.'

'And that was it?' asked DeDe.

'What?'

'Nothing else peculiar?'

'Not until Sitka,' said Prue, her face contorting to a look of naked terror. 'Not until . . . he took them . . . and . . .' She clamped her hand against her mouth, choking on her sobs.

'And *what*?' demanded DeDe.

'The . . . the rabbits.'

DeDe exploded. '*The rabbits?*'

'Your mother didn't tell you?' Prue stared at her aghast.

'No.'

'Oh, God,' said the columnist.

A Delicate Matter

'*What* rabbits?' asked DeDe.

Prue looked away, her lower lip trembling violently. 'When he took the children we were in a restaurant not far from here. I went to the little girls' room and . . . when I came out, he was gone.'

DeDe nodded impatiently. 'Mother told us that already.'

'Anyway,' continued the columnist, 'I looked up and down the street . . .'

'And you found Anna in an alleyway.' This was Mary Ann, trying to move the story along. DeDe's annoyance with Prue was obviously escalating.

Prue nodded funereally. 'After I saw him drag her off, I sat down in this vacant lot . . .'

'*What?*' thundered DeDe.

'I was *hurt*. I ran after him, but I cut my ankle.' She lifted her foot as evidence. 'This man came along and started yelling at me, because he thought I was with Lu . . . Mr Starr. I told him I . . .'

'Wait just a goddamn minute! What did you just say?'

Prue blinked at her balefully. 'Nothing.'

'Yes you did, goddamnit! You started to call him something else!'

Mary Ann caught DeDe's eye and said quietly: 'Why don't we let her finish?'

Prue took that as her cue to continue. 'So he dragged me over to his backyard . . .'

'Who?'

'This man . . . the one who . . .'

'O.K., O.K.'

'He had these rabbit cages . . . hutches . . . and there was blood all over the place . . . and he made me . . .' Something seemed to catch in her throat. She pressed her hand against her mouth and closed her eyes. When she opened them again, she was almost whimpering. 'He made me look at these two little rabbits that had been . . . skinned.'

'Jesus,' murmured Mary Ann.

DeDe remained cool. 'Your friend did that?'

Prue nodded, fighting back the tears. 'It's so awful. I've never known anyone who could . . .'

'Were the skins still there?' asked DeDe. Mary Ann shuddered. What on earth was she getting at?

Prue thought for a moment. 'I don't think so. There was so much blood that I . . .'

'And you know nothing about this *elegant* man, as you call him, except that he was an American stockbroker living in London? What was he doing on *that* cruise, anyway?'

'I don't understand,' said Prue.

'Doesn't it strike you as just a teensy bit out of his way?'

The columnist shook her head slowly. 'No, I mean . . . he seemed to have enough money to . . .'

'Was he your lover?'

Prue's mouth dropped open.

'*Was* he?'

'I don't see what business that is of . . .'

'*I have a reason for asking. Did you ever see him with his clothes off?*'

Prue's indignation was monumental. 'Look here, I'm sorry about your children, but you have no right to . . .'

'You'll be even sorrier when we talk to the police. Not to mention the press.'

Prue began sniffling. 'I had no way of knowing he would do a thing like that . . .'

'I know.' DeDe's tone was kinder now. She reached over and took the columnist's hand. 'No one ever does.'

Prue continued to weep until DeDe's message sank in. 'You *know* him?' she asked dumbfoundedly.

'I think so,' said DeDe softly. She turned to Mary Ann. 'This is kind of delicate. Would you excuse us for a moment?'

Mary Ann shot to her feet. 'Of course . . . I . . . what time shall we . . . ?'

'I'll meet you in our room,' said DeDe. 'Half-an-hour?'

'Fine,' said Mary Ann.

It was more like an hour.

When DeDe appeared, she looked thoroughly exhausted.

'Think we could get a drink somewhere?'

'Sure. Are you O.K.?'

'Sure.'

'Could you find out if . . .'

'It's him,' said DeDe.

'How do you know?'

DeDe moved to the window and stared out at the blackness. 'Does it matter?'

Mary Ann hesitated. 'Sooner or later it will.'

'Then . . . could we make it later?'

An awkward silence followed. Then Mary Ann said: 'I've been thinking about those rabbits.'

'Yeah?'

'That nursery rhyme he used to sing. "Bye baby bunting, Daddy's gone a-hunting . . ."'

DeDe finished it. '"Gone to get a rabbit skin to wrap the baby bunting in."'

'You thought of that,' said Mary Ann.

'Yeah,' DeDe replied listlessly. 'I thought of it.'

On the Home Front

Mary Ann's phone was ringing off the hook.

Brian stood on the landing outside her doorway and debated his responsibility. She hadn't *asked* him to tend to her affairs in her absence. What's more, she hadn't even told him where she was going, and he resented that more than he would admit to anyone.

The caller, however, was persistent.

So it was curiosity, more than anything, that sent him up the stairs to his tiny studio, where he conducted a frantic search for his keys to Mary Ann's apartment.

Finding them, he bounded downstairs again, opened the door and lunged for the wall phone in Mary Ann's kitchen.

'Yeah, yeah.'

'Who is this?' asked a male voice.

'This is Sid Vicious. Who is *this*?' It really pissed him off when people didn't identify themselves on the telephone.

A long silence and then: 'Is this Mary Ann Singleton's apartment?' The guy was annoyed, Brian noted with some degree of pleasure.

'She's out of town right now. I suggest you try again in a few days.'

'Do you know where she went?'

That did it. 'Look . . . who the hell is this?'

673

'Larry Kenan,' replied the caller. 'Ms Singleton's boss.' His voice was dripping with sarcasm.

'Oh . . . I see. Mary Ann's mentioned you. The news director, right?'

'Right.'

'This is Brian Hawkins. Her fiancé.' It was the first time he had ever used that word to describe himself. It had a curiously old-fashioned sound, but he enjoyed the hell out of it. Things were official now, he realized.

'Good,' said the news director. 'Then you can tell her she's in deep shit.'

'What's the problem?' asked Brian, trying to change his tone to one of responsible concern.

'The problem,' snapped Larry, 'is that she skipped out on us yesterday – twenty minutes before the show. That's the problem, Mr Hawkins.'

Brian thought fast. 'She didn't tell you?'

'What?'

'Her grandmother died. Unexpectedly. In Cleveland.' Brian winced at this hackneyed alibi. There was practically nothing that hadn't been blamed on a dead grandmother.

'Well . . . I'm sorry about that . . . but she didn't say a word to anybody . . . not a goddamn word. There's such a thing as professionalism, after all. We were stuck. We had to get Father Paddy to announce the movie.'

'I saw that,' said Brian. 'I thought he was rather good.'

'Well, you tell your friend that she'd better report to me on Friday or she's out on her ass. Got that?'

Brian longed to tell him to shove it. Instead, he said: 'I'm sure she'll be back by then. She should be checking in with me, so I'll be glad to tell her. I'm sorry. I know she wouldn't intentionally . . .'

'Friday,' said Larry Kenan. 'After that, *finito*.'

Brian's face was hot with rage when he hung up. While most of his anger was directed towards the news director, he was also upset with Mary Ann for not giving him enough information to cover for her properly.

What could have prompted such an abrupt exit, anyway? He presumed it involved her story about DeDe Day's return from Guyana. That could even mean she was still in town – in Hillsborough, perhaps, putting the finishing touches on the piece.

674

'I'm going away,' was all she had told him. 'I'll probably be gone a few days, so please don't worry about me. I'll call as soon as I get a chance. I'm so glad we're getting married.'

Swell. But where was she?

He found her address book and looked up the number of the Halcyon residence in Hillsborough. When he dialed it, he reached a maid who was straight out of *Gone With the Wind*. There was no one there, she said.

As soon as he had hung up, the phone rang again. He answered it, trying to sound a little nicer this time.

'Is Mary Ann there?' came a woman's voice that sounded strangely familiar.

'She's in Cleveland,' he replied, opting for consistency. 'She should be back by Friday.'

'Will you give her a message for me?'

'Sure.'

'Tell her I found the notes she left behind at the station. It's vitally important that I talk to her.'

'Right. Who is this, please?'

'Bambi Kanetaka. Shall I spell it?'

'No,' said Brian. 'I know it. You're the anchorperson, right? You're famous.'

'Tell her I can't sit on this.'

Brian suppressed a laugh. To hear Mary Ann tell it, this must be the *only* thing that Bambi Kanetaka couldn't sit on.

'Tell her that I won't tell Larry until she calls me . . . but she *must* call me as soon as possible. From Cleveland, if necessary. Do you understand?'

'I think so,' said Brian.

Now what? he thought. *Now what?*

Dire Needs

Mary Ann slept fitfully at the Potlatch House. Twice during the night she awoke to DeDe's screams, only to fall victim to her own nightmares when she plunged into sleep again. Morning came as a reprieve at 7:30.

DeDe was already up, studying a map as she sipped a cup of black coffee. When she realized that Mary Ann's eyes were opened, she smiled apologetically and said: '*Night of the Living Dead*, huh?'

Mary Ann smiled back at her. 'We can handle it.'

'Want some coffee?'

'I think I'll wait,' said Mary Ann. 'I'm wired enough as it is.'

DeDe looked down at the map again. 'We're having breakfast with Prue, if that's O.K. with you. I want her to take us to the man with the rabbits. Later, I thought we could check the car rental agencies and airplane people.'

A long silence followed while Mary Ann wrestled with the monstrous futility of their search. Then she said: 'DeDe . . . don't you think . . . ?' She cut herself off, suddenly wary of seeming disloyal to the undertaking.

'What?' said DeDe. 'Say it.'

'Well . . . it just seems to me that we're losing time by doing this ourselves. If we told the police, they could be issuing all-points bulletins, or whatever it is that they do.'

'Issuing press releases is more like it.'

'But we don't have to tell them who we think he is . . . just that he took the children.' From Mary Ann's standpoint, that was all that mattered, anyway: *someone* had kidnapped the twins.

DeDe poured herself more coffee. 'The point is not what the police know, but what *he* knows.'

'But surely he can't expect us to . . . ?'

'I *know* this man, Mary Ann. You keep forgetting that.'

'But how can you be so sure he won't . . . Surely, those rabbits were proof enough of his . . .'

'Those rabbits were a little bit of bad symbolism and nothing more. He has a weakness for grand gestures. That was just his way of . . . being Daddy.'

'But what makes you think he won't harm the children?'

DeDe shrugged. 'Because he loves them.'

'You can't be serious!'

'Well, that's the way *he* sees it. What happened in Jonestown, anyway? When did the killing start? When the outside world invaded his private fantasy of peace and love. I missed the massacre, Mary Ann, and I'm not going to let it happen again. If I want my children back alive, I've got to find them before the media find out about Jones. It's as simple as that.'

*

Breakfast was a harrowing affair. Prue was a wreck, and Mrs Halcyon was a worse wreck. DeDe, to her credit, stayed calm throughout, absolving her mother and the columnist of all guilt in exchange for their absolute silence on the subject. Prue had no trouble consenting to this condition; Mrs Halcyon did so with great reluctance.

DeDe, of course, gave no indication that she knew who the kidnapper was.

On the way to the airport, Prue pointed out the house of the man with the rabbits. Mary Ann made a quick note of the address, feeling weirder by the minute. Half-an-hour later, Prue and Mrs Halcyon were airborne, bound for San Francisco, while Mary Ann and DeDe conferred with the last known witness of the abduction.

'I was in the kitchen when it happened,' said the rabbit fancier. 'He was out here with the kids at the hutches. I couldn't tell what was happening until I got out here, and then it was too late.'

Mary Ann looked contrite. 'We're awfully sorry about the . . .'

'He didn't say anything?' interrupted DeDe. 'Nothing at all?'

'Hell, no. He hightailed it. I found a book of matches out here later in the day. He must've dropped it, I guess. They were from the Red Dog Saloon in Juneau. That help you any?'

'Do you still have them?' asked DeDe.

'Hang on,' said the man. He went into the house, returning seconds later with the matchbook. DeDe turned it over in her hand, then opened it. Written in felt-tip pen on the inside was this word: DIOMEDES.

'"Diomedes",' said DeDe, turning to the man. 'Do you know what that means?'

The man shook his head. 'Sorry.'

DeDe frowned, discarding the matchbook. 'It probably doesn't mean a damn thing.'

'Wait,' blurted Mary Ann.

'Yeah?'

'Diomedes. *That's* what Prue heard. Not dire needs – Diomedes!'

Definitions

Diomedes.

It had a vaguely scientific sound to it, chemical perhaps. It also suggested a classical figure, like Diogenes and Archimedes. Mary Ann, however, deduced that its roots were geographical, since Mr Starr had been heard using the word in conversation with a pilot.

'You're probably right,' said DeDe, pocketing the matchbook. 'It's not like him, though, to be so careless about leaving a clue behind. I think it's best to check our logical sources first.'

Their first stop, via cab, was a car rental agency near the waterfront. There, sounding remarkably nonchalant, DeDe confronted a fastidiously groomed young woman in a two-tone green uniform.

'A friend of ours may have rented a car here yesterday. We were wondering if you'd mind checking . . . if it's no trouble.'

The young woman's smile fell. 'We don't normally give out that kind of information.'

'Why the hell not?'

Mary Ann stepped forward, touching the small of DeDe's back. 'Uh . . . it's kind of stupid, really. He told us to be sure to use the same rental agency he used, and we forgot to ask him the name. Dumb, huh?'

The woman refused to thaw. 'Customer records are confidential. If I gave out that kind of information, I'm afraid it would be an invasion of privacy. If you'd like to rent a car, I'd be glad . . .'

'This isn't a fucking missile station, you know!' DeDe was edgier than ever.

This time Mary Ann gripped her elbow. 'We don't need you to check the computer, actually. They'd be easy to recognize.'

'I thought it was one person.'

'One adult,' amended Mary Ann, before DeDe could speak. 'A nice-looking man about fifty and four-year-old twins, a boy and a girl.'

'Eurasian,' added DeDe.

'I'm *what?*' snapped the woman.

DeDe groaned. Before she could retaliate, Mary Ann said: 'The children are part Chinese. They were wearing fur-lined parkas. I

678

think you would've remembered them if . . .' The woman had become an obelisk; it was futile to continue. Mary Ann addressed DeDe, who was smoldering. 'I think we'd better go.'

DeDe shot daggers at her adversary until she was out of sight.

At the next agency, DeDe did all the talking, while Mary Ann looked for a dictionary at a neighboring motel. The desk clerk produced a battered volume which Mary Ann consulted while standing in the lobby.

She found this:

Diomedes n. Class. Myth. 1. the son of Tydeus, next in prowess to Achilles at the siege of Troy. 2. a Thracian king who fed his wild mares on human flesh and was himself fed to them by Hercules.

When DeDe emerged from the rental agency, Mary Ann was waiting for her on the street.

'Any luck?' asked DeDe.

'Afraid not.'

'They didn't have a dictionary?'

'They had one. Diomedes wasn't in it.'

'There's a book store over there. Maybe they would know.'

Mary Ann shook her head. 'I think we're beating a dead horse.' Clever girl, she told herself. You have a cliché for every occasion.

DeDe persisted. 'The sign says: "Specializing in Alaska Lore." If anybody would know, they would. It's worth a try, at any rate. C'mon.'

Hundreds of musty volumes were stacked everywhere in the tiny book store: on shelves, on tables, on the floor. But there wasn't a person in sight.

'Hello,' hollered DeDe.

No answer.

'I think we should check the float plane places,' said Mary Ann, inching towards the door.

'Hold it . . . I hear somebody.'

The proprietor, an Ichabod Crane look-alike, emerged from the back room. 'Yes, ladies. May I help you?'

'I hope so,' said DeDe. 'We need some information. Do you know what the word "Diomedes" means?'

The man smiled instantly, unveiling the sizable gap between his front teeth. 'You mean, *The* Diomedes.' He might have been talking about old friends, like The Martins or The Browns. 'What would you like to know about 'em?'

'For starters,' said DeDe, 'what are they?'

'Islands,' replied the bookseller.

'Thank God!' said Mary Ann.

DeDe turned and scrutinized her. 'Why thank God?'

Mary Ann reddened. 'I . . . well, I'm just glad somebody knows.'

'Where are they?' asked DeDe, addressing the proprietor again.

'Way north of here. In the Bering Strait. Cute little buggers. Little Diomede and Big Diomede. The little one's about four square miles. The other's . . . oh, twenty or so. No trees. Lots of rocks and Eskimos. The two of 'em are just a few miles apart.'

'Is anything . . . special there?' asked Mary Ann.

The man grinned like a jack o' lantern. 'It's not *what* they are, but *where.*'

'How so?' said DeDe.

'Well,' said the man. 'Little Diomede's in the United States and Big Diomede's in Russia.'

Revising the Itinerary

'That son of a bitch,' muttered DeDe, back in their room at the Potlatch House, 'that two-bit Bolshevik son of a bitch. Jesus H. Christ . . . Russia!'

Mary Ann felt more ineffectual than ever. 'I'd forgotten how close we were,' she said.

'He probably *lives* there,' added DeDe. 'He's got what he wanted and he's heading home.'

'But the trip was *our* idea, DeDe. How could he have known we were doing it? How could he . . .?'

'Maybe he just lucked into it. How the hell do I know? What does it matter, this speculation? He could be back in Moscow by now!'

'Not really,' said Mary Ann, perusing DeDe's map of Alaska. 'Not unless they made terrific airline connections. The closest big city to the Diomedes is Nome and that's over eleven hundred miles from here. Then he'd have to get a smaller plane to take them to the

680

Diomedes. Plus, there must be some sort of restriction on travel between Little Diomede and Big Diomede. It's a pretty complicated scheme.'

'If anybody could do it, he could.'

'It would take money,' countered Mary Ann.

'Prue said he had lots of it. He had lots of it in Jonestown – trunks of it – enough to last him the rest of his life. He could bribe his way from here to Timbuktu if he wanted to.'

Mary Ann rummaged for a word of consolation. 'In one way, you know, this helps us. I mean . . . it narrows the focus of our search. The man at the book store said Little Diomede is only four square miles. Any airplane trying to land there would be noticed immediately . . . if he's trying to make a jump into Russia.'

'Yeah,' said DeDe dourly. 'I suppose so.'

'So, if we call the authorities in Nome, they could relay . . .'

'No. No police!'

'We wouldn't have to tell them . . .'

'No. I told you how I feel about that.' DeDe grabbed her tote bag and headed for the door. 'There's a travel agent two blocks away. I'll check on the flights to Nome. Be back in twenty minutes.'

'DeDe . . .'

'All we've got to do is beat him there. We can hire people, if we have to. Once he lands on that island, we've got him cornered. Jesus, we've gotta hurry!'

DeDe stopped when she reached the door. 'Oh . . . I'm assuming you're going with me?'

Mary Ann hesitated, then smiled as confidently as possible. 'You assumed right,' she said.

As soon as DeDe had gone, Mary Ann called Brian at Perry's.

'It's me,' she said, perhaps a little too blithely. 'Alive and well.'

'And living where?' He was understandably miffed.

'I'm sorry, Brian. I didn't count on this.'

A long pause and then: 'I've heard of brides-to-be getting cold feet, but this is ridiculous.'

She laughed uneasily. 'You know it isn't that.'

'Is it . . . the Jonestown business?'

'Yeah.'

'Christ! You aren't *in* Jonestown, are you?'

Another laugh. 'God, no. I'm fine. DeDe's with me, and we should be back in a few days. I'm sorry to be so mysterious about all this, but I gave DeDe my word I wouldn't talk for a while.'

'I miss the hell out of you.'

'I miss you, too.' For a moment, she thought she might cry. Instead, she said brightly: 'It's gonna be wonderful being Mrs Hawkins!'

'Yeah?'

'You bet.'

'You don't have to take my name, you know.'

'Fuck that,' she said. 'I'm from Cleveland, remember?'

Finally, he laughed. 'Get home, hear?'

'I will. Soon. How's everybody?'

'O.K., I guess. Michael says he's not getting laid these days. But who is? Jesus . . . I almost forgot. That asshole from the station called. He says you're . . . let me get this right . . . "out on your ass" if you're not back to work on Friday.'

'Larry Kenan?'

'Uh-huh. And I think he meant it.'

'Breaks my heart.'

'I thought you might say that. Also, Bambi Kanetaka called to say that you left some notes at the station. She says she'll give them to Larry if you don't call her right away. What's that all about?'

It took a moment for the catastrophe to sink in. 'Oh, *no*,' groaned Mary Ann. 'Those were my notes on DeDe and the whole . . . oh God, this is awful, Brian. Look, I have to call her right away. I'll call you soon, O.K.?'

'Sure, but . . .'

'I love you. Bye-bye.'

Rough Treatment

It was such a stupid mistake – such a stupid, conventional, deadly mistake. Even in her panic and excitement, how could she have rushed off to Alaska, leaving those incriminating notes behind at the station?

At least Larry hadn't found them. That was some consolation. Bambi was bad enough, of course, but there was some hope that her simplemindedness and/or vanity might be activated to prevent her from leaking the story to the world at large.

She pondered the problem for a minute or so, then looked up Bambi's number in her address book and dialed her direct.

'Hello.' Bambi's voice, vapid and breezy as ever, was accompanied by the sound of Andy Gibb's falsetto.

'Bambi, it's Mary Ann.'

'Aha! You still in Cleveland?'

Cleveland? Is that what Brian told her? 'Uh . . . yeah . . . what's up?'

'Didn't your boyfriend tell you?'

'Well . . . he said something about some notes, but I wasn't exactly sure what he meant.'

'Does Jonestown ring a bell?'

Mary Ann counted. One . . . two . . . three . . . four. 'Oh,' she exclaimed, 'my treatment. How embarrassing! I hope you didn't *read* it. It's hopelessly corny at this point.'

'*Treatment?*'

'For a movie. I had this dumb idea for a thriller, and a friend of mine who knows this agent in Hollywood said I should work up some notes before making a formal presentation.'

'Oh.'

'It's kind of moonlighting, I guess. I'd appreciate it if you wouldn't mention it to . . .'

'You *made up* a story about Jim Jones?'

'Why not?' said Mary Ann. 'Lots of writers make up stories about . . . say, Jack the Ripper. He was the boogeyman of his time; Jones is ours.'

'And that stuff about him having a double . . . ?'

'Pretty dumb, huh?'

Silence.

'Oh well,' sighed Mary Ann. 'This is my first crack at it. I guess I'll get better as . . .'

'I like your casting,' said Bambi.

'Huh?'

'DeDe Day as the one who escapes from Guyana with her twins in tow. It's ingenious, really, using a real-life person like that. It's so outlandish that it could almost be true, couldn't it?'

Silence.

'*Couldn't it, Mary Ann?*'

The jig was obviously up. 'Bambi, look . . .'

'No, *you* look. I have an obligation to give those notes to Larry,

Mary Ann. I wanted you to know that. Frankly, I'm surprised you would sit on a story of this magnitude without seeking some sort of professional journalistic guidance.'

Meaning *her*, of course. 'I had planned on consulting the news department,' said Mary Ann. 'In fact, I thought you would be the ideal person to . . .' The lie caught in her throat like a bad oyster. 'The story is yours, Bambi. I promise you that. Only we have to wait . . . just a little while.'

'Forget it. News doesn't wait. Larry Layton's trial is going full tilt right now. Don't you think this might have *some* bearing on the case?'

'Not really,' replied Mary Ann. 'He's charged with murdering the congressman at the airstrip. DeDe left before any of that even happened.'

'Ah . . . this treatment gets better all the time.'

Desperate, Mary Ann threw caution to the winds. 'Bambi . . . DeDe's children are in great danger. *Any* public notice of this . . . situation could result in their death. I wish I could give you the details, but I can't. I'm begging you . . . please give me a week to . . .'

The newswoman laughed derisively.

'Three days, then.'

'Mary Ann . . . you have *got* to learn a little detachment, if you ever want to be a practicing newsperson. If those kids are in some sort of trouble, it's a crying shame, but the public has a right to know about it. You can't just pick and choose when it comes to news.'

This was a load of crap, and Mary Ann knew it. The journalists she dealt with were picking and choosing all the time. 'Can we at least talk before you tell Larry about it?'

'We're talking now.'

'I mean, in person.'

'Terrific. But you're in Cleveland.'

'My plane gets in tomorrow afternoon,' said Mary Ann. 'I could meet you at my apartment at . . . say, three o'clock. This would help *you*, actually. I could clarify the things you're not clear on before you present it to Larry.'

'All right. But I'm definitely telling him about it on Friday.'

'Fine. I really appreciate it, Bambi. Got a pencil handy?'

'Go ahead.'

'I'm at 28 Barbary Lane, apartment 3. If my plane should be a little late or something, my friend Brian will let you in. Please don't say a word till then, O.K.?'

'O.K.,' said Bambi.

After hanging up, Mary Ann placed another call to Brian.

'Hi,' she said grimly, 'I've got a big favor to ask you.'

Clerical Error

As soon as he recognized Prue's voice, Father Paddy tittered throught the grille in the confessional: 'Really, darling, we can't go on meeting like this!'

Prue answered him soberly. 'I want this to be . . . official, Father.'

'Meaning, zip the old lip, huh?'

'It *must* be confidential,' whispered Prue. 'I promised Frannie Halcyon I wouldn't tell anybody. Apparently, it's a matter of life and death.'

'My God, girl! What happened on that ship? I *thought* you were back a little early. Don't tell me that you and Luke had some sort of . . . ?'

'Luke is gone, Father!'

'What!'

The cleric stirred audibly in the confessional.

'What are you doing?' asked Prue.

'Getting a cigaret,' he replied. 'Bear with me, darling.' There was more moving about, then Prue heard the cat-like hiss of Father Paddy's lighter. 'All right,' he said finally, expelling smoke. 'Take it from the top, darling.'

It took her ten minutes to outline the disaster for him. When she had finished, Father Paddy uttered a faint moan of disbelief.

'Well?' said Prue.

'Does he still have my ID?' inquired the priest.

'I'm afraid so, I'm sorry, Father . . . I . . .'

'Don't apologize, darling. It was my stupid idea in the first place. What about Frannie Halcyon? Did she make any connection between *that* Sean Starr and me?'

'None, as far as I know,' said Prue. 'I doubt if she realizes your first name is Sean. She was too upset about the children to be functioning in a rational . . .'

'Mary Ann might figure it out, though.'

'You *know* her?' asked Prue.

'We work at the same station. I tape my *Honest to God* show just before she does the afternoon movie. I had to stand in for her on Tuesday when she didn't show up. No one had any idea where she was, and I certainly had no idea she was . . . Lord, this is getting sticky!'

'The thing that upsets me,' said Prue, 'is that DeDe appears to have . . . known Luke.' The very thought of this made her eyes well up with tears again.

Father Paddy must have heard her sniffling. 'Darling . . . you don't mean . . . biblically?'

'Yes!' sobbed the columnist.

'Oh my,' said the priest. 'She *told* you they had been lovers?'

'Not exactly. But she knew something about him that she couldn't possibly have known if she hadn't been . . . intimate with him.'

The priest sucked air in noisily. '*What?*'

Prue hesitated. 'I don't see how that matters. She just *did*, that's all.'

A long silence. 'Very well, then . . . I guess it's time for my next customer.'

'But Father . . . what should I *do*?'

'You've already done it, my child. You told them what you know.'

'I didn't tell them about the shack in the park . . . or the fake ID. I didn't tell them I had known Luke before the cruise.'

'Purely extraneous, darling. It's obvious you've stumbled on some private romantic squabble between DeDe and Luke. I know it must be painful to accept that, but you can't let your emotions drive you into doing something rash. If I were you, I'd lay low for a . . .'

'Father, he took her children, for God's sake!'

'Well, of course, that's dreadful . . . and she deserves our prayers . . . but your little interlude with Luke is hardly pertinent to her dilemma. Where did she know him, anyway? I thought you said she'd been hiding out at Frannie's place since her return from Cuba.'

'I don't know for sure. I guess she could have . . . you don't think she knew him in Guyana, do you?'

'I was wondering when you'd get to that.'

'You mean . . . a Temple member?'

'It's certainly possible,' said the cleric. 'Now, is that really the sort of thing you want to get mixed up in, darling?'

'But I *am* mixed up in it, Father. If they find him and he's carrying your ID . . .'

'But . . .'

'I'll tell them that I lost my wallet in the park about a month ago. And you'll confirm it, because you were with me at the time. And that will be the end of that. Do you read me, darling?'

'I think so,' said Prue.

'Good. Now run along and be a good girl. This will all come out in the wash . . . I promise you.'

'But . . . what if he tells them about me?'

'Then, they'll just have to choose between the word of a reputable columnist and the word of a kidnapper. That shouldn't be too tough. Scoot, now! I've got customers waiting. And, Prue . . . put this all behind you, darling.'

'All right.'

'That means: *stay away from that shack.*'

'O.K.,' said Prue defeatedly.

'God bless,' said Father Paddy.

Tea

She arrived right on the dot, as Brian had expected.

'You're Bambi,' he said as cordially as possible, extending his hand. 'I'm Brian, Mary Ann's friend. I watch you on TV all the time.'

She barely returned his handshake. 'She's not here, huh?' She scanned the room as she spoke, as if she might spot Mary Ann peering out from under a tablecloth or crouching behind a curtain. 'I haven't got a lot of time, you know.'

'She just called from the airport,' said Brian. 'Apparently, she had a little trouble making a connection in Denver – the traffic controllers' strike. Here, let me take your coat. I'm sure she won't be long.'

Bambi slid out of her bronze metallic windbreaker but retained control of the matching shoulder bag. Hanging the jacket on a chair, Brian grinned with calculated boyishness and said: 'You look even better in person.'

'Thanks,' said Bambi.

Another grin, this time ducking his head. 'I guess you hear that a lot?'

The newswoman shrugged. 'It's nice to hear it, anyway.'

Brian sprawled on the sofa, letting his denimed legs fall open carelessly. 'I liked your stuff on the gas leak, by the way. Very cool-headed and thorough.'

'You saw that?'

Brian nodded. 'On three channels, as a matter of fact. Yours was the only one that made sense. Sit down. You might as well get comfortable.'

Bambi pulled up a Breuer chair and sat down, keeping the handbag in her lap. 'They almost didn't send me on that story,' she said.

'Really?'

The newswoman nodded. 'You'd be surprised what prejudice there is against letting women do any of the really hard-hitting disaster stuff. I just keep pushing, though.' She smiled valiantly.

'Good for you!' said Brian. 'Look . . . I'm gonna have a cup of tea. Will you join me?'

Bambi shook her head. 'I can't handle the caffeine.'

'It's herbal,' said Brian. 'Our landlady makes it. Incredibly soothing. You should try a cup.'

'Oh . . . all right.'

He was back in five minutes, his hand shaking slightly as he handed her the cup. She sipped it tentatively, then unleashed her best six o'clock smile. 'It's *marvelous* . . . What's in it?'

'Uh . . . hibiscus flowers, orange peels . . . stuff like that.'

'Does she have a name for it?'

'Oh . . . Alaskan Twilight, I think.'

Bambi took another sip. 'Mmmm . . .'

Brian kept up the idle chatter for another five minutes until the newscaster's speech began to slur. For one terrifying moment, she seemed to realize what had happened, staring at him in confusion and anger. Then her eyelids dropped shut, and she slumped forward in the chair.

'Jesus,' murmured Brian. He rose and checked the body: she was out cold but still breathing. When he tilted the head back, a pearl of saliva rolled from the corner of the newscaster's mouth.

'O.K.,' he said aloud.

The door to the hallway swung open. Michael's head appeared first, then Mrs Madrigal's. The landlady's brow was creased with concern. 'Are you sure she's . . . ?'

'She's all right,' Brian assured her. 'What's in that stuff, anyway?'

'Never mind,' said Mrs Madrigal. 'It's organic.'

'And it lasts fifteen minutes?'

688

'More or less,' replied the landlady. 'I wouldn't push it. Michael dear, if you'll grab the feet, Brian take her arms. I'll make sure the coast is clear.'

Michael knelt by the body and grasped the newscaster's ankles. 'We *could* just finish her off.'

'Michael!' Mrs Madrigal was in no mood for joking.

Hoisting their quarry until she was waist high, Brian and Michael staggered into the hallway.

'Alaskan Twilight,' grinned Michael. 'Gimme a break!'

The New Boarder

Night had fallen by the time Mrs Madrigal rejoined her 'boys' on the roof of 28 Barbary Lane.

'Well,' she said, slipping between them and squeezing their waists, 'her temper's as foul as ever, but her appetite's improved considerably.'

Brian looked relieved. 'For a while there, I was sure she was going for a hunger strike.'

'Has she stopped yelling?' asked Michael.

The landlady nodded. 'I think I convinced her the basement is soundproof. We don't need to worry about the neighbors, really. Even when she's making noise, you can't hear her beyond the foyer. Visitors are another story.'

Michael gazed out at the lights on the bay. 'It's like *The Collector*,' he said.

'She has all the amenities,' insisted the landlady. 'A comfy bed, a space heater, all my Agatha Christies. I even gave her Mona's old TV set.' She turned to Michael. 'What did you do with her car?'

'I parked it down on Leavenworth. Five or six blocks away.'

Brian frowned. 'That doesn't exactly cover our tracks.'

'Well,' shrugged Michael, 'if you know of a swamp nearby . . .'

'Leavenworth is fine,' said Mrs Madrigal. 'I don't expect we'll be keeping her longer than two or three days. I hope not, anyway. She says she's due at the station on Friday afternoon. Somebody's bound to start getting suspicious.'

'Mary Ann took care of that,' said Brian.

'How?' asked Michael.

'She called the station and said that she and Bambi are on the trail of a big story and that they won't be back until the weekend. The news director was plenty pissed, but he bought it. He didn't have much choice.'

'So no one else knows that DeDe and the kids are alive?'

'No one except the kidnapper,' said Brian.

'And they've got no idea whatsoever who he is?'

Brian shook his head. 'Just some guy Mrs Halcyon met on the ship. Mary Ann is convinced that any media attention at all would seriously jeopardize their chances of getting the kids back alive.'

'That's quite enough for me,' said Mrs Madrigal.

'She wouldn't have asked us to do this,' added Brian, 'if the situation wasn't desperate.' He turned to the landlady. 'Did you get Mary Ann's notes, by the way?'

Mrs Madrigal nodded. 'I locked them in my safe.'

'Good. We'll come out of this O.K. I mean . . . it isn't like we're torturing her or holding her for ransom or something.'

'You're right,' Michael deadpanned. 'Maybe we're not thinking big enough.'

'Michael, dear.' Mrs Madrigal remonstrated with her eyes.

Brian addressed the landlady: 'I think you're great to be doing this. Mary Ann says she'll take full responsibility when she gets back.'

Mrs Madrigal smile was understandably weary. 'It's not just for her, you know.'

'What do you mean?'

'Those children,' explained the landlady. 'I wept for a week when I read about their disappearance in Guyana.'

'You *knew* them?' asked Michael.

Mrs Madrigal smiled wanly and shook her head. 'I knew their grandfather.'

'Mary Ann's old boss?'

Another nod.

'You mean you . . . ?'

'We had a rather friendly little affair just before he died. Nothing earth-shattering, but . . . nice.'

Both men stared at her in amazement.

The landlady took ladylike delight in their confusion. 'If I'm not mistaken, one of the twins was named after me. The little girl, I presume.'

'That's right,' laughed Brian. 'Her name is Anna. Mary Ann told me. Jesus, you're a trip!'

'The little boy is Edgar,' added Mrs Madrigal. 'Edgar and Anna. Isn't that lovely symbolism? Our affair was memorialized by those children. They're coming home safe and sound if I have to *strangle* that ridiculous woman in the basement.'

Michael regarded her with admiration. 'What a fabulous ulterior motive!'

The landlady gave both of her boys a jaunty shake. 'How about some brownies for my partners in crime?'

'When did you have time for *that?*' asked Michael.

'Well . . . I made a batch for our houseguest, and there are plenty of leftovers.'

'You got *her* loaded?'

Mrs Madrigal's face was resolute. 'I want her to be comfortable.'

'This woman knows how to take prisoners,' said Brian.

The Diomedes

After several hours of searching in Nome, Mary Ann and DeDe found an Eskimo bush pilot who filled their requirements exactly. His name was Willie Omiak, and his cousin Andy had served for the past four years as a National Guardsman on Little Diomede.

'He can have it,' declared Willie, shouting over the engine noise. 'Nome's small enough for me, I tried living in Wales for a while and even that drove me crazy.'

'You mean . . . the British Isles?' Mary Ann couldn't picture this round-faced, brown-skinned youth living among Welshmen.

The Eskimo grinned. 'Wales, Alaska. The nearest mainland town to the Diomedes. We'll be stopping there to refuel and check weather conditions. You sure you want to stay overnight on Little Diomede?'

'We may,' said DeDe. 'It depends.'

'They don't have a Holiday Inn,' smiled Willie.

'We'll manage.'

'Sure,' said the pilot. 'Maybe Andy's family can put you up.' He winked, apparently sensing the first question that occurred to Mary Ann. 'Don't sweat it. They've never lived in igloos – mostly sod huts propped up on stilts. The Bureau of Indian Affairs built 'em some new houses about six or seven years ago. Polyurethane walls . . . much warmer.'

'I'll bet,' said Mary Ann, privately saddened that even the Eskimos had been reduced to using plastics.

'What about defenses?' asked DeDe, as the tiny, single-engine Cessna skirted the coastline northwest of Nome.

'What about 'em?'

'Well, I mean . . . with Russia only two-and-a-half miles away?'

'According to Andy,' said Willie Omiak, 'they've got three M–14 rifles, one grenade launcher and one grenade. It isn't exactly a full-time job, being a scout.'

'A scout?'

'Eskimo Scouts,' explained the pilot. 'That's the official name for Alaska National Guardsmen. They do most of their work in the winter, I guess, when you can walk right across the ice. Most people know better these days. Back in '47, the Russians held Andy's dad for almost two months when he crossed the strait to visit relatives. Hell, it was just family. Nobody even knew about the Cold War.'

'Do the Russians have forces on Big Diomede?' asked Mary Ann.

Willie Omiak grinned. 'About as scary as ours. A guy in a little shack on the highest part of the island.'

'What does he do?'

'Watches,' answered the pilot. 'While our guy watches back. Nobody has much reason to visit Big Diomede anymore. Most of our cousins were shipped to the Siberian mainland back in the fifties. For that matter, nobody goes to Little Diomede either. What got *you* interested?'

'We're looking for someone,' said DeDe.

'An Eskimo?'

'No,' DeDe replied. 'An American.'

Willie Omiak looked at his passenger, then turned and winked at Mary Ann. 'We'll forget she said that, won't we?'

They appeared out of nowhere it seemed – two granite crags united by their isolation, but divided by politics. On the smaller one, a village was visible, a cluster of clapboard and tarpaper houses snuggled against the base of a sixteen-hundred-foot cliff.

'That's Ingaluk,' said Willie Omiak, making a low pass between the islands. 'It's Thursday down there. Over there on Big Diomede it's Friday already.'

692

Mary Ann peered down. 'You mean . . . ?'

'We're flying directly over the International Date Line.' He grinned at her over his shoulder. 'This place confusing enough for you?'

It was eerie, all right. Two continents, two ideologies, two nations – neatly bisected by today and tomorrow. What better place to search for two frightened little children teetering perilously between two fates?

As the Cessna swooped lower, Mary Ann could make out a school-house and a church. Then the airstrip materialized: a rectangle of asphalt near the shore, delineated by oil drums and half-a-dozen people awaiting their arrival.

'There's Andy,' yelled Willie Omiak, as the plane bumped the runway.

'He looks awfully glad to see you,' said Mary Ann.

The pilot patted the leather satchel on the seat next to him. 'I've got the new *Playboy*,' he grinned.

Mary Ann's giggling stopped when she saw the naked dread in DeDe's eyes. They had chased their quarry to the end of the world. What if it was too late?

Deadline

Prue sat at her Coronamatic and wept softly to herself. Her maid, her secretary and her chauffeur were all in the house, so a visible (or audible) display of grief was completely out of the question.

She slipped a piece of paper into the typewriter. It hung there listlessly, like a surrender flag, a horrid metaphor for the emptiness she felt now that Luke was gone. What was there to write about, really? What was there to live for?

She yanked the paper out again, just as the phone rang.

'Yes?'

'All right, Prudy Sue, let's have it.'

'Have what?' Getting right to the point was Victoria Lynch's annoy-ing device for flaunting her intuitive powers. Prue refused to play along.

'You know. True confessions. What the hell's been going on? You've been in the most morbid funk ever since you got back fom Alaska.'

Silence.

'You looked like holy hell last night at the placenta party.'

Prue almost bit her head off. 'I don't *like* placenta parties, all right?'

693

(The party had been held in the spacious Pacific Heights garden of John and Eugenia Stonecypher. In keeping with a hallowed family tradition, the couple had planted Eugenia's most recent afterbirth in the same hole as a flowering plum sapling, a ritual intended to ensure long life and happiness for the Stonecypher's baby girl. Prue had almost thrown up.)

'It isn't my idea of a fun time,' she added.

'You haven't even called me,' countered her friend.

'I'm a little blue,' said Prue. 'What can I say?'

'You can say you'll call me. You can lean on your pal, Prudy Sue. Look, I've got the most marvelous news. I've found a place that sells Rioco!'

'What's that?'

'You remember. That Brazilian cola Binky told us about last spring.'

'She didn't tell *me*.'

'Well, it's full of jungle speed or something. Half of Rio is buzzed on it. Guarana. It sounds like bat shit, but it's fabulous stuff. They've got it at the Twin Peaks Grocery. What say we dash out there?'

'I'm on deadline, Vicky.'

'We could go this afternoon.'

'Vicky . . .'

'All right, *be* in your funk, then.'

'You're sweet to think of me.'

'I'm not trying to be sweet, Prudy Sue. I want my friend back.'

A long pause, then a sigh from the columnist. 'I'm trying, Vickie. Give me a little time, O.K.?'

'You got it. Just don't mope, Prudy Sue. Get out and get some air, at least. Take Vuitton for a walk.'

That was what did it: a little sisterly advice from an old friend.

Despite repeated warnings from Father Paddy, she had known that this moment would come. How could she have avoided it? How could she not return, however briefly, to the scene of her happiest moments on earth?

Besides, she might find a clue there – something to aid DeDe in her search for Luke and the twins. She wouldn't have to tell DeDe everything – just enough to point her in the right direction. That couldn't hurt, could it?

She also wanted some answers herself. Maybe the truth, however painful, would free her from this crippling melancholy. It was worth a try, anyway.

And Vuitton needed the walk.

Ingaluk

The first thing Mary Ann noticed about Little Diomede was the row of crude wooden boxes perched on the rocks above the village. She asked Andy Omiak about them.

'Coffins,' he replied amiably. 'Most of the year the ground's frozen solid. We have to bury people above ground.' Seeing Mary Ann's grimace, he added: 'It's not as bad as it sounds. It's so dry here that the boxes last longer than . . . their contents. The dogs scatter whatever's left.'

The dogs were the next thing she noticed. Dozens of them – thick-coated and yellow-eyed – roaming the island in ominous packs. 'We're glad to have 'em,' insisted Andy Omiak. 'They function as our radar. If anybody comes over from the other island the dogs will let us know.'

DeDe, who had been silent during the trek from the airfield, turned to the Eskimo Scout. 'What about the other way around?'

Andy Omiak frowned at her. 'You mean . . . ?'

'If somebody tried to cross over to the Russian island, would you have any way of knowing it?'

'Oh . . . well . . . there it is. It wouldn't be too hard to *see* anybody who might try to cross over. This time of year it never gets dark, so . . . why do you ask, anyway?'

DeDe maintained her stride, looking straight ahead. 'We think somebody may be trying to cross over. He may have already, in fact.'

'From the mainland?'

DeDe nodded. 'A man about fifty and two four-year-olds, a boy and a girl. They were Eurasian and dressed in parkas, so they might have been mistaken for Eskimos.'

Andy Omiak smiled. 'Not around here. Everybody knows everybody. We'd see that for sure.'

Mary Ann asked: 'If they came from the mainland, would they have to arrive by airplane?'

The Eskimo Scout shrugged. 'Probably. That's the usual way. I guess he could come in by boat . . . from Wales or something. There wouldn't be much point in stopping here, though. Why wouldn't he go straight to Big Diomede?'

It was a good question – one that cast a shadow on the validity of their search. In light of the roving dogs and Eskimo Scouts, a stopover on Little Diomede would be almost foolhardy. Why not go directly to Big Diomede, if you were going to go at all?

Willie Omiak, Andy's pilot cousin, parted company with them as soon as they reached Andy's house, a sturdy wood-and-tarpaper structure near the waterfront. 'I'll be back at the airstrip,' he said. 'Give a holler if you need me.'

'Thanks,' said DeDe, looking genuinely grateful. 'You've been very kind.'

'No sweat. You leaving tomorrow, by the way?'

'I think so,' said DeDe. 'Can I let you know later?'

'Sure. Nana will take good care of you.'

Nana was his grandmother, a rotund and wrinkled crone who reminded Mary Ann of the dried apple dolls sold at the Renaissance Pleasure Faire. Having little command of English, she simply smiled at them toothlessly when she arrived with mugs of steaming cocoa.

Mary Ann made an exaggerated bow to show her appreciation. 'How lovely,' she said, addressing Andy Omiak.

'We don't get much company,' he grinned. He turned to his grandmother, speaking to her in their common language. The old lady looked at Mary Ann, giggled, and scurried out of the room.

'So,' said Andy Omiak, 'maybe you'd better tell me what this is all about.'

An awkward silence followed. Then DeDe said. 'Someone has kidnapped my children.'

The Eskimo Scout frowned. 'Someone you know?'

'Yes.'

'But . . . why?'

'He wants them for himself,' she replied. 'He's crazy. We think he plans to take them to Russia.'

'Have you notified the mainland police?'

'No,' said DeDe. 'No one.'

'Why not?'

'It's complicated,' DeDe replied. 'If he knows we're involved with the police, he might hurt the children.'

696

'You must be very worried,' said Andy Omiak.

'I'm desperate.'

'And you want to find out if he's taken them to Big Diomede?'

'Yes.'

The Eskimo started to speak, then stopped, looking away from DeDe. 'I could get into a lot of trouble,' he said at last.

'I'm afraid I don't . . .'

'If I help you . . . you can't tell *anybody*.'

'I promise you,' said DeDe.

Andy Omiak leaned closer, speaking in a furtive tone. 'I can take you,' he said.

'To . . . ?'

He nodded. 'I've done it before.'

Mary Ann looked up from her cocoa. 'Wait a minute. You don't mean . . . ?'

'It's all right,' said the Eskimo. 'It can be done.'

'*Without being shot at?*'

Andy Omiak grinned. 'It's possible.'

Anna and Bambi

Mrs Madrigal was preparing Bambi Kanetaka's tray when Michael bounced into the kitchen.

'What's for din-din?' he asked, lifting the lid on a covered dish. 'Mmmm . . . parakeet . . . my favorite!'

The landlady snapped at him. 'It's five-spice chicken, Michael! And I'll thank you not to be so flip!'

Michael ducked his head repentantly. 'Hey . . . sorry.'

Mrs Madrigal placed a pink rose in the bud vase on the tray. 'I'm worried about her,' she said. 'She seems to be getting . . . desperate. I've told her time and again that we mean her no harm, but she just won't relax.'

'I'm surprised your brownies didn't do the trick.'

'She wants out,' said the landlady, 'Period. She even promised she'd keep quiet about DeDe if I'd set her free.'

'You don't believe that, do you?'

'I can't afford to,' replied Mrs Madrigal, 'not if there's the slightest chance of endangering those children. Besides, if I release her before there's *some* resolution, we'll only be in worse trouble. We need proof that we had a good reason to . . . detain her.'

'Good point,' said Michael.

Mrs Madrigal lifted the tray. 'I suppose things will work themselves out. They always do. I can't help worrying, though.'

Michael looked at her earnestly. 'We're in this together, you know. Brian and I have talked about it. If they haul you off to jail, then they're taking us, too. And we'll insist on the same cell.'

The landlady smiled back at him, then pecked him on the cheek. 'I'm sorry I barked at you, dear. This is all a bit new to me. I feel like such an *outlaw*.'

Michael winked at her. 'But you *are*, Blanche . . . you *are*.'

Somewhat more at peace with herself, Mrs Madrigal descended the stairs to the basement.

She listened for a moment outside the door, then set the tray down on the floor and undid the padlock. Bambi was sitting in the rumpsprung armchair that the landlady had retired when Mona moved to Seattle.

'Suppertime,' chimed Mrs Madrigal, trying to sound cheerful without patronizing her. She placed the tray on an ancient laundry hamper that Burke Andrew had left behind.

Bambi didn't stir.

'I checked the TV listings,' said the landlady. '*The Barretts of Wimpole Street* is on tonight. I thought you might enjoy watching it.'

A low growl from the newscaster.

'I know it isn't easy,' continued Mrs Madrigal, 'but it won't be long now. We're all terribly sorry that it had to come to this, but . . .'

In a single lightning-swift movement, Bambi sprang to her feet and lunged at her captor, knocking the landlady backwards until she was pinned against the board where the house keys were hung. Mrs Madrigal screamed in agony as the nails in the key board pressed into her back.

Crumpling to her knees, she looked up to see the newscaster's triumphant sneer as Bambi kicked her once . . . twice . . . three times in the stomach. On the third kick, Mrs Madrigal seized Bambi's ankle and twisted it sharply, eliciting a scream of Samurai intensity. Bambi toppled to the concrete floor, then raised herself to her hands and knees and began crawling for the door.

Wheezing in pain, Mrs Madrigal reached for a loop of garden hose and hoisted herself to a near-standing position. Something warm and wet – presumably blood – was trickling down her spine, pasting her kimono to her back. Her fingers found the handle of a shovel, which she wielded like a mace, bringing it down squarely on Bambi's backside.

For a moment, and only a moment, the newscaster was splayed against the floor like a swastika. Then she lurched to her feet and made her way through the doorway and up the steps.

Mrs Madrigal staggered after her, still brandishing the shovel. When Bambi reached the top of the stairs, the landlady swung wildly, clipping her adversary in the back of the knees. Bambi fell forward ingloriously, then slid back down the steps until her ankles were once more within the landlady's grasp.

Mrs Madrigal dragged the newscaster back into the basement, wrapped her ankles hastily with a length of electrical cord, and hurried out the door, locking it behind her.

Gasping for breath, she leaned against the door for almost a minute. Inside, Bambi was screaming bloody murder. Upstairs, someone was ringing the door buzzer.

She made her way slowly up the stairs, hoping to God that the visitor hadn't heard the ruckus.

When she saw the man at the door, she wanted to weep in his arms.

It was Jon Fielding.

House Call

The doctor knelt next to his patient, who was lying face down on the red velvet sofa in her parlor. 'O.K. now . . . bite the bullet, Mrs M. This'll sting a little.'

Her body tensed as he daubed gently at the puncture in her back. 'Good girl,' he said. 'It's not nearly as bad as it looked. How did you do this, anyway?'

'It was silly,' replied Mrs Madrigal. 'I slipped and fell against a nail.'

'Where?'

'Uh . . . in the basement. Does it need stitches?'

'Not really. A Band-Aid will fix you up just fine. Got any?'

'In the bathroom cabinet,' said the landlady. 'Why don't I just . . . ?'

'Sit tight. You're indisposed.'

He was back moments later, smoothing the bandage into place. 'There,' he said, rising to his feet. 'I think you'll pull through just fine.'

Mrs Madrigal adjusted the bloodied kimono as she shifted to a sitting position and retied the silken cord around her waist. 'Well,' she said, smiling lovingly at Jon, 'what did we ever do without a doctor in the house?'

Jon shrugged. 'I was kind of hoping you'd tell me.'

Mrs Madrigal studied him for a moment, reassessing the Arrow Collar blond who had lived with Michael for almost three years. He seemed thinner now, a little haggard even, but his classically Nordic face was more beautiful than ever. 'How old are you now?' she asked.

He replied with a smile. 'Thirty-three.'

'It suits you,' she said.

'Thanks. You look pretty good yourself. Aside from the wound, that is.'

She bowed graciously. 'It's good to see you, Jon. It really is. Michael's upstairs, if you want to see him.' She patted her hair to regain some sense of order. 'I'm sure you didn't plan this detour.'

'Actually,' said Jon, 'I did. It was your buzzer I rang, remember?'

'Then, I'm honored.'

'I was hoping you could tell me the lay of the land.'

'Oh . . . I see.' She fussed with a wisp of hair over her ear.

'I haven't talked to Michael for a long time, and I'm not sure if . . .' He stopped talking and jerked his head sharply, like an animal picking up a scent. 'What was that?' he asked.

'What was what?'

'I'm not sure . . . somebody yelling, I think. You didn't hear it?'

'It could be the children,' said Mrs Madrigal.

'Children?'

'Down on Leavenworth . . . skateboarding. It's quite bloodcurdling sometimes.'

'It sounded closer than that.'

'Look, dear . . . if you want to have a little chat, why don't we just stroll down to North Beach. It's such a balmy evening, and we could have a lovely little dinner somewhere.'

'All right,' said Jon, 'but on me, O.K.?'

'You've got a date,' said Mrs Madrigal.

*

After changing clothes, she hurried him through the foyer, chattering as noisily as possible. Bambi's outburst seemed to have subsided, but Mrs Madrigal breathed a secret sigh of relief when they were finally out of earshot on the lane.

They dined in a window seat at the Washington Square Bar and Grill.

'So how is he?' asked Jon, after they had placed their orders.

Mrs Madrigal pursed her lips in thought. 'A little restless, I suppose.'

'How so?'

'Well, he makes a lot of fuss about his independence, but I don't think he really enjoys it very much.'

'But he has friends,' said the doctor.

'Plenty,' said the landlady.

'That's good.'

'Friends,' smiled the landlady, 'but no capital F Friend. That's what you wanted to know, isn't it?'

The doctor reddened. 'I guess it was.'

'Good.'

'It's been a long time, though . . . almost two years.'

'And you think you can pick up where you left off?'

'No,' said Jon, 'I just . . .'

'It's all right, dear. I think you can, too.'

He smiled at her almost timidly. 'I'm not sure either one of us could handle it at this point.'

'Why not?'

The doctor shrugged. 'Things change.'

'Do they now? Do you know what I think?'

'What?'

'I think you should stop beating around the bush, because you came here to get him back.'

'You do, huh?'

'Uh-huh. And I think I'm going to help you.' Her big blue eyes flowed into his.

Embarrassed, the doctor looked down.

'I'm a cranky old hen,' said Mrs Madrigal. 'I like all my eggs in one basket.'

701

To Russia with DeDe

Andy Omiak's proposal struck Mary Ann as exceptionally foolhardy, and she told DeDe so as soon as they were alone.

'What choice do we have?' countered DeDe.

'Well . . . we could notify the mainland police, and *they* could conduct the search.'

'And go charging in there with guns and bullhorns, loaded for bear. If we tell them who he is, my children will be the last thing they'll worry about.'

'Then we won't tell them. We'll just say . . . well, we could tell them the truth.'

'Which is?'

'That a man from the ship kidnapped your children in Sitka . . . and we think he brought them up here.'

'Do you seriously believe *he'll* think that's what we told them? Look . . . there's no reason for you to go with me, really. Andy'll be there, with a gun and all. It isn't fair to ask you . . .'

'Forget that,' said Mary Ann. 'I'm going.'

'I'd feel awful if . . .'

'Don't. This is my decision.'

DeDe squeezed her hand. 'Thanks.'

'Besides,' added Mary Ann, 'I've never been to Russia.'

They napped for several hours, after which Andy returned.

'Have you had a chance to think it over?' he asked.

'We're game,' said DeDe. Mary Ann nodded her agreement.

'O.K.,' said Andy. 'We should leave about an hour from now.'

Mary Ann made a face. 'In broad daylight?'

The Eskimo grinned. 'We don't have much else.'

'Oh . . . right.'

'Anyway,' continued Andy, 'this'll be almost as safe as darkness. Between eight and ten o'clock the whole town's at the school-house.'

'*Everybody?*' asked DeDe.

'All eighty-two of 'em,' smiled Andy.

'For classes or what?'

The Eskimo shook his head. 'We get a movie from the mainland once a week.'

'Oh.'

'Tonight they're showing *Superman II*. I think we're safe.'

'At least as far as Ingaluk is concerned.'

'What do you mean?' asked Andy.

'The *Russians*,' said DeDe. 'Don't tell me they're watching a movie, too?'

'Oh,' said Andy drily. 'Don't worry about *them*.'

As predicted, Ingaluk looked like a ghost town when the trip left the dock in Andy's fifteen-foot motor launch. Mary Ann stared up in awe at the dark cliffs above the village, the sun-bleached coffins flecking the rocks like seagull droppings. Then she turned her attention to the Russian island, only two miles away.

'What about that sentry shack?' she asked the Eskimo. 'Won't he see us cross the strait?'

'He usually does,' said Andy. 'Every week at this time.'

'I don't understand.'

Andy smiled. 'Neither would my C.O. That's why I'd appreciate it if you kept this under your hat.'

'Of course.'

'A friend of mine lives on Big Diomede.'

'I see.'

'My girlfriend, actually.'

DeDe and Mary Ann cast quick glances at each other. It was Mary Ann who sought further details. 'You mean she . . . ?'

'She's a radar technician. The guy in the lookout shack is her brother-in-law. We're kind of a family operation out here. If your kidnapper made it to Big Diomede, Jane will know about it.'

Half-an-hour later, Andy docked the boat on the far side of the big island, out of sight of Little Diomede.

'Wait here,' he told the women. 'You'll be O.K. If there's any news, you can come ashore with me later.' He leaped out of the boat and bolted down the dock to the shore.

Presently, a female figure appeared on the rocky ridge above the harbor, jumping from boulder to boulder until she reached the sand. Then Andy and Jane were in each other's arms, spinning like a couple in a corny commercial.

703

Mary Ann felt a curious kinship with them, seeing herself suddenly as Deborah Kerr in *The King and I.*

Cling very close to each other tonight – I've had a love of my own, like yours . . .

As usual, Brian was there when she needed him, nestled cozily in her heart.

The Eskimo lovers talked for several minutes, well out of earshot of DeDe and Mary Ann. When Andy returned, his face conveyed the news. 'I'm sorry,' he told DeDe.

'Nothing?'

'I'm afraid not,' he replied. 'They just haven't been here.'

'Could she let us know if . . .'

'Of course. She'll keep an eye out.'

There was a long agonizing silence. Then Mary Ann turned to DeDe. 'What do you want to do?' she asked.

A single tear rolled down DeDe's face. 'I want to go home,' she said.

'We will, then,' said Mary Ann. She searched in her windbreaker for a Kleenex, handing it to her friend. 'We won't give up on this, DeDe. I promise you we'll find them.'

As Andy shoved off from the dock, Mary Ann cast a final glance at the shores of the Soviet Union.

Jane was still standing there. Seeing Mary Ann, she smiled shyly, then lifted her hand and waved.

Mary Ann, of course, waved back.

Eden Revisited

A thick summer fog had settled over Golden Gate Park by the time Prue arrived at the tree ferns. Shuddering slightly at the eerie familiarity of it all, she turned up the collar of her Montodoro trench coat and plunged into the wilderness.

Vuitton ran ahead of her up the path, chasing a squirrel to the edge of the U-shaped ridge. When she called to him, he made a rapid decision to ignore her altogether.

'Vuitton!' she called. 'Come back here this second!' She was terrified of being left alone.

The wolfhound turned, wagged a cursory greeting to her, and bounded into the green-black depths of the rhododendron dell.

She ran after him, yelling 'Vuitton! COME BACK, GOD-DAMNIT!'

It was pointless, of course. Vuitton knew where he wanted to go. He even knew where *she* wanted to go. He would simply get there before she did. Why should that strike such fear in her heart?

She found the familiar path through the rhododendron dell and maintained a brisk pace, catching occasional glimpses of Vuitton's champagne-colored fur amid the foliage. As she searched for the bush that marked the entrance to Luke's secret enclave, a foghorn bleated mournfully in the distance.

Vuitton, as usual, led the way. Barking deliriously, the wolf-hound doubled back, burst through the gateway shrub and danced in circles around his mistress.

'Stay here!' she ordered him. 'Heel, Vuitton, heel!'

But he was off again, scampering down the crumbly slope that led to the shack. When Prue caught sight of the dwelling, she had second thoughts about the search she had planned to conduct. She was reminded of a summer years ago in Grass Valley when she had explored her father's bedside table and found a package of Trojans there. Some mysteries were better left alone.

Vuitton, however, was outside the door of the shack, yapping his silly head off.

When no one responded to his bark, Prue stumbled down the slope and listened outside the door. Trying the latch, she found that the door wasn't locked.

Inside, it seemed that nothing had been touched. The big chunk of foam rubber was still there. Likewise, the army cot, the map of the city, and Luke's beloved motto hanging on the wall.

There weren't that many places to search, she realized. Her first choice was the handmade wooden box where Luke had stored his gear for Vuitton. Only now it wasn't on the floor; it was on the shelf above the foam rubber.

When Prue reached for it, her hand touched something cold and slimy. She screamed hysterically and dropped the box, thereby crushing a large banana slug that had affixed itself to the box's backside.

She stood there shaking, wiping her fingers frantically against her coat. Vuitton crouched at her feet and whimpered in sympathy. 'It's O.K., baby,' murmured Prue. 'We're gonna leave in a minute.'

'*I think that's a good idea.*'

Prue's eyes shot to the door of the shack, where she was confronted by a uniformed policeman, staring down at her from the back of a large chestnut stallion.

'Oh . . . officer,' she said. 'I . . . uh, my dog ran in here, and I . . .'

The policeman smiled at her. 'Pretty dog.'

'Oh . . . well, thank you. He's such a nuisance sometimes.'

The officer leaned forward in the saddle, peering into the shack. 'Some place, huh?'

Prue nodded wordlessly. How long had he been watching her?

'It used to be a tool shed for the park, until a bum moved in about a year ago. I sort of keep an eye on things for him.'

Prue sidled out of the shack with Vuitton by her side. If Prue was intimidated by the policeman, the wolfhound was more intimidated by the horse.

'I apologize, officer,' said the columnist. 'It's just so . . . fascinating.'

The policeman smiled. 'Isn't it?' He seemed much less foreboding now that Prue could see that he was young and darkly handsome, Latino probably.

And he was wearing a Walkman.

A Man Called Mark

'He's quite a character,' said the mounted policeman.

Prue drew a momentary blank, still flushed with guilt over being caught in the act of searching Luke's shack. 'Uh . . . I'm sorry. What did you say?'

The officer smiled forgivingly. 'The guy who lives here. He's something else. One of those characters you find only in San Francisco.'

'I suppose so,' she said.

'You know him?'

'No,' she replied hastily. 'I mean . . . I *assume* he's a character . . . judging by this place. It's so . . . quaint. And he seems to keep it fairly neat.'

'I'm surprised it hasn't been vandalized,' said the policeman.

'Oh?'

'He's been gone for a couple of weeks . . . the longest time yet. I guess he's coming back, though; he left his stuff here. He was weird, but domestic, if you know what I mean.'

'I think so,' said Prue.

'Maybe I'd better take a look.' The officer dismounted, tethering his horse to a tree. As the stallion shifted, Vuitton whimpered nervously to his mistress. The policeman reached down and petted the wolfhound. 'What's his name?'

'Vuitton,' answered Prue.

'Uh . . . French?'

'Uh-huh.'

'What does it mean?'

Prue saw no point in explaining it. 'It's just a proper name.'

'He looks a lot like a dog that used to hang out with Mark.'

'Who's Mark?' asked Prue.

'The guy who lives here. I don't know his last name.' He smiled at the columnist. 'For all I know, *he* doesn't know his last name.'

Prue tried not to show her confusion. 'You don't know very much about him, I take it?'

The officer shrugged. 'What's to know? He's a drifter. Decent enough guy. Says he used to live in Hawaii. Ate mangoes on the beach, scrounged a lot. Same as here.'

'Really?'

'Sure. There are lots of guys like that in San Francisco. Sleeping in packing crates, bumming free food when the restaurants close. It's been going on since Emperor Norton.'

Prue frowned. 'But this man . . . well, he seems to be sort of intelligent.'

'How can you tell?'

'Well . . . that motto on his wall, for one thing . . . and those pencils and the map.'

The policeman grinned. 'He's probably trying to take over the world or something.'

'You think he's crazy?'

The officer shrugged. 'Maybe we're the crazy ones.'

'Yeah,' Prue replied vaguely. 'Maybe so.'

'He's educated, I know that. He studied at Harvard before he moved to Australia.'

'*Australia?*'

The policeman enjoyed her amazement. 'That came before Hawaii. He was foreman of a sheep ranch. Then he moved to Sydney and opened a travel agency. He hasn't had a bad life, I guess . . . all things considered.'

'No,' said Prue, 'I guess not.'

The officer made a quick inventory of the shack's contents. 'Most of his stuff seems O.K. I guess I'd better finish my rounds. It was nice talking to you, Miss Giroux.'

Prue was flabbergasted. 'How did you know my name?'

'C'mon,' smiled the policeman. 'You're a star. I saw you on TV once.'

'Oh,' said Prue feebly.

The officer mounted his horse, then leaned down and offered her his hand. 'I'm Bill Rivera, by the way. Have a nice day.'

Then the stallion and his rider were gone.

Prue stood there for a moment in mild shock.

When the silence had engulfed her again, she reentered the shack for a final appraisal of its contents. She had come this far, she decided, so she might as well play out the drama to the end.

The slug-smeared box lay on its side on the earthen floor. To avoid touching it, Prue poked it with her toe, but the latch was firmly secured. So she knelt beside it and prodded it with one of Luke's pencils until the lid creaked open.

Inside were two lumps of grayish fur.

Two little rabbit skins.

Behind, oblivious to this discovery, Vuitton spotted an old friend approaching through the underbrush and ran out into the fog to greet him.

Catching Up

When Jon and Mrs Madrigal returned to Barbary Lane, they sat on the bench in the courtyard and smoked a joint.

'Just like old times,' said the doctor.

The landlady gave him a drowsy smile. 'Almost.'

He smiled back, knowing what she meant.

'His light's still on,' she said.

'Yeah, I see.'

The joint was so resinous that it went out. Mrs Madrigal relit it and handed it to Jon. 'Am I pushing too much?' she asked.

'A little,' he said.

'Sorry.'

'I'll bet,' he grinned.

She tugged his earlobe affectionately. 'I want what's best for my children.'

A long pause, and then: 'I didn't know I was still part of the family.'

The landlady chuckled. 'Listen, dear . . . when you get this old lady, you get her for life.'

'That's good to know,' said the doctor.

'Funny thing,' added Mrs Madrigal, nodding towards the lighted window. 'That one's the same way.'

Jon turned and looked at her in silence.

'He is,' she said softly. 'I'm sure of it. He just has to be reminded of it sometimes . . . by the people who love him. If you catch my drift.'

'If I didn't,' smiled Jon, 'you'd rent a sound truck and broadcast it.' He rose, pecking her on the cheek. 'Are you sure he doesn't have company?'

'I'm sure,' said the landlady.

'You don't miss a trick, do you?'

She shook her head, smiling. 'Not one. And I'm sure you didn't mean it that way.'

Michael stood in the doorway, dumbfounded. 'Jon . . . my God . . . I didn't even hear you ring.'

'I didn't. Mrs Madrigal let me in. We just had dinner together.'

'Oh . . . great.'

'Can I come in?'

'Sure . . . of course. It's great to see you.'

'Thanks. Same to you.'

'Great . . . great.'

'I think we've agreed on that,' smiled Jon. He stepped across the threshold and embraced Michael clumsily. 'It's rotten notice. I'm sorry.'

'No problem. It's great to see you.' Michael winced and slapped his own face. 'I promise the patter will improve.'

Jon laughed and looked around the room. 'I like this color.'

'Can I get you a drink or something? Or a Diet Pepsi? I'm out of grass, but I'm sure I could bum one off . . .'

'I just did,' grinned Jon. 'I'm ripped to the tits.'

'No wonder you like this color.'

Another laugh, more nervous than the first. 'No . . . really.'

'You'll hate the bedroom,' said Michael. 'I got rid of the egg-plant.'

Jon made a mock-fierce expression. 'What color is it now?'

'Crayfish.'

'What color is that??'

'Sort of . . . cream.'

'Crayfish are cream-colored?'

Michael laughed and pointed to a chair. 'Sit down. God, where do we start?'

'Well . . . I know about Mary Ann and Brian. Mrs M. told me. She invited me to the wedding, in fact.'

'Great.'

'Are you sure? This isn't exactly . . . my territory anymore. I don't want you to be uncomfortable, Michael.'

Michael rolled his eyes. 'Do I *look* uncomfortable?'

'It's a family thing, though . . .'

'You *are* family, Jon. Mary Ann would be crushed if you were in town and didn't come to the wedding. How long are you here for?'

'A week or ten days.'

'Great. Which hotel?'

The doctor pointed out the window to the bay. 'You can see it from here, actually.'

'You're on the water?' asked Michael.

'*In* it,' said Jon. 'I'm a ship's doctor now.'

'You mean like . . . in the Navy?'

'God, no. A cruise ship . . . Norwegian.'

Michael's mouth fell open. 'Which one?'

'The *Sagafjord*.'

'I don't believe this!' Michael spun around and peered down at the great white ship. 'That it? It's back? This is really unbelievable!'

'It's a job,' said Jon, obviously unsettled by Michael's reaction.

'Does Mrs Madrigal know this?'

'Should she?' asked Jon.'

'Yeah,' said Michael. 'I think she should.'

Shipmates

Michael left Jon in his apartment and hurried downstairs to Mrs Madrigal's under the pretext of bumming a joint.

'Look,' he said. 'How much did you tell him, anyway?'

'About what?'

'For starters, that media geisha we've got locked in the basement.'

'We didn't discuss any of that,' said the landlady.

'Does he know where Mary Ann is? Does he know about DeDe and the twins? He was on the *Sagafjord*, Mrs Madrigal! He's the ship's doctor!'

'*What?*'

'I can't believe it either. Jesus . . . what are we gonna do?'

Mrs Madrigal studied him for a moment. 'That's up to you, dear.'

'*Me?*'

'Well . . . if he's no longer a member of the family, I don't think it's fair to implicate him in our shenanigans. I think you should ask him to leave as soon as possible.'

Silence.

'Unless, of course, you want him to stay.'

Michael glowered at her. 'He says you invited him to the wedding.'

'I did. I think Mary Ann and Brian would like that. Where is Brian, anyway? Has Jon talked to him?'

'He's working,' said Michael.

'I could put Jon in Burke's old room,' offered Mrs Madrigal. 'If you don't mind, that is?'

'What makes you think he'd *want* to stay in a house with a kidnapped anchorwoman in the basement?'

'We could ask and find out.'

Michael sighed resignedly. 'Do what you want, O.K.?'

'Well,' said the landlady, 'I think we owe him an explanation. He brought those children into the world, remember?'

The explanation was a monumental task. When Michael had finished, Jon's confusion was obvious.

'Now, wait a minute! This makes no sense at all.'

'Tell *me*,' said Michael.

'You mean . . . those four-year-olds were DeDe's *children*?'

Michael and the landlady nodded in unison.

'But . . . I thought they were Mrs Halcyon's foster grandchildren . . . Vietnamese orphans.'

'That's what DeDe told her to say,' said Michael. 'They were trying to avoid publicity until Mary Ann could release the story properly.'

'But they weren't *kidnapped*,' said Jon.

Mrs Madrigal blinked at him. 'What on earth are you talking about, Jon?'

'They weren't kidnapped,' the doctor repeated. 'I watched a movie with them yesterday.'

'Where?' asked Michael.

'On the ship. And Sean Starr was with them. They were getting along famously, too.'

Mrs Madrigal leaned closer to the doctor. 'Jon, dear . . . are you sure we're talking about the same children?'

'We must be. I didn't even see them on the trip up . . . I suppose Mrs Halcyon didn't want me to . . . but I saw them several times on the trip back. There can't be that many Oriental four-year-olds on a cruise ship. Besides, Sean *told* me they were Mrs Halcyon's foster grandchildren.'

'Jesus,' murmured Michael.

'What do you mean?'

'Well . . . didn't you think it was strange that Mrs Halcyon wasn't there?'

'A little,' said Jon, 'but Sean said that she and Prue Giroux had decided to spend more time in Sitka. He also said he was an old friend of the family, so I figured . . . well, I figured he *was*. He was a nice guy.'

'Did he say where he was taking the children?' asked Michael.

Jon shook his head. 'I assumed he was delivering them to Halcyon Hill.'

Michael shook his head, groaning softly. Mrs Madrigal looked deathly ill. 'Are you thinking what I'm thinking?' asked Michael.

The landlady nodded. 'Bambi.'

'Who's Bambi?' asked Jon.

Michael regarded him for a moment, then turned to Mrs Madrigal. 'Your turn,' he said.

Family Man

Prue was so horrified by the sight of the rabbit skins that she didn't look up until Vuitton's yelping disturbed her.

'Hush, Vuitton. We're going soon . . . I promise.'

'I hope you don't,' said a voice just outside the door.

The columnist's heart caught in her throat. She spun around to see Luke crouched in the doorway, stroking the wolfhound's muzzle. He looked up and gave her the sunniest smile. 'Welcome home, my love.'

'Luke, I . . .'

'Don't say a word, O.K.? I don't care where you've been, I'm just glad you're back.'

Disbelieving silence.

'I knew you'd be back,' Luke continued, rising to his feet. 'I knew you'd come here to find me, if I waited long enough.' He extended his arms in a posture of crucifixion. 'Doesn't Dad get a hug?'

Some nameless instinct told her to do it.

'You're shivering,' he said, holding her in his arms. 'That fog's pretty bad, huh?'

She nodded against his chest.

'How did you do it?' he asked.

'What?'

'Miss the ship.'

She pulled away from him. 'Luke . . . what on earth are you talking about? This is . . . crazy. I've practically had a nervous breakdown this week. I can't take this anymore, Luke . . . I can't. Where are those children?'

'They're here,' he smiled. 'They're fine.'

'*Where?*'

'Huh-uh. You answer my question first.'

'Luke . . . uh, what question?'

He traced her eyebrow with his beefy forefinger. 'I waited for you,' he said quietly. 'Two hours, at least. I was mighty worried, Prue.'

'When? Where?'

'Back in Sitka. After we had our . . . little tiff at the café, I took the children back to the ship and waited for you in my room.' His finger slid down the side of her face, stopping at her chin. 'But no Prue. The ship sailed without you.'

'You mean . . . *you were on it?*'

'You deserted me, Prue. No one's ever done that before. I hope you realize that.'

'*I* deserted *you*? Listen to me, Luke . . . you dragged those children off under your arm! I saw you do it!'

Luke shrugged. 'I was angry. I didn't want them to be around you . . . no, not you, your principles . . . all the bourgeois babble. Your world doesn't *work*, Prue. I realized that in Sitka. There's a reason I live the way I do. Surely you can see that now.'

She jerked away from him and snatched up one of the rabbit skins. 'I see *this*, Luke! I saw what you did to those poor little things!'

He took the skin from her and stroked its fur gently. 'Didn't your brother ever skin rabbits back in Grass Valley?'

'Don't be ridiculous!'

'Well, didn't he?'

Prue looked away. 'Why on earth would you . . . ? Those rabbits weren't yours, Luke. You had no right to . . . This is insane! What am I even discussing this for?'

His hand moved down the long curve of her neck and came to rest on her shoulder blade. 'You still haven't told me why you didn't come back to the ship.'

'But I *did*. I spent half-an-hour searching for you in Sitka, and then I came back to tell Frannie Halcyon that . . . you and the children were missing.'

'You didn't check my room?'

'Twice. It was locked both times.'

'I must've been off with the children. I was still a little angry, hardly in a mood to seek you out. It simply never occurred to me that you might not be on board when the ship sailed. When I realized you weren't on board, I couldn't even ask for help, Prue . . . or report you missing. I was traveling with a phony ID. Anyway, why didn't *you* put out a missing persons notice?'

'We were going to,' blurted Prue, 'but Frannie called DeDe when we realized that the ship was about to sail . . . and DeDe said to get off the ship immediately and not to say a . . .'

'Wait a minute. She called who?'

'DeDe. Her daughter.'

'I thought you said she died in Guyana.'

'No . . . lost. I said she was lost. She's home now. Oh, Luke . . . we really thought you were ashore. I never dreamed you'd come back to the ship after . . .' She cut herself off.

'After what?'

'It doesn't matter. Really.'

He leaned down and kissed her softly on the mouth. 'What matters, my precious one . . . is that we're together again.'

'Luke, I don't . . .'

'We're together in body *and* spirit. A unity.'

Silence.

'This time it'll work, Prue. I know it. Everything is so much easier when you have a family.'

Four on the Phone

'Mother?'

'DeDe! Thank God! Where are you?'

'Nome. Listen, Mother . . .'

'Did you find them?'

'No. Not yet. I'm coming home, Mother. I just wanted you to know . . .'

'This is awful! Oh God, this is *awful*, DeDe. I thought you said you could . . .'

'I *tried*, Mother. I was sure we could . . .'

'You're insane! I'm calling the police right now. We can't go on handling this thing on our own. I don't *care* about the publicity anymore, I don't . . .'

'It isn't the publicity, Mother. It's Mr Starr. We can't afford to have him hear about this from the media.'

'So you just let him ride off with your children? I've never heard such madness! You've lost all sense of judgment, DeDe. Anyone who distrusts the police so much that . . .'

'I don't distrust the police. I just know your Mr Starr.'

'You've never met him!'

Silence.

'DeDe?'

'I think I *have* met him, Mother.'

'What on earth are you talking about? DeDe . . . please, darling . . . you're scaring me to death!'

'I'm sorry, Mother. I've tried to protect you, but I need your help now. I want you to be brave. Can you do that for me?'

'Of course I can. What are you talking about?'

'Is Emma there?'

'Of course. She's always here.'

'You've got company, then. Are any of these Quaaludes left?'

'DeDe . . .'

'I want you to take one after we hang up.'

'DeDe, I'm calling the police after we hang up. You're not responsible for your actions anymore. That's become perfectly clear, and I *won't* be . . .'

'*Sit down, Mother!*'

'I *am* sitting down.'

'Good. Now listen to me . . . Mother, please don't cry.'

'I can't help it.'

'I'll be back tomorrow morning, Mother. We'll talk about the police then.'

Silence.

'In the meantime, I want you to know about Mr Starr, so we can discuss this rationally when I get home tomorrow. You've won, Mother. I'll do whatever you want. Only hear me out. There isn't time to waste.'

'Mouse, it's Mary Ann.'

'Thank God! Where are you?'

'Nome. We didn't find them. The whole damn thing has been a wild goose chase.'

'They're *here*, Babycakes! Somewhere.'

'What!'

'Jon saw them come back on the ship. Jon Fielding. He's the doctor on the *Sagafjord*!'

'You're making this up!'

'I wish I were! Didn't somebody *check* to see if they were on the ship? I mean . . . this doesn't sound like a kidnapping at all. Meanwhile, we've got a fairly pissed-off lady living in the basement.'

'I know. I'll take care of that. Is Jon *sure*?'

'He's sure.'

Silence.

716

'What now, my love?'

'God!'

'That isn't an answer, I'm afraid.'

'Listen, Mouse . . . did Jon know where they were going?'

'He assumed they were being delivered to Halcyon Hill.'

'Forget that.'

'Jon said he was a friend of the family.'

'Well, he's *not*, Mouse. He's lying. The man went berserk. He kidnapped those children!'

'And then cruised leisurely back to San Francisco.'

'Mouse . . . I know it sounds crazy . . . but that's because *he's* crazy. Something's not right here.'

'You'll get no argument from me.'

'At least the kids are O.K.'

'Mmm. Bambi will be relieved to know that, too.'

'Jesus, Mouse . . . I'm really sorry.'

'Do we let her out, then?'

'Well . . . no. I mean, the kids are still missing and . . . God, I can't think straight anymore. You might as well keep her until I get back tomorrow. I'd rather do my explaining there. Please tell Mrs Madrigal not to worry . . . and tell Brian I love him. I tried to reach him, but the line was busy at Perry's.'

'I'll tell him you called. Take care, Babycakes.'

'You too. I miss you.'

'Same here,' said Michael.

'By the way, ask Jon . . .'

'He's staying for the wedding,' said Michael.'

'Fabulous.'

'In Burke's room.'

'Less than fabulous.'

'Don't *you* start,' said Michael.

When the Children Are Asleep

'You asked about the children,' said Luke, still holding Prue tight against his chest.

'Yes.'

He studied her at arm's length for a moment, then beamed like a doting father. 'Come along. It's getting dark. We should fetch them.'

He led her up the slope and into the rhododendron dell, grasping her arm as he steered her through the labyrinthine thicket.

Emerging from the dell, they followed the U-shaped ridge until the swamp below was visible through a clearing in the underbrush. There, frolicking along the water's edge, two tiny figures were visible.

'Edgar!' called Luke. 'Anna! Come along, children. Time for bed.'

The twins looked up and squealed in protest.

'No arguments!' shouted Luke. 'It's almost dark.'

So the children scampered up the steep path to the ridge. When they caught sight of Prue, they shouted her name gleefully. She knelt to them and accepted their hugs, feeling curiously maternal.

'They look fine,' she said to Luke. It was true.

'They can't stay out of the dirt,' he said, tousling Edgar's hair. 'Isn't that right, roughneck?'

Prue picked a twig out of Anna's sweater. 'They'll be so relieved,' she said.

'Who?' asked Luke.

'Frannie and DeDe.'

Silence.

'We can call a cab from that phone booth outside the de Young,' said Prue. 'We can get them home in an hour. Oh, Luke . . . this is like a great weight being lifted off . . .'

'*I don't want you talking like that in front of the children!*'

That quicksilver rage had come back into his eyes.

'I didn't . . .'

'They *are* home, Prue! I thought you, of all people, would understand that!'

'Luke . . .'

'Shut up, Prue! We'll talk about it later. After the K-I-D-S are A-S-L-E-E-P. Understand?'

Back at the shack, she watched as the twins curled up on pallets on the floor. Luke tucked them in, giving each a rabbit pelt to hold. Then he tiptoed out into the fog, taking Prue with him.

'We're going away,' he whispered.

'We can't just leave them . . .'

'No. The four of us, I mean. The family. We're complete now. We have everything we need. We'll move to South America and start a new life, Prue. God almighty! I'm so happy!'

718

'Luke . . . those children don't belong to us.'

'And who do they belong to? That old society vulture? They aren't her flesh and blood. She got them at an agency, Prue. She told you so herself.'

'I know, but . . .'

'Haven't you always wanted children?'

Silence.

'*Haven't you?*'

'Luke, that has nothing to . . .'

'It's too late to have them yourself. Well . . . now you have them! And a lover who adores you more than life itself. Don't you see how right this is? We're getting exactly what we deserve, Prue! Look into my eyes and behold your destiny!'

She looked into his eyes and beheld madness.

After a moment's hesitation, she said: 'All right.'

'All right what?'

'I'll go with you. It sounds wonderful, Luke.'

He almost crushed her with his embrace. 'Thank God . . . thank God!'

'We can leave in the morning,' she said. 'I'll need to pick up a few things . . . and some credit cards. We can charter a jet. We'll manage.'

He sniffed back the tears. 'It'll be paradise. You'll see.'

Prue inched towards the ledge. 'Wonderful. Then I'll meet you back here in the . . .'

'No. I want you to stay here with the children. I'm going out for a few hours.'

'Oh.'

'I shouldn't be long. I'll tuck you in with the children. I have a few . . . loose ends to tie up.'

'I see.' Prue's skin grew prickly with anticipation. Was this her chance to escape? Or would he simply lock the door when he left?

'Children can be so insistent,' said Luke, caressing Prue's neck in the darkness.

'How's that?'

A low chuckle. 'He wants his fire engine.'

'The little boy?'

'Uh-huh. It's in the garden at the old lady's house. He's been missing it since Sitka. I promised him I'd get it for him. I guess that's the least his Dad can do.'

Silence.

'Do you think that's foolish?'

'No. Not at all. I think it's sweet.'

'I found the address on his luggage. I hope it's the right one.'

'In Hillsborough?'

'Uh-huh. Do you think the old lady will be there?'

'I don't know.'

'What about . . . whatshername . . . DeDe?'

'It's hard to say.'

'I'll be careful, then.'

'Do you have a way?' asked Prue. 'Do you need cab fare? It's some distance.'

He touched her cheek gently. 'I can manage.'

Then he led her back into the shack, tucked her into bed, and kissed her tenderly on the eyelids.

'Soon,' he whispered.

When he left, closing the door behind him, she listened carefully for a click of the padlock.

It never came.

She felt, already, as if she had betrayed him.

Escape

Prue crouched there in the blackness, the sound of her own breathing roaring in her ears like a hurricane.

The twins were already fast asleep, snuggled in the corner with their rabbit skins.

Luke's footsteps receded into the night.

Prue counted slowly to sixty, then pressed her ear to the door of the shack.

Nothing.

She eased the door open several inches and peered out into the darkness.

She could see very little, only the fresh footprints in the sandy slope that marked Luke's exodus. Overhead, in the eucalyptus trees, the wind made a sound like tissue paper being crumpled.

She tugged the door shut again, wincing as it creaked, then knelt by the children and shook them gently. 'Anna . . . Edgar . . . wake up, darlings.'

The little girl stirred first. 'What's the matter?' she asked loudly.

'Shhh,' said Prue. 'We've got to whisper.'

Edgar sat up, rubbing his eyes. 'Where's Dad?' he asked.

'Uh . . . he's out for a while.' She found the little boy's jacket and helped him into it. 'We're going for a little ride. Won't that be fun?'

'Where?' asked Anna.

'To my house,' said Prue. 'You've never seen my house.'

Edgar began whining. 'I don't want to! I'm sleepy!'

Prue felt around in the shadows for Anna's coat, her dread mounting every moment. Short of gagging the children, there was not much she could do about the noise. 'We've got to be quiet, darling. Can you do that for Prue?'

Edgar persisted. 'Why do we have to go?'

'Well . . . it's a surprise . . . for Dad.'

'What kind of a surprise?'

'You'll see,' whispered Prue.

The whimpering continued.

'Don't you want to see your mommy?' asked Prue.

Edgar fell silent.

'Don't you?'

'Is she at your house?' asked Anna.

'She will be,' whispered Prue. 'Very soon. C'mon now . . . let's see how quiet we can be.'

She guided them up the slope into the dell, jumping at the sound of every twig that cracked underfoot. Once they entered the thicket of rhododendrons the darkness was so total that she was forced to find the way from memory.

'I'm scared,' said Anna, clutching at Prue's hand.

'It's all right, darling. It'll only be dark for a little bit.'

The child began to cry noisily.

'Anna . . . please, darling . . . everything's O.K. Edgar, tell your sister not to be scared.'

Silence.

'Edgar?'

No answer.

'*Edgar!* My God . . . Edgar, where are you?'

Anna broke into a full wail. Prue knelt and scooped her into her arms, stroking her hair. 'Shhh . . . it's O.K., darling . . . it's O.K. We've just got to find Edgar, that's all.' She rose, holding the child against her chest, and retraced her steps along the invisible path.

'Edgar!' she called, shouting in a whisper.

'Where are you?' came a tiny voice.

'Over here,' she said. Not the most useful piece of information, she realized.

'Where?' cried the child.

'Walk towards my voice, darling.'

She was relieved to hear something moving through the underbrush, until she noticed the speed with which it was approaching. A branch cracked, then slapped her brutally across the face. She and little Anna shrieked together as an unseen form lunged through the bushes, knocked her to the ground and thrust a huge wet tongue in her ear.

'Vuitton!'

The wolfhound barked excitedly, grateful to be reunited with his mistress. In her consternation over Luke, Prue had completely forgotten about him.

'It's just my puppy,' she told Anna. 'Are you all right, darling?'

'I wanna go back,' sobbed the child.

'It's gonna be all right . . . I promise. Edgar . . . is that you?'

A tiny hand was clutching at her leg.

'Is that your dog?' asked Edgar.

'Yes, darling. He's a nice dog.' She staggered to her feet, holding the children's hands. 'We're gonna be just fine now.'

Where was the nearest telephone, anyway?'

The de Young Museum?

If Luke was on his way to Halcyon Hill, somebody should warn Frannie Halcyon.

Crazy Talk

It was almost nine P.M. when Emma took stock of her mistress and realized that something was wrong.

'Miss Frannie?'

The matriarch looked up with heavy-lidded eyes – a symptom that Emma had long ago learned to recognize. 'Yes . . . Emma, dear?'

722

'I brought you some hot milk,' scowled the maid. 'I thought you might need some help gettin' to sleep.'

'Oh . . . no, thank you, Emma.'

The maid set the tray down on the dresser and moved closer to the bed. 'You been takin' them pills again?'

Silence.

Emma's lower lip plumped angrily. 'You answer me that, Miss Frannie!'

The matriarch looked away. 'Miss DeDe told me to!'

'Where is it?'

'Where's what?'

'The bottle. How many you take?'

'Only three . . . like aspirin.'

'That ain't aspirin, Miss Frannie! You gimme that bottle, hear?'

The matriarch made a fluttery gesture towards the bedside table. 'That was the last of 'em. I'm all right . . . really. Don't you worry, dear.' Her pathetic little smile was belied by the tear that rolled down her face.

Emma blinked at her for several seconds, then sat down on the edge of the bed and took her mistress' hand. 'What's the matter?' she asked sweetly.

'Emma . . . I can't . . .'

'Yes you can. You can talk to Emma 'bout it. If you don't know that, you don't know nothin'.'

The matriarch's lips parted in a silent sob. Then she pressed her palms to her face and rocked slowly back and forth, never making a sound. It was only when the maid leaned forward and hugged her that a low animal moan escaped from somewhere deep inside Frannie Halcyon.

'You go right ahead,' said Emma. 'You just go right ahead and cry.'

So Frannie wept for several minutes, cradled in the old woman's arms.

Then she said: 'DeDe thinks Jim Jones has got them.'

Emma pulled away and stared at her mistress. 'What you talkin' 'bout?'

'Jim Jones,' repeated Frannie. 'From Guyana.'

'That's crazy talk, Miss Frannie! Jim Jones is dead!'

Frannie shook her head lethargically. 'Miss DeDe . . . she thinks . . . she says he didn't die . . . she says . . .'

'You hush now. You get some sleep.'

'No . . . you should know this, Emma. Somebody else died in Guyana. Mr Starr . . . *he's* Jim Jones. He . . .'

'Shhh.'

'Those poor little babies! I gave them away to Jim Jones, Emma. I just gave them . . .'

'Now you listen to me, Miss Frannie! You *saw* Mr Starr, didn't you? He didn't look like no Jim Jones, did he? Any fool could recognize Jim Jones in a minute! Jim Jones is *dead*, Miss Frannie!'

'No . . . he had plastic . . .'

'Hush, now.'

'. . . plastic surgery . . . he had . . . Emma . . .'

And then the matriarch passed out.

Twenty minutes later, the phone rang.

Emma picked it up in the kitchen. 'Halcyon Hill.'

'Oh . . . is this Edna?'

'Emma.'

'This is Ms Giroux, Emma. It's urgent that I speak to Mrs Halcyon.'

'I'm sorry, Miz Giroux. She's asleep.'

'*Emma, I must speak . . .*'

'I'll give her the message, Miz Giroux. She's dead to the world.'

'Emma . . . please . . . you must wake her up . . . *immediately*! Tell her that the children are at my place and they're safe . . .'

'Praise the Lord!' exclaimed Emma.

'But she's got to leave the house immediately. Mr Starr is heading that way.'

'*Here?*'

'Any minute, Edna! He's crazy . . . he's lost his mind completely. I'm so afraid he'll . . . just get out of there, please. Does Mrs Halcyon have her car there?'

'Yes'm, but I don't think . . .'

'Tell her not to get dressed or anything. Just *leave . . . get out of that house!* Do you understand me, Edna?'

'Yes'm.'

She understood only too well.

The Way They Were

When Jon and Michael returned to Michael's apartment shortly after ten o'clock, Michael was considerably more relaxed.

'Frankly,' he said, dropping onto the sofa, 'I was surprised you took it so well.'

'What?' asked Jon, choosing the armchair.

'You know . . . Bambi-in-the-basement.'

The doctor shrugged. 'I lived here, remember?'

Michael smiled. 'Nothing's changed, huh?'

'Not much. I was prepared for almost anything.'

'That's sound thinking.'

A long silence.

'So,' said Jon, 'the nursery's working out O.K.?'

'Great . . . terrific, in fact.'

'It's been . . . how long?'

Michael thought for a moment. 'Over three years . . . three years at the same place. God . . . is it time to call the Guinness Book?'

The doctor smiled. 'I'm glad you like it. That's important.'

Michael nodded. 'It's the only way. Doing *anything* over and over again is boring enough as it is.'

The doctor regarded him for a moment. 'Or *anyone*, huh?'

'Hey . . .'

'Sorry. That was low.'

'I'll say.' Michael was stinging worse than he might have expected.

'Is Ned still running the nursery?' asked Jon, obviously attempting a retreat to the impersonal.

Michael nodded. 'He's been talking about making me a full partner.'

'Good. That's good to hear. You should be putting some money away.'

'I know,' said Michael. 'Don't nag.'

Jon smiled beseechingly. 'Did it sound like that?'

Michael shook his head, smiling back. 'It's just . . . you know . . . a tender spot.'

'It always was,' said Jon.

Michael drummed his fingers on the arm of the sofa. 'Well . . . that's not something you have to worry about anymore, is it?'

Jon said nothing for a moment, then shook his head slowly in amazement. 'It's still so damned convincing, you know.'

'What?'

'You and that brave-waif-in-the-storm routine. Little Michael against the world. You've even got Mrs Madrigal buffaloed. She thinks *I'm* the one who left you.'

Michael stiffened. 'I never told her that.'

'You didn't have to,' said the doctor. 'You just ducked your eyes and looked pitiful, as usual. Someday he'll come along tra la. I've got news for you Michael: he *did* come along and you tossed him out on his butt, because you didn't have the balls to get past your fantasy.'

'*What* fantasy?' Michael was almost speechless.

'You tell me. Young Dr Kildare, maybe? I don't know . . . whatever it was, I couldn't live up to it anymore . . . and you couldn't stand the thought of being loved by just another guy like yourself. You're tough, Michael – despite all that sad young man bullshit – but you're not tough enough to handle that one!'

Michael stared at him, stupefied. 'You're so wrong it's not even . . .'

'Am I? How's the cop working out, by the way?'

Michael's mouth fell open. 'What *didn't* Mrs Madrigal tell you?'

'She told me about the cop,' said Jon. 'And the movie star. And the construction worker. You're not having a life, Michael – you're fucking the Village People, one at a time.'

'Now wait a minute!'

'It's the truth,' said Jon.

'What business is it of . . . ?'

'It *isn't* my business. You're right about that. It hasn't been my business for a long time . . . and I shouldn't have said anything. Except that Mrs M. asked me to . . . and I wanted to . . . and I'm tired of hearing this crap about how nobody wants you. Somebody wants you, Michael . . . as if you didn't know it. And he knows the very worst there is to know about you.'

'Jon . . . I'm sorry if . . .'

The doctor rose. 'There isn't anything to apologize for.'

Michael sat in silence as he headed for the door.

'I'll stay through the wedding,' said Jon. 'There won't be any scenes, I promise you.'

'Do you . . . ? Is Burke's room O.K.? Do you need clean sheets or anything?'

726

'Thanks, Mrs M. took care of that.'

'I love you,' said Michael.

'I know,' said the doctor. 'Isn't that the hell of it?'

Dead to the World

Hardly believing her ears, Emma set the receiver down, then hurried back upstairs to her mistress' bedroom. Frannie Halcyon was out cold and snoring, one arm dangling inelegantly off the edge of the four-poster.

'Miss Frannie,' whispered the maid, bending over the matriarch. 'Wake up, Miss Frannie!'

No response.

'Law', Miss Frannie, *you wake up now!*' Emma grasped her mistress by the shoulders and shook gently. 'He's comin', Miss Frannie . . . Jim Jones is comin'!'

Still no response.

'Sweet Jesus!' murmured Emma. Those unholy pills, she realized, had done their job but good.

She fetched a glass of water from the bathroom and tossed half of it onto the matriarch's face. Frannie Halcyon's features contorted momentarily. Then she uttered a half-hearted groan and rolled over on to her stomach.

'Please . . . oh Lord, *please*, Miss Frannie . . . you gotta wake up! Jim Jones is comin'!'

Ripping off the bedclothes, Emma rolled the matriarch over again and pulled her feet off the bed. Then she hoisted her into a sitting position.

The matriarch's head hung slack. She mumbled something unintelligible into her own cleavage.

'Do you hear me?' asked Emma.

'Grdlarmarelup.'

'You just sit there,' panted Emma. 'I'll get you out of here.'

She dashed to the closet and conducted a frantic search for her mistress' floor-length black mink. Finding it, she rushed back to the bed and began pulling it onto the matriarch's arms.

'C'mon now . . . c'mon, Miss Frannie . . . we gotta walk. Can you do that for Emma now? C'mon . . .' Facing her mistress, she slid her hands under the mink-sheathed arms and lifted with all her might.

'Herpledarnover.'

'Help me, Miss Frannie . . . you can do it. Stand on them feet for me . . .'

For a moment, the matriarch seemed to be doing just that.

'Good,' said Emma. 'That's real good. Now just start walkin'. It's O.K. Emma's got you.'

Seconds later, Frannie toppled like a felled bear, pinning Emma painfully against the Chinese carpet. The maid somehow managed to dislodge herself, gasping for breath.

'Miss Frannie,' she wept. 'God help us both.' She stared at her mistress in despair before taking a pillow from the bed and sliding it under Frannie Halcyon's head. The matriarch snorted noisily, rolled over and fell asleep.

Emma went directly to the bathroom and removed the bottle of rum that her mistress kept hidden in the toilet tank. She took two burning swigs, then returned it to its hiding place.

She had never done that before, but she knew what would soon be required of her.

The matriarch kept her pistol in the bottom drawer of the bedside table. It was a recent acquisition, Emma knew – purchased only days after Mrs Reagan announced her own reliance on a 'tiny little gun.'

The maid lifted it gingerly by the butt and crept out of the room, closing the door behind her.

Then she moved from room to room downstairs, turning off the lights as she went.

She checked the lock on the front door.

Then the one in the kitchen.

Then the one on the sunporch.

As she crossed the sunporch, heading for the living room, she heard a noise in the garden.

She ducked behind a big wicker chair, peering over the edge long enough to see a man push his way through the shrubbery and cross the lawn.

He stood in the middle of the lawn, assessing the house, looking from left to right.

Emma made a dash for the kitchen, then let herself out into the garage. The garage door was still open, so she slipped into the darkness, ran across the front lawn, and crept through the arbor in the side yard until the intruder was once again in view.

This time she was behind him.

The man moved closer to the house.

Then he tried to open the door to the sunporch.

'*You!*' shouted Emma. '*Jim Jones!*'

The intruder spun on his heels, locking eyes with the rail-thin old woman who stood on the lawn with a pistol in her hand. He raised his arms in a gesture of supplication and uttered his last word in a surprisingly placid tone of voice.

'Sister,' he said.

Then Emma shot him between the eyes.

Not Gay

Only minutes after Jon left Michael's apartment, Brian showed up on the doorstep.

'How's the media widow?' asked Michael.

'Rotten,' replied Brian. 'You feel like a walk?'

'Sure,' said Michael, 'but only if misery loves company.'

'Oh, no . . . what is it this time?'

Michael rolled his eyes. 'What is it every time?'

'Uh . . . Jon?'

'You win the cigar.'

'I saw him upstairs,' said Brian. 'Is he back for good?'

Michael shook his head. 'Just the wedding . . . as far as I know.'

'Do you want him to stay?'

Michael sighed wearily. 'You aren't, by any chance, a spy for Mrs Madrigal?'

'I just thought things might get complicated.'

'More complicated?'

'I mean . . . with Bambi and all.'

'Oh God,' said Michael, suddenly remembering. 'Things have already gotten more complicated. You haven't heard the latest!'

As they walked to the Marina Green, Michael told Brian about Jon's sighting of the 'kidnapped' twins.

'Does Mary Ann know this?' asked Brian.

Michael nodded. 'She called while you were at work. She's coming home in the morning, by the way.'

'Thank God. What the hell are we gonna do about Bambi?'

'You got me. Jon says she's already had a knock-down-drag-out fight with Mrs Madrigal.'

'When?'

'Tonight.'

'Christ.' Brian shook his head. 'That place is a madhouse.'

Michael smiled. 'Jon said the same thing.'

A period of silence followed. Then Brian said: 'Is he here to get you back?'

'Yeah,' said Michael. 'I guess he is.'

'Is that what you want?'

Michael turned and looked at his friend. 'Can I pass on that one right now?'

Brian laid his arm on Michael's shoulder. 'You bet, I wouldn't rule it out, though . . . just because he needs you a little bit more than you need him.'

Silence.

'That's it, isn't it? It's that way with me and Mary Ann . . . and *she* didn't rule it out, thank God.'

'Brian . . . she loves you very much.'

Brian gave his shoulder a brotherly shake. 'Needing and loving are two different things.'

Another period of silence ensued as they skirted the dark rectangle of the newly-named Moscone Playground. A large car passed them, screeched to a halt, and backed up until it was even with them.

A man in the passenger seat rapped his hand noisily against the side of the car. 'Hey faggots! You a couple of cocksuckers?'

Brian kept his arm on Michael's shoulder. 'What's it to you, fella?'

'Hey,' Michael whispered, 'you're supposed to say "yes, thank you" and smile.'

The man leaned out the window as the car kept pace with them. '*What did you say to me, cocksucker?*'

'Just keep walking,' muttered Michael.

'Huh, faggot . . . *huh?* Would you like to suck my cock, cocksucker? Is that what you want?'

Michael noted that this witticism provoked raucous laughter from the back seat. There were at least four people in the car; one of them was a woman.

'Hey,' said Michael. 'I think it's time to run for it.'

'Fuck that,' said Brian.

'*What did you say, faggot?*'

Brain wheeled around and raised his middle finger to the heckler. 'I said fuck you, buddy. Piss off!'

The car lurched to a stop. People spilled out of it like circus clowns from a fire engine. The first one went straight for Michael, kicking him squarely in the groin. He toppled backwards, his head striking the sidewalk with an audible thud.

He opened his eyes to see someone's hands moving in on his throat. The man raised him from the sidewalk almost gently . . . then slammed his head back down against the pavement. The noise this time was muffled, liquid.

'Hey,' someone shouted, 'over here!'

The man released Michael's throat and ran to join the other two. One of them was straddling Brian's chest; the other was holding his ankles. 'O.K.,' said the man who had jumped Michael, 'you ready to die, faggot?'

When Michael saw the sudden flash of steel, he screamed in disbelief. 'Please . . . please don't . . . he's not gay! *He's not gay!*'

But the knife came down again and again.

Home Again

When Mary Ann spotted her Le Car in the long-term parking lot at San Francisco International, she felt an unexplainable surge of optimism.

'You know,' she said, taking DeDe's arm, 'somehow I think the worst part is over.'

DeDe's expression was hollow, devoid of hope. 'Please don't try to make things better,' she said. 'You've done enough already. Really.'

'I'm not trying to make things better. I really feel that way. If he came back with them on the ship . . . in full view of everybody . . . then, he must not have intended to kidnap them. Not in the usual sense, anyway. I mean . . . he may be crazy, but it doesn't sound like he's dangerous.'

'Sure,' said DeDe. 'That's what they said back in '78.'

Mary Ann proceeded cautiously. 'But . . . we don't really know for sure if this Starr guy was really . . .'

'Stop saying that. *I* know. I know he is. He acted out that nursery rhyme, didn't he? And Prue's description seems perfectly compatible with . . .' She stopped in mid-sentence.

'With what?' asked Mary Ann.

'With . . . the way he looked.'

'What did she tell you, anyway?'

'Who?'

'Prue. When you talked to her alone.'

DeDe looked away. 'This isn't the time for that.'

Mary Ann unlocked the door of the car, climbed in and unlocked DeDe's door.

DeDe got in, saying nothing.

'When *will* it be?' asked Mary Ann.

Hesitating, DeDe looked directly at her friend, 'Later . . . all right?'

'All right,' said Mary Ann.

It was simple fatigue that prompted the long silence on the drive to Hillsborough. They needed time for healing. Mary Ann realized – time to be free from the crisis at hand . . . and each other. When they pulled into the circular drive at Halcyon Hill, Mary Ann approached the subject directly.

'I think we need a break,' she said, 'and some sleep. Why don't you let your mother pamper you for a while? I'll call in the morning and we'll talk.'

DeDe leaned over and hugged her. 'You've been great. I can't imagine anyone doing what you've done.'

'That's O.K.,' said Mary Ann.

'I hope they aren't mad at you.'

'Who?'

'The station. For missing your show.'

'Oh.' She hadn't told DeDe about Bambi Kanetaka, and this was no time to start. 'I think I can patch things up.'

'I hope so.' DeDe climbed out of the car and closed the door. 'Sleep tight. I'll talk to you tomorrow.'

'DeDe?'

'Yeah?'

'I think it's time to call the police.'

DeDe remained surprisingly calm. 'Yeah. So do I.'

732

'Thank God.'

'Well . . . it's come to that, I guess. We'll map it out tomorrow.'

Mary Ann peered up at the house. 'You're sure your mother is here?'

'Her car's here,' said DeDe.

'Shall I wait for you to see?'

'No. I'm fine. Go home, Mary Ann. Climb in bed with Brian.'

Mary Ann checked her watch. 7:57 A.M. 'It might not be too late,' she smiled.

DeDe winked at her. 'It's never too late for that.'

Pulling away from the house, Mary Ann watched DeDe in the rear-view mirror until she saw Emma appear at the front door. With that question resolved, she settled herself behind the wheel and began composing her explanation to Bambi.

This was the anchorwoman's third day of captivity, she realized.

Unless, of course, Mrs Madrigal had been unable – or unwilling – to hold her that long.

She hadn't checked the newspapers at the airport. It was entirely possible that Bambi had *already* released the story. And what if Bambi had brought criminal action against Mrs Madrigal and the others . . . ?'

She had almost reached the gates to Halcyon Hill when she heard the commotion behind her. She looked in the mirror again to see DeDe running down the driveway, screaming at the top of her lungs.

'STOP! COME BACK, MARY ANN! COME BACK! . . .'

Corpus Delicti

The maid sat in a straight-back chair, her hands folded regally in her lap, while DeDe and Mary Ann encircled her frantically.

'Where is he?' asked DeDe.

'Out back,' answered Emma. 'I drug him behind the garage.' Seeing Mary Ann frown, she added: 'He creeped right up in the dark, Miss DeDe. Miz Giroux . . . she called and said he was on the way, and your mama, she already tol' me he was Jim Jones . . . and I couldn't wake her up for nothin'.'

'The children weren't . . . ?'

'Miz Giroux has 'em.'

'They're . . . ?'

'He didn't harm a hair, Miss DeDe!'

DeDe closed her eyes and swallowed. She reached out and took Mary Ann's hand, sharing the moment with her. Emma looked at both of them with tears in her eyes. 'The Lord looks out for us,' she said.

DeDe rushed forward and knelt next to the old woman, embracing her vigorously. 'It wasn't the Lord, Emma; it was *you*. God bless you, Emma. God bless my wonderful Emma!'

The maid pressed her hand against DeDe's cheek. 'He was messin' with my family,' she said.

DeDe laughed and hugged her again. 'Is Mother all right?'

Emma shrugged. 'She ain't woke up yet.'

'You mean . . . she doesn't know?'

'Not a blessed thing,' said Emma. 'She took three more o' them pills last night.'

'Jesus,' muttered DeDe. 'I told her to take one.'

'I tried to wake her,' said Emma. 'When Miz Giroux called, I . . .'

'Does *she* know?'

Emma shook her head. 'She never called back.'

'And did you call the police?'

'No'm. I knew you was comin' back. I reckoned you'd want to call 'em yourself . . . after you knew the babies was safe.'

'Exactly right.' DeDe turned to Mary Ann. 'I'm going out to the garage. Why don't you stay here and keep Emma company?'

Mary Ann was relieved, but she felt a nominal protest was in order. 'You don't want me to go with you?'

'Actually,' replied DeDe, 'I'd rather you didn't.'

She was gone for ten minutes. When she returned, her face was virtually expressionless. 'Can I talk to you?' she asked quietly.

They conferred in the library, leaving Emma in the living room.

'I have to know something,' said DeDe.

Mary Ann felt horribly uneasy. 'Yeah?'

'What do you plan to do with this?'

'You mean . . . the story?'

DeDe nodded.

'Well . . . I hadn't really . . . DeDe, is it *him*?'

'Put that aside for a minute. We've got some fast decisions to make. She shot him in cold blood, Mary Ann – he wasn't even in the house, and he was unarmed. There's bound to be a murder trial, and that old woman is gonna go through hell all over again . . .'

'But surely . . . if he's who you think he is . . .'

'Then Emma and Mother and the children . . . all of us . . . will be subjected to the most hideous kind of public scrutiny. I've had it, Mary Ann. I'm tired of torturing my family. This is as close as I've ever gotten to a happy ending. I'll do anything I can to hang onto it.'

'DeDe . . . what are you saying? What do you want?'

'I want you to tell only part of the story. You can say all you want about my escape . . . and the Cuban stuff. I just don't want you to mention anything after that. You offered to do that once. I need to know if the offer still holds.'

'DeDe . . . you know I would, but . . .'

'But what?'

'Well . . . there are other people who know about it.'

'Just Mother, really. And she slept through the bad stuff.'

'And Prue,' added Mary Ann.

'Are you kidding? She was sleeping with him, Mary Ann! She'd like nothing better than to forget it ever happened. She didn't even call back after she warned Emma. Forget about that bitch.'

'DeDe . . . we can't just forget a body in the backyard. We can't just pretend it never happened.'

DeDe looked at her long and hard. 'Why not?' she asked.

'You mean . . . ?'

DeDe nodded. 'If we hurry, we can do it before Mother wakes up.'

A Tangled Web

Mary Ann noticed, with some dismay, that there were still traces of mud on her shoes when she and DeDe arrived at Prue Giroux's townhouse on Nob Hill.

'God,' she said, frowning down at them. 'I thought I'd cleaned all that off.'

DeDe rang Prue's doorbell. 'She won't notice. What's a little mud, anyway? It could happen to anybody. How's your back, by the way?'

'Better,' said Mary Ann.

'Good.'

'I'm not used to that kind of exercise.'

DeDe's smile was sardonic. 'I'm glad to hear that.'

At this point, Mary Ann could only smile back. 'What did you tell her?' she asked.

'Who?'

'Prue.'

DeDe shrugged. 'Just that we were coming over to pick up the kids.' Then, hearing the door open, she squeezed Mary Ann's arm and whispered: 'Don't worry. Let me do the talking.'

There was little talking, however, when DeDe caught sight of her children. She fell to her knees and scooped them into her arms, weeping copiously.

Mary Ann and Prue watched in silence, also crying.

Only the children were free from tears, accepting the reunion as a matter of joyful inevitability. Released from their mother's embrace, they gamboled about her ecstatically, attempting to recount their adventures in DeDe's absence.

'Now, now,' said Prue. 'Your mommy's tired right now, so why don't you . . . ?'

'It's all right,' beamed DeDe. 'Let them yammer all they want.' She reached out for Edgar again and hugged him. 'It's sheer music.' Looking up at Prue, she asked: 'How . . . how did it happen?'

Prue flushed noticeably. 'He . . . well, it's silly, but he came back on the ship.'

'We know,' said DeDe, standing up again.

Prue was obviously thrown. '*How?*' she asked.

'A friend of Mary Ann's saw him.'

'Oh . . . then you . . . ?'

'How did he get *here?*' asked DeDe. 'That's what I meant.'

'Oh . . . well, he just brought them by the house.'

DeDe frowned. '*When?*'

'Uh . . . last night. I called your mother's house immediately. That's when Emma took the message.'

DeDe's brow furrowed. 'But the ship got in yesterday.'

'It did?'

'Yes,' said DeDe darkly. 'It did.'

Silence.

DeDe studied the columnist's face. 'He didn't suggest to you where he might have been for a day?'

'No,' replied Prue. 'Nothing.'

'Why did you tell Emma he had lost his mind?'

Prue looked away. 'I don't think I phrased it exactly that way. He was *upset*, of course . . . mostly because he'd been stuck with the kids for the rest of the trip. He waited for us back on the ship that day. When we didn't show up, he was angry. And worried.'

'But it didn't occur to him to tell anybody? The ship's officials, for instance?'

Silence.

'Prue . . . why did you tell Emma that Mr Starr had lost his mind?'

'I told you . . . I . . .'

'You told them to leave the house immediately!'

'Well . . . he was extremely upset. I'm sorry if I gave her the impression that . . .'

'Why didn't he bring the children directly to Halcyon Hill?'

'Uh . . . well, he didn't know the address. He knew *mine*, so he brought them here . . .'

'And then *you* called Halcyon Hill and told Emma to get my mother out of the house immediately. What sense does that make, Prue?'

'Well . . . he was furious at your mother, and I didn't want her to be subjected to . . .'

DeDe rolled her eyes impatiently. 'If he was coming to Halcyon Hill anyway, why didn't he bring the children with him?'

Prue's eyes welled with tears again. 'DeDe . . . please . . . I don't know . . . He wasn't making any sense. I thought you'd be grateful to have your children back.'

DeDe employed a more lenient tone. 'I'm just trying to get at the truth. You can understand that.'

Prue nodded, wiping her eyes. 'He was acting funny. That's all I can say. It was just an instinct I had. If your mother had stayed at Halcyon Hill, she would have *seen* that!'

DeDe heaved a long sigh. 'She did stay, Prue.'

'What?'

'She was sound asleep,' said DeDe.

'Then, maybe Emma . . .'

'That's right,' said DeDe. 'He never showed up.'

Buffaloes in London

After leaving Prue's apartment, DeDe and Mary Ann took the twins to breakfast at Mama's in Gramercy Towers. A hot meal and the sound of laughing children did wonders for Mary Ann's faltering spirits.

The ordeal, she realized, was finally over.

'It's a great story,' she remarked, 'even without . . . him.'

DeDe wiped a blob of jelly off Edgar's chin. 'I'll do all I can to help. Give us a few days, O.K.?'

'Sure.'

'Do you still want to do it on your movie show?' asked DeDe.

'I'm not sure about that,' said Mary Ann. 'Do you mind including the children, by the way?'

DeDe hesitated, then smiled. 'Of course not. Not after what you've done.' She turned to the twins. 'Hey, you guys . . . wanna be on TV with Mary Ann?'

The children cheered.

'There's your answer,' smiled DeDe.

'Great,' said Mary Ann.

Edgar tugged on his mother's arm. 'Can Dad be on TV, too?'

After a pregnant pause, DeDe said: 'Dad?'

'*Can* he?' asked Anna, lending support to her brother.

DeDe looked from one child to the other, then said quietly. 'Do you mean Mr Starr?'

Both heads nodded, eyes wider than ever. Mary Ann turned and waited with them for DeDe's answer.

'Darling,' said DeDe, 'Mr Starr has gone back to London. We won't be seeing him for a while.'

'*Why?*' asked Anna.

Well . . . because that's where he lives. He was just on vacation when you met him on the ship. His house is in London.'

'His house is *neat*,' said Anna.

DeDe stared at the little girl. '*What*, darling?'

'He has chipmunkies,' said Anna.

Edgar corrected her. '*Chipmunks*.'

738

Anna stuck her tongue out at her brother. 'And buffaloes,' she added defiantly.

'And a great big windmill,' said Edgar, upping her one.

'It's in Japan,' Anna revealed. 'He has a bridge in his yard that goes way high up in the air.'

'Right,' said DeDe. She cast a wry glance in Mary Ann's direction. 'There's no telling *what* that bastard told them.' Then she turned back to the children. 'You guys ready to go home?'

'Where?' asked Edgar. A damn good point, thought Mary Ann.

'To Gangie's house,' replied DeDe.

The children said yes.

They spoke their parting words in the garage next to L'Etoile. DeDe waited there for her Mercedes – Mary Ann, her Le Car.

'You've been an angel,' said DeDe, sounding oddly like a club-woman from the peninsula.

Mary Ann smiled ruefully. 'Glad to help.'

'Right,' grinned DeDe.

The Mercedes arrived. DeDe held the door while the twins scrambled into the front seat. When she slid behind the wheel, Mary Ann leaned down and spoke to her.

'You're not going to tell me, are you?'

'What?' asked DeDe.

'You know. If we got the right guy.'

DeDe shook her head.

'Why? Because we didn't?'

DeDe smiled. 'If we didn't, I don't want you to suffer because of it. You've done enough already.'

'What if we did?'

DeDe shrugged. 'I don't want you to be tempted.'

'Tempted?'

'You know,' said DeDe. 'By the story.'

'DeDe . . . I'm your friend. I would never betray the trust . . .'

'I know. And you'd never forgive yourself either. How could you? You're a journalist.'

'I am?'

DeDe grabbed her hand and kissed it. 'You are.'

'Thanks,' said Mary Ann.

'Don't mention it,' said DeDe.

*

739

It was almost noon when Mary Ann dragged herself up the stairway at 28 Barbary Lane. As she slipped her key into the lock, she heard Mrs Madrigal's distinctive footsteps behind her.

'Dear . . . is that you?'

'It's me,' said Mary Ann.

The landlady's eyes were bloodshot.

'Good God,' said Mary Ann. 'Is something . . . ?'

'I'm sorry,' said Mrs Madrigal. 'I have something unpleasant to tell you.'

Lucking Out

A sense of *déjà vu*, almost indistinguishable from nausea, swept over Mary Ann as she and Mrs Madrigal strode through the lobby of St Sebastian's Hospital.

It was here that Michael had been treated for Guillain-Barré almost five years before. Here, too, was the sinister flower shop where the man with the transplant had secreted body parts for the cannibal cult at Grace Cathedral.

The most macabre memory, however, was a fixture of the hospital itself: an antique portrait of St Sebastian, shot through with arrows, proudly displayed on the wall above the reception desk.

Mrs Madrigal took Mary Ann's arm and steered her away from the holy man. 'C'mon, dear. I know the way. This place is too Catholic for words.'

They rode the elevator to the third floor. When they emerged, Jon was waiting for them. The very sight of him cracked the bland veneer that Mary Ann had assumed for the ride to the hospital.

She fell into his arms, weeping.

'A helluva way to come home, huh?' He laid his hand gently on the crown of her head.

'Are they awake?' she asked.

'Brian is,' said the doctor. 'Michael nodded off about an hour ago.' He turned to Mrs Madrigal. 'Did you fill her in on the particulars?'

'As best I could,' said the landlady.

'His lung was punctured,' Jon told Mary Ann. 'That was the worst part. It was a surprisingly small puncture, though . . . all things considered.'

It sounded awful to Mary Ann. 'Did they sew it up or what?'

Jon shook his head. 'It wasn't that bad. It should heal on its own. He's got a tube in him so that can happen. It isn't as bad as it looks, Mary Ann. That's the main thing you should know.'

'But I thought they . . . did it three times.' She couldn't bring herself to say the word.

'Two of the blows glanced off his ribs,' said Jon. 'There were plenty of stitches, but they were all in the chest wall. He's breathing normally now . . .' He smiled at her. 'I expect that'll change when he sees you.'

'What about Michael?'

'An enormous goose egg, mostly. Half-a-dozen stitches. He's O.K. . . . or he will be soon.' He looked at Mary Ann earnestly. 'We lucked out, didn't we?'

'If you can call it that,' said Mary Ann.

'We can,' said Jon. 'We have to.'

Brian's head was turned towards the window when Mary Ann entered the room. His chest was a mass of bandages. The tubes sprouting from the hole in his side led to a sort of suction cannister on the floor beside the bed.

As he breathed, a thing that looked oddly like a Ping-Pong ball bobbed about erratically in the cannister. Another tube (an IV, she presumed) led from a bedside pole into Brian's arm.

Michael was sleeping in the other bed, an enormous bandage crowning his head.

'It's me,' said Mary Ann.

Brian rolled his head over and smiled at her. 'Hi, sweetheart.'

Mary Ann moved cautiously towards the bed, feeling his wounds with every step. 'Is there anything I can kiss?' she asked.

A large tear rolled down Brian's cheek. 'Just stand there and let me look at you.'

She stood there awkwardly, hands at her sides. 'How's this?'

'Just fine,' he smiled.

'Shall I show a little leg?'

She had never seen a grown man laugh and cry at the same time. 'Jesus,' he sobbed, 'I love you so much!'

'Brian, damnit . . . if I start blubbering . . .'

'I can't help it. I've never been so goddamn glad to see somebody in my whole life!'

She grabbed a Kleenex from the bedside table and stood over him, blotting his cheeks. 'Hush now . . . I'm back. I'm so sorry I wasn't here, Brian.'

'What are you talking about? How could you have known?'

'I know, but you needed me and . . .'

'To hell with that. Did you find the kids?'

Mary Ann nodded. 'We found them.'

'They're O.K.?'

'They're fine,' said Mary Ann.

'Then you did good.'

Mary Ann turned the Kleenex on her own face and blew her nose noisily. 'How long will they keep you here?' she asked.

'Two weeks,' said Brian. 'Maybe three.'

'Then, let's do it here.'

'What?'

'The wedding,' said Mary Ann. 'Remember?'

'Sure . . . but . . .'

'Yeah?'

'Well, you wanted a garden wedding.'

'Fuck the garden. I wanna be married to you. Do you wanna be married to me?'

'I do,' said Brian.

Mary Ann beamed. 'I'll tell Mrs Madrigal.'

Michael's Doctor

Michael slipped into the hallway to find Jon reading a *Highlights* magazine next to the nurse's station.

'Hey,' said the doctor, 'you're supposed to be prone, sport.'

Michael sat down next to him, wearing only his hospital smock. 'Whoa!' he yelped, stiffening as his bare butt collided with cold plastic.

Jon grinned. 'They're not for patients.'

'What? The chair or the dress?'

The doctor pointed to Michael's room, admonishing him with his eyes.

'In a minute,' said Michael. 'I thought the lovebirds could use a little privacy. Anyway . . . stop being such a doctor.'

Jon shrugged. 'I'm not in white, am I?'

'You're on the verge . . . I can tell. Why don't you get some sleep, Jon? How long have you been here, anyway?'

'I'm all right,' said Jon. 'I'll go home with Mary Ann when she leaves.'

'Did Mrs Madrigal go home?'

Jon nodded. 'It's past time for Bambi's lunch.'

'Jesus,' groaned Michael. 'I completely forgot about that little drama!'

'Didn't we all?'

'Mary Ann says that's next on her agenda . . . now that the twins are back. Did you hear from the police, by the way? Anything new, I mean?'

Jon shook his head. 'I don't expect there will be. No license number, no solid description. The people who found you didn't reach the police until half-an-hour after the attack. I think we've got to write it off, Michael.'

Michael's eyes glazed over.

'Hey,' said Jon. 'You with me, sport?'

'Yeah.'

'It was an awful thing, Michael, but you can't let it get the best of you. Don't let those bastards change the way you look at life. Hey, sport . . . look at me.'

Michael's lower lip was trembling uncontrollably. Tears flooded his face. 'I know, Jon . . . it isn't that. It's just . . .'

'What?'

'Do you think they blame me?'

Jon blinked at him, uncomprehending. 'Who?'

'Mary Ann and Brian.'

'Michael . . . what in the world are you talking about?'

'Well,' answered Michael, his voice quavering. 'Those guys who jumped us . . . they thought we were *both* gay . . . and . . . if I hadn't been there . . .'

'Jesus,' muttered Jon.

'No, listen . . . they were just plain wrong about Brian. They had even less reason to attack him than me. But he got the worst of it. He . . .'

'Even *less* reason, huh? Meaning, I suppose, that they had at least a marginal reason to attack you? Is that what you think, Michael? Do you really believe that you deserved to get it more than Brian did?'

743

'Jon . . . I don't . . .'

'Goddamnit, Michael! How dare you talk like that? Brian doesn't think that. Mary Ann certainly doesn't. You're the biggest hom-ophobe in the family. What the hell does gay have to do with anything?'

Michael looked at him imploringly, eyes brimming with tears. 'Jon . . . please . . . I came out here for a hug.'

A hug was what he got. 'Listen to me,' said Jon, speaking directly into Michael's ear, 'you taught me everything I know about being happy with myself. Don't poop out on me now, kiddo.'

'Jon, I just can't keep . . .'

'Yes you can,' said the doctor. 'You're the toughest little fucker I know. You're right out there on the battle lines . . . and that's where I want you to stay. Christ, Michael . . . I'm the guy who wouldn't let you kiss him in airports.'

Silence.

'I'm different now,' Jon added. 'You're the one who changed me.'

Michael pulled away from him and looked into his eyes. 'Who have you been kissing in airports?'

Jon faked nonchalance. 'Oh . . . lots of people.'

'I'll bet.'

'Wanna try for a hospital?'

They kissed for almost half-a-minute until the head nurse returned to her station.

She cleared her throat noisily. 'If you don't mind, gentlemen.'

Jon looked up at her and smiled. 'It's all right,' he said. 'I'm a doctor.'

Options

When Mary Ann descended the stairs to the basement, she found Bambi curled – no, *coiled* – on an ancient sofa Mrs Madrigal had provided for her comfort.

She looked up sullenly, a long shadow falling across her face.

'You're gonna pay for this,' she said ominously.

'I suppose so,' said Mary Ann.

'I'm not talking job, lady – I'm talking criminal action. Your ass is grass, Mary Ann.'

It was creepy to see how much of Larry Kenan's pig lingo Bambi could appropriate for her own use.

Mary Ann pulled up a chair. A safe distance away. 'I thought we should . . . discuss things first.'

'Tell it to the police,' snarled Bambi.

'Do it yourself,' countered Mary Ann. 'The door is open.'

The anchorwoman cast a quick glance up the stairs.

'You're free to go,' said Mary Ann.

Bambi's eyes narrowed suspiciously. 'This is still a kidnapping, you know. Just because you're turning me loose doesn't mean . . .'

'I know.'

'And just because somebody else did it for you . . .'

'I know that, too.' Mary Ann smiled sweetly. 'So, haul ass, lady.' She jerked her head jauntily towards the stairs, 'Give my love to Larry . . . while you're at it. The poor jerk thinks you're out on a hot story. I'd hate to be the one to disillusion him.'

'You're gonna hate it even more when . . . What did you tell him?'

'Just that,' shrugged Mary Ann. 'That you and I were out chasing the scoop of the year.'

'DeDe Day?'

Mary Ann nodded, smiling.

'I Xeroxed those notes, you know.' Bambi's sneer was almost obscene. 'Stealing my purse was the stupidest thing you could've done. That story is still ours, Mary Ann. All it takes is a phone call to the station.'

'What a coincidence,' said Mary Ann. 'Those were my exact words to DeDe.'

Silence.

'We were talking about a different station, of course.'

Bambi glared at her murderously. 'You wouldn't do that.'

'Why not?' said Mary Ann blithely. 'My ass is grass, right? I'd get a much warmer reception at Channel 5. And let's face it . . . there *is* no story without DeDe and the kids. *Is there?*'

Silence.

'That's why I thought we should have a little discussion first. I wanted you to know what your options are . . . before you screw this up completely.' Another smile, more sugary than the first.

'Go ahead,' muttered Bambi.

'Well,' said Mary Ann, 'you can press charges, like you said. That'll simply force me to explain publicly why we felt a moral obligation to

745

hold you here until DeDe was certain that her children were out of harm's way. That won't look very pretty, Bambi. It wasn't your story in the first place. That's easy enough to prove.'

'A story is a story,' growled the newscaster.

'Exactly,' said Mary Ann. 'And I'm prepared to share this one with you.'

Bambi gave her a long distrusting look. 'You are?'

'With you or Wendy Tokuda. Take your pick.'

The coil tightened. 'I wanna know what "harm's way" was.'

Mary Ann blinked at her. 'Huh?'

'You said, "when the children were out of harm's way." What possible threat could justify your locking me in a cellar for three days?'

'The threat was *you*! The press! DeDe is my friend. She's made some dumb mistakes, but she's a good woman and I like her. She wanted time to breathe, that's all. A month of serenity with her mother and children. Is that too much to ask for a woman who escaped from Guyana in a fish barrel?'

'What about that double, then?'

'What about him? She says an imposter was trained while she was still in Jonestown . . . but she left days before the massacre. It's definitely worth mentioning. I'd count on being shot down, though.'

'Why?'

Mary Ann nailed her with a glance. 'Do *you* think Jim Jones is still alive?'

Bambi scowled and looked away. 'So what do you want to do about this?'

'All right: I want you to sign a paper certifying your willing tenancy at 28 Barbary Lane over the past few days . . .'

'Just a second!'

'I'm not finished. Since it's obvious that you and I have been out interviewing DeDe for the past few days – got that – you couldn't possibly have been locked in the basement of 28 Barbary Lane. This was simply your command post. I think that sounds pretty damn glamorous myself.'

'What about air time?'

'We'll share that,' said Mary Ann. 'I don't care if you do the announcing. You can interview me.'

'I'm ever so grateful.'

'You should be. I've been leaning towards Wendy lately. The book rights are mine, incidentally.' Mary Ann smiled. 'Not that you'd pose any threat there.'

'So . . . you weren't in Cleveland, then?'

'Of course I was in Cleveland!' Mary Ann's indignation was heroic. 'Do you think I would lie about my own grandmother?'

A Garden Wedding

After sleeping for almost fifteen hours, Mary Ann awoke at 9:00 A.M. and hurried downstairs to Mrs Madrigal's apartment. The landlady was in her kitchen, baking a cake.

Baking *the* cake.

Mary Ann pecked her on the cheek. 'You're so sweet to be doing that. What are those little brown specks in the batter?'

'Carrots,' said Mrs Madrigal.

'You're lying.'

'Then don't ask impertinent questions. I take it you worked things out with Bambi?'

'Completely.'

'Good girl. Have you called your mother yet?'

'After the ceremony,' said Mary Ann. 'I want this to be just family. I mean . . . my family here.'

The landlady smiled lovingly. 'I knew what you meant.' She held out a spoon for Mary Ann to lick.

'Yum-yum,' said Mary Ann. 'Carrots!'

DeDe phoned at eleven o'clock.

'I just saw the papers,' she said breathlessly. 'I'm so sorry about Brian!'

'Thanks.'

'You poor thing! You must think this week will *never* end!'

'It can't,' said Mary Ann, 'until tonight.'

'Jesus. I'm afraid to ask.'

Mary Ann laughed. 'No. It's good this time. We're getting married tonight. At the hospital. I'd love it if you could come.'

'Of course! How exciting! Can I bring the children?'

'That would be marvelous!'

'What about the show?'

'You mean our debut on the news?'

DeDe laughed. 'Yeah.'

'Is Monday all right with you?'

'Sure,' said DeDe. 'Fine.'

Mary Ann giggled. 'It sounds like we just made a date for lunch or something.'

'Well . . . we can do that, too.'

By mid-afternoon, Mary Ann was back at the hospital. When she opened the door to Brian and Michael's room, the sight that confronted her took her breath away.

'My God!'

Michael beamed at her from his bed. 'Pretty neat, huh?' The room was a veritable jungle of greenery and flowers – most of which were obviously not indigenous to the hospital florist. Both beds were framed by boxwood bushes, passion vines trailed along the window sill, and a bright pink fuchsia drooped luxuriantly from Brian's IV pole.

'They're on loan,' said Brian. 'Ned and a friend brought them by a little while ago.'

Mary Ann was undone. 'What a sweet thing!'

Brian nodded. 'You get your garden wedding, after all.'

'Where is he?'

'Who?'

'Ned. I want to call and thank him.'

'They'll be back in a minute,' said Brian. 'They went to get coffee.'

'Anyway,' said Michael, 'we've got some questions to ask you.'

'If you mean Bambi, I've taken care of that.'

'What did you tell her? That the whole damn thing was a wild goose chase?'

'She doesn't know about the kidnapping,' said Mary Ann. 'She doesn't even know about my trip to Alaska. She thinks we locked her up to prevent early release of the story.' She looked earnestly at both men. 'I don't want her – or anybody – to know about Mr Starr.'

'Why?' asked Michael.

'Because that whole thing was a big fiasco. It's embarrassing. It makes DeDe and me both look a little drifty.'

A smile flickered across Brian's face. 'What were you doing up there, anyway? Chartering dog sleds? Chasing Eskimos across the ice?'

'Brian . . .'

'And this Starr guy?' asked Michael. 'You have no idea where he went after he dropped the kids off at Prue Giroux's house?'

'None,' said Mary Ann.

'In other words, it was just Mrs Halcyon's dumb mistake. There was never a kidnapping. There was never a real threat of any kind. Slow curtain . . . The End.'

Mary Ann nodded vaguely. 'That's about it. I'm afraid.'

Michael addressed his next question to Brian. 'Why do I have such a hard time believing that?'

Brian gazed lovingly at Mary Ann. 'It's all right,' he said. 'She never lies to us about the important stuff.'

A bald head poked through the doorway.

'Ned!' exclaimed Mary Ann, grateful for the interruption. 'This is the sweetest thing anyone has ever done! We've *definitely* got to get a photographer now! Those fuchsias are the most wonderful . . .' Her gushing stopped when she saw the man shambling into the room behind Ned.

Brian took it from there. 'Mary Ann, this is _____ _____.'

'Yes,' she said, 'I see.'

'He and Ned are staying for the wedding.' Brian winked at his bride-to-be. 'I figured you wouldn't mind.'

Back in her Own Backyard

Frannie Halcyon was helping herself to more cinnamon toast when her daughter joined her for breakfast on the terrace at Halcyon Hill.

'How was the wedding, darling? Did everything go off all right?'

DeDe sat down and poured herself a cup of coffee. 'Very sweet,' she said. 'In some ways, a lot like mine. The minister even read from Gibran.'

The matriarch's brow wrinkled. 'Oh, dear. Are they *still* doing that?'

DeDe smiled. '_____ _____ was there, by the way.'

'Really? What on earth for?'

'He's a friend of the family,' smiled DeDe.

'Oh.'

'And Mary Ann sent you a piece of the wedding cake . . . along with her love.'

'Bless her heart,' said Frannie. 'She's had a dreadful time of it, hasn't she? All that frantic dashing about with you . . . and then her fiancé is mistaken for a homosexual.'

DeDe scowled at her. 'That is hardly the point, Mother.'

'Well,' said Frannie merrily, 'all's well that ends well, I always say. One look at my grandchildren is proof enough of that.'

'Are they up yet?' said DeDe.

Frannie pointed to the edge of the garden. 'They're out there keeping Emma company.' She smiled benevolently at the distant figures, then turned to her daughter with a sigh. 'You know . . . I feel awfully silly about all that.'

'All what?' asked DeDe, buttering a piece of toast.

'Well . . . not checking to see if Mr Starr had come back to the ship. We maligned him dreadfully . . . when you come to think of it. We assumed the very worst about him.'

DeDe took a bite out of the toast. 'That was a perfectly natural reaction.'

'I know. Just the same, I wish I could write him a thank-you note. Do you think he left a forwarding address with Prue?'

DeDe shook her head and continued to eat.

'He must think us awfully stupid,' added Frannie. 'I mean . . . leaving the children like that. Think how it must have looked to *him*.'

'I wouldn't worry about it,' said DeDe.

'He was always such a gentleman,' said Frannie, closing the subject once and for all. She turned her gaze to the garden again, then shook her head in admiration. 'Emma's such a marvel, isn't she? Just look at her out there! She's absolutely obsessed with that new azalea bed of hers.'

'Uh-huh,' said DeDe.

'You can't help admiring her,' said Frannie. 'Starting a new hobby at *her* age.'

DeDe nodded. 'She loves this family very much.'

'I don't care what they say,' declared the matriarch. 'You can't get help like *that* anymore.'

When the phone rang, DeDe took it in the kitchen.

'Halcyon Hill.'

'Uh . . . Emma?'

'No. This is DeDe.' *At last*, she could say that.

'I thought so! Thank God!'

750

'Who is this?'

'Who else? The Red Menace.'

'D'or! Where are you? You sound different.'

'It must be the ambience. I'm in Miami.'

'*What?*'

'At the Fontainebleau, no less. When I sell out, I don't fuck around!'

DeDe laughed. 'I've missed you so much.'

'Yeah? Wanna see me?'

'Are you kidding? How soon can you get here?'

'Gimme a day or so. Listen, hon . . . what about your mother?'

'I'll take care of that,' said DeDe.

Five minutes later, she hung up the phone and went out to take care of it.

Six Weeks Later . . .

Mary Ann and Brian chose Golden Gate Park as the site of their unofficial 'honeymoon' – a lavish picnic lunch that marked their first venture into the outdoors since the knife attack. At the last minute, they asked Michael to join them.

'You know,' said Mary Ann, smearing Brie on a chunk of sourdough bread, 'there's only one thing missing today.'

'What's that?' asked Michael.

Mary Ann smiled and handed him the morsel. 'Jon,' she said.

Michael popped the bread into his mouth and turned to Brian. 'Will you please tell the Little Woman to lay off for a while? She's determined to make us Lucy & Ricky & Fred & Ethel.'

Brian grinned. 'Does that make me Fred or Ricky?'

'Don't press your luck,' said Michael. 'You might be Ethel.'

'When does Jon's ship get back?' asked Mary Ann.

'Tomorrow,' said Michael. 'Pass the smoky cheddar, please.'

Brian shoved the cheese board in Michael's direction. 'Remember when you and I were here last?'

'Yeah?'

'You told me to hurry up and marry Mary Ann.'

'He *did*?' Mary Ann stopped spreading Brie and looked up. 'That's so sweet, Mouse.'

751

'Well,' continued Brian, still talking to Michael, 'I think it's time you married Jon.'

Michael lopped a strawberry into his mouth. 'I've done that already.'

'Then, *remarry* him.' This was Mary Ann, putting in her own two cents' worth.

Michael looked at them in succession. 'You guys want *everybody* to be married.'

'But, it would be so wonderful, Mouse. We could all plan trips to Yosemite together . . . and *family* things. You've been looking for two years, Mouse. Have you ever found *anybody* better than Jon?'

Michael pretended to search for another strawberry.

'Everybody but you can see that. Jon is your Christmas tree man.'

'My *what*?'

'You told me that, once. Before you met Jon. You said you didn't expect that much from a relationship . . . just somebody nice to buy a Christmas tree with. That's Jon, Mouse! He doesn't even mind it when you sleep around.'

'Oh?'

Mary Ann nodded. 'He told me so himself. He *loves* you.'

'He sleeps around himself,' said Michael. 'Why do you think he's on that ship?'

'Then you're *perfect* for each other! Like me and Brian.'

Brian gave his wife a funny look. She squeezed his leg to reassure him.

'Are you meeting his ship?' she asked Michael.

A long pause, and then: 'Yeah.'

Mary Ann smiled triumphantly, giving Brian's knee a healthy shake. 'You see . . . you see?'

'See what?' asked Michael.

'Nothing,' grinned Mary Ann.

'You're impossible,' grumped Michael. 'What did you do with the Dijon?'

But his smile betrayed him again.

High on the ridge above them, Prue Giroux made her way carefully through the rhododendron dell, disregarding once again the admonitions of her priest.

She had not set foot in Luke's shack since her escape with the children.

Something strangely akin to remorse engulfed her as she pushed open the door of the little house and perused its scattered contents.

The walls had been horribly vandalized with spray paint. The foam rubber 'sofa,' once the scene of her happiest moments, was littered with alien condoms.

'Animals,' she muttered.

Very little remained except the handmade plaque, now rudely splashed with crimson:

THOSE WHO DO NOT
REMEMBER THE PAST
ARE CONDEMNED
TO REPEAT IT

She couldn't bear the thought of leaving that sentiment behind, so she removed the plaque from the wall and slipped it lovingly into her tote bag. Before the tears could come, she hurried out into the sunlight again and scaled the slope to the rhododendron dell.

She was halfway across the dell when she spied a familiar figure emerging from one of the enormous bushes.

'Oh . . . uh . . . Prue, darling.' It was Father Paddy, looking unusually flustered.

Prue tried to sound breezy, hoping he hadn't deduced the reason for her visit to the dell. 'Isn't it a gorgeous day, Father?'

'Yes, indeed . . . God's in his heaven, all right!'

'Mmm.'

'What are you . . . uh . . . doing in this neck of the woods?'

'Just walking Vuitton,' said Prue.

'Oh . . . well, it's a lovely day for . . .' Before he could finish, another man emerged from the huge shrub. He greeted Prue by name, winked at Father Paddy, and sauntered off down the path, whistling contentedly.

'I didn't know you knew Officer Rivera,' said Prue.

Father Paddy hesitated. 'Actually . . . we just met.'

'He's so conscientious,' observed the columnist. 'It's nice to know that there are policemen like that.'

'Yes,' said the cleric. 'Yes, it is.' He took Prue's arm suddenly. 'I don't know about you, darling, but I'm *famished*. How about a little lunch somewhere?'

'I'd adore lunch,' said Prue. 'Help me find Vuitton.'

The priest scolded her with a glance. 'You've lost him again?'

'Of course not,' said Prue. 'He's around here somewhere. Vuiiiton. Here, boy! *Vuiiiiton! . . .*'

THE END

A Note about the Author

Armistead Maupin was born in Washington D.C. in 1944 but was brought up in Raleigh, North Carolina. A graduate of the University of North Carolina, he served as a naval officer in Vietnam before moving to California in 1971. Maupin lives in San Francisco with gay rights activist Terry Anderson.